PENGUIN  CLASSICS

THE COMPLETE SHORT NOVELS

DAVID HERBERT LAWRENCE was born at Eastwood, Nottinghamshire, in 1885, fourth of the five children of a miner and his middle-class wife. He attended Nottingham High School and Nottingham University College. His first novel, *The White Peacock*, was published in 1911, just a few weeks after the death of his mother, to whom he had been abnormally close. At this time he finally ended his relationship with Jessie Chambers (the Miriam of *Sons and Lovers*) and became engaged to Louie Burrows. His career as a school-teacher was ended in 1911 by the illness which was ultimately diagnosed as tuberculosis.

In 1912 Lawrence eloped to Germany with Frieda Weekley, the German wife of his former modern languages tutor. They were married on their return to England in 1914. Lawrence was now living, precariously, by his writing. His greatest novels, *The Rainbow* and *Women in Love*, were completed in 1915 and 1916. The former was suppressed, and he could not find a publisher for the latter.

After the war Lawrence began his 'savage pilgrimage' in search of a more fulfilling mode of life than industrial Western civilization could offer. This took him to Sicily, Ceylon, Australia and, finally, New Mexico. The Lawrences returned to Europe in 1925. Lawrence's last novel, *Lady Chatterley's Lover*, was banned in 1928, and his paintings confiscated in 1929. He died in Vence in 1930 at the age of 44.

Lawrence spent most of his short life living. Nevertheless, he produced an amazing quantity of work – novels, stories, poems, plays, essays, travel books, translations and letters ... After his death Frieda wrote: 'What he had seen and felt and known he gave in his writing to his fellow men, the splendour of living, the hope of more and more life ... a heroic and immeasurable gift.'

KEITH SAGAR is Reader in English Literature in the Extra-Mural Department of the University of Manchester. Dr Sagar is the author of *The Art of D. H. Lawrence* (1966), *The Art of Ted Hughes* (1975 and 1978), *D. H. Lawrence – a Calendar of His Works* (1979), *The Life of D. H. Lawrence* (1980), *The Reef and Other Poems* (1980) and *D. H. Lawrence: Life into Art* (Penguin, 1985). He has also edited several books, including Lawrence's *Sons and Lovers* for Penguin Classics. He is now editing volume seven of Lawrence's letters for the Cambridge edition, and working on a *magnum opus*, *Worshippers of Nature*.

MELISSA PARTRIDGE ... *wilight in* *Italy* for the Cambri ...

D1425128

Short Words for my Big Favourite
To Caryl with love - December 88.
Kein.
xx

The Complete Short Novels

D. H. LAWRENCE

EDITED WITH AN
INTRODUCTION AND NOTES
BY KEITH SAGAR
AND MELISSA PARTRIDGE

PENGUIN BOOKS

PENGUIN BOOKS

Published by the Penguin Group
27 Wrights Lane, London w8 5tz, England
Viking Penguin Inc., 40 West 23rd Street, New York, New York 10010, USA
Penguin Books Australia Ltd, Ringwood, Victoria, Australia
Penguin Books Canada Ltd, 2801 John Street, Markham, Ontario, Canada l3r 1b4
Penguin Books (NZ) Ltd, 182–190 Wairau Road, Auckland 10, New Zealand

Penguin Books Ltd, Registered Offices: Harmondsworth, Middlesex, England

This selection first published in the Penguin English Library 1982
Reprinted 1984
Reprinted in Penguin Classics 1987, 1988

Introduction and notes copyright © Keith Sagar and Melissa Partridge, 1982
All rights reserved

Printed and bound in Great Britain by
Richard Clay Ltd, Bungay, Suffolk
Filmset in Monophoto Ehrhardt

Contents

Lawrence's Life and Works: a Chronology

1885	David Herbert Richards Lawrence born in Eastwood, Nottinghamshire, the fourth child of Arthur Lawrence, miner, and Lydia, *née* Beardsall, formerly a schoolmistress.
1891–8	He attends Beauvale Board School and becomes the first boy from that school to win a County Council Scholarship to
1898–1901	Nottingham High School, which he attends until 1901.
1901	Begins frequent visits to Chambers family at Haggs Farm, and his relationship with Jessie Chambers (the Miriam of *Sons and Lovers*) which was to develop into an 'unofficial engagement'.
1901–2	Works as a clerk at Haywood's surgical appliances factory. Has to leave after severe attack of pneumonia.
1902–6	Pupil–teacher at British School, Eastwood. Sits the King's Scholarship examination in December 1904 and is placed in the first division of the first class. A few months later he matriculates and qualifies himself to take a two-year teachers' certificate course at Nottingham University College, beginning in September 1906.
1906–8	Writes his first poems and stories and begins his first novel *Laetitia* (later *The White Peacock*). Wins *Nottinghamshire Guardian* Christmas 1907 short story competition with 'A Prelude'. Loses his faith in 'a personal, human God'.
1908–11	Teaches at Davidson Road School, Croydon. Meets Ford Madox Hueffer who begins to publish his poems and stories in the *English Review* and introduces him to the London literary world. In 1910 he writes his second novel, *The Trespasser*, in conjunction with Helen Corke, and begins *Paul Morel* (later *Sons and Lovers*). His relationship with Jessie Chambers comes to an end. He has a brief affair with Alice Dax, wife of an Eastwood chemist, then becomes engaged to Louie Burrows, who had been a fellow-student at college. In December 1910 Mrs Lawrence dies of cancer. In January 1911 *The White Peacock* is published by Heinemann. Edward Garnett becomes Lawrence's mentor. Lawrence becomes seriously ill with pneumonia and has to give up school-teaching.
1912	In March Lawrence meets Frieda Weekley, wife of his former modern languages tutor, and six weeks later elopes with her

to Germany. Lawrence records the vicissitudes of their relationship in '*Look! We Have Come Through!*'. They walk over the Alps into Italy and settle at Gargnano, where Lawrence finishes *Sons and Lovers* and begins *The Insurrection of Miss Houghton* (later to be rewritten as *The Lost Girl*).

1913   Begins *The Sisters*, eventually to be split into *The Rainbow* and *Women in Love*, and *Italian Sketches* (later *Twilight in Italy*). They return to England in June and begin friendship with John Middleton Murry and Katherine Mansfield. They return to Italy (Lerici) in September. Lawrence works mainly on *The Sisters* until June, when they return to England to

1914   marry (Frieda having at last obtained her divorce) and to find a publisher for *The Rainbow*. The wedding takes place at Kensington Registry Office on 13 July 1914. Lawrence works on revising his short stories for *The Prussian Officer*. The outbreak of war the following month prevents the Lawrences from returning to Italy. At Chesham and Greatham during the next six months, Lawrence rewrites *The Rainbow*. He

1915   begins important friendships with Lady Cynthia Asquith, Lady Ottoline Morrell, Bertrand Russell and E. M. Forster. In August they move to Hampstead. Lawrence develops his idea of an ideal community, Rananim, envisaged, at this stage, in Florida. His plans to form a revolutionary anti-war party with Russell and Murry collapse. *The Rainbow* is published by Methuen and immediately suppressed. This blow, together with the war, ill-health, increasing poverty, the defection of several friends, humiliating examinations for military service, and his inability to get permission to leave the country, brings Lawrence close to despair and misanthropy – his 'nightmare'.

1916   The Lawrences move to Cornwall where Lawrence writes *Women in Love*.

1917   He begins *Studies in Classic American Literature*. The Lawrences are evicted from Cornwall on suspicion of spying. In London Lawrence begins *Aaron's Rod*.

1918   They move to Newbury, in Berkshire, then to Mountain Cottage, Middleton-by-Wirksworth, Derbyshire. Lawrence writes *Movements in European History*.

1919   Lawrence is very ill with influenza. Moves back to Berkshire. In November the Lawrences leave for Italy and settle in Capri.

1920   Moves to Fontana Vecchia, Taormina, Sicily. Visits Maurice Magnus at Monte Cassino.

1920–21   Writes *The Lost Girl*, *Mr Noon*, *Sea and Sardinia* and the two psychoanalysis books; begins *Birds, Beasts and Flowers*;

finishes *Aaron's Rod*. Revises stories for *England, My England* and *The Ladybird*.

1922   Translates Verga. Visits the Brewsters in Ceylon on the way to Australia, where he spends the summer at Thirroul, N.S.W., writing *Kangaroo*. Goes to New Mexico in September at the invitation of Mabel Dodge Luhan. In December settles at Del Monte ranch, Questa, near Taos. Finishes *Studies in Classic American Literature*.

1923   Finishes *Birds, Beasts and Flowers*. Spends the summer at Chapala in Mexico where he writes *Quetzalcoatl* (the first version of *The Plumed Serpent*). Rewrites Mollie Skinner's novel *The House of Ellis* as *The Boy in the Bush*. Frieda returns to England in August; Lawrence follows in December.

1924   Dinner at the Café Royal where Lawrence invites his friends to form a community at the ranch in Taos. Only Dorothy Brett accepts and accompanies the Lawrences to New Mexico in March. Frieda acquires Lobo ranch, later renamed Kiowa, from Mabel in exchange for the manuscript of *Sons and Lovers*. That summer at the ranch Lawrence writes *The Woman Who Rode Away*, *St Mawr*, *The Princess* and the New Mexico sections of *Mornings in Mexico*. Lawrence's father dies. In November the Lawrences move to Oaxaca, Mexico, where Lawrence writes the Mexican sections of *Mornings in Mexico* and rewrites *Quetzalcoatl*.

1925   In February Lawrence almost dies of malaria. In Mexico City a doctor tells Frieda that he is dying of consumption. He puts rouge on his cheeks to get back across the border. Recuperates at the ranch and writes *David* and *Reflections on the Death of a Porcupine*. In September the Lawrences return to Europe and settle at Spotorno in Italy, where Lawrence writes *Sun*.

1926   Writes *The Virgin and the Gipsy*. Quarrels with Frieda and leaves her for several weeks. Has an abortive affair with Dorothy Brett. In May the Lawrences move to the Villa Mirenda, Scandicci, near Florence. In the late summer Lawrence makes his last visit to England. On his return he writes *The First Lady Chatterley*. Takes up painting seriously.

1927   Writes second version of *Lady Chatterley's Lover*. Makes Etruscan pilgrimage with Earl Brewster. Writes *The Escaped Cock* and *Etruscan Places*. Begins final version of *Lady Chatterley's Lover*. Prepares *The Woman Who Rode Away and Other Stories* for publication.

1928   In June the Lawrences move to Switzerland and settle at Gsteig. Lawrence is too weak to work, except on newspaper articles and paintings. In October he visits Richard Aldington on Port Cros, then settles in Bandol. Begins *Pansies. Lady Chatterley's Lover* published, with consequent furore.

1929
Visits Paris in the spring, then Mallorca. Lawrence's paintings exhibited at the Warren Gallery in London. On the day the show is raided by the police Lawrence collapses at Forte dei Marmi. He goes to Bavaria for treatment, but returns, no better, to Bandol in September. Writes *Nettles* and *Last Poems*. Begins *Apocalypse*.

1930
On Dr Morland's recommendation Lawrence enters Ad Astra sanatorium at Vence in February. After three weeks with no improvement, he is moved by Frieda and Aldous and Maria Huxley to a nearby villa where he dies the following night. He is buried at Vence.

1935
Lawrence's body exhumed, cremated, and the ashes taken to Taos where Frieda's third husband, Angelo Ravagli, has built a small shrine above the ranch.

1956
Frieda dies and is buried outside the shrine.

KEITH SAGAR

Introduction

'The Captain's Doll', 'The Fox', 'The Ladybird'

These stories were written during the last three months of 1921, and published together under the title *The Ladybird* in England, and *The Captain's Doll* in America, in 1923. Each story made use of earlier material, 'The Fox' being a much extended version of the short story with the same title written in November 1918 and published in *Hutchinson's Story Magazine* for July 1919; while 'The Captain's Doll' and 'The Ladybird' were new approaches to themes and material from two earlier short stories, 'The Mortal Coil' and 'The Thimble' respectively.

When Lawrence had completed the first two short novels, he wrote to his American publisher Thomas Seltzer: ' "The Fox" and "The Captain's Doll" are so modern, so new: a new manner.'* He clearly felt that the short novels shared qualities which distinguished them from either his novels or short stories, and required a different name – 'novelettes'. What, then, were these qualities? Only a sensitive reading of the stories in the context of Lawrence's other works can yield a full answer; but we can note here some of the more striking features.

The most obvious of these is the use of a central, symbolically charged image or emblem, as the organizing principle of the whole work. It was by no means new for Lawrence to extract an important symbol from a work as its title; but in no previous work had the story's development and exploration of its themes been so exclusively and explicitly linked with a single dominating motif.

'The Captain's Doll' was the first of the short novels to be completed. The doll directs the story from beginning to end. On the first page Hannele is making the doll; on the last she burns the painting of it. The story is skilfully organized, and the

* D. H. Lawrence, *Letters to Thomas and Adele Seltzer*, ed. G. M. Lacy (Black Sparrow Press, 1976), p. 29.

significance of the title left in no doubt. Very near the end Hepburn asserts: 'If a woman loves you, she'll make a doll out of you.' This story, like both the others, is about the right relation between men and women. The doll represents what Lawrence finds wrong in most sexual relationships.

'The Captain's Doll' certainly cannot be called simply a later version of 'The Mortal Coil', yet there are closer links between the two stories than mere similarity of theme. The plot of 'The Mortal Coil' (which Lawrence had written in 1913 and revised in 1916) had derived from a real experience of Frieda's father, and is quite different from that of 'The Captain's Doll'. It concerns a young army officer called Friedeburg, who is strikingly similar to Anton Skrebensky in *The Rainbow*. Friedeburg is deeply in debt from gambling, and sinks into despair because he knows that this will ruin his army career; and his army life, the life he shares with his men and fellow-officers, is everything to him, giving him purpose and his sense of self. He is unable or unwilling to be comforted by his mistress Marta, who, as the story opens, is waiting for him in his room, as Hannele waits for Hepburn. When he comes, they have a fierce argument, Marta pouring scorn on her lover for his weakness and his dependence on the army, and bitterly hurt because he does not see their relationship as giving any meaning to his life. But when she makes to leave, he prevents her, exercising his will and sexual power to keep her with him through the night. Apparently, she heals him with her love and passion; but in the morning, though she is triumphant and deeply satisfied, he seems destroyed: 'He felt as if someone had stolen away his being in the night.'* The cold morning and strenuous physical activity with his men at first restore and exhilarate him, but with the progress of the day his despair returns bringing thoughts of suicide. When he returns home, full of the idea of his own death, he discovers that Marta and her woman friend, who had joined her for companionship when he had left in the early morning, are dead, asphyxiated by fumes from the stove.

It is a puzzling story, which draws no moral, about a young

* D. H. Lawrence, *The Mortal Coil and Other Stories* (Penguin, 1971), p. 227.

man who 'felt himself nothing' and a girl who tries to fill him with her own abundant vitality. He refuses responsibility both for himself and for her; and she, trying to be what he will not be, succeeds only in smothering him:

'You'd never shoot yourself, because you're mine, aren't you!' she said, knowing the fine quivering of his body, in mastery.
'Yes,' he said.
'Quite mine?' she said, her voice rising in ecstasy.
'Yes.'
'Nobody else but mine – nothing at all –?'
'Nothing at all,' he re-echoed.
'But me?' came her last words of ecstasy.
'Yes.'*

But it is she who suffocates in the poisonous heat of the too-cosy room. The deaths are purely accidental, yet it is clear that the weak and purposeless man can bring good neither to himself nor to his woman, and she cannot take the place that should be his. Friedeburg fails to be 'the free indomitable self-sufficient being which a man must be in his relation to a woman who loves him'.†

In 'The Captain's Doll' Lawrence rewrites the story, but with a man who is to be just that 'free indomitable self-sufficient being'. 'The Mortal Coil' has no doll motif, at least not explicitly; but Friedeburg, without the army, is described as 'a palpitating rag of meaningless human life'. In the army he is a puppet, the army holding the strings which keep him upright and putting him through the motions of life. It is, however, a life supported entirely from the outside. Those strings once cut, the puppet becomes a rag doll with no support or motive power. Though the woman here did not create the doll, she pushes him closer to destruction with her overweening love.

'The Captain's Doll' stands as an answer to the earlier story; a prescription for success in reply to the earlier delineation of failure. Hepburn is not a doll. We may have doubts about a man who could have behaved so abjectly with his first wife, but his strength (though never adequately defined) and his integrity are

* ibid., p. 226.
† ibid., pp. 218–19.

constantly emphasized. The doll here is not the man, but a travesty of him. His assertion of his own un-doll-like being, and his insistence that his woman should recognize it, is the burden of the story, and its prescription for a successful relationship.

'The Captain's Doll' has been much praised; but there are considerable problems for the reader. One disturbing element is the over-convenient death of Mrs Hepburn, and the comic tone in which Lawrence seeks to pass it off: 'And then a dreadful thing happened: really a very dreadful thing.' The ending, too, raises problems. Again the mode is comic, with the crucial discussion taking place in a car bumping and rattling down the mountain-side; but the comedy does not obscure the serious import of the discussion. Hepburn defines what he is looking for in a wife: 'I want a sort of patient Griselda. I want to be honoured and obeyed.' When Hannele, who loves him, assuming that his assertions are less than fully serious, replies: 'I'll come to Africa with you. But I won't promise to honour and obey you', he answers: 'I don't want you otherwise.' Half a page later, though Hannele has not agreed to his conditions in so many words, she has tacitly capitulated, and the story ends with her planning to marry him and accompany him to Africa.

What the reader who objects to this ending must decide is whether his objections derive from outside the story – from the reader's own prior commitments and beliefs – and are insisted on in spite of the story's own internal integrity and artistic success, or whether the story itself shows any evidence of strain, any suggestion that Lawrence was forcing it towards a willed conclusion. That he was conscious of some difficulty in writing the ending is evident:

> I suddenly wrote a very funny long story called 'The Captain's Doll', which I haven't finished yet. But I have just got it high up in the mountains of the Tyrol, and don't quite know how to get it down without breaking its neck.*

Did he break its neck?

The ending of the story as it stands depends on a confusion;

---

* *The Collected Letters of D. H. Lawrence*, ed. H. T. Moore (Heinemann, 1962), p. 670.

for the Hannele Lawrence has created *cannot* accept Hepburn's terms as he interprets them, that is, not just as forms of expression lifted from the marriage service, but absolutely literally, and as constituting an ultimatum. Yet her acceptance of his terms is the ending Lawrence requires, so she is made to accept them in a non-committal way, as a few words she will agree to say at the wedding, to humour him, which makes nonsense of the seriousness of his proposals. He is not seeking merely freedom from the tyranny of idealized and smothering love and the falsity of conventional ideas of marriage. He wants to impose another, equally fixed idea of marriage – that implied by the allusion to Griselda. Griselda did not merely respect her husband. Her obedience was total and unquestioning, acquiescing in her husband's most outrageous demands and entirely resigning her judgement and responsibility to him. Hepburn's allusion to 'patient Griselda' implies the same idea of what a woman should undertake in marriage as Count Dionys, in 'The Ladybird', expresses in defining what a man should undertake when he swears fealty to a chosen leader:

'My chosen aristocrat would say to those who chose him: "If you choose me, you give up forever your right to judge me. If you have truly chosen to follow me, you have therefore rejected all your right to criticize me. You can no longer either approve or disapprove of me. You have performed the sacred act of choice. Henceforth you can only obey." '

To agree in any real way to this, Hannele would have to be a different woman; perhaps such a woman as we find in March in 'The Fox', mesmerized and entirely under the domination of her man, or Lady Daphne in 'The Ladybird', eagerly accepting the hypnotic mastery of Count Dionys as an escape from the emptiness of her life with her husband. But those two stories use strategies of non-realistic self-enclosure, isolating themselves in an autonomous world by the use of extended animal analogy and of myth. 'The Captain's Doll' differs from them in being much closer to the realistic mode of the earlier novels, and its realism defeats its purpose. Unlike a novel such as *Women in Love*, it insists on a closed ending, with a definite prescriptive message; but it tries to impose this on a story which, like *Women in Love*,

incorporates lively resistance to some of its ideas. The result is
willed distortion. Perhaps it was his desire to remove the last
remaining resistance to his ideas, his message, which impelled
Lawrence to move into less realistic modes in 'The Fox' and 'The
Ladybird'.

Immediately after finishing 'The Captain's Doll', Lawrence
'put a long tail to "The Fox", which was a bobbed short story.
Now he careers with a strange and fiery brush.'* The story takes
its outward circumstances from life. In 1918 and 1919 the
Lawrences had stayed intermittently at Chapel Farm Cottage,
Hermitage, near Newbury, in Berkshire, and made the acquaintance of two young women at nearby Grimsbury Farm. After the
death of its owner, Grimsbury Farm was being run by his
granddaughters, two cousins named Cecily Lambert and Violet
Monk. Cecily Lambert's memoir reveals how much Lawrence
drew on Violet Monk's manner and appearance when he created
March:

> My cousin was a good-looking girl with dark wavy hair and velvety
> brown eyes, but an undefinable personality ... [She] was a strange
> mixture of overwhelming conceit and arrogance allied to a kind of
> meekness and unsureness in direct contradiction. In appearance she was
> very feminine except for a flat boyish figure, which was graceful ... She
> loved doing mannish jobs – carpenting, digging and rough jobs generally
> ... In her very scarce spare moments as a complete contrast she would
> crochet lace with very fine white cotton and seemed to enjoy this hobby.
> If by any chance visitors came, she would leave the entertaining entirely
> to me while she would go off and wash up or do jobs outside – anything
> to avoid the bother of talking.
>
> At this time also a brother of mine was home on sick leave from the
> East Africa War Zone ... But far from having any amorous feelings
> towards the lady (my cousin), he actively disliked her ... I believe
> between them they mutilated a tree.†

Cecily Lambert also recalled that they were infested with foxes
at that period, but added: 'regarding the short story attributed
to us: it was sheer fantasy really.' She considered the story
offensive, and a breach of hospitality.

* ibid., p. 678.

† *D. H. Lawrence: A Composite Biography*, ed. E. Nehls (Madison: University
of Wisconsin Press, 1957–9), Vol. 1, pp. 465–6.

Lawrence rarely invented anything entirely, but used his own experiences and those of his friends and casual acquaintances for his material. The friends frequently recognized themselves in his fiction, portrayed often in unflattering ways, and many of them regarded this as a betrayal. But such instances were not meant to be portraits. Lawrence saw individuals in direct relation to the largest issues, and discovered universal significance in the details of everyday life. His offence was not so much his use of people (though this was often ruthless), but his misuse of them by distorting reality to fit his preconceived theories.

Lawrence claimed that all serious art must have behind it a metaphysic, a body of ideas:

> Every work of art adheres to some system of morality. But if it be really a work of art it must contain the essential criticism on the morality to which it adheres.*

The short novel, as Lawrence now developed it, is a form in which it is all too easy to protect his metaphysic from such criticism, to create an autonomous fictional world. This 'The Fox' and 'The Ladybird' progressively do.

'The Fox', in its original short story version, ended with Henry's proposal of marriage, his almost immediate success, and Banford's shocked acquiescence. The analogy between the boy and the fox was strongly present, but the more unpleasant uses of that analogy were developed with the expansion of the story to almost three times its original length in 1921. By identifying the boy with the fox, Lawrence removes him from the human frame of moral reference and releases him into an amoral world of wildness and predation. This non-human order of things is supported by a story which funnels all opposition to Henry into the unsympathetic figure of Banford. March's 'Don't try any of your tomfoolery on me' is the brief struggle of the trapped prey. She is pursued with almost supernatural inevitability:

> It's no good walking out into the forest and saying to the deer: 'Please fall to my gun' ... You have to be subtle and cunning and absolutely

---

* D. H. Lawrence, *Phoenix* (Heinemann, 1936), p. 476.

fatally ready. It becomes like a fate. Your own fate overtakes and determines the fate of the deer you are hunting ... there is a strange battle, like mesmerism.

March's submission to the boy becomes a fatal necessity because it is relentlessly presented in these terms. The mode of the story, itself mesmeric, does not allow for the objection that this description of pursuit to kill is being used to describe the pursuit of a woman by a man for the purpose of marriage. The story has no place for such objections from beyond the limits of its own strange, circumscribed and displaced reality.

In this closed world, the murder of Banford is presented as an inevitable natural event. It is effectively and convincingly done, like so much else in the story. We believe that Henry and Banford might both have acted as they did, and the 'accident' is thoroughly prepared for, so that in that sense it is not arbitrary, as the death of Mrs Hepburn had been arbitrary. The death has also a clear symbolic function as the death of an old unfruitful way of life: the tree being felled is already dead. It is none the less a real death, which can never be analogous to a fox taking a chicken or the felling of a tree.

After the death of Banford, the story has virtually ended, and the objective, impersonal prose gives way to a more direct address from the author, instructing the reader to take the whole story as an endorsement of Henry. The major part has had little to do with the moral reality of the world we actually inhabit, yet the story claims to prescribe for that world when it confronts the future which awaits March and Henry as man and wife. As the result of the hunt is to be marriage, not death, Lawrence seeks an image of the new life this marriage is to be; yet the new images Lawrence here introduces suggest death much more strongly than life:

No, she had to be passive, to acquiesce, and to be submerged under the surface of love. She had to be like the seaweeds ... swaying forever delicately under water ... never looking forth from the water until they died, only then washing, corpses, upon the surface. But while they lived, always submerged, always beneath the wave ... But it was always under-water, always under-water. And she, being a woman, must be like that.

At the very end of 'The Fox' we can see the difficulty Lawrence had in opening out the world of the tale into the reader's own world, where a living future must be contemplated. The final page does not leave us with the image of March submerged like the swaying seaweed, but shows her struggling to resist this state. That sleep–like submergence is still the tale's ideal, but it is an ideal which Lawrence leaves for possible future fulfilment, unable to realize it in the concrete present of his story.

'The Ladybird', ending with 'the thought of eternity', avoids the problem of moving from the story's note of mysticism to the contemplation of a human and worldly future. It also builds for itself a different world within and running counter to the familiar world; but here it is done gradually, and not through the development of the animal analogue. The ladybird is merely an emblem of Count Dionys, not a fully developed analogy, and its significance remains fixed throughout the novella, though it is only fully revealed towards the end. The story distances itself from familiar daily life largely by its use of mythology. Analogies are developed between the central characters and figures from myth, so that by the end, the story's reality is in its dark, underground, mythic world, the familiar world of daylight and ordinary incident having withdrawn and become shadowy.

The known world in which both 'The Ladybird' and 'The Fox' are set is the England of the latter part of the war and the first months afterwards. 'The Ladybird' takes up a note sounded at the end of 'The Fox' when Henry speaks of leaving 'this England which he so hated, because in some way it seemed to have stung him with poison'. It is an England 'tight with innumerable little houses', in which wild things like the fox have little chance among the 'loudly barking dogs'. In 'The Ladybird', the England we see through the eyes of the German prisoner Count Dionys Psanek is even more claustrophobic:

'Little houses like little boxes, each with its domestic Englishman and his domestic wife, each ruling the world because all are alike, so alike ... Little fields with innumerable hedges. Like a net with an irregular mesh, pinned down over this island and everything under the net.'

In both 'The Fox' and 'The Ladybird', running parallel with the major preoccupation with individual human relationships and closely bound up with it, is Lawrence's fear of the increasing degree to which life was becoming standardized, undifferentiated. The language of this passage reflects his own feelings about his native country where he had been forced to remain against his will for five years. All three novelettes express to some extent his sense of post-war Europe. 'The Captain's Doll' is set in Allied-occupied Germany and economically collapsed Austria, and many incidental observations are interesting in relation to his prophetic 1924 'Letter from Germany', in which he was to describe stirrings of dangerous and uncontrollable energy which he detected in the young Germans he met. It is in 'The Ladybird', however, that the war and its effects impinge most strongly. A comparison with the earlier story 'The Thimble' is interesting for what it reveals of Lawrence's changing response to the war.

'The Thimble' was written in October 1915. The story is quite different from that of 'The Ladybird', having only two characters, unnamed, but recognizably the same couple who become Lady Daphne and her husband Basil in 'The Ladybird'. Count Dionys, the ladybird itself, and almost all the classical allusions are absent, and the thimble itself has a very different significance. However, the situation at the start is more or less the same in each story. The woman in both cases is based on Lady Cynthia Asquith. Lawrence sent her 'The Thimble', calling it 'a rather good word-sketch of you'.* This time the word-sketch caused no offence:

> Lawrence's story arrived by the morning post. It is called 'The Thimble' and it is extremely well written, I think, though the symbolism of the thimble is somewhat obscure ... I think some of his character hints are damnably good. He has kept fairly close to the model in the circumstances.†

It is the story of a woman's first meeting with her badly disfigured husband on his return from the war. It opens with her thinking back over their past relationship as she awaits his imminent arrival. They had married in the excitement of the

* *Collected Letters*, p. 372.
† Lady Cynthia Asquith, *Diaries: 1915–1918* (Hutchinson, 1968), p. 95.

early days of the war, he, who had been a 'slack and unconvinc-
ing' man, suddenly gaining a new and 'fascinating importance'
from his soldier's uniform.* Their fortnight's honeymoon before
his departure to France had been a 'Bacchic revel', but during
his absence she had fallen ill, and on recovery had realized with
fear how little she knew the man she had married. As she muses
in this way, she nervously pushes her hand down the side of the
sofa, and, in a long and highly charged passage, Lawrence
describes how she finds an old and rather valuable thimble.
When her husband arrives, it is clear that he has suffered an ego
death, having been shattered in body and mind by the war.
Although at first she is hard and unresponsive, he silent and
inert, they gradually realize that this can be a new beginning, a
rebirth after the death of their old false life. During their conversation, the woman has shown the thimble, her 'treasure-
trove', to her husband. At the end he throws it away in renuncia-
tion of the past it represents.

It is a tale of resurrection, but not the Christian resurrection
to a life beyond literal death and beyond this world; rather a
rebirth in this life from the ashes of an old dead life, the life of
'this Europe now, this England'.†

Much of Lawrence's creative energy during the early part of
the war went into philosophical writings in which he tried to
clarify to himself what had happened in private and public life
to produce the 'colossal idiocy' of the war. The latest of these was
'The Crown', written in the summer of 1915, and from which
emerges the conviction that the war was so fearful and devastating that there could be no patching up of the old way of life, but
only a sweeping away and a completely new start: resurrection
on an individual, national and universal scale. Lawrence saw
individuals as microcosms of the larger social units to which they
belonged; the larger units as merely aggregates of individuals. He
therefore believed that as the war brought such profound change
in the individuals who experienced it, the values and institutions
of Edwardian England would also be destroyed.

* *The Mortal Coil*, p. 196.
† *Collected Letters*, p. 338.

Lady Cynthia Asquith was the recipient of many impassioned letters on this theme, one of which, on 30 October 1915, accompanied 'The Thimble':

> This is the story: I don't know what you'll think of it. The fact of resurrection, in this life, is all in all to me now. I don't know what the story is like, as a story. I don't want to read it over – not yet ... The fact of resurrection is everything now: whether we dead can rise from the dead and love, and live, in a new life, here.
>
> I tremble very much in front of this. If it could come to pass, one would give anything. If it cannot come to pass, one must go away: you and your husband also. Having known this death, one cannot remain in death. That were profanity. One must go away.
>
> If the war could but end this winter, we might rise to life again, here in this our world. If it sets in for another year, all is lost. One should give anything now, give the Germans England and the whole empire, if they want it, so we may save the hope of a resurrection from the dead, we English, all Europe. What is the whole empire, and kingdom, save the thimble in my story? If we could but bring our souls through, to life.*

This letter shows what a great weight of generalizing intention this story carried. Only two characters are involved, and there are no references to public life, Europe or the empire; yet their case is to be paradigmatic, their hope the image of a great hope. The thimble is not 'the whole empire and kingdom', but that in the individual which corresponds to these forms of public pride and possession. It is a hard, resistant relic of the past, a hard shell over the natural sensitivity of the body, and valuable because of its precious metal. The pursuit of such possessions is linked with a concentrated masturbatory sexuality in the description of the woman's fingers thrusting purposefully down the side of the sofa to find it. There is, therefore, complex and considerable symbolic force in the gesture of throwing away the thimble which ends the story.

'The Ladybird' starts from the same point, but moves in a quite different direction. It was written out of the bitterness and disillusion of crushed hope. By 1921, indeed long before that, Lawrence's trembling optimism had died. His efforts to involve

*ibid., pp. 372–3.

himself in public life had given way to a fierce withdrawal. He had seen the clamping down on private freedom which the continuation of the war brought with it, and had suffered personally from this with the banning of *The Rainbow*, his expulsion from Cornwall on suspicion of spying, his failure to find a publisher for *Women in Love*, humiliating medical examinations, and the refusal of passports to America.

Through it all, Lawrence had poured out his hopes and fears to Lady Cynthia because he felt her to be a natural aristocrat, capable of standing outside the merely local and temporal. In 1917, however, he had written to her:

I feel angry with you, the way you have betrayed everything that is real, by admitting the superiority of that which is merely temporal and foul and external upon us. If all the aristocrats have sold the vital principle of life to the mere current of foul affairs, what good are the aristocrats? As for the people, they will serve to make a real bust-up, quite purposeless and aimless. But when the bust-up is made and the place more or less destroyed we can have a new start.*

In 'The Ladybird' the idea that destruction is a necessary prelude to resurrection is still very strongly present, but the process of destruction is now seen to be far from complete. No easy gesture can get rid of the past. The thimble gives way to the ladybird, descendant of the Egyptian scarab, which, the story tells us, is not the symbol of 'the creative principle' but of 'the principle of decomposition'. The ladybird shares this very different thimble with a snake, bringing with it all the snake's suggestion of dark sexuality, and the 'king in exile' lord of the underworld from Lawrence's poem 'Snake', written the previous year.

Basil, the husband, returns, not changed and ready for a new life, but deathly, clinging more tightly than ever to his old ideals, emptied of warmth and vitality. His place as instigator of a new life is taken by Count Dionys Psanek, the dark little stranger with his mystic emblem and new ideas of power and mastery.

Of the three short novels it is in 'The Ladybird' that Lawrence most explicitly expounds his belief that a new approach to the

*ibid., p. 510.

question of power was the necessary cure for the emptiness of individual lives and the dangerous friction of public life. Lawrence had just completed *Aaron's Rod*, where the effects of war are rendered through pervasive imagery of explosion and fragmentation, and where he developed his idea that women and the majority of men must surrender their lives to those with the innate strength to bear such responsibility. But Dionys, like Lilly in *Aaron's Rod*, has no thought of bringing about this desired state of affairs in the public sphere. In fact, 'The Ladybird' moves towards a complete rejection of the world, withdrawing to an underworld the other side of death. Lawrence arrives at this perplexing conclusion by a process of transforming what we take to be merely mythological allusions at the beginning of the story, into the story's only 'reality' at the end.

The classical allusions with which the story is thickly studded have both a generalized significance and also a very specific and detailed relevance. Thus it is clear that the references to Isis, Astarte, Venus, Aphrodite, Cybele, are to their character as moon-goddesses, as in the 'Moony' chapter of *Women in Love*. But the individual myths of these different goddesses are also powerfully suggestive in the context of the story: Isis, the earth-goddess searching out and reassembling the dismembered body of her husband Osiris; Aphrodite, the love-goddess born from the foam of corrosive sea water; the frenzied rites of self-castration among the followers of Cybele. Proserpine, or Persephone, is well known as the stolen bride of Hades, Lord of the Underworld, whose yearly return to the daylight world brought the earth to fruitfulness again; but the myth in which she is linked with Dionysos is much less well known, and has far greater resonance in 'The Ladybird'. Finally, there is the figure of Dionysos himself, whose centrality in the story is explicit in the name Count Dionys. Dionysos, again, is a familiar figure in mythology. He is Bacchus, god of wine and revelry, commonly pictured as a wild figure, clothed in vines, surrounded by animals and frenzied women. The story of his birth, nursed in Zeus' thigh, is also relatively well known;* yet none of the familiar

---

* See note 38 to 'The Ladybird'; also *Phoenix*, p. 60.

attributes of Dionysos gives any clear sense of his relevance to Count Dionys, who is far removed from the world of Bacchic revelry.

In 'The Thimble', the honeymoon of the Lady Daphne figure and her husband had been a 'Bacchic revel', and again in 'The Ladybird', Lady Daphne says of her husband: 'He was the Dionysos, full of sap, milk and honey, and northern golden wine: he, her husband. Not that little unreal Count.' What Lawrence is doing is playing against each other two distinct Dionysos myths, rejecting the familiar figure and embracing the Dionysos of the Orphic mysteries, Dionysos Zagreus, son and spouse of Persephone, torn apart by the jealous titans but resurrected to be god of the underworld, and, like Persephone, a promise of the continual renewal of life. This was the Dionysos of whom Herakleitos said: 'Hades and Dionysos are one.' By identifying his hero with this Dionysos, Lawrence creates a dark lord of the underworld that Daphne worships as a true god; not as her husband had falsely worshipped her, but as a god of power. In this way, all Dionys' claims are underpinned. Even more than Hepburn or Henry he has the right to dominate, for he is a god-man.

Nowhere else in his fiction does Lawrence make such full use of classical mythology, or expect so much esoteric knowledge from his readers. The device is hardly successful. Classical references which began as metaphors have taken on a life of their own. Lawrence uses similar allusions very beautifully and movingly in his late poetry, but in a work of fiction with a story to tell, with some residue of moral and psychological realism, the mythic and realistic elements become incongruous.

How literally are we to take the ending, where Dionys and Daphne appear to have no future but to wait for physical death and reunion in the underworld? This story is perhaps the least successful example of a form which Lawrence was later to use with a much surer touch.

MELISSA PARTRIDGE

'St Mawr', 'The Princess', 'The Virgin and the Gipsy', 'The Escaped Cock'

Lawrence's discovery of the short novel form in 1921 seems to me to have been disastrous for his art. In a short story there is little room for anything but story-telling. In a full-length novel there are checks and balances, the obligation to pay one's debts to reality. But the short novel form enabled Lawrence to conceive stories as mere vehicles for his current ideas – ideas which were, at that particular phase of his life, misanthropic and desperate – or, in the case of 'The Ladybird', for the merest wish-fulfilment, arrogating to himself in his fictional underworld the power he had so completely failed to achieve in the real world, with a surrogate Lady Cynthia Asquith as his resistless bride in place of the all too resistant Frieda. The 1921 novelettes are doctrinaire, ruthless, and humanly thin, by Lawrence's own best standards.

The phase of Lawrence's belief in leadership, male supremacy, and the sexually passive role of women lasted from the end of the war until about 1925. It reached its culmination in *The Plumed Serpent*, the first version of which was written in the early summer of 1923, where Lawrence attempted to develop those ideas into a full-blown religious and political system preached by Don Ramon Carrasco, Lawrence's representative in the novel: 'I do believe what Ramon means – for all of us'.*

In the second version of the novel, however, written at the end of 1924 and beginning of 1925, we find many hints of reservations and scepticism which, the following year, were to grow into a repudiation of Don Ramon (and with him Hepburn, Henry and Count Dionys):

The hero is obsolete, and the leader of men is a back number. After all, at the back of the hero is the militant ideal: and the militant ideal, or the ideal militant, seems to me also a cold egg. We're sort of sick of all forms of militarism and militantism ... The leader-cum-follower relationship is a bore. And the new relationship will be some sort of

* *Collected Letters*, p. 859.

tenderness, sensitive, between men and men and men and women, and not the one up one down, lead on I follow, ich dien sort of business.*

Lawrence returned to the short novel form in the summer of 1924 (that is, between the two drafts of *The Plumed Serpent*), at his ranch in New Mexico, to write 'St Mawr' and 'The Princess'. Fortunately, having got his 'hero' theme out of his system in *The Plumed Serpent*, he felt free to take up other themes in these stories. 'St Mawr' is about a woman who does *not* meet a man capable of transforming her life, but who manages, nevertheless, to bring about its transformation, with the help of first a horse, then a landscape. No other Lawrence heroine is denied her saving man. Lou's phrase 'since the mystic new man will never come to me' gives her story a dimension lacking in all those stories where Lawrence is able to take the easy option of resolving his heroine's problems by producing a 'mystic new man' for her out of his hat. Here, for the only time in his major fiction, Lawrence denies himself the opportunity to approach his religious vision – his vision of the truly human and therefore truly religious life – through sexual metaphor.

Lou Carrington, like so many Lawrence heroines, is living in a world so empty, false and trivial that she cannot believe it is real. It can only be a bad dream from which she waits to be woken. The style of the opening is ironic, flippant, undercutting, its life all on the surface. The arrival of St Mawr changes everything. He seems to inhabit a different world and cannot be accommodated in Rico's world of 'attitude'. To describe him, a language other than that appropriate to Rico is demanded of Lawrence, a highly charged poetic language which erupts through the brittle irony:

She could not bear the triviality and superficiality of her human relationships. Looming like some god out of the darkness was the head of that horse, with the wide, terrible, questioning eyes. And she felt that it forbade her to be her ordinary, commonplace self. It forbade her to be just Rico's wife, young Lady Carrington, and all that.

The questions St Mawr silently asks her are: 'What is real?' and 'Are you alive?' and 'What in you can answer to my horseness?'.

* ibid., p. 1045.

He challenges her to meet him half-way – 'half-way across from our human world to that terrific equine twilight'. St Mawr's role in the story is exactly that of Evangelist in *Pilgrim's Progress*, who awakens Christian to the realization that he inhabits the city of destruction, strengthens his resolve to sever all the ties which bind him to it, and shows him the way towards the new life. Once Christian has begun his spiritual journey, Evangelist's role is done, and we hear no more of him. Lawrence, too, uses the archetypal myth of the spiritual journey, and once Lou is embarked upon it, St Mawr can lapse back into being an ordinary horse, rather than a messenger from the gods.

Why should Lawrence cast a splendid and dangerous stallion in the role of Evangelist? The image of Major Thomas Philip Barber, the local coal-owner, making his horse's mouth bleed as he forced it to stand at Moorgreen crossing while a colliery engine clanked past, had imprinted itself on Lawrence's imagination as a child, so that horse and rider became for him a symbol of the human will bullying the body, or the instincts, or the life of nature, long before he knew what a symbol was. The Bible confirmed the symbol: 'Be ye not as the horse, or as the mule, which have no understanding: whose mouth must be held in with bit and bridle.'* His early acquaintance with Plato's dialogues would have given him the same symbol developed into an allegory of the soul as charioteer (intellect) driving a team of horses, one white and compliant (spirit), the other black and hardly to be controlled (passion). There comes a point where the black horse, long frustrated and reined in, 'takes the bit between his teeth and pulls shamelessly':

The driver, however, experiences even more intensely what he experienced before; he falls back like a racing charioteer at the barrier, and with a still more violent backward pull, jerks the bit from between the teeth of the lustful horse, drenches his abusive tongue and jaws with blood, and forcing his legs and haunches against the ground reduces him to torment.†

* Psalms xxxii, 9.
† Plato, *Phaedrus* (Penguin, 1973), p. 63.

His acquaintance, through Frieda, with the work of European psychologists no doubt gave Lawrence further understanding of horse symbolism. There is no space here to survey the rich use he made of it in *The Rainbow* and *Women in Love*. Certainly he already knew much of what he was to read in Jung's *Psychology of the Unconscious* in 1918:

> Legend attributes properties to the horse which psychologically belong to the unconscious of man: there are clairvoyant and clairaudient horses, pathfinding horses who show the way when the wanderer is lost, horses with mantic powers ... Horses also see ghosts. All these things are typical manifestations of the unconscious. We can therefore see why the horse, as a symbol of the animal component in man, has numerous connections with the devil ... The sexual nature of the devil is imparted to the horse as well, so that this symbol is found in contexts where the sexual interpretation is the only one that fits ... Lightning, too, is represented theriomorphically as a horse.*

The first version of Lawrence's essay on Fenimore Cooper's Anglo-American novels was published in February 1919. It begins:

> It is quite certain that the pre-Christian priesthoods understood the process of *dynamic* consciousness, which is pre-cerebral consciousness. It is certain that St John gives us in the *Apocalypse* a cypher-account of the process of the conquest of the lower or sensual dynamic centres by the upper or spiritual dynamic consciousness.†

One of the most important cyphers in that account is the horse. It was probably his reading of this essay which prompted Frederick Carter to write to Lawrence about his own work, in December 1922, and to send him, the following April, a manuscript of his unpublished *Dragon of the Alchemists*. On his next visit to England Lawrence spent two days, 3–5 January 1924, visiting Carter at Pontesbury in Shropshire, discussing Apocalyptic symbols, including the four horsemen, and walking several miles into the hills:

* Jung, C. G. *Psychology of the Unconscious*, now called *Symbols of Transformation* (Routledge & Kegan Paul, 1952): chapter called 'The Battle for Deliverance from the Mother'.

† D. H. Lawrence, *The Symbolic Meaning*, ed. Armin Arnold (Centaur Press, 1962), p. 75.

Lawrence liked the name – the Devil's Chair – for the stone on which we stood. And there we talked of the great hilltop rocks with similar names that are found all over Europe as seats of the changeful gods.*

Whether or not Lawrence had already conceived 'St Mawr', this landscape, the place-names, the house in the churchyard looking over gravestones, the good-natured curate, and Carter himself, all were fixed in his memory and ready for use in the novel.

A week later Lawrence wrote his London Letter to Spud Johnson for the periodical *The Laughing Horse*. Here Lawrence associates the horse with the centaur and with Pan, dead in Europe, but alive and kicking in the blue air of the Rockies:

> In modern symbolism, the Horse is supposed to stand for the passions. Passions be blowed. What does the Centaur stand for, Chiron or any other of that quondam four-footed gentry? Sense! Horse-sense! Sound, powerful, four-footed *sense*, that's what the Horse stands for. Horse-sense, I tell you. That's the Centaur. That's the blue Horse of the ancient Mediterranean, before the pale Galilean or the extra-pale German or Nordic gentleman conquered. First of all, Sense, Good Sense, Sound Sense, Horse Sense. And then, a laugh, a loud, sensible Horse Laugh. After that, these same passions, glossy and dangerous in the flanks. And after these again, hoofs, irresistible, splintering hoofs, that can kick the walls of the world down.†

In March Lawrence escaped from the 'dreadful mummy sarcophagus of Europe' back to New Mexico, where he knew the horse in us was not dead:

> In Lobo, in Taos, in Santa Fe the Turquoise Horse is waving snow out of his tail, and trotting gaily to the blue mountains of the far distance. And in Mexico his mane is bright yellow on his blue body, so streaming with sun, and he's lashing out again like the devil, till his hoofs are red.‡

In May the Lawrences moved two thousand feet higher up Lobo mountain to a new ranch, which Lawrence described to his niece:

> Forty years ago a man came out looking for gold, and staked here. There was some gold in the mountains. Then he got poor, and a man

---

* Frederick Carter, *D. H. Lawrence and the Body Mystical* (Denis Archer, 1932), p. 40: extract reprinted in Nehls, Vol. 2, pp. 313–19.

† *Collected Letters*, p. 769.

‡ ibid., p. 769.

called McClure had the place. He had 500 white goats here, raised alfalfa, and let his goats feed wild in the mountains. But the water supply is too bad, and we are too far from anywhere. So he gave up ... So we leave the ranch quite wild – only there's abundant feed for the five horses. And if we wanted to take the trouble, we could bring the water here as McClure did, and have a little farm ... If we ride two miles, we can get no farther. Beyond, all savage, unbroken mountains ... We went to get Frieda's grey horse – the Azul – shod. They call him in Spanish *el Azul* – the Blue ... I want a Mexican to come and live here while we are away, to keep the place from going wild, squirrels and bushy-tailed pack-rats from coming in, and to see the water doesn't freeze for the horses.*

The first thing Lawrence wrote at the new ranch was 'Pan in America', where he defines his pantheism as 'a vivid relatedness between the man and the living universe that surrounds him':†

The contact between all things is keen and wary: for wariness is also a sort of reverence, or respect. And nothing, in the world of Pan, may be taken for granted.‡

There was indeed real danger up there. Three horses on the neighbouring ranch were killed by lightning.

There was much work to be done at the ranch that summer, but Lawrence found time in June to write 'The Woman Who Rode Away' and, in July and August, 'St Mawr'.

It can be seen from this skeletal account of the genesis of 'St Mawr' how the horse came to focus so many of Lawrence's deepest and most lasting preoccupations; how, with a minimum of overt reference to mythology or psychology or any abstract ideas imported from outside the novel, rather through vivid scenes and through the perfect control of evocative language, Lawrence is able to endow his stallion with such a range and depth of significance. Yet this account of the genesis of the novel has left out a whole cluster of themes every bit as central to it. It is a measure of the complexity of the story, not as story but as pattern of meanings, that its genesis could be described convincingly in terms which have nothing to do with horses.

* ibid., pp. 805–6.
† *Phoenix*, p. 27.
‡ ibid., p. 30.

Lawrence had always been highly ambivalent about the monastic ideal, which fascinated him. Despite his allegiance to the body, he led a relatively ascetic life, and his hatred of the human world often led him to explore various possibilities of withdrawal from it. On 31 July 1915, thanking Viola Meynell for the loan of her cottage at Greatham, he had written:

> I feel as if I had been born afresh there, got a new, sure, separate soul: as a monk in a monastery, or St John in the wilderness. Now we must go back into the world to fight. We must set about cleaning the face of the earth a bit, or everything will perish.*

A year later he wrote:

> I have been reading *St Bernard's Letters*, and I realize that the greatest thing the world has seen is Christianity.†

Throughout this period Lawrence consistently thought of his projected ideal community – Rananim – as overtly monastic. By 1917 he was already locating it in the American west:

> And what I want is for us to have sufficient to go far west, to California or the South Seas, and live apart, away from the world. I hope in the end other people will come, and we can be a little community, a monastery, a school – a little Hesperides of the soul and body.‡

This recurrent imagery of monasticism was brought into clear focus for Lawrence by his visit to an actual monastery, the Abbey of Monte Cassino, the birthplace of European monasticism, in February 1920. Lawrence's account of that visit, in his introduction to the Maurice Magnus memoirs, reveals how closely his response to the monastic ideal was bound up with his sense of the past and of the spirit of place:

> That hill-top must have been one of man's intense sacred places for three thousand years.§

As soon as Lawrence arrived in Taos in 1922, the Indian pueblo affected him 'like one of the old monasteries': here he

---

* *Collected Letters*, p. 357.
† ibid., p. 466.
‡ ibid., p. 497.
§ D. H. Lawrence, *Phoenix II* (Heinemann, 1968), p. 326.

recognized another of those 'choice spots of the earth, where the spirit dwelt'. It reminded him of what happened in Europe in the Dark Ages:

Then those whose souls were still alive withdrew together and gradually built monasteries, and these monasteries and convents, little communities of quiet labour and courage, isolated, helpless, and yet never overcome in a world flooded with devastation, these alone kept the human spirit from disintegration, from going quite dark, in the Dark Ages.*

In January 1924, in the essay 'Books', Lawrence returned to the theme:

The flood of barbarism rose and covered Europe from end to end. But, bless your life, there was Noah in his Ark with the animals. There was young Christianity. There were the lonely fortified monasteries, like little arks floating and keeping the adventure afloat. There is no break in the great adventure in consciousness. Throughout the howlingest deluge, some few brave souls are steering the ark under the rainbow ... But now I live in 1924, and the Christian venture is done. The adventure is gone out of Christianity. We must start on a new venture towards God.†

Lou in 'St Mawr' starts out on just such a new venture. In 1922 Lawrence had written:

I think one must for the moment withdraw from the world, away towards the inner realities that *are* real: and return, maybe, to the world later, when one is quiet and sure.‡

In the New Mexico Rockies Lou is face to face with those realities. They are not wholly beautiful. If Lou allows herself to be dazzled by the glamour, she will be crushed like the New England woman before her. They are also sordid and destructive:

The gods of those inner mountains were grim and invidious and relentless, huger than man, and lower than man.

You do not serve these gods and expect them to love you. You

* *Phoenix*, p. 100.
† ibid., pp. 733-4.
‡ *Collected Letters*, p. 687.

fight them 'to win from the crude, wild nature the victory and the power to make another start'.

Lawrence's new venture, in which Lou is his and our representative, is in a sense a return to paganism, or more particularly, Pantheism. His primary effort, from now on, is to be to resanctify the world, to reawaken in his readers their long-lost power to recognize and respond appropriately to the sacred in themselves and the living environment on which they totally depend. It was a Herculean undertaking in 1924, when nature seemed to be disappearing under 'the century-deep deposits of layer upon layer of refuse: even of tin cans'; when the machine seemed to have triumphed utterly; when H. G. Wells and the vast majority for whom he spoke could complacently and arrogantly assume that history was man's progress towards the triumph of 'mind' over both nature and human nature. Pantheism, at that time, had come to mean nothing more than the Wordsworthian pieties. It was not a serious option as a religion for the twentieth century. Lawrence took it upon himself to make it so; not just an option, but a necessity for sanity and survival.

Up to this time, Lawrence's thinking had been thoroughly dualistic. He had been torn by contradictory impulses and mutually exclusive needs. In 'The Crown' he saw all creation in the image of the lion of the body (Plato's black horse) and the unicorn of the spirit (Plato's white horse) fighting for the crown of life, never to be reconciled. He could not at that time have reconciled in himself that which identified itself with everything we have seen to attach to the image of the horse, and that which identified itself with everything attaching to the image of the monk. In a central passage in his friend E. M. Forster's novel *Howards End*, the author had spoken of 'the rainbow bridge that should connect the prose in us with the passion. Without it we are meaningless fragments, half monks, half beasts, unconnected arches that have never joined into a man.'* In 'St Mawr' Lawrence attempts to connect and reconcile the monk and the beast in us. He finds there a perfect fictional vehicle for drawing together these two hitherto diverse currents of his thought into a single stream.

* E. M. Forster, *Howards End* (Penguin, 1941), p. 174.

That Lawrence knew exactly what he was doing is evident in his choice of the name St Mawr for his stallion. It is a strange name for a horse. St Mawr comes from Wales, and his name is first pronounced in the story 'with a Welsh twist'. 'Mawr' in Welsh is the masculine form of the adjective meaning 'big' or 'great'; but according to Dorothy Brett, who was living with the Lawrences at the time and typed out 'St Mawr' page by page as Lawrence wrote it, Lawrence himself pronounced the name 'Seymour'. 'Seymour' is a common English surname which derives from the Norman French 'de St Maur'. The village of St Maur in Normandy is named after St Maur or Maurus, the disciple of St Benedict. Chaucer's monk ('a good man to horse') has no time for the traditional monastic life:

> The Rule of good St Benet or St Maur
> As old and strict he tended to ignore.*

St Benedict, the father of western monasticism, established his great monastery at Monte Cassino in 529. The monk at Monte Cassino with whom Lawrence had become particularly friendly on his visit there in 1920, and to whom he had later sent a copy of *The Lost Girl*, was called Don Mauro Iguanez.

St Mawr represents not only the life of the body and the senses, but also the life of the spirit which modern barbarism seeks to extinguish. The whole meaning of the story is encapsulated in its title.

'The Princess', which Lawrence wrote immediately after 'St Mawr', is in a way its shadow or negative.

During their stay in London the previous December and January, the Lawrences had stayed with Catherine and Donald Carswell, whom they had met before the war. Catherine told Lawrence of a novel she had in mind:

> The theme had been suggested to me by reading of some savages who took a baby girl, and that they might rear her into a goddess for themselves, brought her up on a covered river boat, tending her in all respects, but never letting her mix with her kind and leading her to believe that she was herself no mortal, but a goddess.†

* G. Chaucer, *The Canterbury Tales*, trans. N. Coghill (Penguin, 1951), p. 30.
† Catherine Carswell, *The Savage Pilgrimage* (Chatto & Windus, 1932), p. 201.

Lawrence was fired by the idea, and offered to collaborate. Indeed, he sketched an outline the same day. Catherine felt inadequate, and left the story to Lawrence, who later completed it as 'The Princess'.

According to his original outline, Lawrence had at first intended to begin with the story of the girl's parents – material he later dropped. After the death of the mother, leaving a baby girl, the outline continues:

Then it seems to him [the father] the mother was not mortal. She was a mysterious woman from the faery, and the child, he secretly believes, is one of the Tuatha De Danaan.* This idea he gradually inculcates into the people round him, and into the child herself. It steals over them all gradually, almost unawares.

The girl accepts from the start a difference between herself and the rest of people. She does not feel quite mortal. Men are only men to her: she is of another race, the Tuatha De Danaan. She doesn't talk about it: nobody talks about it. But there it is, tacit, accepted.

Her father hires a poor scholar to be her tutor, and she has an ordinary education. But she has no real friends. There is no one of her race. Sometimes she goes to Glasgow, to Edinburgh, to London with her father. The world interests her, but she doesn't belong to it. She is a little afraid of it. It is not of her race.

When she is seventeen her father is suddenly killed, and she is alone, save for her tutor. She has an income of about three hundred a year. She decides to go to London. The war has broken out – she becomes a nurse. She nurses men, and knows their wounds and their necessities. But she tends them as if they were lambs or other delicate and lovable

---

* 'In the epics of ancient Ireland, the Celtic warrior kings and their brilliant chariot fighters move in a landscape beset with invisible fairy forts, wherein abide a race of beings of an earlier mythological age: the wonderful Tuatha De Danaan, children of the Goddess Dana, who retired, when defeated, into wizard hills of glass. And these are the very people of the *sidhe* or Shee, the Fairy Host, the Fairy Cavalcade, of the Irish peasantry to this day.

'"Who are they?" asks the poet Yeats. And he gives a trilogy of answers: "Fallen angels who were not good enough to be saved, nor bad enough to be lost," say the peasantry. "The gods of the earth," says the Book of Armagh. "The gods of pagan Ireland," say the antiquarians, "the *Tuatha De Danän*, who, when no longer worshipped and fed with offerings, dwindled away in the popular imagination, and now are only a few spans high."' (Joseph Campbell, *Occidental Mythology*, Souvenir Press, 1974, pp. 40–41.)

animals. Their blood is not her blood, their needs are not the needs of her race.

Men fall in love with her, and that is terrible to her. She is waiting for one of her own race. Her tutor supports her in the myth. Wait, he says, wait for the Tuatha De Danaan to send you your mate. You can't mate with a man. Wait till you see a demon between his brows.

At last she saw him in the street. She knew him at once, knew the demon between his brows. And she was afraid. For the first time in her life, she was afraid of her own nature, the mystery of herself. Because it seemed to her that her race, the Tuatha, had come back to destroy the race of men. She was terrified of her own destiny. She wanted never again to see the man with the demon between his brows.

So for a long time she did not see him again. And then her fear that she would never see him any more was deeper than anything else. Whatever she wanted, she wanted her own destiny with him, let happen what might.*

It is not at all clear from this outline whether the woman's destiny is to be an escape into a more real world, 'the man with the demon between his brows' being the 'mystic new man' who will perform for her the function performed for Lou by St Mawr, or whether it is to be suicidal, like that of the Princess or the woman who rode away. Certainly, the other world from which St Mawr is a messenger could easily have been linked to that of the Tuatha De Danaan, the pre-Christian nature deities of Ireland, as it is linked by Lewis to Celtic folklore. The outline could have gone either way, towards rebirth or madness.

In August 1924 Lawrence was away for ten days on his trip to see the Hopi Snake Dance. During his absence a neighbour, Bill Hawk, took Brett riding much further into the mountains behind the ranch than she or Lawrence had ever been. On his return Lawrence needed little persuading to make the same journey, with Brett and Rachel Hawk. In *Lawrence and Brett*, Brett records the trip with great enthusiasm:

We reach a flat spot and dismount. Around and about us are the mountain ridges, running hither and thither in wild, strange lines. It is immense and fierce and dynamic. The pink and white rocks of Red River shine across the valley; and below, far below in the valley, lies a

* Carswell, op. cit., pp. 203-4.

tiny green lake, blue green and dark: Columbine Lake, round which the
drama of your story 'The Princess' is written.

It seems not to have occurred to Brett how much of herself
Lawrence had put into the character of his princess, brilliantly
fusing what he knew of Brett's life with the princess he had
inherited from Catherine Carswell. It was the identification with
Brett which determined the final negative outcome.

Thus Catherine Carswell's story could be seen as the germ of
all three stories Lawrence wrote in the summer of 1924. In Lou
Carrington it is given its most positive development. Her sense
of what makes her different from other people is her sanity, her
openness to life, her deep need for a meaningful relationship with
the living universe. But the story itself is open to life: we cannot
predict what will happen to Lou. In a sense, however, the very
fact that she has answered the call is her salvation, although
Lawrence was well aware of the dangers of cutting oneself off
from one's fellow men and retiring to some wilderness place. It
could be escapist. It could be a temptation to egotism, narcissism
or solipsism; a way of closing oneself to life until one becomes
a sealed monad and goes mad like the Princess, or dies of it like
the man who loved islands.

In September 1925, Lawrence left America for the last time, to
spend the remaining five years of his life in Europe. At last he was
reconciled with Frieda's daughters. Barby, in particular, stayed
often with the Lawrences in Spotorno, and told Lawrence many
stories of her life in the Weekley household. In January 1926 he
wrote 'The Virgin and the Gipsy', based largely on those stories.

'The Virgin and the Gipsy' is more like a conventional novel
than the other novelettes, full of 'characters', family and social
relationships presented in 'scenes', and moral judgements
evinced through a finely modulated ironic tone, like a more
direct, barbed and colloquial Jane Austen. The mode is realistic,
with no dominant symbol, emblem or myth, except insofar as the
gipsy himself may be regarded as a symbol. Indeed, he functions
on two levels, like St Mawr. He is a real gipsy, hawking his
brooms, saucepans and copperware, with several brats to maintain; but for Yvette he is much more than that, much more than

any mere man. He is messenger from a world free from all the stifling hypocrisies of her home, class and religion, a projection of her hope of a fulfilled life as a woman free from guilt. Having given her the courage to assert her independent womanhood, he reverts to being just the semi-literate Joe Boswell.

The integrity of the story can be measured by the extent to which it does not fulfil the expectations aroused by its perhaps unfortunate title. The relationship between virgin and gipsy never becomes overtly sexual. We do not know, and it does not matter, whether at the end she is still a virgin or not. Nor is the gipsy blown up to figure as a 'mystic new man', a man with a demon between his brows or a noble savage, except to a slight degree in Yvette's adolescent imagination. Lawrence beautifully captures that phase of a girl's life – the infuriating selfishness, the sulks and outbursts of revolt, the general vagueness and wryly romantic longings.

Again, the ending is open. It is unlikely Yvette will ever see her gipsy again; certainly she pins no hopes upon him. There is no doubt much conflict and suffering ahead for her; but she has found the courage to live her own life, and is unlikely to let go of that.

Lawrence had for several years been fascinated by the Etruscans. In March 1927, in the company of his American Buddhist friend Earl Brewster, he undertook a tour of several of the major Etruscan sites, ending at Volterra on Easter Sunday, 10 April:

> I was really happy looking at Etruscan tombs by the coast north of Rome – Cerveteri, Tarquinia etc. No rush there! Even the ass brays slowly and leisurely, and the tombs are far more twinkling and alive than the houses of men.*

He returned home to the Villa Mirenda, near Florence, but not to write *Etruscan Places*. What he wrote first was 'a story of the Resurrection – what sort of a man "rose up", after all that other pretty little experience'.† Earl Brewster recalled:

*D. H. Lawrence, *The Centaur Letters* (Texas, 1970), p. 29.
† D. H. Lawrence, *The Escaped Cock*, ed. G. M. Lacy (Black Sparrow Press, 1973), p. 65.

My memory is that Easter morning found us at Grosseto [in fact Volterra]: there we passed a little shop, in the window of which was a toy rooster escaping from an egg. I remarked that it suggested a title – The Escaped Cock – a story of the Resurrection. Lawrence replied that he had been thinking about writing a story of the Resurrection.*

Thus 'The Escaped Cock'† is a direct product of Lawrence's Etruscan experience. In the tombs the egg was also a frequent resurrection symbol. The man who has died 'holds up the egg of resurrection, within which the germ sleeps as the soul sleeps in the tomb, before it breaks the shell and emerges again'.‡ The shell, in Lawrence's interpretation, is the old dead life, hardened into habit and egotism. The 'germ' which emerges is 'the soul itself, the conscious spark of every creature'.§ It is also life itself, inextinguishable, 'the fiery spark of procreation'.‖ Resurrection, for Lawrence, is as always a metaphor for a spiritual death and rebirth, which is envisaged as a recovery, through the body, of a lost connection with everything else that lives.

The cock in Lawrence's story escapes not from a shell, but from the cord which ties him by the leg. He represents the dauntless life-urge – 'resplendent with arched and orange neck by the time the fig trees were letting out leaves from their end-tips' – denied its full expression. He crows for the kingdom, power and glory which is his birthright:

* Earl and Achsah Brewster, *D. H. Lawrence: Reminiscences and Correspondence* (Secker, 1934), p. 124.

† 'The Escaped Cock' was always Lawrence's preferred title. The story was published under that title by the Black Sun Press in September 1929. In the last month of his life, February 1930, Lawrence was negotiating with the London bookseller Charles Lahr about publishing the first unlimited edition. Apparently Lahr was unhappy about the title, and suggested 'The Man Who Had Died', which Lawrence reluctantly approved, insisting on retaining 'The Escaped Cock' as a subtitle. The Lahr edition never appeared. The first English edition was published by Secker in March 1931, under the title 'The Man Who Died', a title never approved by Lawrence, which has nevertheless been retained in every subsequent edition until Gerald Lacy's definitive edition in 1973.

‡ D. H. Lawrence, *Mornings in Mexico* and *Etruscan Places* (Penguin, 1960), p. 142.

§ ibid., p. 154.

‖ ibid., p. 151.

Body, soul and spirit were tied by that string. Underneath, however, the life in him was grimly unbroken. It was the cord that should break.

His crow wakes the man who had died. Again, he is a messenger, crowing from the world Christ had denied, as he had denied 'the greater life of the body':

The world, the same as ever, the natural world, thronging with greenness, a nightingale singing winsomely, wistfully, coaxingly calling from the bushes beside a runnel of water, in the world, the natural world of morning and evening, forever undying, from which he had died.

The bird, herald of a new day, is already risen. The man, recognizing in the cock 'the necessity to live, and even to cry out the triumph of life', must rediscover and re-establish his connection with the phenomenal world, must learn to ride the 'wave of life of which the bird was the crest'. His earlier denial of that world he now sees was an evasion of the life issue, leading inevitably to the Crucifixion.

Lawrence summarized 'The Escaped Cock' to Earl Brewster in these words:

I wrote a story of the Resurrection, where Jesus gets up and feels very sick about everything, and can't stand the old crowd any more – so cuts out – and as he heals up, he begins to find what an astonishing place the phenomenal world is, far more marvellous than any salvation or heaven – and thanks his stars he needn't have a 'mission' any more.*

In *Etruscan Places* Lawrence takes up the contrast between the preacher and the nightingale:

And before Buddha or Jesus spoke the nightingale sang, and long after the words of Jesus and Buddha are gone into oblivion the nightingale will sing. Because it is neither preaching nor teaching nor commanding nor urging. It is just singing. And in the beginning was not a Word, but a chirrup.†

In the story, as in the travel book, the villains are the Romans, who trample on the rose of life and burden the earth with their monuments:

* *Collected Letters*, p. 975.
† *Etruscan Places*, p. 126.

Because a fool kills a nightingale with a stone, is he therefore greater than the nightingale? Because the Roman took the life out of the Etruscan, was he therefore greater than the Etruscan? Not he! Rome fell, and the Roman phenomenon with it.*

Lawrence recognized in the Etruscans a people who 'lived their own lives without wanting to dominate the lives of others'.† Jesus, in his way, had wanted to dominate as much as the Romans. Both conquering and saving are forms of domination. The man who had died does not see his crucifixion as a triumph:

My triumph is that I am not dead, I have outlived my mission and know no more of it. It is my triumph. I have survived the day and the death of my interference, and am still a man ... The teacher and the saviour are dead in me; now I can go about my business, into my own single life ... For my reach ends in my finger-tips, and my stride is no longer than the ends of my toes. Yet I would embrace multitudes, I who have never truly embraced even one.

He is rediscovering the Etruscan insouciance. The Etruscans knew the gods 'in their very finger-tips'; they danced to the very ends of their fingers and toes; they entered into the flow of touch which comes not from pawing and laying hold, but 'from the middle of the human being'.‡

'The Escaped Cock' is the story of how Jesus becomes an Etruscan. At the end he is letting the current carry him, and smiling the enigmatic Etruscan smile.

Lawrence wrote only the first part of 'The Escaped Cock' in the spring of 1927. It was almost a year before he had the idea of adding a second, and this was actually written in Switzerland in the summer of 1928. The cock had now fulfilled his role of messenger and pointer of the way. The challenge remaining for Lawrence was to imagine Christ's resurrection in the flesh and atonement with his own body, with woman, and with the natural world, the 'living, incarnate cosmos'.§ It seems likely that

---

* ibid., p. 126.
† Nehls, op. cit., Vol. 3, p. 137.
‡ *Etruscan Places*, p. 144.
§ D. H. Lawrence, *Apocalypse*, ed. Mara Kalnins (Cambridge University Press, 1980), p. 149.

Lawrence had been reading Frazer yet again. In any case, he was already familiar with *The Golden Bough*, where Frazer's accounts of the mutilation, death and resurrection of the pagan fertility gods, particularly Adonis, Attis and Osiris, cannot fail to impress the reader with their similarity to the story of Christ. Frazer himself trod warily here, but allowed himself to say that 'Christians and pagans alike were struck by the remarkable coincidence between the death and resurrection of their respective deities.'* Starting from this hint of Frazer's, Lawrence brilliantly saw how he could solve his problem by completing the identification of Christ with Osiris. Christ is crucified, and resurrected as a young fertility god at the hands of the priestess of Isis in Search.

It was a daring undertaking in 1928, risking blasphemy, and indeed it caused much outrage at the time. But such is the tact and sensitivity with which it is carried through that many Christians have subsequently responded warmly to it as a corrective to the tendency of orthodox Christianity to be life-denying, and to evade the implications of the phrase 'the resurrection of the body'.

It would perhaps have been an even greater challenge to Lawrence to follow his hero still further, and imagine a life for him wherever he is heading at the end. The essay 'The Risen Lord', written in August 1929, might almost be regarded as an outline for a third part to 'The Escaped Cock':

If Jesus rose in the full flesh, He rose to know the tenderness of a woman, and the great pleasure of her, and to have children by her. He rose to know the responsibility and the peculiar delight of children, and also the exasperation and nuisance of them. If Jesus rose as a full man, in the flesh, He rose to have friends, to have a man-friend whom He would hold sometimes to His breast, in strong affection, and who would be dearer to Him than a brother, just out of the sheer mystery of sympathy. And how much more wonderful, this, than having disciples! If Jesus rose a full man in the flesh, He rose to do His share in the world's work, something He really liked doing. And if He remembered His first life, it would be neither teaching nor preaching, but probably carpentering again, with joy, among the shavings. If Jesus rose a full

* J. G. Frazer, *The Golden Bough*, abridged edition (Macmillan, 1957), p. 475.

man in the flesh, He rose to continue His fight with the hard-boiled conventionalists like Roman judges and Jewish priests and money-makers of every sort. But this time, it would no longer be the fight of self-sacrifice that would end in crucifixion. This time it would be a freed man fighting to shelter the rose of life from being trampled on by the pigs.*

But Lawrence had only six months to live, and wrote no more fiction.

A NOTE ON THE TEXT

'The Fox' was written in its first, short story version in November 1918. In July 1919 Lawrence's agent, Pinker, asked him to shorten it for magazine publication, but he felt able to make only very small cuts without mutilating it. This version appeared in *Hutchinson's Story Magazine* in November 1920. In November 1921, working from his original manuscript, not the slightly shorter published version, Lawrence revised the story and extended it to three times its original length. At that time Lawrence had just finished 'The Captain's Doll', and the following month he wrote 'The Ladybird'. The three novelettes were published by Secker in March 1923 as *The Ladybird*, and by Seltzer in America in November 1923 as *The Captain's Doll*. Lawrence corrected Seltzer's proofs, so the Seltzer edition represents his latest intentions, and has been used here.

As Brian Finney discovered, a whole page of the manuscript of 'The Ladybird' is missing from the printed text. The likeliest explanation is that the printer inadvertently turned over two pages of manuscript, and that, since the resulting text still made perfect sense, Lawrence did not notice the omission when proof-correcting. However, it is possible that the page was left out intentionally, or that Lawrence condoned the accidental pruning. The missing page is indeed one of the worst and most repetitive. It has not been restored here.

Lawrence wrote 'St Mawr' in the summer of 1924 and 'The Princess' in September/October 1924 at his New Mexico ranch.

* *Phoenix II*, p. 575.

'The Princess' was serialized in three numbers of *The Calendar of Modern Letters*, March–May 1925. The two stories were published together by Secker in May 1925, and Knopf published 'St Mawr' by itself in America the following month. Lawrence corrected Secker's proofs, but was too ill to correct Knopf's properly. We have therefore used the Secker edition here.

'The Virgin and the Gipsy' was written in Spotorno in January 1926. It seems that Secker wanted to do another book of three novelettes like *The Ladybird*, possibly combining 'The Virgin and the Gipsy' with 'Glad Ghosts' and 'Sun'; but for some reason this was never done, and Secker did not publish *The Virgin and the Gipsy* (by itself) until November 1930, after Lawrence's death. Six months earlier it had been published in Florence by Orioli. Both these editions carry the note: 'This work lacks the author's final revision, and has been printed from the manuscript exactly as it stands.' This is misleading, since these editions were not printed from the holograph manuscript, which survives, but from a revised typescript which has not survived. The Orioli text has been used here.

Lawrence wrote the first part of 'The Escaped Cock' in April 1927; this was published in *Forum* in February 1928, and the second part was added in June/July 1928. The complete story was published by the Black Sun Press in Paris in September 1929. There was no English edition until Secker's in 1931 under the title *The Man Who Died*. The Black Sun Press text has been used here.

KEITH SAGAR

The Captain's Doll

I

'HANNELE –'
  'Ja – a!'
'Wo bist du?'
  'Hier.'
'Wo denn?'[1]
Hannele did not lift her head from her work. She sat in a low
chair under a reading-lamp, a basket of coloured silk pieces
beside her, and in her hands a doll, or mannikin, which she was
dressing. She was doing something to the knee of the mannikin,
so that the poor little gentleman flourished head downwards with
arms wildly tossed out. And it was not at all seemly, because the
doll was a Scotch soldier in tight-fitting tartan trews.[2]

There was a tap at the door, and the same voice, a woman's,
calling:
  'Hannele!'
  'Ja – a!'
'Are you here? – Are you alone?' asked the voice, in German.
  'Yes – come in.'

Hannele did not sound very encouraging. She turned round
her doll as the door opened, and straightened his coat. A dark-
eyed young woman peeped in through the door, with a roguish
coyness. She was dressed fashionably for the street, in a thick
cape-wrap, and a little black hat pulled down to her ears.

'Quite, quite alone!' said the new-comer, in a tone of wonder.
'Where is he then?'

'That I don't know,' said Hannele.

'And you sit here alone, and wait for him? But no! That I call
courage! Aren't you afraid?' Mitchka strolled across to her friend.

'Why shall I be afraid?' said Hannele curtly.

'But no –! And what are you doing? Another puppet? He is

a good one, though! Ha – ha – ha! *Him!* It is him! No – no –
that is too beautiful! Now – that is too beautiful, Hannele. It is
him – exactly him. Only the trousers.'

'He wears those trousers, too,' said Hannele, standing her doll
on her knee. It was a perfect portrait of an officer of a Scottish
regiment, slender, delicately made, with a slight, elegant stoop
of the shoulders, and close-fitting tartan trousers. The face was
beautifully modelled, and a wonderful portrait, dark-skinned,
with a little close-cut moustache, and wide-open dark eyes, and
that air of aloofness and perfect diffidence which marks an officer
and a gentleman.

Mitchka bent forward, studying the doll. She was a handsome
woman with a warm, dark golden skin and clear black eyebrows
over her russet-brown eyes.

'No,' she whispered to herself, as if awestruck. 'That is him.
That is him. Only not the trousers. Beautiful, though, the
trousers. Has he really such beautiful fine legs?'

Hannele did not answer.

'Exactly him. Just as finished as he is. Just as complete. He
is just like that: finished off. – Has he seen it?'

'No,' said Hannele.

'What will he say then?' She started. Her quick ear had caught
a sound on the stone stairs. A look of fear came to her face. She
flew to the door and out of the room, closing the door to behind
her.

'Who is it?' her voice was heard calling anxiously down the
stairs.

The answer came in German. Mitchka immediately opened
the door again and came back to join Hannele.

'Only Martin,' she said.

She stood waiting. A man appeared in the doorway – erect,
military.

'Ah! – Countess Hannele,' he said in his quick, precise way,
as he stood on the threshold in the distance. 'May one come in?'

'Yes, come in,' said Hannele.

The man entered with a quick, military step, bowed, and
kissed the hand of the woman who was sewing the doll. Then,
much more intimately, he touched Mitchka's hand with his lips.

Mitchka meanwhile was glancing round the room. It was a very large attic, with the ceiling sloping and then bending in two handsome movements towards the walls. The light from the dark-shaded reading-lamp fell softly on the huge whitewashed vaulting of the ceiling, on the various objects round the walls, and made a brilliant pool of colour where Hannele sat in her soft red dress, with her basket of silks.

She was a fair woman with dark-blond hair and a beautiful fine skin. Her face seemed luminous, a certain quick gleam of life about it as she looked up at the man. He was handsome, clean-shaven, with very blue eyes strained a little too wide. One could see the war in his face.

Mitchka was wandering round the room, looking at everything, and saying: 'Beautiful! But beautiful! Such good taste! A man, and such good taste! No, they don't need a woman. No, look here, Martin, the Captain Hepburn has arranged all this room himself. Here you have the man. Do you see? So simple, yet so elegant. He needs no woman —'

The room was really beautiful, spacious, pale, soft-lighted. It was heated by a large stove of dark-blue tiles, and had very little furniture save large peasant cupboards or presses of painted wood, and a huge writing-table, on which were writing materials and some scientific apparatus and a cactus plant with fine scarlet blossoms. But it was a man's room. Tobacco and pipes were on a little tray, on the pegs in the distance hung military overcoats and belts, and two guns on a bracket. Then there were two telescopes, one mounted on a stand near a window. Various astronomical apparatus lay upon the table.

'And he reads the stars. Only think — he is an astronomer and reads the stars. Queer, queer people, the English!'

'He is Scottish,' said Hannele.

'Yes, Scottish,' said Mitchka. — 'But, you know, I am afraid when I am with him. He is at a closed end. I don't know where I can get to with him. Are you afraid of him, too, Hannele? Ach, like a closed road!'

'Why should I be?'

'Ah, you! Perhaps you don't know when you should be afraid. But if he were to come and find us here? — No, no — let us go.

Let us go, Martin. Come, let us go. I don't want the Captain Hepburn to come and find me in his room. Oh, no!' – Mitchka was busily pushing Martin to the door, and he was laughing with the queer mad laugh in his strained eyes. 'Oh, no! I don't like. I don't like it,' said Mitchka, trying her English now. She spoke a few sentences prettily. 'Oh, no, Sir Captain, I don't want that you come. I don't like it, to be here when you come. Oh, no. Not at all. I go. I go, Hannele. I go, my Hannele. – And you will really stay here and wait for him? – But when will he come? You don't know? – Oh, dear, I don't like it, I don't like it. I do not wait in the man's room. No, no – Never – jamais – jamais, voyez vous.[3] – Ach, you poor Hannele! And he has got wife and children in England? – Nevair! No, nevair shall I wait for him.'

She had bustlingly pushed Martin through the door, and settled her wrap and taken a mincing elegant pose, ready for the street, and waved her hand and made wide, scared eyes at Hannele, and was gone. The Countess Hannele picked up the doll again and began to sew its shoe. What living she now had she earned making these puppets.

But she was restless. She pressed her arms into her lap, as if holding them bent had wearied her. Then she looked at the little clock on his writing-table. It was long after dinner-time – why hadn't he come? She sighed rather exasperated. She was tired of her doll.

Putting aside her basket of silks, she went to one of the windows. Outside the stars seemed white, and very near. Below was the dark agglomeration of the roofs of houses, a fume of light came up from beneath the darkness of roofs, and a faint breakage of noise from the town far below. The room seemed high, remote, in the sky.

She went to the table and looked at his letter-clip with letters in it and at his sealing-wax and his stamp-box, touching things and moving them a little, just for the sake of the contract, not really noticing what she touched. Then she took a pencil, and in stiff Gothic characters began to write her name – Johanna zu Rassentlow – time after time her own name – and then once, bitterly, curiously, with a curious sharpening of her nose: Alexander Hepburn.

But she threw the pencil down, having no more interest in her writing. She wandered to where the large telescope stood near a further window, and stood for some minutes with her fingers on the barrel, where it was a little brighter from his touching it. Then she drifted restlessly back to her chair. She had picked up her puppet when she heard him on the stairs. She lifted her face and watched as he entered.

'Hello, you there!' he said quietly, as he closed the door behind him. She glanced at him swiftly, but did not move nor answer.

He took off his overcoat with quick, quiet movements, and went to hang it up on the pegs. She heard his step, and looked again. He was like the doll, a tall, slender, well-bred man in uniform. When he turned, his dark eyes seemed very wide open. His black hair was growing grey at the temples – the first touch.

She was sewing her doll. Without saying anything, he wheeled round the chair from the writing-table, so that he sat with his knees almost touching her. Then he crossed one leg over the other. He wore fine tartan socks. His ankles seemed slender and elegant, his brown shoes fitted as if they were part of him. For some moments he watched her as she sat sewing. The light fell on her soft, delicate hair, that was full of strands of gold and of tarnished gold and shadow. She did not look up.

In silence he held out his small, naked-looking brown hand, for the doll. On his forearm were black hairs.

She glanced up at him. Curious how fresh and luminous her face looked in contrast to his.

'Do you want to see it?' she asked, in natural English.

'Yes,' he said.

She broke off her thread of cotton and handed him the puppet. He sat with one leg thrown over the other, holding the doll in one hand, and smiling inscrutably with his dark eyes. His hair, parted perfectly on one side, was jet black and glossy.

'You've got me,' he said at last, in his amused, melodious voice.

'What?' she said.

'You've got me,' he repeated.

'I don't care,' she said.

'What? – You don't care?' – His face broke into a smile. He had an odd way of answering, as if he were only half attending, as if he were thinking of something else.

'You are very late, aren't you?' she ventured.

'Yes. I am rather late.'

'Why are you?'

'Well, as a matter of fact, I was talking with the Colonel.'

'About me?'

'Yes. It was about you.'

She went pale as she sat looking up into his face. But it was impossible to tell whether there was distress on his dark brow, or not.

'Anything nasty?' she said.

'Well, yes. It was rather nasty. Not about you, I mean. But rather awkward for me.'

She watched him. But still he said no more.

'What was it?' she said.

'Oh, well – only what I expected. They seem to know rather too much about you – about you and me, I mean. Not that anybody cares one bit, you know, unofficially. The trouble is, they are apparently going to have to take official notice.'

'Why?'

'Oh, well – it appears my wife has been writing letters to the Major-General. He is one of her family acquaintances – known her all his life. And I suppose she's been hearing rumours. In fact I know she has. She said so in her letter to me.'

'And what do you say to her then?'

'Oh, I tell her I'm all right – not to worry.'

'You don't expect *that* to stop her worrying, do you?' she asked.

'Oh, I don't know. Why should she worry?' he said.

'I think she might have some reason,' said Hannele. 'You've not seen her for a year. And if she adores you –'

'Oh, I don't think she adores me. I think she quite likes me.'

'Do you think you matter as little as that to her?'

'I don't see why not. – Of course she likes to feel *safe* about me –'

'But now she doesn't feel safe?'

'No – exactly. Exactly. That's the point. That's where it is. The Colonel advises me to go home on leave.'

He sat gazing with curious bright, dark, unseeing eyes at the doll which he held by one arm. It was an extraordinary likeness of himself, true even to the smooth parting of his hair and his peculiar way of fixing his dark eyes.

'For how long?' she asked.

'I don't know. – For a month,' he replied, first vaguely, then definitely.

'For a month!' She watched him, and seemed to see him fade from her eyes.

'And will you go?' she asked.

'I don't know. I don't know.' His head remained bent, he seemed to muse rather vaguely. 'I don't know,' he repeated. 'I can't make up my mind what I shall do.'

'Would you like to go?' she asked.

He lifted his brows and looked at her. Her heart always melted in her when he looked straight at her with his black eyes, and that curious, bright unseeing look that was more like second sight than direct human vision. She never knew what he saw when he looked at her.

'No,' he said simply. 'I don't *want* to go. I don't think I've any desire at all to go to England.'

'Why not?' she asked.

'I can't say.' – Then again he looked at her, and a curious white light seemed to shine on his eyes, as he smiled slowly with his mouth, and said: 'I suppose you ought to know, if anybody does.'

A glad, half-frightened look came on her face.

'You mean you don't want to leave me?' she asked, breathless.

'Yes. I suppose that's what I mean.'

'But you aren't sure?'

'Yes, I am, I'm quite sure,' he said, and the curious smile lingered on his face, and the strange light shone in his eyes.

'That you don't want to leave me?' she stammered, looking aside.

'Yes, I'm quite sure I don't want to leave you,' he repeated. He had a curious, very melodious Scottish voice. But it was the incomprehensible smile on his face, that convinced and frightened her. It was almost a gargoyle smile, a strange, lurking, changeless-seeming grin.

She was frightened, and turned aside her face. When she looked at him again, his face was like a mask, with strange, deep-graven lines and a glossy dark skin and a fixed look – as if carved half grotesque in some glossy stone. His black hair on his smooth, beautifully-shaped head seemed changeless.

'Are you rather tired?' she asked him.

'Yes, I think I am.' He looked at her with black, unseeing eyes, and a mask-like face. Then he glanced aside as if he heard something. Then he rose with his hand on his belt, saying: 'I'll take off my belt, and change my coat, if you don't mind.'

He walked across the room, unfastening his broad brown belt. He was in well-fitting, well-cut khaki. He hung up his belt and came back to her wearing an old light tunic, which he left unbuttoned. He carried his slippers in one hand. When he sat down to unfasten his shoes, she noticed again how black and hairy his forearm was, how naked his brown hand seemed. His hair was black and smooth and perfect on his head, like some close helmet, as he stooped down.

He put on his slippers, carried his shoes aside, and resumed his chair, stretching luxuriously.

'There,' he said. 'I feel better now.' And he looked at her. 'Well,' he said, 'and how are you?'

'Me?' she said. 'Do I matter?' She was rather bitter.

'Do you matter?' he repeated, without noticing her bitterness. 'Why, what a question! Of course you are of the very highest importance. What? Aren't you?' And smiling his curious smile – it made her for a moment think of the fixed sadness of monkeys, of those Chinese carved soapstone apes – he put his hand under her chin, and gently drew his finger along her cheek. She flushed deeply.

'But I'm not as important as you, am I?' she asked defiantly.

'As important as me! Why, bless you, I'm not important a bit. I'm not important a bit!' – the odd, straying sound of his words mystified her. What did he really mean?

'And I'm even less important than that,' she said bitterly.

'Oh, no, you're not. Oh, no, you're not. You're very important. You're very important indeed, I assure you.'

'And your wife?' — the question came rebelliously. 'Your wife? Isn't she important?'

'My wife? My wife?' He seemed to let the word stray out of him as if he did not quite know what it meant. 'Why, yes, I suppose she is important in her own sphere.'

'What sphere?' blurted Hannele, with a laugh.

'Why, her own sphere, of course. Her own house, her own home, and her two children: that's her sphere.'

'And you? – where do you come in?'

'At present I don't come in,' he said.

'But isn't that just the trouble?' said Hannele. 'If you have a wife and a home, it's your business to belong to it, isn't it?'

'Yes, I suppose it is, if I want to,' he replied.

'And you *do* want to?' she challenged.

'No, I don't,' he replied.

'Well then –?' she said.

'Yes, quite,' he answered. 'I admit, it's a dilemma.'

'But what will you *do*?' she insisted.

'Why, I don't know. I don't know yet. I haven't made up my mind what I'm going to do.'

'Then you'd better begin to make it up,' she said.

'Yes, I know that. I know that.'

He rose, and began to walk uneasily up and down the room. But the same vacant darkness was on his brow. He had his hands in his pockets. Hannele sat feeling helpless. She couldn't help being in love with the man; with his hands, with his strange, fascinating physique, with his incalculable presence. She loved the way he put his feet down, she loved the way he moved his legs as he walked, she loved the mould of his loins, she loved the way he dropped his head a little, and the strange dark vacancy of his brow, his not-thinking. But now his restlessness only made her unhappy. Nothing would come of it. Yet she had driven him to it.

He took his hands out of his pockets and returned to her like a piece of iron returning to a magnet. He sat down again in front of her and put his hands to her, looking into her face.

'Give me your hands,' he said softly, with that strange, mind-less soft suggestive tone which left her powerless to disobey. 'Give me your hands, and let me feel that we are together. Words mean so little. They mean nothing. And all that one thinks and plans doesn't amount to anything. Let me feel that we are together, and I don't care about all the rest.'

He spoke in his slow, melodious way, and closed her hands in his. She struggled still for voice.

'But you'll *have* to care about it. You'll *have* to make up your mind. You'll just *have* to,' she insisted.

'Yes, I suppose I shall. I suppose I shall. But now that we are together, I won't bother. Now that we are together, let us forget it.'

'But when we *can't* forget it any more?'

'Well – then I don't know. But – to-night – it seems to me – we might just as well forget it.'

The soft, melodious, straying sound of his voice made her feel helpless. She felt that he never answered her. Words of reply seemed to stray out of him, in the need to say *something*. But he himself never spoke. There he was, a continual blank silence in front of her.

She had a battle with herself. When he put his hand again on her cheek, softly, with the most extraordinary soft half-touch, as a kitten's paw sometimes touches one, like a fluff of living air, then, if it had not been for the magic of that almost indiscernible caress of his hand, she would have stiffened herself and drawn away and told him she could have nothing to do with him, while he was so half-hearted and unsatisfactory. She wanted to tell him these things. But when she began he answered invariably in the same soft, straying voice, that seemed to spin gossamer threads all over her, so that she could neither think nor act nor even feel distinctly. Her soul groaned rebelliously in her. And yet, when he put his hand softly under her chin, and lifted her face and smiled down on her with that gargoyle smile of his – she let him kiss her.

'What are you thinking about to-night?' he said. 'What are you thinking about?'

'What did your Colonel say to you, exactly?' she replied, trying to harden her eyes.

'Oh, that!' he answered. 'Never mind that. That is of no significance whatever.'

'But what *is* of any significance?' she insisted. She almost hated him.

'What is of any significance? Well, nothing, to me, outside of this room, at this minute. Nothing in time or space matters to me.'

'Yes, *this minute*!' she repeated bitterly. 'But then there's the future. *I've* got to live in the future.'

'The future! The future! The future is used up every day. The future to me is like a big tangle of black thread. Every morning you begin to untangle one loose end – and that's your day. And every evening you break off and throw away what you've untangled and the heap is so much less: just one thread less, one day less. That's all the future matters to me.'

'Then nothing matters to you. And I don't matter to you. As you say, only an end of waste thread,' she resisted him.

'No, there you're wrong. You aren't the future to me.'

'What am I then? – the past?'

'No, not any of those things. You're nothing. As far as all that goes, you're nothing.'

'Thank you,' she said sarcastically, 'if I'm nothing.'

But the very irrelevancy of the man overcame her. He kissed her with half discernible, dim kisses, and touched her throat. And the meaninglessness of him fascinated her and left her powerless. She could ascribe no meaning to him, none whatever. And yet his mouth, so strange in kissing, and his hairy forearms and his slender, beautiful breast with black hair – it was all like a mystery to her, as if one of the men from Mars were loving her. And she was heavy and spell-bound, and she loved the spell that bound her. But also she didn't love it.

II

Countess zu Rassentlow had a studio in one of the main streets. She was really a refugee. And nowadays you can be a Grand Duke and a pauper, if you are a refugee. But Hannele was not a pauper, because she and her friend Mitchka had the studio where they made these dolls, and beautiful cushions of embroidered coloured wools, and such-like objects of feminine art. The dolls were quite famous, so the two women did not starve.

Hannele did not work much in the studio. She preferred to be alone in her own room, which was another fine attic, not quite so large as the Captain's, under the same roof. But often she went to the studio in the afternoon, and if purchasers came, then they were offered a cup of tea.

The Alexander doll was never intended for sale. What made Hannele take it to the studio one afternoon, we do no know. But she did so, and stood it on a little bureau. It was a wonderful little portrait of an officer and gentleman, the physique modelled so that it made you hold your breath.

'And *that* – that is genius!' cried Mitchka. 'That is a *chef d'œuvre*! That is thy masterpiece, Hannele. That is really marvellous. And beautiful! A beautiful man, what! But no, that is *too* real. I don't understand how you *dare*. I always thought you were *good*, Hannele, so much better-natured than I am. But now you frighten me, I am afraid you are wicked, do you know? It frightens me to think that you are wicked. Aber nein![4] – But you won't leave him there?'

'Why not?' said Hannele, satiric.

Mitchka made big dark eyes of wonder, reproach, and fear.

'But you *must* not,' she said.

'Why not?'

'No, that you *may* not do. You love the man.'

'What then?'

'You can't leave his puppet standing there.'

'Why can't I?'

'But you are really wicked. Du bist *wirklich* bös. Only think! – and he is an English officer.'

'He isn't sacrosanct even then.'

'They will expel you from the town. They will deport you.'[5]

'Let them then.'

'But no! What will you do? That would be horrible if we had to go to Berlin or to Munich and begin again. Here everything has happened so well.'

'I don't care,' said Hannele.

Mitchka looked at her friend and said no more. But she was angry. After some time she turned and uttered her ultimatum.

'When you are not there,' she said, 'I shall put the puppet away in a drawer, I shall show it to nobody, nobody. And I must tell you, it makes me afraid to see it there. It makes me afraid. And you have no right to get me into trouble, do you see? It is not I who look at the English officers. I don't like them, they are too cold and finished off for me. I shall never bring trouble on *myself* because of the English officers.'

'Don't be afraid,' said Hannele. 'They won't trouble *you*. They know everything we do, well enough. They have their spies everywhere. Nothing will happen to you.'

'But if they make you go away – and I am planted here with the studio –'

It was no good, however; Hannele was obstinate.

So, one sunny afternoon there was a ring at the door: a little lady in white, with a wrinkled face that still had its prettiness.

'Good-afternoon!' – in rather lardy-dardy middle-class English. 'I wonder if I may see your things in your studio?'

'Oh, yes!' said Mitchka. 'Please come in.'

Entered the little lady in her finery and her crumpled prettiness. She would not be very old: perhaps younger than fifty. And it was odd that her face had gone so crumpled, because her figure was very trim, her eyes were bright, and she had pretty teeth when she laughed. She was very fine in her clothes: a dress of thick knitted white silk, a large ermine scarf with the tails only at the ends, and a black hat over which dripped a trail of green feathers of the osprey sort. She wore rather a lot of jewellery, and two bangles tinkled over her white kid gloves as she put up her fingers to touch her hair, whilst she stood complacently and looked round.

'You've got a *charming* studio – *charming* – perfectly delightful. I couldn't imagine anything more delightful.'

Mitchka gave a slight ironic bow, and said, in her odd, plangent English:

'Oh, yes. We like it very much also.'

Hannele, who had dodged behind a screen, now came quickly forth.

'Oh, how do you do!' smiled the elderly lady. 'I heard there were two of you. Now which is which, if I may be so bold? This' – and she gave a winsome smile and pointed a white kid finger at Mitchka – 'is the –?'

'Annamaria von Prielau-Carolath,' said Mitchka, slightly bowing.

'Oh! –' and the white kid finger jerked away. 'Then this –'

'Johanna zu Rassentlow,' said Hannele, smiling.

'Ah, yes! Countess von Rassentlow! And this is Baroness von – von – but I shall never remember even if you tell me, for I'm awful at names. Anyhow, I shall call one *Countess* and the other *Baroness*. That will do, won't it, from poor me! Now I should like awfully to see your things, if I may. I want to buy a little present to take back to England with me. I suppose I shan't have to pay the world in duty on things like these, shall I?'

'Oh, no,' said Mitchka. 'No duty. Toys, you know, they – there is –' Her English stammered to an end, so she turned to Hannele.

'They don't charge duty on toys, and the embroideries they don't notice,' said Hannele.

'Oh, well. Then I'm all right,' said the visitor. 'I hope I can buy something really nice! I see a perfectly lovely jumper over there, perfectly delightful. But a little too gay for me, I'm afraid. I'm not quite so young as I was, alas.' She smiled her winsome little smile, showing her pretty teeth, and the old pearls in her ears shook.

'I've heard so much about your dolls. I hear they're perfectly exquisite, quite works of art. May I see some, please?'

'Oh, yes,' came Mitchka's invariable answer, this exclamation being the foundation stone of all her English.

There were never more than three or four dolls in stock. This time there were only two. The famous Captain was hidden in his drawer.

'Perfectly beautiful! Perfectly wonderful!' murmured the little lady, in an artistic murmur. 'I think they're perfectly delightful. It's wonderful of you, Countess, to make them. It is you who make them, is it not? Or do you both do them together?'

Hannele explained, and the inspection and the rhapsody went

on together. But it was evident that the little lady was a cautious buyer. She went over the things very carefully, and thought more than twice. The dolls attracted her – but she thought them expensive, and hung fire.

– 'I do wish,' she said wistfully, 'there had been a larger selection of the dolls. I feel, you know, there might have been one which I *just loved*. Of course these are *darlings* – darlings they are; and worth every *penny*, considering the work there is in them. And the *art*, of course. But I have a feeling, don't you know how it is, that if there had been just one or two more, I should have found one which I *absolutely* couldn't live without. – Don't you know how it is? – One is so foolish, of course. – What does Goethe say – "Dort wo du nicht bist[6] . . ."? – My German isn't even a beginning, so you must excuse it. But it means you always feel you would be happy somewhere else, and not just where you are. Isn't that it? – Ah, well, it's so very often true – so very often. But not always, thank goodness.' – She smiled an odd little smile to herself, pursed her lips, and resumed: 'Well now, that's how I feel about the dolls. If only there had been one or two more. Isn't there a single one?'

She looked winsomely at Hannele.

'Yes,' said Hannele, 'there is one. But it is ordered. It isn't for sale.'

'Oh, do you think I might see it? I'm sure it's lovely. Oh, I'm dying to see it. – You know what woman's curiosity is, don't you?' – she laughed her tinkling little laugh. 'Well, I'm afraid I'm all woman, unfortunately. One is so much harder if one has a touch of the man in one, don't you think, and more able to bear things. But I'm afraid I'm all woman.' She sighed and went silent.

Hannele went quietly to the drawer and took out the Captain. She handed him to the little woman. The latter looked frightened. Her eyes became round and childish, her face went yellowish. Her jewels tinkled nervously as she stammered:

'Now *that* – isn't that –' and she laughed a little hysterical laugh.

She turned round, as if to escape.

'Do you mind if I sit down?' she said. 'I think the standing –'

and she subsided into a chair. She kept her face averted. But she held the puppet fast, her small white fingers with their heavy jewelled rings clasped round his waist.

'You know,' rushed in Mitchka, who was terrified, 'you know, that is a life-picture of one of the Englishmen, of a gentleman, you know. A life-picture, you know.'

'A portrait,' said Hannele brightly.

'Yes,' murmured the visitor vaguely. 'I'm sure it is a very clever portrait indeed.'

She fumbled with a chain, and put up a small gold lorgnette before her eyes, as if to screen herself. And from behind the screen of her lorgnette she peered at the image in her hand.

'But,' she said, 'do any of the English officers wear the tartan trews?'

Her voice was vague and distant.

'No, they don't now,' said Hannele. 'But that is the correct dress. I think they are so handsome, don't you?'

'Well. I don't know. It depends –' and the little woman laughed shakily.

'Oh, yes,' said Hannele. 'It needs well-shapen legs.'

'Such as the original of your doll must have had – quite,' said the lady.

'Oh, yes,' said Hannele. 'I think his legs are very handsome.'

'Quite!' said the lady. 'Judging from his portrait, as you call it. – May I ask the name of the gentleman – if it is not too indiscreet?'

'Captain Hepburn,' said Hannele.

'Yes, of course it is. I knew him at once. – I've known him for many years.'

'Oh, please,' broke in Mitchka. 'Oh, please do not tell him you have seen it! Oh, please! Please not to tell anyone!'

The visitor looked up with a grey little smile.

'But why not?' she said. 'Anyhow, I can't tell him at once, because I hear he is away at present. You don't happen to know when he will be back?'

'I believe to-morrow,' said Hannele.

'To-morrow!'

'And please!' pleaded Mitchka, who looked lovely in her

pleading distress. 'Please not to tell anybody that you have seen it.'

'Must I promise?' smiled the little lady wanly. 'Very well, then, I won't tell him I've seen it. – And now I think I must be going. Yes, I'll just take the cushion-cover, thank you. Tell me again how much it is, please –'

III

That evening Hannele was restless. He had been away on some duty for three days. He was returning that night – should have been back in time for dinner. But he had not arrived, and his room was locked and dark. Hannele had heard the servant light the stove some hours ago. Now the room was locked and blank as it had been for three days.

Hannele was most uneasy because she seemed to have forgotten him in the three days whilst he had been away. He seemed to have quite disappeared out of her. She could hardly even remember him. He had become so insignificant to her she was dazed.

Now she wanted to see him again, to know if it was really so. She felt that he was coming. She felt that he was already putting out some influence towards her. But what? And was he real? Why had she made his doll? Why had his doll been so important, if he was nothing? Why had she shown it to that funny little woman this afternoon? Why was she herself such a fool, getting herself into tangles in this place where it was so unpleasant to be entangled? Why was she entangled, after all? It was all so unreal. And particularly *he* was unreal, as unreal as a person in a dream, whom one has never heard of in actual life. In actual life, her own German friends were real. Martin was real; German men were real to her. But this other, he was simply not there. He didn't really exist. He was a nullus, in reality. A nullus – and she had somehow got herself complicated with him.

Was it possible? Was it possible she had been so closely entangled with an absolute nothing? Now he was absent she couldn't even *imagine* him. He had gone out of her imagination, and even when she looked at his doll she saw nothing but a barren puppet. And yet for this dead puppet she had been compromising herself, now, when it was so risky for her to be compromised.

Her own German friends – her own German men – they were men, they were real beings. But this English officer, he was neither fish, flesh, fowl, nor good red herring, as they say. He was just a hypothetical presence. – She felt that if he never came back, she would be just as if she had read a rather peculiar but false story, a *tour de force*[7] which works up one's imagination all falsely.

Nevertheless she was uneasy. She had a lurking suspicion that there might be something else. So she kept uneasily wandering out onto the landing, and listening to hear if he might be coming.

Yes – there was a sound. Yes, there was his slow step on the stairs, and the slow, straying purr of his voice. And instantly she heard his voice she was afraid again. She knew there *was* something there. And instantly she felt the reality of his presence, she felt the unreality of her own German men-friends. The moment she heard the peculiar slow melody of his foreign voice everything seemed to go changed in her, and Martin and Otto and Albrecht, her German friends, seemed to go pale and dim as if one could almost see through them, like unsubstantial things.

This is what she had to reckon with, this recoil from one to the other. When he was present, he seemed so terribly real. When he was absent he was completely vague, and her own men of her own race seemed so absolutely the only reality.

But he was talking. Whom was he talking to? She heard the steps echo up the hollows of the stone staircase, slowly, as if wearily, and voices slowly, confusedly mingle. The slow, soft trail of his voice – and then the peculiar quick tones – yes, of a woman. And not one of the maids, because they were speaking English. She listened hard. The quick, and yet slightly hushed, slightly sad-sounding voice of a woman who talks a good deal, as if talking to herself. Hannele's quick ears caught the sound of what she was saying: 'Yes, I thought the Baroness a perfectly beautiful creature, perfectly lovely. But so extraordinarily like a Spaniard. – Do you remember, Alec, at Malaga? I always thought they fascinated you then, with their mantillas. Perfectly lovely she would look in a mantilla. Only perhaps she is too open-hearted, too impulsive, poor thing. She lacks the Spanish reserve. Poor thing, I feel sorry for her. For them both, indeed. It must be very hard to have to do these things for a living, after you've been accustomed to be made much of for your own sake and for your aristocratic title. It's very hard for them, poor things. Baroness, Countess, it sounds just a little ridiculous, when you're buying woollen embroideries from them. But I suppose, poor things, they can't help it. Better drop the titles altogether, I think –'

'Well, they do, if people will let them. Only English and American people find it so much easier to say Baroness or Countess than Fräulein von Prielau-Carolath, or whatever it is.'

'They could say simply Fräulein, as we do to our governesses – or as we used to, when we *had* German governesses,' came the voice of *her*.

'Yes, we *could* –' said the voice of him.

'After all, what is the good, what is the good of titles if you have to sell dolls and woollen embroideries – not so *very* beautiful, either –'

'Oh, quite! Oh, quite! I think titles are perhaps a mistake, anyhow. But they've always had them,' came his slow musical voice, with its singsong note of hopeless indifference. He sounded rather like a man talking out of his sleep.

Hannele caught sight of the tail of blue-green crane feathers veering round a turn in the stairs away below, and she beat a hasty retreat.

IV

There was a little platform out on the roof, where he used sometimes to stand his telescope and observe the stars or the moon: the moon when possible. It was not a very safe platform, just a little ledge of the roof, outside the window at the end of the top corridor: or rather, the top landing, for it was only the space between the attics. Hannele had the one attic-room at the back, he had the room we have seen, and a little bedroom which was really only a lumber-room. Before he came, Hannele had been alone under the roof. His rooms were then lumber-room and laundry-room, where the clothes were dried. But he had wanted to be high up, because of his stars, and this was the place that pleased him.

Hannele heard him quite late in the night, wandering about. She heard him also on the ledge outside. She could not sleep. He disturbed her. The moon was risen, large and bright in the sky. She heard the bells from the cathedral slowly strike two: two great drops of sound in the livid night. And again, from outside on the roof, she heard him clear his throat. Then a cat howled.

She rose, wrapped herself in a dark wrap, and went down the landing to the window at the end. The sky outside was full of moonlight. He was squatted like a great cat peering up his telescope, sitting on a stool, his knees wide apart. Quite motionless he sat in that attitude, like some leaden figure on the roof. The moonlight glistened with a gleam of plumbago on the great slope of black tiles. She stood still in the window, watching. And he remained fixed and motionless at the end of the telescope.

She tapped softly on the window-pane. He looked round – like some tom-cat staring round with wide night-eyes. Then he reached down his hand and pulled the window open.

'Hello,' he said quietly. 'You not asleep?'

'Aren't *you* tired?' she replied, rather resentful.

'No, I was as wide awake as I could be. *Isn't* the moon fine to-night! What? Perfectly amazing. Wouldn't you like to come up and have a look at her?'

'No, thank you,' she said hastily, terrified at the thought.

He resumed his posture, peering up the telescope.

'Perfectly amazing,' he said, murmuring. She waited for some time, bewitched likewise by the great October moon and the sky full of resplendent white-green light. It seemed like another sort of daytime. And there he straddled on the roof like some cat! It was exactly like day in some other planet.

At length he turned round to her. His face glistened faintly, and his eyes were dilated like a cat's at night.

'You know I had a visitor?' he said.

'Yes.'

'My wife.'

'Your *wife* –!' She looked up really astonished. She had

thought it might be an acquaintance – perhaps his aunt – or even an elder sister. – 'But she's years older than you,' she added.

'Eight years,' he said. 'I'm forty-one.'

There was a silence.

'Yes,' he mused. 'She arrived suddenly, by surprise, yesterday, and found me away. She's staying in the hotel, in the Vier Jahreszeiten.'

There was a pause.

'Aren't you going to stay with her?' asked Hannele.

'Yes, I shall probably join her to-morrow.'

There was a still longer pause.

'Why not to-night?' asked Hannele.

'Oh, well – I put it off for to-night. – It meant all the bother of my wife changing her room at the hotel – and it was late – and I was all mucky after travelling.'

'But you'll go to-morrow?'

'Yes, I shall go to-morrow. For a week or so. – After that I'm not sure what will happen.'

There was quite a long pause. He remained seated on his stool on the roof, looking with dilated, blank black eyes at nothingness. She stood below in the open window-space, pondering.

'Do you want to go to her at the hotel?' asked Hannele.

'Well, I don't particularly. But I don't mind, really. We're very good friends. Why, we've been friends for eighteen years – we've been married seventeen. Oh, she's a nice little woman. I don't want to hurt her feelings. – I wish her no harm, you know. – On the contrary, I wish her all the good in the world.'

He had no idea of the blank amazement in which Hannele listened to these stray remarks.

'But –' she stammered. 'But doesn't she expect you to make *love* to her?'

'Oh, yes, she expects that. You bet she does; woman-like.'

'And you –?' – the question had a dangerous ring.

'Why, I don't mind, really, you know, if it's only for a short time. I'm used to her. I've always been fond of her, you know – and so if it gives her any pleasure – why, I like her to get what pleasure out of life she can.'

'But *you* – you *yourself*? Don't *you* feel anything?' Hannele's amazement was reaching the point of incredulity. She began to feel that he was making it up. It was all so different from her own point of view. To sit there so quiet and to make such statements in all good faith: no, it was impossible.

'I don't consider I count,' he said, naïvely.

Hannele looked aside. If that wasn't lying, it was imbecility, or worse. She had for the moment nothing to say. She felt he was a sort of psychic phenomenon like a grasshopper or a tadpole or an ammonite. Not to be regarded from a human point of view. No, he just wasn't normal. And she had been fascinated by him! – It was only sheer, amazed curiosity that carried her on to her next question.

'But do you *never* count, then?' she asked, and there was a touch of derision, of laughter in her tone. He took no offence.

'Well – very rarely,' he said. 'I count very rarely. That's how life appears to me. One matters so *very* little.'

She felt quite dizzy with astonishment. – And he called himself a man!

'But if you matter so very little, what do you do anything at all for?' she asked.

'Oh, one has to. And then, why not? Why not do things, even if oneself hardly matters. – Look at the moon. It doesn't matter in the least to the moon whether I exist or whether I don't. So why should it matter to me?'

After a blank pause of incredulity she said:

'I could die with laughter. It seems to me all so ridiculous – no, I can't believe it.'

'Perhaps it is a point of view,' he said.

There was a long and pregnant silence: we should not like to say pregnant with what.

'And so I don't mean anything to you at all?' she said.

'I didn't say that,' he replied.

'Nothing means anything to you,' she challenged.

'I don't say that.'

'Whether it's your wife – or me – or the moon – toute la même chose.'[8]

'No – no – that's hardly the way to look at it –'

She gazed at him in such utter amazement that she felt

something would really explode in her if she heard another word. Was this a man? – or what was it? It was too much for her, that was all.

'Well, good-bye,' she said. 'I hope you will have a nice time at the Vier Jahreszeiten.'

So she left him still sitting on the roof.

'I suppose,' she said to herself, 'that is love *à l'anglaise*. But it's more than I can swallow.'

v

'Won't you come and have tea with me – do! Come right along now. Don't you find it bitterly cold? Yes – well now – come in with me and we'll have a cup of nice hot tea in our little sitting-room. The weather changes so suddenly, and really, one needs a little reinforcement. But perhaps you don't take tea?'

'Oh, yes. I got so used to it in England,' said Hannele.

'Did you now! Well, now, were you long in England?'

'Oh, yes –'

The two women had met in the Domplatz. Mrs Hepburn was looking extraordinarily like one of Hannele's dolls, in a funny little cape of odd striped skins, and a little dark-green skirt, and a rather fuzzy sort of hat. Hannele looked almost huge beside her.

'But now you will come in and have tea, won't you? Oh, please do. Never mind whether it's *de rigueur*⁹ or not. I *always* please myself *what* I do. I'm afraid my husband gets some shocks sometimes – but that we can't help. I won't have anybody laying down the law to me.' She laughed her winsome little laugh. 'So now come along in, and we'll see if there aren't hot scones as well. I love a hot scone for tea in cold weather. And I hope you do. – That is, if there are any. We don't know yet.' She tinkled her little laugh. 'My husband may or may not be in. But that makes no difference to you and me, does it? – There, it's just striking half-past four. In England we always have tea at half past. My husband *adores* his tea. I don't suppose our man is five minutes off the half-past, ringing the gong for tea, not once in twelve months. My husband doesn't mind at all if dinner is a little late. But he gets – quite –well, quite "ratty" if tea is late.' She tinkled a laugh. 'Though I shouldn't say that. He is the soul of kindness and patience. I don't think I've ever known him do an unkind thing – or hardly say an unkind word. – But I doubt if he will be in to-day.'

He *was* in, however, standing with his feet apart and his hands in his trouser pockets in the little sitting-room upstairs in the hotel. He raised his eyebrows the smallest degree, seeing Hannele enter.

'Ah, Countess Hannele – my wife has brought you along! Very nice, very nice! Let me take your wrap. – Oh, yes, certainly.'

'Have you rung for tea, dear?' asked Mrs Hepburn.

'Er – yes. I said as soon as you came in they were to bring it.'

'Yes – well – Won't you ring again, dear, and say for *three* –'

'Yes – certainly. Certainly.'

He rang, and stood about with his hands in his pockets waiting for tea.

'Well, now,' said Mrs Hepburn, as she lifted the tea-pot, and her bangles tinkled, and her huge rings of brilliants twinkled, and her big ear-rings of clustered seed-pearls bobbed against her rather withered cheek, 'isn't it charming of Countess zu – Countess zu –'

'Rassentlow,' said he. 'I believe most people say Countess Hannele. I know we always do among ourselves. We say Countess Hannele's shop –'

'Countess Hannele's shop! Now isn't that perfectly delightful: such a romance in the very sound of it. – You take cream –?'

'Thank you,' said Hannele.

The tea passed in a cloud of chatter, while Mrs Hepburn manipulated the tea-pot, and lit the spirit flame, and blew it out, and peeped into the steam of the tea-pot, and couldn't see whether there was any more tea or not – and – 'At home I *know* – I was going to say to a teaspoonful – how much tea there is in the pot. But this tea-pot – I don't know what it's made of – it isn't silver, I know that – it is so heavy in itself that it's deceived me several times already. And my husband is a greedy man, a greedy man – he likes at least three cups – and four if he can get them – or five! Yes, dear, I've plenty of tea today –. You shall have even five, if you don't mind the last two weak. – Do let

me fill your cup, Countess Hannele. – I think it's a *charming*
name –'

'There's a play called *Hannele*, isn't there?' said he.[10]

When he had had his five cups, and his wife had got her
cigarette perched in the end of a long, long slim, white holder,
and was puffing like a little China woman from the distance,
there was a little lull.

'Alec, dear,' said Mrs Hepburn. 'You won't forget to leave that
message for me at Mrs Rackham's. I'm so afraid it will be
forgotten.'

'No, dear, I won't forget. – Er – would you like me to go round
now?'

Hannele noticed how often he said 'er', when he was beginning
to speak to his wife. But they *were* such good friends, the two of
them.

'Why, if you *would*, dear, I should feel perfectly comfortable.
– But I don't want you to hurry one bit.'

'Oh, I may as well go now.'

And he went. Mrs Hepburn detained her guest.

'He *is* so charming to me,' said the little woman. 'He's really
wonderful. And he always has been the same – invariably. So that
if he *did* make a little slip – well, you know, I don't have to take
it so seriously.'

'No,' said Hannele, feeling as if her ears were stretching with
astonishment.

'It's the war. It's just the war. It's had a terribly deteriorating
effect on the men.'

'In what way?' said Hannele.

'Why, morally. Really, there's hardly one man left the same
as he was before the war. Terribly degenerated.'

'Is that so?' said Hannele.

'It is indeed. Why, isn't it the same with the German men and
officers?'

'Yes, I think so,' said Hannele.

'And I'm sure so, from what I hear. – But of course it is the
women who are to blame in the first place. We poor women! We
are a guilty race, I am afraid. But I never throw stones. I know
what it is myself to have temptations. I have to flirt a little – and

when I was younger – well, the men didn't escape me, I assure you. And I was *so* often scorched. But never *quite* singed. My husband never minded. He knew I was *really* safe. Oh, yes, I have always been faithful to him. But still – I have been *very* near the flame –' And she laughed her winsome little laugh.

Hannele put her fingers to her ears, to make sure they were not falling off.

'Of course during the war it was terrible. I know that in a certain hospital it was quite impossible for a girl to stay on if she kept straight. The matrons and sisters just turned her out. They wouldn't have her unless she was one of themselves. And you know what that means. – Quite like the convent in Balzac's story[11] – you know which I mean, I'm sure –' And the laugh tinkled gaily.

'But then, what can you expect, when there aren't enough men to go round! – Why, I had a friend in Ireland. She and her husband had been an *ideal* couple, an ideal couple. Real playmates. And you can't say more than that, can you? – Well then, he became a major during the war. And she was so looking forward, poor thing, to the perfectly lovely times they would have together when he came home. She is like me, and is lucky enough to have a little income of her own – not a great fortune – but – well – Well now, what was I going to say? Oh, yes, she was looking forward to the perfectly lovely times they would have when he came home: building on her dreams, poor thing, as we unfortunate women always do. I suppose we shall never be cured of it –' A little tinkling laugh. 'Well now, not a bit of it. Not a bit of it.' Mrs Hepburn lifted her heavily-jewelled little hand in a motion of protest. It was curious, her hands were pretty and white, and her neck and breast, now she wore a little tea-gown, were also smooth and white and pretty, under the medley of twinkling chains and little coloured jewels. Why should her face have played her this nasty trick of going all crumpled? However, it was so. –

'Not one bit of it,' reiterated the little lady. 'He came home quite changed. She said she could hardly recognize him for the same man. Let me tell you one little incident. Just a trifle, but significant. – He was coming home – this was some time after he was free from the army – he was coming home from London, and he told her to meet him at the boat: gave her the time and everything. Well, she went to the boat, poor thing, and he didn't come. She waited, and no word of explanation or anything. So she couldn't make up her mind whether to go next day and meet the boat again. – However, she decided she wouldn't. So, of course, on that boat he arrived. When he got home, he said to her, "Why didn't you meet the boat?" – "Well," she said, "I went yesterday, and you didn't come –" – "Then why didn't you meet it again to-day?" – Imagine it, the sauce! And they had been real playmates. Heartbreaking, isn't it? – "Well," she said in self-defence, "why didn't you come yesterday?" – "Oh," he said, "I met a woman in town whom I liked, and she asked me to spend the night with her, so I did." – Now what do you think of that? – Can you conceive of such a thing?'

'Oh, no,' said Hannele. 'I call that unnecessary brutality.'

'Exactly! So terrible to say such a thing to her! The brutality of it! – Well, that's how the world is to-day. – I'm thankful my husband isn't that sort. I don't say he's perfect. But whatever else he did, he'd never be unkind, and he *couldn't* be brutal. He just couldn't. He'd never tell me a lie – I know *that*. But callous brutality, no, thank goodness, he hasn't a spark of it in him. I'm the wicked one, if either of us is wicked. –' The little laugh tinkled. 'Oh, but he's been perfect to me, perfect. Hardly a cross word. Why, on our wedding night, he kneeled down in front of me and promised, with God's help, to make my life happy. And I must say, as far as possible, he's kept his word. It has been his one aim in life, to make my life happy.'

The little lady looked away with a bright, musing look, towards the window. She was being a heroine in a romance. Hannele could see her being a heroine, playing the chief part in her own life-romance. It is such a feminine occupation, that no woman takes offence when she is made audience.

'I'm afraid I've more of the woman than the mother in my composition,' resumed the little heroine. 'I adore my two children. The boy is at Winchester, and my little girl is in a convent in Brittany. Oh, they are perfect darlings, both of them. But the man is first in my mind, I'm afraid. I fear I'm rather old-

fashioned. But never mind. I can see the attractions in other men
– can't I, indeed! There was a perfectly exquisite creature – he
was a very clever engineer – but much, much more than *that* –
But never mind.' The little heroine sniffed as if there were
perfume in the air, folded her jewelled hands, and resumed:
'However – I know what it is myself to flutter round the flame.
You know I'm Irish myself, and we Irish can't help it. Oh, I
wouldn't be English for anything. Just that little touch of
imagination, you know . . .'

The little laugh tinkled. 'And that's what makes me able to
sympathize with my husband even when, perhaps, I shouldn't.
Why, when he was at home with me, he never gave a thought,
not a thought, to another woman. I must say, he used to make
me feel a little guilty sometimes – But there! – I don't think he
ever thought of another woman as being flesh and blood, after
he knew me. I could tell. Pleasant, courteous, charming – but
other women were not flesh and blood to him, they were just
people, callers – that kind of thing. It used to amaze me, when
some perfectly lovely creature came, whom I should have been
head over heels in love with in a minute – and he, he was
charming, delightful, he could see her points, but she was no
more to him than, let me say, a pot of carnations, or a beautiful
old piece of punto di Milano.[12] Not flesh and blood. – Well,
perhaps one can feel too safe. Perhaps one needs a tiny pinch of
salt of jealousy. I believe one does. And I have not had one jealous
moment for seventeen years. – So that, *really*, when I heard a
whisper of something going on here, I felt almost pleased. I felt
exonerated for my own little peccadilloes, for one thing. And I
felt he was perhaps a little more human. Because, after all, it is
nothing but human to fall in love, if you are alone for a long time
and in the company of a beautiful woman – and if you're an
attractive man yourself. –'

Hannele sat with her eyes propped open and her ears buttoned
back with amazement, expecting the next revelations.

'Why, of course,' she said, knowing she was expected to say
something.

'Yes, of course,' said Mrs Hepburn, eyeing her sharply . . . 'So
I thought I'd better come and see how far things had gone. I had

nothing but a hint to go on. I knew no name – nothing. I had just a hint that she was German, and a refugee aristocrat – and that he used to call at the studio –' The little lady eyed Hannele sharply, and gave a breathless little laugh, clasping her hands nervously. Hannele sat absolutely blank: really dazed.

'Of course,' resumed Mrs Hepburn, 'that was enough. That was quite a sufficient clue. I'm afraid my intentions when I called at the studio were not as pure as they might have been. I'm afraid I wanted to see something more than the dolls. – But when you showed me *his* doll, then I knew. Of course there wasn't a shadow of doubt after that. And I saw at once that she loved him, poor thing. She was *so* agitated. And no idea who I was. And you were so unkind to show me the doll. Of course you had no idea who you were showing it to. But for her, poor thing, it was such a trial. I could see how she suffered. And I must say she's very lovely – she's very, very lovely, with her golden skin and her reddish amber eyes and her beautiful, beautiful carriage. And such a naïve impulsive nature. Gives everything away in a minute. And then her deep voice – "*Oh, yes – Oh, please.*" – Such a child. And such an aristocrat, that lovely turn of her head, and her simple, elegant dress. Oh, she's very charming. And she's just the type I always knew would attract him, if he hadn't got me. I've thought about it many a time – many a time. When a woman is older than a man, she does think these things – especially if he has his attractive points too. And when I've dreamed of the woman he would love if he hadn't got me, it has always been a Spanish type. And the Baroness is extraordinarily Spanish in her appearance. She must have had some noble Spanish ancestor. Don't you think so?'

'Oh, yes,' said Hannele. 'There were such a lot of Spaniards in Austria, too, with the various emperors.'

'With Charles V,[13] exactly. Exactly. That's how it must have been. And so she has all the Spanish beauty, and all the German feeling. Of course, for myself, I miss the *reserve*, the haughtiness. But she's very, very lovely, and I'm sure I could never *hate* her. I couldn't even if I tried. And I'm not going to try. But I think she's much too dangerous for my husband to see much of her. Don't you agree, now?'

'Oh, but really,' stammered Hannele. 'There's nothing in it, really.'

'Well,' said the little lady, cocking her head shrewdly aside, 'I shouldn't like there to be any *more* in it.'

And there was a moment's dead pause. Each woman was reflecting. Hannele wondered if the little lady was just fooling her.

'Anyhow,' continued Mrs Hepburn, 'the spark is there, and I don't intend the fire to spread. – I am going to be very, very careful, myself, not to fan the flames. The last thing I should think of would be to make my husband scenes. I believe it would be fatal.'

'Yes,' said Hannele, during the pause.

'I am going very carefully. – You think there isn't much in it – between him and the Baroness –?'

'No – no – I'm sure there isn't,' cried Hannele, with a full voice of conviction. She was almost indignant at being slighted so completely herself, in the little lady's suspicions.

'Hm! – mm!' hummed the little woman, sapiently nodding her head slowly up and down. 'I'm not so sure! I'm not so sure that it hasn't gone pretty far –'

'Oh *no* – !' cried Hannele, in real irritation of protest.

'Well,' said the other. – 'In any case, I don't intend it to go any further.'

There was dead silence for some time.

'There's more in it than you say. There's more in it than you say,' ruminated the little woman. 'I know *him*, for one thing. I know he's got a cloud on his brow. And I know it hasn't left his brow for a single moment. – And when I told him I had been to the studio, and showed him the cushion-cover, I knew he felt guilty. I am not so easily deceived. We Irish all have a touch of second sight, I believe. – Of course I haven't challenged him. I haven't even mentioned the doll – By the way, *who* ordered the doll? Do you mind telling me –?'

'No, it wasn't ordered,' confessed Hannele.

'Ah – I thought not – I thought not!' said Mrs Hepburn, lifting her finger. 'At least, I knew no outsider had ordered it. Of course I knew. –' And she smiled to herself.

'So,' she continued, 'I had too much sense to say anything about it. I don't believe in stripping wounds bare. I believe in gently covering them and letting them heal. – But I *did* say I thought her a lovely creature –' The little lady looked brightly at Hannele.

'Yes,' said Hannele.

'And he was very vague in his manner. "Yes, not bad," he said. I thought to myself, Aha, my boy, you don't deceive me with your *not bad*. She's very much more than not bad. I said so, too. I wanted, of course, to let him know I had a suspicion.'

'And do you think he knew?'

'Of course he did. Of course he did. – "She's much too dangerous," I said, "to be in a town where there are so many strange men: married and unmarried." And then he turned round to me and gave himself away, oh, so plainly. "Why?" he said. But such a haughty, distant tone. I said to myself, "It's time, my dear boy, you were removed out of the danger-zone." But I answered him: "Surely somebody is bound to fall in love with her." – "Not at all," – he said, – "she keeps to her own countrymen." – "You don't tell *me*," – I answered him, – "with her pretty broken English! It is a wonder the two of them are allowed to stay in the town." – And then again he rounded on me. "Good gracious!" he said. "Would you have them turned out just because they're beautiful to look at, when they have nowhere else to go, and they make their bit of a livelihood here?" – I assure you, he hasn't rounded on me in that overbearing way, not once before in all our married life. So I just said quietly: – "I should like to protect *our own men*." – And he didn't say anything more. But he looked at me under his brows, and went out of the room.'

There was a silence. Hannele waited with her hands in her lap, and Mrs Hepburn mused, with her hands in her lap. Her face looked yellow, and *very* wrinkled.

'Well now,' she said, breaking again suddenly into life. 'What are we to do? – I mean what is to be done? – You are the Baroness's nearest friend. And I wish her *no* harm, none whatsoever –'

'What can we do?' said Hannele, in the pause.

'I have been urging my husband for some time to get his discharge from the army,' said the little woman. 'I know he could have it in three months' time. But like so many more men, he has no income of his own, and he doesn't want to feel dependent. Perfect nonsense! — So he says he wants to stay on in the army. — I have never known him before go against my real wishes —'

'But it *is* better for a man to be independent,' said Hannele.

'I know it is. But it is also better for him to be *at home*. — And I could get him a post in one of the observatories. He could do something in meteorological work.'

Hannele refused to answer any more.

'Of course,' said Mrs Hepburn, 'if he *does* stay on here, it would be much better if the Baroness left the town.'

'I'm sure she will never leave of her own choice,' said Hannele.

'I'm sure she won't either. But she might be made to see that it would be very much *wiser* of her to move of her own free will.'

'Why?' said Hannele.

'Why because, she might any time be removed by the British authorities.'

'Why should she?' said Hannele.

'I think the women who are a menace to our men should be removed.'

'But she is *not* a menace to your men.'

'Well, I have my own opinion on that point.'

Which was a decided deadlock.

'I'm sure I've kept you an awful long time with my chatter,' said Mrs Hepburn. 'But I did want to make everything as simple as possible. As I said before, I can't feel any ill-will against her. Yet I can't let things just go on. Heaven alone knows when they may end. — Of course if I can persuade my husband to resign his commission and come back to England — Anyhow, we will see. — I'm sure I am the last person in the world to bear malice.'

The tone in which she said it conveyed a dire threat.

Hannele rose from her chair.

'Oh, and one other thing,' said her hostess, taking out a tiny lace handkerchief and touching her nose delicately with it. 'Do you think —' dab, dab, — 'that I might have that *doll* - you know —?'

'That —?'

'Yes, of my husband' – the little lady rubbed her nose with her handkerchief.

'The price is three guineas –' said Hannele.

'Oh, indeed!' – the tone was very cold. 'I thought it was not for sale.'

Hannele put on her wrap.

'You'll send it round – will you? – if you will be so kind.'

'I must ask my friend, first.'

'Yes, of course. – But I'm sure she will be so kind as to send it me. It is a little – er – indelicate, don't you think!'

'No,' said Hannele. 'No more than a painted portrait.'

'Don't you?' said her hostess coldly. 'Well, even a painted portrait I think I should like in my own possession. This *doll* –'

Hannele waited, but there was no conclusion.

'Anyhow,' she said, 'the price is three guineas: or the equivalent in marks.'

'Very well,' said the little lady, 'you shall have your three guineas when I get the doll.'

VI

Hannele went her way pondering. A man never is quite such an abject specimen as his wife makes him look, talking about 'my husband'. Therefore, if any woman wishes to rescue her husband from the clutches of another female, let her only invite this female to tea and talk quite sincerely about 'my husband, you know'. Every man has made a ghastly fool of himself with a woman, at some time or other. No woman ever forgets. And most women will give the show away, with real pathos, to another woman. For instance, the picture of Alec at his wife's feet on his wedding night, vowing to devote himself to her lifelong happiness – this picture strayed across Hannele's mind time after time, whenever she thought of her dear captain. With disastrous consequences to the captain. Of course if he had been at her own feet, then Hannele would have thought it almost natural: almost a necessary part of the show of love. But at the feet of that other little woman! – And what was that other little woman wearing? – Her wedding night! Hannele hoped before heaven it wasn't some awful little nightie of frail flowered silk. Imagine it, that little lady! Perhaps in a chic little boudoir cap of 'punto di Milano', and this slip of frail flowered silk: and the man, perhaps, in his braces! Oh, merciful heaven, save us from other people's indiscretions. – No, let us be sure it was in proper evening dress – twenty years ago – very low cut, with a full skirt gathered behind and trailing a little, and a little feather-erection in her high-dressed hair, and all those jewels; pearls of course; and he in a dinner-jacket and a white waistcoat: probably in an hotel bedroom in Lugano, or Biarritz. And she? Was she standing with one small hand on his shoulder? – or was she seated on the couch in the bedroom? Oh, dreadful thought! – And yet it was almost inevitable, that scene. – Hannele had never been married, but she had come quite near enough to the realization of the event, to know that such a scene *was* practically inevitable. An indispensable part of any honeymoon. Him on his knees, with his heels up!

And how black and tidy his hair must have been then! and no grey at the temples at all. Such a good-looking bridegroom. Perhaps with a white rose in his buttonhole still. – And she could see him kneeling there, in his new black trousers, and a wing collar. And she could see his head bowed. And she could hear his plangent, musical voice saying: 'With God's help, I will make your life happy. I will live for that and for nothing else.' And then the little lady must have had tears in her eyes, and she must have said, rather superbly: 'Thank you, dear. I'm perfectly sure of it.'

Ach! Ach! Husbands should be left to their own wives: and wives should be left to their own husbands. And *no* stranger should ever be made a party to these terrible bits of connubial staging. Nay, thought Hannele, that scene was really true. It actually took place. And with the man of that scene I have been in love! With the devoted husband of that little lady. Oh, God, oh, God, how was it possible! Him on his knees, on his knees, with his heels up!

Am I a perfect fool? she thought to herself. Am I really just an idiot, gaping with love for him? How *could* I? How could I? The very way he says 'Yes, dear!' to her! The way he does what she tells him! The way he fidgets about the room with his hands in his pockets! The way he goes off when she sends him away because she wants to talk to me. And he knows she wants to talk to me. And he knows what she *might* have to say to me. Yet he goes off on his errand without a question, like a servant. 'I will do exactly whatever you wish, darling.' He must have said those words time after time, to the little lady. And fulfilled them, also. Performed all his pledges and his promises.

Ach! Ach! Hammele wrung her hands to think of *herself* being mixed up with him. And he had seemed to her so manly. He seemed to have so much silent male passion in him. And yet – the little lady! 'My husband has *always* been *perfectly sweet* to me.' Think of it! On his knees, too. And his 'Yes, dear! Certainly. Certainly.' Not that he was afraid of the little lady. He was just committed to her, as he might have been committed to gaol, or committed to paradise.

Had she been dreaming, to be in love with him? Oh, she wished so much she had never been it. She *wished* she had never given herself away. To him! – given herself away to him! – and so abjectly! Hung upon his words and his motions, and looked up to him as if he were Caesar. So he had seemed to her: like a mute Caesar. Like Germanicus.[14] Like – she did not know what –

How had it all happened? What had taken her in? Was it just his good looks? – No, not really. Because they were the kind of staring good looks she didn't really care for. – He must have had charm. He must have charm. Yes, he *had* charm. – When it worked.

His charm had not worked on her now for some time – never since that evening after his wife's arrival. Since then he had seemed to her – rather awful. Rather awful – stupid – an ass – a limited, rather vulgar person. That was what he seemed to her when his charm wouldn't work. A limited, rather inferior person. And in a world of *Schiebers* and profiteers and vulgar, pretentious persons, this was the worst thing possible. A limited, inferior, slightly pretentious individual! The husband of the little lady! – And oh heaven, she was so deeply implicated with him. He had not, however, spoken with her in private since his wife's arrival. Probably he would never speak with her in private again. She hoped to heaven, never again. The awful thing was the past, that which had been between him and her. She shuddered when she thought of it. The husband of the little lady!

But surely there was something to account for it! Charm, just charm. He had a charm. And then, oh heaven, when the charm left off working! It had left off so completely at this moment, in Hannele's case, that her very mouth tasted salt. What *did* it all amount to?

What was his charm, after all? How could it have affected her? – She began to think of him again, at his best: his presence, when they were alone high up in that big, lonely attic near the stars. His room! – the big white-washed walls, the first scent of tobacco, the silence, the sense of the stars being near, the telescopes, the cactus with fine scarlet flowers: and above all the strange, remote, insidious silence of his presence, that was so congenial to her also. The curious way he had of turning his head to listen – to listen to what? – as if he heard something in the stars. The strange look, like destiny, in his wide-open, almost staring dark eyes. The beautiful line of his brow, that seemed always to have a certain cloud on it. The slow elegance of his straight beautiful legs as he walked, and the exquisiteness of his dark slender chest! Ah, she could feel the charm mounting over her again. She could feel the snake biting her heart. She could feel the arrows of desire rankling.

But then – and she turned from her thoughts, back to this last little tea-party in the Vier Jahreszeiten. She thought of his voice: 'Yes, dear. Certainly. Certainly I will.' – And she thought of the stupid, inferior look on his face. And the something of a servant-like way in which he went out to do his wife's bidding.

And then the charm was gone again, as the glow of sunset goes off a burning city and leaves it a sordid industrial hole. So much for charm!

So much for charm. She had better have stuck to her own sort of men, Martin, for instance, who was a gentleman and a daring soldier and a queer soul and pleasant to talk to. Only he hadn't any *magic*. Magic? The very word made her writhe. Magic? Swindle. Swindle, that was all it amounted to. Magic!

*

And yet – let us not be too hasty. If the magic had *really* been there, on those evenings in that great lofty attic. – Had it? Yes. Yes, she was bound to admit it. There had been magic. If there had been magic in his presence and in his contact, the husband of the little lady. – But the distaste was in her mouth again.

So she started afresh, trying to keep a tight hold on the tail of that all-too evanescent magic of his. Dear, it slipped so quickly into disillusion. Nevertheless, if it had existed, it did exist. And if it did exist, it was worth having. You could call it an illusion if you liked. But an illusion which is a real experience worth having. Perhaps this disillusion was a greater illusion than the illusion itself. Perhaps all this disillusion of the little lady and the husband of the little lady was falser than the illusion and magic of those few evenings. Perhaps the long disillusion of life was falser than the brief moments of real illusion. After all – the delicate darkness of his breast, the mystery that seemed to come with him as he trod slowly across the floor of his room, after changing his tunic – Nay, nay, if she could keep the illusion of his charm, she would give all disillusion to the devils. Nay, only let her be under the spell of his charm. Only let the spell be upon her. It was all she yearned for. And the thing she had to fight was the vulgarity of disillusion. The vulgarity of the little lady, the vulgarity of the husband of the little lady, the vulgarity of his insincerity, his 'Yes, dear. Certainly! Certainly!' – this was what she had to fight. He *was* vulgar and horrible, then. But also, the queer figure that sat alone on the roof watching the stars! The wonderful red flower of the cactus. The mystery that advanced with him as he came across the room after changing his tunic. The glamour and sadness of him, his silence, as he stooped unfastening his boots. And the strange gargoyle smile, fixed, when he caressed her with his hand under the chin! – Life is all a choice. And if she chose the glamour, the magic, the charm, the illusion, the spell! – Better death than that other, the husband of the little lady. When all was said and done, was he as much the husband of the little lady as he was that other, queer, delicate-breasted Caesar of her own knowledge? Which was he?

No, she was *not* going to send her the doll. The little lady should never have the doll.

What a doll she would make herself! Heavens, what a wizened jewel!

VII

Captain Hepburn still called occasionally at the house for his post. The maid always put his letters in a certain place in the hall, so that he should not have to climb the stairs.

Among his letters – that is to say, along with another letter, for his correspondence was very meagre – he one day found an envelope with a crest. Inside this envelope two letters.

Dear Captain Hepburn,

I had the enclosed letter from Mrs Hepburn. I don't intend her to have the doll which is your portrait, so I shall not answer this note. Also I don't see why she should try to turn us out of the town. She talked to me after tea that day, and it seems she believes that Mitchka is your lover. I didn't say anything at all except that it wasn't true. But she needn't be afraid of me. I don't want you to trouble yourself. But you may as well *know* how things are.

Johanna z. R.

The other letter was on his wife's well-known heavy paper, and in her well-known, large, 'aristocratic' hand.

My dear Countess,

I wonder if there has been some mistake, or some mis-understanding. Four days ago you said you would send round that *doll* we spoke of, but I have seen no sign of it yet. I thought of calling at the studio, but did not wish to disturb the Baroness. I should be very much obliged if you could send the doll at once, as I do not feel easy while it is out of my possession. You may rely on having a cheque by return.

Our old family friend, Major General Barlow, called on me yesterday, and we had a most interesting conversation on our *Tommies*,[15] and the protection of their morals here. It seems we have full power to send away any person or persons deemed undesirable, with twenty-four hours' notice to leave. But of course all this is done as quietly and with the intention of causing as little scandal as possible.

Please let me have the doll by to-morrow, and perhaps some hint as to your future intentions.

With very best wishes from one who seeks only to be your friend,

Yours very sincerely,

Evangeline Hepburn.

VIII

And then a dreadful thing happened: really a very dreadful thing. Hannele read of it in the evening newspaper of the town – the *Abendblatt*. Mitchka came rushing up with the paper at ten o'clock at night, just when Hannele was going to bed.

Mrs Hepburn had fallen out of her bedroom window, from the third floor of the hotel, down on to the pavement below, and was killed. She was dressing for dinner. And apparently she had in the morning washed a certain little camisole, and put it on the window-sill to dry. She must have stood on a chair, reaching for it, when she fell out of the window. Her husband, who was in the dressing-room, heard a queer little noise, a sort of choking cry, and came into her room to see what it was. And she wasn't there. The window was open and the chair by the window. He looked round, and thought she had left the room for a moment, so returned to his shaving. He was half shaved when one of the maids rushed in. – When he looked out of the window down into the street he fainted, and would have fallen, too, if the maid had not pulled him in in time.

IX

The very next day the captain came back to his attic. Hannele did not know, until quite late at night when he tapped on her door. She knew his soft tap immediately.

'Won't you come over for a chat?' he said.

She paused for some moments before she answered. And then perhaps surprise made her agree: surprise and curiosity.

'Yes, in a minute,' she said, closing her door in his face.

She found him sitting quite still, not even smoking, in his quiet attic. He did not rise, but just glanced round with a faint smile. And she thought his face seemed different, more flexible. But in the half-light she could not tell. She sat at some little distance from him.

'I suppose you've heard,' he said.

'Yes.'

After a long pause, he resumed:

'Yes. It seems an impossible thing to have happened. Yet it *has* happened.'

Hannele's ears were sharp. But strain them as she might she could not catch the meaning of his voice.

'A terrible thing. A very terrible thing,' she said.

'Yes.'

'Do you think she fell quite accidentally?' she said.

'Must have done. The maid was in just a minute before, and she seemed as happy as possible. – I suppose reaching over that broad window-ledge, her brain must suddenly have turned. I can't imagine why she didn't call me. She could never bear even to look out of a high window. Turned her ill instantly if she saw a space below her. She used to say she couldn't really look at the moon, it made her feel as if she would fall down a dreadful height. She never dared do more than glance at it. She always had the feeling, I suppose, of the awful space beneath her, if she were on the moon.'

Hannele was not listening to his words, but to his voice. There was something a little automatic in what he said. But then that is always so when people have had a shock.

'It must have been terrible for you too,' she said.

'Ah, yes. At the time it was awful. Awful. I felt the smash right inside me, you know.'

'Awful!' she repeated.

'But now,' he said, 'I feel very strangely happy about it. I feel happy about it. I feel happy for her sake, if you can understand that. I feel she has got out of some great tension. I feel she's free now for the first time in her life. She was a gentle soul, and an original soul, but she was like a fairy who is condemned to live in houses and sit on furniture and all that, don't you know. It was never her nature.'

'No?' said Hannele, herself sitting in blank amazement.

'I always felt she was born in the wrong period – or on the wrong planet. Like some sort of delicate creature you take out of a tropical forest the moment it is born and from the first moment teach it to perform tricks. You know what I mean. All her life she performed the tricks of life, clever little monkey she was at it too. Beat me into fits. But her own poor little soul, a sort of fairy soul, those queer Irish creatures, was cooped up inside her all her life, tombed in. There it was, tombed in, while she went through all the tricks of life, that you have to go through if you are born to-day.'

'But –' stammered Hannele – 'what would she have done if she *had* been free?'

'Why, don't you see, there *is* nothing for her to do in the world to-day. Take her language, for instance. She never ought to have been speaking English. I don't know what language she ought to have spoken. Because if you take the Irish language, they only learn it back from English. They think in English, and just put Irish words on top. – But English was never her language. It bubbled off her lips, so to speak. And she had no other language. Like a starling that you've made talk from the very beginning, and so it can only shout these talking noises, don't you know. It can't whistle its own whistling to save its life. Couldn't do it. It's lost it. All its own natural mode of expressing itself has collapsed, and it can only be artificial.'

There was a long pause.

'Would she have been wonderful, then, if she had been able to talk in some unknown language?' said Hannele jealously.

'I don't say she would have been wonderful. As a matter of fact we think a talking starling is much more wonderful than an ordinary starling. I don't myself, but most people do. And she would have been a sort of starling. And she would have had her own language and her own ways. As it was, poor thing, she was always arranging herself and fluttering and chattering inside a cage. And she never knew she was in the cage, any more than we know we are inside our own skins.'

'But,' said Hannele, with a touch of mockery, 'how do you know you haven't made it all up – just to console yourself?'

'Oh, I've thought it long ago,' he said.

'Still,' she blurted, 'you may have invented it all – as a sort of consolation for – for – for your life.'

'Yes, I may,' he said. 'But I don't think so. It was her eyes. Did you ever notice her eyes? I often used to catch her eyes. And she'd be talking away, all the language bubbling off her lips. And her eyes were so clear and bright and different. Like a child's, that is listening to something, and is going to be frightened. She was always listening – and waiting – for something else. I tell you what, she was exactly like that fairy in the Scotch song, who is in love with a mortal, and sits by the high road in terror waiting for him to come, and hearing the plovers and the curlews. – Only nowadays motor lorries go along the moor roads and the poor thing is struck unconscious, and carried into our world in a state of unconsciousness, and when she comes round, she tries to talk our language and behave as we behave, and she can't remember anything else, so she goes on and on, till she falls with a crash, back to her own world.'

Hannele was silent, and so was he.

'You loved her then?' she said at length.

'Yes. But in this way. When I was a boy I caught a bird, a black-cap, and I put it in a cage. And I loved that bird. I don't know why, but I loved it. I simply loved that bird. All the gorse, and the heather, and the rock, and the hot smell of yellow gorse-blossoms, and the sky that seemed to have no end to it, when I was a boy, everything that I almost was *mad* with as boys are, seemed to me to be in that little, fluttering black-cap. And it would peck its seed as if it didn't quite know what else to do; and look round about, and begin to sing. But in quite a few days it turned its head aside and died. Yes, it died. – I never had the feeling again, that I got from that black-cap when I was a boy – not until I saw her. And then I felt it all again. I felt it all again. And it was the same feeling. I knew, quite soon I knew, that she would die. She would peck her seed and look round in the cage just the same. But she would die in the end. – Only it would last much longer. – But she would die in the cage, like the black-cap.'

'But she loved the cage. She loved her clothes and her jewels. She must have loved her house and her furniture and all that with a perfect frenzy.'

'She did. She did. But like a child with playthings. Only they were big, marvellous playthings to her. Oh, yes, she was never away from them. She never forgot her things – her trinkets and her furs and her furniture. She never got away from them for a minute. And everything in her mind was mixed up with them.'

'Dreadful!' said Hannele.

'Yes, it was dreadful,' he answered.

'Dreadful,' repeated Hannele.

'Yes, quite. Quite! And it got worse. And her way of talking got worse. As if it bubbled off her lips. – But her eyes never lost their brightness, they never lost that fairy look. Only I used to see fear in them. Fear of everything – even all the things she surrounded herself with. Just like my black-cap used to look out of his cage – so bright and sharp, and yet as if he didn't know that it was just the cage that was between him and the outside. He thought it was inside himself, the barrier. He thought it was part of his own nature, to be shut in. And she thought it was part of her own nature. – And so they both died.'

'What I can't see,' said Hannele, 'is what she would have done outside her cage. What other life could she have, except her *bibelots*[16] and her furniture, and her talk –?'

'Why, none. There *is* no life outside, for human beings.'

'Then there's nothing,' said Hannele.

'That's true. In a great measure, there's nothing.'

'Thank you,' said Hannele.

There was a long pause.

'And perhaps I was to blame. Perhaps I ought to have made some sort of a move. But I didn't know what to do. For my life, I didn't know what to do, except try to make her happy. She had enough money – and I didn't think it mattered if she shared it with me. I always had a garden – and the astronomy. It's been an immense relief to me, watching the moon. It's been wonderful. Instead of looking inside the cage, as I did at my bird, or at her – I look right out – into freedom – into freedom.'

'The moon, you mean?' said Hannele.

'Yes, the moon.'

'And that's your freedom?'

'That's where I've found the greatest sense of freedom,' he said.

'Well, I'm not going to be jealous of the moon,' said Hannele at length.

'Why should you? It's not a thing to be jealous of.'

In a little while, she bade him good-night, and left him.

x

The chief thing that the Captain knew, at this juncture, was that a hatchet had gone through the ligatures and veins that connected him with the people of his affection, and that he was left with the bleeding ends of all his vital human relationships. Why it should be so, he did not know. But then one never can know the whys and the wherefores of one's passional changes.

He only knew that it was so. The emotional flow between him and all the people he knew and cared for was broken, and for the time being he was conscious only of the cleavage. The cleavage that had occurred between him and his fellow men, the cleft that was now between him and them. It was not the fault of anybody or anything. He could reproach neither himself nor them. What had happened had been preparing for a long time. Now suddenly the cleavage. There had been a long slow weaning away: and now this sudden silent rupture.

What it amounted to principally was that he did not want even to see Hannele. He did not want to think of her even. But neither did he want to see anybody else or to think of anybody else. He shrank with a feeling almost of disgust from his friends and acquaintances, and their expressions of sympathy. It affected him with instantaneous disgust, when anybody wanted to share emotions with him. He did not want to share emotions or feelings of any sort. He wanted to be by himself, essentially, even if he was moving about among other people.

So he went to England, to settle his own affairs, and out of duty to see his children. He wished his children all the well in the world – everything except any emotional connexion with himself. He decided to take his girl away from the convent at once, and to put her into a jolly English school. His boy was all right where he was.

The Captain had now an income sufficient to give him his independence, but not sufficient to keep up his wife's house. So he prepared to sell the house and most of the things in it. He decided also to leave the Army as soon as he could be free. And he thought he would wander about for a time, till he came upon something he wanted.

So the winter passed, without his going back to Germany. He was free of the army. He drifted along, settling his affairs. They were of no very great importance. And all the time he never wrote once to Hannele. He could not get over his disgust that people insisted on his sharing their emotions. He could not bear their emotions, neither their activities. Other people might have all the emotions and feelings and earnestnesses and busy activities they liked. Quite nice even that they had such a multifarious commotion for themselves. But the moment they approached him to spread their feelings over him or to entangle him in their activities a helpless disgust came up in him, and until he could get away, he felt sick, even physically.

This was no state of mind for a lover. He could not even think of Hannele. Anybody else he felt he need not think about. He was deeply, profoundly thankful that his wife was dead. It was an end of pity now: because, poor thing, she had escaped and gone her own way into the void, like a flown bird.

XI

Nevertheless, a man hasn't finished his life at forty. He may, however, have finished one great phase of his life.

And Alexander Hepburn was not the man to live alone. All our troubles, says somebody wise, come upon us because we cannot be alone. And that is all very well. We must all be *able* to be alone, otherwise we are just victims. But when we *are* able to be alone, then we realize that the only thing to do is to start a new relationship with another – or even the same – human being. That people should all be stuck up apart, like so many telegraph poles, is nonsense.

So with our dear Captain. He had his convulsion into a sort of telegraph-pole isolation: which was absolutely necessary for him. But then he began to bud with a new yearning for – what? For love?

It was a question he kept nicely putting to himself. And really, the nice young girls of eighteen or twenty attracted him very much: so fresh, so impulsive, and looking up to him as if he were something wonderful. If only he could have married two or three of them, instead of just one!

Love! – When a man has no particular ambition, his mind turns back perpetually, as a needle towards the pole. That tiresome word Love. It means so many things. It meant the feeling he had for his wife. He had loved her. But he shuddered at the thought of having to go through such love again. – It meant also the feeling he had for the awfully nice young things he met here and there: fresh, impulsive girls ready to give all their hearts away. Oh, yes, he could fall in love with half a dozen of them. But he knew he'd better not.

At last he wrote to Hannele: and got no answer. So he wrote to Mitchka and still got no answer. So he wrote for information – and there was none forthcoming, except that the two women had gone to Munich.

For the time being, he left it at that. To him, Hannele did not exactly represent rosy love. Rather a hard destiny. He did not adore her. He did not feel one bit of adoration for her. As a matter of fact, not all the beauties and virtues of woman put together with all the gold in the Indies would have tempted him into the business of adoration any more. He had gone on his knees once, vowing with faltering tones to try and make the adored one happy. And now – never again. Never.

The temptation this time was, to be adored. One of those fresh young things would have adored him as if he were a god. And there was something *very* alluring about the thought. Very. Very alluring. To be god-almighty in your own house, with a lovely young thing adoring you, and you giving off beams of bright effulgence like a Gloria![17] Who wouldn't be tempted: at the age of forty? And this was why he dallied.

But in the end he suddenly took the train to Munich. And when he got there he found the town beastly uncomfortable, the Bavarians rude and disagreeable, and no sign of the missing females, not even in the Café Stéphanie. He wandered round and round.

And then one day, oh, heaven, he saw his doll in a shop-window: a little art shop; he stood and stared quite spellbound.

'Well, if that isn't the devil,' he said. 'Seeing yourself in a shop-window!'

He was so disgusted that he would not go into the shop.

Then, every day for a week did he walk down that little street and look at himself in the shop-window. Yes, there he stood, with one hand in his pocket. And the figure had one hand in its pocket. There he stood, with his cap pulled rather low over his brow. And the figure had its cap pulled low over its brow. But thank goodness his own cap now was a civilian tweed. But there he stood, his head rather forward, gazing with fixed dark eyes. And himself in little, that wretched figure, stood there with its head rather forward, staring with fixed dark eyes. It was such a real little *man*, that it fairly staggered him. The oftener he saw it, the more it staggered him. And the more he hated it. Yet it fascinated him, and he came again to look.

And it was always there. A lonely little individual lounging there with one hand in its pocket, and nothing to do, among the bric-à-brac and the *bibelots*. Poor devil, stuck so incongruously in the world. And yet losing none of his masculinity.

A male little devil, for all his forlornness. But such an air of isolation, of not belonging. Yet taut and male, in his tartan trews. And what a situation to be in: – lounging with his back against a little Japanese lacquer cabinet, with a few old pots on his right hand and a tiresome brass ink-tray, on his left, while pieces of not-very-nice filet lace hung their length up and down the background. Poor little devil: it was like a deliberate satire.

And then one day it was gone. There was the cabinet and the filet lace and the tiresome ink-stand tray: and the little gentleman wasn't there. The Captain at once walked into the shop.

'Have you sold that doll? – that unknown soldier?' he added, without knowing quite what he was saying.

The doll was sold.

'Do you know who bought it?'

The girl looked at him very coldly, and did not know.

'I once knew the lady who made it. In fact the doll was *me*,' he said.

The girl now looked at him with sudden interest.

'Don't you think it was like me?' he said.

'Perhaps –' she began to smile.

'It was me. And the lady who made it was a friend of mine. Do you know her name?'

'Yes.'

'Gräfin[18] zu Rassentlow,' he cried, his eyes shining.

'Oh, yes. But her dolls are famous.'

'Do you know where she is? Is she in Munich?'

'That I don't know.'

'Could you find out?'

'I don't know. I can ask.'

'Or the Baroness von Prielau-Carolath.'

'The Baroness is dead.'

'Dead!'

'She was shot in a riot in Salzburg. They say a lover –'

'How do you know?'

'From the newspapers.'

'Dead! Is it possible? Poor Hannele.'

There was a pause.

'Well,' he said, 'if you would inquire about the address – I'll call again.'

Then he turned back from the door.

'By the way, do you mind telling me how much you sold the doll for?'

The girl hesitated. She was by no means anxious to give away any of her trade details. But at length she answered reluctantly:

'Five hundred marks.'

'So cheap,' he said. 'Good-day. Then I will call again.'

XII

Then again he got a trace. It was in the Chit-Chat column of the *Münchener Neue Zeitung*: under Studio-Comments. 'Theodor Worpswede's latest picture is a still-life, containing an entertaining group of a doll, two sun-flowers in a glass jar, and a poached egg on toast. The contrast between the three substances is highly diverting and instructive, and this is perhaps one of the most interesting of Worpswede's works. The doll, by the way, is one of the creations of our fertile Countess Hannele. It is the figure of an English, or rather Scottish officer in the famous tartan trousers which, clinging closely to the legs of the lively Gaul, so shocked the eminent Julius Caesar and his cohorts. We, of course, are no longer shocked, but full of admiration for the creative genius of our dear Countess. The doll itself is a masterpiece, and has begotten another masterpiece in Theodor Worpswede's Still-life. – We have heard, by the way, a rumour of Countess zu Rassentlow's engagement. Apparently the Herr Regierungsrat[19] Trepte, of that most beautiful of summer-resorts, Kaprun, in the Tyrol, is the fortunate man –'

XIII

The Captain bought the still-life. This new version of himself along with the poached egg and the sun-flowers was rather frightening. So he packed up for Austria, for Kaprun, with his picture, and had a fight to get the beastly thing out of Germany, and another fight to get it into Austria. Fatigued and furious he arrived in Salzburg, seeing no beauty in anything. Next day he was in Kaprun.

It was an elegant and fashionable watering-place before the war: a lovely little lake in the midst of the Alps, an old Tyrolese town on the water-side, green slopes sheering up opposite, and away beyond, a glacier. It was still crowded and still elegant. But alas, with a broken, bankrupt, desperate elegance and almost empty shops.

The Captain felt rather dazed. He found himself in an hotel

full of Jews of the wrong rich sort, and wondered what next. The place was beautiful, but the life wasn't.

XIV

The Herr Regierungsrat was not at first sight prepossessing. He was approaching fifty, and had gone stout and rather loose, as so many men of his class and race do. Then he wore one of those dreadful full-bottom coats, a kind of poor relation to our full-skirted frock-coat: it would best be described as a family coat. It flapped about him as he walked, and he looked at first glance lower middle-class.

But he wasn't. Of course, being in office in the collapsed Austria, he was a republican. But by nature he was a monarchist, nay, an imperialist, as every true Austrian is. And he was a true Austrian. And as such he was much finer and subtler than he looked. As one got used to him, his rather fat face with its fine nose and slightly bitter, pursed mouth came to have a resemblance to the busts of some of the late Roman emperors. And as one was with him one came gradually to realize that out of all his baggy bourgeois appearance came something of a *grand geste.*[20] He could not help it. There was something sweeping and careless about his soul: big, rather assertive, and ill-bred-seeming; but in fact, not ill-bred at all, only a little bitter and a good deal indifferent to his surroundings. He looked at first sight so common and parvenu.[21] And then one had to realize that he was a member of a big old empire, fallen into a sort of epicure-anism, and a little bitter. – There was no littleness, no meanness, and no real coarseness. But he was a great talker, and relentless towards his audience.

Hannele was attracted to him by his talk. He began as soon as dinner appeared: and he went on, carrying the decanter and the wine-glass with him out on to the balcony of the villa, over the lake, on and on until midnight. The summer night was still and warm: the lake lay deep and full, and the old town twinkled away across. There was the faintest tang of snow in the air, from the great glacier-peaks that were hidden in the night opposite. Sometimes a boat with a lantern twanged a guitar. The clematis flowers were quite black like leaves, dangling from the terrace.

It was so beautiful, there in the very heart of the Tyrol. The hotels glittered with lights: electric light was still cheap. There seemed a fullness and a loveliness in the night. And yet for some reason it was all terrible and devastating: the life-spirit seemed to be squirming, bleeding all the time.

And on and on talked the Herr Regierungsrat, with all the witty volubility of the more versatile Austrian. He was really very witty, very human, and with a touch of salty cynicism that reminded one of a real old Roman of the Empire. That subtle stoicism, that unsentimental epicureanism, that kind of reckless hopelessness of course fascinated the women. And particularly Hannele. He talked on and on – about his work before the war, when he held an important post and was one of the governing class – then about the war – then about the hopelessness of the present: and in it all there seemed a bigness, a carelessness based on indifference, and hopelessness that laughed at its very self. The real old Austria had always fascinated Hannele. As represented in the witty, bitter-indifferent Herr Regierungsrat it carried her away.

And he, of course, turned instinctively to her, talking in his rapid, ceaseless fashion with a laugh and a pause to drink and a new start taken. She liked the sound of his Austrian speech: its racy carelessness, its salty indifference to standards of correctness. Oh yes, here was the *grand geste* still lingering.

He turned his large breast towards her, and made a quick gesture with his fat, well-shapen hand, blurted out another subtle, rough-seeming romance, pursed his mouth, and emptied his glass once more. Then he looked at his half-forgotten cigar and started again.

There was something almost boyish and impulsive about him: the way he turned to her, and the odd way he seemed to open his big breast to her. And again, he seemed almost eternal, sitting there in his chair with knees planted apart. It was as if he would never rise again, but would remain sitting for ever, and talking. He seemed as if he had no legs, save to sit with. As if to stand on his feet and walk would not be natural to him.

Yet he rose at last, and kissed her hand with the grand gesture that France or Germany have never acquired: carelessness, profound indifference to other people's standards, and then such a sudden stillness, as he bent and kissed her hand. Of course she felt a queen in exile.

And perhaps it is more dangerous to feel yourself a queen in exile than a queen *in situ*. She fell in love with him, with this large, stout, loose widower of fifty, with two children. He had no money except some Austrian money that was worth nothing outside Austria. He could not even go to Germany. There he was, fixed in this hollow in the middle of the Tyrol.

But he had an ambition still, old Roman of the decadence that he was. He had year by year and without making any fuss collected the material for a very minute and thorough history of his own district: the Chiemgau and the Pinzgau. Hannele found that his fund of information on this subject was inexhaustible, and his intelligence was so delicate, so human and his scope seemed so wide, that she felt a touch of reverence for him. He wanted to write this history. And she wanted to help him.

For of course, as things were he would never write it. He was Regierungsrat: that is, he was the petty local governor of his town and immediate district. The Amthaus[22] was a great old building, and there young ladies in high heels flirted among masses of papers with bare-kneed young gentlemen in Tyrolese costume, and occasionally they parted, to take a pleasant, interesting attitude and write a word or two, after which they fluttered together for a little more interesting diversion. It was extraordinary how many finely built, handsome young people of an age fitted for nothing but love affairs, ran the governmental business of this department. And the Herr Regierungsrat sailed in and out of the big old room, his wide coat flying like wings and making the papers flutter, his rather wine-reddened, old-Roman face smiling with its bitter look. And of course it was a witticism he uttered first, even if Hungary was invading the frontier or cholera was in Vienna.

When he was on his legs, he walked nimbly, briskly, and his coat bottoms always flew. So he waved through the town, greeting somebody at every few strides, and grinning, and yet with a certain haughty reserve. Oh yes, there was a certain salty *hauteur* about him, which made the people trust him. And he spoke the vernacular so racily.

Hannele felt she would like to marry him. She would like to be near him. She would like him to write his history. She would like him to make her feel a queen in exile. No one had ever *quite* kissed her hand as he kissed it: with that sudden stillness and strange, chivalric abandon of himself. How he would abandon himself to her! – terribly – wonderfully – perhaps a little horribly. His wife, whom he had married late, had died after seven years of marriage. Hannele could understand that too. One or the other must die.

She became engaged. But something made her hesitate before marriage. Being in Austria was like being on a wrecked ship, that *must* sink after a certain short length of time. And marrying the Herr Regierungsrat was like marrying the doomed captain of the doomed ship. The sense of fatality was part of the attraction.

And yet she hesitated. The summer weeks passed. The strangers flooded in and crowded the town, and ate up the food like locusts. People no longer counted the paper money, they weighed it by the kilogram. Peasants stored it in a corner of the meal-bin, and mice came and chewed holes in it. Nobody knew where the next lot of food was going to come from: and yet it always came. And the lake teemed with bathers. When the Captain arrived he looked with amazement on the crowds of strapping, powerful fellows who bathed all day long, magnificent blond flesh of men and women. No wonder the old Romans stood in astonishment before the huge blond limbs of the savage Germans.

Well, the life was like a madness. The hotels charged fifteen-hundred kronen a day: the women, old and young, paraded in the peasant-costume, in flowery cotton dresses with gaudy, expensive silk aprons: the men wore the Tyrolese costume, bare knees and little short jackets. And for the men, the correct thing was to have the leathern hose and the blue linen jacket as old as possible. If you had a hole in your leathern seat, so much the better.

Everything so physical. Such magnificent naked limbs and

naked bodies, and in the streets, in the hotels, everywhere, bare white arms of women and bare, brown, powerful knees and thighs of men. The sense of flesh everywhere, and the endless ache of flesh. Even in the peasants who rowed across the lake, standing and rowing with a slow, heavy, gondolier motion at the one curved oar, there was the same endless ache of physical yearning.

XV

It was August when Alexander met Hannele. She was walking under a chintz parasol, wearing a dress of blue cotton with little red roses, and a red silk apron. She had no hat, her arms were bare and soft, and she had white stockings under her short dress. The Herr Regierungsrat was at her side, large, nimble, and laughing with a new witticism.

Alexander, in a light summer suit and Panama, was just coming out of the bank, shoving twenty thousand kronen into his pocket. He saw her coming across from the Amtsgericht, with the Herr Regierungsrat at her side, across the space of sunshine. She was laughing, and did not notice him.

She did not notice till he had taken off his hat and was saluting her. Then what she saw was the black, smooth, shining head, and she went pale. His black, smooth, close head – and all the blue Austrian day seemed to shrivel before her eyes.

'How do you do, Countess! I hoped I should meet you.'

She heard his slow, sad-clanging, straying voice again, and she pressed her hand with the umbrella stick against her breast. She had forgotten it – forgotten his peculiar slow voice. And now it seemed like a noise that sounds in the silence of night. Ah, how difficult it was, that suddenly the world could split under her eyes, and show this darkness inside. She wished he had not come.

She presented him to the Herr Regierungsrat, who was stiff and cold. She asked where the Captain was staying. And then, not knowing what else to say, she said:

'Won't you come to tea?'

She was staying in a villa across the lake. Yes, he would come to tea.

He went. He hired a boat and a man to row him across. It was not far. There stood the villa, with its brown balconies one above the other, the bright red geraniums and white geraniums twinkling all round, the tress of purple clematis tumbling at one corner. All the green window-doors were open: but nobody about. In the little garden by the water's edge the rose-trees were tall and lank, drawn up by the dark green trees of the background. A white table with chairs and garden seats stood under the shadow of a big willow tree, and a hammock with cushions swung just behind. But no one in sight. There was a little landing bridge on to the garden: and a fairly large boat-house at the garden end.

The Captain was not sure that the boat-house belonged to the villa. Voices were shouting and laughing from the water's surface, bathers swimming. A tall, naked youth with a little red cap on his head and a tiny red loin-cloth round his slender young hips was standing on the steps of the boat-house calling to the three women who were swimming near. The dark-haired woman with the white cap swam up to the steps and caught the boy by the ankle. He cried and laughed and remonstrated, and poked her in the breast with his foot.

'Nein, nein, Hardu!' she cried as he tickled her with his toe. 'Hardu! Hardu! Hör' auf! – Leave off!' and she fell with a crash back into the water. The youth laughed a loud, deep laugh of a lad whose voice is newly broken.

'Was macht er denn?' cried a voice from the waters. 'What is he doing?' It was a dark-skinned girl swimming swiftly, her big dark eyes watching amused from the water-surface.

'Jetzt Hardu hör' auf. Nein. Jetzt ruhig! Now leave off! Now be quiet.' And the dark-haired woman was climbing out in the sunshine onto the pale, raw-wood steps of the boat-house, the water glistening on her dark-blue, stockinette, soft-moulded back and loins: while the boy, with his foot stretched out, was trying to push her back into the water. She clambered out, however, and sat on the steps in the sun, panting slightly. She was dark and attractive-looking, with a mature beautiful figure, and handsome, strong woman's legs.

In the garden appeared a black-and-white maid-servant with a trav

'Kaffee, gnädige Frau!'[23]

The voice came so distinct over the water.

'Hannele! Hannele! Kaffee!' called the woman on the steps of the bathing-house.

'Tante Hannele! Kaffee!' called the dark-eyed girl, turning round in the water, then swimming for home.

'Kaffee! Kaffee!' roared the youth, in anticipation.

'Ja – a! Ich kom – m,'[24] sang Hannele's voice from the water.

The dark-eyed girl, her hair tied up in a silk bandana, had reached the steps and was climbing out, a slim young fish in her close dark suit. The three stood clustered on the steps, the elder woman with one arm over the naked shoulders of the youth, the other arm over the shoulders of the girl. And all in chorus they sang:

'Hannele! Hannele! Hannele! – Wir warten auf dich.'[25]

The boat-man had left off rowing, and the boat was drifting slowly in. The family became quiet, because of the intrusion. The attractive-looking woman turned and picked up her blue bath-robe, of a mid-blue colour that became her. She swung it round her as if it were an opera cloak. The youth stared at the boat.

The Captain was watching Hannele. With a white kerchief tied round her silky, brownish hair, she was swimming home. He saw her white shoulders, and her white wavering legs below in the clear water. Round the boat fishes were suddenly jumping.

The three on the steps beyond stood silent, watching the intruding boat with resentment. The boat-man twisted his head round and watched them. The Captain, who was facing them, watched Hannele. She swam slowly and easily up, caught the rail of the steps, and stooping forward, climbed slowly out of the water. Her legs were large and flashing white and looked rich, the rich white thighs with the blue veins behind, and the full, rich softness of her sloping loins.

'Ach – ! Schön! 'S war schön! Das Wasser ist gut,'[26] her voice was heard, half singing as she took her breath – 'It was lovely.'

'Heiss,'[27] said the woman above. 'Zu warm. – Too warm.'

The youth made way for Hannele, who drew herself erect at the top of the steps, looking round, panting a little, and putting

up her hands to the knot of her kerchief on her head. Her legs
were magnificent and white.

'Kuck de Leut die da bleiben,' said the woman in the blue
wrap, in a loud voice. 'Look at the people stopping there.'

'Ja!' said Hannele negligently. Then she looked. She started
as if in fear, looked round, as if to run away, looked back again,
and met the eyes of the Captain, who took off his hat.

She cried, in a loud frightened voice:

'Oh, but – I thought it was *to-morrow*!'

'No – to-day,' came the quiet voice of the Captain over the
water.

'*To-day*! Are you *sure* – ?' she cried, calling to the boat.

'Quite sure. But we'll make it to-morrow if you like,' he said.

'To-day! To-day!' she repeated in bewilderment. 'No! Wait
a minute.' And she ran into the boat-house.

'Was ist es?' asked the dark woman, following her. 'What is
it?'

'A friend – a visitor – Captain Hepburn,' came Hannele's
voice.

The boat-man now rowed slowly to the landing stage. The
dark woman, huddled in her blue wrap as in an opera-cloak,
walked proudly and unconcernedly across the background of the
garden, and up the steps to the first balcony. Hannele, her feet
slip-slopping in loose slippers, clutching an old yellow wrap
round her, came to the landing stage and shook hands.

'I am so sorry. It is so stupid of me. I was sure it was to-
morrow,' she said.

'No, it was to-day. But I wish for your sake it had been to-
morrow,' he replied.

'No. No. It doesn't matter. You won't mind waiting a minute,
will you? You mustn't be angry with me for being so stupid.'

So she went away, the heel-less slippers flipping up to her
naked heels. Then the big-eyed, dusky girl stole into the house:
and then the naked youth, who went with sang-froid.[28] He
would make a fine, handsome man: and he knew it.

XVI

Hepburn and Hannele were to make a small excursion to the glacier which stood there always in sight, coldly grinning in the sky. The weather had been very hot, but this morning there were loose clouds in the sky. The Captain rowed over the lake soon after dawn. Hannele stepped into the little craft, and they pulled back to the town. There was a wind ruffling the water, so that the boat leaped and chuckled. The glacier, in a recess among the folded mountains, looked cold and angry. But morning was very sweet in the sky, and blowing very sweet with a faint scent of the second hay, from the low lands at the head of the lake. Beyond stood naked grey rock like a wall of mountains, pure rock, with faint thin slashes of snow. Yesterday it had rained on the lake. The sun was going to appear from behind the Breitsteinhorn, the sky with its clouds floating in blue light and yellow radiance was lovely and cheering again. But dark clouds seemed to spout up from the Pinzgau valley. And once across the lake, all was shadow, when the water no longer gave back the sky-morning.

The day was a feast day, a holiday. Already so early three young men from the mountains, were bathing near the steps of the Badeanstalt. Handsome, physical fellows, with good limbs rolling and swaying in the early morning water. They seemed to enjoy it too. But to Hepburn it was always as if a dark wing were stretched in the sky, over these mountains, like a doom. And these three young, lusty naked men swimming and rolling in the shadow.

Hepburn's was the first boat stirring. He made fast in the hotel boat-house, and he and Hannele went into the little town. It was deep in shadow, though the light of the sky, curdled with cloud, was bright overhead. But dark and chill and heavy lay the shadow in the black-and-white town, like a sediment.

The shops were all shut, but peasants from the hills were already strolling about, in their holiday dress: the men in their short leather trousers, like foot-ball drawers, and bare brown knees, and great boots: their little grey jackets faced with green, and their green hats with the proud chamois-brush behind. They seemed to stray about like lost souls, and the proud chamois-brush behind their hats, this proud, cocky, perking-up tail, like a mountain-buck with his tail up, was belied by the lost-soul look of the men, as they loitered about with their hands shoved in the front pockets of their trousers. – Some women also were creeping about: peasant women, in the funny little black hats that had thick gold under the brim and long black streamers of ribbon, broad black water-wave ribbon starting from a bow under the brim behind and streaming right to the bottom of the skirt. These women in their thick dark dresses with tight bodices, and massive heavy full skirts, and bright or dark aprons, strode about with the heavy stride of the mountain women, the heavy, quick, forward-leaning motion. They were waiting for the town-day to begin.

Hepburn had a knapsack on his back, with food for the day. But bread was wanting. They found the door of the bakery open, and got a loaf: a long, hot loaf of pure white bread, beautiful sweet bread. It cost seventy kronen. To Hepburn it was always a mystery where this exquisite bread came from, in a lost land.

In the little square where the clock stood were bunches of people, and a big motor-omnibus, and a motor-car that would hold about eight people. Hepburn had paid his seven hundred kronen for the two tickets. Hannele tied up her head in a thin scarf, and put on her thick coat. She and Hepburn sat in front by the peaked driver. And at seven o'clock away went the car, swooping out of the town, past the handsome old Tyrolese Schloss, or manor, black-and-white, with its little black spires pricking up, past the station, and under the trees by the lakeside. The road was not good, but they ran at a great speed, out past the end of the lake, where the reeds grew, out into the open valley-mouth, where the mountains opened in two clefts. It was cold in the car. Hepburn buttoned himself up to the throat and pulled his hat down on his ears. Hannele's scarf fluttered. She sat without saying anything, erect, her face fine and keen, watching ahead. From the deep Pinzgau valley came the river roaring and raging, a glacier river of pale, seething ice-water. Over went the car, over the log bridge, darting towards the great slopes opposite. And then a sudden immense turn, a swerve under the height of the mountainside, and again a darting lurch forward, under the pear-trees of the high road, past the big old ruined castle that so magnificently watched the valley mouth, and the foaming river, on, rushing under the huge roofs of the balconied peasant houses of a village, then swinging again to take another valley mouth, there where a little village clustered all black and white on a knoll, with a white church that had a black steeple, and a white castle with black spines, and clustering, ample black-and-white houses of the Tyrol. There is a grandeur even in the peasant houses, with their great wide passage halls where the swallows build, and where one could build a whole English cottage.

So the motor-car darted up this new, narrow, wilder, more sinister valley. A herd of almost wild young horses, handsome reddish things, burst around the car, and one great mare with full flanks went crashing up the road ahead, her heels flashing to the car, while her foal whinneyed and screamed from behind. But no, she could not turn from the road. On and on she crashed, forging ahead, the car behind her. And then at last she did swerve aside, among the thin alder trees by the wild river-bed.

'If it isn't a cow, it's a horse,' said the driver, who was thin and weaselish and silent, with his ear-flaps over his ears.

But the great mare had shaken herself in a wild swerve, and screaming and whinneying was plunging back to her foal. Hannele had been frightened.

The car rushed on, through water-meadows, along a naked white bit of mountain road. Ahead was a darkness of mountain front and pine trees. To the right was the stony, furious, lion-like river, tawny-coloured here, and the slope up beyond. But the road for the moment was swinging fairly level through the stunned water-meadows of the savage valley. There were gates to open, and Hepburn jumping down to open them, as if he were the foot-boy. The heavy Jews of the wrong sort, seated behind, of course did not stir.

At a house on a knoll the driver sounded his horn, and out rushed children crying Papa! Papa! – then a woman with a basket. A few brief words from the weaselish man, who smiled with warm, manly blue eyes at his children, then the car leaped forward. The whole bearing of the man was so different, when he was looking at his own family. He could not even say thank-you when Hepburn opened the gates. He hated and even despised his human cargo of middle-class people. Deep, deep is class-hatred, and it begins to swallow all human feeling in its abyss. So, stiff, silent, thin, capable, and neuter towards his fares sat the little driver with the flaps over his ears, and his thin nose cold.

The car swept round, suddenly, into the trees: and into the ravine. The river shouted at the bottom of a gulf. Bristling pine-trees stood around. The air was black and cold and forever sunless. The motor-car rushed on, in this blackness, under the rock-walls and the fir-trees.

Then it suddenly stopped. There was a huge motor-omnibus ahead, drab and enormous looking. Tourists and trippers of last night coming back from the glacier. It stood like a great rock. And the smaller motor-car edged past, tilting into the rock-gutter under the face of stone.

So, after a while of this valley of the shadow of death, lurching in steep loops upwards, the motor-car scrambling wonderfully, struggling past trees and rock upwards, at last they came to the end. It was a huge inn or tourist-hotel of brown wood: and here the road ended in a little wide bay surrounded and overhung by trees. Beyond was a garage and a bridge over a roaring river, and always the overhung darkness of trees and the intolerable steep slopes immediately above.

Hannele left her big coat. The sky looked blue above the gloom. They set out across the hollow-sounding bridge, over the everlasting mad rush of ice-water, to the immediate upslope of the path, under dark trees. But a little old man in a sort of sentry-box wanted fifty or sixty kronen: apparently for the upkeep of the road, a sort of toll.

The other tourists were coming – some stopping to have a drink first. The second omnibus had not yet arrived. Hannele and Hepburn were the first two, treading slowly up that dark path, under the trees. The grasses hanging on the rock face were still dewy. There were a few wild raspberries, and a tiny tuft of bilberries with black berries here and there, and a few tufts of unripe cranberries. The many hundreds of tourists who passed up and down did not leave much to pick. Some mountain hare-bells, like bells of blue water, hung coldly glistening in their darkness. Sometimes the hairy mountain-bell, pale-blue and bristling, stood alone, curving his head right down, stiff and taut. There was an occasional big, moist, lolling daisy.

So the two climbed slowly up the steep ledge of a road. This valley was just a mountain cleft, cleft sheer in the hard, living rock, with black trees like hair flourishing in this secret, naked place of the earth. At the bottom of the open wedge for ever roared the rampant, insatiable water. The sky from above was like a sharp wedge forcing its way into the earth's cleavage, and that eternal ferocious water was like the steel edge of the wedge, the terrible tip biting in into the rocks' intensity. Who could have thought that the soft sky of light, and the soft foam of water could thrust and penetrate into the dark strong earth? – But so it was. Hannele and Hepburn, toiling up the steep little ledge of a road that hung half-way down the gulf, looked back, time after time, back down upon the brown timbers and shingle roofs of the hotel, that now, away below, looked damp and wedged in like boulders. Then back at the next tourists struggling up. Then down at the water, that rushed like a beast of prey. And then, as they rose higher, they looked up also, at the livid great sides of rock, livid bare rock that sloped from the sky-ridge in a hideous sheer swerve downwards.

In his heart of hearts Hepburn hated it. He hated it, he loathed it, it seemed almost obscene, this livid naked slide of rock, unthinkably huge and massive, sliding down to this gulf where bushes grew like hair in the darkness, and water roared. Above, there were thin slashes of snow.

So the two climbed slowly on, up the eternal side of that valley, sweating with the exertion. Sometimes the sun, now risen high, shone full on their side of the gulley. Tourists were trickling down-hill too: two maidens with bare arms and bare heads and huge boots: men tourists with great knapsacks and edelweiss in their hats: giving Bergheil[29] for a greeting. But the Captain said Good-day. He refused this Bergheil business. People swarming touristy on these horrible mountains made him feel almost sick.

He and Hannele also were not in good company together. There was a sort of silent hostility between them. She hated the effort of climbing; but the high air, the cold in the air, the savage cat-howling sound of the water, those awful flanks of livid rock, all this thrilled and excited her to another sort of savageness. And he, dark, rather slender and feline, with something of the physical suavity of a delicate-footed race, he hated beating his way up the rock, he hated the sound of the water, it frightened him, and the high air bit him in the chest, like a viper.

'Wonderful! Wonderful!' she cried, taking great breaths in her splendid chest.

'Yes. – And horrible. Detestable,' he said, as if lurking among it all and trying to retain a certain invisibility.

She turned with a flash, and the high strident sound of the mountain in her voice.

'If you don't like it,' she said, rather jeering, 'why did you come?'

'I had to try,' he said.

'And if you don't like it,' she said, 'why should you try to spoil it for me?'

'I hate it,' he answered.

They were climbing more into the height, more into the light, into the open, in the full sun. The valley-cleft was sinking below them. Opposite was only the sheer livid slide of the naked rock, tipping from the pure sky. At a certain angle they could see away beyond, the lake lying far off and small, the wall of those other rocks like a curtain of stone, dim and diminished to the horizon. And the sky with curdling clouds and blue sunshine intermittent.

'Wonderful, wonderful, to be high up,' she said, breathing great breaths.

'Yes,' he said. 'It *is* wonderful. But very detestable. I want to live near the sea-level. I am no mountain-topper.'

'Evidently not,' she said.

'Bergheil!' cried a youth with bare arms and bare chest, bare head, terrific fanged boots, a knapsack and an alpenstock, and all the bronzed wind and sun of the mountain snow in his skin and his faintly bleached hair. With his great heavy knapsack, his rumpled thick stockings, his ghastly fanged boots, Hepburn found him repulsive.

'Guten Tag,' he answered coldly.[30]

'Grüss Gott,' said Hannele.[31]

And the young Tannhäuser, the young Siegfried, this young
Balder beautiful,[32] strode climbing down the rocks, marching
and swinging with his alpenstock. And immediately after the
youth came a maiden, with hair on the wind and her shirt-breast
open, striding in corduroy breeches, rumpled worsted stockings,
thick boots, a knapsack and an alpenstock. She passed without
greeting. And our pair stopped in angry silence and watched her
dropping down the mountainside.

XVII

Ah, well, everything comes to an end, even the longest up-climb.
So, after much sweat and effort and crossness, Hepburn and
Hannele emerged on to the rounded bluff where the road wound
out of that hideous great valley-cleft, into upper regions. So they
emerged more on the level, out of the trees as out of something
horrible, on to a naked great bank of rock and grass.

'Thank the Lord!' said Hannele.

So they trudged on round the bluff, and then in front of them
saw what is always, always wonderful, one of those shallow upper
valleys, naked, where the first waters are rocked. A flat, shallow,
utterly desolate valley, wide as a wide bowl under the sky, with
rock slopes and grey stone-slides and precipices all around, and
the zig-zag of snow-stripes and ice-roots descending, and then
rivers, streams and rivers rushing from many points downwards,
down out of the ice-roots and the snow-dagger-points, waters
rushing in newly-liberated frenzy downwards, down in waterfalls and cascades and threads, down into the wide shallow bed
of the valley, strewn with rocks and stones innumerable, and not
a tree, not a visible bush.

Only, of course, two hotels or restaurant places. But these no
more than low, sprawling, peasant-looking places lost among the
stones, with stones on their roofs so that they seemed just a part
of the valley bed. There was the valley, dotted with rock and
rolled-down stone, and these two house-places, and woven with
innumerable new waters, and one hoarse stone-tracked river in
the desert, and the thin road-track winding along the desolate

flat, past first one house, then the other, over one stream, then another, on to the far rock-face above which the glacier seemed to loll like some awful great tongue put out.

'Ah, it is wonderful!' he said, as if to himself.

And she looked quickly at his face, saw the queer, blank, sphinx-look with which he gazed out beyond himself. His eyes were black and set, and he seemed so motionless, as if he were eternal facing these upper facts.

She thrilled with triumph. She felt he was overcome.

'It *is* wonderful,' she said.

'Wonderful. And forever wonderful,' he said.

'Ah, in *winter* –' she cried.

His face changed, and he looked at her.

'In winter you couldn't get up here,' he said.

They went on. Up the slopes cattle were feeding: came that isolated tong-tong-tong of cowbells, dropping like the slow clink of ice on the arrested air. The sound always woke in him a primeval, almost hopeless melancholy. Always made him feel *navré*.[33] He looked round. There was no tree, no bush, only great grey rocks and pale boulders scattered in place of trees and bushes. – But yes, clinging on one side like a dark close beard were the Alpenrose shrubs.

'In May,' he said, 'that side there must be all pink with Alpenroses.'

'I *must* come. I *must* come!' she cried.

There were tourists dotted along the road: and two tiny low carts drawn by silky long-eared mules. These carts went right down to meet the motor-cars, and to bring up provisions for the Glacier Hotel: for there was still another big hotel ahead. Hepburn was happy in that upper valley, that first rocking cradle of early water. He liked to see the great fangs and slashes of ice and snow thrust down into the rock, as if the ice had bitten into the flesh of the earth. And from the fang-tips the hoarse water crying its birth-cry, rushing down.

By the turfy road and under the rocks were many flowers: wonderful hare-bells, big and cold and dark, almost black, and seeming like purple-dark ice: then little tufts of tiny pale-blue bells, as if some fairy frog had been blowing spume-bubbles out

of the ice: then the bishops-crosier of the stiff, bigger, hairy
mountain-bell: then many stars of pale-lavender gentian,
touched with earth-colour: and then monkshood, yellow,
primrose yellow monkshood, and sudden places full of dark
monkshood. That dark-blue, black-blue, terrible colour of the
strange rich monkshood made Hepburn look and look and look
again. How did the ice come by that lustrous blue-purple intense
darkness? – and by that royal poison? – that laughing-snake
gorgeousness of much monkshood.

XVIII

By one of the loud streams, under a rock in the sun, with scented
minty or thyme flowers near, they sat down to eat some lunch.
It was about eleven o'clock. A thin bee went in and out the
scented flowers and the eyebright. The water poured with all the
lust and greed of unloosed water over the stones. He took a cupful
for Hannele, bright and icy, and she mixed it with the red
Hungarian wine.

Down the road strayed the tourists like pilgrims, and at the
closed end of the valley they could be seen, quite tiny, climbing
the cut-out road that went up like a stairway. Just by their
movements you perceived them. But on the valley-bed they went
like rolling stones, little as stones. A very elegant mule came
stepping by, following a middle-aged woman in tweeds and a tall,
high-browed man in knickerbockers. The mule was drawing a
very amusing little cart, a chair, rather like a round office-chair
upholstered in red velvet, and mounted on two wheels. The red
velvet had gone gold and orange and like fruit-juice, being old:
really a lovely colour. And the muleteer, a little shabby creature,
waddled beside excitedly.

'Ach,' cried Hannele, 'that looks almost like before the war:
almost as peaceful.'

'Except that the chair is too shabby, and that they all feel
exceptional,' he remarked.

There in that upper valley, there was no sense of peace. The
rush of the waters seemed like weapons, and the tourists all

seemed in a sort of frenzy, in a frenzy to be happy, or to be thrilled. It was a feeling that desolated the heart.

The two sat in the changing sunshine under their rock, with the mountain flowers scenting the snow-bitter air, and they ate their eggs and sausage and cheese, and drank the bright-red Hungarian wine. It seemed lovely: almost like before the war: almost the same feeling of eternal holiday, as if the world was made for man's everlasting holiday. But not quite. Never again quite the same. The world is not made for man's everlasting holiday.

As Alexander was putting the bread back into his shoulder-sack, he exclaimed:

'Oh, look here!'

She looked, and saw him drawing out a flat package wrapped in paper: evidently a picture.

'A picture!' she cried.

He unwrapped the thing, and handed it to her. It was Theodor Worpswede's Still-eben: not very large, painted on a board.

Hannele looked at it, and went pale.

'It's good,' she cried, in an equivocal tone.

'Quite good,' he said.

'Especially the poached egg,' she said.

'Yes, the poached egg is almost living.'

'But where did you find it?'

'Oh, I found it in the artist's studio –' And he told her how he had traced her.

'How extraordinary!' she cried. 'But why did you buy it?'

'I don't quite know.'

'Did you *like* it?'

'No, not quite that.'

'You could *never* hang it up.'

'No, never,' he said.

'But do you think it is good as a work of art?'

'I think it is quite clever as a painting. I don't like the spirit of it, of course. I'm too catholic for that.'

'No – No –' she faltered. 'It's rather horrid really. That's why I wonder why you bought it.'

'Perhaps to prevent anyone else's buying it,' he said.

'Do you mind very much, then?' she asked.

'No, I don't mind very much. – I didn't quite like it that you sold the doll,' he said.

'I needed the money,' she said quietly.

'Oh, quite.'

There was a pause for some moments.

'I felt you'd sold *me*,' she said, quiet and savage.

'When?'

'When your wife appeared. And when you *disappeared*.'

Again there was a pause: his pause this time.

'I did write to you,' he said.

'When?'

'Oh – March, I believe.'

'Oh yes. I had that letter.' Her tone was just as quiet, and even savager.

So there was a pause that belonged to both of them. Then she rose.

'I want to be going,' she said. 'We shall never get to the glacier at this rate.'

He packed up the picture, slung on his knapsack, and they set off. She stooped now and then to pick the starry, earth-lavender gentians from the road-side. As they passed the second of the valley hotels, they saw the man and wife sitting at a little table outside eating bread and cheese, while the mule-chair with its red velvet waited aside on the grass. They passed a whole grove of black-purple nightshade – monkshood – on the left, and some long, low cattle-huts which, with the stones on their roof, looked as if they had grown up as stones grow in such places through the grass. In the wild, desert place some black pigs were snouting.

So they wound into the head of the valley, and saw the steep face ahead, and high up, like vapour or foam dripping from the fangs of a beast, waterfalls vapouring down from the deep fangs of ice. And there was one end of the glacier, like a great bluey-white fur just slipping over the slope of the rock.

As the valley closed in again the flowers were very lovely, especially the big, dark, icy bells, like hare-bells, that would sway so easily, but which hung dark and with that terrible motionless-ness of upper mountain flowers. And the road turned to get on the long slant in the cliff-face, where it climbed like a stair. Slowly, slowly the two climbed up. Now again they saw the valley below, behind. The mule-chair was coming, hastening, the lady seated tight facing backwards, as the chair faced, and wrapped in rugs. The tall, fair, middle-aged husband in knickerbockers strode just behind, bare-headed.

Alexander and Hannele climbed slowly, slowly up the slant, under the dripping rock-face where the white and veined flowers of the grass of Parnassus still rose straight and chilly in the shadow, like water which had taken on itself white flower-flesh. Above they saw the slipping edge of the glacier, like a terrible great paw, bluey. And from the skyline dark grey clouds were fuming up, fuming up as if breathed black and icily out from some ice-cauldron.

'It is going to rain,' said Alexander.

'Not much,' said Hannele shortly.

'I hope not,' said he.

And still she would not hurry up that steep slant, but insisted on standing to look. So the dark, ice-black clouds fumed solid, and the rain began to fly on a cold wind. The mule-chair hastened past, the lady sitting comfortably with her back to the mule, a little pheasant-trimming in her tweed hat, while her Tannhäuser husband reached for his dark, cape-frilled mantle.

Alexander had his dust-coat, but Hannele had nothing but a light knitted jersey-coat, such as women wear indoors. Over the hollow crest above came the cold steel rain. They pushed on up the slope. From behind came another mule, and a little old man hurrying, and a little cart like a hand barrow, on which were hampers with cabbage and carrots and peas and joints of meat, for the hotel above.

'Wird es viel sein?' asked Alexander of the little gnome. 'Will it be much?'

'Was meint der Herr?' replied the other. 'What does the gentleman say?'

'Der Regen, wird es lang dauern? – Will the rain last long?'

'Nein. Nein. Dies ist kein langer Regen.'[34]

So, with his mule which had to stand exactly at that spot to make droppings, the little man resumed his way, and Hannele and Alexander were the last on the slope. The air smelt steel-cold of rain, and of hot mule-droppings. Alexander watched the rain beat on the shoulders and on the blue skirt of Hannele.

'It is a pity you left your big coat down below,' he said.

'What good is it saying so now!' she replied, pale at the nose with anger.

'Quite,' he said, as his eyes glowed and his brow blackened. 'What good suggesting anything at any time, apparently!'

She turned round on him in the rain, as they stood perched nearly at the summit of that slanting cliff-climb, with a glacier-paw hung almost invisible above, and waters gloating aloud in the gulf below. She faced him, and he faced her.

'What have you ever suggested to me?' she said, her face naked as the rain itself with an ice-bitter fury. 'What have you ever suggested to me?'

'When have you ever been open to suggestion?' he said, his face dark and his eyes curiously glowing.

'I? I? Haven't I waited for you to suggest something? – And all you can do is to come here with a picture to reproach me for having sold your doll. Ha! I'm glad I sold it. A foolish empty figure it was too, a foolish staring thing. What should I do but sell it? Why should I keep it, do you imagine?'

'Why do you come here with me to-day, then?'

'Why do I come here with you to-day?' she replied. 'I come to see the mountains, which are wonderful, and give me strength. And I come to see the glacier. Do you think I come here to see *you*? Why should I? You are always in some hotel or other away below.'

'You came to see the glacier and the mountains *with* me,' he replied.

'Did I? Then I made a mistake. You can do nothing but find fault even with God's mountains.'

A dark flame suddenly went over his face.

'Yes,' he said, 'I hate them, I hate them. I hate their snow and their affectations.'

'Affectation!' she laughed. 'Oh! Even the mountains are affected for you, are they?'

'Yes,' he said. 'Their loftiness and their uplift. I hate their uplift. I hate people prancing on mountain-tops and feeling exalted. I'd like to make them all stop up there, on their mountain-tops, and chew ice to fill their stomachs. I wouldn't let them down again, I wouldn't. I hate it all, I tell you, I hate it.'

She looked in wonder on his dark, glowing, ineffectual face. It seemed to her like a dark flame burning in the daylight and in the ice-rains: very ineffectual and unnecessary.

'You must be a little mad,' she said superbly, 'to talk like that about the mountains. They are so much bigger than you.'

'No,' he said. 'No! They are not.'

'What!' she laughed aloud. 'The mountains are not bigger than you? But you are extraordinary.'

'They are not bigger than me,' he cried. 'Any more than you are bigger than me if you stand on a ladder. They are not bigger than me. They are less than me.'

'Oh! Oh!' she cried in wonder and ridicule. 'The mountains are less than you.'

'Yes,' he cried, 'they are less.'

He seemed suddenly to go silent and remote as she watched him. The speech had gone out of his face again, he seemed to be standing a long way off from her, beyond some border-line. And in the midst of her indignant amazement she watched him with wonder and a touch of fascination. To what country did he belong then? – to what dark, different atmosphere.

'You must suffer from megalomania,' she said. And she said what she felt.

But he only looked at her out of dark, dangerous, haughty eyes.

They went on their way in the rain in silence. He was filled with a passionate silence and imperiousness, a curiousness, a curious, dark, masterful force that supplanted thought in him. And she, who always pondered, went pondering: 'Is he mad? What does he mean? Is he a madman? – He wants to bully me. He wants to bully me into something. What does he want to bully me into? Does he want me to love him?'

At this final question she rested. She decided that what he wanted was that she should love him. And this thought flattered her vanity and her pride and appeased her wrath against him. She felt quite mollified towards him.

But what a way he went about it! He wanted her to love him. Of this she was sure. He had always wanted her to love him even from the first. Only he had not made up his *mind* about it. He had not made up his mind. After his wife had died he had gone away to make up his mind. Now he had made it up. He wanted her to love him. And he was offended, mortally offended, because she had sold his doll.

So, this was the conclusion to which Hannele came. And it pleased her, and it flattered her. And it made her feel quite warm towards him, as they walked in the rain. The rain, by the way, was abating. The spume over the hollow crest to which they were approaching was thinning considerably. They could again see the glacier paw hanging out, a little beyond. The rain was going to pass. And they were not far now from the hotel, and the third level of Lammerboden.

He wanted her to love him. She felt again quite glowing and triumphant inside herself, and did not care a bit about the rain on her shoulders. He wanted her to love him. Yes, that was how she had to put it. He didn't want to *love* her. No. He wanted *her* to love *him*.

But then, of course, woman-like, she took his love for granted. So many men had been so very ready to love her. And this one – to her amazement, to her indignation, and rather to her secret satisfaction – just blackly insisted that *she* must love *him*. Very well – she would give him a run for his money. That was it: he blackly insisted that *she* must love *him*. What he felt was not to be considered. *She* must love *him*. And be bullied into it. That was what it amounted to. In his silent, black, overbearing soul, he wanted to compel her, he wanted to have power over her. He wanted to make her love him so that he had power over her. He wanted to bully her, physically, sexually, and from the inside.

And she! Well, she was just as confident that she was not going to be bullied. She would love him: probably she would: most probably she did already. But she was not going to be bullied by him in any way whatsoever. No, he must go down on his knees to her if he wanted her love. And then she would love him.

Because she did love him. But a dark-eyed little master and bully she would never have.

And this was her triumphant conclusion. Meanwhile the rain had almost ceased, they had almost reached the rim of the upper level, towards which they were climbing, and he was walking in that silent diffidence which made her watch him because she was not sure what he was feeling, what he was thinking, or even what he was. He was a puzzle to her: eternally incomprehensible in his feelings and even his sayings. There seemed to her no logic and no reason in what he felt and said. She could never tell what his next mood would come out of. And this made her uneasy, made her watch him. And at the same time it piqued her attention. He had some of the fascination of the incomprehensible. And his curious inscrutable face – it wasn't really only a meaningless mask, because she had seen it half an hour ago melt with a quite incomprehensible and rather, to her mind, foolish passion. Strange, black, inconsequential passion. Asserting with that curious dark ferocity that he was bigger than the mountains. Madness! Madness! Megalomania.

But because he gave himself away, she forgave him and even liked him. And the strange passion of his, that gave out incomprehensible flashes, *was* rather fascinating to her. She felt just a tiny bit sorry for him. But she wasn't going to be bullied by him. She wasn't going to give in to him and his black passion. No, never. It must be love on equal terms, or nothing. For love on equal terms she was quite ready. She only waited for him to offer it.

XIX

In the hotel was a buzz of tourists. Alexander and Hannele sat in the restaurant drinking hot coffee and milk, and watching the maidens in cotton frocks and aprons and bare arms, and the fair youths with maidenly necks and huge voracious boots, and the many Jews of the wrong sort and the wrong shape. These Jews were all being very Austrian, in Tyrol costume that didn't sit on them, assuming the whole gesture and intonation of aristocratic Austria, so that you might think they *were* Austrian aristocrats, if you weren't properly listening, or if you didn't look twice. Certainly they were lords of the Alps, or at least lords of the Alpine hotels this summer, let prejudice be what it might. Jews of the wrong sort. And yet even they imparted a wholesome breath of sanity, disillusion, unsentimentality to the excited 'Bergheil' atmosphere. Their dark-eyed, sardonic presence seemed to say to the maidenly-necked mountain youths: 'Don't sprout too much wings of the spirit, my dears.'

The rain had ceased. There was a wisp of sunshine from a grey sky. Alexander left the knapsack, and the two went out into the air. Before them lay the last level of the up-climb, the Lammerboden. It was a rather gruesome hollow between the peaks, a last shallow valley about a mile long. At the end the enormous static stream of the glacier poured in from the blunt mountain-top of ice. The ice was dull, sullen-coloured, melted on the surface by the very hot summer: and so it seemed a huge, arrested, sodden flood, ending in a wave-wall of stone-speckled ice upon the valley bed of rocky débris. A gruesome descent of stone and blocks of rock, the little valley bed, with a river raving through. On the left rose the grey rock, but the glacier was there, sending down great paws of ice. It was like some great, deep-furred ice-bear lying spread upon the top heights, and reaching down terrible paws of ice into the valley: like some immense sky-bear fishing in the earth's solid hollows, from above. Hepburn it just filled with terror. Hannele, too, it scared, but it gave her a sense of ecstasy. Some of the immense, furrowed paws of ice held down between the rock were vivid blue in colour, but of a frightening, poisonous blue, like crystal copper-sulphate. Most of the ice was a sullen, semi-translucent greeny grey.

The two set off to walk through the massy desolate stone-bed, under rocks and over waters, to the main glacier. The flowers were even more beautiful on this last reach. Particularly the dark hare-bells were large and almost black and ice-metallic – one could imagine they gave a dull ice-chink. And the grass of Parnassus stood erect, white-veined big cups held terribly naked and open to their ice-air.

From behind the great blunt summit of ice that blocked the distance at the end of the valley a pale-grey, woolly mist or cloud was fusing up, exhaling huge like some grey-dead aura into the sky, and covering the top of the glacier. All the way along the valley people were threading, strangely insignificant, among the grey dishevel of stone and rock, like insects. Hannele and Alexander went ahead quickly, along the tiring track.

'Are you glad now that you came?' she said, looking at him triumphant.

'Very glad I came,' he said. His eyes were dilated with excitement that was ordeal or mystic battle rather than the Bergheil ecstasy. The curious vibration of his excitement made the scene strange, rather horrible to her. She, too, shuddered. But it still seemed to her to hold the key to all glamour and ecstasy, the great silent, living glacier. It seemed to her like a grand beast.

As they came near they saw the wall of ice: the glacier end, thick crusted and speckled with stone and dirt débris. From underneath, secret in stones, water rushed out. When they came quite near, they saw the great monster was sweating all over, trickles and rivulets of sweat running down his sides of pure, slush-translucent ice. There it was, the glacier, ending abruptly in the wall of ice under which they stood. Near to, the ice was pure, but waterlogged, all the surface rather rotten from the hot summer. It was sullenly translucent, and of a watery, darkish bluey-green colour. But near the earth it became again bright coloured, gleams of green like jade, gleams of blue like thin, pale sapphire, in little caverns above the wet stones where the walls trickled for ever.

Alexander wanted to climb on to the glacier. It was his one desire – to stand upon it. So under the pellucid wet wall they toiled among rock upwards, to where the guide-track mounted the ice. Several other people were before them – mere day-tourists – and all uncertain about venturing any further. For the ice-slope rose steep and slithery, pure, sun-licked, sweating ice. Still, it was like a curved back. One could scramble on to it, on and on up to the first level, like the flat on top of some huge paw.

There stood the little cluster of people, facing the uphill of sullen, pure, sodden-looking ice. They were all afraid: naturally. But being human, they all wanted to go beyond their fear. It was strange that the ice looked so pure, like flesh. Not bright, because the surface was soft like a soft, deep epidermis. But pure ice away down to immense depths.

Alexander, after some hesitation, began gingerly to try the ice. He was frightened of it. And he had no stick, and only smooth-soled boots. But he had a great desire to stand on the glacier. So, gingerly and shakily, he began to struggle a few steps up the pure slope. The ice was soft on the surface, he could kick his heel in it and get a little sideways grip. So, staggering and going sideways he got up a few yards, and was on the naked ice-slope.

Immediately the youths and the fat man below began to tackle it, too: also two maidens. For some time, however, Alexander gingerly and scramblingly led the way. The slope of ice was steeper, and rounded, so that it was difficult to stand up in any way. Sometimes he slipped, and was clinging with burnt finger-ends to the soft ice-mass. Then he tried throwing his coat down, and getting a foot-hold on that. Then he went quite quickly by bending down and getting a little grip with his fingers, and going ridiculously as on four legs.

Hannele watched from below, and saw the ridiculous exhibition, and was frightened, and amused, but more frightened. And she kept calling, to the great joy of the Austrians down below:

'Come back. Do come back.'

But when he got on to his feet again he only waved his hand at her, half crossly, as she stood away down there in her blue frock. – The other fellows with sticks and nail-boots had now taken heart and were scrambling like crabs past our hero, doing better than he.

He had come to a rift in the ice. He sat near the edge and looked down. Clean, pure ice, fused with pale colour, and fused into intense copper-sulphate blue away down in the crack. It was not like crystal, but fused as one fuses a borax bead under a blow-flame.[35] And keenly, wickedly blue in the depths of the crack.

He looked upwards. He had not half mounted the slope. So on he went, upon the huge body of the soft-fleshed ice, slanting his way sometimes on all fours, sometimes using his coat, usually hitting-in with the side of his heel. Hannele down below was crying him to come back. But two other youths were now almost level with him.

So he struggled on till he was more or less over the brim. There he stood and looked at the ice. It came down from above in a great hollow world of ice. A world, a terrible place of hills and valleys and slopes, all motionless, all of ice. Away above the grey mist-cloud was looming bigger. And near at hand were long huge cracks, side by side, like gills in the ice. It would seem as if the ice breathed through these great ridged gills. One could look down into the series of gulfs, fearful depths, and the colour burning that acid, intense blue, intenser as the crack went deeper. And the crests of the open gills ridged and grouped pale blue above the crevices. It seemed as if the ice breathed there.

The wonder, the terror, and the bitterness of it. Never a warm leaf to unfold, never a gesture of life to give off. A world sufficient unto itself in lifelessness, all this ice.

He turned to go down, though the youths were passing beyond him. And seeing the naked translucent ice heaving downwards in a vicious curve, always the same dark translucency underfoot, he was afraid. If he slipped, he would certainly slither the whole way down, and break some of his bones. Even when he sat down he had to cling with his finger-nails in the ice, because if he had started to slide he would have slid the whole way down on his trouser-seat, precipitously, and landed heaven knows how.

Hannele was watching from below. And he was frightened, perched seated on the shoulder of ice and not knowing how to get off. Above he saw the great blue gills of ice ridging the air. Down below were two blue cracks – then the last wet level claws of ice upon the stones. And there stood Hannele and the three or four people who had got so far.

However, he found that by striking in his heels sideways with sufficient sharpness he could keep his footing no matter how steep the slope. So he started to jerk his way zigzag downwards.

As he descended, arrived a guide with a black beard and all the paraphernalia of ropes and pole and bristling boots. He and his gentleman began to strike their way up the ice. With those bristling nails like teeth in one's boots, and a pole to press on to it was quite easy.

Hannele, who had got sick of waiting, and who was also frightened, had gone scuttling on the return journey. He hurried after her, thankful to be off the ice, but excited and gratified. Looking round, he saw the guide and the man on the ice watching the ice-world and the weather. Then they, too, turned to come down. The day wasn't safe.

XX

Pondering, rather thrilled, they threaded their way through the desert of rock and rushing water back to the hotel. The sun was shining warmly for a moment, and he felt happy, though his finger-ends were bleeding a little from the ice.

'But one day,' said Hannele, 'I should love to go with a guide right up, high, right into the glacier.'

'No,' said he. 'I've been far enough. I prefer the world where cabbages will grow on the soil. Nothing grows on glaciers.'

'They say there are glacier-fleas, which only live on glaciers,' she said.

'Well, to me the ice didn't look good to eat, even for a flea.'

'You never know,' she laughed. – 'But you're glad you've been, aren't you?'

'Very glad. Now I need never go again.'

'But you *did* think it wonderful?'

'Marvellous. And awful, to my mind.'

XXI

They ate venison and spinach in the hotel, then set off down again. Both felt happier. She gathered some flowers and put them in her handkerchief so they should not die. And again they sat by the stream, to drink a little wine.

But the fume of cloud was blowing up again thick from behind the glacier. Hannele was uneasy. She wanted to get down. So they went fairly quickly. Many other tourists were hurrying downwards also. The rain began – a sharp handful of drops flung from beyond the glacier. So Hannele and he did not stay to rest, but dropped easily down the steep dark valley towards the motor-car terminus.

There they had tea, rather tired but comfortably so. The big hotel restaurant was hideous, and seemed sordid. So in the gloom of a grey, early twilight they went out again and sat on a seat, watching the tourists and the trippers and the motor-car men. There were three Jews from Vienna: and the girl had a huge white woolly dog, as big as a calf, and white and woolly and silky and amiable as a toy. The men of course came patting it and admiring it, just as men always do, in life and in novels. And the girl, holding the leash, posed and leaned backwards in the attitude of heroines on novel-covers. She said the white wool monster was a Siberian steppe-dog. Alexander wondered what the steppes made of such a wuffer. And the three Jews pretended they were elegant Austrians out of popular romances.

'Do you think,' said Alexander, 'you will marry the Herr Regierungsrat?'

She looked round, making wide eyes.

'It looks like it, doesn't it!' she said.

'Quite,' he said.

Hannele watched the woolly white dog. So of course it came wagging its ever-amiable hindquarters towards her. She looked at it still, but did not touch it.

'What makes you ask such a question?' she said.

'I can't say. But even so, you haven't really answered. Do you really fully intend to marry the Herr Regierungsrat? Is that your final intention at this moment?'

She looked at him again.

'But before I answer,' she said, 'oughtn't I to know why you ask?'

'Probably you know already,' he said.

'I assure you I don't.'

He was silent for some moments. The huge woolly dog stood in front of him and breathed enticingly, with its tongue out. He only looked at it blankly.

'Well,' he said, 'if you were not going to marry the Herr Regierungsrat, I should suggest that you marry me.'

She stared away at the auto-garage, a very faint look of amusement, or pleasure, or ridicule on her face: or all three. And a certain shyness.

'But why?' she said.

'Why what?' he returned.

'Why should you suggest that I should marry you?'

'*Why?*' he replied, in his lingering tones. '*Why?* – Well, for what purpose does a man usually ask a woman to marry him?'

'For what *purpose!*' she repeated, rather haughtily.

'For what reason, then!' he corrected.

She was silent for some moments. Her face was closed and a little numb-looking, her hands lay very still in her lap. She looked away from him, across the road.

'There is usually only one reason,' she replied, in a rather small voice.

'Yes?' he replied curiously. 'What would you say that was?'

She hesitated. Then she said, rather stiffly:

'Because he really loved her, I suppose. That seems to me the only excuse for a man asking a woman to marry him.'

Followed a dead silence, which she did not intend to break. He knew he would have to answer, and for some reason he didn't want to say what was obviously the thing to say.

'Leaving aside the question of whether you love me or I love you –' he began.

'I certainly *won't* leave it aside,' she said.

'And I certainly won't consider it,' he said, just as obstinately.

She turned now and looked full at him, with amazement, ridicule, and anger in her face.

'I really think you must be mad,' she said.

'I doubt if you do think that,' he replied. 'It is only a method of retaliation, that is. I think you understand my point very clearly.'

'Your point!' she cried. 'Your point! Oh, so you have a point in all this palavering?'

'Quite!' said he.

She was silent with indignation for some time. Then she said angrily:

'I assure you I do *not* see your point. I don't see any point at all. I see only impertinence.'

'Very good,' he replied. 'The point is whether we marry on a basis of love.'

'Indeed! Marry! We, marry! I don't think that is by any means the point.'

He took his knapsack from under the seat, between his feet. And from the knapsack he took the famous picture.

'When,' he said, 'we were supposed to be in love with one another, you made that doll of me, didn't you?' And he sat looking at the odious picture.

'I never for one moment deluded myself that you *really* loved me,' she said bitterly.

'Take the other point, whether *you* loved *me*, or not,' said he.

'How could I love you, when I couldn't believe in your love for me?' she cried.

He put the picture down between his knees again.

'All this about love,' he said, 'is very confusing, and very complicated.'

'Very! In *your* case. Love to me is simple enough,' she said.

'Is it? Is it? And was it simple love which made you make that doll of me?'

'Why shouldn't I make a doll of you? Does it do you any harm?'

'Yes, it does. It does me the greatest possible damage,' he replied.

She turned on him with wide-open eyes of amazement and rage.

'Why? Pray why? Can you tell me why?'

'Not quite, I can't,' he replied, taking up the picture and holding it in front of him. She turned her face from it as a cat turns its nose away from a lighted cigarette. 'But when I look at it – when I look at this – then I *know* that there is no love between you and me.'

'Then why are you talking at me in this shameful way?' she flashed at him, tears of anger and mortification rising to her eyes. 'You want your little revenge on me, I suppose, because I made that doll of you.'

'That may be so, in a small measure,' he said.

'That is *all*. That is all and everything,' she cried. 'And that is all you came back to me for – for this petty revenge. – Well, you've had it now. – But please don't speak to me any more. I shall see if I can go home in the big omnibus.'

She rose and walked away. He saw her hunting for the motor-bus conductor. He saw her penetrate into the yard of the garage.

And he saw her emerge again, after a time, and take the path to the river. He sat on in front of the hotel. There was nothing else to do.

The tourists who had arrived in the big bus now began to collect. And soon the huge drab vehicle itself rolled up and stood big as a house before the hotel door. The passengers began to scramble in to their seats. The two men of the white dog were going: but the woman of the white dog, and the dog, were staying behind. Hepburn wondered if Hannele had managed to get herself transferred. He doubted it, because he knew the omnibus was crowded.

Moreover, he had her ticket.

The passengers were packed in. The conductor was collecting the tickets. And at last the great bus rolled away. The bay of the road-end seemed very empty. Even the woman with the white dog had gone. Soon the other car, the Luxus, so-called, must appear. Hepburn sat and waited. The evening was falling chilly, the trees looked gruesome.

At last Hannele sauntered up again, unwillingly.

'I think,' she said, 'you have my ticket.'

'Yes, I have,' he replied.

'Will you give it me, please?'

He gave it to her. She lingered a moment. Then she walked away.

There was the sound of a motor-car. With a triumphant purr the Luxus came steering out of the garage yard, and drew up at the hotel door. Hannele came hastening also. She went straight to one of the hinder doors – she and Hepburn had their seats in front, beside the driver. She had her foot on the step of the back seat. And then she was afraid. The little sharp-faced driver – there was no conductor – came round looking at the car. He looked at her with his sharp, metallic eye of a mechanic.

'Are all the people going back, who came?' she asked, shrinking.

'Jawohl.'[36]

'It is full? – this car?'

'Jawohl.'

'There's no other place?'

'Nein'

Hannele shrank away. The driver was absolutely laconic.

Six of the passengers were here: four were already seated. Hepburn sat still by the hotel door, Hannele lingered in the road by the car, and the little driver, with a huge woollen muffler round his throat, was running round and in and out looking for the two missing passengers. Of course there were two missing passengers. No, he could not find them. And off he trotted again, silently, like a weasel after two rabbits. And at last, when everybody was getting cross, he unearthed them and brought them scuttling to the car.

Now Hannele took her seat, and Hepburn beside her. The driver snapped up the tickets and climbed in past them. With a vindictive screech the car glided away down the ravine. Another beastly trip was over, another infernal joyful holiday done with.

'I think,' said Hepburn, 'I may as well finish what I had to say?'

'What?' cried Hannele, fluttering in the wind of the rushing car.

'I may as well finish what I had to say,' shouted he, his breath blown away.

'Finish then,' she screamed, the ends of her scarf flickering behind her.

'When my wife died,' he said loudly, 'I knew I couldn't love any more.'

'Oh – h!' she screamed ironically.

'In fact,' he shouted, 'I realized that, as far as I was concerned, love was a mistake.'

'*What* was a mistake?' she screamed.

'Love,' he bawled.

'Love!' she screamed. 'A mistake?' Her tone was derisive.

'For me personally,' he said, shouting.

'Oh, only for you personally,' she cried, with a pouf of laughter.

The car gave a great swerve, and she fell on the driver. Then she righted herself. It gave another swerve, and she fell on Alexander. She righted herself angrily. And now they ran straight on: and it seemed a little quieter.

'I realized,' he said, 'that I had always made a mistake, undertaking to love.'

'It must have been an undertaking, *for you*,' she cried.

'Yes, I'm afraid it was. I never really wanted it. But I thought I did. And that's where I made my mistake.'

'Whom have you ever loved? – even as an undertaking?' she asked.

'To begin with, my mother: and that was a mistake. Then my sister: and that was a mistake. Then a girl I had known all my life: and that was a mistake. Then my wife: and that was my most terrible mistake. And then I began the mistake of loving you.'

'Undertaking to love me, you mean,' she said. 'But then you never did properly undertake it. You never really *undertook* to love me.'

'Not quite, did I?' said he.

And she sat feeling angry that he had never made the undertaking.

'No,' he continued. 'Not quite. That is why I came back to you. I don't want to love you. I don't want marriage on a basis of love.'

'On a basis of what, then?'

'I think you know without my putting it into words,' he said.

'Indeed I assure you I don't. You are much too mysterious,' she replied.

Talking in a swiftly-running motor-car is a nerve-racking business. They both had a pause, to rest, and to wait for a quieter stretch of road.

'It isn't very easy to put it into words,' he said. – 'But I tried marriage once on a basis of love: and I must say, it was a ghastly affair in the long run. And I believe it would be so, for me, *whatever* woman I had.'

'There must be something wrong with you, then,' said she.

'As far as love goes. – And yet I want marriage – I want marriage. I want a woman to honour and obey me –'

'If you are quite reasonable and *very* sparing with your commands,' said Hannele. 'And very careful how you give your orders.'

'In fact, I want a sort of patient Griselda.[37] I want to be honoured and obeyed. I don't want love.'

'How Griselda managed to honour that fool of a husband of hers, even if she obeyed him, is more than I can say,' said Hannele. 'I'd like to know what she *really* thought of him. – Just what any woman thinks of a bullying fool of a husband.'

'Well,' said he, 'that's no good to me.'

They were silent now until the car stopped at the station. There they descended and walked on under the trees by the lake.

'Sit on a seat,' he said, 'and let us finish.'

Hannele, who was really anxious to hear what he should say, and who, woman-like, was fascinated by a man when he began to give away his own inmost thoughts – no matter how much she might jeer afterwards – sat down by his side. It was a grey evening, just falling dark. Lights twinkled across the lake, the hotel over there threaded its strings of light. Some little boats came rowing quietly to shore. It was a grey, heavy evening, with that special sense of dreariness with which a public holiday usually winds up.

'Honour, and obedience: and the proper physical feelings,' he said. 'To me that is marriage. Nothing else.'

'But what are the proper physical feelings, but love?' asked Hannele.

'No,' he said. 'A woman wants you to adore her, and be in love with her – and I shan't. I will not do it again, if I live a monk for the rest of my days. I will neither adore you nor be in love with you.'

'You won't get a chance, thank you. – And what do you call the proper physical feelings, if you are not in love? I think you want something vile.'

'If a woman honours me – absolutely from the bottom of her nature honours me – and obeys me because of that, I take it, my desire for her goes very much deeper than if I was in love with her, or if I adored her.'

'It's the same thing. If you love, then everything is there – all the lot: your honour and obedience and everything. And if love isn't there, nothing is there,' she said.

'That isn't true,' he replied. 'A woman may love you, she may adore you, but she'll never honour you nor obey you. The most loving and adoring woman to-day could any minute start and make a doll of her husband – as you made of me.'

'Oh, that eternal doll! What makes it stick so in your mind?'

'I don't know. But there it is. It wasn't malicious. It was flattering, if you like. But it just sticks in me like a thorn: like a thorn. – And there it is, in the world, in Germany somewhere. – And you can say what you like, but *any* woman, to-day, no matter *how* much she loves her man – she could start any minute and make a doll of him. And the doll would be her hero: and her hero would be no more than her doll. – My wife might have done it. She did do it, in her mind. She had her doll of me right enough. Why, I've heard her talk about me to other women. And her doll was a great deal sillier than the one you made. – But it's all the same. – If a woman loves you, she'll make a doll out of you. She'll never be satisfied till she's made your doll. And when she's got your doll, that's all she wants. – And that's what love means. – And so, I won't be loved. And I won't love. I won't have anybody loving me. It is an insult. I feel I've been insulted for forty years: by love, and the women who've loved me. I won't be loved. And I won't love. – I'll be honoured and I'll be obeyed: or nothing.'

'Then it'll most probably be nothing,' said Hannele sarcastically. 'For I assure you, I've nothing but love to offer.'

'Then keep your love,' said he.

She laughed shortly.

'And you?' she cried. 'You! Even suppose you *were* honoured and obeyed. I suppose all you've got to do is to sit there like a sultan and sup it up.'

'Oh, no, I have many things to do. And woman or no woman, I'm going to start to do them.'

'What, pray?'

'Why, nothing very exciting. I'm going to East Africa to join a man who's breaking his neck to get his three thousand acres of land under control.[38] And when I've done a few more experiments and observations, and got all the necessary facts, I'm going to do a book on the moon. Woman or no woman, I'm going to do that.'

'And the woman? – supposing you got the poor thing.'

'Why, she'll come along with me, and we'll set ourselves up out there.'

'And she'll do all the honouring and obeying and house-keeping incidentally, while you ride about in the day and stare at the moon in the night.'

He did not answer. He was staring away across the lake.

'What will you do for the woman, poor thing, while she's racking herself to pieces honouring you and obeying you and doing frightful house-keeping in Africa: because I know it can be *awful*: awful.'

'Well' – he said slowly, 'she'll be my wife, and I shall treat her as such. If the marriage service says love and cherish – well, in that sense I shall do so –'

'Oh!' cried Hannele. 'What, *love* her? Actually love the poor thing?'

'Not in that sense of the word, no. I shan't adore her or be in love with her. But she'll be my wife, and I shall love and cherish her as such.'

'Just because she's your wife. Not because she's herself. Ghastly fate for any miserable woman,' said Hannele.

'I don't think so. I think it's her highest fate.'

'To be your wife?'

'To be a wife – and to be loved and shielded as a wife – not as a flirting woman.'

'To be loved and cherished just because you're his wife! No, thank you. All I can admire is the conceit and impudence of it.'

'Very well, then – there it is,' he said, rising.

She rose too, and they went on towards where the boat was tied.

As they were rowing in silence over the lake, he said:

'I shall leave to-morrow.'

She made no answer. She sat and watched the lights of the villa draw near. And then she said:

'I'll come to Africa with you. But I won't promise to honour and obey you.'

'I don't want you otherwise,' he said, very quietly.

The boat was drifting to the little landing-stage. Hannele's friends were hallooing to her from the balcony.

'Hallo!' she cried. 'Ja! Da bin ich. Ja –'s war wunderschön.'[39]

Then to him she said:

'You'll come in?'

'No,' he said, 'I'll row straight back.'

From the villa they were running down the steps to meet Hannele.

'But won't you have me even if I love you?' she asked him.

'You must promise the other,' he said. 'It comes in the marriage service.'

'Hat's geregnet? Wie war das Wetter? Warst du auf dem Gletscher?'[40] cried the voices from the garden.

'Nein – kein Regen. Wunderschön! Ja, er war ganz auf dem Gletscher,'[41] cried Hannele in reply. And to him, *sotto voce*:

'Don't be a solemn ass. Do come in.'

'No,' he said, 'I don't want to come in.'

'Do you want to go away to-morrow? Go if you *do*. But anyway I won't say it *before* the marriage service. I needn't, need I?'

She stepped from the boat on to the plank.

'Oh,' she said, turning round, 'give me that picture, please, will you? I want to burn it.'

He handed it to her.

'And come to-morrow, will you?' she said.

'Yes, in the morning.'

He pulled back quickly into the darkness.

The Fox

THE two girls were usually known by their surnames, Banford and March. They had taken the farm together, intending to work it all by themselves: that is, they were going to rear chickens, make a living by poultry, and add to this by keeping a cow, and raising one or two young beasts. Unfortunately things did not turn out well.

Banford was a small, thin, delicate thing with spectacles. She, however, was the principal investor, for March had little or no money. Banford's father, who was a tradesman in Islington, gave his daughter the start, for her health's sake, and because he loved her, and because it did not look as if she would marry. March was more robust. She had learned carpentry and joinery at the evening classes in Islington. She would be the man about the place. They had, moreover, Banford's old grandfather living with them at the start. He had been a farmer. But unfortunately the old man died after he had been at Bailey Farm for a year. Then the two girls were left alone.

They were neither of them young: that is, they were near thirty. But they certainly were not old. They set out quite gallantly with their enterprise. They had numbers of chickens, black Leghorns and white Leghorns, Plymouths and Wyandottes; also some ducks; also two heifers in the fields. One heifer, unfortunately, refused absolutely to stay in the Bailey Farm closes. No matter how March made up the fences, the heifer was out, wild in the woods, or trespassing on the neighbouring pasture, and March and Banford were away, flying after her, with more haste than success. So this heifer they sold in despair. Then, just before the other beast was expecting her first calf, the old man died, and the girls, afraid of the coming event, sold her in a panic, and limited their attentions to fowls and ducks.

In spite of a little chagrin, it was a relief to have no more cattle on hand. Life was not made merely to be slaved away. Both girls

agreed in this. The fowls were quite enough trouble. March had
set up her carpenter's bench at the end of the open shed. Here
she worked, making coops and doors and other appurtenances.
The fowls were housed in the bigger building, which had served
as barn and cowshed in old days. They had a beautiful home, and
should have been perfectly content. Indeed, they looked well
enough. But the girls were disgusted at their tendency to strange
illnesses, at their exacting way of life, and at their refusal,
obstinate refusal to lay eggs.

March did most of the outdoor work. When she was out and
about, in her puttees and breeches, her belted coat and her loose
cap, she looked almost like some graceful, loose-balanced young
man, for her shoulders were straight, and her movements easy
and confident, even tinged with a little indifference, or irony. But
her face was not a man's face, ever. The wisps of her crisp dark
hair blew about her as she stooped, her eyes were big and wide
and dark, when she looked up again, strange, startled, shy and
sardonic at once. Her mouth, too, was almost pinched as if in pain
and irony. There was something odd and unexplained about her.
She would stand balanced on one hip, looking at the fowls
pattering about in the obnoxious fine mud of the sloping yard,
and calling to her favourite white hen, which came in answer to
her name. But there was an almost satirical flicker in March's big,
dark eyes as she looked at her three-toed flock pottering about
under her gaze, and the same slight dangerous satire in her voice
as she spoke to the favoured Patty, who pecked at March's boot
by way of friendly demonstration.

Fowls did not flourish at Bailey Farm, in spite of all that
March did for them. When she provided hot food for them, in
the morning, according to rule, she noticed that it made them
heavy and dozy for hours. She expected to see them lean against
the pillars of the shed in their languid processes of digestion. And
she knew quite well that they ought to be busily scratching and
foraging about, if they were to come to any good. So she decided
to give them their hot food at night, and let them sleep on it.
Which she did. But it made no difference.

War conditions, again, were very unfavourable to poultry
keeping. Food was scarce and bad. And when the Daylight

Saving Bill[1] was passed, the fowls obstinately refused to go to bed as usual, about nine o'clock in the summer-time. That was late enough, indeed, for there was no peace till they were shut up and asleep. Now they cheerfully walked around, without so much as glancing at the barn, until ten o'clock or later. Both Banford and March disbelieved in living for work alone. They wanted to read or take a cycle-ride in the evening, or perhaps March wished to paint curvilinear swans on porcelain, with green background, or else make a marvellous fire-screen by processes of elaborate cabinet work. For she was a creature of odd whims and unsatis-fied tendencies. But from all these things she was prevented by the stupid fowls.

One evil there was greater than any other. Bailey Farm was a little homestead, with ancient wooden barn and two-gabled farm-house, lying just one field removed from the edge of the wood. Since the War the fox was a demon. He carried off the hens under the very noses of March and Banford. Banford would start and stare through her big spectacles with all her eyes, as another squawk and flutter took place at her heels. Too late! Another white Leghorn gone. It was disheartening.

They did what they could to remedy it. When it became permitted to shoot foxes, they stood sentinel with their guns, the two of them, at the favoured hours. But it was no good. The fox was too quick for them. So another year passed, and another, and they were living on their losses, as Banford said. They let their farm-house one summer, and retired to live in a railway-carriage that was deposited as a sort of out-house in a corner of the field. This amused them, and helped their finances. None the less, things looked dark.

Although they were usually the best of friends, because Banford, though nervous and delicate, was a warm, generous soul, and March, though so odd and absent in herself, had a strange magnanimity, yet, in the long solitude, they were apt to become a little irritable with one another, tired of one another. March had four-fifths of the work to do, and though she did not mind, there seemed no relief, and it made her eyes flash curiously sometimes. Then Banford, feeling more nerve-worn than ever, would become despondent, and March would speak sharply to her. They seemed to be losing ground, somehow, losing hope as the months went by. There alone in the fields by the wood, with the wide country stretching hollow and dim to the round hills of the White Horse[2], in the far distance, they seemed to have to live too much off themselves. There was nothing to keep them up – and no hope.

The fox really exasperated them both. As soon as they had let the fowls out, in the early summer mornings, they had to take their guns and keep guard: and then again, as soon as evening began to mellow, they must go once more. And he was so sly. He slid along in the deep grass, he was difficult as a serpent to see. And he seemed to circumvent the girls deliberately. Once or twice March had caught sight of the white tip of his brush, or the ruddy shadow of him in the deep grass, and she had let fire at him. But he made no account of this.

One evening March was standing with her back to the sunset, her gun under her arm, her hair pushed under her cap. She was half watching, half musing. It was her constant state. Her eyes were keen and observant, but her inner mind took no notice of what she saw. She was always lapsing into this odd, rapt state, her mouth rather screwed up. It was a question, whether she was there, actually consciously present, or not.

The trees on the wood-edge were a darkish, brownish green in the full light – for it was the end of August. Beyond, the naked, copper-like shafts and limbs of the pine-trees shone in the air. Nearer the rough grass, with its long brownish stalks all agleam, was full of light. The fowls were round about – the ducks were still swimming on the pond under the pine trees. March looked at it all, saw it all, and did not see it. She heard Banford speaking to the fowls, in the distance – and she did not hear. What was she thinking about? Heaven knows. Her consciousness was, as it were, held back.

She lowered her eyes, and suddenly saw the fox. He was looking up at her. His chin was pressed down, and his eyes were looking up. They met her eyes. And he knew her. She was spell-bound – she knew he knew her. So he looked into her eyes, and her soul failed her. He knew her, he was not daunted.

She struggled, confusedly she came to herself, and saw him

making off, with slow leaps over some fallen boughs, slow, impudent jumps. Then he glanced over his shoulder, and ran smoothly away. She saw his brush held smooth like a feather, she saw his white buttocks twinkle. And he was gone, softly, soft as the wind.

She put her gun to her shoulder, but even then pursed her mouth, knowing it was nonsense to pretend to fire. So she began to walk slowly after him, in the direction he had gone, slowly, pertinaciously. She expected to find him. In her heart she was determined to find him. What she would do when she saw him again she did not consider. But she was determined to find him. So she walked abstractedly about on the edge of the wood, with wide, vivid dark eyes, and a faint flush in her cheeks. She did not think. In strange mindlessness she walked hither and thither.

At last she became aware that Banford was calling her. She made an effort of attention, turned, and gave some sort of screaming call in answer. Then again she was striding off towards the homestead. The red sun was setting, the fowls were retiring towards their roost. She watched them, white creatures, black creatures, gathering to the barn. She watched them spell-bound, without seeing them. But her automatic intelligence told her when it was time to shut the door.

She went indoors to supper, which Banford had set on the table. Banford chatted easily. March seemed to listen, in her distant, manly way. She answered a brief word now and then. But all the time she was as if spell-bound. And as soon as supper was over, she rose again to go out, without saying why.

She took her gun again and went to look for the fox. For he had lifted his eyes upon her, and his knowing look seemed to have entered her brain. She did not so much think of him: she was possessed by him. She saw his dark, shrewd, unabashed eye looking into her, knowing her. She felt him invisibly master her spirit. She knew the way he lowered his chin as he looked up, she knew his muzzle, the golden brown, and the greyish white. And again she saw him glance over his shoulder at her, half inviting, half contemptuous and cunning. So she went, with her great startled eyes glowing, her gun under her arm, along the wood edge. Meanwhile the night fell, and a great moon rose above the pine trees. And again Banford was calling.

So she went indoors. She was silent and busy. She examined her gun, and cleaned it, musing abstractedly by the lamplight. Then she went out again, under the great moon, to see if everything was right. When she saw the dark crests of the pine-trees against the blood-red sky, again her heart beat to the fox, the fox. She wanted to follow him, with her gun.

It was some days before she mentioned the affair to Banford. Then suddenly, one evening she said:

'The fox was right at my feet on Saturday night.'

'Where?' said Banford, her eyes opening behind her spectacles.

'When I stood just above the pond.'

'Did you fire?' cried Banford.

'No, I didn't.'

'Why not?'

'Why, I was too much surprised, I suppose.'

It was the same old, slow, laconic way of speech March always had. Banford stared at her friend for a few moments.

'You saw him?' she cried.

'Oh yes! He was looking up at me, cool as anything.'

'I tell you,' cried Banford – 'the cheek! – They're not afraid of us, Nellie.'

'Oh, no,' said March.

'Pity you didn't get a shot at him,' said Banford.

'Isn't it a pity! I've been looking for him ever since. But I don't suppose he'll come so near again.'

'I don't suppose he will,' said Banford.

And she proceeded to forget about it, except that she was more indignant than ever at the impudence of the beggars. March was also not conscious that she thought of the fox. But whenever she fell into her half-musing, when she was half rapt, and half intelligently aware of what passed under her vision, then it was the fox which somehow dominated her unconsciousness, possessed the blank half of her musing. And so it was for weeks, and months. No matter whether she had been climbing the trees for the apples, or beating down the last of the damsons, or whether she had been digging out the ditch from the duck-pond, or clearing out the barn, when she had finished, or when she straightened herself, and pushed the wisps of hair away again from her forehead, and pursed up her mouth again in an odd, screwed fashion, much too old for her years, there was sure to come over her mind the old spell of the fox, as it came when he was looking at her. It was as if she could smell him at these times. And it always recurred, at unexpected moments, just as she was going to sleep at night, or just as she was pouring the water into the tea-pot, to make tea – it was the fox, it came over her like a spell.

So the months passed. She still looked for him unconsciously when she went towards the wood. He had become a settled effect in her spirit, a state permanently established, not continuous, but always recurring. She did not know what she felt or thought: only the state came over her, as when he looked at her.

The months passed, the dark evenings came, heavy, dark November, when March went about in high boots, ankle deep in mud, when the night began to fall at four o'clock, and the day never properly dawned. Both girls dreaded these times. They dreaded the almost continuous darkness that enveloped them on their desolate little farm near the wood. Banford was physically afraid. She was afraid of tramps, afraid lest someone should come prowling around. March was not so much afraid, as uncomfortable, and disturbed. She felt discomfort and gloom in all her physique.

Usually the two girls had tea in the sitting room. March lighted a fire at dusk, and put on the wood she had chopped and sawed during the day. Then the long evening was in front, dark, sodden, black outside, lonely and rather oppressive inside, a little dismal. March was content not to talk, but Banford could not keep still. Merely listening to the wind in the pines outside, or the drip of water, was too much for her.

One evening the girls had washed up the tea-things in the kitchen, and March had put on her house-shoes, and taken up a roll of crochet-work, which she worked at slowly from time to time. So she lapsed into silence. Banford stared at the red fire, which, being of wood, needed constant attention. She was afraid to begin to read too early, because her eyes would not bear any strain. So she sat staring at the fire, listening to the distant sounds, sound of cattle lowing, of a dull, heavy moist wind, of the rattle of the evening train on the little railway not far off. She was almost fascinated by the red glow of the fire.

Suddenly both girls started, and lifted their heads. They heard a footstep – distinctly a footstep. Banford recoiled in fear. March stood listening. Then rapidly she approached the door that led into the kitchen. At the same time they heard the footsteps approach the back door. They waited a second. The back door opened softly. Banford gave a loud cry. A man's voice said softly:

'Hello!'

March recoiled, and took a gun from a corner.

'What do you want?' she cried, in a sharp voice.

Again the soft, softly-vibrating man's voice said:

'Hello! What's wrong?'

'I shall shoot!' cried March. 'What do you want?'

'Why, what's wrong? What's wrong?' come the soft, wondering, rather scared voice: and a young soldier, with his heavy kit on his back, advanced into the dim light.

'Why,' he said, 'who lives here then?'

'We live here,' said March. 'What do you want?'

'Oh!' came the long, melodious, wonder-note from the young soldier. 'Doesn't William Grenfel live here then?'

'No – you know he doesn't.'

'Do I? – Do I? I don't, you see. – He *did* live here, because he was my grandfather, and I lived here myself five years ago. What's become of him then?'

The young man – or youth, for he would not be more than twenty, now advanced and stood in the inner doorway. March, already under the influence of his strange, soft, modulated voice, stared at him spell-bound. He had a ruddy, roundish face, with fairish hair, rather long, flattened to his forehead with sweat. His eyes were blue, and very bright and sharp. On his cheeks, on the fresh ruddy skin were fine, fair hairs, like a down, but sharper. It gave him a slightly glistening look. Having his heavy sack on his shoulders, he stooped, thrusting his head forward. His hat was loose in one hand. He stared brightly, very keenly from girl to girl, particularly at March, who stood pale, with great dilated eyes, in her belted coat and puttees, her hair knotted in a big crisp knot behind. She still had the gun in her hand. Behind her, Banford, clinging to the sofa-arm, was shrinking away, with half-averted head.

'I thought my grandfather still lived here? – I wonder if he's dead.'

'We've been here for three years,' said Banford, who was beginning to recover her wits, seeing something boyish in the round head with its rather long sweaty hair.

'Three years! You don't say so! – And you don't know who was here before you?'

'I know it was an old man, who lived by himself.'

'Ay! Yes, that's him! – And what became of him then?'

'He died. – I know he died –'

'Ay! He's dead then!'

The youth stared at them without changing colour or expression. If he had any expression, besides a slight baffled look of wonder, it was one of sharp curiosity concerning the two girls; sharp, impersonal curiosity, the curiosity of that round young head.

But to March he was the fox. Whether it was the thrusting forward of his head, or the glisten of fine whitish hairs on the ruddy cheek-bones, or the bright, keen eyes, that can never be said: but the boy was to her the fox, and she could not see him otherwise.

'How is it you didn't know if your grandfather was alive or dead?' asked Banford, recovering her natural sharpness.

'Ay, that's it,' replied the softly-breathing youth. 'You see, I joined up in Canada, and I hadn't heard for three or four years. – I ran away to Canada.'

'And now have you just come from France?'

'Well – from Salonika really.'

There was a pause, nobody knowing quite what to say.

'So you've nowhere to go now?' said Banford rather lamely.

'Oh, I know some people in the village. Anyhow, I can go to the "Swan".'

'You came on the train, I suppose. – Would you like to sit down a bit?'

'Well – I don't mind.'

He gave an odd little groan as he swung off his kit. Banford looked at March.

'Put the gun down,' she said. 'We'll make a cup of tea.'

'Ay,' said the youth. 'We've seen enough of rifles.'

He sat down rather tired on the sofa, leaning forward.

March recovered her presence of mind, and went into the kitchen. There she heard the soft young voice musing:

'Well, to think I should come back and find it like this!' He did not seem sad, not at all – only rather interestedly surprised.

'And what a difference in the place, eh?' he continued, looking round the room.

'You see a difference, do you?' said Banford.

'Yes, – don't I!'

His eyes were unnaturally clear and bright, though it was the brightness of abundant health.

March was busy in the kitchen preparing another meal. It was about seven o'clock. All the time, while she was active, she was attending to the youth in the sitting-room, not so much listening to what he said, as feeling the soft run of his voice. She primmed up her mouth tighter and tighter, puckering it as if it were sewed, in her effort to keep her will uppermost. Yet her large eyes dilated and glowed in spite of her, she lost herself. Rapidly and carelessly she prepared the meal, cutting large chunks of bread and margarine – for there was no butter. She racked her brain to think of something else to put on the tray – she had only bread, margarine, and jam, and the larder was bare. Unable to conjure anything up, she went into the sitting-room with her tray.

She did not want to be noticed. Above all, she did not want him to look at her. But when she came in, and was busy setting the table just behind him, he pulled himself up from his sprawling, and turned and looked over his shoulder. She became pale and wan.

The youth watched her as she bent over the table, looked at her slim, well-shapen legs, at the belted coat dropping around her thighs, at the knot of dark hair, and his curiosity, vivid and widely alert, was again arrested by her.

The lamp was shaded with a dark-green shade, so that the light was thrown downwards, the upper half of the room was dim. His face moved bright under the light, but March loomed shadowy in the distance.

She turned round, but kept her eyes sideways, dropping and lifting her dark lashes. Her mouth unpuckered, as she said to Banford:

'Will you pour out?'

Then she went into the kitchen again.

'Have your tea where you are, will you?' said Banford to the youth – 'unless you'd rather come to the table.'

'Well,' said he, 'I'm nice and comfortable here, aren't I? I will have it here, if you don't mind.'

'There's nothing but bread and jam,' she said. And she put his plate on a stool by him. She was very happy now, waiting on him. For she loved company. And now she was no more afraid of him than if he were her own younger brother. He was such a boy.

'Nellie,' she called. 'I've poured you a cup out.'

March appeared in the doorway, took her cup, and sat down in a corner, as far from the light as possible. She was very sensitive in her knees. Having no skirts to cover them, and being forced to sit with them boldly exposed, she suffered. She shrank and shrank, trying not to be seen. And the youth, sprawling low on the couch, glanced up at her, with long, steady, penetrating looks, till she was almost ready to disappear. Yet she held her cup balanced, she drank her tea, screwed up her mouth and held her head averted. Her desire to be invisible was so strong that it quite baffled the youth. He felt he could not see her distinctly. She seemed like a shadow within the shadow. And ever his eyes came back to her, searching, unremitting, with unconscious fixed attention.

Meanwhile he was talking softly and smoothly to Banford, who loved nothing so much as gossip, and who was full of perky interest, like a bird. Also he ate largely and quickly and voraciously, so that March had to cut more chunks of bread and margarine, for the roughness of which Banford apologized.

'Oh, well,' said March, suddenly speaking, 'if there's no butter to put on it, it's no good trying to make dainty pieces.'

Again the youth watched her, and he laughed, with a sudden, quick laugh, showing his teeth and wrinkling his nose.

'It isn't, is it,' he answered in his soft, near voice.

It appeared he was Cornish by birth and upbringing. When he was twelve years old he had come to Bailey Farm with his grandfather, with whom he had never agreed very well. So he had run away to Canada, and worked far away in the West. Now he was here – and that was the end of it.

He was very curious about the girls, to find out exactly what they were doing. His questions were those of a farm youth; acute, practical, a little mocking. He was very much amused by their attitude to their losses: for they were amusing on the score of heifers and fowls.

'Oh, well,' broke in March, 'we don't believe in living for nothing but work.'

'Don't you?' he answered. And again the quick young laugh came over his face. He kept his eyes steadily on the obscure woman in the corner.

'But what will you do when you've used up all your capital?' he said.

'Oh, I don't know,' answered March laconically. 'Hire ourselves out for landworkers, I suppose.'

'Yes, but there won't be any demand for women landworkers now the war's over,' said the youth.

'Oh, we'll see. We shall hold on a bit longer yet,' said March, with a plangent, half-sad, half-ironical indifference.

'There wants a man about the place,' said the youth softly. Banford burst out laughing.

'Take care what you say,' she interrupted. 'We consider ourselves quite efficient.'

'Oh,' came March's slow, plangent voice, 'it isn't a case of efficiency, I'm afraid. If you're going to do farming you must be at it from morning till night, and you might as well be a beast yourself.'

'Yes, that's it,' said the youth. 'You aren't willing to put yourselves into it.'

'We aren't,' said March, 'and we know it.'

'We want some of our time for ourselves,' said Banford.

The youth threw himself back on the sofa, his face tight with laughter, and laughed silently but thoroughly. The calm scorn of the girls tickled him tremendously.

'Yes,' he said, 'but why did you begin then?'

'Oh,' said March, 'we had a better opinion of the nature of fowls then, than we have now.'

'Of Nature altogether, I'm afraid,' said Banford. 'Don't talk to me about Nature.'

Again the face of the youth tightened with delighted laughter.

'You haven't a very high opinion of fowls and cattle, have you?' he said.

'Oh no – quite a low one,' said March.

He laughed out.

'Neither fowls nor heifers,' said Banford, 'nor goats nor the weather.'

The youth broke into a sharp yap of laughter, delighted. The girls began to laugh too, March turning aside her face and wrinkling her mouth in amusement.

'Oh, well,' said Banford, 'we don't mind, do we, Nellie?'

'No,' said March, 'we don't mind.'

The youth was very pleased. He had eaten and drunk his fill. Banford began to question him. His name was Henry Grenfel – no, he was not called Harry, always Henry. He continued to answer with courteous simplicity, grave and charming. March, who was not included, cast long, slow glances at him from her recess, as he sat there on the sofa, his hands clasping his knees, his face under the lamp bright and alert, turned to Banford. She became almost peaceful, at last. He was identified with the fox – and he was here in full presence. She need not go after him any more. There in the shadow of her corner she gave herself up to a warm, relaxed peace, almost like sleep, accepting the spell that was on her. But she wished to remain hidden. She was only fully at peace whilst he forgot her, talking to Banford. Hidden in the shadow of the corner, she need not any more be divided in herself, trying to keep up two planes of consciousness. She could at last lapse into the odour of the fox.

For the youth, sitting before the fire in his uniform, sent a faint but distinct odour into the room, indefinable, but something like a wild creature. March no longer tried to reserve herself from it. She was still and soft in her corner like a passive creature in its cave.

At last the talk dwindled. The youth relaxed his clasp of his knees, pulled himself together a little, and looked round. Again he became aware of the silent, half-invisible woman in the corner.

'Well,' he said, unwillingly, 'I suppose I'd better be going, or they'll be in bed at the Swan.'

'I'm afraid they're in bed anyhow,' said Banford. 'They've all got this influenza.'

'Have they!' he exclaimed. And he pondered. 'Well,' he continued, 'I shall find a place somewhere.'

'I'd say you could stay here, only —' Banford began.

He turned and watched her, holding his head forward.

'What —?' he asked.

'Oh, well,' she said, 'propriety, I suppose —' She was rather confused.

'It wouldn't be improper, would it?' he said, gently surprised.

'Not as far as we're concerned,' said Banford.

'And not as far as *I'm* concerned,' he said, with grave naïveté. 'After all, it's my own home, in a way.'

Banford smiled at this.

'It's what the village will have to say,' she said.

There was a moment's blank pause.

'What do you say, Nellie?' asked Banford.

'I don't mind,' said March, in her distinct tone. 'The village doesn't matter to me, anyhow.'

'No,' said the youth, quick and soft. 'Why should it? — I mean, what should they say?'

'Oh, well,' came March's plangent, laconic voice, 'they'll easily find something to say. But it makes no difference, what they say. We can look after ourselves.'

'Of course you can,' said the youth.

'Well then, stop if you like,' said Banford. 'The spare room is quite ready.'

His face shone with pleasure.

'If you're quite sure it isn't troubling you too much,' he said, with that soft courtesy which distinguished him.

'Oh, it's no trouble,' they both said.

He looked, smiling with delight, from one to another.

'It's awfully nice not to have to turn out again, isn't it?' he said gratefully.

'I suppose it is,' said Banford.

March disappeared to attend the room. Banford was as pleased and thoughtful as if she had her own brother home from France. It gave her just the same kind of gratification to attend on him, to get out the bath for him, and everything. Her natural warmth and kindliness had now an outlet. And the youth luxuriated in her sisterly attention. But it puzzled him slightly to know that March was silently working for him too. She was so curiously silent and obliterated. It seemed to him he had not really seen her. He felt he should not know her if he met her in the road.

That night March dreamed vividly. She dreamed she heard a singing outside, which she could not understand, a singing that roamed round the house, in the fields and in the darkness. It moved her so, that she felt she must weep. She went out, and suddenly she knew it was the fox singing. He was very yellow and bright, like corn. She went nearer to him, but he ran away and ceased singing. He seemed near, and she wanted to touch him. She stretched out her hand, but suddenly he bit her wrist, and at the same instant, as she drew back, the fox, turning round to bound away, whisked his brush across her face, and it seemed his brush was on fire, for it seared and burned her mouth with a great pain. She awoke with the pain of it, and lay trembling as if she were really seared.

In the morning, however, she only remembered it as a distant memory. She arose and was busy preparing the house and attending to the fowls. Banford flew into the village on her bicycle, to try and buy food. She was a hospitable soul. But alas, in the year 1918 there was not much food to buy. The youth came downstairs in his shirt-sleeves. He was young and fresh, but he walked with his head thrust forward, so that his shoulders seemed raised and rounded, as if he had a slight curvature of the spine. It must have been only a manner of bearing himself, for he was young and vigorous. He washed himself and went outside, whilst the women were preparing breakfast.

He saw everything, and examined everything. His curiosity was quick and insatiable. He compared the state of things with that which he remembered before, and cast over in his mind the effect of the changes. He watched the fowls and the ducks, to see their condition, he noticed the flight of wood-pigeons overhead: they were very numerous; he saw the few apples high up, which March had not been able to reach; he remarked that they had borrowed a draw-pump, presumably to empty the big soft-water cistern which was on the north side of the house.

'It's a funny, dilapidated old place,' he said to the girls, as he sat at breakfast.

His eyes were wise and childish, with thinking about things. He did not say much, but ate largely. March kept her face averted. She, too, in the early morning, could not be aware of him, though something about the glint of his khaki reminded her of the brilliance of her dream-fox.

During the day the girls went about their business. In the morning, he attended to the guns, shot a rabbit and a wild duck that was flying high, towards the wood. That was a great addition to the empty larder. The girls felt that already he had earned his keep. He said nothing about leaving, however. In the afternoon he went to the village. He came back at tea-time. He had the same alert, forward-reaching look on his roundish face. He hung his hat on a peg with a little swinging gesture. He was thinking about something.

'Well,' he said to the girls, as he sat at table. 'What am I going to do?'

'How do you mean – what are you going to do?' said Banford.

'Where am I going to find a place in the village, to stay?' he said.

'I don't know,' said Banford. 'Where do you think of staying?'

'Well –' he hesitated – 'at the Swan they've got this flu, and at the Plough and Harrow they've got the soldiers who are collecting the hay for the army: besides in the private houses, there's ten men and a corporal altogether billeted in the village, they tell me. I'm not sure where I could get a bed.'

He left the matter to them. He was rather calm about it. March sat with her elbows on the table, her two hands supporting her chin, looking at him unconsciously. Suddenly he lifted his clouded blue eyes, and unthinking looked straight into March's eyes. He was startled as well as she. He, too, recoiled a little. March felt the same sly, taunting, knowing spark leap out of his eyes as he turned his head aside, and fall into her soul, as it had fallen from the dark eyes of the fox. She pursed her mouth as if in pain, as if asleep too.

'Well, I don't know –' Banford was saying. She seemed reluctant, as if she were afraid of being imposed upon. She looked at March. But, with her weak, troubled sight, she only saw the usual semi-abstraction on her friend's face. 'Why don't you speak, Nellie?' she said.

But March was wide-eyed and silent, and the youth, as if fascinated, was watching her without moving his eyes.

'Go on – answer something,' said Banford. And March turned her head slightly aside, as if coming to consciousness, or trying to come to consciousness.

'What do you expect me to say?' she asked automatically.

'Say what you think,' said Banford.

'It's all the same to me,' said March.

And again there was silence. A pointed light seemed to be on the boy's eyes, penetrating like a needle.

'So it is to me,' said Banford. 'You can stop on here if you like.'

A smile like a cunning little flame came over his face, suddenly and involuntarily. He dropped his head quickly to hide it, and remained with his head dropped, his face hidden.

'You can stop on here if you like. You can please yourself, Henry,' Banford concluded.

Still he did not reply, but remained with his head dropped. Then he lifted his face. It was bright with a curious light, as if exultant, and his eyes were strangely clear as he watched March. She turned her face aside, her mouth suffering as if wounded, and her consciousness dim.

Banford became a little puzzled. She watched the steady, pellucid gaze of the youth's eyes, as he looked at March, with the invisible smile gleaming on his face. She did not know how he was smiling, for no feature moved. It seemed only in the gleam, almost the glitter of the fine hairs on his cheeks. Then he looked with quite a changed look, at Banford.

'I'm sure,' he said in his soft, courteous voice, 'you're awfully good. You're too good. You don't want to be bothered with me, I'm sure.'

'Cut a bit of bread, Nellie,' said Banford uneasily; adding: 'It's no bother, if you like to stay. It's like having my own brother here for a few days. He's a boy like you are.'

'That's awfully kind of you,' the lad repeated. 'I should like to stay, ever so much, if you're sure I'm not a trouble to you.'

'No, of course you're no trouble. I tell you, it's a pleasure to have somebody in the house beside ourselves,' said warm-hearted Banford.

'But Miss March?' he said in his soft voice, looking at her.

'Oh, it's quite all right as far as I'm concerned,' said March vaguely.

His face beamed, and he almost rubbed his hands with pleasure.

'Well then,' he said, 'I should love it, if you'd let me pay my board and help with the work.'

'You've no need to talk about board,' said Banford.

One or two days went by, and the youth stayed on at the farm. Banford was quite charmed by him. He was so soft and courteous in speech, not wanting to say much himself, preferring to hear what she had to say, and to laugh in his quick, half-mocking way. He helped readily with the work – but not too much. He loved to be out alone with the gun in his hands, to watch, to see. For his sharp-eyed, impersonal curiosity was insatiable, and he was most free when he was quite alone, half-hidden, watching.

Particularly he watched March. She was a strange character to him. Her figure, like a graceful young man's, piqued him. Her dark eyes made something rise in his soul, with a curious elate excitement, when he looked into them, an excitement he was afraid to let be seen, it was so keen and secret. And then her odd, shrewd speech made him laugh outright. He felt he must go further, he was inevitably impelled. But he put away the thought of her, and went off towards the wood's edge with the gun.

The dusk was falling as he came home, and with the dusk, a

fine, late November rain. He saw the fire-light leaping in the window of the sitting-room, a leaping light in the little cluster of the dark buildings. And he thought to himself, it would be a good thing to have this place for his own. And then the thought entered him shrewdly: why not marry March? He stood still in the middle of the field for some moments, the dead rabbit hanging still in his hand, arrested by this thought. His mind waited in amazement – it seemed to calculate – and then he smiled curiously to himself in acquiescence. Why not? Why not, indeed? It was a good idea. What if it was rather ridiculous? What did it matter? What if she was older than he? It didn't matter. When he thought of her dark, startled, vulnerable eyes he smiled subtly to himself. He was older than she, really. He was master of her.

He scarcely admitted his intention even to himself. He kept it as a secret even from himself. It was all too uncertain as yet. He would have to see how things went. Yes, he would have to see how things went. If he wasn't careful, she would just simply mock at the idea. He knew, sly and subtle as he was, that if he went to her plainly and said: 'Miss March, I love you and want you to marry me,' her inevitable answer would be: 'Get out. I don't want any of that tomfoolery.' This was her attitude to men and their 'tomfoolery'. If he was not careful, she would turn round on him with her savage, sardonic ridicule, and dismiss him from the farm and from her own mind, for ever. He would have to go gently. He would have to catch her as you catch a deer or a woodcock when you go out shooting. It's no good walking out into the forest and saying to the deer: 'Please fall to my gun.' No, it is a slow, subtle battle. When you really go out to get a deer, you gather yourself together, you coil yourself inside yourself, and you advance secretly, before dawn, into the mountains. It is not so much what you do, when you go out hunting, as how you feel. You have to be subtle and cunning and absolutely fatally ready. It becomes like a fate. Your own fate overtakes and determines the fate of the deer you are hunting. First of all, even before you come in sight of your quarry, there is a strange battle, like mesmerism. Your own soul, as a hunter, has gone out to fasten on the soul of the deer, even before you see any deer. And the soul of the deer fights to escape. Even before the deer has any wind of you, it is so. It is a subtle, profound battle of wills, which takes place in the invisible. And it is a battle never finished till your bullet goes home. When you are *really* worked up to the true pitch, and you come at last into range, you don't then aim as you do when you are firing at a bottle. It is your own *will* which carries the bullet into the heart of your quarry. The bullet's flight home is a sheer projection of your own fate into the fate of the deer. It happens like a supreme wish, a supreme act of volition, not as a dodge of cleverness.

He was a huntsman in spirit, not a farmer, and not a soldier stuck in a regiment. And it was as a young hunter, that he wanted to bring down March as his quarry, to make her his wife. So he gathered himself subtly together, seemed to withdraw into a kind of invisibility. He was not quite sure how he would go on. And March was suspicious as a hare. So he remained in appearance just the nice, odd stranger-youth, staying for a fortnight on the place.

He had been sawing logs for the fire, in the afternoon. Darkness came very early. It was still a cold, raw mist. It was getting almost too dark to see. A pile of short sawed logs lay beside the trestle. March came to carry them indoors, or into the shed, as he was busy sawing the last log. He was working in his shirt-sleeves, and did not notice her approach. She came unwillingly, as if shy. He saw her stooping to the bright-ended logs, and he stopped sawing. A fire like lightning flew down his legs in the nerves.

'March?' he said, in his quiet young voice.

She looked up from the logs she was piling.

'Yes!' she said.

He looked down on her in the dusk. He could see her not too distinctly.

'I wanted to ask you something,' he said.

'Did you? What was it?' she said. Already the fright was in her voice. But she was too much mistress of herself.

'Why –' his voice seemed to draw out soft and subtle, it penetrated her nerves – 'why, what do you think it is?'

She stood up, placed her hands on her hips, and stood looking at him transfixed, without answering. Again he burned with a sudden power.

'Well,' he said and his voice was so soft it seemed rather like a subtle touch, like the merest touch of a cat's paw, a feeling rather than a sound. 'Well – I wanted to ask you to marry me.'

March felt rather than heard him. She was trying in vain to turn aside her face. A great relaxation seemed to have come over her. She stood silent, her head slightly on one side. He seemed to be bending towards her, invisibly smiling. It seemed to her fine sparks came out of him.

Then very suddenly, she said:

'Don't try any of your tomfoolery on me.'

A quiver went over his nerves. He had missed. He waited a moment to collect himself again. Then he said, putting all the strange softness into his voice, as if he were imperceptibly stroking her:

'Why, it's not tomfoolery. It's not tomfoolery. I mean it. I mean it. What makes you disbelieve me?'

He sounded hurt. And his voice had such a curious power over her; making her feel loose and relaxed. She struggled somewhere for her own power. She felt for a moment that she was lost – lost – lost. The word seemed to rock in her as if she were dying. Suddenly again she spoke.

'You don't know what you are talking about,' she said, in a brief and transient stroke of scorn. 'What nonsense! I'm old enough to be your mother.'

'Yes, I do know what I'm talking about. Yes, I do,' he persisted softly, as if he were producing his voice in her blood. 'I know quite well what I'm talking about. You're not old enough to be my mother. That isn't true. And what does it matter even if it was. You can marry me whatever age we are. What is age to me? And what is age to you! Age is nothing.'

A swoon went over her as he concluded. He spoke rapidly – in the rapid Cornish fashion – and his voice seemed to sound in her somewhere where she was helpless against it. 'Age is nothing!' The soft, heavy insistence of it made her sway dimly out there in the darkness. She could not answer.

A great exultance leaped like fire over his limbs. He felt he had won.

'I want to marry you, you see. Why shouldn't I?' he pro-

ceeded, soft and rapid. He waited for her to answer. In the dusk
he saw her almost phosphorescent. Her eyelids were dropped,
her face half-averted and unconscious. She seemed to be in his
power. But he waited, watchful. He dared not yet touch her.

'Say then,' he said. 'Say then you'll marry me. Say – say?' He
was softly insistent.

'What?' she asked, faint, from a distance, like one in pain. His
voice was now unthinkably near and soft. He drew very near to
her.

'Say yes.'

'Oh, I can't,' she wailed helplessly, half articulate, as if semi-
conscious, and as if in pain, like one who dies. 'How can I?'

'You can,' he said softly, laying his hand gently on her
shoulder as she stood with her head averted and dropped, dazed.
'You can. Yes, you can. What makes you say you can't? You can.
You can.' And with awful softness he bent forward and just
touched her neck with his mouth and his chin.

'Don't!' she cried, with a faint mad cry like hysteria, starting
away and facing round on him. 'What do you mean?' But she had
no breath to speak with. It was as if she was killed.

'I mean what I say,' he persisted softly and cruelly. 'I want
you to marry me. I want you to marry me. You know that, now,
don't you? You know that, now? Don't you? Don't you?'

'What?' she said.

'Know,' he replied.

'Yes,' she said. 'I know you say so.'

'And you know I mean it, don't you?'

'I know you say so.'

'You believe me?' he said.

She was silent for some time. Then she pursed her lips.

'I don't know what I believe,' she said.

'Are you out there?' came Banford's voice, calling from the
house.

'Yes, we're bringing in the logs,' he answered.

'I thought you'd gone lost,' said Banford disconsolately.
'Hurry up, do, and come and let's have tea. The kettle's boiling.'

He stooped at once, to take an armful of little logs and carry
them into the kitchen, where they were piled in a corner. March

also helped, filling her arms and carrying the logs on her breast as if they were some heavy child. The night had fallen cold.

When the logs were all in, the two cleaned their boots noisily on the scraper outside, then rubbed them on the mat. March shut the door and took off her old felt hat — her farm-girl hat. Her thick, crisp black hair was loose, her face was pale and strained. She pushed back her hair vaguely, and washed her hands. Banford came hurrying into the dimly-lighted kitchen, to take from the oven the scones she was keeping hot.

'Whatever have you been doing all this time?' she asked fretfully. 'I thought you were never coming in. And it's ages since you stopped sawing. What were you doing out there?'

'Well,' said Henry, 'we had to stop that hole in the barn, to keeps the rats out.'

'Why, I could see you standing there in the shed. I could see your shirt-sleeves,' challenged Banford.

'Yes, I was just putting the saw away.'

They went in to tea. March was quite mute. Her face was pale and strained and vague. The youth, who always had the same ruddy, self-contained look on his face, as though he were keeping himself to himself, had come to tea in his shirt-sleeves as if he were at home. He bent over his plate as he ate his food.

'Aren't you cold?' said Banford spitefully. 'In your shirt-sleeves.'

He looked up at her, with his chin near his plate, and his eyes very clear, pellucid, and unwavering as he watched her.

'No, I'm not cold,' he said with his usual soft courtesy. 'It's much warmer in here than it is outside, you see.'

'I hope it is,' said Banford, feeling nettled by him. He had a strange, suave assurance, and a wide-eyed bright look that got on her nerves this evening.

'But perhaps,' he said softly and courteously, 'you don't like me coming to tea without my coat. I forgot that.'

'Oh, I don't mind,' said Banford: although she *did*.

'I'll go and get it, shall I?' he said.

March's eyes turned slowly down to him.

'No, don't you bother,' she said in her queer, twanging tone.

'If you feel all right as you are, stop as you are.' She spoke with a crude authority.

'Yes,' said he, 'I *feel* all right, if I'm not rude.'

'It's usually considered rude,' said Banford. 'But we don't mind.'

'Go along, "considered rude",' ejaculated March. 'Who considers it rude?'

'Why you do, Nellie, in anybody else,' said Banford, bridling a little behind her spectacles, and feeling her food stick in her throat.

But March had again gone vague and unheeding, chewing her food as if she did not know she was eating at all. And the youth looked from one to another, with bright, watchful eyes.

Banford was offended. For all his suave courtesy and soft voice, the youth seemed to her impudent. She did not like to look at him. She did not like to meet his clear, watchful eyes, she did not like to see the strange glow in his face, his cheeks with their delicate fine hair, and his ruddy skin that was quite dull and yet which seemed to burn with a curious heat of life. It made her feel a little ill to look at him: the quality of his physical presence was too penetrating, too hot.

After tea the evening was very quiet. The youth rarely went into the village. As a rule he read: he was a great reader, in his own hours. That is, when he did begin, he read absorbedly. But he was not very eager to begin. Often he walked about the fields and along the hedges alone in the dark at night, prowling with a queer instinct for the night, and listening to the wild sounds.

Tonight, however, he took a Captain Mayne Reid[3] book from Banford's shelf and sat down with knees wide apart and immersed himself in his story. His brownish fair hair was long, and lay on his head like a thick cap, combed sideways. He was still in his shirt-sleeves, and bending forward under the lamplight, with his knees stuck wide apart and the book in his hand and his whole figure absorbed in the rather strenuous business of reading, he gave Banford's sitting-room the look of a lumber-camp. She resented this. For on her sitting-room floor she had a red Turkey rug and dark stain round, the fire-place had fashionable green tiles, the piano stood open with the latest dance-music: she played quite well: and on the walls were March's hand-painted swans and water-lilies. Moreover, with the logs nicely, tremulously burning in the grate, the thick curtains drawn, the doors all shut, and the pine-trees hissing and shuddering in the wind outside, it was cosy, it was refined and nice. She resented the big, raw, long-legged youth sticking his khaki knees out and sitting there with his soldier's shirt-cuffs buttoned on his thick red wrists. From time to time he turned a page, and from time to time he gave a sharp look at the fire, settling the logs. Then he immersed himself again in the intense and isolated business of reading.

March, on the far side of the table, was spasmodically crocheting. Her mouth was pursed in an odd way, as when she had dreamed the fox's brush burned it, her beautiful, crisp black hair strayed in wisps. But her whole figure was absorbed in its bearing, as if she herself was miles away. In a sort of semi-dream she seemed to be hearing the fox singing round the house in the wind, singing wildly and sweetly and like a madness. With red but well-shaped hands she slowly crocheted the white cotton, very slowly, awkwardly.

Banford was also trying to read, sitting in her low chair. But between those two she felt fidgety. She kept moving and looking round and listening to the wind, and glancing secretly from one to the other of her companions. March, seated on a straight chair, with her knees in their close breeches crossed, and slowly, laboriously crocheting, was also a trial.

'Oh dear!' said Banford. 'My eyes are bad tonight.' And she pressed her fingers on her eyes.

The youth looked up at her with his clear bright look, but did not speak.

'Are they, Jill?' said March absently.

Then the youth began to read again, and Banford perforce returned to her book. But she could not keep still. After a while she looked up at March, and a queer, almost malignant little smile was on her thin face.

'A penny for them, Nell,' she said suddenly.

March looked round with big, startled black eyes, and went pale as if with terror. She had been listening to the fox singing so tenderly, so tenderly, as he wandered round the house.

'What?' she said vaguely.

'A penny for them,' said Banford sarcastically. 'Or two-pence, if they're as deep as all that.'

The youth was watching with bright clear eyes from beneath the lamp.

'Why,' came March's vague voice, 'what do you want to waste your money for?'

'I thought it would be well spent,' said Banford.

'I wasn't thinking of anything except the way the wind was blowing,' said March.

'Oh dear,' replied Banford, 'I could have had as original thoughts as that myself. I'm afraid I *have* wasted my money this time.'

'Well, you needn't pay,' said March.

The youth suddenly laughed. Both women looked at him: March rather surprised-looking, as if she had hardly known he was there.

'Why, do you ever pay up on these occasions?' he asked.

'Oh yes,' said Banford. 'We always do. I've sometimes had to pass a shilling a week to Nellie, in the wintertime. It costs much less in summer.'

'What, paying for each other's thoughts?' he laughed.

'Yes, when we've absolutely come to the end of everything else.'

He laughed quickly, wrinkling his nose sharply like a puppy and laughing with quick pleasure, his eyes shining.

'It's the first time I ever heard of that,' he said.

'I guess you'd hear of it often enough if you stayed a winter on Bailey Farm,' said Banford lamentably.

'Do you get so tired, then?' he asked.

'So bored,' said Banford.

'Oh!' he said gravely. 'But why should you be bored?'

'Who wouldn't be bored?' said Banford.

'I'm sorry to hear that,' he said gravely.

'You must be, if you were hoping to have a lively time here,' said Banford.

He looked at her long and gravely.

'Well,' he said, with his odd young seriousness, 'it's quite lively enough for me.'

'I'm glad to hear it,' said Banford.

And she returned to her book. In her thin, frail hair were already many threads of grey, though she was not yet thirty. The boy did not look down, but turned his eyes to March, who was sitting with pursed mouth laboriously crocheting, her eyes wide and absent. She had a warm, pale, fine skin, and a delicate nose. Her pursed mouth looked shrewish. But the shrewish look was contradicted by the curious lifted arch of her dark brows, and the wideness of her eyes; a look of startled wonder and vagueness. She was listening again for the fox, who seemed to have wandered farther off into the night.

From under the edge of the lamp-light the boy sat with his face looking up, watching her silently, his eyes round and very clear and intent. Banford, biting her fingers irritably, was glancing at him under her hair. He sat there perfectly still, his ruddy face tilted up from the low level under the light, on the edge of the dimness, and watching with perfect abstract intentness. March suddenly lifted her great dark eyes from her crocheting, and saw him. She started, giving a little exclamation.

'There he *is!*' she cried involuntarily, as if terribly startled.

Banford looked round in amazement, sitting up straight.

'Whatever has got you, Nellie?' she cried.

But March, her face flushed a delicate rose colour, was looking away to the door.

'Nothing! Nothing!' she said crossly. 'Can't one speak?'

'Yes, if you speak sensibly,' said Banford. 'What ever did you mean?'

'I don't know what I meant,' cried March testily.

'Oh, Nellie, I hope you aren't going jumpy and nervy. I feel I can't stand another *thing*! – Whoever did you mean? Did you mean Henry?' cried poor frightened Banford.

'Yes. I suppose so,' said March laconically. She would never confess to the fox.

'Oh dear, my nerves are all gone for tonight,' wailed Banford.

At nine o'clock March brought in a tray with bread and cheese and tea – Henry had confessed that he liked a cup of tea. Banford drank a glass of milk, and ate a little bread. And soon she said:

'I'm going to bed, Nellie. I'm all nerves tonight. Are you coming?'

'Yes, I'm coming the minute I've taken the tray away,' said March.

'Don't be long then,' said Banford fretfully. 'Good-night, Henry. You'll see the fire is safe, if you come up last, won't you?'

'Yes, Miss Banford, I'll see it's safe,' he replied in his reassuring way.

March was lighting the candle to go to the kitchen. Banford took her candle and went upstairs. When March came back to the fire she said to him:

'I suppose we can trust you to put out the fire and everything?' She stood there with her hand on her hip, and one knee loose, her head averted shyly, as if she could not look at him. He had his face lifted, watching her.

'Come and sit down a minute,' he said softly.

'No, I'll be going. Jill will be waiting, and she'll get upset if I don't come.'

'What made you jump like that this evening?' he asked.

'When did I jump?' she retorted, looking at him.

'Why, just now you did,' he said. 'When you cried out.'

'Oh!' she said. 'Then! – Why, I thought you were the fox!' And her face screwed into a queer smile, half ironic.

'The fox! Why the fox?' he asked softly.

'Why, one evening last summer when I was out with the gun I saw the fox in the grass nearly at my feet, looking straight up at me. I don't know – I suppose he made an impression on me.' She turned aside her head again, and let one foot stray loose, self-consciously.

'And did you shoot him?' asked the boy.

'No, he gave me such a start, staring straight at me as he did, and then stopping to look back at me over his shoulder with a laugh on his face.'

'A laugh on his face!' repeated Henry, also laughing. 'He frightened you, did he?'

'No, he didn't frighten me. He made an impression on me, that's all.'

'And you thought I was the fox, did you?' he laughed, with

the same queer, quick little laugh, like a puppy wrinkling its nose.

'Yes, I did, for the moment,' she said. 'Perhaps he'd been in my mind without my knowing.'

'Perhaps you think I've come to steal your chickens or something,' he said, with the same young laugh.

But she only looked at him with a wide, dark, vacant eye.

'It's the first time,' he said, 'that I've ever been taken for a fox. Won't you sit down for a minute?' His voice was very soft and cajoling.

'No,' she said. 'Jill will be waiting.' But still she did not go, but stood with one foot loose and her face turned aside, just outside the circle of light.

'But won't you answer my question?' he said, lowering his voice still more.

'I don't know what question you mean.'

'Yes, you do. Of course you do. I mean the question of you marrying me.'

'No, I shan't answer that question,' she said flatly.

'Won't you?' The queer young laugh came on his nose again. 'Is it because I'm like the fox? Is that why?' And still he laughed.

She turned and looked at him with a long, slow look.

'I wouldn't let that put you against me,' he said. 'Let me turn the lamp low, and come and sit down a minute.'

He put his red hand under the glow of the lamp, and suddenly made the light very dim. March stood there in the dimness quite shadowy, but unmoving. He rose silently to his feet, on his long legs. And now his voice was extraordinarily soft and suggestive, hardly audible.

'You'll stay a moment,' he said. 'Just a moment.' And he put his hand on her shoulder. – She turned her face from him. 'I'm sure you don't really think I'm like the fox,' he said, with the same softness and with a suggestion of laughter in his tone, a subtle mockery. 'Do you now?' – and he drew her gently towards him and kissed her neck, softly. She winced and trembled and hung away. But his strong young arm held her, and he kissed her softly again, still on the neck, for her face was averted.

'Won't you answer my question? Won't you now?' came his

soft, lingering voice. He was trying to draw her near to kiss her face. And he kissed her cheek softly, near the ear.

At that moment Banford's voice was heard calling fretfully, crossly from upstairs.

'There's Jill!' cried March, starting and drawing erect.

And as she did so, quick as lightning he kissed her on the mouth, with a quick brushing kiss. It seemed to burn through her every fibre. She gave a queer little cry.

'You will, won't you? You will?' he insisted softly.

'Nellie! *Nellie!* What ever are you so long for?' came Banford's faint cry from the outer darkness.

But he held her fast, and was murmuring with that intolerable softness and insistency:

'You will, won't you? Say yes! Say yes!'

March, who felt as if the fire had gone through her and scathed her, and as if she could do no more, murmured:

'Yes! Yes! Anything you like! Anything you like! Only let me go! Only let me go! Jill's calling.'

'You know you've promised,' he said insidiously.

'Yes! Yes! I do! –' Her voice suddenly rose into a shrill cry. 'All right, Jill, I'm coming.'

Startled, he let her go, and she went straight upstairs.

In the morning at breakfast, after he had looked round the place and attended to the stock and thought to himself that one could live easily enough here, he said to Banford:

'Do you know what, Miss Banford?'

'Well, what?' said the good-natured, nervy Banford.

He looked at March, who was spreading jam on her bread.

'Shall I tell?' he said to her.

She looked up at him, and a deep pink colour flushed over her face.

'Yes, if you mean Jill,' she said. 'I hope you won't go talking all over the village, that's all.' And she swallowed her dry bread with difficulty.

'Whatever's coming?' said Banford, looking up with wide, tired, slightly reddened eyes. She was a thin, frail little thing, and her hair, which was delicate and thin, was bobbed, so it hung softly by her worn face in its faded brown and grey.

'Why, what do you think?' he said, smiling like one who has a secret.

'How do I know!' said Banford.

'Can't you guess?' he said, making bright eyes, and smiling, pleased with himself.

'I'm sure I can't. What's more, I'm not going to try.'

'Nellie and I are going to be married.'

Banford put down her knife, out of her thin, delicate fingers, as if she would never take it up to eat any more. She stared with blank, reddened eyes.

'You what?' she exclaimed.

'We're going to get married. Aren't we, Nellie?' and he turned to March.

'You say so, anyway,' said March laconically. But again she flushed with an agonized flush. She, too, could swallow no more.

Banford looked at her like a bird that has been shot: a poor little sick bird. She gazed at her with all her wounded soul in her face, at the deep-flushed March.

'Never!' she exclaimed, helpless.

'It's quite right,' said the bright and gloating youth.

Banford turned aside her face, as if the sight of the food on the table made her sick. She sat like this for some moments, as if she were sick. Then, with one hand on the edge of the table, she rose to her feet.

'I'll *never* believe it, Nellie,' she cried. 'It's absolutely impossible!'

Her plaintive, fretful voice had a thread of hot anger and despair.

'Why? Why shouldn't you believe it?' asked the youth, with all his soft, velvety impertinence in his voice.

Banford looked at him from her wide vague eyes, as if he were some creature in a museum.

'Oh,' she said languidly, 'because she can never be such a fool. She can't lose her self-respect to such an extent.' Her voice was cold and plaintive, drifting.

'In what way will she lose her self-respect?' asked the boy.

Banford looked at him with vague fixity from behind her spectacles.

'If she hasn't lost it already,' she said.

He became very red, vermilion, under the slow vague stare from behind the spectacles.

'I don't see it at all,' he said.

'Probably you don't. I shouldn't expect you would,' said Banford, with that straying mild tone of remoteness which made her words even more insulting.

He sat stiff in his chair, staring with hot blue eyes from his scarlet face. An ugly look had come on his brow.

'My word, she doesn't know what she's letting herself in for,' said Banford, in her plaintive, drifting, insulting voice.

'What has it got to do with you, anyway?' said the youth in a temper.

'More than it has to do with you, probably,' she replied, plaintive and venomous.

'Oh, has it! I don't see that at all,' he jerked out.

'No, you wouldn't,' she answered, drifting.

'Anyhow,' said March, pushing back her hair and rising uncouthly, 'it's no good arguing about it.' And she seized the bread and the tea-pot, and strode away to the kitchen.

Banford let her fingers stray across her brow and along her hair, like one bemused. Then she turned and went away upstairs.

Henry sat stiff and sulky in his chair, with his face and his eyes on fire. March came and went, clearing the table. But Henry sat on, stiff with temper. He took no notice of her. She had regained her composure and her soft, even, creamy complexion. But her mouth was pursed up. She glanced at him each time as she came to take things from the table, glanced from her large, curious eyes, more in curiosity than anything. Such a long, red-faced sulky boy! That was all he was. He seemed as remote from her as if his red face were a red chimney-pot on a cottage across the fields, and she looked at him just as objectively, as remotely.

At length he got up and stalked out into the fields with the gun. He came in only at dinner-time, with the devil still in his face, but his manners quite polite. Nobody said anything particular: they sat each one at the sharp corner of a triangle, in obstinate remoteness. In the afternoon he went out again at once with the gun. He came in at nightfall with a rabbit and a pigeon.

He stayed in all evening, but hardly opened his mouth. He was in the devil of a temper, feeling he had been insulted.

Banford's eyes were red, she had evidently been crying. But her manner was more remote and supercilious than ever, the way she turned her head if he spoke at all, as if he were some tramp or inferior intruder of that sort, made his blue eyes go almost black with rage. His face looked sulkier. But he never forgot his polite intonation, if he opened his mouth to speak.

March seemed to flourish in this atmosphere. She seemed to sit between the two antagonists with a little wicked smile on her face, enjoying herself. There was even a sort of complacency in the way she laboriously crocheted, this evening.

When he was in bed, the youth could hear the two women talking and arguing in their room. He sat up in bed and strained his ears to hear what they said. But he could hear nothing, it was too far off. Yet he could hear the soft, plaintive drip of Banford's voice, and March's deeper note.

The night was quiet, frosty. Big stars were snapping outside, beyond the ridge-tops of the pine-trees. He listened and listened. In the distance he heard a fox yelping: and the dogs from the farms barking in answer. But it was not that he wanted to hear. It was what the two women were saying.

He got stealthily out of bed, and stood by his door. He could hear no more than before. Very, very carefully he began to lift the door-latch. After quite a time he had his door open. Then he stepped stealthily out into the passage. The old oak planks were cold under his feet, and they creaked preposterously. He crept very, very gently up the one step, and along by the wall, till he stood outside their door. And there he held his breath and listened. Banford's voice:

'No, I simply couldn't stand it. I should be dead in a month. Which is just what he would be aiming at, of course. That would just be his game, to see me in the churchyard. No, Nellie, if you were to do such a thing as marry him, you could never stop here. I couldn't, I couldn't live in the same house with him. Oh – ! I feel quite sick with the smell of his clothes. And his red face simply turns me over. I can't eat my food when he's at the table. What a fool I was ever to let him stop. One ought *never* to try to do a kind action. It always flies back in your face like a boomerang.'

'Well, he's only got two more days,' said March.

'Yes, thank heaven. And when he's gone he'll never come in this house again. I feel so bad while he's here. And I know, I know he's only counting what he can get out of you. I *know* that's all it is. He's just a good-for-nothing, who doesn't want to work, and who thinks he'll live on us. But he won't live on me. If you're such a fool, then it's your own lookout. Mrs Burgess knew him all the time he was here. And the old man could never get him to do any steady work. He was off with the gun on every occasion, just as he is now. Nothing but the gun! Oh, I do hate it. You don't know what you're doing, Nellie, you don't. If you marry him he'll just make a fool of you. He'll go off and leave you stranded. I know he will, if he can't get Bailey Farm out of us – and he's not going to, while I live. While I live he's never going to set foot here. I know what it would be. He'd soon think he was master of both of us, as he thinks he's master of you already.'

'But he isn't,' said Nellie.

'He thinks he is, anyway. And that's what he wants: to come and be master here. Yes, imagine it! That's what we've got the place together for, is it, to be bossed and bullied by a hateful red-faced boy, a beastly labourer. Oh we *did* make a mistake when we let him stop. We ought never to have lowered ourselves. And I've had such a fight with all the people here, not to be pulled down to their level. No, he's not coming here. – And then you see – if he can't have the place, he'll run off to Canada or somewhere again, as if he'd never known you. And here you'll be, absolutely ruined and made a fool of. I know I shall never have any peace of mind again.'

'We'll tell him he can't come here. We'll tell him that,' said March.

'Oh, don't you bother, I'm going to tell him that, and other things as well, before he goes. He's not going to have all his own way, while I've got the strength left to speak. Oh, Nellie, he'll despise you, he'll despise you like the awful little beast he is, if you give way to him. I'd no more trust him than I'd trust a cat not to steal. He's deep, he's deep, and he's bossy, and he's selfish through and through, as cold as ice. All he wants is to make use of you. And when you're no more use to him, then I pity you.'

'I don't think he's as bad as all that,' said March.

'No, because he's been playing up to you. But you'll find out, if you see much more of him. Oh, Nellie, I can't bear to think of it.'

'Well, it won't hurt you, Jill darling.'

'Won't it! Won't it! I shall never know a moment's peace again while I live, nor a moment's happiness. No, Nellie –' and Banford began to weep bitterly.

The boy outside could hear the stifled sound of the woman's sobbing, and could hear March's soft, deep, tender voice comforting, with wonderful gentleness and tenderness, the weeping woman.

His eyes were so round and wide that he seemed to see the whole night, and his ears were almost jumping off his head. He was frozen stiff. He crept back to bed, but felt as if the top of his head were coming off. He could not sleep. He could not keep still. He rose, quietly dressed himself, and crept out on to the landing once more. The women were silent. He went softly downstairs and out to the kitchen.

Then he put on his boots and overcoat, and took the gun. He did not think to go away from the farm. No, he only took the gun. As softly as possible he unfastened the door and went out into the frosty December night. The air was still, the stars bright, the pine-trees seemed to bristle audibly in the sky. He went stealthily away down a fence-side, looking for something to shoot. At the same time he remembered that he ought not to shoot and frighten the women.

So he prowled round the edge of the gorse cover, and through the grove of tall old hollies, to the woodside. There he skirted the fence, peering through the darkness with dilated eyes that seemed to be able to grow black and full of sight in the dark, like a cat's. An owl was slowly and mournfully whooing round a great oak tree. He stepped stealthily with his gun, listening, listening, watching.

As he stood under the oaks of the wood-edge he heard the dogs from the neighbouring cottage, up the hill, yelling suddenly and startlingly, and the wakened dogs from the farms around barking answer. And suddenly, it seemed to him England was little and tight, he felt the landscape was constricted even in the dark, and that there were too many dogs in the night, making a noise like a fence of sound, like the network of English hedges netting the view. He felt the fox didn't have a chance. For it must be the fox that had started all this hullabaloo.

Why not watch for him, anyhow! He would no doubt be coming sniffing round. The lad walked downhill to where the farmstead with its few pine-trees crouched blackly. In the angle of the long shed, in the black dark, he crouched down. He knew the fox would be coming. It seemed to him it would be the last of the foxes in this loudly-barking, thick-voiced England, tight with innumerable little houses.

He sat a long time with his eyes fixed unchanging upon the open gateway, where a little light seemed to fall from the stars or from the horizon, who knows. He was sitting on a log in a dark corner with the gun across his knees. The pine-trees snapped. Once a chicken fell off its perch in the barn, with a loud crawk and cackle and commotion that startled him, and he stood up, watching with all his eyes, thinking it might be a rat. But he *felt* it was nothing. So he sat down again with the gun on his knees and his hands tucked in to keep them warm, and his eyes fixed unblinking on the pale reach of the open gateway. He felt he could smell the hot, sickly, rich smell of live chickens on the cold air.

And then – a shadow. A sliding shadow in the gateway. He gathered all his vision into a concentrated spark, and saw the shadow of the fox, the fox creeping on his belly through the gate. There he went, on his belly like a snake. The boy smiled to himself and brought the gun to his shoulder. He knew quite well what would happen. He knew the fox would go to where the fowl-door was boarded up, and sniff there. He knew he would lie there for a minute, sniffing the fowls within. And then he would start again prowling under the edge of the old barn, waiting to get in.

The fowl-door was at the top of a slight incline. Soft, soft as a shadow the fox slid up this incline, and crouched with his nose to the boards. And at the same moment there was the awful crash of a gun reverberating between the old buildings, as if all the night had gone smash. But the boy watched keenly. He saw even the white belly of the fox as the beast beat his paws in death. So he went forward.

There was a commotion everywhere. The fowls were scuffling and crawking, the ducks were quark-quarking, the pony had stamped wildly to his feet. But the fox was on his side, struggling in his last tremors. The boy bent over him and smelt his foxy smell.

There was a sound of a window opening upstairs, then March's voice calling:

'Who is it?'

'It's me,' said Henry; 'I've shot the fox.'

'Oh, goodness! You nearly frightened us to death.'

'Did I? I'm awfully sorry.'

'Whatever made you get up?'

'I heard him about.'

'And have you shot him?'

'Yes, he's here,' and the boy stood in the yard holding up the warm, dead brute. 'You can't see, can you? Wait a minute.' And he took his flash-light from his pocket, and flashed it on to the dead animal. He was holding it by the brush. March saw, in the middle of the darkness, just the reddish fleece and the white belly and the white underneath of the pointed chin, and the queer, dangling paws. She did not know what to say.

'He's a beauty,' he said. 'He will make you a lovely fur.'

'You don't catch me wearing a fox fur,' she replied.

'Oh!' he said. And he switched off the light.

'Well, I should think you'll come in and go to bed again now,' she said.

'Probably I shall. What time is it?'

'What time is it, Jill?' called March's voice. It was a quarter to one.

That night March had another dream. She dreamed that Banford was dead, and that she, March, was sobbing her heart out. Then she had to put Banford into her coffin. And the coffin was the rough wood-box in which the bits of chopped wood were kept in the kitchen, by the fire. This was the coffin, and there was no other, and March was in agony and dazed bewilderment, looking for something to line the box with, something to make it soft with, something to cover up the poor dead darling. Because she couldn't lay her in there just in her white thin nightdress, in the horrible wood-box. So she hunted and hunted, and picked up thing after thing, and threw it aside in the agony of dream-frustration. And in her dream-despair all she could find that would do was a fox-skin. She knew that it wasn't right, that this was not what she could have. But it was all she could find. And so she folded the brush of the fox, and laid her darling Jill's head on this, and she brought round the skin of the fox and laid it on the top of the body, so that it seemed to make a whole ruddy, fiery coverlet, and she cried and cried and woke to find the tears streaming down her face.

The first thing that both she and Banford did in the morning was to go out to see the fox. He had hung it up by the heels in the shed, with its poor brush falling backwards. It was a lovely dog-fox in its prime with a handsome thick winter coat: a lovely golden-red colour, with grey as it passed to the belly, and belly all white, and a great full brush with a delicate black and grey and pure white tip.

'Poor brute!' said Banford. 'If it wasn't such a thieving wretch, you'd feel sorry for it.'

March said nothing, but stood with her foot trailing aside, one hip out; her face was pale and her eyes big and black, watching the dead animal that was suspended upside down. White and soft as snow his belly: white and soft as snow. She passed her hand softly down it. And his wonderful black-glinted brush was full and frictional, wonderful. She passed her hand down this also, and quivered. Time after time she took the full fur of that thick tail between her hand and passed her hand slowly downwards. Wonderful sharp thick splendour of a tail! And he was dead! She pursed her lips, and her eyes went black and vacant. Then she took the head in her hand.

Henry was sauntering up, so Banford walked rather pointedly away. March stood there bemused, with the head of the fox in her hand. She was wondering, wondering, wondering over his long fine muzzle. For some reason it reminded her of a spoon or a spatula. She felt she could not understand it. The beast was a strange beast to her, incomprehensible, out of her range. Wonderful silver whiskers he had, like ice-threads. And pricked ears with hair inside. – But that long, long slender spoon of a nose! – and the marvellous white teeth beneath! It was to thrust forward and bite with, deep, deep into the living prey, to bite and bite the blood.

'He's a beauty, isn't he?' said Henry, standing by.

'Oh yes, he's a fine big fox. I wonder how many chickens he's responsible for,' she replied.

'A good many. Do you think he's the same one you saw in the summer?'

'I should think very likely he is,' she replied.

He watched her, but he could make nothing of her. Partly she was so shy and virgin, and partly she was so grim, matter-of-fact, shrewish. What she said seemed to him so different from the look of her big, queer dark eyes.

'Are you going to skin him?' she asked.

'Yes, when I've had breakfast, and got a board to peg him on.'

'My word, what a strong smell he's got! Pooo! – It'll take some washing off one's hands. I don't know why I was so silly as to handle him.' – And she looked at her right hand, that had passed down his belly and along his tail, and had even got a tiny streak of blood from one dark place in his fur.

'Have you seen the chickens when they smell him, how frightened they are?' he said.

'Yes, aren't they!'

'You must mind you don't get some of his fleas.'

'Oh, fleas!' she replied, nonchalant.

Later in the day she saw the fox's skin nailed flat on a board, as if crucified. It gave her an uneasy feeling.

The boy was angry. He went about with his mouth shut, as if he had swallowed part of his chin. But in behaviour he was polite and affable. He did not say anything about his intention. And he left March alone.

That evening they sat in the dining-room. Banford wouldn't have him in her sitting-room any more. There was a very big log on the fire. And everybody was busy. Banford had letters to write, March was sewing a dress, and he was mending some little contrivance.

Banford stopped her letter-writing from time to time to look round and rest her eyes. The boy had his head down, his face hidden over his job.

'Let's see,' said Banford. 'What train do you go by, Henry?'

He looked up straight at her.

'The morning train. In the morning,' he said.

'What, the eight-ten or the eleven-twenty?'

'The eleven-twenty, I suppose,' he said.

'That is the day after tomorrow?' said Banford.

'Yes, the day after tomorrow.'

'Mmm!' murmured Banford, and she returned to her writing. But as she was licking her envelope, she asked:

'And what plans have you made for the future, if I may ask?'

'Plans?' he said, his face very bright and angry.

'I mean about you and Nellie, if you are going on with this business. When do you expect the wedding to come off?' She spoke in a jeering tone.

'Oh, the wedding!' he replied. 'I don't know.'

'Don't you know anything?' said Banford. 'Are you going to clear out on Friday and leave things no more settled than they are?'

'Well, why shouldn't I? We can always write letters.'

'Yes, of course you can. But I wanted to know because of this place. If Nellie is going to get married all of a sudden, I shall have to be looking round for a new partner.'

'Couldn't she stay on here if she was married?' he said. He knew quite well what was coming.

'Oh,' said Banford, 'this is no place for a married couple. There's not enough work to keep a man going, for one thing. And there's no money to be made. It's quite useless your thinking of staying on here if you marry. Absolutely!'

'Yes, but I wasn't thinking of staying on here,' he said.

'Well, that's what I want to know. And what about Nellie, then? How long is *she* going to be here with me, in that case?'

The two antagonists looked at one another.

'That I can't say,' he answered.

'Oh, go along,' she cried petulantly. 'You must have some idea what you are going to do, if you ask a woman to marry you. Unless it's all a hoax.'

'Why should it be a hoax? – I am going back to Canada.'

'And taking her with you?'

'Yes, certainly.'

'You hear that, Nellie?' said Banford.

March, who had had her head bent over her sewing, now looked up with a sharp pink blush on her face and a queer, sardonic laugh in her eyes and on her twisted mouth.

'That's the first time I've heard that I was going to Canada,' she said.

'Well, you have to hear it for the first time, haven't you?' said the boy.

'Yes, I suppose I have,' she said nonchalantly. And she went back to her sewing.

'You're quite ready, are you, to go to Canada? Are you, Nellie?' asked Banford.

March looked up again. She let her shoulders go slack, and let her hand that held the needle lie loose in her lap.

'It depends on *how* I'm going,' she said. 'I don't think I want to go jammed up in the steerage, as a soldier's wife. I'm afraid I'm not used to that way.'

The boy watched her with bright eyes.

'Would you rather stay over here while I go first?' he asked.

'I would, if that's the only alternative,' she replied.

'That's much the wisest. Don't make it any fixed engagement,' said Banford. 'Leave yourself free to go or not after he's got back and found you a place, Nellie. Anything else is madness, madness.'

'Don't you think,' said the youth, 'we ought to get married before I go – and then go together, or separate, according to how it happens?'

'I think it's a *terrible* idea,' cried Banford.

But the boy was watching March.

'What do you think?' he asked her.

She let her eyes stray vaguely into space.

'Well, I don't know,' she said. 'I shall have to think about it.'

'Why?' he asked, pertinently.

'Why?' – She repeated his question in a mocking way and looked at him laughing, though her face was pink again. 'I should think there's plenty of reasons why.'

He watched her in silence. She seemed to have escaped him. She had got into league with Banford against him. There was again the queer sardonic look about her; she would mock stoically at everything he said or which life offered.

'Of course,' he said, 'I don't want to press you to do anything you don't wish to do.'

'I should think not, indeed,' cried Banford indignantly.

At bedtime Banford said plaintively to March:

'You take my hot bottle up for me, Nellie, will you?'

'Yes, I'll do it,' said March, with the kind of willing unwillingness she so often showed towards her beloved but uncertain Jill.

The two women went upstairs. After a time March called from the top of the stairs: 'Good-night, Henry. I shan't be coming down. You'll see to the lamp and the fire, won't you?'

The next day Henry went about with the cloud on his brow and his young cub's face shut up tight. He was cogitating all the time. He had wanted March to marry him and go back to Canada with him. And he had been sure she would do it. Why he wanted her he didn't know. But he did want her. He had set his mind on her. And he was convulsed with a youth's fury at being thwarted. To be thwarted, to be thwarted! It made him so furious inside, that he did not know what to do with himself. But he kept himself in hand. Because even now things might turn out differently. She might come over to him. Of course she might. It was her business to do so.

Things drew to a tension again towards evening. He and Banford had avoided each other all day. In fact Banford went in to the little town by the 11.20 train. It was market day. She arrived back on the 4.25. Just as the night was falling Henry saw her little figure in a dark-blue coat and a dark-blue tam-o'-shanter hat crossing the first meadow from the station. He stood under one of the wild pear trees, with the old dead leaves round his feet. And he watched the little blue figure advancing per-

sistently over the rough winter-ragged meadow. She had her
arms full of parcels, and advanced slowly, frail thing she was, but
with that devilish little certainty which he so detested in her. He
stood invisible under the pear-tree, watching her every step. And
if looks could have affected her, she would have felt a log of iron
on each of her ankles as she made her way forward. 'You're a
nasty little thing, you are,' he was saying softly, across the
distance. 'You're a nasty little thing. I hope you'll be paid back
for all the harm you've done me for nothing. I hope you will –
you nasty little thing. I hope you'll have to pay for it. You will,
if wishes are anything. You nasty little creature that you are.'

She was toiling slowly up the slope. But if she had been
slipping back at every step towards the Bottomless Pit, he would
not have gone to help her with her parcels. Aha, there went
March, striding with her long land stride in her breeches and her
short tunic! Striding downhill at a great pace, and even running
a few steps now and then, in her great solicitude and desire to
come to the rescue of the little Banford. The boy watched her
with rage in his heart. See her leap a ditch, and run, run as if
a house was on fire, just to get to that creeping dark little object
down there! So, the Banford just stood still and waited. And
March strode up and took *all* the parcels except a bunch of yellow
chrysanthemums. These the Banford still carried – yellow
chrysanthemums!

'Yes, you look well, don't you,' he said softly into the dusk air.
'You look well, pottering up there with a bunch of flowers, you
do. I'd make you eat them for your tea, if you hug them so tight.
And I'd give them you for breakfast again, I would. I'd give you
flowers. Nothing but flowers.'

He watched the progress of the two women. He could hear
their voices: March always outspoken and rather scolding in her
tenderness, Banford murmuring rather vaguely. They were
evidently good friends. He could not hear what they said till they
came to the fence of the home meadow, which they must climb.
Then he saw March manfully climbing over the bars with all her
packages in her arms, and on the still air he heard Banford's
fretful:

'Why don't you let me help you with the parcels?' She had a

queer plaintive hitch in her voice. – Then came March's robust and reckless:

'Oh, I can manage. Don't you bother about me. You've all you can do to get yourself over.'

'Yes, that's all very well,' said Banford fretfully. 'You say *Don't you bother about me*, and then all the while you feel injured because nobody thinks of you.'

'When do I feel injured?' said March.

'Always. You always feel injured. Now you're feeling injured because I won't have that boy to come and live on the farm.'

'I'm not feeling injured at all,' said March.

'I know you are. When he's gone you'll sulk over it. I know you will.'

'Shall I?' said March. 'We'll see.'

'Yes, we *shall* see, unfortunately. – I can't think how you can make yourself so cheap. I can't *imagine* how you can lower yourself like it.'

'I haven't lowered myself,' said March.

'I don't know what you call it, then. Letting a boy like that come so cheeky and impudent and make a mug of you. I don't know what you think of yourself. How much respect do you think he's going to have for you afterwards? – My word, I wouldn't be in your shoes, if you married him.'

'Of course you wouldn't. My boots are a good bit too big for you, and not half dainty enough,' said March, with rather a mis-fire sarcasm.

'I thought you had too much pride, really I did. A woman's got to hold herself high, especially with a youth like that. Why, he's impudent. Even the way he forced himself on us at the start.'

'We asked him to stay,' said March.

'Not till he'd almost forced us to. – And then he's so cocky and self-assured. My word, he puts my back up. I simply can't imagine how you can let him treat you so cheaply.'

'I don't let him treat me cheaply,' said March. 'Don't you worry yourself, nobody's going to treat me cheaply. And even you aren't, either.' She had a tender defiance, and a certain fire in her voice.

'Yes, it's sure to come back to me,' said Banford bitterly.

'That's always the end of it. I believe you only do it to spite me.'

They went now in silence up the steep grassy slope and over the brow through the gorse-bushes. On the other side the hedge the boy followed in the dusk, at some little distance. Now and then, through the huge ancient hedge of hawthorn, risen into trees, he saw the two dark figures creeping up the hill. As he came to the top of the slope he saw the homestead dark in the twilight, with a huge old pear-tree leaning from the near gable, and a little yellow light twinkling in the small side windows of the kitchen. He heard the clink of the latch and saw the kitchen door open into light as the two women went indoors. So, they were at home.

And so! – this was what they thought of him. It was rather in his nature to be a listener, so he was not at all surprised whatever he heard. The things people said about him always missed him personally. He was only rather surprised at the women's way with one another. And he disliked the Banford with an acid dislike. And he felt drawn to the March again. He felt again irresistibly drawn to her. He felt there was a secret bond, a secret thread between him and her, something very exclusive, which shut out everybody else and made him and her possess each other in secret.

He hoped again that she would have him. He hoped with his blood suddenly firing up that she would agree to marry him quite quickly: at Christmas, very likely. Christmas was not far off. He wanted, whatever else happened, to snatch her into a hasty marriage and a consummation with him. Then for the future, they could arrange later. But he hoped it would happen as he wanted it. He hoped that tonight she would stay a little while with him, after Banford had gone upstairs. He hoped he could touch her soft, creamy cheek, her strange, frightened face. He hoped he could look into her dilated, frightened dark eyes, quite near. He hoped he might even put his hand on her bosom and feel her soft breasts under her tunic. His heart beat deep and powerful as he thought of that. He wanted very much to do so. He wanted to make sure of her soft woman's breasts under her tunic. She always kept the brown linen coat buttoned so close up to her throat. It seemed to him like some perilous secret, that her soft woman's breasts must be buttoned up in that uniform. It seemed to him moreover that they were so much softer, tenderer, more lovely and lovable, shut up in that tunic, than were the Banford's breasts, under her soft blouses and chiffon dresses. The Banford would have little iron breasts, he said to himself. For all her frailty and fretfulness and delicacy, she would have tiny iron breasts. But March, under her crude, fast, workman's tunic, would have soft white breasts, white and unseen. So he told himself, and his blood burned.

When he went in to tea, he had a surprise. He appeared at the inner door, his face very ruddy and vivid and his blue eyes shining, dropping his head forward as he came in, in his usual way, and hesitating in the doorway to watch the inside of the room, keenly and cautiously, before he entered. He was wearing a long-sleeved waistcoat. His face seemed extraordinarily a piece of the out-of-doors come indoors: as holly-berries do. In his second of pause in the doorway he took in the two women sitting at table, at opposite ends, saw them sharply. And to his amazement March was dressed in a dress of dull, green silk crape. His mouth came open in surprise. If she had suddenly grown a moustache he could not have been more surprised.

'Why,' he said, 'do you wear a dress, then?'

She looked up, flushing a deep rose colour, and twisting her mouth with a smile, said:

'Of course I do. What else do you expect me to wear, but a dress?'

'A land girl's uniform, of course,' said he.

'Oh,' she cried nonchalant, 'that's only for this dirty mucky work about here.'

'Isn't it your proper dress, then?' he said.

'No, not indoors it isn't,' she said. But she was blushing all the time as she poured out his tea. He sat down in his chair at table, unable to take his eyes off her. Her dress was a perfectly simple slip of bluey-green crape, with a line of gold stitching round the top and round the sleeves, which came to the elbow. It was cut just plain, and round at the top, and showed her white soft throat. Her arms he knew, strong and firm muscled, for he had often seen her with her sleeves rolled up. But he looked her up and down, up and down.

Banford, at the other end of the table, said not a word, but piggled with the sardine on her plate. He had forgotten her existence. He just simply stared at March, while he ate his bread and margarine in huge mouthfuls, forgetting even his tea.

'Well, I never knew anything make such a difference!' he murmured, across his mouthfuls.

'Oh, goodness!' cried March, blushing still more. 'I might be a pink monkey!'

And she rose quickly to her feet and took the tea-pot to the fire, to the kettle. And as she crouched on the hearth with her green slip about her, the boy stared more wide-eyed than ever. Through the crape her woman's form seemed soft and womanly. And when she stood up and walked he saw her legs move soft within her moderately short skirt. She had on black silk stockings and small patent shoes with little gold buckles.

No, she was another being. She was something quite different. Seeing her always in the hard-cloth breeches, wide on the hips, buttoned on the knee, strong as armour, and in the brown puttees and thick boots, it had never occurred to him that she had a woman's legs and feet. Now it came upon him. She had a woman's soft, skirted legs, and she was accessible. He blushed to the roots of his hair, shoved his nose in his teacup and drank his tea with a little noise that made Banford simply squirm: and strangely, suddenly he felt a man, no longer a youth. He felt a man, with all a man's grave weight of responsibility. A curious quietness and gravity came over his soul. He felt a man, quiet, with a little of the heaviness of male destiny upon him.

She was soft and accessible in her dress. The thought went home in him like an everlasting responsibility.

'Oh for Goodness' sake, say something, somebody,' cried Banford fretfully. 'It might be a funeral.' The boy looked at her, and she could not bear his face.

'A funeral!' said March, with a twisted smile. 'Why, that breaks my dream.'

Suddenly she had thought of Banford in the wood-box for a coffin.

'What, have you been dreaming of a wedding?' said Banford sarcastically.

'Must have been,' said March.

'Whose wedding?' asked the boy.

'I can't remember,' said March.

She was shy and rather awkward that evening, in spite of the fact that, wearing a dress, her bearing was much more subdued than in her uniform. She felt unpeeled and rather exposed. She felt almost improper.

They talked desultorily about Henry's departure next morning, and made the trivial arrangement. But of the matter on their minds, none of them spoke. They were rather quiet and friendly this evening; Banford had practically nothing to say. But inside herself she seemed still, perhaps kindly.

At nine o'clock March brought in the tray with the everlasting tea and a little cold meat which Banford had managed to procure. It was the last supper, so Banford did not want to be disagreeable. She felt a bit sorry for the boy, and felt she must be as nice as she could.

He wanted her to go to bed. She was usually the first. But she sat on in her chair under the lamp, glancing at her book now and then, and staring into the fire. A deep silence had come into the room. It was broken by March asking, in a rather small tone:

'What time is it, Jill?'

'Five past ten,' said Banford, looking at her wrist.

And then not a sound. The boy had looked up from the book he was holding between his knees. His rather wide, cat-shaped face had its obstinate look, his eyes were watchful.

'What about bed?' said March at last.

'I'm ready when you are,' said Banford.

'Oh, very well,' said March. 'I'll fill your bottle.'

She was as good as her word. When the hot-water bottle was ready, she lit a candle and went upstairs with it. Banford remained in her chair, listening acutely. March came downstairs again.

'There you are then,' she said. 'Are you going up?'

'Yes, in a minute,' said Banford. But the minute passed, and she sat on in her chair under the lamp.

Henry, whose eyes were shining like a cat's as he watched from under his brows, and whose face seemed wider, more chubbed and cat-like with unalterable obstinacy, now rose to his feet to try his throw.

'I think I'll go and look if I can see the she-fox,' he said. 'She may be creeping round. Won't you come as well for a minute, Nellie, and see if we see anything?'

'Me!' cried March, looking up with her startled, wondering face.

'Yes. Come on,' he said. It was wonderful how soft and warm and coaxing his voice could be, how near. The very sound of it made Banford's blood boil. 'Come on for a minute,' he said, looking down into her uplifted, unsure face.

And she rose to her feet as if drawn up by this young, ruddy face that was looking down on her.

'I should think you're never going out at this time of night, Nellie!' cried Banford.

'Yes, just for a minute,' said the boy, looking round on her, and speaking with an odd sharp yelp in his voice.

March looked from one to the other, as if confused, vague. Banford rose to her feet for battle.

'Why, it's ridiculous. It's bitter cold. You'll catch your death in that thin frock. And in those slippers. You're not going to do any such thing.'

There was a moment's pause. Banford turtled up like a little fighting cock, facing March and the boy.

'Oh, I don't think you need worry yourself,' he replied. 'A moment under the stars won't do anybody any damage. I'll get the rug off the sofa in the dining-room. You're coming, Nellie.'

His voice had so much anger and contempt and fury in it as he spoke to Banford: and so much tenderness and proud authority as he spoke to March, that the latter answered:

'Yes, I'm coming.'

And she turned with him to the door.

Banford, standing there in the middle of the room, suddenly burst into a long wail and a spasm of sobs. She covered her face with her poor thin hands, and her thin shoulders shook in an agony of weeping. March looked back from the door.

'Jill!' she cried in a frantic tone, like someone just coming awake. And she seemed to start towards her darling.

But the boy had March's arm in his grip, and she could not move. She did not know why she could not move. It was as in a dream when the heart strains and the body cannot stir.

'Never mind,' said the boy softly. 'Let her cry. Let her cry. She will have to cry sooner or later. And the tears will relieve her feelings. They will do her good.'

So he drew March slowly through the doorway. But her last look was back to the poor little figure which stood in the middle of the room with covered face and thin shoulders shaken with bitter weeping.

In the dining-room he picked up the rug and said:

'Wrap yourself up in this.'

She obeyed – and they reached the kitchen door, he holding her soft and firm by the arm, though she did not know it. When she saw the night outside she started back.

'I must go back to Jill,' she said. 'I *must*! Oh yes, I must.'

Her tone sounded final. The boy let go of her and she turned indoors. But he seized her again and arrested her.

'Wait a minute,' he said. 'Wait a minute. Even if you go you're not going yet.'

'Leave go! Leave go!' she cried. 'My place is at Jill's side. Poor little thing, she's sobbing her heart out.'

'Yes,' said the boy bitterly. 'And your heart too, and mine as well.'

'Your heart?' said March. He still gripped her and detained her.

'Isn't it as good as her heart?' he said. 'Or do you think it's not?'

'Your heart?' she said again, incredulous.

'Yes, mine! Mine! Do you think I haven't *got* a heart?' – And with his hot grasp he took her hand and pressed it under his left breast. 'There's my heart,' he said, 'if you don't believe in it.'

It was wonder which made her attend. And then she felt the deep, heavy, powerful stroke of his heart, terrible, like something from beyond. It was like something from beyond, something awful from outside, signalling to her. And the signal paralysed her. It beat upon her very soul, and made her helpless. She forgot Jill. She could not think of Jill any more. She could not think of her. That terrible signalling from outside!

The boy put his arm round her waist.

'Come with me,' he said gently. 'Come and let us say what we've got to say.'

And he drew her outside, closed the door. And she went with him darkly down the garden path. That he should have a beating heart! And that he should have his arm round her, outside the blanket! She was too confused to think who he was or what he was.

He took her to a dark corner of the shed, where there was a tool-box with a lid, long and low.

'We'll sit here a minute,' he said.

And obediently she sat down by his side.

'Give me your hand,' he said.

She gave him both her hands, and he held them between his own. He was young, and it made him tremble.

'You'll marry me. You'll marry me before I go back, won't you?' he pleaded.

'Why, aren't we both a pair of fools?' she said.

He had put her in the corner, so that she should not look out and see the lighted window of the house, across the dark garden. He tried to keep her all there inside the shed with him.

'In what way a pair of fools?' he said. 'If you go back to Canada with me, I've got a job and a good wage waiting for me, and it's a nice place, near the mountains. Why shouldn't you marry me? Why shouldn't we marry? I should like to have you there with me. I should like to feel I'd got somebody there, at the back of me, all my life.'

'You'd easily find somebody else, who'd suit you better,' she said.

'Yes, I might easily find another girl. I know I could. But not one I really wanted. I've never met one I really wanted, for good. You see, I'm thinking of all my life. If I marry, I want to feel it's for all my life. Other girls: well, they're just girls, nice enough to go a walk with now and then. Nice enough for a bit of play.

But when I think of my life, then I should be very sorry to have to marry one of them, I should indeed.'

'You mean they wouldn't make you a good wife.'

'Yes, I mean that. But I don't mean they wouldn't do their duty by me. I mean – I don't know what I mean. Only when I think of my life, and of you, then the two things go together.'

'And what if they didn't?' she said, with her odd sardonic touch.

'Well, I think they would.'

They sat for some time silent. He held her hands in his, but he did not make love to her. Since he had realized that she was a woman, and vulnerable, accessible, a certain heaviness had possessed his soul. He did not want to make love to her. He shrank from any such performance, almost with fear. She was a woman, and vulnerable, accessible to him finally, and he held back from that which was ahead, almost with dread. It was a kind of darkness he knew he would enter finally, but of which he did not want as yet even to think. She was the woman, and he was responsible for the strange vulnerability he had suddenly realized in her.

'No,' she said at last, 'I'm a fool. I know I'm a fool.'

'What for?' he asked.

'To go on with this business.'

'Do you mean me?' he asked.

'No, I mean myself. I'm making a fool of myself, and a big one.'

'Why, because you don't want to marry me, really?'

'Oh, I don't know whether I'm against it, as a matter of fact. That's just it. I don't know.'

He looked at her in the darkness, puzzled. He did not in the least know what she meant.

'And don't you know whether you like to sit here with me this minute, or not?' he asked.

'No, I don't, really. I don't know whether I wish I was somewhere else, or whether I like being here. I don't know, really.'

'Do you wish you were with Miss Banford? Do you wish you'd gone to bed with her?' he asked, as a challenge.

She waited a long time before she answered:

'No,' she said at last. 'I don't wish that.'

'And do you think you would spend all your life with her – when your hair goes white, and you are old?' he said.

'No,' she said, without much hesitation. 'I don't see Jill and me two old women together.'

'And don't you think, when I'm an old man, and you're an old woman, we might be together still, as we are now?' he said.

'Well, not as we are now,' she replied. 'But I could imagine – no, I can't. I can't imagine you an old man. Besides, it's dreadful!'

'What, to be an old man?'

'Yes, of course.'

'Not when the time comes,' he said. 'But it hasn't come. Only it will. And when it does, I should like to think you'd be there as well.'

'Sort of old age pensions,' she said dryly.

Her kind of witless humour always startled him. He never knew what she meant. Probably she didn't quite know herself.

'No,' he said, hurt.

'I don't know why you harp on old age,' she said. 'I'm not ninety.'

'Did anybody ever say you were?' he asked, offended.

They were silent for some time, pulling different ways in the silence.

'I don't want you to make fun of me,' he said.

'Don't you?' she replied, enigmatic.

'No, because just this minute I'm serious. And when I'm serious, I believe in not making fun of it.'

'You mean nobody else can make fun of you,' she replied.

'Yes, I mean that. And I mean I don't believe in making fun of it myself. When it comes over me so that I'm serious, then – there it is, I don't want it to be laughed at.'

She was silent for some time. Then she said, in a vague, almost pained voice:

'No, I'm not laughing at you.'

A hot wave rose in his heart.

'You believe me, do you?' he asked.

'Yes, I believe you,' she replied, with a twang of her old tired nonchalance, as if she gave in because she was tired. – But he didn't care. His heart was hot and clamorous.

'So you agree to marry me before I go? – perhaps at Christmas?'

'Yes, I agree.'

'There!' he exclaimed. 'That's settled it.'

And he sat silent, unconscious, with all the blood burning in all his veins, like fire in all the branches and twigs of him. He only pressed her two hands to his chest, without knowing. When the curious passion began to die down, he seemed to come awake to the world.

'We'll go in, shall we?' he said: as if he realized it was cold.

She rose without answering.

'Kiss me before we go, now you've said it,' he said.

And he kissed her gently on the mouth, with a young, frightened kiss. It made her feel so young, too, and frightened, and wondering: and tired, tired, as if she were going to sleep.

They went indoors. And in the sitting-room, there, crouched by the fire like a queer little witch, was Banford. She looked round with reddened eyes as they entered, but did not rise. He thought she looked frightening, unnatural, crouching there and looking round at them. Evil he thought her look was, and he crossed his fingers.

Banford saw the ruddy, elate face of the youth: he seemed strangely tall and bright and looming. And March had a delicate look on her face, she wanted to hide her face, to screen it, to let it not be seen.

'You've come at last,' said Banford uglily.

'Yes, we've come,' said he.

'You've been long enough for anything,' she said.

'Yes, we have. We've settled it. We shall marry as soon as possible,' he replied.

'Oh, you've settled it, have you! Well, I hope you won't live to repent it,' said Banford.

'I hope so too,' he replied.

'Are you going to bed *now*, Nellie?' said Banford.

'Yes, I'm going now.'

'Then for goodness sake come along.'

March looked at the boy. He was glancing with his very bright eyes at her and at Banford. March looked at him wistfully. She wished she could stay with him. She wished she had married him already, and it was all over. For oh, she felt suddenly so safe with him. She felt so strangely safe and peaceful in his presence. If only she could sleep in his shelter, and not with Jill. She felt afraid of Jill. In her dim, tender state, it was agony to have to go with Jill and sleep with her. She wanted the boy to save her. She looked again at him.

And he, watching with bright eyes, divined something of what she felt. It puzzled and distressed him that she must go with Jill.

'I shan't forget what you've promised,' he said, looking clear into her eyes, right into her eyes, so that he seemed to occupy all herself with his queer, bright look.

She smiled to him, faintly, gently. She felt safe again – safe with him.

But in spite of all the boy's precautions, he had a set-back. The morning he was leaving the farm he got March to accompany him to the market-town, about six miles away, where they went to the registrar and had their names stuck up as two people who were going to marry. He was to come at Christmas, and the wedding was to take place then. He hoped in the spring to be able to take March back to Canada with him, now the war was really over. Though he was so young, he had saved some money.

'You never have to be without *some* money at the back of you, if you can help it,' he said.

So she saw him off in the train that was going West: his camp was on Salisbury plains. And with big dark eyes she watched him go, and it seemed as if everything real in life was retreating as the train retreated with his queer, chubby, ruddy face, that seemed so broad across the cheeks, and which never seemed to change its expression, save when a cloud of sulky anger hung on the brow, or the bright eyes fixed themselves in their stare. This was what happened now. He leaned there out of the carriage window as the train drew off, saying good-bye and staring back at her, but his face quite unchanged. There was no emotion on his face. Only his eyes tightened and became fixed and intent in their watching, as a cat when suddenly she sees something and stares. So the boy's eyes stared fixedly as the train drew away, and she was left feeling intensely forlorn. Failing his physical presence, she seemed to have nothing of him. And she had nothing of anything. Only his face was fixed in her mind: the full, ruddy, unchanging cheeks, and the straight snout of a nose, and the two eyes staring above. All she could remember was how he suddenly wrinkled his nose when he laughed, as a puppy does when he is playfully growling. But him, himself, and what he was she knew nothing, she had nothing of him when he left her.

On the ninth day after he had left her he received this letter.

"Dear Henry,

I have been over it all again in my mind, this business of me and you, and it seems to me impossible. When you aren't there I see what a fool I am. When you are there you seem to blind me to things as they actually are. You make me see things all unreal and I don't know what. Then when I am alone again with Jill I seem to come to my own senses and realize what a fool I am making of myself and how I am treating you unfairly. Because it must be unfair to you for me to go on with this affair when I can't feel in my heart that I really love you. I know people talk a lot of stuff and nonsense about love, and I don't want to do that. I want to keep to plain facts and act in a sensible way. And that seems to me what I'm not doing. I don't see on what grounds I am going to marry you. I know I am not head over heels in love with you, as I have fancied myself to be with fellows when I was a young fool of a girl. You are an absolute stranger to me, and it seems to me you will always be one. So on what grounds am I going to marry you? When I think of Jill she is ten times more real to me. I know her and I'm awfully fond of her and I hate myself for a beast if I ever hurt her little finger. We have a life together. And even if it can't last for ever, it is a life while it does last. And it might last as long as either of us lives. Who knows how long we've got to live? She is a delicate little thing, perhaps nobody but me knows how delicate. And as for me, I feel I might fall down the well any day. What I don't seem to see at all is you. When I think of what I've been and what I've done with you I'm afraid I am a few screws loose. I should be sorry to think that softening of the brain is setting in so soon, but that is what it seems like. You are such an absolute stranger and so different from what I'm used to and we don't seem to have a thing in common. As for love the word seems impossible. I know what love means even in Jill's case, and I know that in this affair with you it's an absolute impossibility. And then going to Canada. I'm sure I must have been clean off my chump when I promised such a thing. It makes me feel fairly frightened of myself. I feel I might do something really silly that I wasn't responsible for. And end my days in a lunatic asylum. You may think that's all I'm fit for after the way I've gone on, but it isn't a very nice thought for me. Thank goodness Jill is here and her being here makes me feel sane again, else I don't know what I might do, I might have an accident with the gun one evening. I love Jill and she makes me feel safe and sane, with her loving anger against me for being such a fool. Well what I want to say is won't you let us cry the whole thing off? I can't marry you, and really, I won't do such a thing if it seems to me wrong. It is all a great mistake. I've made a complete fool of myself, and all I can do is to apologise to you and ask you please to forget it and please to take no further notice of me. Your fox skin is nearly ready and seems all right. I will post it to you if you will let me know if this address is still right, and if you will accept my apology for the awful and lunatic way I have behaved with you, and then let the matter rest.

Jill sends her kindest regards. Her mother and father are staying with us over Christmas.

Yours very sincerely,

Ellen March."

The boy read this letter in camp as he was cleaning his kit. He set his teeth and for a moment went almost pale, yellow round the eyes with fury. He said nothing and saw nothing and felt nothing but a livid rage that was quite unreasoning. Balked! Balked again! Balked! He wanted the woman, he had fixed like doom upon having her. He felt that was his doom, his destiny, and his reward, to have this woman. She was his heaven and hell on earth, and he would have none elsewhere. Sightless with rage and thwarted madness he got through the morning. Save that in his mind he was lurking and scheming towards an issue, he would have committed some insane act. Deep in himself he felt like roaring and howling and gnashing his teeth and breaking things. But he was too intelligent. He knew society was on top of him, and he must scheme. So with his teeth bitten together and his nose curiously slightly lifted, like some creature that is vicious, and his eyes fixed and staring, he went through the morning's affairs drunk with anger and suppression. In his mind was one thing – Banford. He took no heed of all March's outpouring: none. One thorn rankled, stuck in his mind. Banford. In his mind, in his soul, in his whole being, one thorn rankling to insanity. And he would have to get it out. He would have to get the thorn of Banford out of his life, if he died for it.

With this one fixed idea in his mind, he went to ask for twenty-four hours leave of absence. He knew it was not due to him. His consciousness was supernaturally keen. He knew where he must go – he must go to the Captain. But how could he get at the Captain? In that great camp of wooden huts and tents he had no idea where his captain was.

But he went to the officers' canteen. There was his captain standing talking with three other officers. Henry stood in the doorway at attention.

'May I speak to Captain Berryman?' The captain was Cornish like himself.

'What do you want?' called the captain.

'May I speak to you, Captain?'

'What do you want?' replied the captain, not stirring from among his group of fellow officers.

Henry watched his superior for a minute without speaking.

'You won't refuse me, sir, will you?' he asked gravely.

'It depends what it is.'

'Can I have twenty-four hours leave?'

'No, you've no business to ask.'

'I know I haven't. But I must ask you '

'You've had your answer.'

'Don't sent me away, Captain.'

There was something strange about the boy as he stood there so everlasting in the doorway. The Cornish Captain felt the strangeness at once, and eyed him shrewdly.

'Why, what's afoot?' he said, curious.

'I'm in trouble about something. I must go to Blewbury,' said the boy.

'Blewbury, eh? After the girls?'

'Yes, it is a woman, Captain.' And the boy, as he stood there with his head reaching forward a little, went suddenly terribly pale, or yellow, and his lips seemed to give off pain. The captain saw and paled a little also. He turned aside.

'Go on then,' he said. 'But for God's sake don't cause any trouble of any sort.'

'I won't, Captain, thank you.'

He was gone. The captain, upset, took a gin and bitters. Henry managed to hire a bicycle. It was twelve o'clock when he left the camp. He had sixty miles of wet and muddy cross-roads to ride. But he was in the saddle and down the road without a thought of food.

At the farm, March was busy with a work she had had some time in hand. A bunch of Scotch-fir-trees stood at the end of the open shed, on a little bank where ran the fence between two of the gorse-shaggy meadows. The furthest of these trees was dead – it had died in the summer and stood with all its needles brown and sere in the air. It was not a very big tree. And it was absolutely dead. So March determined to have it, although they were not allowed to cut any of the timber. But it would make such splendid firing, in these days of scarce fuel.

She had been giving a few stealthy chops at the trunk for a week or more, every now and then hacking away for five minutes, low down, near the ground, so no one should notice. She had not tried the saw, it was such hard work, alone. Now the tree stood with a great yawning gap in his base, perched as it were on one sinew, and ready to fall. But he did not fall.

It was late in the damp December afternoon, with cold mists creeping out of the woods and up the hollows, and darkness waiting to sink in from above. There was a bit of yellowness where the sun was fading away beyond the low woods of the distance. March took her axe and went to the tree. The small thud-thud of her blows resounded rather ineffectual about the wintry homestead. Banford came out wearing her thick coat, but with no hat on her head, so that her thin, bobbed hair blew on the uneasy wind that sounded in the pines and in the wood.

'What I'm afraid of,' said Banford, 'is that it will fall on the shed and we s'll have another job repairing that.'

'Oh, I don't think so,' said March, straightening herself and wiping her arm over her hot brow. She was flushed red, her eyes were very wide – open and queer, her upper lip lifted away from her two white front teeth with a curious, almost rabbit-look.

A little stout man in a black overcoat and a bowler hat came pottering across the yard. He had a pink face and a white beard and smallish, pale-blue eyes. He was not very old, but nervy, and he walked with little short steps.

'What do you think, father?' said Banford. 'Don't you think it might hit the shed in falling?'

'Shed, no!' said the old man. 'Can't hit the shed. Might as well say the fence.'

'The fence doesn't matter,' said March, in her high voice.

'Wrong as usual, am I!' said Banford, wiping her straying hair from her eyes.

The tree stood as it were on one spelch of itself, leaning, and creaking in the wind. It grew on the bank of a little dry ditch between the two meadows. On the top of the bank straggled one fence, running to the bushes uphill. Several trees clustered there in the corner of the field near the shed and near the gate which led into the yard. Towards this gate, horizontal across the weary meadows came the grassy, rutted approach from the high road. There trailed another rickety fence, long split poles joining the short, thick, wide-apart uprights.

The three people stood at the back of the tree, in the corner of the shed meadow, just above the yard gate. The house with its two gables and its porch stood tidy in a little grassed garden across the yard. A little stout rosy-faced woman in a little red woollen shoulder shawl had come and taken her stand in the porch.

'Isn't it down yet?' she cried, in a high little voice.

'Just thinking about it,' called her husband. His tone towards the two girls was always rather mocking and satirical. March did not want to go on with her hitting while he was there. As for him, he wouldn't lift a stick from the ground if he could help it, complaining, like his daughter, of rheumatics in his shoulder. So the three stood there a moment silent in the cold afternoon, in the bottom corner near the yard.

They heard the far-off taps of a gate, and craned to look. Away across, on the green horizontal approach, a figure was just swinging on to a bicycle again, and lurching up and down over the grass, approaching.

'Why it's one of our boys – it's Jack,' said the old man.

'Can't be,' said Banford.

March craned her head to look. She alone recognized the khaki figure. She flushed, but said nothing.

'No, it isn't Jack, I don't think,' said the old man, staring with little round blue eyes under his white lashes.

In another moment the bicycle lurched into sight, and the rider dropped off at the gate. It was Henry, his face wet and red and spotted with mud. He was altogether a muddy sight.

'Oh!' cried Banford, as if afraid. 'Why, it's Henry!'

'What!' muttered the old man. He had a thick, rapid, muttering way of speaking, and was slightly deaf. 'What? What? Who is it? Who is it do you say? That young fellow? That young fellow of Nellie's? Oh! Oh!' And the satiric smile came on his pink face and white eyelashes.

Henry, pushing the wet hair off his steaming brow, had caught sight of them and heard what the old man said. His hot young face seemed to flame in the cold light.

'Oh, are you all there!' he said, giving his sudden, puppy's little laugh. He was so hot and dazed with cycling he hardly knew where he was. He leaned the bicycle against the fence and climbed over into the corner on to the bank, without going in to the yard.

'Well, I must say, we weren't expecting *you*,' said Banford laconically.

'No, I suppose not,' said he, looking at March.

She stood aside, slack, with one knee drooped and the axe resting its head loosely on the ground. Her eyes were wide and vacant, and her upper lip lifted from her teeth in that helpless, fascinated rabbit-look. The moment she saw his glowing red face it was all over with her. She was as helpless as if she had been bound. The moment she saw the way his head seemed to reach forward.

'Well, who is it? Who is it, anyway?' asked the smiling, satiric old man in his muttering voice.

'Why, Mr Grenfel, whom you've heard us tell about, father,' said Banford coldly.

'Heard you tell about, I should think so. Heard of nothing else practically,' muttered the elderly man with his queer little jeering smile on his face. 'How do you do,' he added, suddenly reaching out his hand to Henry.

The boy shook hands just as startled. Then the two men fell apart.

'Cycled over from Salisbury Plain have you?' asked the old man.

'Yes.'

'Hm! Longish ride. How long d'it take you, eh? Some time, eh? Several hours, I suppose.'

'About four.'

'Eh? Four! Yes, I should have thought so. When are you going back then?'

'I've got till tomorrow evening.'

'Till tomorrow evening, eh? Yes. Hm! Girls weren't expecting you, were they?'

And the old man turned his pale-blue, round little eyes under their white lashes mockingly towards the girls. Henry also looked round. He had become a little awkward. He looked at March, who was still staring away into the distance as if to see where the cattle were. Her hand was on the pommel of the axe, whose head rested loosely on the ground.

'What were you doing there?' he asked in his soft, courteous voice. 'Cutting a tree down?'

March seemed not to hear, as if in a trance.

'Yes,' said Banford. 'We've been at it for over a week.'

'Oh! And have you done it all by yourselves then?'

'Nellie's done it all, I've done nothing,' said Banford.

'Really! – You must have worked quite hard,' he said, addressing himself in a curious gentle tone direct to March. She did not answer, but remained half averted staring away towards the woods above as if in a trance.

'*Nellie!*' cried Banford sharply. 'Can't you answer?'

'What – me?' cried March starting round, and looking from one to the other. 'Did anyone speak to me?'

'Dreaming!' muttered the old man, turning aside to smile. 'Must be in love, eh, dreaming in the daytime!'

'Did you say anything to me?' said March, looking at the boy as from a strange distance, her eyes wide and doubtful, her face delicately flushed.

'I said you must have worked hard at the tree,' he replied courteously.

'Oh, that! Bit by bit. I thought it would have come down by now.'

'I'm thankful it hasn't come down in the night, to frighten us to death,' said Banford.

'Let me just finish it for you, shall I?' said the boy.

March slanted the axe-shaft in his direction.

'Would you like to?' she said.

'Yes, if you wish it,' he said.

'Oh, I'm thankful when the thing's down, that's all,' she replied, nonchalant.

'Which way is it going to fall?' said Banford. 'Will it hit the shed?'

'No, it won't hit the shed,' he said. 'I should think it will fall there – quite clear. Though it might give a twist and catch the fence.'

'Catch the fence!' cried the old man. 'What, catch the fence! When it's leaning at that angle? – Why it's farther off than the shed. It won't catch the fence.'

'No,' said Henry, 'I don't suppose it will. It has plenty of room to fall quite clear, and I suppose it will fall clear.'

'Won't tumble backwards on top of *us*, will it?' asked the old man, sarcastic.

'No, it won't do that,' said Henry, taking off his short overcoat and his tunic. 'Ducks! Ducks! Go back!'

A line of four brown-speckled ducks led by a brown-and-green drake were stemming away downhill from the upper meadow, coming like boats running on a ruffled sea, cackling their way top speed downwards towards the fence and towards the little group of people, and cackling as excitedly as if they brought the news of the Spanish Armada.

'Silly things! Silly things!' cried Banford going forward to turn them off. But they came eagerly towards her, opening their yellow-green beaks and quacking as if they were so excited to say something.

'There's no food. There's nothing here. You must wait a bit,' said Banford to them. 'Go away. Go away. Go round to the yard.'

They didn't go, so she climbed the fence to swerve them round under the gate and into the yard. So off they waggled in an excited string once more, wagging their rumps like the stems of little gondolas, ducking under the bar of the gate. Banford stood on the top of the bank, just over the fence, looking down on the other three.

Henry looked up at her, and met her queer, round-pupilled, weak eyes staring behind her spectacles. He was perfectly still. He looked away, up at the weak, leaning tree. And as he looked into the sky, like a huntsman who is watching a flying bird, he thought to himself: 'If the tree falls in just such a way, and spins just so much as it falls, then the branch there will strike her exactly as she stands on top of that bank.'

He looked at her again. She was wiping the hair from her brow again, with that perpetual gesture. In his heart he had decided her death. A terrible still force seemed in him, and a power that was just his. If he turned even a hair's breadth in the wrong direction, he would lose the power.

'Mind yourself, Miss Banford,' he said. And his heart held perfectly still, in the terrible pure will that she should not move.

'Who, me, mind myself?' she cried, her father's jeering tone in her voice. 'Why, do you think you might hit me with the axe?'

'No, it's just possible the tree might, though,' he answered soberly. But the tone of his voice seemed to her to imply that he was only being falsely solicitous and trying to make her move because it was his will to move her.

'Absolutely impossible,' she said.

He heard her. But he held himself icy still, lest he should lose his power.

'No, it's just possible. You'd better come down this way.'

'Oh, all right. Let us see some crack Canadian tree felling,' she retorted.

'Ready then,' he said, taking the axe, looking round to see he was clear.

There was a moment of pure, motionless suspense, when the world seemed to stand still. Then suddenly his form seemed to flash up enormously tall and fearful, he gave two swift, flashing blows, in immediate succession, the tree was severed, turning slowly, spinning strangely in the air and coming down like a sudden darkness on the earth. No one saw what was happening except himself. No one heard the strange little cry which Banford gave as the dark end of the bough swooped down, down on her. No one saw her crouch a little and receive the blow on the back of the neck. No one saw her flung outwards and laid, a little twitching heap, at the foot of the fence. No one except the boy. And he watched with intense bright eyes, as he would watch a wild goose he had shot. Was it winged, or dead? Dead!

Immediately he gave a loud cry. Immediately March gave a wild shriek that went far, far down the afternoon. And the father started a strange bellowing sound.

The boy leapt the fence and ran to the figure. The back of the neck and head was a mass of blood, of horror. He turned it over. The body was quivering with little convulsions. But she was dead really. He knew it, that it was so. He knew it in his soul and his blood. The inner necessity of his life was fulfilling itself, it was he who was to live. The thorn was drawn out of his bowels. So, he put her down gently, she was dead.

He stood up. March was standing there petrified and absolutely motionless. Her face was dead white, her eyes big black pools. The old man was scrambling horribly over the fence.

'I'm afraid it's killed her,' said the boy.

The old man was making curious, blubbering noises as he huddled over the fence.

'What!' cried March, starting electric.

'Yes, I'm afraid,' repeated the boy.

March was coming forward. The boy was over the fence before she reached it.

'What do you say, killed her?' she asked in a sharp voice.

'I'm afraid so,' he answered softly.

She went still whiter, fearful. The two stood facing one another. Her black eyes gazed on him with the last look of resistance. And then in a last agonized failure she began to grizzle, to cry in a shivery little fashion of a child that doesn't want to cry, but which is beaten from within, and gives that little first shudder of sobbing which is not yet weeping, dry and fearful.

He had won. She stood there absolutely helpless, shuddering her dry sobs and her mouth trembling rapidly. And then, as in a child, with a little crash came the tears and the blind agony of sightless weeping. She sank down on the grass and sat there with her hands on her breast and her face lifted in sightless, convulsed weeping. He stood above her, looking down on her, mute, pale, and everlasting seeming. He never moved, but looked down on her. And among all the torture of the scene, the torture of his own heart and bowels, he was glad, he had won.

After a long time he stooped to her and took her hands.

'Don't cry,' he said softly. 'Don't cry.'

She looked up at him with tears running from her eyes, a senseless look of helplessness and submission. So she gazed on him as if sightless, yet looking up to him. She would never leave him again. He had won her. And he knew it and was glad, because he wanted her for his life. His life must have her. And now he had won her. It was what his life must have.

But if he had won her, he had not yet got her. They were married at Christmas as he had planned, and he got again ten days leave. They went to Cornwall, to his own village, on the sea. He realized that it was awful for her to be at the farm any more.

But though she belonged to him, though she lived in his

shadow, as if she could not be away from him, she was not happy. She did not want to leave him: and yet she did not feel free with him. Everything round her seemed to watch her, seemed to press on her. He had won her, he had her with him, she was his wife. And she – she belonged to him, she knew it. But she was not glad. And he was still foiled. He realized that though he was married to her and possessed her in every possible way, apparently, and though she *wanted* him to possess her, she wanted it, she wanted nothing else, now, still he did not quite succeed.

Something was missing. Instead of her soul swaying with new life, it seemed to droop, to bleed, as if it were wounded. She would sit for a long time with her hand in his, looking away at the sea. And in her dark, vacant eyes was a sort of wound, and her face looked a little peaked. If he spoke to her, she would turn to him with a faint new smile, the strange, quivering little smile of a woman who has died in the old way of love, and can't quite rise to the new way. She still felt she ought to *do* something, to strain herself in some direction. And there was nothing to do, and no direction in which to strain herself. And she could not quite accept the submergence which his new love put upon her. If she was in love, she ought to *exert* herself, in some way, loving. She felt the weary need of our day to *exert* herself in love. But she knew that in fact she must no more exert herself in love. He would not have the love which exerted itself towards him. It made his brow go black. No, he wouldn't let her exert her love towards him. No, she had to be passive, to acquiesce, and to be submerged under the surface of love. She had to be like the seaweeds she saw as she peered down from the boat, swaying forever delicately under water, with all their delicate fibrils put tenderly out upon the flood, sensitive, utterly sensitive and receptive within the shadowy sea, and never, never rising and looking forth above water while they lived. Never. Never looking forth from the water until they died, only then washing, corpses, upon the surface. But while they lived, always submerged, always beneath the wave. Beneath the wave they might have powerful roots, stronger than iron, they might be tenacious and dangerous in their soft waving within the flood. Beneath the water they might be stronger, more indestructible than resistant oak trees are on land. But it was always under-water, always under-water. And she, being a woman, must be like that.

And she had been so used to the very opposite. She had had to take all the thought for love and for life, and all the responsibility. Day after day she had been responsible for the coming day, for the coming year: for her dear Jill's health and happiness and well-being. Verily, in her own small way, she had felt herself responsible for the well-being of the world. And this had been her great stimulant, this grand feeling that, in her own small sphere, she was responsible for the well-being of the world.

And she had failed. She knew that, even in her small way, she had failed. She had failed to satisfy her own feeling of responsibility. It was so difficult. It seemed so grand and easy at first. And the more you tried, the more difficult it became. It had seemed so easy to make one beloved creature happy. And the more you tried, the worse the failure. It was terrible. She had been all her life reaching, reaching, and what she reached for seemed so near, until she had stretched to her utmost limit. And then it was always beyond her.

Always beyond her, vaguely, unrealizably beyond her, and she was left with nothingness at last. The life she reached for, the happiness she reached for, the well-being she reached for all slipped back, became unreal, the further she stretched her hand. She wanted some goal, some finality – and there was none. Always this ghastly reaching, reaching, striving for something that might be just beyond. Even to make Jill happy. She was glad Jill was dead. For she had realized that she could never make her happy. Jill would always be fretting herself thinner and thinner, weaker and weaker. Her pains grew worse instead of less. It would be so for ever. She was glad she was dead.

And if she had married a man it would have been just the same. The woman striving, striving to make the man happy, striving within her own limits for the well-being of her world. And always achieving failure. Little, foolish successes in money or in ambition. But at the very point where she most wanted success, in the anguished effort to make some one beloved human being happy and perfect, there the failure was almost catastrophic. You wanted to make your beloved happy, and his happiness seemed always achievable. If only you did just this, that and the other. And you did this, that, and the other, in all good faith, and every time the failure became a little more ghastly. You could love yourself to ribbons, and strive and strain yourself to the bone, and things would go from bad to worse, bad to worse, as far as happiness went. The awful mistake of happiness.

Poor March, in her goodwill and her responsibility, she had strained herself till it seemed to her that the whole of life and everything was only a horrible abyss of nothingness. The more you reached after the fatal flower of happiness, which trembles so blue and lovely in a crevice just beyond your grasp, the more fearfully you became aware of the ghastly and awful gulf of the precipice below you, into which you will inevitably plunge, as into the bottomless pit, if you reach any further. You pluck flower after flower – it is never *the* flower. The flower itself – its calyx is a horrible gulf, it is the bottomless pit.

That is the whole history of the search for happiness, whether it be your own or somebody else's that you want to win. It ends, and it always ends, in the ghastly sense of the bottomless nothingness into which you will inevitably fall if you strain any further.

And women? – what goal can any woman conceive, except happiness? Just happiness, for herself and the whole world. That, and nothing else. And so, she assumes the responsibility and sets off towards her goal. She can see it there, at the foot of the rainbow. Or she can see it a little way beyond, in the blue distance. Not far, not far.

But the end of the rainbow is a bottomless gulf down which you can fall forever without arriving, and the blue distance is a void pit which can swallow you and all your efforts into its emptiness, and still be no emptier. You and all your efforts. So, the illusion of attainable happiness!

Poor March, she had set off so wonderfully, towards the blue goal. And the further and further she had gone, the more fearful had become the realization of emptiness. An agony, an insanity at last.

She was glad it was over. She was glad to sit on the shore and look westwards over the sea, and know the great strain had ended. She would never strain for love and happiness any more. And Jill was safely dead. Poor Jill, poor Jill. It must be sweet to be dead.

For her own part, death was not her destiny. She would have to leave her destiny to the boy. But then, the boy. He wanted more than that. He wanted her to give herself without defences, to sink and become submerged in him. And she – she wanted to sit still, like a woman on the last milestone, and watch. She wanted to see, to know, to understand. She wanted to be alone: with him at her side.

And he! He did not want her to watch any more, to see any more, to understand any more. He wanted to veil her woman's spirit, as Orientals veil the woman's face. He wanted her to commit herself to him, and to put her independent spirit to sleep. He wanted to take away from her all her effort, all that seemed her very *raison d'être*. He wanted to make her submit, yield, blindly pass away out of all her strenuous consciousness. He wanted to take away her consciousness, and make her just his woman. Just his woman.

And she was so tired, so tired, like a child that wants to go to sleep, but which fights against sleep as if sleep were death. She seemed to stretch her eyes wider in the obstinate effort and tension of keeping awake. She *would* keep awake. She *would* know. She *would* consider and judge and decide. She *would* have the reins of her own life between her own hands. She *would* be an independent woman to the last. But she was so tired, so tired of everything. And sleep seemed near. And there was such rest in the boy.

Yet there, sitting in a niche of the high wild cliffs of West Cornwall, looking over the westward sea, she stretched her eyes wider and wider. Away to the West, Canada, America. She *would* know and she *would* see what was ahead. And the boy, sitting beside her staring down at the gulls, had a cloud between his brows and the strain of discontent in his eyes. He wanted her asleep, at peace in him. He wanted her at peace, asleep in him. And *there* she was, dying with the strain of her own wakefulness. Yet she would not sleep: no, never. Sometimes he thought bitterly that he ought to have left her. He ought never to have killed Banford. He should have left Banford and March to kill one another.

But that was only impatience: and he knew it. He was waiting, waiting to go west. He was aching almost in torment to leave England, to go west, to take March away. To leave this shore! He believed that as they crossed the seas, as they left this England which he so hated, because in some way it seemed to have stung him with poison, she would go to sleep. She would close her eyes at last, and give in to him.

And then he would have her, and he would have his own life at last. He chafed, feeling he hadn't got his own life. He would never have it till she yielded and slept in him. Then he would have all his own life as a young man and a male, and she would have all her own life as a woman and a female. There would be no more of this awful straining. She would not be a man any more, an independent woman with a man's responsibility. Nay, even the responsibility for her own soul she would have to commit to him. He knew it was so, and obstinately held out against her, waiting for the surrender.

'You'll feel better when once we get over the seas, to Canada, over there,' he said to her as they sat among the rocks on the cliff.

She looked away to the sea's horizon, as if it were not real. Then she looked round at him, with the strained, strange look of a child that is struggling against sleep.

'Shall I?' she said.

'Yes,' he answered quietly.

And her eyelids dropped with the slow motion, sleep weighing them unconscious. But she pulled them open again to say:

'Yes, I may. I can't tell. I can't tell what it will be like over there.'

'If only we could go soon!' he said, with pain in his voice.

The Ladybird

HOW many swords had Lady Beveridge in her pierced heart! Yet there always seemed room for another. Since she had determined that her heart of pity and kindness should never die. If it had not been for this determination she herself might have died of sheer agony, in the years 1916 and 1917, when her boys were killed, and her brother, and death seemed to be mowing with wide swathes through her family. But let us forget.

Lady Beveridge loved humanity, and come what might, she would continue to love it. Nay, in the human sense, she would love her enemies. Not the criminals among the enemy, the men who committed atrocities. But the men who were enemies through no choice of their own. She would be swept into no general hate.

Somebody had called her the soul of England. It was not ill said; though she was half Irish. But of an old, aristocratic, loyal family famous for its brilliant men. And she, Lady Beveridge, had for years as much influence on the tone of English politics as any individual alive. The close friend of the real leaders in the House of Lords and in the Cabinet, she was content that the men should act, so long as they breathed from her as from the rose of life the pure fragrance of truth and genuine love. She had no misgivings regarding her own spirit.

She, she would never lower her delicate silken flag. For instance, throughout all the agony of the war she never forgot the enemy prisoners, she was determined to do her best for them. During the first years she still had influence. But during the last years of the war power slipped out of the hands of her and her sort, and she found she could do nothing any more: almost nothing. Then it seemed as if the many swords had gone home into the heart of this little, unyielding Mater Dolorosa.[1] The new generation jeered at her. She was no longer a fashionable little aristocrat. Since the war her drawing-room was out of date.

But we anticipate. The years 1916 and 1917 were the years when the old spirit died for ever in England. But Lady Beveridge struggled on. She was being beaten.

It was in the winter of 1917 – or in the late autumn. She had been for a fortnight sick, stricken, paralysed by the fearful death of her youngest boy. She felt she *must* give in, and just die. And then she remembered how many others were lying in agony.

So she rose, trembling, frail, to pay a visit to the hospital where lay the enemy sick and wounded, near London. Countess Beveridge was still a privileged woman. Society was beginning to jeer at this little, worn bird of an out-of-date righteousness and aesthetic. But they dared not think ill of her.

She ordered the car and went alone. The Earl, her husband, had taken his gloom to Scotland. So, on a sunny, wan November morning Lady Beveridge descended at the hospital, Hurst Place. The guard knew her, and saluted as she passed. Ah, she was used to such deep respect! It was strange that she felt it so bitterly, when the respect became shallower. But she did. It was the beginning of the end to her.

The matron went with her into the ward. Alas, the beds were all full, and men were even lying on pallets on the floor. There was a desperate, crowded dreariness and helplessness in the place: as if nobody wanted to make a sound or utter a word. Many of the men were haggard and unshaven, one was delirious, and talking fitfully in the Saxon dialect. It went to Lady Beveridge's heart. She had been educated in Dresden, and had had many dear friendships in the city. Her children also had been educated there. She heard the Saxon dialect with pain.

She was a little, frail, bird-like woman, elegant, but with that touch of the blue-stocking of the nineties which was unmistakable. She fluttered delicately from bed to bed, speaking in perfect German, but with a thin, English intonation: and always asking if there was anything she could do. The men were mostly officers and gentlemen. They made little requests which she wrote down in a book. Her long, pale, rather worn face and her nervous little gestures somehow inspired confidence.

One man lay quite still, with his eyes shut. He had a black beard. His face was rather small and sallow. He might be dead.

Lady Beveridge looked at him earnestly, and fear came into her face.

'Why, Count Dionys!' she said, fluttered. 'Are you asleep?'

It was Count Johann Dionys Psanek, a Bohemian. She had known him when he was a boy, and only in the spring of 1914 he and his wife had stayed with Lady Beveridge in her country house in Leicestershire.

His black eyes opened: large, black, unseeing eyes, with curved black lashes. He was a small man, small as a boy, and his face too was rather small. But all the lines were fine, as if they had been fired with a keen male energy. Now the yellowish swarthy paste of his flesh seemed dead, and the fine black brows seemed drawn on the face of one dead. The eyes, however, were alive: but only just alive, unseeing and unknowing.

'You know me, Count Dionys? You know me, don't you?' said Lady Beveridge, bending forward over the bed.

There was no reply for some time. Then the black eyes gathered a look of recognition, and there came the ghost of a polite smile.

'Lady Beveridge.' The lips formed the words. There was practically no sound.

'I am so glad you can recognize me. – And I am so sorry you are hurt. I am so sorry.'

The black eyes watched her from that terrible remoteness of death, without changing.

'There is nothing I can do for you? Nothing at all?' she said, always speaking German.

And after a time, and from a distance, came the answer from his eyes, a look of weariness, of refusal, and a wish to be left alone; he was unable to strain himself into consciousness. His eyelids dropped.

'I am so sorry,' she said. 'If ever there is anything I can do –'

The eyes opened again, looking at her. He seemed at last to hear, and it was as if his eyes made the last weary gesture of a polite bow. Then slowly his eyelids closed again.

Poor Lady Beveridge felt another sword-thrust of sorrow in her heart, as she stood looking down at the motionless face, and at the black fine beard. The black hairs came out of his skin thin and fine, not very close together. A queer, dark, aboriginal little face he had, with a fine little nose: not an Aryan, surely. And he was going to die.

He had a bullet through the upper part of his chest, and another bullet had broken one of his ribs. He had been in hospital five days.

Lady Beveridge asked the matron to ring her up if anything happened. Then she drove away, saddened. Instead of going to Beveridge House, she went to her daughter's flat near the park – near Hyde Park. Lady Daphne was poor. She had married a commoner, son of one of the most famous politicians in England, but a man with no money. And Earl Beveridge had wasted most of the large fortune that had come to him, so that the daughter had very little, comparatively.

Lady Beveridge suffered, going in the narrow doorway into the rather ugly flat. Lady Daphne was sitting by the electric fire in the small yellow drawing-room, talking to a visitor. She rose at once, seeing her little mother.

'Why, mother, ought you to be out? I'm sure not.'

'Yes, Daphne darling. Of course I ought to be out.'

'How are you?' The daughter's voice was slow and sonorous, protective, sad. Lady Daphne was tall, only twenty-five years old. She had been one of the beauties, when the war broke out, and her father had hoped she would make a splendid match. Truly, she had married fame: but without money. Now, sorrow, pain, thwarted passion had done her great damage. Her husband was missing in the East. Her baby had been born dead. Her two darling brothers were dead. And she was ill, always ill.

A tall, beautifully-built girl, she had the fine stature of her father. Her shoulders were still straight. But how thin her white throat! She wore a simple black frock stitched with coloured wool round the top, and held in a loose coloured girdle: otherwise no ornaments. And her face was lovely, fair, with a soft exotic white complexion and delicate pink cheeks. Her hair was soft and heavy, of a pallid gold quality, ash-blonde. Her hair, her complexion were so perfectly cared for as to be almost artificial, like a hot-house flower.

But alas! her beauty was a failure. She was threatened with

phthisis, and was far too thin. Her eyes were the saddest part of her. They had slightly reddened rims, nerve-worn, with heavy, veined lids that seemed as if they did not want to keep up. The eyes themselves were large and of a beautiful green-blue colour. But they were dull, languid, almost glaucous.

Standing as she was, a tall, finely built girl, looking down with affectionate care on her mother, she filled the heart with ashes. The little pathetic mother, so wonderful in her way, was not really to be pitied for all her sorrow. Her life was in her sorrows, and her efforts on behalf of the sorrows of others. But Daphne was not born for grief and philanthropy. With her splendid frame, and her lovely, long, strong legs she was Artemis or Atlanta rather than Daphne.[2] There was a certain width of brow and even of chin that spoke a strong, reckless nature, and the curious, distraught slant of her eyes told of a wild energy dammed up inside her.

That was what ailed her: her own wild energy. She had it from her father, and from her father's desperate race. The earldom had begun with a riotous, daredevil border soldier, and this was the blood that flowed on. And alas, what was to be done with it?

Daphne had married an adorable husband: truly an adorable husband. Whereas she needed a daredevil. But in her *mind* she hated all daredevils; she had been brought up by her mother to admire only the good.

So, her reckless, anti-philanthropic passion could find no outlet – and *should* find no outlet, she thought. So her own blood turned against her, beat on her own nerves, and destroyed her. It was nothing but frustration and anger which made her ill, and made the doctors fear consumption. There it was, drawn on her rather wide mouth: frustration, anger, bitterness. There it was the same in the roll of her green-blue eyes, a slanting, averted look: the same anger furtively turning back on itself. This anger reddened her eyes and shattered her nerves. And yet, her whole will was fixed in her adoption of her mother's creed, and in condemnation of her handsome, proud, brutal father, who had made so much misery in the family. Yes, her will was fixed in the determination that life should be gentle and good and benevolent. Whereas her blood was reckless, the blood of daredevils. Her will was the stronger of the two. But her blood had its revenge on her. So it is with strong natures to-day: shattered from the inside.

'You have no news, darling?' asked the mother.

'No. My father-in-law had information that British prisoners had been brought into Hasrun, and that details would be forwarded by the Turks. And there was a rumour from some Arab prisoners that Basil was one of the British brought in wounded.'

'When did you hear this?'

'Primrose came in this morning.'

'Then we can hope, dear.'

'Yes.'

Never was anything more dull and bitter than Daphne's affirmative of hope. Hope had become almost a curse to her. She wished there need be no such thing. Ha, the torment of hoping, and the *insult* to one's soul. Like the importunate widow dunning for her deserts. Why could it not all be just clean disaster, and have done with it? This dilly-dallying with despair was worse than despair. She had hoped so much: ah, for her darling brothers she had hoped with such anguish. And the two she loved best were dead. So were most others she had hoped for, dead. Only this uncertainty about her husband still rankling.

'You feel better, dear?' said the little, unquenched mother.

'Rather better,' came the resentful answer.

'And your night?'

'No better.'

There was a pause.

'You are coming to lunch with me, Daphne darling?'

'No, mother dear. I promised to lunch at the Howards' with Primrose. But I needn't go for a quarter of an hour. Do sit down.'

Both women seated themselves near the electric fire. There was that bitter pause, neither knowing what to say. Then Daphne roused herself to look at her mother.

'Are you sure you were fit to go out?' she said. 'What took you out so suddenly?'

'I went to Hurst Place, dear. I had the men on my mind, after the way the newspapers had been talking.'

'Why ever do you read the newspapers!' blurted Daphne, with a certain burning, acid anger. 'Well,' she said, more composed. 'And do you feel better now you've been?'

'So many people suffer besides ourselves, darling.'

'I know they do. Makes it all the worse. It wouldn't matter if it were only just us. At least, it would matter, but one could bear it more easily. To be just one of a crowd all in the same state –'

'And some even worse, dear –'

'Oh, quite! And the worse it is for all, the worse it is for one.'

'Is that so, darling? Try not to see too darkly. I feel if I can give just a little bit of myself to help the others – you know – it alleviates me. I feel that what I can give to the men lying there, Daphne, I give to my own boys. I can only help them now through helping others. But I can still do that, Daphne, my girl.'

And the mother put her little white hand into the long, white, cold hand of her daughter. Tears came to Daphne's eyes, and a fearful stony grimace to her mouth.

'It's so wonderful of you that you can feel like that,' she said.

'But you feel the same, my love. I know you do.'

'No, I don't. Everyone I see suffering these same awful things, it makes me wish more for the end of the world. And I quite see that the world won't end –'

'But it will get better, dear. This time is like a great sickness – like a terrible pneumonia tearing the breast of the world.'

'Do you believe it will get better? I don't.'

'It will get better. Of course it will get better. It is perverse to think otherwise, Daphne. Remember what *has* been before, even in Europe. Ah, Daphne, we must take a bigger view.'

'Yes, I suppose we must.'

The daughter spoke rapidly, from the lips, in a resonant, monotonous tone. The mother spoke from the heart.

'And Daphne, I found an old friend among the men at Hurst Place.'

'Who?'

'Little Count Dionys Psanek. You remember him?'

'Quite. What's wrong?'

'Wounded rather badly – through the chest. So ill.'

'Did you speak to him?'

'Yes. I recognized him in spite of his beard.'

'Beard!'

'Yes – a black beard. I suppose he could not be shaven. It seems strange that he is still alive, poor man.'

'Why strange? He isn't old. How old is he?'

'Between thirty and forty. But so ill, so wounded, Daphne. And so small. So small, so sallow – *smorto*,[3] you know the Italian word. The way dark people look. There is something so distressing in it.'

'Does he look *very* small now? – uncanny?' asked the daughter.

'No, not uncanny. Something of the terrible far-awayness of a child that is very ill and can't tell you what hurts it. Poor Count Dionys, Daphne. I didn't know, dear, that his eyes were so black, and his lashes so curved and long. I had never thought of him as beautiful.'

'Nor I. Only a little comical. Such a dapper little man.'

'Yes. And yet now, Daphne, there is something remote and in a sad way heroic in his dark face. Something primitive.'

'What did he say to you?'

'He couldn't speak to me. Only with his lips, just my name.'

'So bad as that?'

'Oh yes. They are afraid he will die.'

'Poor Count Dionys. I liked him. He was a bit like a monkey, but he had his points. He gave me a thimble on my seventeenth birthday. Such an amusing thimble.'

'I remember, dear.'

'Unpleasant wife, though. Wonder if he minds dying far away from her. Wonder if she knows.'

'I think not. They didn't even know his name properly. Only that he was a colonel of such-and-such a regiment –'

'Fourth Cavalry,' said Daphne. 'Poor Count Dionys. Such a lovely name, I always thought: Count Johann Dionys Psanek. Extraordinary dandy he was. And an amazingly good dancer, small, yet electric. Wonder if he minds dying.'

'He was so full of life, in his own little animal way. They say small people are always conceited. But he doesn't look conceited now, dear. Something ages old in his face – and, yes, a certain beauty, Daphne.'

'You mean long lashes –'

'No. So still, so solitary – and ages old, in his race. I suppose he must belong to one of those curious little aboriginal races of Central Europe. I felt quite new beside him.'

'How nice of you!' said Daphne.

Nevertheless, next day Daphne telephoned to Hurst Place to ask for news of him. He was about the same. She telephoned every day. Then she was told he was a little stronger. The day she received the message that her husband was wounded and a prisoner in Turkey, and that his wounds were healing, she forgot to telephone for news of the little enemy Count. And the following day she telephoned that she was coming to the hospital to see him.

He was awake, more restless, more in physical excitement. They could see the nausea of pain round his nose. His face seemed to Daphne curiously hidden behind the black beard, which nevertheless was thin, each hair coming thin and fine, singly, from the sallow, slightly translucent skin. In the same way his moustache made a thin black line round his mouth. His eyes were wide open, very black, and of no legible expression. He watched the two women coming down the crowded, dreary room, as if he did not see them. His eyes seemed too wide.

It was a cold day, and Daphne was huddled in a black sealskin coat with a skunk collar pulled up to her ears, and a dull gold cap with wings pulled down on her brow. Lady Beveridge wore her sable coat, and had that odd, untidy elegance which was natural to her, rather like a ruffled chicken.

Daphne was upset by the hospital. She looked from right to left in spite of herself, and everything gave her a dull feeling of horror: the terror of these sick, wounded enemy men. She loomed tall and obtrusive in her furs by the bed, her little mother at her side.

'I hope you don't mind my coming,' she said in German to the sick man. Her tongue felt rusty, speaking the language.

'Who is it, then?' he asked.

'It is my daughter, Lady Daphne. You remember *me*, Lady

Beveridge. This is my daughter, whom you knew in Saxony. She was so sorry to hear you were wounded.'

The black eyes rested on the little lady. Then they returned to the looming figure of Daphne. And a certain fear grew on the low sick brow. It was evident the presences loomed and frightened him. He turned his face aside. Daphne noticed how his fine black hair grew uncut over his small, animal ears.

'You don't remember me, Count Dionys?' she said dully.

'Yes,' he said. But he kept his face averted.

She stood there feeling confused and miserable, as if she had made a *faux pas*[4] in coming.

'Would you rather be left alone?' she said. 'I'm sorry.'

Her voice was monotonous. She felt suddenly stifled in her closed furs, and threw her coat open, showing her thin white throat and plain black slip dress on her flat breast. He turned again unwillingly to look at her. He looked at her as if she were some strange creature standing near him.

'Good-bye,' she said. 'Do get better.'

She was looking at him with a queer, slanting, downward look of her heavy eyes, as she turned away. She was still a little red round the eyes, with nervous exhaustion.

'You are so tall!' he said, still frightened.

'I was always tall,' she replied, turning half to him again.

'And I small,' he said.

'I am so glad you are getting better,' she said.

'I am not glad,' he said.

'Why? I'm sure you are. Just as we are glad because we want you to get better.'

'Thank you,' he said. 'I have wished to die.'

'Don't do that, Count Dionys. Do get better,' she said, in the rather deep, laconic manner of her girlhood. He looked at her with a farther look of recognition. But his short, rather pointed nose was lifted with the disgust and weariness of pain, his brows were tense. He watched her with that curious flame of suffering which is forced to give a little outside attention, but which speaks only to itself.

'Why did they not let me die?' he said. 'I wanted death now.'

'No,' she said. 'You mustn't. You must live. If we *can* live we must.'

'I wanted death,' he said.

'Ah, well,' she said, 'even death we can't have when we want it, or when we think we want it.'

'That is true,' he said, watching her with the same wide black eyes. 'Please to sit down. You are so tall as you stand.'

It was evident he was a little frightened still by her looming, overhanging figure.

'I am sorry I am too tall,' she said, smiling, taking a chair which a man-nurse had brought her. Lady Beveridge had gone away to speak with the men. Daphne sat down, not knowing what to say further. The pitch-black look in the Count's wide eyes puzzled her.

'Why do you come here? Why does your lady mother come?' he said.

'To see if we can do anything,' she answered.

'When I am well, I will thank your ladyship.'

'All right,' she replied. 'When you are well I will let my lord the Count thank me. Please do get well.'

'We are enemies,' he said.

'Who? You and I and my mother?'

'Are we not? The most difficult thing is to be sure of anything. If they had let me die!'

'That is at least ungrateful, Count Dionys.'

'*Lady Daphne!* Yes! *Lady Daphne!* Beautiful, the name is. You are always called Lady Daphne? I remember you were so bright a maiden.'

'More or less,' she said, answering his question.

'Ach! We should all have new names now. I thought of a name for myself, but I have forgotten it. No longer Johann Dionys. That is shot away. I am Karl or Wilhelm or Ernst or Georg. Those are names I hate. Do you hate them?'

'I don't like them – but I don't hate them. And you mustn't leave off being Count Johann Dionys. If you do I shall have to leave off being Daphne. I like your name so much.'

'Lady Daphne! Lady Daphne!' he repeated. 'Yes, it rings well, it sounds beautiful to me. – I think I talk foolishly. I hear myself talking foolishly to you.' – He looked at her anxiously.

'Not at all,' she said.

'Ach! I have a head on my shoulders that is like a child's windmill, and I can't prevent it making foolish words. Please to go away, not to hear me. I can hear myself.'

'Can't I do anything for you?' she asked.

'No, no! No, no! If I could be buried deep, very deep down, where everything is forgotten! But they draw me up, back to the surface. I would not mind if they buried me alive, if it were very deep, and dark, and the earth heavy above.'

'Don't say that,' she replied, rising.

'No, I am saying it when I don't wish to say it. Why am I here? Why am I here? Why have I survived into this? Why can I not stop talking?'

He turned his face aside. The black, fine, elvish hair was so long, and pushed up in tufts from the smooth brown nape of his neck. Daphne looked at him in sorrow. He could not turn his body. He could only move his head. And he lay with his face hard averted, the fine hair of his beard coming up strange from under his chin and from his throat, up to the socket of his ear. He lay quite still, in this position. And she turned away, looking for her mother. She had suddenly realized that the bonds, the connexions between him and his life in the world had broken, and he lay there a bit of loose, palpitating humanity, shot away from the body of humanity.

It was ten days before she went to the hospital again. She had wanted never to go again, to forget him, as one tries to forget incurable things. But she could not forget him. He came again and again into her mind. She had to go back. She had heard that he was recovering very slowly.

He looked really better. His eyes were not so wide open, they had lost that black, inky exposure which had given him such an unnatural look, unpleasant. He watched her guardedly. She had taken off her furs, and wore only her dress and a dark, soft feather cap.

'How are you?' she said, keeping her face averted, unwilling to meet his eyes.

'Thank you, I am better. The nights are not so long.'

She shuddered, knowing what long nights meant. He saw the worn look in her face, too; the reddened rims of her eyes.

'Are you not well? Have you some trouble?' he asked her.

'No, no,' she answered.

She had brought a handful of pinky, daisy-shaped flowers.

'Do you care for flowers?' she asked.

He looked at them. Then he slowly shook his head.

'No,' he said. 'If I am on horseback, riding through the marshes or through the hills, I like to see them below me. But not here. Not now. Please do not bring flowers into this grave. Even in gardens, I do not like them. When they are upholstery to human life!'

'I will take them away again,' she said.

'Please do. Please give them to the nurse.'

Daphne paused.

'Perhaps,' she said, 'you wish I would not come to disturb you.'

He looked into her face.

'No,' he said. 'You are like a flower behind a rock, near an icy water. No, you do not live too much. – I am afraid I cannot talk sensibly. I wish to hold my mouth shut. If I open it, I talk this absurdity. It escapes from my mouth.'

'It is not so very absurd,' she said.

But he was silent – looking away from her.

'I want you to tell me if there is really nothing I can do for you,' she said.

'Nothing,' he answered.

'If I can write any letter for you.'

'None,' he answered.

'But your wife and your two children – do they know where you are?'

'I should think not.'

'And where are they?'

'I do not know. Probably they are in Hungary.'

'Not at your home?'

'My castle was burnt down in a riot. My wife went to Hungary with the children. She has her relatives there. She went away from me. I wished it, too. Also for her, I wished to be dead. Pardon me the personal tone –'

Daphne looked down at him – the queer, obstinate little fellow.

'But you have somebody you wish to tell – somebody you want to hear from?'

'Nobody. Nobody. I wish the bullet had gone through my heart. I wish to be dead. It is only I have a devil in my body, that will not die.'

She looked at him as he lay with closed, averted face.

'Surely it is not a devil which keeps you alive,' she said. 'It is something good.'

'No, a devil!' he said.

She sat looking at him with a long, slow, wondering look.

'Must one hate a devil that makes one live?' she asked.

He turned his eyes to her with a touch of a satiric smile.

'If one lives, no –' he said.

She looked away from him the moment he looked at her. For her life she would not have met his dark eyes direct.

She left him, and he lay still. He neither read nor talked, throughout the long winter nights and the short winter days. He only lay for hours with black, open eyes, seeing everything around with a touch of disgust, and heeding nothing.

Daphne went to see him now and then. She never forgot him for long. He seemed to come into her mind suddenly, as if by sorcery.

One day he said to her:

'I see you are married. May I ask you who is your husband?'

She told him. She had had a letter also from Basil. The Count smiled slowly.

'You can look forward,' he said, 'to a happy reunion, and new, lovely children, Lady Daphne. Is it not so?'

'Yes, of course,' she said.

'But you are ill,' he said to her.

'Yes – rather ill.'

'Of what –?'

'Oh –!' she answered fretfully, turning her face aside. 'They talk about lungs.' She hated speaking of it. 'Why, how do you know I am ill?' she added quickly.

Again he smiled slowly.

'I see it in your face, and hear it in your voice. One would say the Evil One had cast a spell on you.'

'Oh, no,' she said hastily. 'But do I look ill?'

'Yes. You look as if something had struck you across the face, and you could not forget it.'

'Nothing has,' she said. 'Unless it's the war.'

'The war!' he repeated.

'Oh, well, don't let us talk of it,' she said.

Another time he said to her:

'The year has turned – the sun must shine at last, even in England. I am afraid of getting well too soon. I am a prisoner, am I not? But I wish the sun would shine. I wish the sun would shine on my face.'

'You won't always be a prisoner. The war will end. And the sun *does* shine even in the winter in England,' she said.

'I wish it would shine on my face,' he said.

So that when in February there came a blue, bright morning, the morning that suggests yellow crocuses and the smell of a mezereon tree and the smell of damp, warm earth, Daphne hastily got a taxi and drove out to the hospital.

'You have come to put me in the sun,' he said the moment he saw her.

'Yes, that's what I came for,' she said.

She spoke to the matron, and had his bed carried out where there was a big window that came low. There he was put full in the sun. Turning, he could see the blue sky, and the twinkling tops of purplish, bare trees.

'The world! The world!' he murmured.

He lay with his eyes shut, and the sun on his swarthy, transparent, immobile face. The breath came and went through his nostrils invisibly. Daphne wondered how he could lie so still, how he could look so immobile. It was true as her mother had said: he looked as if he had been cast in the mould when the metal was white hot, all his lines were so clean. So small, he was, and in his way perfect.

Suddenly his dark eyes opened and caught her looking.

'The sun makes even anger open like a flower,' he said.

'Whose anger?' she said.

'I don't know. But I can make flowers, looking through my eyelashes. Do you know how?'

'You mean rainbows?'

'Yes, flowers.'

And she saw him, with a curious smile on his lips, looking through his almost closed eyelids at the sun.

'The sun is neither English nor German nor Bohemian,' he said. 'I am a subject of the sun. I belong to the fire-worshippers.'

'Do you?' she replied.

'Yes, truly, by tradition.' He looked at her smiling. 'You stand there like a flower that will melt,' he added.

She smiled slowly at him, with a slow, cautious look of her eyes, as if she feared something.

'I am much more solid than you imagine,' she said.

Still he watched her.

'One day,' he said, 'before I go, let me wrap your hair round my hands, will you?' He lifted his thin, short dark hands. 'Let me wrap your hair round my hands, like a bandage. They hurt me. I don't know what it is. I think it is all the gun explosions. But if you let me wrap your hair round my hands. You know, it is the hermetic gold – but so much of water in it, of the moon. That will soothe my hands. – One day, will you?'

'Let us wait till the day comes,' she said.

'Yes,' he answered, and was still again.

'It troubles me,' he said after a while, 'that I complain like a child, and ask for things. I feel I have lost my manhood for the time being. The continual explosions of guns and shells! It seems to have driven my soul out of me like a bird frightened away at last. But it will come back, you know. And I am so grateful to you, you are good to me when I am soulless, and you don't take advantage of me. Your soul is quiet and heroic.'

'Don't,' she said. 'Don't talk!'

The expression of shame and anguish and disgust crossed his face.

'It is because I can't help it,' he said. 'I have lost my soul, and I can't stop talking to you. I can't stop. But I don't talk to anyone else. I try not to talk, but I can't prevent it. Do you draw the words out of me?'

Her wide, green-blue eyes seemed like the heart of some curious, full-open flower, some Christmas rose with its petals of snow and flush. Her hair glinted heavy, like water-gold. She stood there passive and indomitable with the wide-eyed persistence of her wintry, blond nature.

Another day when she came to see him, he watched her for a time, then he said:

'Do they all tell you you are lovely, you are beautiful?'

'Not quite all,' she replied.

'But your husband?'

'He has said so.'

'Is he gentle? Is he tender? Is he a dear lover?'

She turned her face aside, displeased.

'Yes,' she replied curtly.

He did not answer. And when she looked again he was lying with his eyes shut, a faint smile seeming to curl round his short, transparent nose. She could faintly see the flesh through his beard, as water through reeds. His black hair was brushed smooth as glass, his black eyebrows glinted like a curve of black glass on the swarthy opalescence of his brow.

Suddenly he spoke, without opening his eyes.

'You have been very kind to me,' he said.

'Have I? Nothing to speak of.'

He opened his eyes and looked at her.

'Everything finds its mate,' he said. 'The ermine and the pole-cat and the buzzard. One thinks so often that only the dove and the nightingale and the stag with his antlers have gentle mates. But the pole-cat and the ice-bears of the north have their mates. And a white she-bear lies with her cubs under a rock as a snake lies hidden, and the male-bear slowly swims back from the sea, like a clot of snow or a shadow of white cloud passing on the speckled sea. I have seen her too, and I did not shoot her, nor him when he landed with fish in his mouth, wading wet and slow and yellow-white over the black stones.'

'You have been in the north sea?'

'Yes. And with the Eskimo in Siberia, and across the Tundras. And a white sea-hawk makes a nest on a high stone, and sometimes looks out with her white head, over the edge of the rocks. It is not only a world of men, Lady Daphne.'

'Not by any means,' said she.

'Else it were a sorry place.'

'It is bad enough,' said she.

'Foxes have their holes. They have even their mates, Lady Daphne, that they bark to and are answered. And an adder finds his female. Psanek means an outlaw, did you know?'

'I did not.'

'Outlaws, and brigands, have often the finest woman-mates.'

'They do,' she said.

'I will be Psanek, Lady Daphne. I will not be Johann Dionys any more. I will be Psanek. The law has shot me through.'

'You might be Psanek and Johann and Dionys as well,' she said.

'With the sun on my face? – Maybe –' he said, looking to the sun.

There were some lovely days in the spring of 1918. In March the Count was able to get up. They dressed him in a simple, dark-blue uniform. He was not very thin, only swarthy-transparent, now his beard was shaven and his hair was cut. His smallness made him noticeable, but he was masculine, perfect in his small stature. All the smiling dapperness that had made him seem like a monkey to Daphne when she was a girl had gone now. His eyes were dark and haughty, he seemed to keep inside his own reserves, speaking to nobody if he could help it, neither to the nurses nor the visitors nor to his fellow-prisoners, fellow-officers. He seemed to put a shadow between himself and them, and from across this shadow he looked with his dark, beautifully-fringed eyes, as a proud little beast from the shadow of its lair. Only to Daphne he laughed and chatted.

She sat with him one day in March on the terrace of the hospital, on a morning when white clouds went endlessly and magnificently about a blue sky, and the sunshine felt warm after the blots of shadow.

'When you had a birthday, and you were seventeen, didn't I give you a thimble?' he asked her.

'Yes. I have it still.'

'With a gold snake at the bottom, and a Mary-beetle of green stone at the top, to push the needle with?'

'Yes.'

'Do you ever use it?'

'No. I sew so rarely.'

'Would it displease you to sew something for me?'

'You won't admire my stitches. What would you wish me to sew?'

'Sew me a shirt that I can wear. I have never before worn shirts from a shop, with a maker's name inside. It is very distasteful to me.'

She looked at him – his haughty little brows.

'Shall I ask my maid to do it?' she said.

'Oh please no! Oh please no, do not trouble. No, please, I would not want it unless you sewed it yourself, with the Psanek thimble.'

She paused before she answered. Then came her slow: 'Why?'

He turned and looked at her with dark, searching eyes.

'I have no reason,' he said, rather haughtily.

She left the matter there. For two weeks she did not go to see him. Then suddenly one day she took the bus down Oxford Street and bought some fine white flannel. She decided he must wear flannel.

That afternoon she drove out to Hurst Place. She found him sitting on the terrace, looking across the garden at the red suburb of London smoking fumily in the near distance, interrupted by patches of uncovered ground and a flat, tin-roofed laundry.

'Will you give me measurements for your shirt?' she said.

'The number of the neck-band of this English shirt is fifteen. If you ask the matron she will give you the measurement. It is a little too large, too long in the sleeves, you see –' and he shook his shirt cuff over his wrist. 'Also too long altogether.'

'Mine will probably be unwearable when I've made them,' said she.

'Oh no. Let your maid direct you. But please do not let her sew them.'

'Will you tell me why you want me to do it?'

'Because I am a prisoner, in other people's clothes, and I have nothing of my own. All the things I touch are distasteful to me. If your maid sews for me, it will still be the same. Only you might give me what I want, something that buttons round my throat and on my wrists.'

'And in Germany – or in Austria –'

'My mother sewed for me. And after her, my mother's sister who was the head of my house.'

'Not your wife?'

'Naturally not. She would have been insulted. She was never more than a guest in my house. In my family there are old traditions – but with me they have come to an end. I had best try to revive them.'

'Beginning with traditions of shirts?'

'Yes. In our family the shirt should be made and washed by a woman of our own blood: but when we marry, by the wife. So when I married I had sixty shirts, and many other things – sewn by my mother and my aunt, all with my initial, and the ladybird, which is our crest.'

'And where did they put the initial?'

'Here –' He put his finger on the back of his neck, on the swarthy, transparent skin. 'I fancy I can feel the embroidered ladybird still. On our linen we had no crown: only the ladybird.'

She was silent, thinking.

'You will forgive what I ask you?' he said, 'since I am a prisoner and can do no other, and since fate has made you so that you understand the world as I understand it. It is not really indelicate, what I ask you. There will be a ladybird on your finger when you sew, and those who wear the ladybird understand.'

'I suppose,' she mused, 'it is as bad to have your bee in your shirt as in your bonnet.'

He looked at her with round eyes.

'Don't you know what it is to have a bee in your bonnet?' she said.

'No.'

'To have a bee buzzing among your hair! to be out of your wits,' she smiled at him.

'So!' he said. 'Ah, the Psaneks have had a ladybird in their bonnets for many hundred years.'

'Quite, quite mad,' she said.

'It may be,' he answered. 'But with my wife I was quite, quite sane for ten years. Now give me the madness of the ladybird. The world I was sane about has gone raving. The ladybird I was mad with is wise still.'

'At least, when I sew the shirts, if I sew them,' she said, 'I shall have the ladybird at my finger's end.'

'You want to laugh at me.'

'But surely you know you are funny, with your family insect.'

'My family insect? Now you want to be rude to me.'

'How many spots must it have?'

'Seven.'

'Three on each wing. And what do I do with the odd one?'

'You put that one between its teeth, like the cake for Cerberus.'[5]

'I'll remember that.'

When she brought the first shirt, she gave it to the matron. Then she found Count Dionys sitting on the terrace. It was a beautiful spring day. Near at hand were tall elm trees and some rooks cawing.

'What a lovely day!' she said. 'Are you liking the world any better?'

'The world?' he said, looking up at her with the same old discontent and disgust on his fine, transparent nose.

'Yes,' she replied, a shadow coming over her face.

'Is this the world – all those little red-brick boxes in rows, where couples of little people live, who decree my destiny –?'

'You don't like England?'

'Ah, England! Little houses like little boxes, each with its domestic Englishman and his domestic wife, each ruling the world because all are alike, so alike –'

'But England isn't all houses.'

'Fields then! Little fields with innumerable hedges. Like a net with an irregular mesh, pinned down over this island, and everything under the net. Ah, Lady Daphne, forgive me. I am ungrateful. I am so full of bile, of spleen, you say. My only wisdom is to keep my mouth shut.'

'Why do you hate everything?' she said, her own face going bitter.

'Not everything. If I were free! If I were outside the law. Ah, Lady Daphne, how does one get outside the law?'

'By going inside oneself,' she said. 'Not outside.'

His face took on a greater expression of disgust.

'No, no. I am a man, I am a man, even if I am little. I am not a spirit, that coils itself inside a shell. In my soul is anger, anger, anger. Give me room for my anger. Give me room for that.'

His black eyes looked keenly into her. She rolled her eyes as if in a half-trance. And in a monotonous, tranced voice she said:

'Much better get over your anger. And *why* are you angry?'

'There is no why. If it were love, you would not ask me, *why do you love*? But it is anger, anger, anger. What else can I call it? And there is no why.'

Again he looked at her with his dark, sharp, questioning, tormented eyes.

'Can't you get rid of it?' she said, looking aside.

'If a shell exploded and blew me into a thousand fragments,' he said, 'it would not destroy the anger that is in me. I know that. No, it will never dissipate. And to die is no release. The anger goes on gnashing and whimpering in death. Lady Daphne, Lady Daphne, we have used up all the love, and this is what is left.'

'Perhaps *you* have used up all your love,' she replied. 'You are not everybody.'

'I know it. I speak for me and you.'

'Not for me,' she said rapidly.

He did not answer, and they remained silent.

At length she turned her eyes slowly to him.

'Why do you say you speak for me?' she said, in an accusing tone.

'Pardon me. I was hasty.'

But a faint touch of superciliousness in his tone showed he meant what he had said. She mused, her brow cold and stony.

'And why do you tell *me* about your anger?' she said. 'Will that make it better?'

'Even the adder finds his mate. And she has as much poison in her mouth as he.'

She gave a little sudden squirt of laughter.

'Awfully poetic thing to say about me,' she said.

He smiled, but with the same corrosive quality.

'Ah,' he said, 'you are not a dove. You are a wild-cat with open eyes, half dreaming on a bough, in a lonely place, as I have seen her. And I ask myself – What are her memories then?'

'I wish I were a wild-cat,' she said suddenly.

He eyed her shrewdly, and did not answer.

'You want more war?' she said to him bitterly.

'More trenches? More Big Berthas,[6] more shells and poison-gas, more machine-drilled science-manoeuvred so-called armies? Never. Never. I would rather work in a factory that makes boots and shoes. And I would rather deliberately starve to death than work in a factory that makes boots and shoes.'

'Then what do you want?'

'I want my anger to have room to grow.'

'How?'

'I do not know. That is why I sit here, day after day. I wait.'

'For your anger to have room to grow?'

'For that.'

'Good-bye, Count Dionys.'

'Good-bye, Lady Daphne.'

She had determined never to go and see him again. She had no sign from him. Since she had begun the second shirt, she went on with it. And then she hurried to finish it, because she was starting a round of visits that would end in the summer sojourn in Scotland. She intended to post the shirt. But after all, she took it herself.

She found Count Dionys had been removed from Hurst Place to Voynich Hall, where other enemy officers were interned. The being thwarted made her more determined. She took the train next day to go to Voynich Hall.

When he came into the ante-room where he was to receive her, she felt at once the old influence of his silence and his subtle power. His face had still that swarthy-transparent look of one who is unhappy, but his bearing was proud and reserved. He kissed her hand politely, leaving her to speak.

'How are you?' she said. 'I didn't know you were here. I am going away for the summer.'

'I wish you a pleasant time,' he said. They were speaking English.

'I brought the other shirt,' she said. 'It is finished at last.'

'That is a greater honour than I dared expect,' he said.

'I'm afraid it may be more honourable than useful. The other didn't fit, did it?'

'Almost,' he said. 'It fitted the spirit, if not the flesh,' he smiled.

'I'd rather it had been the reverse, for once,' she said. 'Sorry.'

'I would not have it one stitch different.'

'Can we sit in the garden?'

'I think we may.'

They sat on a bench. Other prisoners were playing croquet not far off. But these two were left comparatively alone.

'Do you like it better here?' she said.

'I have nothing to complain of,' he said.

'And the anger?'

'It is doing well, I thank you,' he smiled.

'You mean getting better?'

'Making strong roots,' he said, laughing.

'Ah, so long as it only makes roots – !' she said.

'And your ladyship, how is she?'

'My ladyship is rather better,' she replied.

'Much better, indeed,' he said, looking into her face.

'Do you mean I *look* much better?' she asked quickly.

'Very much. – It is your beauty you think of. Well, your beauty is almost itself again.'

'Thanks.'

'You brood on your beauty as I on my anger. Ah, your ladyship, be wise, and make friends with your anger. That is the way to let your beauty blossom.'

'I was not unfriendly with you, was I?' she said.

'With me?' His face flickered with a laugh. 'Am I your anger? Your wrath incarnate? So then, be friends with the angry me, your ladyship. I ask nothing better.'

'What is the use,' she said, 'being friends with the *angry* you? I would much rather be friends with the happy you.'

'That little animal is extinct,' he laughed. 'And I am glad of it.'

'But what remains? Only the angry you? Then it is no use my trying to be friends.'

'You remember, dear Lady Daphne, that the adder does not suck his poison all alone, and the pole-cat knows where to find his she-pole-cat. You remember that each one has his own dear mate,' he laughed. 'Dear, deadly mate.'

'And what if I do remember those bits of natural history, Count Dionys?'

'The she-adder is dainty, delicate, and carries her poison lightly. The wild-cat has wonderful green eyes that she closes with memory like a screen. The ice-bear hides like a snake with her cubs, and her snarl is the strangest thing in the world.'

'Have you ever heard me snarl?' she asked suddenly.

He only laughed, and looked away.

They were silent. And immediately the strange thrill of secrecy was between them. Something had gone beyond sadness into another, secret, thrilling communion which she would never admit.

'What do you do all day here?' she asked.

'Play chess – play this foolish croquet – play billiards – and read – and wait – and remember.'

'What do you wait for?'

'I don't know.'

'And what do you remember?'

'Ah, that – Shall I tell you what amuses me? Shall I tell you a secret?'

'Please don't, if it's anything that matters.'

'It matters to nobody but me. Will you hear it?'

'If it does not implicate me in any way.'

'It does not. Well, I am a member of a certain old secret society – no, don't look at me, nothing frightening – only a society like the free-masons.'

'And – ?'

'And – well, as you know, one is initiated into certain so-called secrets and rites. My family has always been initiated. So I am an initiate too. Does it interest you?'

'Why, of course.'

'Well – I was always rather thrilled by these secrets. Or some of them. Some seemed to me far-fetched. The ones that thrilled me even never had any relation to actual life. When you knew me in Dresden and Prague, you would not have thought me a man invested with awful secret knowledge, now would you?'

'Never.'

'No. It was just a little exciting side-show. And I was a grimacing little society man. But now they become true. It becomes true.'

'The secret knowledge?'

'Yes.'

'What, for instance?'

'Take actual fire. It will bore you. Do you want to hear?'

'Go on.'

'This is what I was taught. The true fire is invisible. Flame, and the red fire we see burning, has its back to us. It is running away from us – does that mean anything to you?'

'Yes.'

'Well, then, the yellowness of sunshine – light itself – that is only the glancing aside of the real original fire. You know that is true. There would be no light if there was no refraction, no bits of dust and stuff to turn the dark fire into visibility. – You know that's a fact. – And that being so, even the sun is dark. It is only his jacket of dust that makes him visible. You know that too. – And the true sunbeams coming towards us flow darkly, a moving darkness of the genuine fire. The sun is dark, the sunshine flowing to us is dark. And light is only the inside-out of it all, the lining, and the yellow beams are only the turning away of the sun's directness that was coming to us. – Does that interest you at all?'

'Yes,' she said dubiously.

'Well, we've got the world inside out. The true living world of fire is dark, throbbing, darker than blood. Our luminous world that we go by is only the white lining of this.'

'Yes, I like that,' she said.

'Well! Now listen. The same with love. This white love that we have is the same. It is only the reverse, the whited sepulchre of the true love. True love is dark, a throbbing together in darkness, like the wild-cat in the night, when the green screen opens and her eyes are on the darkness.'

'No, I don't see that,' she said in a slow, clanging voice.

'You, and your beauty – that is only the inside-out of you. The real you is the wild-cat invisible in the night, with red fire perhaps coming out of its wide, dark eyes. Your beauty is your whited sepulchre.'

'You mean cosmetics,' she said. 'I've used none at all to-day – not even powder.'

He laughed.

'Very good,' he said. 'Consider me. I used to think myself small but handsome, and the ladies used to admire me moderately, never very much. A smart little fellow, you know. Well, that was just the inside-out of me. I am a black tom-cat howling in the night, and it is then that fire comes out of me. This me you look at is my whited sepulchre. What do you say –'

She was looking into his eyes. She could see the darkness swaying in the depths. She perceived the invisible, cat-like fire stirring deep inside them, felt it coming towards her. She turned her face aside. Then he laughed, showing his strong white teeth, that seemed a little too large, rather dreadful.

She rose to go.

'Well,' she said. 'I shall have the summer in which to think about the world inside-out. Do write if there is anything to say. Write to Thoresway. – Good-bye!'

'Ah, your eyes!' he said. 'They are like jewels of stone.'

Being away from the Count, she put him out of her mind. Only she was sorry for him a prisoner in that sickening Voynich Hall. But she did not write. Nor did he.

As a matter of fact, her mind was now much more occupied with her husband. All arrangements were being made to effect his exchange. From month to month she looked for his return. And so she thought of him.

Whatever happened to her, she thought about it, thought and thought a great deal. The consciousness of her mind was like tablets of stone weighing her down. And whoever would make a new entry into her must break these tablets of stone piece by piece. So it was that in her own way she thought often enough of the Count's world inside-out. A curious latency stirred in her consciousness, that was not yet an idea.

He said her eyes were like jewels of stone. What a horrid thing to say! What did he want her eyes to be like? – He wanted them to dilate and become all black pupil, like a cat's at night. She shrank convulsively from the thought, and tightened her breast.

He said her beauty was her whited sepulchre. Even that, she knew what he meant. The fluid invisibility of her he wanted to love. But ah, her pearl-like beauty was so dear to her, and it was so famous in the world.

He said her white love was like moonshine, harmful, the reverse of love. He meant Basil, of course. Basil always said she was the moon. But then Basil loved her for that. The ecstasy of it! She shivered, thinking of her husband. But it had also made her nerve-worn, her husband's love. Ah, nerve-worn.

What then would the Count's love be like? Something so secret and different. She would not be lovely and a queen to him. He hated her loveliness. The wild-cat has its mate. The little wild-cat that he was. Ah – !

She caught her breath, determined not to think. When she thought of Count Dionys she felt the world slipping away from her. She would sit in front of a mirror, looking at her wonderful cared-for face, that had appeared in so many society magazines. She loved it so, it made her feel so vain. And she looked at her blue-green eyes – the eyes of the wild-cat on a bough. Yes, the lovely blue-green iris drawn tight like a screen. Supposing it should relax. Supposing it should unfold, and open out the dark depths, the dark, dilated pupil! Supposing it should?

Never! She always caught herself back. She felt she might be killed, before she could give way to that relaxation that the Count wanted of her. She could not. She just could not. At the very thought of it some hypersensitive nerve started with a great twinge in her breast, she drew back, forced to keep her guard. Ah, no, Monsieur le Comte, you shall never take her ladyship off her guard.

She disliked the thought of the Count. An impudent little fellow. An impertinent little fellow! A little madman, really. A little outsider. – No, no. She would think of her husband: an adorable, tall, well-bred Englishman, so easy and simple, and with the amused look in his blue eyes. She thought of the cultured, casual trail of his voice. It set her nerves on fire. She thought of his strong, easy body – beautiful, white-fleshed, with the fine sprinkling of warm-brown hair like tiny flames. He was the Dionysos,[7] full of sap, milk and honey and northern golden wine: he, her husband. Not that little unreal Count. – Ah, she dreamed of her husband, of the love-days, and the honeymoon, the lovely, simple intimacy. Ah, the marvellous revelation of that intimacy, when he left himself to her so generously. Ah, she was his wife for this reason, that he had given himself to her so greatly, so generously. Like an ear of corn he was there for her gathering – her husband, her own lovely English husband. Ah, when would he come again, when would he come again!

She had letters from him – and how he loved her. Far away, his life was all hers. All hers, flowing to her as the beam flows from a white star right down to us, to our heart. Her lover, her husband.

He was now expecting to come home soon. It had all been arranged. 'I hope you won't be disappointed in me when I do get back,' he wrote. 'I am afraid I am no longer the plump and well-looking young man I was. I've got a big scar at the side of my mouth, and I'm as thin as a starved rabbit, and my hair's going grey. Doesn't sound attractive, does it? And it isn't attractive. But once I can get out of this infernal place, and once I can be with you again, I shall come in for my second blooming. The very thought of being quietly in the same house with you, quiet and in peace, makes me realize that if I've been through hell, I have known heaven on earth and can hope to know it again. I am a miserable brute to look at now. But I have faith in you. You will forgive my appearance, and that alone will make me feel handsome –'

She read this letter many times. She was not afraid of his scar or his looks. She would love him all the more.

Since she had started making shirts – those two for the Count had been an enormous labour, even though her maid had come to her assistance forty times: but since she had started making shirts, she thought she might continue. She had some good suitable silk: her husband liked silk underwear.

But still she used the Count's thimble. It was gold outside and silver inside, and was too heavy. A snake was coiled round the base, and at the top, for pressing the needle, was inlet a semi-translucent apple-green stone, perhaps jade, carved like a scarab, with little dots. It was too heavy. But then she sewed so slowly. And she liked to feel her hand heavy, weighted. And as she sewed she thought about her husband, and she felt herself in love with him. She thought of him, how beautiful he was, and how she would love him now he was thin, she would love him all the more. She would love to trace his bones, as if to trace his living skeleton. The thought made her rest her hands in her lap, and drift into a muse. Then she felt the weight of the thimble on her finger, and took it off, and sat looking at the green stone. The ladybird. The ladybird. And if only her husband would come soon, soon. It was wanting him that made her so ill. Nothing but that. She had wanted him so badly. She wanted him now. Ah, if she could go to him now, and find him, wherever he was, and see him and touch him and take all his love.

As she mused, she put the thimble down in front of her, took up a little silver pencil from her work-basket, and on a bit of blue paper that had been the band of a small skein of silk she wrote the lines of the silly little song

> 'Wenn ich ein Vöglein wär'
> Und auch zwei Flüglein hätt',
> Flög' ich zu dir —'[8]

That was all she could get on her bit of pale-blue paper.

> 'If I were a little bird
> And had two little wings
> I'd fly to thee —'

Silly enough, in all conscience. But she did not translate it, so it did not seem quite so silly.

At that moment her maid announced Lady Bingham – her husband's sister. Daphne crumpled up the bit of paper in a flurry, and in another minute Primrose, his sister, came in. The newcomer was not a bit like a primrose, being long-faced and clever, smart, but not a bit elegant, in her new clothes.

'Daphne, dear, what a domestic scene! I suppose it's rehearsal. Well, you may as well rehearse, he's with Admiral Burns on the *Ariadne*. Father just heard from the Admiralty: quite fit. He'll be here in a day or two. Splendid, isn't it? And the war is going to end. At least it seems like it. You'll be safe of your man now, dear. Thank heaven when it's all over. What are you sewing?'

'A shirt,' said Daphne.

'A shirt! Why, how clever of you. I should never know which end to begin. Who showed you?'

'Millicent.'

'And how did *she* know? She's no business to know how to sew shirts: nor cushions nor sheets, either. Do let me look. Why, how perfectly marvéllous you are! – every bit by hand, too. Basil isn't worth it, dear, really he isn't. Let him order his shirts in Oxford Street. Your business is to be beautiful, not to sew shirts. What a dear little pin-poppet, or rather needle-woman! I say, a satire on us, that is. But what a darling, with mother of pearl wings to her skirts! And darling little gold-eyed needles inside her. You screw her head off, and you find she's full of pins and needles. Woman for you! – Mother says won't you come to lunch to-morrow. And won't you come to Brassey's to tea with me at this minute. Do, there's a dear. I've got a taxi –'

Daphne bundled her sewing loosely together.

When she tried to do a bit more, two days later, she could not find her thimble. She asked her maid, whom she could absolutely trust. The girl had not seen it. She searched every-where. She asked her nurse – who was now her housekeeper and footman. No, nobody had seen it. Daphne even asked her sister-in-law.

'Thimble, darling? No, I don't remember a thimble. I remember a dear little needle lady, whom I thought such a precious satire on us women. I didn't notice a thimble.'

Poor Daphne wandered about in a muse. She did not want to believe it lost. It had been like a talisman to her. She tried to forget it. Her husband was coming, quite soon, quite soon. But she could not raise herself to joy. She had lost her thimble. It was as if Count Dionys accused her in her sleep, of something, she did not quite know what.

And though she did not really want to go to Voynich Hall, yet like a fatality she went, like one doomed. It was already late autumn, and some lovely days. This was the last of the lovely days. She was told that Count Dionys was in the small park, finding chestnuts. She went to look for him. Yes, there he was in his blue uniform, stooping over the brilliant yellow leaves of the sweet chestnut tree that lay around him like a fallen nimbus of glowing yellow, under his feet as he kicked and rustled looking for the chestnut burrs. And with his short brown hands he was pulling out the small chestnuts and putting them in his pockets. But as she approached he peeled a nut to eat it. His teeth were white and powerful.

'You remind me of a squirrel laying in a winter store,' said she.

'Ah, Lady Daphne – I was thinking, and did not hear you.'

'I thought you were gathering chestnuts – even eating them.'

'Also!' he laughed. He had a dark, sudden charm when he laughed, showing his rather large white teeth. She was not quite sure whether she found him a little repulsive.

'Were you *really* thinking?' she said, in her slow, resonant way.

'Very truly.'

'And weren't you enjoying the chestnut a bit?'

'Very much. Like sweet milk. Excellent, excellent –' He had the fragments of the nut between his teeth, and bit them freely. 'Will you take one too – He held out the little, pointed brown nuts on the palm of his hand.

She looked at them doubtfully.

'Are they as tough as they always were?' she said.

'No, they are fresh and good. Wait, I will peel one for you.'

They strayed about through the thin clump of trees.

'You have had a pleasant summer? You are strong?'

'Almost *quite* strong,' said she. 'Lovely summer, thanks. I suppose it's no good asking you if you have been happy?'

'Happy? –' He looked at her direct. His eyes were black, and seemed to examine her. She always felt he had a little contempt of her. 'Oh, yes,' he said, smiling. 'I have been very happy.'

'So glad.'

They drifted a little farther, and he picked up an apple-green chestnut burr out of the yellow-brown leaves, handling it with sensitive fingers that still suggested paws to her.

'How did you succeed in being happy?' she said.

'How shall I tell you? I felt that the same power which put up the mountains could pull them down again – no matter how long it took.'

'And was that all?'

'Was it not enough?'

'I should say decidedly too little.'

He laughed broadly, showing the strong, negroid teeth.

'You do not know all it means,' he said.

'The thought that the mountains were going to be pulled down?' she said. 'It will be so long after my day –'

'Ah, you are bored,' he said. 'But I – I found the God who pulls things down: especially the things that men have put up. Do they not say that life is a search after God, Lady Daphne? I have found my God.'

'The God of destruction,' she said, blanching.

'Yes – not the devil of destruction, but the God of destruction. The blessed God of Destruction. It is strange –' he stood before her, looking up at her – 'but I have found my God. The God of anger, who throws down the steeples and the factory chimneys. Ah, Lady Daphne, he is a man's God, he is a man's God. I have found my God, Lady Daphne.'

'Apparently. And how are you going to serve him?'

A naïve glow transfigured his face.

'Oh, I will help. With my heart I will help while I can do nothing with my hands. I say to my heart: Beat, hammer, beat with little strokes. Beat, hammer of God, beat them down. Beat it all down.'

Her brows knitted, her face took on a look of discontent.

'Beat what down?' she asked harshly.

'The world, the world of man. Not the trees – these chestnuts, for example –' he looked up at them, at the tufts and loose pinions of yellow – 'not these – nor the chattering sorcerers, the squirrels – nor the hawk that comes. Not those.'

'You mean beat England?' she said.

'Ah, no! Ah, no! Not England any more than Germany – perhaps not as much. Not Europe any more than Asia.'

'Just the end of the world?'

'No, no. No, no. What grudge have I against a world where little chestnuts are so sweet as these! Do you like yours? Will you take another?'

'No, thanks.'

'What grudge have I against a world where even the hedges are full of berries, bunches of black berries that hang down, and red berries that thrust up. Never would I hate the world. But the world of man. Lady Daphne –' his voice sank to a whisper. '*I hate it. Zzz!*' he hissed. '*Strike, little heart! Strike, strike, hit, smite!* Oh, Lady Daphne!' – his eyes dilated with a ring of fire.

'What?' she said, scared.

'I believe in the power of my red, dark heart. God has put the hammer in my breast – the little eternal hammer. Hit – hit – hit! It hits on the world of man. It hits, it hits! And it hears the thin sound of cracking. The thin sound of cracking. Hark!'

He stood still and made her listen. It was late afternoon. The strange laugh of his face made the air seem dark to her. And she could easily have believed that she heard a faint fine shivering, cracking, through the air, a delicate crackling noise.

'You hear it? Yes? – Oh, may I live long! May I live long, so that my hammer may strike and strike, and the cracks go deeper, deeper! Ah, the world of man! Ah, the joy, the passion in every heart-beat! Strike home, strike true, strike sure. Strike to destroy it. Strike! Strike! To destroy the world of man. Ah, God. Ah, God, prisoner of peace. Do I not know you, Lady Daphne? Do I not? Do I not?'

She was silent for some moments, looking away at the twinkling lights of a station beyond.

'Not the white plucked lily of your body. I have gathered no flower for my ostentatious life. – But in the cold dark, your lily root, Lady Daphne. Ah, yes, you will know it all your life, that I know where your root lies buried, with its sad, sad quick of life. – What does it matter!'

They had walked slowly towards the house. She was silent. Then at last she said, in a peculiar voice:

'And you would never want to kiss me?'

'Ah, no!' he answered sharply.

She held out her hand.

'Good-bye, Count Dionys,' she drawled, fashionably. He bowed over her hand, but did not kiss it.

'Good-bye, Lady Daphne.'

She went away, with her brow set hard. And henceforth she thought only of her husband, of Basil. She made the Count die out of her. – Basil was coming, he was near. He was coming back from the east, from war and death. Ah, he had been through awful fire of experience. He would be something new, something she did not know. He was something new, a stranger lover who had been through terrible fire, and had come out strange and new, like a god. Ah, new and terrible his love would be, pure and intensified by the awful fire of suffering. A new lover – a new bridegroom – a new, superhuman wedding-night. She shivered in anticipation, waiting for her husband. She hardly noticed the wild excitement of the Armistice. She was waiting for something more wonderful to her.

And yet the moment she heard his voice on the telephone, her heart contracted with fear. It was his well-known voice, deliberate, diffident, almost drawling, with the same subtle suggestion of deference, and the rather exaggerated Cambridge intonation, up and down. But there was a difference, a new icy note that went through her veins like death.

'Is that you, Daphne? I shall be with you in half an hour. Is that all right for you? Yes, I've just landed, and shall come straight to you. Yes, a taxi. Shall I be too sudden for you, darling? No? Good, oh, good! half an hour, then! – I say, Daphne? – There won't be anyone else there, will there? Quite alone! Good! I can ring up Dad afterwards. – Yes, splendid, splendid. Sure you're all right, my darling? I'm at death's door till I see you. – Yes. Good-bye – half an hour. Good-bye.'

When Daphne had hung up the receiver she sat down almost in a faint. What was it that so frightened her? His terrible, terrible altered voice, like cold blue steel. She had no time to think. She rang for her maid.

'Oh, my lady, it isn't bad news?' cried Millicent when she caught sight of her mistress white as death.

'No, good news. Major Apsley will be here in half an hour. Help me to dress. Ring to Murry's first to send in some roses, red ones, and some lilac-coloured iris – two dozen of each, at once.'

Daphne went to her room. She didn't know what to wear, she didn't know how she wanted her hair dressed. She spoke hastily to her maid. She chose a violet-coloured dress. She did not know what she was doing. In the middle of dressing the flowers came, and she left off to put them in the bowls. So that when she heard his voice in the hall, she was still standing in front of the mirror reddening her lips and wiping it away again.

'Major Apsley, my lady!' murmured the maid, in excitement.

'Yes, I can hear. Go and tell him I shall be *one* minute.'

Daphne's voice had become slow and sonorous, like bronze, as it always did when she was upset. Her face looked almost haggard, and in vain she dabbed with the rouge.

'How does he look?' she asked curtly when her maid came back.

'A long scar here –' said the maid, and she drew her finger from the left hand corner of her mouth into her cheek, slanting downwards.

'Make him look very different?' asked Daphne.

'Not so *very* different, my lady,' said Millicent gently. 'His eyes are the same, I think.' The girl also was distressed.

'All right,' said Daphne. She looked at herself a long last look as she turned away from the mirror. The sight of her own face made her feel almost sick. She had seen so much of herself. And yet even now she was fascinated by the heavy droop of her lilac-veined lids over her slow, strange, large, green-blue eyes. They *were* mysterious-looking. And she gave herself a long, sideways glance, curious and Chinese. How was it possible there was a touch of the Chinese in her face? – she so purely an English blonde, an Aphrodite of the foam,[9] as Basil had called her in poetry. Ah, well! – She left off her thoughts and went through the hall to the drawing-room.

He was standing nervously in the middle of the room, in his

uniform. She hardly glanced at his face – and saw only the scar.

'Hullo, Daphne –' he said, in a voice full of the expected emotion. He stepped forward and took her in his arms, and kissed her forehead.

'So glad! So glad it's happened at last,' she said, hiding her tears.

'So glad what has happened, darling?' he asked in his deliberate manner.

'That you're back.' Her voice had the bronze resonance, she spoke rather fast.

'Yes, I'm back, Daphne, darling – as much of me as there is to bring back.'

'Why?' she said. 'You've come back whole, surely!' She was frightened.

'Yes, apparently I have. Apparently. But don't let's talk of that. Let's talk of you, darling. How are you? Let me look at you. You are thinner, you are older. But you are more wonderful than ever. Far more wonderful.'

'How?' said she.

'I can't exactly say how. You were only a girl. Now you are a woman. I suppose it's all that's happened. But you are wonderful as a woman, Daphne, darling – more wonderful than all that's happened. I couldn't have believed you'd be so wonderful. I'd forgotten – or else I'd never known. I say, I'm a lucky chap really. Here I am, alive and well, and I've got you for a wife. – It's brought you out like a flower. – I say, darling, there is more now than Venus of the foam – grander. How beautiful you are! But you look like the beauty of all life – as if you were moon-mother of the world – Aphrodite. – God is good to me after all, darling. I ought never to utter a single complaint. – How lovely you are – how lovely you are, my darling! I'd forgotten you – and I thought I knew you so well. – Is it true, that you belong to me? Are you really mine?'

They were seated on the yellow sofa. He was holding her hand, and his eyes were going up and down, from her face to her throat and her breast. The sound of his words, and the strong, cold desire in his voice excited her, pleased her, and made her heart freeze. She turned and looked into his light blue eyes. They had no longer the amused light, nor the young look. They burned with a hard, focused light, whitish.

'It's all right. You are mine, aren't you, Daphne, darling?' came his cultured, musical voice, that had always the well-bred twang of diffidence.

She looked back into his eyes.

'Yes, I am yours,' she said, from the lips.

'Darling! Darling!' he murmured, kissing her hand.

Her heart beat suddenly so terribly, as if her breast would be ruptured, and she rose in one movement and went across the room. She leaned her hand on the mantelpiece and looked down at the electric fire. She could hear the faint, faint noise of it. There was silence for a few moments.

Then she turned and looked at him. He was watching her intently. His face was gaunt, and there was a curious deathly sub-pallor, though his cheeks were not white. The scar ran livid from the side of his mouth. It was not so very big. But it seemed like a scar in him himself, in his brain, as it were. In his eyes was that hard, white, focused light that fascinated her and was terrible to her. He was different. He was like death; like risen death. She felt she dared not touch him. White death was still upon him. She could tell that he shrank with a kind of agony from contact. 'Touch me not, I am not yet ascended unto the Father.' – Yet for contact he had come. Something, someone seemed to be looking over his shoulder. His own young ghost looking over his shoulder. Oh, God! She closed her eyes, seeming to swoon. He remained leaning forward on the sofa, watching her.

'Aren't you well, darling?' he asked. There was a strange, incomprehensible coldness in his very fire. He did not move to come near her.

'Yes, I'm well. It is only that after all it is so sudden. Let me get used to you,' she said, turning aside her face from him. She felt utterly like a victim of his white, awful face.

'I suppose I must be a bit of a shock to you,' he said. 'I hope you won't leave off loving me. It won't be that, will it?'

The strange coldness in his voice! And yet the white, uncanny fire.

'No, I shan't leave off loving you,' she admitted, in a low tone, as if almost ashamed. She *dared* not have said otherwise. And the saying it made it true.

'Ah, if you're sure of that,' he said. 'I'm a rather unlovely sight to behold, I know, with this wound-scar. But if you can forgive it me, darling. – Do you think you can?' There was something like compulsion in his tone.

She looked at him, and shivered slightly.

'I love you – more than before,' she said hurriedly.

'Even the scar?' – came his terrible voice, inquiring.

She glanced again, with that slow, Chinese side-look, and felt she would die.

'Yes,' she said, looking away at nothingness. It was an awful moment to her. A little, slightly imbecile smile widened on her face.

He suddenly knelt at her feet, and kissed the toe of her slipper, and kissed the instep, and kissed the ankle in the thin black stocking.

'I knew,' he said in a muffled voice. 'I knew you would make good. I knew if I had to kneel, it was before you. I knew you were divine, you were the one – Cybele – Isis.[10] I knew I was your slave. I knew. It has all been just a long initiation. I had to learn how to worship you.'

He kissed her feet again and again, without the slightest self-consciousness, or the slightest misgiving. Then he went back to the sofa, and sat there looking at her, saying:

'It isn't love, it is worship. Love between me and you will be a sacrament, Daphne. That's what I had to learn. You are beyond me. A mystery to me. My God, how great it all is! How marvellous!'

She stood with her hand on the mantelpiece, looking down and not answering. She was frightened – almost horrified: but she was thrilled deep down to her soul. She really felt she could glow white and fill the universe like the moon, like Astarte,[11] like Isis, like Venus. The grandeur of her own pale power. The man religiously worshipped her, not merely amorously. She was ready for him – for the sacrament of his supreme worship.

He sat on the sofa with his hands spread on the yellow brocade and pushing downwards behind him, down between the deep upholstery of the back and the seat. He had long, white hands with pale freckles. And his fingers touched something. With his long white fingers he groped and brought it out. It was the lost thimble. And inside it was the bit of screwed-up blue paper.

'I say, is that *your* thimble?' he asked, delighted.

She started, and went hurriedly forward for it.

'Where was it?' she said, agitated.

But he did not give it to her. He turned it round and pulled out the bit of blue paper. He saw the faint pencil marks on the screwed-up ball, and unrolled the band of paper, and slowly deciphered the verse.

> 'Wenn ich ein Vöglein wär'
> Und auch zwei Flüglein hätt'
> Flög' ich zu dir –'

'How awfully touching that is,' he said. 'A *Vöglein* with two little *Flüglein*! But what a precious darling child you are! – Whom did you want to fly to, if you were a *Vöglein*?' He looked up at her with a curious smile.

'I can't remember,' she said, turning aside her head.

'I hope it was to me,' he said. 'Anyhow, I shall consider it was, and shall love you all the more for it. What a darling child! A *Vöglein* if you please, with two little wings! Why, how beautifully absurd of you, darling!'

He folded the scrap of paper carefully, and put it in his pocket-book, keeping the thimble all the time between his knees.

'Tell me when you lost it, Daphne,' he said, examining the bauble.

'About a month ago – or two months.'

'About a month ago – or two months. – And what were you sewing? Do you mind if I ask? I like to think of you then. I was still in that beastly El Hasrun. What were you sewing, darling, two months ago, when you lost your thimble?'

'A shirt.'

'I say, a shirt! Whose shirt?'

'Yours.'

'There. Now we've run it to earth. Were you really sewing a shirt for me! Is it finished? Can I put it on at this minute?'

'That one isn't finished, but the first one is.'

'I say, darling – let me go and put it on. To think I should have it next my skin! I shall feel you all round me, all over me. I say, how marvellous that will be! Won't you come?'

'Won't you give me the thimble?' she said.

'Yes, of course. What a noble thimble, too! Who gave it to you?'

'Count Dionys Psanek.'

'Who was he?'

'A Bohemian Count, in Dresden. He once stayed with us in Thoresway – with a tall wife. Didn't you meet them?'

'I don't think I did. I don't think I did. I don't remember. What was he like?'

'A little man with black hair and a rather low dark forehead – rather dressy.'

'No, I don't remember him at all. – So he gave it you. – Well, I wonder where he is now? – Probably rotted, poor devil.'

'No, he's interned in Voynich Hall. Mother and I have been to see him several times. He was awfully badly wounded.'

'Poor little beggar! In Voynich Hall! I'll look at him before he goes. Odd thing, to give you a thimble. Odd gift! You were a girl then, though. Do you think he had it made, or do you think he found it in a shop?'

'I think it belonged to the family. The ladybird at the top is part of their crest – and the snake as well, I think.'

'A ladybird! Funny thing for a crest. Americans would call it a bug. I must look at him before he goes. – And you were sewing a shirt for me! And then you posted me this little letter into the sofa. Well, I'm jolly glad I received it, and that it didn't go astray in the post, like so many things. *"Wenn ich ein Vöglein wär'"* – you perfect child! But that is the beauty of a woman like you: you are so superb and beyond worship, and then such an exquisite naïve child. Who could help worshipping you and loving you: immortal and mortal together. What, you want the thimble? Here! – Wonderful, wonderful white fingers. Ah, darling, you are more goddess than child, you long limber Isis with sacred hands. White, white, and immortal! Don't tell me your hands could die, darling: your wonderful Proserpine fingers.[12] They are immortal as February and snowdrops. If you lift your hands the spring comes. I *can't* help kneeling before you, darling. I am no more than a sacrifice to you, an offering. I *wish* I could die in giving myself to you, give you all my blood on your altar, for ever.'

She looked at him with a long, slow look, as he turned his face to her. His face was white with ecstacy. And she was not afraid. Somewhere, saturnine, she knew it was absurd. But she chose not to know. A certain swoon-sleep was on her. With her slow, green-blue eyes she looked down on his ecstasized face, almost benign. But in her right hand unconsciously she held the thimble fast, she only gave him her left hand. He took her hand and rose to his feet in that curious priestly ecstasy which made him more than a man or a soldier, far, far more than a lover to her.

Nevertheless, his homecoming made her begin to be ill again. Afterwards, after his love, she had to bear herself in torment. To her shame and her heaviness, she knew she was not strong enough, or pure enough, to bear this awful out-pouring adoration-lust. It was not her fault she felt weak and fretful afterwards, as if she wanted to cry and be fretful and petulant, wanted someone to save her. She could not turn to Basil, her husband. After his ecstasy of adoration-lust for her, she recoiled from him. Alas, she was not the goddess, the superb person he named her. She was flawed with the fatal humility of her age. She could not harden her heart and burn her soul pure of this humility, this misgiving. She could not finally believe in her own woman-godhead – only in her own female mortality.

That fierce power of continuing alone, even with your lover, the fierce power of the woman *in excelsis*[13] – alas, she could not keep it. She could rise to the height for the time, the incandescent, transcendent, moon-fierce womanhood. But, alas, she could not stay intensified and resplendent in her white, womanly powers, her female mystery. She relaxed, she lost her glory, and became fretful. Fretful and ill and never to be soothed. And then naturally her man became ashy and somewhat acrid, while she ached with nerves, and could not eat.

Of course, she began to dream about Count Dionys: to yearn wistfully for him. And it was absolutely a fatal thought to her, that he was going away. When she thought that, that he was leaving England soon – going away into the dark for ever – then the last spark seemed to die in her. She felt her soul perish, whilst she herself was worn and soulless like a prostitute. A prostitute goddess. And her husband, the gaunt, white, intensified priest of her, who never ceased from being before her, like a lust.

'Tomorrow,' she said to him, gathering her last courage and looking at him with a side look, 'I want to go to Voynich Hall.'

'What, to see Count Psanek? Oh, good! Yes, very good! I'll come along as well. I should like very much to see him. I suppose he'll be getting sent back before long.'

It was a fortnight before Christmas, very dark weather. Her husband was in khaki. She wore black furs and a black lace veil over her face, so that she seemed mysterious. But she lifted the veil and looped it behind, so that it made a frame for her face. She looked very lovely like that – her face pure like the most white hellebore flower, touched with winter pink, amid the blackness of her drapery and furs. Only she was rather too much like the picture of a modern beauty; too much the actual thing. She had half an idea that Dionys would hate her for her effective loveliness. He would see it and hate it. The thought was like a bitter balm to her. For herself, she loved her loveliness almost with obsession.

The Count came cautiously forward, glancing from the lovely figure of Lady Daphne to the gaunt, well-bred Major at her side. Daphne was so beautiful in her dark furs, the black lace of her veil thrown back over her close-fitting, dull-gold-threaded hat, and her face fair like a winter flower in a cranny of darkness. But on her face, that was smiling with a slow self-satisfaction of beauty and of knowledge that she was dangling the two men, and setting all the imprisoned officers wildly on the alert, the Count could read that acrid dissatisfaction and inefficiency. And he looked away to the livid scar on the Major's face.

'Count Dionys, I wanted to bring my husband to see you. May I introduce him to you? Major Apsley – Count Dionys Psanek.'

The two men shook hands, rather stiffly.

'I can sympathize with you being fastened up in this place,' said Basil in his slow, easy fashion. 'I hated it, I assure you, out there in the east.'

'But your conditions were much worse than mine,' smiled the Count.

'Well, perhaps they were. But prison is prison, even if it were heaven itself.'

'Lady Apsley has been the one angel of my heaven,' smiled the Count.

'I'm afraid I was as inefficient as most angels,' said she.

The small smile never left the Count's dark face. It was true as she said, he was low-browed, the black hair growing low on his brow, and his eyebrows making a thick bow above his dark eyes, which had again long black lashes, so that the upper part of his face seemed very dusky-black. His nose was small and somewhat translucent. There was a touch of mockery about him, which was intensified even by his small, energetic stature. He was still carefully dressed in the dark-blue uniform, whose shabbiness could not hinder the dark flame of life which seemed to glow through the cloth from his body. He was not thin – but still had a curious swarthy translucency of skin in his low-browed face.

'What would you have been more?' he laughed, making equivocal dark eyes at her.

'Oh, of course, a delivering angel – a cinema heroine,' she replied, closing her eyes and turning her face aside.

All the while the white-faced, tall Major watched the little man with a fixed, half-smiling scrutiny. The foreigner seemed not to notice. He turned to the Englishman.

'I am glad that I can congratulate you, Major Apsley, on your safe and happy return to your home.'

'Thanks. I hope I may be able to congratulate you in the same way before long.'

'Oh, yes,' said the Count. 'Before long I shall be shipped back.'

'Have you any news of your family?' interrupted Daphne.

'No news,' he replied briefly, with sudden gravity.

'It seems you'll find a fairish mess out in Austria,' said Basil.

'Yes, probably. It is what we had to expect,' replied the Count.

'Well, I don't know. Sometimes things do turn out for the

best – I feel that's as good as true in my case,' said the Major.

'Things have turned out for the best?' said the Count, with an intonation of polite inquiry.

'Yes. Just for me personally, I mean – to put it quite selfishly. After all, what we've learned is that a man can only speak for himself. And I feel it's been dreadful, but it's not been lost. It was an ordeal one had to go through,' said Basil.

'You mean the war?'

'The war and everything that went with it.'

'And when you've been through the ordeal?' politely inquired the Count.

'Why, you arrive at a higher state of consciousness, and therefore of life. And so, of course, at a higher plane of love. A surprisingly higher plane of love, that you had never suspected the existence of, before.'

The Count looked from Basil to Daphne – who was posing her head a little self-consciously.

'Then indeed the war has been a valuable thing,' he said.

'Exactly!' cried Basil. 'I am another man.'

'And Lady Apsley?' queried the Count.

'Oh' – her husband faced round to her – 'she is *absolutely* another woman – and *much* more wonderful, more marvellous.'

The Count smiled and bowed slightly.

'When we knew her ten years ago, we should have said then that it was impossible,' said he – 'for her to be more wonderful.'

'Oh, quite!' returned the husband. 'It always seems impossible. And the impossible is always happening. – As a matter of fact, I think the war has opened another cycle of life to us – a wider ring.'

'It may be so,' said the Count.

'You don't feel it so yourself?' The Major looked with his keen, white attention into the dark, low-browed face of the other man. The Count looked smiling at Daphne.

'I am only a prisoner still, Major, therefore I feel my ring quite small.'

'Yes, of course you do. Of course. – Well, I do hope you won't be a prisoner much longer. You must be dying to get back into your own country.'

'I shall be glad to be free. Also,' he smiled, 'I shall miss my prison and my visits from the angels.'

Even Daphne could not be sure he was mocking her. It was evident the visit was unpleasant to him. She could see he did not like Basil. Nay, more, she could feel that the presence of her tall, gaunt, idealistic husband was hateful to the little swarthy man. Bu he passed it all off in smiles and polite speeches.

On the other hand, Basil was as if fascinated by the Count. He watched him absorbedly all the time, quite forgetting Daphne. She knew this. She knew that she was quite gone out of her husband's consciousness, like a lamp that has been carried away into another room. There he stood completely in the dark, as far as she was concerned, and all his attention focused on the other man. On his pale, gaunt face was a fixed smile of amused attention.

'But don't you get awfully bored?' he said – 'between the visits?'

The Count looked up with an affectation of frankness.

'No, I do not,' he said. 'I can brood, you see, on the things that come to pass.'

'I think that's where the harm comes in,' replied the Major. 'One sits and broods, and is cut off from everything, and one loses one's contact with reality. That's the effect it had on me, being a prisoner.'

'Contact with reality – what is that?'

'Well – contact with anybody, really – or anything –'

'Why must one have contact?'

'Well, because one must,' said Basil.

The Count smiled slowly.

'But I can sit and watch fate flowing, like black water, deep down in my own soul,' he said. 'I feel that there, in the dark of my own soul, things are happening.'

'That may be. But whatever happens, it is only one thing, really. It is a contact between your own soul and the soul of one other being, or of many other beings. Nothing else can happen to man. – That's how I figured it out for myself. I may be wrong. But that's how I figured it out, when I was wounded and a prisoner.'

The Count's face had gone dark and serious.

'But is this contact an aim in itself?' he asked.

'Well,' said the Major – he had taken his degree in philosophy – 'it seems to me it is. It results inevitably in some form of activity. But the cause and the origin and the life-impetus of all action, activity, whether constructive or destructive, seems to me to be in the dynamic contact between human beings. You bring to pass a certain dynamic contact between men, and you get war. Another sort of dynamic contact, and you get them all building a cathedral, as they did in the Middle Ages –'

'But was not the war, or the cathedral, the real aim, and the emotional contact just the means?' said the Count.

'I don't think so,' said the Major, his curious white passion beginning to glow through his face. The three were seated in a little card-room, left alone by courtesy by the other men. Daphne was still draped in her dark, too-becoming drapery. But alas, she sat now ignored by both men. She might just as well have been an ugly little nobody, for all the notice that was taken of her. She sat in the window-seat of the dreary small room with a look of discontent on her exotic, rare face, that was like a delicate white and pink hot-house flower. From time to time she glanced with long, slow looks from man to man: from her husband, whose pallid, intense, white glowing face was pressed forward across the table; to the Count, who sat back in his chair, as if in opposition, and whose dark face seemed clubbed together in a dark, unwilling stare. Her husband was *quite* unaware of anything but his own white identity. But the Count still had a grain of secondary consciousness which hovered round and remained aware of the woman in the window-seat. The whole of his face, and his forward-looking attention was concentrated on Basil. But somewhere at the back of him he kept track of Daphne. She sat uneasy, in discontent, as women always do sit when men are consumed together in a combustion of words. At the same time, she followed the argument. It was curious that, while her sympathy at this moment was with the Count, it was her husband whose words she believed to be true. The contact, the emotional contact was the real thing, the so-called 'aim' was only a by-product. Even wars and cathedrals, in her mind, were only by-products.

The real thing was what the warriors and cathedral-builders had had in common, as a great uniting feeling: the thing they felt for one another: and for their women in particular, of course.

'There are a great many kinds of contact, nevertheless,' said Dionys.

'Well, do you know,' said the Major, 'it seems to me there is really only one supreme contact, the contact of love. Mind you, the love may take on an infinite variety of forms. And in my opinion, no form of love is wrong, so long as it *is* love, and you yourself *honour* what you are doing. Love has an extraordinary variety of forms! And that is all that there is in life, it seems to me. — But I grant you, if you deny the *variety* of love you deny love altogether. If you try to specialize love into one set of accepted feelings, you wound the very soul of love. Love *must* be multiform, else it is just tyranny, just death.'

'But why call it all *love*?' said the Count.

'Because it seems to me it *is* love: the great power that draws human beings together, no matter what the result of the contact may be. Of course there is hate, but hate is only the recoil of love.'

'Do you think the old Egypt was established on love?' asked Dionys.

'Why, of course! And perhaps the most multiform, the most comprehensive love that the world has seen. All that we suffer from now is that our way of love is narrow, exclusive, and therefore not love at all; more like death and tyranny.'

The Count slowly shook his head, smiling slowly and as if sadly.

'No,' he said. 'No. It is no good. You must use another word than love.'

'I don't agree at all,' said Basil.

'What word then?' blurted Daphne.

The Count looked at her.

'How shall I say? I know no word. But to a man something is absolute. His will, his good-will is absolute to him. Beyond the interference of any other creature.' He looked with his obstinate dark eyes into her eyes. It was curious, she disliked his words intensely, but she liked him. On the other hand, she believed absolutely what her husband said, yet her physical sympathy was against him.

'Do you agree, Daphne?' asked Basil.

'Not a bit,' she replied, with a heavy look at her husband.

'Nor I,' said Basil. 'It seems to me, if you love, you abandon your will, give it up to the soul of love. If you mean your will is the will to love, I quite agree. But if you mean that your will, your good-will, is purely autocratic – I don't agree, and never shall. It seems to me just there where we have gone wrong. Kaiser Wilhelm II wanted power –'[14]

'No, no,' said the Count. 'He was a mountebank. He had no conception of the sacredness of power.'

'He proved himself very dangerous.'

'Oh, yes. But peace can be even more dangerous still.'

'Tell me, then. Do you believe that you, as an aristocrat, should have feudal power over a few hundreds of other men, who happen to be born serfs, or not aristocrats?'

'Not as a hereditary aristocrat, but as a *man* who is by nature an aristocrat,' said the Count, 'it is my sacred duty to hold the destiny of other men in my hands, and to shape the issue. But I can never fulfil that duty till men willingly put their lives in my hands.'

'You don't expect them to, do you?' smiled Basil.

'At this moment, no.'

'Or at any moment!' The Major was sarcastic.

'At a certain moment the men who are really living will come beseeching to put their lives into the hands of the greater men among them, beseeching the greater men to take the sacred responsibility of power.'

'Do you think so? – Perhaps you mean men will at last begin to choose leaders whom they will *love*,' said Basil. 'I wish they would.'

'No, I mean that they will at last yield themselves before men who are greater than they: become vassals, by choice.'

'Vassals!' exclaimed Basil, smiling. 'You are still in the feudal ages, Count.'

'Vassals. Not to any hereditary aristocrat – Hohenzollern or Hapsburg or Psanek,' smiled the Count.[15] 'But to the man whose soul is born able, able to be alone, to choose and to command. At last the masses will come to such men and say, "You are greater than we. Be our lords. Take our life and our death in your hands, and dispose of us according to your will. Because we see a light in your face, and a burning on your mouth." '

The Major smiled for many moments, really piqued and amused, watching the Count, who did not turn a hair.

'I say, you must be awfully naïve, Count, if you believe the modern masses are ever going to behave like that. I assure you, they never will.'

'If they did,' said the Count, 'would you call it a new reign of love, or something else?'

'Well, of course, it would contain an element of love. There would have to be an element of love in their feeling for their leaders.'

'Do you think so? I thought that love assumed an equality in difference. I thought that love gave to every man the right to judge the acts of other men – "This was not an act of love, therefore it was wrong." Does not democracy, and love, give to every man that right?'

'Certainly,' said Basil.

'Ah, but my chosen aristocrat would say to those who chose him: "If you choose me, you give up forever your right to judge me. If you have truly chosen to follow me, you have thereby rejected all your right to criticize me. You can no longer either approve or disapprove of me. You have performed the sacred act of choice. Henceforth you can only obey." '

'They wouldn't be able to help criticizing, for all that,' said Daphne, blurting in her say.

He looked at her slowly, and for the first time in her life she was doubtful of what she was saying.

'The day of Judas,' he said, 'ends with the day of love.'[16]

Basil woke up from a sort of trance.

'I think, of course, Count,' he said, 'that it's an awfully amusing idea. A retrogression slap back to the Dark Ages.'

'Not so,' said the Count. 'Men – the mass of men – were never before free to perform the sacred act of choice. To-day – soon – they may be free.'

'Oh, I don't know. Many tribes chose their kings and chiefs.'

'Men have never before been quite free to choose: and to know what they are doing –'

'You mean they've only made themselves free in order voluntarily to saddle themselves with new lords and masters?'

'I do mean that.'

'In short, life is just a vicious circle –'

'Not at all. An ever-widening circle, as you say. Always more wonderful.'

'Well, it's all frightfully interesting and amusing – don't you think so, Daphne? By the way, Count, where would women be? Would they be allowed to criticize their husbands?'

'Only before marriage,' smiled the Count. 'Not after.'

'Splendid!' said Basil. 'I'm all for that bit of your scheme, Count. I hope you're listening, Daphne.'

'Oh, yes. But, then, I've only married *you*. I've got my right to criticize all the other men,' she said, in a dull, angry voice.

'Exactly. Clever of you! So the Count won't get off! Well now, what do you think of the Count's aristocratic scheme for the future, Daphne? Do you approve?'

'Not at all. But, then, little men have always wanted power,' she said cruelly.

'Oh, big men as well, for that matter,' said Basil, conciliatory.

'I have been told before,' smiled the Count, 'little men are always bossy. – I am afraid I have offended Lady Daphne?'

'No,' she said. 'Not really. I'm amused, really. But I always dislike any suggestion of bullying.'

'Indeed, so do I,' said he.

'The Count didn't mean bullying, Daphne,' said Basil. 'Come, there is really an allowable distinction between responsible power and bullying.'

'When men put their heads together about it,' said she.

She was haughty and angry, as if she were afraid of losing something. The Count smiled mischievously at her.

'You are offended, Lady Daphne? But why? You are safe from any spark of my dangerous and extensive authority.'

Basil burst into a roar of laughter.

'It *is* rather funny, you to be talking of power and of not being criticized,' he said. 'But I should like to hear more: I would like to hear more.'

As they drove home, he said to his wife:

'You know I like that little man. He's a quaint little bantam. And he sets one thinking.'

Lady Daphne froze to four degrees below zero, under the north-wind of this statement, and not another word was to be thawed out of her.

Curiously enough, it was now Basil who was attracted by the Count, and Daphne who was repelled. Not that she was so bound up in her husband. Not at all. She was feeling rather sore against men altogether. But as so often happens, in this life based on the wicked triangle, Basil could only follow his enthusiasm for the Count in his wife's presence. When the two men were alone together, they were awkward, resistant, they could hardly get out a dozen words to one another. When Daphne was there, however, to complete the circuit of the opposing currents, things went like a house on fire.

This, however, was not much consolation to Lady Daphne. Merely to sit as a passive medium between two men who are squibbing philosophical nonsense to one another: no, it was not good enough! She almost hated the Count: low-browed little man, belonging to the race of prehistoric slaves. But her grudge against her white-faced, spiritually intense husband was sharp as vinegar. Let down: she was let down between the pair of them.

What next? Well, what followed was entirely Basil's fault. The winter was passing: it was obvious the war was really over, that Germany was finished. The Hohenzollern had fizzled out like a very poor squib, the Hapsburg was popping feebly in obscurity, the Romanov was smudged out without a sputter.[17] So much for imperial royalty. Henceforth democratic peace.

The Count, of course, would be shipped back now like returned goods that had no market any more. There was a world peace ahead. A week or two, and Voynich Hall would be empty.

Basil, however, could not let matters follow their simple course. He was intrigued by the Count. He wanted to entertain him as a guest before he went. And Major Apsley could get anything in reason, at this moment. So he obtained permission for the poor little Count to stay a fortnight at Thoresway, before being shipped back to Austria. Earl Beveridge, whose soul was black as ink since the war, would never have allowed the little alien enemy to enter his house, had it not been for the hatred which had been aroused in him, during the last two years, by the degrading spectacle of the so-called patriots who had been howling their mongrel indecency in the public face. These mongrels had held the press and the British public in abeyance for almost two years. Their one aim was to degrade and humiliate anything that was proud or dignified remaining in England. It was almost the worst nightmare of all, this coming to the top of a lot of public filth which was determined to suffocate the souls of all dignified men.

Hence, the Earl, who never intended to be swamped by unclean scum, whatever else happened to him, stamped his heels in the ground and stood on his own feet. When Basil said to him, would he allow the Count to have a fortnight's decent peace in Thoresway before all was finished, Lord Beveridge gave a slow consent, scandal or no scandal. Indeed, it was really to defy scandal that he took such a step. For the thought of his dead boys was bitter to him: and the thought of England fallen under the paws of smelly mongrels was bitterer still.

Lord Beveridge was at Thoresway to receive the Count, who arrived escorted by Basil. The English Earl was a big, handsome man, rather heavy, with a dark, sombre face that would have been haughty if haughtiness had not been made so ridiculous. He was a passionate man, with a passionate man's sensitiveness, generosity, and instinctive overbearing. But *his* dark passionate nature, and his violent sensitiveness had been subjected now to fifty-five years' subtle repression, condemnation, repudiation, till he had almost come to believe in his own wrongness. His little, frail wife, all love for humanity, she was the genuine article. Himself, he was labelled selfish, sensual, cruel, etc., etc. So by now he always seemed to be standing aside, in the shadow, letting himself be obliterated by the pallid rabble of the democratic hurry. That was the impression he gave, of a man standing back, half-shamed, half-haughty, semi-hidden in the dark background.

He was a little on the defensive as Basil came in with the Count.

'Ah – how do you do, Count Psanek?' he said, striding largely forward and holding out his hand. Because he was the father of Daphne, the Count felt a certain tenderness for the taciturn Englishman.

'You do me too much honour, my lord, receiving me in your house,' said the small Count proudly.

The Earl looked at him slowly, without speaking: seemed to look down on him, in every sense of the words.

'We are still men, Count. We are not beasts altogether.'

'You wish to say that my countrymen are so very nearly beasts, Lord Beveridge?' smiled the Count, curling his fine nose.

Again the Earl was slow in replying.

'You have a low opinion of my manners, Count Psanek.'

'But perhaps a just appreciation of your meaning, Lord Beveridge,' smiled the Count, with the reckless little look of contempt on his nose.

Lord Beveridge flushed dark, with all his native anger offended.

'I am glad Count Psanek makes my own meaning clear to me,' he said.

'I beg your pardon a thousand times, Sir, if I give offence in doing so,' replied the Count.

The Earl went black, and felt a fool. He turned his back on the Count. And then he turned round again, offering his cigar-case.

'Will you smoke?' he said. There was kindness in his tone.

'Thank you,' said the Count, taking a cigar.

'I dare say,' said Lord Beveridge, 'that all men are beasts in some way. I am afraid I have fallen into the common habit of speaking by rote, and not what I really mean. Won't you take a seat?'

'It is only as a prisoner that I have learned that I am *not* truly a beast. No, I am myself. I am not a beast,' said the Count, seating himself.

The Earl eyed him curiously.

'Well,' he said, smiling, 'I suppose it is best to come to a decision about it.'

'It is necessary, if one is to be safe from vulgarity.'

The Earl felt a twinge of accusation. With his agate-brown, hard-looking eyes he watched the black-browed little Count.

'You are probably right,' he said.

But he turned his face aside.

There were five people at dinner – Lady Beveridge was there as hostess.

'Ah, Count Dionys,' she said with a sigh, 'do you really feel that the war is over?'

'Oh yes,' he replied quickly. '*This* war is over. The armies will go home. *Their* cannon will not sound any more. Never again like this.'

'Ah, I hope so,' she sighed.

'I am sure,' he said.

'You think there'll be no more war?' said Daphne.

For some reason she had made herself very fine, in her newest dress of silver and black and pink-chenille, with bare shoulders, and her hair fashionably done. The Count in his shabby uniform turned to her. She was nervous, hurried. Her slim white arm was near him, with the bit of silver at the shoulder. Her skin was white like a hot-house flower. Her lips moved hurriedly.

'Such a war as this there will never be again,' he said.

'What makes you so sure?' she replied, glancing into his eyes.

'The machine of war has got out of our control. We shall never start it again, till it has fallen to pieces. We shall be afraid.'

'Will everybody be afraid?' said she, looking down and pressing back her chin.

'I think so.'

'We will hope so,' said Lady Beveridge.

'Do you mind if I ask you, Count,' said Basil, 'what you feel about the way the war has ended – The way it has ended for *you*, I mean.'

'You mean that Germany and Austria have lost the war? It was bound to be. We have all lost the war. All Europe.'

'I agree there,' said Lord Beveridge.

'We've all lost the war –?' said Daphne, turning to look at him.

There was pain on his dark, low-browed face. He suffered having the sensitive woman beside him. Her skin had a hot-house

delicacy that made his head go round. Her shoulders were broad,
rather thin, but the skin was white and so sensitive, so hot-house
delicate. It affected him like the perfume of some white, exotic
flower. And she seemed to be sending her heart towards him. It
was as if she wanted to press her breast to his. From the breast
she loved him, and sent out love to him. And it made him
unhappy; he wanted to be quiet, and to keep his honour before
these hosts.

He looked into her eyes, his own eyes dark with knowledge and
pain. She, in her silence and her brief words seemed to be holding
them all under her spell. She seemed to have cast a certain
muteness on the table, in the midst of which she remained
silently master, leaning forward to her plate, and silently master-
ing them all.

'Don't I think we've all lost the war?' he replied, in answer to
her question. 'It was a war of suicide. Nobody could win it. It
was suicide for all of us.'

'Oh, I don't know,' she replied. 'What about America and
Japan?'

'They don't count. They only helped *us* to commit suicide.
They did not enter vitally.'

There was such a look of pain on his face, and such a sound
of pain in his voice, that the other three closed their ears, shut
off from attending. Only Daphne was making him speak. It was
she who was drawing the soul out of him, trying to read the future
in him as the augurs read the future in the quivering entrails of
the sacrificed beast. She looked direct into his face, searching his
soul.

'You think Europe has committed suicide?' she said.

'Morally.'

'Only morally?' came her slow, bronze-like words, so fatal.

'That is enough,' he smiled.

'Quite,' she said, with a slow droop of her eyelids. Then she
turned away her face. But he felt the heart strangling inside his
breast. What was she doing now? What was she thinking? She
filled him with uncertainty and with uncanny fear.

'At least,' said Basil, 'those infernal guns are quiet.'

'For ever,' said Dionys.

'I wish I could believe you, Count,' said the Major.

The talk became more general – or more personal. Lady Beveridge asked Dionys about his wife and family. He knew nothing save that they had gone to Hungary in 1916, when his own house was burnt down. His wife might even have gone to Bulgaria with Prince Bogorik. He did not know.

'But your children, Count!' cried Lady Beveridge.

'I do not know. Probably in Hungary, with their grandmother. I will go when I get back.'

'But have you never *written*? – never inquired?'

'I could not write. I shall know soon enough – everything.'

'You have no son?'

'No. Two girls.'

'Poor things!'

'Yes.'

'I say, isn't it an odd thing to have a ladybird on your crest?' asked Basil, to cheer up the conversation.

'Why queer? Charlemagne had bees. And it is a *Marienkäfer* – a Mary-beetle. The beetle of Our Lady. I think it is quite a heraldic insect, Major,' smiled the Count.

'You're proud of it?' said Daphne, suddenly turning to look at him again, with her slow, pregnant look.

'I am, you know. It has such a long genealogy – our spotted beetle. Much longer than the Psaneks. I think, you know, it is a descendant of the Egyptian scarabeus, which is a very mysterious emblem. So I connect myself with the Pharaohs: just through my ladybird.'

'You feel your ladybird has crept through so many ages,' she said.

'Imagine it!' he laughed.

'The scarab *is* a piquant insect,' said Basil.

'Do you know Fabre?'[18] put in Lord Beveridge. 'He suggests that the beetle rolling a little ball of dung before him, in a dry old field, must have suggested to the Egyptians the First Principle that set the globe rolling. And so the scarab became the symbol of the creative principle – or something like that.'

'That the earth is a tiny ball of dry dung is good,' said Basil.

'Between the claws of a ladybird,' added Daphne.

'That is what it is, to go back to one's origin,' said Lady Beveridge.

'Perhaps they meant that it was the principle of decomposition which first set the ball rolling,' said the Count.

'The ball would have to be *there* first,' said Basil.

'Certainly. But it hadn't started to roll. Then the principle of decomposition started it.' The Count smiled as if it were a joke.

'I am no Egyptologist,' said Lady Beveridge, 'so I can't judge.'

The Earl and Countess Beveridge left next day. Count Dionys was left with the two young people in the house. It was a beautiful Elizabethan mansion, not very large, but with those magical rooms that are all a twinkle of small-paned windows, looking out from the dark panelled interior. The interior was cosy, panelled to the ceiling, and the ceiling moulded and touched with gold. And then the great square bow of the window with its little panes intervening like magic between oneself and the world outside, the crest in stained glass crowning its colour, the broad window-seat cushioned in faded green. Dionys wandered round the house like a little ghost, through the succession of small and large, twinkling sitting-rooms and lounge rooms in front, down the long wide corridor with the wide stair-head at each end, and up the narrow stairs to the bedrooms above, and on to the roof.

It was early spring, and he loved to sit on the leaded, pale-grey roof that had its queer seats and slopes, a little pale world in itself. Then to look down over the garden and the sloping lawn to the ponds massed round with trees, and away to the elms and furrows and hedges of the shires. On the left of the house was the farmstead, with ricks and great-roofed barns and dark-red cattle. Away to the right, beyond the park, was a village among trees, and the spark of a grey church-spire.

He liked to be alone, feeling his soul heavy with its own fate. He would sit for hours watching the elm-trees standing in rows like giants, like warriors across the country. The Earl had told him that the Romans had brought these elms to Britain. And he seemed to see the spirit of the Romans in them still. Sitting there alone in the spring sunshine, in the solitude of the roof, he saw the glamour of this England of hedgerows and elm-trees, and the labourers with slow horses slowly drilling the seed, crossing the brown furrow: and the roofs of the village, with the church-steeple rising beside a big black yew-tree: and the chequer of fields away to the distance.

And the charm of the old manor around him, the garden with its grey stone walls and yew hedges – broad, broad yew hedges – and a peacock pausing to glitter and scream in the busy silence of an English spring, when celandines open their yellow under the hedges, and violets are in the secret, and by the broad paths of the garden polyanthus and crocuses vary the velvet and flame, and bits of yellow wallflower shake raggedly, with a wonderful triumphance, out of the cracks of the wall. There was a fold somewhere near, and he could hear the treble bleat of the growing lambs, and the deeper, contented baa-ing of the ewes.

This was Daphne's home, where she had been born. She loved it with an ache of affection. But now it was hard to forget her dead brothers. She wandered about in the sun, with two old dogs paddling after her. She talked with everybody, gardener, groom, stableman, with the farm-hands. That filled a large part of her life – straying round talking with the work-people. They were of course respectful to her – but not at all afraid of her. They knew she was poor, that she could not afford a car or anything. So they talked to her very freely: perhaps a little too freely. Yet she let it be. It was her one passion at Thoresway, to hear the dependants talk and talk – about everything. The curious feeling of intimacy across a breach fascinated her. Their lives fascinated her: what they thought, what they *felt*. – These, what they felt. That fascinated her. There was a gamekeeper she could have loved – an impudent, ruddy-faced, laughing, ingratiating fellow; she could have loved him, if he had not been isolated beyond the breach of his birth, her culture, her consciousness. Her *consciousness* seemed to make a great gulf between her and the lower classes, the unconscious classes. She accepted it as her doom. She could never meet in real contact anyone but a super-conscious, finished being like herself, or like her husband. Her father had some of the unconscious dark blood-warmth of primitive people. But he was like a man who is damned. And the Count, of course. The Count had something that was hot and invisible, a dark flame of life that might warm the cold white fire of her own blood. But – .

They avoided each other. All three, they avoided one another. Basil, too, went off alone. Or he immersed himself in poetry. Sometimes he and the Count played billiards. Sometimes all three walked in the park. Often Basil and Daphne walked to the village, to post. But truly, they avoided one another, all three. The days slipped by.

At evening they sat together in the small west-room that had books and a piano and comfortable shabby furniture of faded rose-coloured tapestry: a shabby room. Sometimes Basil read aloud. Sometimes the Count played the piano. And they talked. And Daphne stitch by stitch went on with a big embroidered bed-spread, which she might finish if she lived long enough. But they always went to bed early. They were nearly always avoiding one another.

Dionys had a bedroom in the east bay – a long way from the rooms of the others. He had a habit, when he was quite alone, of singing, or rather crooning to himself the old songs of his childhood. It was only when he felt he was quite alone: when other people seemed to fade out of him, and all the world seemed to dissolve into darkness, and there was nothing but himself, his own soul, alive in the middle of his own small night, isolate for ever. Then, half unconscious, he would croon in a small, high-pitched, squeezed voice, a sort of high dream-voice, the songs of his childhood dialect. It was a curious noise: the sound of a man who is alone in his own blood: almost the sound of a man who is going to be executed.

Daphne heard the sound one night when she was going downstairs again with the corridor lantern, to find a book. She was a bad sleeper, and her nights were a torture to her. She, too, like a neurotic, was nailed inside her own fretful self-consciousness. But she had a very keen ear. So she started as she heard the small, bat-like sound of the Count's singing to himself. She stood in the midst of the wide corridor, that was wide as a room, carpeted with a faded lavender-coloured carpet, with a piece of massive dark furniture at intervals by the wall, and an oak arm-chair, and sometimes a faded, reddish oriental rug. The big horn lantern which stood at nights at the end of the corridor she held in her hand. The intense 'peeping' sound of the Count, like a witch-craft, made her forget everything. She could not understand a word, of course. She could not understand the noise even. After listening for a long time, she went on downstairs. When she came back again he was still and the light was gone from under his door.

After this, it became almost an obsession to her to listen for him. She waited with fretful impatience for ten o'clock, when she could retire. She waited more fretfully still, for the maid to leave her, and for her husband to come and say good-night. Basil had the room across the corridor. And then in resentful impatience she waited for the sounds of the house to become still. Then she opened her door to listen.

And far away, as if from far, far away in the unseen, like a ventriloquist sound or a bat's uncanny peeping, came the frail, almost inaudible sound of the Count's singing to himself before he went to bed. It *was* inaudible to anyone but herself. But she, by concentration, seemed to hear supernaturally. She had a low arm-chair by the door, and there, wrapped in a huge old black silk shawl, she sat and listened. At first she could not hear; that is, she could hear the sound. But it was only a sound. And then, gradually, gradually she began to follow the thread of it. It was like a thread which she followed out of the world: out of the world. And as she went, slowly, by degrees, far, far away, down the thin thread of his singing, she knew peace – she knew forgetfulness. She could pass beyond the world, away beyond where her soul balanced like a bird on wings, and was perfected.

So it was, in her upper spirit. But underneath was a wild, wild yearning, actually to go, actually to be given. Actually to go, actually to die the death, actually to cross the border and be gone, to be gone. To be gone from this herself, from this Daphne, to be gone from father and mother, brothers and husband and home and land and world: to be gone. To be gone to the call from the beyond: the call. It was the Count calling. He was calling her. She was sure he was calling her. Out of herself, out of her world, he was calling her.

Two nights she sat just inside her room, by the open door, and listened. Then when he finished she went to sleep, a queer, light, bewitched sleep. In the day she was bewitched. She felt strange and light, as if pressure had been removed from around her. Some pressure had been clamped round her all her life. She had never realized it till now, now it was removed, and her feet felt so light, and her breathing delicate and exquisite. There had always been a pressure against her breathing. Now she breathed delicate and exquisite, so that it was a delight to breathe. Life came in exquisite breaths, quickly, as if it delighted to come to her.

The third night he was silent – though she waited and waited till the small hours of the morning. He was silent, he did not sing. And then she knew the terror and blackness of the feeling that he might never sing any more. She waited like one doomed, throughout the day. And when the night came she trembled. It was her greatest nervous terror, lest her spell should be broken, and she should be thrown back to what she was before.

Night came, and the kind of swoon upon her. Yes, and the call from the night. The call! She rose helplessly and hurried down the corridor. The light was under his door. She sat down in the big oak arm-chair that stood near his door, and huddled herself tight in her black shawl. The corridor was dim with the big, star-studded, yellow lantern-light. Away down she could see the lamp-light in her doorway; she had left her door ajar.

But she saw nothing. Only she wrapped herself close in the black shawl, and listened to the sound from the room. It called. Oh, it called her! Why could she not go? Why could she not cross through the closed door?

Then the noise ceased. And then the light went out, under the door of his room. Must she go back? Must she go back? Oh, impossible! As impossible as that the moon should go back on her tracks, once she has risen. Daphne sat on, wrapped in her black shawl. If it must be so, she would sit on through eternity. Return she never could.

And then began the most terrible song of all. It began with a rather dreary, slow, horrible sound, like death. And then suddenly came a real call – fluty, and a kind of whistling and a strange whirr at the changes, most imperative, and utterly inhuman. Daphne rose to her feet. And at the same moment up rose the whistling throb of a summons out of the death moan.

Daphne tapped low and rapidly at the door. 'Count! Count!' she whispered. The sound inside ceased. The door suddenly opened. The pale, obscure figure of Dionys.

'Lady Daphne!' he said in astonishment, automatically standing aside.

'You called,' she murmured rapidly, and she passed intent into his room.

'No, I did not call,' he said gently, his hand on the door still.

'Shut the door,' she said abruptly.

He did as he was bid. The room was in complete darkness. There was no moon outside. She could not see him.

'Where can I sit down?' she said abruptly.

'I will take you to the couch,' he said, putting out his hand and touching her in the dark. She shuddered.

She found the couch and sat down. It was quite dark.

'What are you singing?' she said rapidly.

'I am so sorry. I did not think anyone could hear.'

'What was it you were singing?'

'A song of my country.'

'Had it any words?'

'Yes, it is a woman who was a swan, and who loved a hunter by the marsh. So she became a woman and married him and had three children. Then in the night, one night the king of the swans called to her to come back, or else he would die. So slowly she turned into a swan again, and slowly she opened her wide, wide wings, and left her husband and her children.'

There was silence in the dark room. The Count had been really startled, startled out of his mood of the song into the day-mood of human convention. He was distressed and embarrassed by Daphne's presence in his dark room. She, however, sat on and did not make a sound. He, too, sat down in a chair by the window. It was everywhere dark. A wind was blowing in gusts outside. He could see nothing inside his room: only the faint, faint strip of light under the door. But he could feel her presence in the darkness. It was uncanny, to feel her near in the dark, and not to see any sign of her, nor to hear any sound.

She had been wounded in her bewitched state, by the contact with the every-day human being in him. But now she began to relapse into her spell, as she sat there in the dark. And he, too, in the silence, felt the world sinking away from him once more, leaving him once more alone on a darkened earth, with nothing between him and the infinite dark space. Except now her presence. Darkness answering to darkness, and deep answering to deep. An answer, near to him, and invisible.

But he did not know what to do. He sat still and silent as she was still and silent. The darkness inside the room seemed alive like blood. He had no power to move. The distance between them seemed absolute.

Then suddenly, without knowing, he went across in the dark, feeling for the end of the couch. And he sat beside her on the couch. But he did not touch her. Neither did she move. The darkness flowed about them thick like blood, and time seemed dissolved in it. They sat with the small, invisible distance between them, motionless, speechless, thoughtless.

Then suddenly he felt her finger-tips touch his arm, and a flame went over him that left him no more a man. He was something seated in flame, in flame unconscious, seated erect, like an Egyptian King-god in the statues. Her finger-tips slid down him, and she herself slid down in a strange silent rush, and he felt her face against his closed feet and ankles, her hands pressing his ankles. He felt her brow and hair against his ankles, her face against his feet, and there she clung in the dark, as if in space below him. He still sat erect and motionless. Then he bent forward and put his hand on her hair.

'Do you come to me?' he murmured. 'Do you come to me?'

The flame that enveloped him seemed to sway him silently.

'Do you really come to me?' he repeated. 'But we have nowhere to go.'

He felt his bare feet wet with her tears. Two things were struggling in him, the sense of eternal solitude, like space, and the rush of dark flame that would throw him out of his solitude, towards her.

He was thinking too. He was thinking of the future. He had no future in the world: of that he was conscious. He had no future in this life. Even if he lived on, it would only be a kind of enduring. – But he felt that in the after-life the inheritance was his. He felt the after-life belonged to him.

Future in the world he could not give her. Life in the world he had not to offer her. Better go on alone. Surely better go on alone.

But then the tears on his feet: and her face that would face him as he left her! No, no. – The next life was his. He was master of the after-life. Why fear for this life? Why not take the soul she offered him? Now and for ever, for the life that would come when they both were dead. Take her into the underworld. Take her into the dark Hades with him, like Francesca and Paolo.[19] And in hell hold her fast, queen of the underworld, himself master of the underworld. Master of the life to come. Father of the soul that would come after.

'Listen,' he said to her softly. 'Now you are mine. In the dark you are mine. And when you die you are mine. But in the day you are not mine, because I have no power in the day. In the night, in the dark, and in death, you are mine. And that is for ever. No matter if I must leave you. I shall come again from time to time. In the dark you are mine. But in the day I cannot claim you. I have no power in the day, and no place. So remember. When the darkness comes, I shall always be in the darkness of you. And as long as I live, from time to time I shall come to find you, when I am able to, when I am not a prisoner. But I shall have to go away soon. So don't forget – you are the night wife of the ladybird, while you live and even when you die.'

Later, when he took her back to her room he saw her door still ajar.

'You shouldn't leave a light in your room,' he murmured.

In the morning there was a curious remote look about him. He was quieter than ever, and seemed very far away. Daphne slept late. She had a strange feeling as if she had slipped off all her cares. She did not care, she did not grieve, she did not fret any more. All that had left her. She felt she could sleep, sleep, sleep – for ever. Her face, too, was very still, with a delicate look of virginity that she had never had before. She had always been Aphrodite, the self-conscious one. And her eyes, the green-blue, had been like slow, living jewels, resistant. Now they had un-folded from the hard flower-bud, and had the wonder, and the stillness of a quiet night.

Basil noticed it at once.

'You're different, Daphne,' he said. 'What are you thinking about?'

'I wasn't thinking,' she said, looking at him with candour.

'What were you doing then?'

'What does one do when one doesn't think? Don't make me puzzle it out, Basil.'

'Not a bit of it, if you don't want to.'

But he was puzzled by her. The sting of his ecstatic love for her seemed to have left him. Yet he did not know what else to do but to make love to her. She went very pale. She submitted to him, bowing her head because she was his wife. But she looked at him with fear, with sorrow, with real suffering. He could feel the heaving of her breast, and knew she was weeping. But there were no tears on her face, she was only death-pale. Her eyes were shut.

'Are you in pain?' he asked her.

'No, no!' She opened her eyes, afraid lest she had disturbed him. She did not want to disturb him.

He was puzzled. His own ecstatic, deadly love for her had received a check. He was out of the reckoning.

He watched her when she was with the Count. Then she seemed so meek – so maidenly – so different from what he had known of her. She was so still, like a virgin girl. And it was this quiet, intact quality of virginity in her which puzzled him most, puzzled his emotions and his ideas. He became suddenly ashamed to make love to her. And because he was ashamed, he said to her as he stood in her room that night:

'Daphne, are you in love with the Count?'

He was standing by the dressing-table, uneasy. She was seated in a low chair by the tiny dying wood-fire. She looked up at him with wide, slow eyes. Without a word, with wide, soft, dilated eyes she watched him. What was it that made him feel all con-fused? He turned his face aside, away from her wide, soft eyes.

'Pardon me, dear. I didn't intend to ask such a question. Don't take any notice of it,' he said. And he strode away and picked up a book. She lowered her head and gazed abstractedly into the fire, without a sound. Then he looked at her again, at her bright hair that the maid had plaited for the night. Her plait hung down over her soft pinkish wrap. His heart softened to her as he saw her sitting there. She seemed like his sister. The excitement of desire had left him, and now he seemed to see clear and feel true for the first time in his life. She was like a dear, dear sister to him. He felt that she was his blood-sister, nearer to him than he had imagined any woman could be. So near – so dear – and all the sex and the desire gone. He didn't want it – he hadn't wanted it. This new pure feeling was so much more wonderful.

He went to her side.

'Forgive me, darling,' he said, 'for having questioned you.'

She looked up at him with the wide eyes, without a word. His face was good and beautiful. Tears came to her eyes.

'You have the right to question me,' she said sadly.

'No,' he said. 'No, darling. I have no right to question you. – Daphne! Daphne darling! It shall be as *you* wish, between us. Shall it? Shall it be as you wish?'

'You are the husband, Basil,' she said sadly.

'Yes, darling. But –' he went on his knees beside her – 'perhaps, darling, something has changed in us. I feel as if I ought never to touch you again – as if I never *wanted* to touch you – in that way – I feel it was wrong, darling. Tell me what you think.'

'Basil – don't be angry with me.'

'It isn't anger – it's pure love, darling – it is.'

'Let us not come any nearer to one another than this, Basil – physically – shall we?' she said. 'And don't be angry with me, will you?'

'Why,' he said. 'I think myself the sexual part has been a mistake. I had rather love you – as I love now. I *know* that this is true love. The other was always a bit whipped up. I *know* I love you now, darling: now I'm free from that other. But what if it comes upon me, that other, Daphne?'

'I am always your wife,' she said quietly. 'I am always your wife. I want always to obey you, Basil: what you wish.'

'Give me your hand, dear.'

She gave him her hand. But the look in her eyes at the same time warned him and frightened him. He kissed her hand and left her.

It was to the Count she belonged. This had decided itself in her down to the depths of her soul. If she could not marry him and be his wife in the world, it had nevertheless happened to her for ever. She could no more question it. Question had gone out of her.

Strange how different she had become – a strange new quiescence. The last days were slipping past. He would be going away – Dionys: he with the still, remote face, the man she belonged to in the dark and in the light, for ever. He would be going away. He said it must be so. And she acquiesced. The grief was deep, deep inside her. He must go away. Their lives could not be one life, in this world's day. Even in her anguish she knew it was so. She knew he was right. He was for her infallible. He spoke the deepest soul in her.

She never *saw* him, as a lover. When she saw him, he was the little officer, a prisoner, quiet, claiming nothing in all the world. And when she went to him as his lover, his wife, it was always dark. She only knew his voice and his contact in darkness. 'My wife in darkness,' he said to her. And in this, too, she believed him. She would not have contradicted him, no, not for anything on earth: lest contradicting him, she should lose the dark treasure of stillness and bliss which she kept in her breast even when her heart was wrung with the agony of knowing he must go.

No, she had found this wonderful thing after she had heard him singing: she had suddenly collapsed away from her old self, into this darkness, this peace, this quiescence that was like a full dark river flowing eternally in her soul. She had gone to sleep from the *nuit blanche* of her days. And Basil, wonderful, had changed almost at once. She feared him, lest he might change back again. She would always have him to fear. But deep inside her she only feared for this love of hers for the Count: this dark, everlasting love that was like a full river flowing for ever inside her. Ah, let that not be broken.

She was so still inside her. She could sit so still, and feel the day slowly, richly changing to night. And she wanted nothing, she was short of nothing. If only Dionys need not go away! If only he need not go away!

But he said to her, the last morning:

'Don't forget me. Always remember me. I leave my soul in your hands and your womb. Nothing can ever separate us, unless we betray one another. If you have to give yourself to your husband, do so, and obey him. If you are true to me, innerly, innerly true, he will not hurt us. He is generous; be generous to him. And never fail to believe in me. Because even on the other side of death I shall be watching for you. I shall be king in Hades when I am dead. And you will be at my side. You will never leave me any more, in the after-death. So don't be afraid in life. Don't be afraid. If you have to cry tears, cry them. But in your heart of hearts know that I shall come again, and that I have taken you for ever. And so, in your heart of hearts be still, be still, since you are the wife of the ladybird.' He laughed as he left her, with his own beautiful, fearless laugh. But they were strange eyes that looked after him.

He went in the car with Basil back to Voynich Hall.

'I believe Daphne will miss you,' said Basil.

The Count did not reply for some moments.

'Well, if she does,' he said, 'there will be no bitterness in it.'

'Are you sure?' smiled Basil.

'Why – if we are sure of anything,' smiled the Count.

'She's changed, isn't she?'

'Is she?'

'Yes, she's quite changed since you came, Count.'

'She does not seem to me so very different from the girl of seventeen, whom I knew.'

'No – perhaps not. I didn't know her then. But she's very different from the wife I have known.'

'A regrettable difference –?'

'Well – no, not as far as she goes. She is much quieter inside herself. You know, Count, something of me died in the war. I feel it will take me an eternity to sit and think about it all.'

'I hope you may think it out to your satisfaction, Major.'

'Yes – I hope so, too. But that is how it has left me – feeling as if I needed eternity now to brood about it all, you know. Without the need to act – or even to love, really. I suppose love is action.'

'Intense action,' said the Count.

'Quite so. I know really how I feel. I only ask of life to spare me from further effort of action of any sort – even love. And then to fulfil myself, brooding through eternity. Of course, I don't mind *work*, mechanical action. That in itself is a form of inaction.'

'A man can only be happy following his own inmost need,' said the Count.

'Exactly!' said Basil. 'I will lay down the law for nobody, not even for myself. And live my day –'

'Then you will be happy in your own way. I find it so difficult to keep from laying the law down for myself,' said the Count. 'Only the thought of death and the after-life saves me from doing it any more.'

'As the thought of eternity helps me,' said Basil. 'I suppose it amounts to the same thing.'

St Mawr

LOU WITT had had her own way so long, that by the age of twenty-five she didn't know where she was. Having one's own way landed one completely at sea.

To be sure for a while she had failed in her grand love affair with Rico. And then she had had something really to despair about. But even that had worked out as she wanted. Rico had come back to her, and was dutifully married to her. And now, when she was twenty-five and he was three months older, they were a charming married couple. He flirted with other women still, to be sure. He wouldn't be the handsome Rico if he didn't. But she had 'got' him. Oh yes! You had only to see the uneasy backward glance at her, from his big blue eyes: just like a horse that is edging away from its master: to know how completely he was mastered.

She, with her odd little *museau*,[1] not exactly pretty, but very attractive; and her quaint air of playing at being well-bred, in a sort of charade game; and her queer familiarity with foreign cities and foreign languages; and the lurking sense of being an outsider everywhere, like a sort of gipsy, who is at home anywhere and nowhere: all this made up her charm and her failure. She didn't quite belong.

Of course she was American: Louisiana family, moved down to Texas. And she was moderately rich, with no close relation except her mother. But she had been sent to school in France when she was twelve, and since she had finished school, she had drifted from Paris to Palermo, Biarritz to Vienna and back via Munich to London, then down again to Rome. Only fleeting trips to her America.

So what sort of American was she, after all?

And what sort of European was she either? She didn't 'belong' anywhere. Perhaps most of all in Rome, among the artists and the Embassy people.

It was in Rome she had met Rico. He was an Australian, son of a government official in Melbourne, who had been made a baronet. So one day Rico would be Sir Henry, as he was the only son. Meanwhile he floated round Europe on a very small allowance – his father wasn't rich in capital – and was being an artist.

They met in Rome when they were twenty-two, and had a love affair in Capri. Rico was handsome, elegant, but mostly he had spots of paint on his trousers and he ruined a necktie pulling it off. He behaved in a most floridly elegant fashion, fascinating to the Italians. But at the same time he was canny and shrewd and sensible as any young poser could be and, on principle, good-hearted, anxious. He was anxious for his future, and anxious for his place in the world, he was poor, and suddenly wasteful in spite of all his tension of economy, and suddenly spiteful in spite of all his ingratiating efforts, and suddenly ungrateful in spite of all his burden of gratitude, and suddenly rude in spite of all his good manners, and suddenly detestable in spite of all his suave, courtier-like amiability.

He was fascinated by Lou's quaint aplomb, her experiences, her 'knowledge', her *gamine*[2] knowingness, her aloneness, her pretty clothes that were sometimes an utter failure, and her southern 'drawl' that was sometimes so irritating. That sing-song which was so American. Yet she used no Americanisms at all, except when she lapsed into her odd spasms of acid irony, when she was very American indeed!

And she was fascinated by Rico. They played to each other like two butterflies at one flower. They pretended to be very poor in Rome – he *was* poor: and very rich in Naples. Everybody stared their eyes out at them. And they had that love affair in Capri.

But they reacted badly on each other's nerves. She became ill. Her mother appeared. He couldn't stand Mrs Witt, and Mrs Witt couldn't stand him. There was a terrible fortnight. Then Lou was popped into a convent nursing-home in Umbria, and Rico dashed off to Paris. Nothing would stop him. He must go back to Australia.

He went to Melbourne, and while there his father died, leaving him a baronet's title and an income still very moderate. Lou

visited America once more, as the strangest of strange lands to
her. She came away disheartened, panting for Europe, and of
course, doomed to meet Rico again.

They couldn't get away from one another, even though in the
course of their rather restrained correspondence he informed her
that he was 'probably' marrying a very dear girl, friend of his
childhood, only daughter of one of the oldest families in Victoria.
Not saying much.

He didn't commit the probability, but reappeared in Paris,
wanting to paint his head off, terribly inspired by Cézanne and
by old Renoir.[3] He dined at the Rotonde with Lou and Mrs Witt,
who, with her queer democratic New Orleans sort of conceit
looked round the drinking-hall with savage contempt, and at
Rico as part of the show. 'Certainly,' she said, 'when these people
here have got any money, they fall in love on a full stomach. And
when they've got no money, they fall in love with a full pocket.
I never was in a more disgusting place. They take their love like
some people take after-dinner pills.'

She would watch with her arching, full, strong grey eyes,
sitting there erect and silent in her well-bought American
clothes. And then she would deliver some such charge of grape-
shot. Rico always writhed.

Mrs Witt hated Paris: 'this sordid, unlucky city', she called it.
'Something unlucky is bound to happen to me in this sinister,
unclean town,' she said. 'I feel *contagion* in the air of this place.
For heaven's sake, Louise, let us go to Morocco or somewhere.'

'No, mother dear, I can't now. Rico has proposed to me,
and I have accepted him. Let us think about a wedding, shall
we?'

'There!' said Mrs Witt. 'I said it was an unlucky city!'

And the peculiar look of extreme New Orleans annoyance
came round her sharp nose. But Lou and Rico were both twenty-
four years old, and beyond management. And anyhow, Lou
would be Lady Carrington. But Mrs Witt was exasperated
beyond exasperation. She would almost rather have preferred
Lou to elope with one of the great, evil porters at Les Halles. Mrs
Witt was at the age when the malevolent male in man, the old
Adam,[4] begins to loom above all the social tailoring. And yet –

and yet – it was better to have Lady Carrington for a daughter, seeing Lou was that sort.

There was a marriage, after which Mrs Witt departed to America, Lou and Rico leased a little old house in Westminster, and began to settle into a certain layer of English society. Rico was becoming an almost fashionable portrait painter. At least, *he* was almost fashionable, whether his portraits were or not. And Lou too was almost fashionable: almost a hit. There was some flaw somewhere. In spite of their appearances, both Rico and she would never quite go down in any society. They were the drifting artist sort. Yet neither of them was content to be of the drifting artist sort. They wanted to fit in, to make good.

Hence the little house in Westminster, the portraits, the dinners, the friends, and the visits. Mrs Witt came and sardonically established herself in a suite in a quiet but good-class hotel not far off. Being on the spot. And her terrible grey eyes with the touch of a leer looked on at the hollow mockery of things. As if *she* knew of anything better!

Lou and Rico had a curious exhausting effect on one another: neither knew why. They were fond of one another. Some inscrutable bond held them together. But it was a strange vibration of nerves, rather than of the blood. A nervous attachment, rather than a sexual love. A curious tension of will, rather than a spontaneous passion. Each was curiously under the domination of the other. They were a pair – they had to be together. Yet quite soon they shrank from one another. This attachment of the will and the nerves was destructive. As soon as one felt strong, the other felt ill. As soon as the ill one recovered strength, down went the one who had been well.

And soon, tacitly, the marriage became more like a friendship, Platonic. It was a marriage, but without sex. Sex was shattering and exhausting, they shrank from it, and became like brother and sister. But still they were husband and wife. And the lack of physical relation was a secret source of uneasiness and chagrin to both of them. They would neither of them accept it. Rico looked with contemplative, anxious eyes at other women.

Mrs Witt kept track of everything, watching as it were from outside the fence, like a potent well-dressed demon, full of uncanny energy and a shattering sort of sense. She said little: but her small, occasionally biting remarks revealed her attitude of contempt for the *ménage*.[5]

Rico entertained clever and well-known people. Mrs Witt would appear, in her New York gowns and few good jewels. She was handsome, with her vigorous grey hair. But, her heavy-lidded grey eyes were the despair of any hostess. They looked too many shattering things. And it was but too obvious that these clever, well-known English people got on her nerves terribly, with their finickiness and their fine-drawn discriminations. She wanted to put her foot through all these fine-drawn distinctions. She thought continually of the house of her girlhood, the planta-tion, the negroes, the planters: the sardonic grimness that under-lay all the big, shiftless life. And she wanted to cleave with some of this grimness of the big, dangerous America, into the safe, finicky drawing-rooms of London. So naturally she was not popular.

But being a woman of energy, she had to do *something*. During the latter part of the war she had worked in the American Red Cross in France, nursing. She loved men – real men. But, on close contact, it was difficult to define what she meant by 'real' men. She never met any.

Out of the *débâcle* of the war she had emerged with an odd piece of *débris*, in the shape of Gerónimo Trujillo. He was an American, son of a Mexican father and a Navajo Indian mother, from Arizona. When you knew him well, you recognized the real half-breed, though at a glance he might pass as a sunburnt citizen of any nation, particularly of France. He looked like a certain sort of Frenchman, with his curiously-set dark eyes, his straight black hair, his thin black moustache, his rather long cheeks, and his almost slouching, diffident, sardonic bearing. Only when you knew him, and looked right into his eyes, you saw that un-forgettable glint of the Indian.

He had been badly shell-shocked, and was for a time a wreck. Mrs Witt, having nursed him into convalescence, asked him where he was going next. He didn't know. His father and mother were dead, and he had nothing to take him back to Phoenix, Arizona. Having had an education in one of the Indian high schools, the unhappy fellow had now no place in life at all. Another of the many misfits.

There was something of the Paris *Apache*⁶ in his appearance: but he was all the time withheld, and nervously shut inside himself. Mrs Witt was intrigued by him.

'Very well, Phoenix,' she said, refusing to adopt his Spanish name, 'I'll see what I can do.'

What she did was to get him a place on a sort of manor farm, with some acquaintances of hers. He was very good with horses, and had a curious success with turkeys and geese and fowls.

Some time after Lou's marriage, Mrs Witt reappeared in London, from the country, with Phoenix in tow, and a couple of horses. She had decided that she would ride in the Park in the morning, and see the world that way. Phoenix was to be her groom.

So, to the great misgiving of Rico, behold Mrs Witt in splendidly tailored habit and perfect boots, a smart black hat on her smart grey hair, riding a grey gelding as smart as she was, and looking down her conceited, inquisitive, scornful, aristocratic-democratic Louisiana nose at the people in Piccadilly, as she crossed to the Row,⁷ followed by the taciturn shadow of Phoenix, who sat on a chestnut with three white feet as if he had grown there.

Mrs Witt, like many other people, always expected to find the real *beau monde* and the real *grand monde*⁸ somewhere or other. She didn't quite give in to what she saw in the Bois de Boulogne,⁹ or in Monte Carlo, or on the Pincio;¹⁰ all a bit shoddy, and not very *beau* and not at all *grand*. There she was, with her grey eagle eye, her splendid complexion and her weapon-like health of a woman of fifty, dropping her eyelids a little, very slightly nervous, but completely prepared to despise the *monde* she was entering in Rotten Row.

In she sailed, and up and down that regatta-canal of horsemen and horsewomen under the trees of the Park. And yes, there were lovely girls with fair hair down their backs, on happy ponies. And awfully well-groomed papas, and tight mamas who looked as if they were going to pour tea between the ears of their horses, and converse with banal skill, one eye on the teapot, one on the visitor with whom she was talking, and all the rest of her hostess' argus-eyes[11] upon everybody in sight. The alert argus capability of the English matron was startling and a bit horrifying. Mrs Witt would at once think of the old negro mammies, away in Louisiana. And her eyes became dagger-like as she watched the clipped, shorn, mincing young Englishmen. She refused to look at the prosperous Jews.

It was still the days before motor-cars were allowed in the Park, but Rico and Lou, sliding round Hyde Park Corner and up Park Lane in their car would watch the steely horsewoman and the saturnine groom with a sort of dismay. Mrs Witt seemed to be pointing a pistol at the bosom of every other horseman or horsewoman, and announcing: *Your virility or your life! Your femininity or your life!* She didn't know herself what she really wanted them to be: but it was something as democratic as Abraham Lincoln[12] and as aristocratic as a Russian Czar, as highbrow as Arthur Balfour,[13] and as taciturn and unideal as Phoenix. Everything at once.

There was nothing for it: Lou had to buy herself a horse and ride at her mother's side, for very decency's sake. Mrs Witt was *so* like a smooth, levelled, gunmetal pistol, Lou had to be a sort of sheath. And she really looked pretty, with her clusters of dark, curly, New Orleans hair, like grapes, and her quaint brown eyes that didn't quite match, and that looked a bit sleepy and vague, and at the same time quick as a squirrel's. She was slight and elegant, and a tiny bit rakish, and somebody suggested she might be on the movies.

Nevertheless, they were in the society columns next morning – *two new and striking figures in the Row this morning were Lady Henry Carrington and her mother Mrs Witt*, etc. And Mrs Witt liked it, let her say what she might. So did Lou. Lou liked it immensely. She simply luxuriated in the sun of publicity.

'Rico dear, you must get a horse.'

The tone was soft and southern and drawling, but the overtone had a decisive finality. In vain Rico squirmed – he had a way of writhing and squirming which perhaps he had caught at Oxford. In vain he protested that he couldn't ride, and that he didn't care for riding. He got quite angry, and his handsome arched nose tilted and his upper lip lifted from his teeth, like a dog that is going to bite. Yet daren't quite bite.

And that was Rico. He daren't quite bite. Not that he was really afraid of the others. He was afraid of himself, once he let himself go. He might rip up in an eruption of life-long anger all this pretty-pretty picture of a charming young wife and a delightful little home and a fascinating success as a painter of fashionable, and at the same time 'great' portraits: with colour, wonderful colour, and at the same time, form, marvellous form. He had composed this little *tableau vivant*[14] with great effort. He didn't want to erupt like some suddenly wicked horse – Rico was really more like a horse than a dog, a horse that might go nasty any moment. For the time, he was good, very good, dangerously good.

'Why, Rico dear, I thought you used to ride so much, in Australia, when you were young? Didn't you tell me all about it, hm?' – and as she ended on that slow, singing *hm?*, which acted on him like an irritant and a drug, he knew he was beaten.

Lou kept the sorrel mare in a mews just behind the house in Westminster, and she was always slipping round to the stables. She had a funny little nostalgia for the place: something that really surprised her. She had never had the faintest notion that she cared for horses and stables and grooms. But she did. She was fascinated. Perhaps it was her childhood's Texas associations come back. Whatever it was, her life with Rico in the elegant little house, and all her social engagements seemed like a dream, the substantial reality of which was those mews in Westminster, her sorrel mare, the owner of the mews, Mr Saintsbury, and the grooms he employed. Mr Saintsbury was a horsey elderly man like an old maid, and he loved the sound of titles.

'Lady Carrington! – well I never! You've come to us for a bit of company again, I see. I don't know whatever we shall do if you go away, we shall be that lonely!' and he flashed his old-maid's smile at her. 'No matter how grey the morning, your ladyship would make a beam of sunshine. Poppy is all right, I think . . .'

Poppy was the sorrel mare with the no white feet and the startled eye, and she was all right. And Mr Saintsbury was smiling with his old-maid's mouth, and showing all his teeth.

'Come across with me, Lady Carrington, and look at a new horse just up from the country. I think he's worth a look, and I believe you have a moment to spare, your Ladyship.'

Her Ladyship had too many moments to spare. She followed the sprightly, elderly, cleanshaven man across the yard to a loose box, and waited while he opened the door.

In the inner dark she saw a handsome bay horse with his clean ears pricked like daggers from his naked head as he swung handsomely round to stare at the open doorway. He had big, black, brilliant eyes, with a sharp questioning glint, and that air of tense, alert quietness which betrays an animal that can be dangerous.

'Is he quiet?' Lou asked.

'Why – yes – my Lady! He's quiet, with those that know how to handle him. *Cup! my boy! Cup, my beauty! Cup then! St Mawr!*'[15]

Loquacious even with the animals, he went softly forward and laid his hand on the horse's shoulder, soft and quiet as a fly settling. Lou saw the brilliant skin of the horse crinkle a little in apprehensive anticipation, like the shadow of the descending hand on a bright red-gold liquid. But then the animal relaxed again.

'Quiet with those that know how to handle him, and a bit of a ruffian with those that don't. Isn't that the ticket, eh, St Mawr?'

'What is his name?' Lou asked.

The man repeated it, with a slight Welsh twist – 'He's from the Welsh borders, belonging to a Welsh gentleman, Mr Griffith Edwards. But they're wanting to sell him.'

'How old is he?' asked Lou.

'About seven years – seven years and five months,' said Mr Saintsbury, dropping his voice as if it were a secret.

'Could one ride him in the Park?'

'Well – yes! I should say a gentleman who knew how to handle him could ride him very well and make a very handsome figure in the Park.'

Lou at once decided that this handsome figure should be Rico's. For she was already half in love with St Mawr. He was of such a lovely red-gold colour, and a dark, invisible fire seemed to come out of him. But in his big black eyes there was a lurking afterthought. Something told her that the horse was not quite happy: that somewhere deep in his animal consciousness lived a dangerous, half-revealed resentment, a diffused sense of hostility. She realized that he was sensitive, in spite of his flaming, healthy strength, and nervous with a touchy uneasiness that might make him vindictive.

'Has he got any tricks?' she asked.

'Not that I know of, my Lady: not tricks exactly. But he's one of these temperamental creatures, as they say. Though *I* say, every horse is temperamental, when you come down to it. But this one, it is as if he was a trifle raw somewhere. Touch this raw spot, and there's no answering for him.'

'Where is he raw?' asked Lou, somewhat mystified. She thought he might really have some physical sore.

'Why, that's hard to say, my Lady. If he was a human being, you'd say something had gone wrong in his life. But with a horse it's not that, exactly. A high-bred animal like St Mawr needs understanding, and I don't know as anybody has quite got the hang of him. I confess I haven't myself. But I do realize that he is a special animal and needs a special sort of touch, and I'm willing he should have it, did I but know exactly what it is.'

She looked at the glowing bay horse that stood there with his ears back, his face averted, but attending as if he were some lightning conductor. He was a stallion. When she realized this, she became more afraid of him.

'Why does Mr Griffith Edwards want to sell him?' she asked.

'Well – my Lady – they raised him for stud purposes – but he didn't answer. There are horses like that: don't seem to fancy the mares, for some reason. Well anyway, they couldn't keep him for the stud. And as you see, he's a powerful, beautiful hackney, clean as a whistle, and eaten up with his own power. But there's no putting him between the shafts. He won't stand it. He's a fine saddle-horse, beautiful action, and lovely to ride. But he's got to be handled, and there you are.'

Lou felt there was something behind the man's reticence.

'Has he ever made a break?' she asked, apprehensive.

'Made a break?' replied the man. 'Well, if I must admit it, he's had two accidents. Mr Griffith Edwards' son rode him a bit wild, away there in the Forest of Dean, and the young fellow had his skull smashed in, against a low oak bough. Last autumn, that was. And some time back, he crushed a groom against the side of the stall – injured him fatally. But they were both accidents, my Lady. Things will happen.'

The man spoke in a melancholy, fatalistic way. The horse, with his ears laid back, seemed to be listening tensely, his face averted. He looked like something finely bred and passionate, that has been judged and condemned.

'May I say *how do you do*?' she said to the horse drawing a little nearer in her white, summery dress, and lifting her hand that glittered with emeralds and diamonds.

He drifted away from her, as if some wind blew him. Then he ducked his head, and looked sideways at her, from his black, full eye.

'I think I'm all right,' she said, edging nearer, while he watched her.

She laid her hand on his side, and gently stroked him. Then she stroked his shoulder, and then the hard, tense arch of his neck. And she was startled to feel the vivid heat of his life come through to her, through the lacquer of red-gold gloss. So slippery with vivid, hot life!

She paused, as if thinking, while her hand rested on the horse's sun-arched neck. Dimly, in her weary young-woman's soul, an ancient understanding seemed to flood in.

She wanted to buy St Mawr.

'I think,' she said to Saintsbury, 'if I can, I will buy him.'

The man looked at her long and shrewdly.

'Well, my Lady,' he said at last, 'there shall be nothing kept from you. But what would your Ladyship do with him, if I may make so bold?'

'I don't know,' she replied, vaguely. 'I might take him to America.'

The man paused once more, then said:

'They say it's been the making of some horses, to take them

over the water, to Australia or such places. It might repay you
– you never know.'

She wanted to buy St Mawr. She wanted him to belong to her.
For some reason the sight of him, his power, his alive, alert
intensity, his unyieldingness, made her want to cry.

She never did cry: except sometimes with vexation, or to get
her own way. As far as weeping went, her heart felt as dry as a
Christmas walnut. What was the good of tears, anyhow? You had
to keep on holding on, in this life, never give way, and never give
in. Tears only left one weakened and ragged.

But now, as if that mysterious fire of the horse's body had split
some rock in her, she went home and hid herself in her room,
and just cried. The wild, brilliant, alert head of St Mawr seemed
to look at her out of another world. It was as if she had had a
vision, as if the walls of her own world had suddenly melted
away, leaving her in a great darkness, in the midst of which the
large, brilliant eyes of that horse looked at her with demonish
question, while his naked ears stood up like daggers from the
naked lines of his inhuman head, and his great body glowed red
with power.

What was it? Almost like a god looking at her terribly out of
the everlasting dark, she had felt the eyes of that horse; great,
glowing, fearsome eyes, arched with a question, and containing
a white blade of light like a threat. What was his non-human
question, and his uncanny threat? She didn't know. He was some
splendid demon, and she must worship him.

She hid herself away from Rico. She could not bear the
triviality and superficiality of her human relationships. Looming
like some god out of the darkness was the head of that horse, with
the wide, terrible, questioning eyes. And she felt that it forbade
her to be her ordinary, commonplace self. It forbade her to be
just Rico's wife, young Lady Carrington, and all that.

It haunted her, the horse. It had looked at her as she had never
been looked at before: terrible, gleaming, questioning eyes arching out of darkness, and backed by all the fire of that great ruddy
body. What did it mean, and what ban did it put upon her? She
felt it put a ban on her heart: wielded some uncanny authority
over her, that she dared not, could not understand.

No matter where she was, what she was doing, at the back of her consciousness loomed a great, over-aweing figure out of a dark background: St Mawr, looking at her without really seeing her, yet gleaming a question at her, from his wide terrible eyes, and gleaming a sort of menace, doom. Master of doom, he seemed to be!

'You are thinking about something, Lou dear!' Rico said to her that evening.

He was so quick and sensitive to detect her moods – so exciting in this respect. And his big, slightly prominent blue eyes, with the whites a little bloodshot, glanced at her quickly, with searching, and anxiety, and a touch of fear, as if his conscience were always uneasy. He, too, was rather like a horse – but for ever quivering with a sort of cold, dangerous mistrust, which he covered with anxious love.

At the middle of his eyes was a central powerlessness, that left him anxious. It used to touch her to pity, that central look of powerlessness in him. But now, since she had seen the full, dark, passionate blaze of power and of different life in the eyes of the thwarted horse, the anxious powerlessness of the man drove her mad. Rico was so handsome, and he was so self-controlled, he had a gallant sort of kindness and a real worldly shrewdness. One had to admire him: at least *she* had to.

But after all, and after all, it was a bluff, an attitude. He kept it all working in himself, deliberately. It was an attitude. She read psychologists who said that everything was an attitude. Even the best of everything. But now she realized that, with men and women, everything is an attitude only when something else is lacking. Something is lacking and they are thrown back on their own devices. That black fiery flow in the eyes of the horse was not 'attitude'. It was something much more terrifying, and real, the only thing that was real. Gushing from the darkness in menace and question, and blazing out in the splendid body of the horse.

'Was I thinking about something?' she replied, in her slow, amused, casual fashion. As if everything was so casual and easy to her. And so it was, from the hard, polished side of herself. But that wasn't the whole story.

'I think you were, Loulina. May we offer the penny?'

'Don't trouble,' she said. 'I was thinking, if I was thinking of anything, about a bay horse called St Mawr.' – Her secret *almost* crept into her eyes.

'The name is awfully attractive,' he said with a laugh.

'Not so attractive as the creature himself. I'm going to buy him.'

'Not really!' he said. 'But why?'

'He *is* so attractive. I'm going to buy him for you.'

'For *me! Darling!* how you do take me for granted. He may not be in the least attractive to me. As you know, I have hardly any feeling for horses at all. – Besides, how much does he cost?'

'That I don't know, Rico dear. But I'm sure you'll love him, for my sake.' – She felt, now, she was merely playing for her own ends.

'Lou dearest, *don't* spend a fortune on a horse for me, which I *don't* want. Honestly, I prefer a car.'

'Won't you ride with me in the Park, Rico?'

'Honestly, dear Lou, I don't want to.'

'Why not, dear boy? You'd look so beautiful. I wish you would. – And anyhow, come with me to look at St Mawr.'

Rico was divided. He had a certain uneasy feeling about horses. At the same time, he *would* like to cut a handsome figure in the Park.

They went across to the mews. A little Welsh groom was watering the brilliant horse.

'Yes dear, he certainly *is* beautiful: such a marvellous colour! Almost orange! But rather large, I should say, to ride in the Park.'

'No, for you he's perfect. You are so tall.'

'He'd be marvellous in a Composition. That colour!'

And all Rico could do was to gaze with the artist's eye at the horse, with a glance at the groom.

'Don't you think the man is rather fascinating too?' he said, nursing his chin artistically and penetratingly.

The groom, Lewis, was a little, quick, rather bow-legged, loosely-built fellow of indeterminate age, with a mop of black hair and a little black beard. He was grooming the brilliant St Mawr, out in the open. The horse was really glorious: like a marigold, with a pure golden sheen, a shimmer of green-gold lacquer, upon a burning red-orange. There on the shoulder you saw the yellow lacquer glisten. Lewis, a little scrub of a fellow, worked absorbedly, unheedingly at the horse, with an absorption that was almost ritualistic. He seemed the attendant shadow of the ruddy animal.

'He goes with the horse,' said Lou. 'If we buy St Mawr we get the man thrown in.'

'They'd be *so* amusing to paint: such an extraordinary contrast! But darling, I *hope* you won't insist on buying the horse. It's so frightfully expensive.'

'Mother will help me. — You'd look so well on him, Rico.'

'If ever I dared take the liberty of getting on his back —!'

'Why not?' She went quickly across the cobbled yard.

'Good morning, Lewis. How is St Mawr?'

Lewis straightened himself and looked at her from under the falling mop of his black hair.

'All right,' he said.

He peered straight at her from under his overhanging black hair. He had pale grey eyes, that looked phosphorescent, and suggested the eyes of a wild cat peering intent from under the darkness of some bush where it lies unseen. Lou, with her brown, unmatched, oddly perplexed eyes, felt herself found out. — 'He's a common little fellow,' she thought to herself. 'But he knows a woman and a horse, at sight.' — Aloud she said, in her southern drawl:

'How do you think he'd be with Sir Henry?'

Lewis turned his remote, coldly watchful eyes on the young baronet. Rico was tall and handsome and balanced on his hips. His face was long and well-defined, and with the hair taken straight back from the brow. It seemed as well-made as his clothing, and as perpetually presentable. You could not imagine his face dirty, or scrubby and unshaven, or bearded, or even moustached. It was perfectly prepared for social purposes. If his head had been cut off, like John the Baptist's, it would have been a thing complete in itself, would not have missed the body in the least. The body was perfectly tailored. The head was one of the famous 'talking heads' of modern youth, with eyebrows a trifle

Mephistophelian, large blue eyes a trifle bold, and curved mouth thrilling to death to kiss.

Lewis, the groom, staring from between his bush of hair and his beard, watched like an animal from the underbrush. And Rico was still sufficiently a colonial to be uneasily aware of the underbrush, uneasy under the watchfulness of the pale grey eyes, and uneasy in that man-to-man exposure which is characteristic of the democratic colonies and of America. He knew he must ultimately be judged on his merits as a man, alone without a background: an ungarnished colonial.

This lack of background, this defenceless man-to-man business which left him at the mercy of every servant, was bad for his nerves. For he was *also* an artist. He bore up against it in a kind of desperation, and was easily moved to rancorous resentment. At the same time he was free of the Englishman's watertight *suffisance*.[16] He really was aware that he would have to hold his own all alone, thrown alone on his own defences in the universe. The extreme democracy of the Colonies had taught him this.

And this, the little aboriginal Lewis recognized in him. He recognized also Rico's curious hollow misgiving, fear of some deficiency in himself, beneath all his handsome, young-hero appearance.

'He'd be all right with anybody as would meet him half-way,' said Lewis, in the quick Welsh manner of speech, impersonal.

'You hear, Rico!' said Lou in her sing-song, turning to her husband.

'Perfectly, darling!'

'Would you be willing to meet St Mawr half-way, hm?'

'All the way, darling! Mahomet would go *all* the way to that mountain.[17] Who would dare do otherwise?'

He spoke with a laughing, yet piqued sarcasm.

'Why, I think St Mawr would understand perfectly,' she said in the soft voice of a woman haunted by love. And she went and laid her hand on the slippery, life-smooth shoulder of the horse. He, with his strange equine head lowered, its exquisite fine lines reaching a little snake-like forward, and his ears a little back, was watching her sideways, from the corner of his eye. He was in a state of absolute mistrust, like a cat crouching to spring.

'St Mawr!' she said. 'St Mawr! What is the matter? Surely you and I are all right!'

And she spoke softly, dreamily stroked the animal's neck. She could feel a response gradually coming from him. But he would not lift up his head. And when Rico suddenly moved nearer, he sprang with a sudden jerk backwards, as if lightning exploded in his four hoofs.

The groom spoke a few low words in Welsh. Lou, frightened, stood with lifted hand arrested. She had been going to stroke him.

'Why did he do that,' she said.

'They gave him a beating once or twice,' said the groom in a neutral voice, 'and he doesn't forget.'

She could hear a neutral sort of judgement in Lewis' voice. And she thought of the 'raw spot'.

Not any raw spot at all. A battle between two worlds. She realized that St Mawr drew his hot breaths in another world from Rico's, from our world. Perhaps the old Greek horses had lived in St Mawr's world. And the old Greek heroes, even Hippolytus,[18] had known it.

With their strangely naked equine heads, and something of a snake in their way of looking round, and lifting their sensitive, dangerous muzzles, they moved in a prehistoric twilight where all things loomed phantasmagoric, all on one plane, sudden presences suddenly jutting out of the matrix. It was another world, an older, heavily potent world. And in this world the horse was swift and fierce and supreme, undominated and unsurpassed. – 'Meet him half-way,' Lewis said. But half-way across from our human world to that terrific equine twilight was not a small step. It was a step, she knew, that Rico would never take. She knew it. But she was prepared to sacrifice Rico.

St Mawr was bought, and Lewis was hired along with him. At first, Lewis rode him behind Lou, in the Row, to get him going. He behaved perfectly.

Phoenix, the half Indian, was very jealous when he saw the black-bearded Welsh groom on St Mawr.

'What horse you got there?' he asked, looking at the other man

with the curious unseeing stare in his hard, Navajo eyes, in which
the Indian glint moved like a spark upon a dark chaos. In
Phoenix's high-boned face there was all the race-misery of the
dispossessed Indian, with an added blankness left by shell-shock.
But at the same time, there was that unyielding, save to death,
which is characteristic of his tribe; his mother's tribe. Difficult
to say what subtle thread bound him to the Navajo, and made
his destiny a Red Man's destiny still.

They were a curious pair of grooms, following the correct, and
yet extraordinary, pair of American mistresses. Mrs Witt and
Phoenix both rode with long stirrups and straight leg, sitting
close to the saddle, without posting. Phoenix looked as if he and
the horse were all one piece, he never seemed to rise in the saddle
at all, neither trotting nor galloping, but sat like a man riding
bareback. And all the time he stared round, at the riders in the
Row, at the people grouped outside the rail, chatting, at the
children walking with their nurses, as if he were looking at a
mirage, in whose actuality he never believed for a moment.
London was all a sort of dark mirage to him. His wide, nervous-
looking brown eyes with a smallish brown pupil, that showed the
white all round, seemed to be focused on the far distance, as if
he could not see things too near. He was watching the pale deserts
of Arizona shimmer with moving light, the long mirage of a
shallow lake ripple, the great pallid concave of earth and sky
expanding with interchanged light. And a horse-shape loom
large and portentous in the mirage, like some prehistoric beast.

That was real to him: the phantasm of Arizona. But this
London was something his eye passed over, as a false mirage.

He looked too smart in his well-tailored groom's clothes, so
smart, he might have been one of the satirized new-rich. Perhaps
it was a sort of half-breed physical assertion that came through
his clothing, the savage's physical assertion of himself. Anyhow,
he looked 'common', rather horsey and loud.

Except his face. In the golden suavity of his high-boned
Indian face, that was hairless, with hardly any eyebrows, there
was a blank, lost look that was almost touching. The same
startled blank look was in his eyes. But in the smallish dark pupils
the dagger-point of light still gleamed unbroken.

He was a good groom, watchful, quick, and on the spot in an instant if anything went wrong. He had a curious quiet power over the horses, unemotional, unsympathetic, but silently potent. In the same way, watching the traffic of Piccadilly with his blank, glinting eye, he would calculate everything instinctively, as if it were an enemy, and pilot Mrs Witt by the strength of his silent will. He threw around her the tense watchfulness of her own America, and made her feel at home.

'Phoenix,' she said, turning abruptly in her saddle as they walked the horses past the sheltering policeman at Hyde Park Corner, 'I can't tell you how glad I am to have something a hundred per cent American at the back of me, when I go through these gates.'

She looked at him from dangerous grey eyes as if she meant it indeed, in vindictive earnest. A ghost of a smile went up to his high cheek-bones, but he did not answer.

'Why, mother?' said Lou, sing-song. 'It feels to me so friendly –!'

'Yes, Louise, it does. *So* friendly! That's why I mistrust it so entirely –'

And she set off at a canter up the Row, under the green trees, her face like the face of Medusa[19] at fifty, a weapon in itself. She stared at everything and everybody, with that stare of cold dynamite waiting to explode them all. Lou posted trotting at her side, graceful and elegant, and faintly amused. Behind came Phoenix, like a shadow, with his yellowish, high-boned face still looking sick. And at his side, on the big brilliant bay horse, the smallish, black-bearded Welshman.

Between Phoenix and Lewis there was a latent, but unspoken and wary sympathy. Phoenix was terribly impressed by St Mawr, he could not leave off staring at him. And Lewis rode the brilliant, handsome-moving stallion so very quietly, like an insinuation.

Of the two men, Lewis looked the darker, with his black beard coming up to his thick black eyebrows. He was swarthy, with a rather short nose, and the uncanny pale-grey eyes that watched everything and cared about nothing. He cared about nothing in the world, except, at the present, St Mawr. People did not matter

to him. He rode his horse and watched the world from the
vantage ground of St Mawr, with a final indifference.

'You have been with that horse long?' asked Phoenix.

'Since he was born.'

Phoenix watched the action of St Mawr as they went. The bay
moved proud and springy, but with perfect good sense, among
the stream of riders. It was a beautiful June morning, the leaves
overhead were thick and green; there came the first whiff of lime-
tree scent. To Phoenix, however, the city was a sort of nightmare
mirage, and to Lewis, it was a sort of prison. The presence of
people he felt as a prison around him.

Mrs Witt and Lou were turning, at the end of the Row, bowing
to some acquaintances. The grooms pulled aside. Mrs Witt
looked at Lewis with a cold eye.

'It seems an extraordinary thing to me, Louise,' she said 'to
see a groom with a beard.'

'It isn't usual, mother,' said Lou. 'Do you mind?'

'Not at all. At least, I think I don't. I get very tired of modern
bare-faced young men, *very!* The clean, pure boy, don't you
know! Doesn't it make you tired? – No, I think a groom with a
beard is quite attractive.'

She gazed into the crowd defiantly, perching her finely shod
toe with warlike firmness on the stirrup-iron. Then suddenly she
reined in, and turned her horse towards the grooms.

'Lewis!' she said. 'I want to ask you a question. Supposing,
now, that Lady Carrington wanted you to shave off that beard,
what should you say?'

Lewis instinctively put up his hand to the said beard.

'They've wanted me to shave it off, Mam,' he said. 'But I've
never done it.'

'But why? Tell me why?'

'It's part of me, Mam.'

Mrs Witt pulled on again.

'Isn't that extraordinary, Louise?' she said. 'Don't you like the
way he says *Mam*? It sounds so impossible to me. Could any
woman think of herself as Mam? Never! – Since Queen Victoria.
But, do you know it hadn't occurred to me that a man's beard
was really part of him. It always seemed to me that men wore

their beards, like they wear their neckties, for show. I shall always remember Lewis for saying his beard was part of him. Isn't it curious, the way he rides? He seems to sink himself in the horse. When I speak to him, I'm not sure whether I'm speaking to a man or to a horse.'

A few days later, Rico himself appeared on St Mawr, for the morning ride. He rode self-consciously, as he did everything, and he was just a little nervous. But his mother-in-law was benevolent. She made him ride between her and Lou, like three ships slowly sailing abreast.

And that very day, who should come driving in an open carriage through the Park but the Queen Mother! Dear old Queen Alexandra,[20] there was a flutter everywhere. And she bowed expressly to Rico, mistaking him, no doubt, for somebody else.

'Do you know,' said Rico, as they sat at lunch, he and Lou and Mrs Witt, in Mrs Witt's sitting-room in the dark, quiet hotel in Mayfair; 'I really like riding St Mawr *so* much. He really is a noble animal. – If ever I am made a Lord – which heaven forbid! – I shall be Lord St Mawr.'

'You mean,' said Mrs Witt, 'his real lordship would be the horse?'

'Very possible, I admit,' said Rico, with a curl of his long upper lip.

'Don't you think, mother,' said Lou, 'there *is* something quite noble about St Mawr? He strikes me as the first noble thing I have ever seen.'

'Certainly I've not seen any *man* that could compare with him. Because these English noblemen – well! I'd rather look at a Negro Pullman-boy,[21] if I was looking for what *I* call nobility.'

Poor Rico was getting crosser and crosser. There was a devil in Mrs Witt. She had a hard, bright devil inside her, that she seemed to be able to let loose at will.

She let it loose the next day, when Rico and Lou joined her in the Row. She was silent but deadly with the horses, balking them in every way. She suddenly crowded over against the rail, in front of St Mawr, so that the stallion had to rear to pull himself up. Then, having a clear track, she suddenly set off at a gallop, like an explosion, and the stallion, all on edge, set off after her.

It seemed as if the whole Park, that morning, were in a state of nervous tension. Perhaps there was thunder in the air. But St Mawr kept on dancing and pulling at the bit, and wheeling sideways up against the railing, to the terror of the children and the onlookers, who squealed and jumped back suddenly, sending the nerves of the stallion into a rush like rockets. He reared and fought as Rico pulled him round.

Then he went on: dancing, pulling, springily progressing sideways, possessed with all the demons of perversity. Poor Rico's face grew longer and angrier. A fury rose in him, which he could hardly control. He hated his horse, and viciously tried to force him to a quiet, straight trot. Up went St Mawr on his hind legs, to the terror of the Row. He got the bit in his teeth, and began to fight.

But Phoenix, cleverly, was in front of him.

'You get off, Rico!' called Mrs Witt's voice, with all the calm of her wicked exultance.

And almost before he knew what he was doing, Rico had sprung lightly to the ground, and was hanging on to the bridle of the rearing stallion.

Phoenix also lightly jumped down, and ran to St Mawr, handing his bridle to Rico. Then began a dancing and a splashing, a rearing and a plunging. St Mawr was being wicked. But Phoenix, the indifference of conflict in his face, sat tight and immovable, without any emotion, only the heaviness of his impersonal will settling down like a weight, all the time, on the horse. There was, perhaps, a curious barbaric exultance in bare, dark will devoid of emotion or personal feeling.

So they had a little display in the Row for almost five minutes, the brilliant horse rearing and fighting. Rico, with a stiff long face, scrambled on to Phoenix's horse, and withdrew to a safe distance. Policemen came, and an officious mounted policeman rode up to save the situation. But it was obvious that Phoenix, detached and apparently unconcerned, but barbarically potent in his will, would bring the horse to order.

Which he did, and rode the creature home. Rico was requested not to ride St Mawr in the Row any more, as the stallion was dangerous to public safety. The authorities knew all about him.

Where ended the first fiasco of St Mawr.

'We didn't get on very well with his lordship this morning,' said Mrs Witt triumphantly.

'No, he didn't like his company *at all*!' Rico snarled back.

He wanted Lou to sell the horse again.

'I doubt if anyone would buy him, dear,' she said. 'He's a known character.'

'Then make a gift of him – to your mother,' said Rico with venom.

'Why to mother?' asked Lou innocently.

'She might be able to cope with him – or he with her!' The last phrase was deadly. Having delivered it, Rico departed.

Lou remained at a loss. She felt almost always a little bit dazed, as if she could not see clear nor feel clear. A curious deadness upon her, like the first touch of death. And through this cloud of numbness, or deadness, came all her muted experiences.

Why was it? She did not know. But she felt that in some way it came from a battle of wills. Her mother, Rico, herself, it was always an unspoken, unconscious battle of wills, which was gradually numbing and paralyzing her. She knew Rico meant nothing but kindness by her. She knew her mother only wanted to watch over her. Yet always there was this tension of will, that was so numbing. As if at the depths of him, Rico were always angry, though he seemed so 'happy' on top. And Mrs Witt was organically angry. So they were like a couple of bombs, timed to explode some day, but ticking on like two ordinary timepieces, in the meanwhile.

She had come definitely to realize this: that Rico's anger was wound up tight at the bottom of him, like a steel spring that kept his works going, while he himself was 'charming', like a bomb-clock with Sèvres paintings or Dresden figures[22] on the outside. But his very charm was a sort of anger, and his love was a destruction in itself. He just couldn't help it.

And she? Perhaps she was a good deal the same herself. Wound up tight inside, and enjoying herself being 'lovely'. But wound up tight on some tension that, she realized now with wonder, was really a sort of anger. This, the main-spring that drove her on the round of 'joys'.

She used really to enjoy the tension, and the *élan*[23] it gave her. While she knew nothing about it. So long as she felt it really was life and happiness, this *élan*, this tension and excitement of 'enjoying oneself'.

Now suddenly she doubted the whole show. She attributed to it the curious numbness that was overcoming her, as if she couldn't feel any more.

She wanted to come unwound. She wanted to escape this battle of wills.

Only St Mawr gave her some hint of the possibility. He was so powerful, and so dangerous. But in his dark eye, that looked, with its cloudy brown pupil, a cloud within a dark fire, like a world beyond our world, there was a dark vitality glowing, and within the fire, another sort of wisdom. She felt sure of it: even when he put his ears back, and bared his teeth, and his great eyes came bolting out of his naked horse's head, and she saw demons upon demons in the chaos of his horrid eyes.

Why did he seem to her like some living background, into which she wanted to retreat? When he reared his head and neighed from his deep chest, like deep wind-bells resounding, she seemed to hear the echoes of another darker, more spacious, more dangerous, more splendid world than ours, that was beyond her. And there she wanted to go.

She kept it utterly a secret, to herself. Because Rico would just have lifted his long upper lip, in his bare face, in a condescending sort of 'understanding'. And her mother would, as usual, have suspected her of side-stepping. People, all the people she knew, seemed so entirely contained within their cardboard let's-be-happy world. Their wills were fixed like machines on happiness, or fun, or the-best-ever. This ghastly cheery-o! touch, that made all her blood go numb.

Since she had really seen St Mawr looming fiery and terrible in an outer darkness, she could not believe the world she lived in. She could not believe it was actually happening, when she was dancing in the afternoon at Claridge's, or in the evening at the Carlton,[24] sliding about with some suave young man who wasn't like a man at all to her. Or down in Sussex for the weekend with the Enderleys: the talk, the eating and drinking, the flirtation, the endless dancing: it all seemed far more bodiless and, in a strange way, wraith-like, than any fairy story. She seemed to be eating Barmecide[25] food, that had been conjured up out of thin air, by the power of words. She seemed to be talking to handsome young bare-faced unrealities, not men at all: as she slid about with them, in the perpetual dance, they too seemed to have been conjured up out of air, merely for this soaring, slithering dance-business. And she could not believe that, when the lights went out, they wouldn't melt back into thin air again, and complete nonentity. The strange nonentity of it all! Everything just conjured up, and nothing real. '*Isn't this the best ever!*' they would beamingly assert, like the wraiths of enjoyment, without any genuine substance. And she would beam back: '*Lots of fun!*'

She was thankful the season was over, and everybody was leaving London. She and Rico were due to go to Scotland, but not till August. In the meantime they would go to her mother.

Mrs Witt had taken a cottage in Shropshire, on the Welsh border, and had moved down there with Phoenix and her horses. The open, heather-and-bilberry-covered hills were splendid for riding.

Rico consented to spend the month in Shropshire, because for near neighbours Mrs Witt had the Manbys, at Corrabach Hall. The Manbys were rich Australians returned to the old country and set up as Squires, all in full blow. Rico had known them in Victoria: they were of good family: and the girls made a great fuss of him.

So down went Lou and Rico, Lewis, Poppy and St Mawr, to Shrewsbury, then out into the country. Mrs Witt's 'cottage' was a tall red-brick Georgian house looking straight on to the Churchyard, and the dark, looming big church.

'I never knew what a comfort it would be,' said Mrs Witt, 'to have grave-stones under my drawing-room windows, and funerals for lunch.'

She really did take a strange pleasure in sitting in her panelled room, that was painted grey, and watching the Dean or one of the curates officiating at the graveside, among a group of

black country mourners with black-bordered handkerchiefs
luxuriantly in use.

'Mother!' said Lou. 'I think it's gruesome!'

She had a room at the back, looking over the walled garden
and the stables. Nevertheless there was the *boom! boom!* of the
passing-bell, and the chiming and pealing on Sundays. The
shadow of the Church, indeed! A very audible shadow, making
itself heard insistently.

The Dean was a big, burly, fat man with a pleasant manner.
He was a gentleman, and a man of learning in his own line. But
he let Mrs Witt know that he looked down on her just a trifle
– as a parvenu American, a Yankee – though she never was a
Yankee: and at the same time he had a sincere respect for her,
as a rich woman. Yes, a sincere respect for her, as a rich woman.

Lou knew that every Englishman, especially of the upper
classes, has a wholesome respect for riches. But then, who hasn't?

The Dean was more *impressed* by Mrs Witt than by little Lou.
But to Lady Carrington he was charming: she was *almost* 'one
of us', you know. And he was very gracious to Rico: 'your father's
splendid colonial service'.

Mrs Witt had now a new pantomime to amuse her: the
Georgian house, her own pew in Church – it went with the old
house: a village of thatched cottages – some of them with cor-
rugated iron over the thatch: the cottage people, farm labourers
and their families, with a few, very few, outsiders: the wicked
little group of cottagers down at Mile End, famous for ill-living.
The Mile-Enders were all Allisons and Jephsons, and in-bred,
the Dean said: result of working through the centuries at the
Quarry, and living isolated there at Mile End.

Isolated! Imagine it! A mile and a half from the railway station,
ten miles from Shrewsbury. Mrs Witt thought of Texas, and said:

'Yes, they are *very* isolated, away down there!'

And the Dean never for a moment suspected sarcasm.

But there she had the whole thing staged complete for her:
English village life. Even miners breaking in to shatter the rather
stuffy, unwholesome harmony. – All the men touched their caps
to her, all the women did a bit of reverence, the children stood
aside for her, if she appeared in the Street.

They were all poor again: the labourers could no longer afford even a glass of beer in the evenings, since the Glorious War.

'Now I think that *is* terrible,' said Mrs Witt. 'Not to be able to get away from those stuffy, squalid, picturesque cottages for an hour in the evening, to drink a glass of beer.'

'It's a pity, I do agree with you, Mrs Witt. But Mr Watson has organized a men's reading-room, where the men can smoke and play dominoes, and read if they wish.'

'But that,' said Mrs Witt, 'is not the same as that cosy parlour in the "Moon and Stars".'

'I quite agree,' said the Dean. 'It isn't.'

Mrs Witt marched to the landlord of the 'Moon and Stars', and asked for a glass of cider.

'I want,' she said, in her American accent, 'these poor labourers to have their glass of beer in the evenings.'

'They want it themselves,' said Harvey.

'Then they must have it —'

The upshot was, she decided to supply one large barrel of beer per week and the landlord was to sell it to the labourers at a penny a glass.

'My own country has gone dry,' she asserted. 'But not because we can't *afford* it.'

By the time Lou and Rico appeared, she was deep in. She actually interfered very little: the barrel of beer was her one public act. But she *did* know everybody by sight, already, and she *did* know everybody's circumstances. And she had attended one prayer-meeting, one mother's meeting, one sewing-bee, one 'social', one Sunday School meeting, one Band of Hope[26] meeting, and one Sunday School treat. She ignored the poky little Wesleyan and Baptist chapels, and was true-blue Episcopalian.[27]

'How strange these picturesque old villages are, Louise!' she said, with a duskiness around her sharp, well-bred nose. 'How *easy* it all seems, all on a definite pattern. And how false! And underneath, *how corrupt*!'

She gave that queer, triumphant leer from her grey eyes, and queer demonish wrinkles seemed to twitter on her face.

Lou shrank away. She was beginning to be afraid of her

mother's insatiable curiosity, that always looked for the snake under the flowers. Or rather, for the maggots.

Always this same morbid interest in other people and their doings, their privacies, their dirty linen. Always this air of alertness for personal happenings, personalities, personalities, personalities. Always this subtle criticism and appraisal of other people, this analysis of other people's motives. If anatomy presupposes a corpse,[28] then psychology pre-supposes a world of corpses. Personalities, which means personal criticism and analysis, presupposes a whole world-laboratory of human psyches waiting to be vivisected. If you cut a thing up, of course it will smell. Hence, nothing raises such an infernal stink, at last, as human psychology.

Mrs Witt was a pure psychologist, a fiendish psychologist. And Rico, in his way, was a psychologist too. But he had a formula. 'Let's *know* the worst, dear! But let's look on the bright side, and believe the best.'

'Isn't the Dean a priceless old darling!' said Rico at breakfast.

And it had begun. Work had started in the psychic vivisection laboratory.

'Isn't he wonderful!' said Lou vaguely.

'So delightfully worldly! – *Some of us are not born to make money, dear boy. Luckily for us, we can marry it.*' – Rico made a priceless face.

'Is Mrs Vyner so rich?' asked Lou.

'She is, quite a wealthy woman – in coal,' replied Mrs Witt. 'But the Dean is surely worth his weight even in gold. And he's a massive figure. I can imagine there would be great satisfaction in having him for a husband.'

'Why, mother?' asked Lou.

'Oh, such a presence! One of these old Englishmen, that nobody can put in their pocket. You can't imagine his wife asking him to thread her needle. Something after all so *robust*! So different from *young* Englishmen, who all seem to me like ladies, perfect ladies.'

'*Somebody* has to keep up the tradition of the perfect lady,' said Rico.

'I know it,' said Mrs Witt. 'And if the women won't do it, the young gentlemen take on the burden. They bear it very well.'

It was in full swing, the cut and thrust. And poor Lou, who had reached the point of stupefaction in the game, felt she did not know what to do with herself.

Rico and Mrs Witt were deadly enemies, yet neither could keep clear of the other. It might have been they who were married to one another, their duel and their duet were so relentless.

But Rico immediately started the social round: first the Manbys: then motor twenty miles to luncheon at Lady Tewkesbury's: then young Mr Burns came flying down in his aeroplane from Chester: then they must motor to the sea, to Sir Edward Edwards' place, where there was a moonlight bathing party. Everything intensely thrilling, and so innerly wearisome, Lou felt.

But back of it all was St Mawr, looming like a bonfire in the dark. He really was a tiresome horse to own. He worried the mares, if they were in the same paddock with him, always driving them round. And with any other horse he just fought with definite intent to kill. So he had to stay alone.

'That St Mawr, he's a bad horse,' said Phoenix.

'Maybe!' said Lewis.

'You don't like quiet horses?' said Phoenix.

'Most horses *is* quiet,' said Lewis. 'St Mawr, he's different.'

'Why don't he never get any foals?'

'Doesn't want to, I should think. Same as me.'

'What good is a horse like that? Better shoot him, before he kill somebody.'

'What good'll they get, shooting St Mawr?' said Lewis.

'If he kills somebody!' said Phoenix.

But there was no answer.

The two grooms both lived over the stables, and Lou, from her window, saw a good deal of them. They were two quiet men, yet she was very much aware of their presence, aware of Phoenix's rather high square shoulders and his fine, straight, vigorous black hair that tended to stand up assertively on his head, as he went quietly drifting about his various jobs. He was not lazy, but he did everything with a sort of diffidence, as if from a distance, and handled his horses carefully, cautiously, and cleverly, but without sympathy. He seemed to be holding something back, all the time, unconsciously, as if in his very being there was some secret. But it was a secret of *will*. His quiet, reluctant movements, as if he never really wanted to do anything; his long flat-stepping stride; the permanent challenge in his high cheek-bones, the Indian glint in his eyes, and his peculiar stare, watchful and yet unseeing, made him unpopular with the women servants.

Nevertheless, women had a certain fascination for him: he would stare at the pretty young maids with an intent blank stare, when they were not looking. Yet he was rather overbearing, domineering with them, and they resented him. It was evident to Lou that he looked upon himself as belonging to the master, not to the servant class. When he flirted with the maids, as he very often did, for he had a certain crude ostentatiousness, he seemed to let them feel that he despised them as inferiors, servants, while he admired their pretty charms, as fresh, country maids.

'I'm fair nervous of that Phoenix,' said Fanny, the fair-haired maid. 'He makes you feel what he'd do to you if he could.'

'He'd better not try with me,' said Mabel. 'I'd scratch his cheeky eyes out. Cheek! – for it's nothing else! He's nobody – Common as they're made!'

'He makes you feel you was there for him to trample on,' said Fanny.

'Mercy, you *are* soft! If anybody's that it's him. Oh my, Fanny, you've no right to let a fellow make you feel like *that*! Make *them* feel that *they're* dirt, for you to trample on: which they are!'

Fanny, however, being a shy little blonde thing, wasn't good at assuming the trampling rôle. She was definitely nervous of Phoenix. And he enjoyed it. An invisible smile seemed to creep up his cheek-bones, and the glint moved in his eyes as he teased her. He tormented her by his very presence, as he knew.

He would come silently up when she was busy, and stand behind her perfectly still, so that she was unaware of his presence. Then, silently, he would *make* her aware. Till she glanced nervously round, and with a scream, saw him.

One day Lou watched this little play. Fanny had been picking over a bowl of black currants, sitting on the bench under the maple tree in a corner of the yard. She didn't look round till she had picked up her bowl to go to the kitchen. Then there was a scream and a crash.

When Lou came out, Phoenix was crouching down silently gathering up the currants, which the little maid, scarlet and trembling, was collecting into another bowl. Phoenix seemed to be smiling down his back.

'Phoenix!' said Lou. 'I wish you wouldn't startle Fanny!'

He looked up, and she saw the glint of ridicule in his eyes.

'Who, me?' he said.

'Yes, you. You go up behind Fanny, to startle her. You're not to do it.'

He slowly stood erect, and lapsed into his peculiar invisible silence. Only for a second his eyes glanced at Lou's, and then she saw the cold anger, the gleam of malevolence and contempt. He could not bear being commanded, or reprimanded, by a woman.

Yet it was even worse with a man.

'What's that, Lou?' said Rico, appearing all handsome and in the picture, in white flannels with an apricot silk shirt.

'I'm telling Phoenix he's not to torment Fanny!'

'Oh!' – and Rico's voice immediately became his father's, the important government official. 'Certainly *not*! Most certainly *not*!' He looked at the scattered currants and the broken bowl. Fanny melted into tears. 'This, I suppose, is some of the results! Now look here, Phoenix, you're to leave the maids strictly alone. I shall ask them to report to me whenever, or *if* ever, you interfere with them. But I hope you *won't* interfere with them – in any way. You understand?'

As Rico became more and more Sir Henry and the government official, Lou's bones melted more and more into discomfort. Phoenix stood in his peculiar silence, the invisible smile on his cheek-bones.

'You understand what I'm saying to you?' Rico demanded, in intensified acid tones.

But Phoenix only stood there, as it were behind a cover of his

own will, and looked back at Rico with a faint smile on his face
and the glint moving in his eyes.

'Do you intend to answer?' Rico's upper lip lifted nastily.

'Mrs Witt is my boss,' came from Phoenix.

The scarlet flew up Rico's throat and flushed his face, his eyes
went glaucous. Then quickly his face turned yellow.

Lou looked at the two men: her husband, whose rages, over-
controlled, were organically terrible: the half-breed, whose dark-
coloured lips were widened in a faint smile of derision, but in
whose eyes caution and hate were playing against one another.
She realized that Phoenix would accept *her* reprimand, or her
mother's, because he could despise the two of them as mere
women. But Rico's bossiness aroused murder pure and simple.

She took her husband's arm.

'Come dear!' she said, in her half plaintive way. 'I'm sure
Phoenix understands. We all understand. Go to the kitchen,
Fanny, never mind the currants. There are plenty more in the
garden.'

Rico was always thankful to be drawn quickly, submissively
away from his own rage. He was afraid of it. He was afraid lest
he should fly at the groom in some horrible fashion. The very
thought horrified him. But in actuality he came very near to it.

He walked stiffly, feeling paralyzed by his own fury. And those
words, *Mrs Witt is my boss*, were like hot acid in his brain. An
insult!

'By the way, Belle-Mère!'[29] he said when they joined Mrs
Witt – she hated being called Belle-Mère, and once said: 'If I'm
the bell-mare, are you one of the colts?' – She also hated his voice
of smothered fury – 'I had to speak to Phoenix about persecuting
the maids. He took the liberty of informing me that you were his
boss, so perhaps you had better speak to him.'

'I certainly will. I believe they're my maids, and nobody else's,
so it's my duty to look after them. Who was he persecuting?'

'I'm the responsible one, mother,' said Lou –

Rico disappeared in a moment. He must get out: get away from
the house. How? Something was wrong with the car. Yet he must
get away, away. He would go over to Corrabach. He would ride
St Mawr. He had been talking about the horse, and Flora Manby

was dying to see him. She had said: 'Oh, I can't *wait* to see that marvellous horse of yours.'

He would ride him over. It was only seven miles. He found Lou's maid Elena, and sent her to tell Lewis. Meanwhile, to soothe himself, he dressed himself most carefully in white riding breeches and a shirt of purple silk crape, with a flowing black tie spotted red like a ladybird, and black riding boots. Then he took a *chic* little white hat with a black band.

St Mawr was saddled and waiting, and Lewis had saddled a second horse.

'Thanks, Lewis, I'm going alone!' said Rico.

This was the first time he had ridden St Mawr in the country, and he was nervous. But he was also in the hell of a smothered fury. All his careful dressing had not really soothed him. So his fury consumed his nervousness.

He mounted with a swing, blind and rough. St Mawr reared.

'Stop that!' snarled Rico, and put him to the gate.

Once out in the village street, the horse went dancing sideways. He insisted on dancing at the sidewalk, to the exaggerated terror of the children. Rico, exasperated, pulled him across. But no, he wouldn't go down the centre of the village street. He began dancing and edging on to the other sidewalk, so the foot-passengers fled into the shops in terror.

The devil was in him. He would turn down every turning where he was not meant to go. He reared with panic at a furniture van. He *insisted* on going down the wrong side of the road. Rico was riding him with a martingale, and he could see the rolling, bloodshot eye.

'Damn you, *go*!' said Rico, giving him a dig with the spurs.

And away they went, down the high road, in a thunderbolt. It was a hot day, with thunder threatening, so Rico was soon in a flame of heat. He held on tight, with fixed eyes, trying all the time to rein in the horse. What he really was afraid of was that the brute would shy suddenly, as he galloped. Watching for this, he didn't care when they sailed past the turning to Corrabach.

St Mawr flew on, in a sort of *élan*. Marvellous the power and life in the creature. There was really a great joy in the motion. If only he wouldn't take the corners at a gallop, nearly swerving

Rico off! Luckily the road was clear. To ride, to ride at this terrific gallop, on into eternity!

After several miles, the horse slowed down, and Rico managed to pull him into a lane that might lead to Corrabach. When all was said and done, it was a wonderful ride. St Mawr could go like the wind, but with that luxurious heavy ripple of life which is like nothing else on earth. It seemed to carry one at once into another world, away from the life of the nerves.

So Rico arrived after all something of a conqueror at Corrabach. To be sure, he was perspiring, and so was his horse. But he was a hero from another, heroic world.

'Oh, such a hot ride!' he said, as he walked on to the lawn at Corrabach Hall. 'Between the sun and the horse, really! – between two fires!'

'Don't you trouble, you're looking dandy, a bit hot and flushed like,' said Flora Manby. 'Let's go and see your horse.'

And her exclamation was: 'Oh, he's *lovely*! He's *fine*! I'd love to try him once –'

Rico decided to accept the invitation to stay overnight at Corrabach. Usually he was very careful, and refused to stay, unless Lou was with him. But they telephoned to the post-office at Chomesbury, would Mr Jones please send a message to Lady Carrington that Sir Henry was staying the night at Corrabach Hall, but would be home next day. Mr Jones received the request with unction, and said he would go over himself to give the message to Lady Carrington.

Lady Carrington was in the walled garden. The peculiarity of Mrs Witt's house was that, for grounds proper, it had the churchyard.

'I never thought, Louise, that one day I should have an old English church-yard for my lawns and shrubbery and park, and funeral mourners for my herds of deer. It's curious. For the first time in my life a funeral has become a real thing to me. I feel I could write a book on them.'

But Louise only felt intimidated.

At the back of the house was a flagged courtyard, with stables and a maple tree in a corner, and big doors opening on to the village street. But at the side was a walled garden, with fruit trees and currant bushes and a great bed of rhubarb, and some tufts of flowers, peonies, pink roses, sweet williams. Phoenix, who had a certain taste for gardening, would be out there thinning the carrots or tying up the lettuce. He was not lazy. Only he would not take work seriously, as a job. He would be quite amused tying up lettuces, and would tie up head after head, quite prettily. Then, becoming bored, he would abandon his task, light a cigarette, and go and stand on the threshold of the big doors, in full view of the street, watching, and yet completely indifferent.

After Rico's departure on St Mawr, Lou went into the garden. And there she saw Phoenix working in the onion bed. He was bending over, in his own silence, busy with nimble, amused fingers among the grassy young onions. She thought he had not seen her, so she went down another path to where a swing bed hung under the apple trees. There she sat with a book and a bundle of magazines. But she did not read.

She was musing vaguely. Vaguely, she was glad that Rico was away for a while. Vaguely, she felt a sense of bitterness, of complete futility: the complete futility of her living. This left her drifting in a sea of utter chagrin. And Rico seemed to her the symbol of the futility. Vaguely, she was aware that something else existed, but she didn't know where it was or what it was.

In the distance she could see Phoenix's dark, rather tall-built head, with its black, fine, intensely-living hair tending to stand on end, like a brush with long, very fine black bristles. His hair, she thought, betrayed him as an animal of a different species. He was growing a little bored by weeding onions: that also she could tell. Soon he would want some other amusement.

Presently Lewis appeared. He was small, energetic, a little bit bow-legged, and he walked with a slight strut. He wore khaki riding-breeches, leather gaiters, and a blue shirt. And, like Phoenix, he rarely had any cap or hat on his head. His thick black hair was parted at the side and brushed over heavily sideways, dropping on his forehead at the right. It was very long, a real mop, under which his eyebrows were dark and steady.

'Seen Lady Carrington?' he asked of Phoenix.

'Yes, she's sitting on that swing over there – she's been there quite a while.'

The wretch – he had seen her from the very first!

Lewis came striding over, looking towards her with his pale-grey eyes, from under his mop of hair.

'Mr Jones from the post office wants to see you, my Lady, with a message from Sir Henry.'

Instantly alarm took possession of Lou's soul.

'Oh! – Does he want to see me personally? – What message? Is anything wrong?' – And her voice trailed out over the last word, with a sort of anxious nonchalance.

'I don't think it's anything amiss,' said Lewis reassuringly.

'Oh! You don't,' the relief came into her voice. Then she looked at Lewis with a slight, winning smile in her unmatched eyes. 'I'm so afraid of St Mawr, you know.' Her voice was soft and cajoling. Phoenix was listening in the distance.

'St Mawr's all right, if you don't do nothing to him,' Lewis replied.

'I'm sure he is! – But how is one to know when one is doing something to him? – Tell Mr Jones to come here, please,' she concluded, on a changed tone.

Mr Jones, a man of forty-five, thick set, with a fresh complexion and rather foolish brown eyes, and a big brown moustache, came prancing down the path, smiling rather fatuously, and doffing his straw hat with a gorgeous bow the moment he saw Lou sitting in her slim white frock on the coloured swing bed under the trees with their hard green apples.

'Good morning Mr Jones!'

'Good morning Lady Carrington. – If I may say so, what a picture you make – a beautiful picture –'

He beamed under his big brown moustache like the greatest lady-killer.

'Do I! – Did Sir Henry say he was all right?'

'He didn't *say* exactly, but I should expect he is all right –' and Mr Jones delivered his message, in the mayonnaise of his own unction.

'Thank you so much, Mr Jones, It's awfully good of you to come and tell me. Now I shan't worry about Sir Henry *at all*.'

'It's a great pleasure to come and deliver a satisfactory message to Lady Carrington. But it won't be kind to Sir Henry if you don't worry about him *at all* in his absence. We all enjoy being worried about by those we love – so long as there is nothing to worry about of course!'

'Quite!' said Lou. 'Now won't you take a glass of port and a biscuit, or a whisky and soda? And thank you ever so much.'

'Thank *you*, my Lady. I might drink a whisky and soda, since you are so good.'

And he beamed fatuously.

'Let Mr Jones mix himself a whisky and soda, Lewis,' said Lou.

'Heavens!' she thought, as the postmaster retreated a little uncomfortably down the garden path, his bald spot passing in and out of the sun, under the trees: 'How ridiculous everything is, how ridiculous, ridiculous!' Yet she didn't really dislike Mr Jones and his interlude.

Phoenix was melting away out of the garden. He had to follow the fun.

'Phoenix!' Lou called. 'Bring me a glass of water, will you? Or send somebody with it.'

He stood in the path looking round at her.

'All right!' he said.

And he turned away again.

She did not like being alone in the garden. She liked to have the men working somewhere near. Curious how pleasant it was to sit there in the garden when Phoenix was about, or Lewis. It made her feel she could never be lonely or jumpy. But when Rico was there, she was all aching nerve.

Phoenix came back with a glass of water, lemon juice, sugar, and a small bottle of brandy. He knew Lou liked a spoonful of brandy in her iced lemonade.

'How thoughtful of you Phoenix!' she said. 'Did Mr Jones get his whisky?'

'He was just getting it.'

'That's right. – By the way, Phoenix, I wish you wouldn't get mad if Sir Henry speaks to you. He is *really* so kind.'

She looked up at the man. He stood there watching her in silence, the invisible smile on his face, and the inscrutable Indian glint moving in his eyes. What was he thinking? There was something passive and almost submissive about him, but underneath this, an unyielding resistance and cruelty: yes, even cruelty. She felt that, on top, he was submissive and attentive, bringing her her lemonade as she liked it, without being told: thinking for her quite subtly. But underneath there was an unchanging hatred. He submitted circumstantially, he worked for a wage. And even circumstantially, he *liked* his mistress – *la patrona* – and her daughter. But much deeper than any circumstance or any circumstantial liking, was the categorical hatred upon which he was founded, and with which he was powerless. His liking for Lou and for Mrs Witt, his serving them and working for a wage, was all side-tracking his own nature, which was grounded on hatred of their very existence. But what was he to do? He had to live. Therefore he had to serve, to work for a wage, and even to be faithful.

And yet *their* existence made his own existence negative. If he was to exist, positively, they would have to cease to exist. At the same time, a fatal sort of tolerance made him serve these women, and go on serving.

'Sir Henry is *so* kind to everybody,' Lou insisted.

The half-breed met her eyes, and smiled uncomfortably.

'Yes, he's a kind man,' he replied, as if sincerely.

'Then why do you mind if he speaks to you?'

'I don't mind,' said Phoenix glibly.

'But you do. Or else you wouldn't make him so angry.'

'Was he angry? I don't know,' said Phoenix.

'He was very angry. And you *do* know.'

'No, I don't know if he's angry. I don't know,' the fellow persisted. And there was a glib sort of satisfaction in his tone.

'That's awfully unkind of you, Phoenix,' she said, growing offended in her turn.

'No, I don't know if he's angry. I don't want to make him angry. I don't know –'

He had taken on a tone of naïve ignorance, which at once gratified her pride as a woman, and deceived her.

'Well, you believe me when I tell you you *did* make him angry, don't you?'

'Yes, I believe when you tell me.'

'And you promise me, won't you, not to do it again? It's *so* bad for him – so bad for his nerves, and for his eyes. It makes them inflamed, and injures his eyesight. And you know, as an artist, it's terrible if anything happens to his eyesight –'

Phoenix was watching her closely, to take it in. He still was not good at understanding continuous, logical statement. Logical connexion in speech seemed to stupefy him, make him stupid. He understood in disconnected assertions of fact. But he had gathered what she said. 'He gets mad at you. When he gets mad, it hurt his eyes. His eyes hurt him. He can't see, because his eyes hurt him. He wants to paint a picture, he can't. He can't paint a picture, he can't see clear –'

Yes, he had understood. She saw he had understood. The bright glint of satisfaction moved in his eyes.

'So now promise me, won't you, you won't make him mad again: you won't make him angry?'

'No, I won't make him angry. I don't do anything to make him angry,' Phoenix answered, rather glibly.

'And you do understand, don't you? You do know how kind he is: how he'd do a good turn to anybody?'

'Yes, he's a kind man,' said Phoenix.

'I'm so glad you realize. There, that's luncheon! How nice it is to sit here in the garden, when everybody is nice to you! No, I can carry the tray, don't you bother.'

But he took the tray from her hand, and followed her to the house. And as he walked behind her, he watched the slim white nape of her neck, beneath the clustering of her bobbed hair, something as a stoat watches a rabbit he is following.

In the afternoon Lou retreated once more to her place in the garden. There she lay, sitting with a bunch of pillows behind her, neither reading nor working, just musing. She had learned the new joy: to do absolutely nothing, but to lie and let the sunshine filter through the leaves, to see the bunch of red-hot-poker flowers pierce scarlet into the afternoon, beside the comparative neutrality of some foxgloves. The mere colour of hard red, like the big oriental poppies that had fallen, and these poker flowers, lingered in her consciousness like a communication.

Into this peaceful indolence, when even the big, dark-grey

tower of the church beyond the wall and the yew-trees was keeping its bells in silence, advanced Mrs Witt, in a broad panama hat and a white dress.

'Don't you want to ride, or do something, Louise?' she asked ominously.

'Don't you want to be peaceful, mother?' retorted Louise.

'Yes – an *active* peace. – I can't *believe* that my daughter can be content to lie on a hammock and do *nothing*, not even read or improve her mind, the greater part of the day.'

'Well, your daughter *is* content to do that. It's her greatest pleasure.'

'I know it. I can see it. And it surprises me *very* much. When I was your age, I was never still. I had so much *go* –'

> 'Those maids, thank God,
> Are 'neath the sod,
> And all their generation.'

'No but, mother, I only take life differently. Perhaps you used up that sort of *go*. I'm the harem type, mother: only I never want the men inside the lattice.'

'Are you really my daughter? – Well! A woman never knows what will happen to her. I'm an *American* woman, and I suppose I've got to remain one, no matter where I am. – What did you want, Lewis?'

The groom had approached down the path.

'If I am to saddle Poppy?' said Lewis.

'No, apparently *not*!' replied Mrs Witt. 'Your mistress prefers the hammock to the saddle.'

'Thank you, Lewis. What mother says is true this afternoon, at least.' And she gave him a peculiar little cross-eyed smile.

'Who,' said Mrs Witt to the man, 'has been cutting at your hair?'

There was a moment of silent resentment.

'I did it myself, Mam! Sir Henry said it was too long.'

'He certainly spoke the truth. But I believe there's a barber in the village on Saturdays – or you could ride over to Shrewsbury. Just turn round, and let me look at the back. Is it the money?'

'No, Mam. I don't like these fellows touching my head.'

He spoke coldly, with a certain hostile reserve that at once piqued Mrs Witt.

'Don't you really!' she said. 'But it's quite *impossible* for you to go about as you are. It gives you a half-witted appearance. Go now into the yard, and get a chair and a dust-sheet. I'll cut your hair.'

The man hesitated, hostile.

'Don't be afraid, I know how it's done. I've cut the hair of many a poor wounded boy in hospital: and shaved them too. *You've got such a touch, nurse*! Poor fellow, he was dying, though none of us knew it. – Those are the compliments I value, Louise. – Get that chair now, and a dust-sheet. I'll borrow your hair-scissors from Elena, Louise.'

Mrs Witt, happily on the war-path, was herself again. She didn't care for work, actual work. But she loved trimming. She loved arranging unnatural and pretty salads, devising new and piquant-looking ice-creams, having a turkey stuffed exactly as she knew a stuffed turkey in Louisiana, with chestnuts and butter and stuff, or showing a servant how to turn waffles on a waffle-iron, or to bake a ham with brown sugar and cloves and a moistening of rum. She liked pruning rose-trees, or beginning to cut a yew hedge into shape. She liked ordering her own and Louise's shoes, with an exactitude and a knowledge of shoe-making that sent the salesman crazy. She was a demon in shoes. Reappearing from America, she would pounce on her daughter. 'Louise, throw those shoes away. Give them to one of the maids.' – 'But, mother, they are some of the best French shoes. I like them.' – 'Throw them away. A shoe has only two excuses for existing: perfect comfort or perfect appearance. Those have neither. I have brought you some shoes.' – Yes, she had brought ten pairs of shoes from New York. She knew her daughter's foot as she knew her own.

So now she was in her element, looming behind Lewis as he sat in the middle of the yard swathed in a dust-sheet. She had on an overall and a pair of wash-leather gloves, and she poised a pair of long scissors like one of the Fates.[30] In her big hat she looked curiously young, but with the youth of a by-gone generation. Her heavy-lidded, laconic grey eyes were alert, studying the groom's black mop of hair. Her eyebrows made thin, uptilting black arches on her brow. Her fresh skin was slightly powdered, and she was really handsome, in a bold, by-gone, eighteenth century style. Some of the curious, adventurous stoicism of the eighteenth century: and then a certain blatant American efficiency.

Lou, who had strayed into the yard to see, looked so much younger and so many thousands of years older than her mother, as she stood in her wisp-like diffidence, the clusters of grape-like bobbed hair hanging beside her face, with its fresh colouring and its ancient weariness, her slightly squinting eyes, that were so disillusioned they were becoming faun-like.

'Not too short, mother, not too short!' she remonstrated, as Mrs Witt, with a terrific flourish of efficiency, darted at the man's black hair, and the thick flakes fell like black snow.

'Now, Louise, I'm right in this job, please don't interfere. Two things I hate to see: a man with his wool in his neck and ears: and a bare-faced young man who looks as if he'd bought his face as well as his hair from a men's beauty-specialist.'

And efficiently she bent down, clip – clip – clipping! while Lewis sat utterly immobile, with sunken head, in a sort of despair.

Phoenix stood against the stable door, with his restless, eternal cigarette. And in the kitchen doorway the maids appeared and fled, appeared and fled in delight. The old gardener, a fixture who went with the house, creaked in and stood with his legs apart, silent in intense condemnation.

'First time I ever see such a thing!' he muttered to himself, as he creaked on into the garden. He was a bad-tempered old soul, who thoroughly disapproved of the household, and would have given notice, but that he knew which side his bread was buttered: and there was butter unstinted on his bread, in Mrs Witt's kitchen.

Mrs Witt stood back to survey her handiwork, holding those terrifying shears with their beak erect. Lewis lifted his head and looked stealthily round, like a creature in a trap.

'Keep still!' she said. 'I haven't finished.'

And she went for his front hair, with vigour, lifting up long layers and snipping off the ends artistically: till at last he sat with a black aureole upon the floor, and his ears standing out with curious new alertness from the sides of his clean-clipped head.

'Stand up,' she said, 'and let me look.'

He stood up, looking absurdly young, with the hair all cut away from his neck and ears, left thick only on top. She surveyed her work with satisfaction.

'You look so much younger,' she said; 'you would be surprised. Sit down again.'

She clipped the back of his neck with the shears, and then, with a very slight hesitation, she said:

'Now about the beard!'

But the man rose suddenly from the chair, pulling the dust-cloth from his neck with desperation.

'No, I'll do that myself,' he said, looking her in the eyes with a cold light in his pale-grey, uncanny eyes.

She hesitated in a kind of wonder at his queer male rebellion.

'Now, listen, I shall do it much better than you – and besides,' she added hurriedly, snatching at the dust-cloth he was flinging on the chair – 'I haven't quite finished round the ears.'

'I think I shall do,' he said, again looking her in the eyes, with a cold, white gleam of finality. 'Thank you for what you've done.'

And he walked away to the stable.

'You'd better sweep up here,' Mrs Witt called.

'Yes, Mam,' he replied, looking round at her again with an odd resentment, but continuing to walk away.

'However!' said Mrs Witt. 'I suppose he'll do.'

And she divested herself of gloves and overall, and walked indoors to wash and to change. Lou went indoors too.

'It is extraordinary what hair that man has!' said Mrs Witt. 'Did I tell you when I was in Paris, I saw a woman's face in the hotel that I thought I knew? I couldn't place her, till she was coming towards me. *Aren't you Rachel Fannière?* she said. *Aren't you Janette Leroy?* We hadn't seen each other since we were girls of twelve and thirteen, at school in New Orleans. *Oh!* she said to me. *Is every illusion doomed to perish? You had such wonderful golden curls! All my life I've said, Oh, if only I had such lovely hair as Rachel Fannière! I've seen those beautiful golden curls of yours all my life. And now I meet you, you're grey!* Wasn't that terrible, Louise? Well, that man's hair made me think of it – so thick and curious. It's strange, what a difference there is in hair; I suppose it's because he's just an animal – no mind! There's nothing I admire in a man like a good *mind*. Your father was a very clever man, and all the men I've admired have been clever. But isn't it curious now, I've never cared much to touch their hair. How strange life is! If it gives one thing, it takes away another. – And even those poor boys in hospital: I have shaved them, or cut their hair, like a mother, never thinking anything of it. Lovely, intelligent, clean boys, most of them were. Yet it never did anything to me. I never knew before that something could happen to one from a person's *hair*! Like to Janette Leroy from my curls when I was a child. And now I'm grey, as she says. – I wonder how old a man Lewis is, Louise! Didn't he look absurdly young, with his ears pricking up?'

'I think Rico said he was forty or forty-one.'

'And never been married?'

'No – not as far as I know.'

'Isn't that curious now! – just an animal! no mind! A man with no mind! I've always thought that the *most* despicable thing. Yet such wonderful hair to touch. Your Henry has quite a good mind, yet I would simply shrink from touching his hair. I suppose one likes stroking a cat's fur, just the same. Just the animal in man. Curious that I never seem to have met it, Louise. Now I come to think of it, he has the eyes of a human cat: a human tom-cat. Would you call him stupid? Yes, he's very stupid.'

'No, mother, he's not stupid. He only doesn't care about most things.'

'Like an animal! But what a strange look he has in his eyes! a strange sort of intelligence! and a confidence in himself. Isn't that curious, Louise, in a man with as little mind as he has? Do you know, I should say he could see through a woman pretty well.'

'Why, mother!' said Lou impatiently. 'I think one gets so tired of your men with mind, as you call it. There are so many of that sort of clever men. And there are lots of men who aren't very clever, but are rather nice: and lots are stupid. It seems to me there's something else besides mind and cleverness, or niceness or cleanness. Perhaps it is the animal. Just think of St Mawr! I've thought so much about him. We call him an animal, but we never know what it means. He seems a far greater mystery to me than a clever man. He's a horse. Why can't one say in the same way, of a man: *He's a man?* There seems no mystery in being a man. But there's a terrible mystery in St Mawr.'

Mrs Witt watched her daughter quizzically.

'Louise,' she said, 'you won't tell me that the mere animal is all that counts in a man. I will never believe it. Man is wonderful because he is able to *think*.'

'But is he?' cried Lou, with sudden exasperation. 'Their thinking seems to me all so childish: like stringing the same beads over and over again. Ah, men! They and their thinking are all so *paltry*. How can you be impressed?'

Mrs Witt raised her eyebrows sardonically.

'Perhaps I'm not – any more,' she said with a grim smile.

'But,' she added, 'I still can't see that I am to be impressed by the mere animal in man. The animals are the same as we are. It seems to me they have the same feelings and wants as we do in a commonplace way. The only difference is that they have no minds: no human minds, at least. And no matter what you say, Louise, lack of mind makes the commonplace.'

Lou knitted her brows nervously.

'I suppose it does, mother. – But men's minds *are* so commonplace: look at Dean Vyner and his mind! Or look at Arthur Balfour,[31] as a shining example. Isn't *that* commonplace, that cleverness? I would hate St Mawr to be spoilt by such a mind.'

'Yes, Louise, so would I. Because the men you mention are really old women, knitting the same pattern over and over again. Nevertheless, I shall never alter my belief that real mind is all that matters in a man, and it's *that* that we women love.'

'Yes, mother! – But what *is* real mind? The old woman who knits the most complicated pattern? Oh, I can hear all their needles clicking, the clever men! As a matter of fact, mother, I believe Lewis has far more real mind than Dean Vyner or any of the clever ones. He has a good intuitive mind, he knows things without thinking them.'

'That may be, Louise! But he is a servant. He is *under*. A real man should never be under. And then you could never be intimate with a man like Lewis.'

'I don't want intimacy, mother. I'm too tired of it all. I love St Mawr because he isn't intimate. He stands where one can't get at him. And he burns with life. And where does his life come from, to him? That's the mystery. That great burning life in him, which never is dead. Most men have a deadness in them, that frightens me so, because of my own deadness. Why can't men get their life straight, like St Mawr, and then think? Why can't they think quick, mother: quick as a woman: only farther than we do? Why isn't men's thinking quick like fire, mother? Why is it so slow, so dead, so deadly dull?'

'I can't tell you, Louise. My own opinion of the men of to-day has grown very small. But I can live in spite of it.'

'No, mother. We seem to be living off old fuel, like the camel when he lives off his hump. Life doesn't rush into us, as it does even into St Mawr, and he's a dependent animal. I can't live, mother. I just can't.'

'I don't see why not? *I'm* full of life.'

'I know you are, mother. But I'm not, and I'm your daughter. – And don't misunderstand me, mother. I don't want to be an animal like a horse or a cat or a lioness, though they all fascinate me, the way they get their life *straight*, not from a lot of old tanks, as we do. I don't admire the cave man, and that sort of thing. But think mother, if we could get our lives straight from the source, as the animals do, and still be ourselves. You don't like men yourself. But you've no idea how men just tire me out: even the very thought of them. You say they are too animal. But they're not, mother. It's the animal in them has gone perverse, or cringing, or humble, or domesticated, like dogs. I don't know one single man who is a proud living animal. I know they've left off really thinking. But then men always do leave off really thinking, when the last bit of wild animal dies in them.'

'Because we have minds –'

'We have no minds once we are tame, mother. Men are all women, knitting and crochetting words together.'

'I can't altogether agree, you know, Louise.'

'I know you don't. – You like clever men. But clever men are mostly such unpleasant *animals*. As animals, so very unpleasant. And in men like Rico, the animal has gone queer and wrong. And in those nice clean boys you liked so much in the war, there is no wild animal left in them. They're all tame dogs, even when they're brave and well-bred. They're all tame dogs, mother, with human masters. There's no mystery in them.'

'What do you want, Louise? You *do* want the cave man, who'll knock you on the head with a club.'

'Don't be silly, mother. That's much more your subconscious line, you admirer of Mind. – I don't consider the cave man is a real human animal at all. He's a brute, a degenerate. A pure animal man would be as lovely as a deer or a leopard, burning like a flame fed straight from underneath. And he'd be part of the unseen, like a mouse is, even. And he'd never cease to wonder, he'd breathe silence and unseen wonder, as the partridges do, running in the stubble. He'd be all the animals in turn, instead of one, fixed, automatic thing, which he is now, grinding on the nerves. – Ah no, mother, I want the wonder back again, or I shall die. I don't want to be like you, just criticizing and annihilating these dreary people, and enjoying it.'

'My dear daughter, whatever else the human animal might be, he'd be a dangerous commodity.'

'I wish he would, mother. I'm dying of these empty dangerless men, who are only sentimental and spiteful.'

'Nonsense, you're not dying.'

'I am, mother. And I should be dead if there weren't St Mawr and Phoenix and Lewis in the world.'

'St Mawr and Phoenix and Lewis! I thought you said they were servants.'

'That's the worst of it. If only they were masters! If only there were some men with as much natural life as they have, and their brave, quick minds that commanded instead of serving!'

'There are no such men,' said Mrs Witt, with a certain grim satisfaction.

'I know it. But I'm young, and I've got to live. And the thing that is offered me as life just starves me, starves me to death, mother. What am I to do? You enjoy shattering people like Dean Vyner. But I am young, I can't live that way.'

'That may be.'

It had long ago struck Lou how much more her mother realized and understood than ever Rico did. Rico was afraid, always afraid of realizing. Rico, with his good manners and his habitual kindness, and that peculiar imprisoned sneer of his.

He arrived home next morning on St Mawr, rather flushed and gaudy, and over-kind, with an *empressé*[32] anxiety about Lou's welfare which spoke too many volumes. Especially as he was accompanied by Flora Manby, and by Flora's sister Elsie, and Elsie's husband, Frederick Edwards. They all came on horseback.

'Such awful ages since I saw you!' said Flora to Lou. 'Sorry if we burst in on you. We're only just saying *How do you do!* and going on to the inn. They've got rooms all ready for us there. We thought we'd stay just one night over here, and ride to-morrow to the Devil's Chair.[33] Won't you come? Lots of fun! Isn't Mrs Witt at home?'

Mrs Witt was out for the moment. When she returned she had on her curious stiff face, yet she greeted the newcomers with a certain cordiality: she felt it would be diplomatic, no doubt.

'There *are* two rooms here,' she said, 'and if you care to poke into them, why we shall be *delighted* to have you. But I'll show them to you first, because they are poor, inconvenient rooms, with no running water and *miles* from the baths.'

Flora and Elsie declared that they were 'perfectly darling sweet rooms – not overcrowded'.

'Well,' said Mrs Witt, 'the conveniences certainly don't fill up much space. But if you like to take them for what they are –'

'Why we feel absolutely overwhelmed, don't we, Elsie! – But we've no clothes –!'

Suddenly the silence had turned into a house-party. The Manby girls appeared to lunch in fine muslin dresses, bought in Paris, fresh as daisies. Women's clothing takes up so little space, especially in summer! Fred Edwards was one of those blond

Englishmen with a little brush moustache and those strong blue
eyes which were always attempting the sentimental, but which
Lou, in her prejudice, considered cruel: upon what grounds she
never analysed. However, he took a gallant tone with her at once,
and she had to seem to simper. Rico, watching her, was so
relieved when he saw the simper coming.

It had begun again, the whole clockwork of 'lots of fun!'

'Isn't Fred flirting perfectly outrageously with Lady Carrington! – She looks so *sweet*!' cried Flora, over her coffee-cup. 'Don't
you mind, Harry!'

They called Rico 'Harry'! His boy-name.

'Only a very little,' said Harry. '*L'uomo è cacciatore*.'

'Oh now, what does that mean?' cried Flora, who always
thrilled to Rico's bits of affectation.

'It means,' said Mrs Witt, leaning forward and speaking in her
most suave voice, 'that man is a hunter.'

Even Flora shrank under the smooth acid of the irony.

'Oh, well now!' she cried. 'If he is, then what is woman?'

'The hunted,' said Mrs Witt, in a still smoother acid.

'At least,' said Rico, 'she is always *game*!'

'Ah, is she though!' came Fred's manly, well-bred tones. 'I'm
not so sure.'

Mrs Witt looked from one man to the other, as if she were
dropping them down the bottomless pit.

Lou escaped to look at St Mawr. He was still moist where the
saddle had been. And he seemed a little bit extinguished, as if
virtue had gone out of him.

But when he lifted his lovely naked head, like a bunch of
flames, to see who it was had entered, she saw he was still himself.
For ever sensitive and alert, his head lifted like the summit of
a fountain. And within him the clean bones striking to the earth,
his hoofs intervening between him and the ground like lesser
jewels.

He knew her and did not resent her. But he took no notice of
her. He would never 'respond'. At first she had resented it. Now
she was glad. He would never be intimate, thank heaven.

She hid herself away till tea-time, but she could not hide from
the sound of voices. Dinner was early, at seven. Dean Vyner

came – Mrs Vyner was an invalid – and also an artist[34] who had a studio in the village and did etchings. He was a man of about thirty-eight, and poor, just beginning to accept himself as a failure, as far as making money goes. But he worked at his etchings and studied esoteric matters like astrology and alchemy. Rico patronized him, and was a little afraid of him. Lou could not quite make him out. After knocking about Paris and London and Munich, he was trying to become staid, and to persuade himself that English village life, with squire and dean in the background, humble artist in the middle and labourer in the common foreground, was genuine life. His self-persuasion was only moderately successful. This was betrayed by the curious arrest in his body: he seemed to have to force himself into movement: and by the curious duplicity in his yellow-grey, twinkling eyes, that twinkled and expanded like a goat's; with mockery, irony, and frustration.

'Your face is curiously like Pan's,' said Lou to him at dinner.

It was true, in a commonplace sense. He had the tilted eyebrows, the twinkling goaty look, and the pointed ears of a goat-Pan.[35]

'People have said so,' he replied. 'But I'm afraid it's not the face of the Great God Pan. Isn't it rather the Great Goat Pan!'

'I say, that's good!' cried Rico. 'The Great Goat Pan!'

'I have always found it difficult,' said the Dean, 'to see the Great God Pan in that goat-legged old father of satyrs. He may have a good deal of influence – the world will always be full of goaty old satyrs. But we find them somewhat vulgar. Even our late King Edward.[36] The goaty old satyrs are too comprehensible to me to be venerable, and I fail to see a Great God in the father of them all.'

'Your ears should be getting red,' said Lou to Cartwright. She, too, had an odd squinting smile that suggested nymphs, so irresponsible and unbelieving.

'Oh no, nothing personal!' cried the Dean.

'I am not sure,' said Cartwright, with a small smile. 'But don't you imagine Pan once *was* a great god, before the anthropomorphic Greeks turned him into half a man?'

'Ah! – maybe. That is very possible. But – I have noticed the limitation in myself – my mind has no grasp whatsoever of Europe before the Greeks arose. Mr Wells' Outline[37] does not help me there, either,' the Dean added with a smile.

'But what was Pan before he was a man with goat legs?' asked Lou.

'Before he looked like me?' said Cartwright, with a faint grin. 'I should say he was the god that is hidden in everything. In those days you saw the thing, you never saw the god in it: I mean in the tree or the fountain or the animal. If you ever saw the God instead of the thing, you died. If you saw it with the naked eye, that is. But in the night you might see the God. And you knew it was there.'

'The modern pantheist not only sees the God in everything, he takes photographs of it,' said the Dean.

'Oh, and the divine pictures he paints!' cried Rico.

'Quite!' said Cartwright.

'But if they never *saw* the God in the thing, the old ones, how did they know he was there? How did they have any Pan at all?' said Lou.

'Pan was the hidden mystery – the hidden cause. That's how it was a Great God. Pan wasn't *he* at all: not even a great God. He was Pan. All: what you see when you see in full. In the daytime you see the thing. But if your third eye is open, which sees only the things that can't be seen, you may see Pan within the thing, hidden: you may see with your third eye, which is darkness.'

'Do you think I might see Pan in a horse, for example?'

'Easily. In St Mawr!' – Cartwright gave her a knowing look.

'But,' said Mrs Witt, 'it would be difficult, I should say, to open the third eye and see Pan in a man.'

'Probably,' said Cartwright, smiling. 'In man he is over-visible: the old satyr: the fallen Pan.'

'Exactly!' said Mrs Witt. And she fell into a muse. 'The fallen Pan!' she re-echoed. 'Wouldn't a man be wonderful in whom Pan hadn't fallen!'

Over the coffee in the grey drawing-room she suddenly asked:

'Supposing, Mr Cartwright, one *did* open the third eye and see Pan in an actual man – I wonder what it would be like?'

She half lowered her eyelids and tilted her face in a strange way, as if she were tasting something, and not quite sure.

'I wonder!' he said, smiling his enigmatic smile. But she could see he did not understand.

'Louise!' said Mrs Witt at bedtime. 'Come into my room for a moment, I want to ask you something.'

'What is it, mother?'

'You, you *get* something from what Mr Cartwright said about seeing Pan with the third eye? Seeing Pan in something?'

Mrs Witt came rather close, and tilted her face with strange insinuating question at her daughter.

'I think I do, mother.'

'In what?' – The question came as a pistol-shot.

'I think, mother,' said Lou reluctantly, 'in St Mawr.'

'In a horse!' – Mrs Witt contracted her eyes slightly. 'Yes, I can see that. I know what you mean. It *is* in St Mawr. It *is*! But in St Mawr it makes me *afraid* –' she dragged out the word. Then she came a step closer. 'But, Louise, did you ever see it in a man?'

'What, mother?'

'Pan. Did you ever see Pan in a man, as you see Pan in St Mawr?'

Louise hesitated.

'No, mother, I don't think I did. When I look at men with my third eye, as you call it – I think I see – mostly – a sort of – pan-cake.' She uttered the last word with a despairing grin, not knowing quite what to say.

'Oh, Louise, isn't that it! Doesn't one always see a pancake! Now listen, Louise. Have you ever been in love?'

'Yes, as far as I understand it.'

'Listen, now. Did you ever see Pan in the man you loved? Tell me if you did.'

'As I see Pan in St Mawr? – no, mother.' And suddenly her lips began to tremble and the tears came to her eyes.

'Listen, Louise. I've been in love innumerable times – and *really* in love twice. Twice! – yet for fifteen years I've left off wanting to have anything to do with a man, really. For fifteen years! And why? Do you know? Because I couldn't see that peculiar hidden Pan in any of them. And I became that I needed to. I needed it. But it wasn't there. Not in any man. Even when I was in love with a man, it was for other things: because I *understood* him so well, or he understood me, or we had such sympathy. Never the hidden Pan. Do you understand what I mean? Unfallen Pan!'

'More or less, mother.'

'But now my third eye is coming open, I believe. I am tired of all these men like breakfast cakes, with a tea-spoonful of mind or a tea-spoonful of spirit in them, for baking powder. Isn't it extraordinary: that young man Cartwright talks about Pan, but he knows nothing of it all. He knows nothing of the unfallen Pan: only the fallen Pan with goat legs and a leer – and that sort of power, don't you know.'

'But what do you know of the unfallen Pan, mother?'

'Don't ask me, Louise! I feel all of a tremble, as if I was just on the verge.'

She flashed a little look of incipient triumph, and said good-night.

An excursion on horseback had been arranged for the next day, to two old groups of rocks, called the Angel's Chair and the Devil's Chair, which crowned the moor-like hills looking into Wales, ten miles away. Everybody was going – they were to start early in the morning, and Lewis would be the guide, since no one exactly knew the way.

Lou got up soon after sunrise. There was a summer scent in the trees of early morning, and monkshood flowers stood up dark and tall, with shadows. She dressed in the green linen riding-skirt her maid had put ready for her, with a close bluish smock.

'Are you going out already, dear?' called Rico from his room.

'Just to smell the roses before we start, Rico.'

He appeared in the doorway in his yellow silk pyjamas. His large blue eyes had that rolling irritable look and the slightly bloodshot whites which made her want to escape.

'Booted and spurred! – the *energy*!' he cried.

'It's a lovely day to ride,' she said.

'A lovely day to do anything *except* ride!' he said. 'Why spoil the day riding!' – A curious bitter-acid escaped into his tone. It was evident he hated the excursion.

'Why, we needn't go if you don't want to, Rico.'

'Oh, I'm sure I shall love it, once I get started. It's all this business of *starting*, with horses and paraphernalia –'

Lou went into the yard. The horses were drinking at the trough under the pump, their colours strong and rich in the shadow of the tree.

'You're not coming with us, Phoenix?' she said.

'Lewis, he's riding my horse.'

She could tell Phoenix did not like being left behind.

By half-past seven everybody was ready. The sun was in the yard, the horses were saddled. They came swishing their tails. Lewis brought out St Mawr from his separate box, speaking to him very quietly in Welsh: a murmuring, soothing little speech. Lou, alert, could see that he was uneasy.

'How is St Mawr this morning?' she asked.

'He's all right. He doesn't like so many people. He'll be all right once he's started.'

The strangers were in the saddle: they moved out to the deep shade of the village road outside. Rico came to his horse to mount. St Mawr jumped away as if he had seen the devil.

'Steady, fool!' cried Rico.

The bay stood with his four feet spread, his neck arched, his big dark eye glancing sideways with that watchful, frightening look.

'You shouldn't be irritable with him, Rico!' said Lou. 'Steady then, St Mawr! Be steady.'

But a certain anger rose also in her. The creature was so big, so brilliant, and so stupid, standing there with his hind legs spread, ready to jump aside or to rear terrifically, and his great eye glancing with a sort of suspicious frenzy. What was there to be suspicious of, after all? – Rico would do him no harm.

'No one will harm you, St Mawr,' she reasoned, a bit exasperated.

The groom was talking quietly, murmuringly, in Welsh. Rico was slowly advancing again, to put his foot in the stirrup. The stallion was watching from the corner of his eye, a strange glare of suspicious frenzy burning stupidly. Any moment his immense physical force might be let loose in a frenzy of panic – or malice. He was really very irritating.

'Probably he doesn't like that apricot shirt,' said Mrs Witt, 'although it tones into him wonderfully well.'

She pronounced it *ap* – ricot, and it irritated Rico terribly.

'Ought we to have *asked* him before we put it on?' he flashed, his upper lip lifting venomously.

'I should say you should,' replied Mrs Witt coolly.

Rico turned with a sudden rush to the horse. Back went the great animal, with a sudden splashing crash of hoofs on the cobble-stones, and Lewis hanging on like a shadow. Up went the forefeet, showing the belly.

'The thing is accursed,' said Rico, who had dropped the reins in sudden shock, and stood marooned. His rage overwhelmed him like a black flood.

'Nothing in the world is so irritating as a horse that is acting up,' thought Lou.

'Say, Harry!' called Flora from the road. 'Come out here into the road to mount him.'

Lewis looked at Rico and nodded. Then soothing the big, quivering animal, he led him springily out to the road under the trees, where the three friends were waiting. Lou and her mother got quickly into the saddle to follow. And in another moment Rico was mounted and bouncing down the road in the wrong direction, Lewis following on the chestnut. It was some time before Rico could get St Mawr round. Watching him from behind, those waiting could judge how the young Baronet hated it.

But at last they set off – Rico ahead, unevenly but quietly, with the two Manby girls, Lou following with the fair young man who had been in a cavalry regiment and who kept looking round for Mrs Witt.

'Don't look round for me,' she called. 'I'm riding behind, out of the dust.'

Just behind Mrs Witt came Lewis. It was a whole cavalcade trotting in the morning sun past the cottages and the cottage gardens, round the field that was the recreation ground, into the deep hedges of the lane.

'Why is St Mawr so bad at starting? Can't you get him into better shape?' she asked over her shoulder.

'Beg your pardon, Mam!'

Lewis trotted a little nearer. She glanced over her shoulder at him, at his dark, unmoved face, his cool little figure.

'I think *Mam* is so ugly. Why not leave it out!' she said. Then she repeated her question.

'St Mawr doesn't trust anybody,' Lewis replied.

'Not you?'

'Yes, he trusts me – mostly.'

'Then why not other people?'

'They're different.'

'All of them?'

'About all of them.'

'How are they different?'

He looked at her with his remote, uncanny grey eyes.

'Different,' he said, not knowing how else to put it.

They rode on slowly, up the steep rise of the wood, then down into a glade where ran a little railway built for hauling some mysterious mineral out of the hill, in war-time, and now already abandoned. Even on this countryside the dead hand of the war lay like a corpse decomposing.

They rode up again, past the foxgloves under the trees. Ahead the brilliant St Mawr and the sorrel and grey horses were swimming like butterflies through the sea of bracken, glittering from sun to shade, shade to sun. Then once more they were on a crest, and through the thinning trees could see the slopes of the moors beyond the next dip.

Soon they were in the open, rolling hills, golden in the morning and empty save for a couple of distant bilberry-pickers, whitish figures pick – pick – picking with curious, rather disgusting assiduity. The horses were on an old trail, which climbed through the pinky tips of heather and ling, across patches of green bilberry. Here and there were tufts of harebells blue as bubbles.

They were out, high on the hills. And there to west lay Wales, folded in crumpled folds, goldish in the morning light, with its moor-like slopes and patches of corn uncannily distinct. Between was a hollow, wide valley of summer haze, showing white farms among trees, and grey slate roofs.

'Ride beside me,' she said to Lewis. 'Nothing makes me want to go back to America like the old look of these little villages. – You have never been to America?'

'No, Mam.'

'Don't you ever want to go?'

'I wouldn't mind going.'

'But you're not just crazy to go?'

'No, Mam.'

'Quite content as you are?'

He looked at her, and his pale, remote eyes met hers.

'I don't fret myself,' he replied.

'Not about anything at all – ever?'

His eyes glanced ahead, at the other riders.

'No, Mam!' he replied, without looking at her.

She rode a few moments in silence.

'What is that over there?' she asked, pointing across the valley. 'What is it called?'

'Yon's Montgomery.'

'Montgomery! And is that *Wales* –?' she trailed the ending curiously.

'Yes, Mam.'

'Where you come from?'

'No, Mam! I come from Merioneth.'

'Not from Wales? I thought you were Welsh?'

'Yes, Mam. Merioneth *is* Wales.'

'And you are Welsh?'

'Yes, Mam.'

'I had a Welsh grandmother. But I come from Louisiana, and when I go back home, the negroes still call me Miss Rachel. *Oh, my, it's little Miss Rachel come back home! Why, ain't I mighty glad to see you – u, Miss Rachel!* That gives me such a strange feeling, you know.'

The man glanced at her curiously, especially when she imitated the negroes.

'Do you feel strange when you go home?' she asked.

'I was brought up by an aunt and uncle,' he said. 'I never want to see them.'

'And you don't have any home?'

'No, Mam.'

'No wife nor anything?'

'No, Mam.'

'But what do you do with your life?'

'I keep to myself.'

'And care about nothing?'

'I mind St Mawr.'

'But you've not always had St Mawr – and you won't always have him. – Were you in the war?'

'Yes, Mam.'

'At the front?'

'Yes, Mam – but I was a groom.'

'And you came out all right?'

'I lost my little finger from a bullet.'

He held up his small, dark left hand, from which the little finger was missing.

'And did you like the war – or didn't you?'

'I didn't like it.'

Again his pale grey eyes met hers, and they looked so non-human and uncommunicative, so without connexion, and inaccessible, she was troubled.

'Tell me,' she said. 'Did you never want a wife and a home and children, like other men?'

'No, Mam. I never wanted a home of my own.'

'Nor a wife of your own?'

'No, Mam.'

'Nor children of your own?'

'No, Mam.'

She reined in her horse.

'Now wait a minute,' she said. 'Now tell me why.'

His horse came to standstill, and the two riders faced one another.

'Tell me why – I must know why you never wanted a wife and children and a home. I must know why you're not like other men.'

'I never felt like it,' he said. 'I made my life with horses.'

'Did you hate people very much? Did you have a very unhappy time as a child?'

'My aunt and uncle didn't like me, and I didn't like them.'

'So you've never liked anybody?'

'Maybe not,' he said. 'Not to get as far as marrying them.'

She touched her horse and moved on.

'Isn't that curious!' she said. 'I've loved people, at various times. But I don't believe *I've* ever liked anybody, except a few of our negroes. I don't like Louise, though she's my daughter and I love her. But I don't really *like* her. – I think you're the first person I've ever liked since I was on our plantation, and we had some *very fine* negroes. – And I think that's very curious. – Now I want to know if you like *me*.'

She looked at him searchingly, but he did not answer.

'Tell me,' she said. 'I don't mind if you say no. But tell me if you like me. I feel I must know.'

The flicker of a smile went over his face – a very rare thing with him.

'Maybe I do,' he said. He was thinking that she put him on a level with a negro slave on a plantation: in his idea, negroes were still slaves. But he did not care where she put him.

'Well, I'm glad – I'm glad if you like me. Because you *don't* like most people, I know that.'

They had passed the hollow where the old Aldecar Chapel hid in damp isolation, beside the ruined mill, over the stream that came down from the moors. Climbing the sharp slope, they saw the folded hills like great shut fingers, with steep, deep clefts between. On the near skyline was a bunch of rocks: and away to the right another bunch.

'Yon's the Angel's Chair,' said Lewis, pointing to the nearer rocks. 'And yon's the Devil's Chair, where we're going.'

'Oh!' said Mrs Witt. 'And aren't we going to the Angel's Chair?'

'No, Mam!'

'Why not?'

'There's nothing to see there. The other's higher, and bigger, and that's where folks mostly go.'

'Is that so! – They give the Devil the higher seat in this country, do they? I think they're right.' And as she got no answer, she added: 'You believe in the Devil, don't you?'

'I never met him,' he answered, evasively.

Ahead, they could see the other horses twinkling in a cavalcade up the slope, the black, the bay, the two greys and the sorrel, sometimes bunching, sometimes straggling. At a gate all waited for Mrs Witt. The fair young man fell in beside her, and talked hunting at her. He had hunted the fox over these hills, and was vigorously excited locating the spot where the hounds first gave cry, etc.

'Really!' said Mrs Witt. '*Really!* Is that so!'

If irony could have been condensed to prussic acid, the fair young man would have ended his life's history with his reminiscences.

They came at last, trotting in file along a narrow track between heather, along the saddle of a hill, to where the knot of pale granite suddenly cropped out. It was one of those places where the spirit of aboriginal England still lingers, the old savage England, whose last blood flows still in a few Englishmen, Welshmen, Cornishmen. The rocks, whitish with weather of all the ages, jutted against the blue August sky, heavy with age-moulded roundnesses.

Lewis stayed below with the horses, the party scrambled rather awkwardly, in their riding-boots, up the foot-worn boulders. At length they stood in the place called the Chair, looking west, west towards Wales, that rolled in golden folds upwards. It was neither impressive nor a very picturesque landscape: the hollow valley with farms, and then the rather bare upheaval of hills, slopes with corn and moor and pasture, rising like a barricade, seemingly high, slantingly. Yet it had a strange effect on the imagination.

'Oh mother,' said Lou, 'doesn't it make you feel old, old, older than anything ever was?'

'It certainly does seem aged,' said Mrs Witt.

'It makes me want to die,' said Lou. 'I feel we've lasted almost too long.'

'Don't say that, Lady Carrington. Why, you're a spring chicken yet: or shall I say an unopened rosebud,' remarked the fair young man.

'No,' said Lou. 'All these millions of ancestors have used all the life up. We're not really alive, in the sense that they were alive.'

'But who?' said Rico. 'Who are *they*?'

'The people who lived on these hills, in the days gone by.'

'But the same people still live on the hills, darling. It's just the same stock.'

'No, Rico. That old fighting stock that worshipped devils among these stones – I'm sure they did –'

'But look here, do you mean they were any better than we are?' asked the fair young man.

Lou looked at him quizzically.

'We don't exist,' she said, squinting at him oddly.

'I jolly well know *I* do,' said the fair young man.

'I consider these days are the best ever, especially for girls,' said Flora Manby. 'And anyhow they're our own days, so I don't jolly well see the use of crying them down.'

They were all silent, with the last echoes of emphatic *joie de vivre*[38] trumpeting on the air, across the hills of Wales.

'Spoken like a brick, Flora,' said Rico. 'Say it again, we may not have the Devil's Chair for a pulpit next time.'

'I do,' reiterated Flora. 'I think this is the best age there ever was for a girl to have a good time in. I read all through H. G. Wells' history, and I shut it up and thanked my stars I live in nineteen-twenty odd, not in some other beastly date when a woman had to cringe before mouldy domineering men.'

After this they turned to scramble to another part of the rocks, to the famous Needle's Eye.

'Thank you so much, I am really better without help,' said Mrs Witt to the fair young man, as she slid downwards till a piece of grey silk stocking showed above her tall boot. But she got her toe in a safe place, and in a moment stood beside him, while he caught her arm protectingly. He might as well have caught the paw of a mountain lion protectingly.

'I should like *so* much to know,' she said suavely, looking into his eyes with a demonish straight look, 'what makes you so certain that you exist?'

He looked back at her, and his jaunty blue eyes went baffled. Then a slow, hot, salmon-coloured flush stole over his face, and he turned abruptly round.

The Needle's Eye was a hole in the ancient grey rock, like a window, looking to England; England at the moment in shadow. A stream wound and glinted in the flat shadow, and beyond that the flat, insignificant hills heaped in mounds of shade. Cloud was coming – the English side was in shadow. Wales was still in the sun, but the shadow was spreading. The day was going to disappoint them. Lou was a tiny bit chilled, already.

Luncheon was still several miles away. The party hastened down to the horses. Lou picked a few sprigs of ling, and some hare-bells, and some straggling yellow flowers: not because she wanted them, but to distract herself. The atmosphere of 'enjoying ourselves' was becoming cruel to her: it sapped all the life out of her. 'Oh, if only I needn't enjoy myself,' she moaned inwardly. But the Manby girls were enjoying themselves so much. 'I think it's frantically lovely up here,' said the other one – not Flora – Elsie.

'It *is* beautiful, isn't it! I'm *so* glad you like it,' replied Rico. And he was really relieved and gratified, because the other one said she was enjoying it so frightfully. He dared not say to Lou, as he wanted to: 'I'm afraid, Lou darling, you don't love it as much as we do.' – He was afraid of her answer: 'No dear, I don't love it at all! I want to be away from these people.'

Slightly piqued, he rode on with the Manby group, and Lou came behind with her mother. Cloud was covering the sky with grey. There was a cold wind. Everybody was anxious to get to the farm for luncheon, and be safely home before rain came.

They were riding along one of the narrow little foot-tracks, mere grooves of grass between heather and bright green bilberry. The blond young man was ahead, then his wife, then Flora, then Rico. Lou, from a little distance, watched the glossy, powerful haunches of St Mawr swaying with life, always too much life, like a menace. The fair young man was whistling a new dance tune.

'That's an awfully attractive tune,' Rico called. 'Do whistle it again, Fred, I should like to memorize it.'

Fred began to whistle it again.

At that moment St Mawr exploded again, shied sideways as if a bomb had gone off, and kept backing through the heather.

'Fool!' cried Rico, thoroughly unnerved: he had been terribly sideways in the saddle, Lou had feared he was going to fall. But he got his seat, and pulled the reins viciously, to bring the horse to order, and put him on the track again. St Mawr began to rear: his favourite trick. Rico got him forward a few yards, when up he went again.

'Fool!' yelled Rico, hanging in the air.

He pulled the horse over backwards on top of him.

Lou gave a loud, unnatural, horrible scream: she heard it herself, at the same time as she heard the crash of the falling horse. Then she saw a pale gold belly, and hoofs that worked and flashed in the air, and St Mawr writhing, straining his head terrifically upwards, his great eyes starting from the naked lines of his nose. With a great neck arching cruelly from the ground, he was pulling frantically at the reins, which Rico still held tight. – Yes, Rico, lying strangely sideways, his eyes also starting from his yellow-white face, among the heather, still clutched the reins.

Young Edwards was rushing forward, and circling round the writhing, immense horse, whose pale-gold, inverted bulk seemed to fill the universe.

'Let him get up, Carrington! Let him get up!' he was yelling, darting warily near, to get the reins. – Another spasmodic convulsion of the horse.

Horror! The young man reeled backwards with his face in his hands. He had got a kick in the face. Red blood running down his chin!

Lewis was there, on the ground, getting the reins out of Rico's hands. St Mawr gave a great curve like a fish, spread his forefeet on the earth and reared his head, looking round in a ghastly fashion. His eyes were arched, his nostrils wide, his face ghastly in a sort of panic. He rested thus, seated with his forefeet planted and his face in panic, almost like some terrible lizard, for several moments. Then he heaved sickeningly to his feet, and stood convulsed, trembling.

There lay Rico, crumpled and rather sideways, staring at the heavens from a yellow, dead-looking face. Lewis, glancing round in a sort of horror, looked in dread at St Mawr again. Flora had been hovering. – She now rushed screeching to the prostrate Rico:

'Harry! Harry! you're not dead! Oh, Harry! Harry! Harry!'
Lou had dismounted. – She didn't know when. She stood a little
way off, as if spellbound, while Flora cried *Harry! Harry!
Harry!*

Suddenly Rico sat up.

'Where is the horse?' he said.

At the same time an added whiteness came on his face, and
he bit his lip with pain, and he fell prostrate again in a faint. Flora
rushed to put her arm round him.

Where was the horse? He had backed slowly away, in an agony
of suspicion, while Lewis murmured to him in vain. His head
was raised again, the eyes still starting from their sockets, and
a terrible guilty, ghost-like look on his face. When Lewis drew
a little nearer he twitched and shrank like a shaken steel spring,
away – not to be touched. He seemed to be seeing legions of
ghosts, down the dark avenues of all the centuries that have
lapsed since the horse became subject to man.

And the other young man? He was still standing, at a little
distance, with his face in his hands, motionless, the blood falling
on his white shirt, and his wife at his side, pleading, distracted.

Mrs Witt too was there, as if cast in steel, watching. She made
no sound and did not move, only, from a fixed, impassive face,
watched each thing.

'Do tell me what you think is the matter?' Lou pleaded,
distracted, to Flora, who was supporting Rico and weeping
torrents of unknown tears.

Then Mrs Witt came forward and began in a very practical
manner to unclose the shirt-neck and feel the young man's heart.
Rico opened his eyes again, said '*Really!*' and closed his eyes once
more.

'It's fainting!' said Mrs Witt. 'We have no brandy.'

Lou, too weary to be able to feel anything, said:

'I'll go and get some.'

She went to her alarmed horse, who stood among the others
with her head down, in suspense. Almost unconsciously Lou
mounted, set her face ahead, and was riding away.

Then Poppy shied too, with a sudden start, and Lou pulled
up. 'Why?' she said to her horse. 'Why did you do that?'

She looked round, and saw in the heather a glimpse of yellow and black.

'A snake!' she said wonderingly.

And she looked closer.

It was a dead adder that had been drinking at a reedy pool in a little depression just off the road, and had been killed with stones. There it lay, also crumpled, its head crushed, its gold-and-yellow back still glittering dully, and a bit of pale-blue belly showing, killed that morning.

Lou rode on, her face set towards the farm. An unspeakable weariness had overcome her. She could not even suffer. Weariness of spirit left her in a sort of apathy.

And she had a vision, a vision of evil. Or not strictly a vision. She became aware of evil, evil, evil, rolling in great waves over the earth. Always she had thought there was no such thing – only a mere negation of good. Now, like an ocean to whose surface she had risen, she saw the dark-grey waves of evil rearing in a great tide.

And it had swept mankind away without mankind's knowing. It had caught up the nations as the rising ocean might lift the fishes, and was sweeping them on in a great tide of evil. They did not know. The people did not know. They did not even wish it. They wanted to be good and to have everything joyful and enjoyable. Everything joyful and enjoyable: for everybody. This was what they wanted, if you asked them.

But at the same time, they had fallen under the spell of evil. It was a soft, subtle thing, soft as water, and its motion was soft and imperceptible, as the running of a tide is invisible to one who is out on the ocean. And they were all out on the ocean, being borne along in the current of the mysterious evil, creatures of the evil principle, as fishes are creatures of the sea.

There was no relief. The whole world was enveloped in one great flood. All the nations, the white, the brown, the black, the yellow, all were immersed in the strange tide of evil that was subtly, irresistibly rising. No one, perhaps, deliberately wished it. Nearly every individual wanted peace and a good time all round: everybody to have a good time.

But some strange thing had happened, and the vast,

mysterious force of positive evil was let loose. She felt that from the core of Asia the evil welled up, as from some strange pole, and slowly was drowning earth.

It was something horrifying, something you could not escape from. It had come to her as in a vision, when she saw the pale gold belly of the stallion upturned, the hoofs working wildly, the wicked curved hams of the horse, and then the evil straining of that arched, fish-like neck, with the dilated eyes of the head. Thrown backwards, and working its hoofs in the air. Reversed, and purely evil.

She saw the same in people. They were thrown backwards, and writhing with evil. And the rider, crushed, was still reining them down.

What did it mean? Evil, evil, and a rapid return to the sordid chaos. Which was wrong, the horse or the rider? Or both?

She thought with horror of St Mawr, and of the look on his face. But she thought with horror, a colder horror, of Rico's face as he snarled *Fool!* His fear, his impotence as a master, as a rider, his presumption. And she thought with horror of those other people, so glib, so glibly evil.

What did they want to do, those Manby girls? Undermine, undermine, undermine. They wanted to undermine Rico, just as that fair young man would have liked to undermine her. Believe in nothing, care about nothing: but keep the surface easy, and have a good time. *Let us undermine one another. There is nothing to believe in, so let us undermine everything. But look out! No scenes, no spoiling the game. Stick to the rules of the game. Be sporting, and don't do anything that would make a commotion. Keep the game going smooth and jolly, and bear your bit like a sport. Never, by any chance, injure your fellow man openly. But always injure him secretly. Make a fool of him, and undermine his nature. Break him up by undermining him, if you can. It's good sport.*

The evil! The mysterious potency of evil. She could see it all the time, in individuals, in society, in the press. There it was in socialism and bolshevism: the same evil. But bolshevism made a mess of the outside of life, so turn it down. Try fascism. Fascism would keep the surface of life intact, and carry on the undermining business all the better. All the better sport. Never draw blood. Keep the haemorrhage internal, invisible.

And as soon as fascism makes a break – which it is bound to, because all evil works up to a break – then turn it down. With gusto, turn it down.

Mankind, like a horse, ridden by a stranger, smooth-faced, evil rider. Evil himself, smooth-faced and pseudo-handsome, riding mankind past the dead snake, to the last break.

Mankind no longer its own master. Ridden by this pseudo-handsome ghoul of outward loyalty, inward treachery, in a game of betrayal, betrayal, betrayal. The last of the gods of our era, Judas supreme!

People performing outward acts of loyalty, piety, self-sacrifice. But inwardly bent on undermining, betraying. Directing all their subtle evil will against any positive living thing. Masquerading as the ideal, in order to poison the real.

Creation destroys as it goes, throws down one tree for the rise of another. But ideal mankind would abolish death, multiply itself million upon million, rear up city upon city, save every parasite alive, until the accumulation of mere existence is swollen to a horror. But go on saving life, the ghastly salvation army of ideal mankind. At the same time secretly, viciously, potently undermine the natural creation, betray it with kiss after kiss, destroy it from the inside, till you have the swollen rottenness of our teeming existences. – But keep the game going. Nobody's going to make another bad break, such as Germany and Russia made.

Two bad breaks the secret evil has made: in Germany and in Russia. Watch it! Let evil keep a policeman's eyes on evil! The surface of life must remain unruptured. Production must be heaped upon production. And the natural creation must be betrayed by many more kisses, yet. Judas is the last God, and, by heaven, the most potent.

But even Judas made a break: hanged himself, and his bowels gushed out. Not long after his triumph.

Man must destroy as he goes, as trees fall for trees to rise. The accumulation of life and things means rottenness. Life must destroy life, in the unfolding of creation. We save up life at the expense of the unfolding, till all is full of rottenness. Then at last, we make a break.

What's to be done? Generally speaking, nothing. The dead will have to bury their dead, while the earth stinks of corpses. The individual can but depart from the mass, and try to cleanse himself. Try to hold fast to the living thing, which destroys as it goes, but remains sweet. And in his soul fight, fight, fight to preserve that which is life in him from the ghastly kisses and poison-bites of the myriad evil ones. Retreat to the desert, and fight. But in his soul adhere to that which is life itself, creatively destroying as it goes: destroying the stiff old thing to let the new bud come through. The one passionate principle of creative being, which recognizes the natural good, and has a sword for the swarms of evil. Fights, fights, fights to protect itself. But with itself, is strong and at peace.

Lou came to the farm, and got brandy, and asked the men to come out to carry in the injured.

It turned out that the kick in the face had knocked a couple of young Edwards' teeth out, and would disfigure him a little.

'To go through the war, and then get this!' he mumbled, with a vindictive glance at St Mawr.

And it turned out that Rico had two broken ribs and a crushed ankle. Poor Rico, he would limp for life.

'I want St Mawr *shot*!' was almost his first word, when he was in bed at the farm and Lou was sitting beside him.

'What good would that do, dear?' she said.

'The brute is evil. I want him *shot*!'

Rico could make the last word sound like the spitting of a bullet.

'Do you want to shoot him yourself?'

'No. But I want to have him shot. I shall never be easy till I know he has a bullet through him. He's got a wicked character. I don't feel you are safe, with him down there. I shall get one of the Manby's gamekeepers to shoot him. You might tell Flora – or I'll tell her myself, when she comes.'

'Don't talk about it now, dear. You've got a temperature.'

Was it true St Mawr was evil? She would never forget him writhing and lunging on the ground, nor his awful face when he reared up. But then that noble look of his: surely he was not mean? Whereas all evil had an inner meanness, mean! Was he mean? Was he meanly treacherous? Did he know he could kill, and meanly wait his opportunity?

She was afraid. And if this were true, then he *should* be shot. Perhaps he ought to be shot.

This thought haunted her. Was there something mean and treacherous in St Mawr's spirit, the vulgar evil? If so, then have him shot. At moments, an anger would rise in her, as she thought of his frenzied rearing, and his mad, hideous writhing on the ground, and in the heat of her anger she would want to hurry down to her mother's house and have the creature shot at once. It would be a satisfaction, and a vindication of human rights. Because after all, Rico was so considerate of the brutal horse. But not a spark of consideration did the stallion have for Rico. No, it was the slavish malevolence of a domesticated creature that kept cropping up in St Mawr. The slave, taking his slavish vengeance, then dropping back into subservience.

All the slaves of this world, accumulating their preparations for slavish vengeance, and then, when they have taken it, ready to drop back into servility. Freedom! Most slaves can't be freed, no matter how you let them loose. Like domestic animals, they are, in the long run, more afraid of freedom than of masters: and freed by some generous master, they will at last crawl back to some mean boss, who will have no scruples about kicking them. Because, for them, far better kicks and servility than the hard, lonely responsibility of real freedom.

The wild animal is at every moment intensely self-disciplined, poised in the tension of self-defence, self-preservation, and self-assertion. The moments of relaxation are rare and most carefully chosen. Even sleep is watchful, guarded, unrelaxing, the wild courage pitched one degree higher than the wild fear. Courage, the wild thing's courage to maintain itself alone and living in the midst of a diverse universe.

Did St Mawr have this courage?

And did Rico?

Ah, Rico! He was one of mankind's myriad conspirators, who conspire to live in absolute physical safety, whilst willing the minor disintegration of all positive living.

But St Mawr? Was it the natural wild thing in him which caused these disasters? Or was it the slave, asserting himself for vengeance?

If the latter, let him be shot. It would be a great satisfaction to see him dead.

But if the former –

When she could leave Rico with the nurse, she motored down to her mother for a couple of days. Rico lay in bed at the farm.

Everything seemed curiously changed. There was a new silence about the place, a new coolness. Summer had passed with several thunderstorms, and the blue, cool touch of autumn was about the house. Dahlias and perennial yellow sunflowers were out, the yellow of ending summer, the red coals of early autumn. First mauve tips of Michaelmas daisies were showing. Something suddenly carried her away to the great bare spaces of Texas, the blue sky, the flat, burnt earth, the miles of sunflowers. Another sky, another silence, towards the setting sun.

And suddenly, she craved again for the more absolute silence of America. English stillness was so soft, like an inaudible murmur of voices, of presences. But the silence in the empty spaces of America was still unutterable, almost cruel.

St Mawr was in a small field by himself: she could not bear that he should be always in stable. Slowly she went through the gate towards him. And he stood there looking at her, the bright bay creature.

She could tell he was feeling somewhat subdued, after his late escapade. He was aware of the general human condemnation: the human damning. But something obstinate and uncanny in him made him not relent.

'Hello! St Mawr!' she said, as she drew near, and he stood watching her, his ears pricked, his big eyes glancing sideways at her.

But he moved away when she wanted to touch him.

'Don't trouble,' she said. 'I don't want to catch you or do anything to you.'

He stood still, listening to the sound of her voice, and giving quick, small glances at her. His underlip trembled. But he did not blink. His eyes remained wide and unrelenting. There was a curious malicious obstinacy in him which roused her anger.

'I don't want to touch you,' she said. 'I only want to look at you, and even you can't prevent that.'

She stood gazing hard at him, wanting to know, to settle the question of his meanness or his spirit. A thing with a brave spirit is not mean.

He was uneasy as she watched him. He pretended to hear something, the mares two fields away, and he lifted his head and neighed. She knew the powerful, splendid sound so well: like bells made of living membrane. And he looked so noble again, with his head tilted up, listening, and his male eyes looking proudly over the distance, eagerly.

But it was all a bluff.

He knew, and became silent again. And as he stood there a few yards away from her, his head lifted and wary, his body full of power and tension, his face slightly averted from her, she felt a great animal sadness come from him. A strange animal atmosphere of sadness, that was vague and disseminated through the air, and made her feel as though she breathed grief. She breathed it into her breast, as if it were a great sigh down the ages, that passed into her breast. And she felt a great woe: the woe of human unworthiness. The race of men judged in the consciousness of the animals they have subdued, and there found unworthy, ignoble.

Ignoble men, unworthy of the animals they have subjugated, bred the woe in the spirit of their creatures. St Mawr, that bright horse, one of the kings of creation in the order below man, it had been a fulfilment for him to serve the brave, reckless, perhaps cruel men of the past, who had a flickering, rising flame of nobility in them. To serve that flame of mysterious further nobility. Nothing matters, but that strange flame, of inborn nobility that obliges men to be brave, and onward plunging. And the horse will bear him on.

But now where is the flame of dangerous, forward-pressing nobility in men? Dead, dead, guttering out in a stink of self-sacrifice whose feeble light is a light of exhaustion and *laissez-faire*.[39]

And the horse, is he to go on carrying man forward into this? – this gutter?

No! Man wisely invents motor-cars and other machines, automobile and locomotive. The horse is superannuated, for man.

But alas, man is even more superannuated, for the horse.

Dimly in a woman's muse, Lou realized this, as she breathed the horse's sadness, his accumulated vague woe from the generations of latter-day ignobility. And a grief and a sympathy flooded her, for the horse. She realized now how his sadness recoiled into these frenzies of obstinacy and malevolence. Underneath it all was grief, an unconscious, vague, pervading animal grief, which perhaps only Lewis understood, because he felt the same. The grief of the generous creature which sees all ends turning to the morass of ignoble living.

She did not want to say any more to the horse: she did not want to look at him any more. The grief flooded her soul, that made her want to be alone. She knew now what it all amounted to. She knew that the horse, born to serve nobly, had waited in vain for some one noble to serve. His spirit knew that nobility had gone out of men. And this left him high and dry, in a sort of despair.

As she walked away from him, towards the gate, slowly he began to walk after her.

Phoenix came striding through the gate towards her.

'You not afraid of that horse?' he asked sardonically, in his quiet, subtle voice.

'Not at the present moment,' she replied, even more quietly, looking direct at him. She was not in any mood to be jeered at.

And instantly the sardonic grimace left his face, followed by the sudden blankness, and the look of race-misery in the keen eyes.

'Do you want me to be afraid?' she said, continuing to the gate.

'No, I don't want it,' he replied, dejected.

'Are you afraid of him yourself?' she said, glancing round. St Mawr had stopped, seeing Phoenix, and had turned away again.

'I'm not afraid of no horses,' said Phoenix.

Lou went on quietly. At the gate, she asked him:

'Don't you like St Mawr, Phoenix?'

'I like him. He's a very good horse.'

'Even after what he's done to Sir Henry?'

'That don't make no difference to him being a good horse.'

'But suppose he'd done it to you?'

'I don't care. I say it my own fault.'

'Don't you think he is wicked?'

'I don't think so. He don't kick anybody. He don't bite anybody. He don't pitch, he don't buck, he don't do nothing.'

'He rears,' said Lou.

'Well, what is rearing!' said the man, with a slow, contemptuous smile.

'A good deal, when a horse falls back on you.'

'That horse don't want to fall back on you, if you don't make him. If you know how to ride him. That horse want his own way sometime. If you don't let him, you got to fight him. Then look out!'

'Look out he doesn't kill you, you mean!'

'Look out you don't let him,' said Phoenix, with his slow, grim, sardonic smile.

Lou watched the smooth, golden face with its thin line of moustache and its sad eyes with the glint in them. Cruel – there was something cruel in him, right down in the abyss of him. But at the same time, there was an aloneness, and a grim little satisfaction in a fight, and the peculiar courage of an inherited despair. People who inherit despair may at last turn it into greater heroism. It was almost so with Phoenix. Three quarters of his blood was probably Indian and the remaining quarter, that came through the Mexican father, had the Spanish-American despair to add to the Indian. It was almost complete enough to leave him free to be heroic.

'What are we going to do with him, though?' she asked.

'Why don't you and Mrs Witt go back to America – you never been west. You go west.'

'Where, to California?'

'No. To Arizona or New Mexico or Colorado or Wyoming, anywhere. Not to California.'

Phoenix looked at her keenly, and she saw the desire dark in him. He wanted to go back. But he was afraid to go back alone, empty-handed, as it were. He had suffered too much, and in that country his sufferings would overcome him, unless he had some other background. He had been too much in contact with the white world, and his own world was too dejected, in a sense, too hopeless for his own hopelessness. He needed an alien contact to give him relief.

But he wanted to go back. His necessity to go back was becoming too strong for him.

'What is it like in Arizona?' she asked. 'Isn't is all pale-coloured sand and alkali, and a few cactuses, and terribly hot and deathly?'

'No!' he cried. 'I don't take you there. I take you to the mountains — trees —' he lifted up his hand and looked at the sky — 'big trees — pine! *Pino-real* and *pinovetes*, smell good. And then you come down, *piñon*,[40] not very tall, and *cedro*, cedar, smell good in the fire. And then you see the desert, away below, go miles and miles, and where the canyon go, the crack where it look red! I know, I been there, working a cattle ranch.'

He looked at her with a haunted glow in his dark eyes. The poor fellow was suffering from nostalgia. And as he glowed at her in that queer mystical way, she too seemed to see that country, with its dark, heavy mountains holding in their lap the great stretches of pale, creased, silent desert that still is virgin of idea, its word unspoken.

Phoenix was watching her closely and subtly. He wanted something of her. He wanted it intensely, heavily, and he watched her as if he could force her to give it him. He wanted her to take him back to America, because, rudderless, he was afraid to go back alone. He wanted her to take him back: avidly he wanted it. She was to be the means to his end.

Why shouldn't he go back by himself? Why should he crave for her to go too? Why should he want her there?

There was no answer, except that he did.

'Why, Phoenix,' she said. 'I might possibly go back to America. But you know, Sir Henry would never go there. He doesn't like America, though he's never been. But I'm sure he'd never go there to live.'

'Let him stay here,' said Phoenix abruptly, the sardonic look on his face as he watched her face. 'You come, and let him stay here.'

'Ah, that's a whole story!' she said, and moved away.

As she went, he looked after her, standing silent and arrested and watching as an Indian watches. It was not love. Personal love counts so little when the greater griefs, the greater hopes, the great despairs and the great resolutions come upon us.

She found Mrs Witt rather more silent, more firmly closed within herself, than usual. Her mouth was shut tight, her brows were arched rather more imperiously than ever, she was revolving some inward problem about which Lou was far too wise to inquire.

In the afternoon Dean Vyner and Mrs Vyner came to call on Lady Carrington.

'What bad luck this is, Lady Carrington!' said the Dean. 'Knocks Scotland on the head for you this year, I'm afraid. How did you leave your husband?'

'He seems to be doing as well as he could do!' said Lou.

'But how *very* unfortunate!' murmured the invalid Mrs Vyner. 'Such a handsome young man, in the bloom of youth! Does he suffer much pain?'

'Chiefly his foot,' said Lou.

'Oh, I *do* so hope they'll be able to restore the ankle. Oh, how dreadful, to be lamed at his age!'

'The doctor doesn't know. There *may* be a limp,' said Lou.

'That horse has certainly left his mark on two good-looking young fellows,' said the Dean. 'If you don't mind my saying so, Lady Carrington, I think he's a bad egg.'

'Who, St Mawr?' said Lou, in her American sing-song.

'Yes, Lady Carrington,' murmured Mrs Vyner, in her invalid's low tone. 'Don't you think he ought to be put away? He seems to me the incarnation of cruelty. His neigh. It goes through me like knives. Cruel! Cruel! Oh, I think he should be put away.'

'How put away?' murmured Lou, taking on an invalid's low tone herself.

'Shot, I suppose,' said the Dean.

'It is quite painless. He'll know nothing,' murmured Mrs Vyner hastily. 'And think of the harm he has done already!

Horrible! Horrible!' she shuddered. 'Poor Sir Henry lame for life, and Eddy Edwards disfigured. Besides all that has gone before. Ah no, such a creature ought not to live!'

'To live, and have a groom to look after him and feed him,' said the Dean. 'It's a bit thick, while he's smashing up the very people that give him bread – or oats, since he's a horse. But I suppose you'll be wanting to get rid of him?'

'Rico does,' murmured Lou.

'Very naturally. So should I. A vicious horse is worse than a vicious man – except that you are free to put him six feet underground, and end his vice finally, by your own act.'

'Do you think St Mawr is vicious?' said Lou.

'Well, of course – if we're driven to definitions! – I *know* he's dangerous.'

'And do you think we ought to shoot everything that is dangerous?' asked Lou, her colour rising.

'But Lady Carrington, have you consulted your husband? Surely his wish should be law, in a matter of this sort! And on such an occasion! For *you*, who are a woman, it is enough that the horse is cruel, cruel, evil! I felt it long before anything happened. That evil male cruelty! Ah!' and she clasped her hands convulsively.

'I suppose,' said Lou slowly, 'that St Mawr is really Rico's horse: I gave him to him, I suppose. But I don't believe I could let him shoot him, for all that.'

'Ah, Lady Carrington,' said the Dean breezily, 'you can shift the responsibility. The horse is a public menace, put it at that. We can get an order to have him done away with, at the public expense. And among ourselves we can find some suitable compensation for you, as a mark of sympathy. Which, believe me, is very sincere! One hates to have to destroy a fine-looking animal. But I would sacrifice a dozen rather than have our Rico limping.'

'Yes, indeed,' murmured Mrs Vyner.

'Will you excuse me one moment, while I see about tea,' said Lou, rising and leaving the room. Her colour was high, and there was a glint in her eye. These people almost roused her to hatred. Oh, these awful, house-bred, house-inbred human-beings, how repulsive they were!

She hurried to her mother's dressing-room. Mrs Witt was very carefully putting a touch of red on her lips.

'Mother, they want to shoot St Mawr,' she said.

'I know,' said Mrs Witt, as calmly as if Lou had said tea was ready.

'Well —' stammered Lou, rather put out. 'Don't you think it cheek?'

'It depends, I suppose, on the point of view,' said Mrs Witt dispassionately, looking closely at her lips. 'I don't think the English climate agrees with me. I need something to stand up against, no matter whether it's great heat or great cold. This climate, like the food and the people, is most always lukewarm or tepid, one or the other. And the tepid and the lukewarm are not really my line.' She spoke with a slow drawl.

'But they're in the drawing-room, mother, trying to force me to have St Mawr killed.'

'What about tea?' said Mrs Witt.

'I don't care,' said Lou.

Mrs Witt worked the bell-handle.

'I suppose, Louise,' she said, in her most beaming eighteenth-century manner, 'that these are your guests, so you will preside over the ceremony of pouring out.'

'No, mother, you do it. I can't smile to-day.'

'I can,' said Mrs Witt.

And she bowed her head slowly, with a faint, ceremoniously-effusive smile, as if handing a cup of tea.

Lou's face flickered to a smile.

'Then you pour out for them. You can stand them better than I can.'

'Yes,' said Mrs Witt. 'I saw Mrs Vyner's hat coming across the churchyard. It looks so like a crumpled cup and saucer, that I have been saying to myself ever since: *Dear Mrs Vyner, can't I fill your cup!* – and then pouring tea into that hat. And I hear the Dean responding: *My head is covered with cream, my cup runneth over.* – That is the way they make *me* feel.'

They marched downstairs, and Mrs Witt poured tea with that devastating correctness which made Mrs Vyner, who was utterly impervious to sarcasm, pronounce her 'indecipherably vulgar'.

But the Dean was the old bull-dog, and he had set his teeth in a subject.

'I was talking to Lady Carrington about that stallion, Mrs Witt.'

'Did you say stallion?' asked Mrs Witt, with perfect neutrality.

'Why, yes, I presume that's what he is.'

'I presume so,' said Mrs Witt colourlessly.

'I'm afraid Lady Carrington is a little sensitive on the wrong score,' said the Dean.

'I beg your pardon,' said Mrs Witt, leaning forward in her most colourless polite manner. 'You mean the stallion's score?'

'Yes,' said the Dean testily. 'The horse St Mawr.'

'The stallion St Mawr,' echoed Mrs Witt, with utmost mild vagueness. She completely ignored Mrs Vyner, who felt plunged like a specimen into methylated spirit. There was a moment's full-stop.

'Yes?' said Mrs Witt naïvely.

'You agree that we can't have any more of these accidents to your young men?' said the Dean rather hastily.

'I certainly do!' Mrs Witt spoke very slowly, and the Dean's lady began to look up. She might find a loop-hole through which to wriggle into the contest. 'You know, Dean, that my son-in-law calls me, for preference, *belle-mère*! It sounds so awfully English when he says it; I always see myself as an old grey mare with a bell round her neck, leading a bunch of horses.' She smiled a prim little smile, *very* conversationally. 'Well!' and she pulled herself up from the aside. 'Now as the bell-mare of the bunch of horses, I shall see to it that my son-in-law doesn't go too near that stallion again. That stallion won't stand mischief.'

She spoke so earnestly that the Dean looked at her with round wide eyes, completely taken aback.

'We all know, Mrs Witt, that the author of the mischief is St Mawr himself,' he said, in a loud tone.

'Really! you think *that*?' Her voice went up in American surprise. 'Why, how *strange* –!' and she lingered over the last word.

'Strange, eh? – After what's just happened?' said the Dean, with a deadly little smile.

'Why, yes! Most strange! I saw with my own eyes my son-in-law pull that stallion over backwards, and hold him down with the reins as tight as he could hold them; pull St Mawr's head backwards on to the ground, till the groom had to crawl up and force the reins out of my son-in-law's hands. Don't you think that was mischievous on Sir Henry's part?'

The Dean was growing purple. He made an apoplectic movement with his hand. Mrs Vyner was turned to a seated pillar of salt, strangely dressed up.

'Mrs Witt, you are playing on words.'

'No, Dean Vyner, I am not. My son-in-law pulled that horse over backwards and pinned him down with the reins.'

'I am sorry for the horse,' said the Dean, with heavy sarcasm.

'I am *very*,' said Mrs Witt, 'sorry for that stallion: *very*!'

Here Mrs Vyner rose as if a chair-spring had suddenly propelled her to her feet. She was streaky pink in the face.

'Mrs Witt,' she panted, 'you misdirect your sympathies. That poor young man – in the beauty of youth.'

'Isn't he *beautiful* –' murmured Mrs Witt, extravagantly in sympathy. 'He's my daughter's husband!' And she looked at the petrified Lou.

'Certainly!' panted the Dean's wife. 'And you can defend that – that –'

'That stallion,' said Mrs Witt. 'But you see, Mrs Vyner,' she added leaning forward female and confidential, 'if the old grey mare doesn't defend the stallion, who will? All the blooming young ladies will defend my beautiful son-in-law. You feel so *warmly* for him yourself! I'm an American woman, and I always have to stand up for the accused. And I stand up for that stallion. I say it is not right. He was pulled over backwards and then pinned down by my son-in-law – who may have meant to do it, or may not. And now people abuse him. – Just tell everybody, Mrs Vyner and Dean Vyner' – she looked round at the Dean – 'that the *belle-mère's* sympathies are with the stallion.'

She looked from one to the other with a faint and gracious little bow, her black eyebrows arching in her eighteenth-century face like black rainbows, and her full, bold grey eyes absolutely incomprehensible.

'Well, it's a peculiar message to have to hand round, Mrs Witt,' the Dean began to boom, when she interrupted him by laying her hand on his arm and leaning forward, looking up into his face like a clinging, pleading female:

'Oh, but *do* hand it, Dean, *do* hand it,' she pleaded, gazing intently into his face.

He backed uncomfortably from that gaze.

'Since you wish it,' he said, in a chest voice.

'I most certainly *do* —' she said, as if she were wishing the sweetest wish on earth. Then turning to Mrs Vyner:

'Good-bye, Mrs Vyner. We *do* appreciate your coming, my daughter and I.'

'I came out of kindness —' said Mrs Vyner.

'Oh, I know it, I know it,' said Mrs Witt. 'Thank you *so* much. Good-bye! Good-bye Dean! Who is taking the morning service on Sunday? I hope it is you, because I want to come.'

'It *is* me,' said the Dean. 'Good-bye! Well, good-bye Lady Carrington. I shall be going over to see our young man to-morrow, and will gladly take you or anything you have to send.'

'Perhaps mother would like to go,' said Lou, softly, plaintively.

'Well, we shall see,' said the Dean. 'Good-bye for the present!'

Mother and daughter stood at the window watching the two cross the churchyard. Dean and wife knew it, but daren't look round, and daren't admit the fact to one another.

Lou was grinning with a complete grin that gave her an odd, dryad or faun look, intensified.

'It was almost as good as pouring tea into her hat,' said Mrs Witt serenely. 'People like that tire me out. I shall take a glass of sherry.'

'So will I, mother. — It was even better than pouring tea in her hat. — You meant, didn't you, if you poured tea in her hat, to put cream and sugar in first?'

'I did,' said Mrs Witt.

But after the excitement of the encounter had passed away, Lou felt as if her life had passed away too. She went to bed, feeling she could stand no more.

In the morning she found her mother sitting at a window

watching a funeral. It was raining heavily, so that some of the mourners even wore mackintosh coats. The funeral was in the poorer corner of the churchyard, where another new grave was covered with wreaths of sodden, shrivelling flowers. The yellowish coffin stood on the wet earth, in the rain: the curate held his hat, in a sort of permanent salute, above his head, like a little umbrella, as he hastened on with the service. The people seemed too wet to weep more wet.

It was a long coffin.

'Mother, do you really *like* watching?' asked Lou irritably, as Mrs Witt sat in complete absorption.

'I do, Louise, I really enjoy it.'

'Enjoy, mother!' – Lou was almost disgusted.

'I'll tell you why. I imagine I'm the one in the coffin – this is a girl of eighteen, who died of consumption – and those are my relatives, and I'm watching them put me away. And you know, Louise, I've come to the conclusion that hardly anybody in the world really lives, and so hardly anybody really dies. They may well say *Oh Death where is thy sting-a-ling-a-ling?*[41] Even Death can't sting those that have never really lived. – I always used to want that – to die without death stinging me. – And I'm sure the girl in the coffin is saying to herself: *Fancy Aunt Emma putting on a drab slicker,*[42] *and wearing it while they bury me. Doesn't show much respect. But then my mother's family always were common!* I feel there should be a solemn burial of a roll of newspapers containing the account of the death and funeral, next week. It would be just as serious: the grave of all the world's remarks –'

'I don't want to think about it, mother. One ought to be able to laugh at it. I want to laugh at it.'

'Well, Louise, I think it's just as great a mistake to laugh at everything as to cry at everything. Laughter's not the one panacea, either. I should *really* like, before I do come to be buried in a box, to know where I am. That young girl in that coffin never was anywhere – any more than the newspaper remarks on her death and burial. And I begin to wonder if I've ever been anywhere. I seem to have been a daily sequence of newspaper remarks, myself. I'm sure I never really conceived you and gave you birth. It all happened in newspaper notices. It's a newspaper fact that you are my child, and that's about all there is to it.'

Lou smiled as she listened.

'I always knew you were philosophic, mother. But I never dreamed it would come to elegies in a country churchyard,[43] written to your motherhood.'

'*Exactly*, Louise! Here I sit and sing the elegy to my own motherhood. I never had any motherhood, except in newspaper fact. I never was a wife, except in newspaper notices. I never was a young girl, except in newspaper remarks. Bury everything I ever said or that was said about me, and you've buried *me*. But since Kind Words Can Never Die, I can't be buried, and death has no sting-a-ling-a-ling for *me!* – Now listen to me, Louise: I want death to be real to me – not as it was to that young girl. I *want* it to hurt me, Louise. If it hurts me enough, I shall know I was alive.'

She set her face and gazed under half-dropped lids at the funeral, stoic, fate-like, and yet, for the first time, with a certain pure wistfulness of a young, virgin girl. This frightened Lou very much. She was so used to the matchless Amazon[44] in her mother, that when she saw her sit there, still, wistful, virginal, tender as a girl who has never taken armour, wistful at the window that only looked on graves, a serious terror took hold of the young woman. The terror of *too late*!

Lou felt years, centuries older than her mother, at that moment, with the tiresome responsibility of youth to protect and guide their elders.

'What can we do about it, mother?' she asked protectively.

'Do nothing, Louise. I'm not going to have anybody wisely steering my canoe, now I feel the rapids are near. I shall go with the river. Don't you pretend to do anything for me. I've done enough mischief myself, that way. I'm going down the stream, at last.'

There was a pause.

'But in actuality, what?' asked Lou, a little ironically.

'I don't quite know. Wait a while.'

'Go back to America?'

'That is possible.'

'I may come too.'

'I've always waited for you to go back of your own will.'

Lou went away, wandering round the house. She was so unutterably tired of everything – weary of the house, the grave-yard, weary of the thought of Rico. She would have to go back to him to-morrow, to nurse him. Poor old Rico, going on like an amiable machine from day to day. It wasn't his fault. But his life was a rattling nullity, and her life rattled in null correspondence. She had hardly strength enough to stop rattling and be still. Perhaps she had not strength enough.

She did not know. She felt so weak, that unless something carried her away she would go on rattling her bit in the great machine of human life, till she collapsed, and her rattle rattled itself out, and there was a sort of barren silence where the sound of her had been.

She wandered out in the rain, to the coach-house where Lewis and Phoenix were sitting facing one another, one on a bin, the other on the inner doorstep.

'Well,' she said, smiling oddly. 'What's to be done?'

The two men stood up. Outside the rain fell steadily on the flagstones of the yard, past the leaves of trees. Lou sat down on the little iron step of the dogcart.

'That's cold,' said Phoenix. 'You sit here.' And he threw a yellow horse-blanket on the box where he had been sit-ting.

'I don't want to take your seat,' she said.

'All right, you take it.'

He moved across and sat gingerly on the shaft of the dog-cart. Lou seated herself, and loosened her soft tartan shawl. Her face was pink and fresh, and her dark hair curled almost merrily in the damp. But under her eyes were the finger-prints of deadly weariness.

She looked up at the two men, again smiling in her odd fashion.

'What are we going to do?' she asked.

They looked at her closely, seeking her meaning.

'What about?' said Phoenix, a faint smile reflecting on his face, merely because she smiled.

'Oh, everything,' she said, hugging her shawl again. 'You know what they want? They want to shoot St Mawr.'

The two men exchanged glances.

'Who want it?' said Phoenix.

'Why – all our *friends*!' she made a little *moue*.⁴⁵ 'Dean Vyner does.'

Again the men exchanged glances. There was a pause. Then Phoenix said, looking aside:

'The boss is selling him.'

'Who?'

'Sir Henry.' – The half-breed always spoke the title with difficulty, and with a sort of sneer. 'He sell him to Miss Manby.'

'How do you know?'

'The man from Corrabach told me last night. Flora, she say it.'

Lou's eyes met the sardonic, empty-seeing eyes of Phoenix direct. There was too much sarcastic understanding. She looked aside.

'What else did he say?' she asked.

'I don't know,' said Phoenix, evasively. 'He say they cut him – else shoot him. Think they cut him – and if he die, he die.'

Lou understood. He meant they would geld St Mawr – at his age.

She looked at Lewis. He sat with his head down, so she could not see his face.

'Do you think it is true?' she asked. 'Lewis? Do you think they would try to geld St Mawr – to make him a gelding?'

Lewis looked up at her. There was a faint deadly glimmer of contempt on his face.

'Very likely, Mam,' he said.

She was afraid of his cold, uncanny pale eyes, with their uneasy grey dawn of contempt. These two men, with their silent, deadly inner purpose, were not like other men. They seemed like two silent enemies of all the other men she knew. Enemies in the great white camp, disguised as servants, waiting the incalculable opportunity. What the opportunity might be, none knew.

'Sir Henry hasn't mentioned anything to me about selling St Mawr to Miss Manby,' she said.

The derisive flicker of a smile came on Phoenix's face.

'He sell him first, and tell you then,' he said, with his deadly impassive manner.

'But do you really think so?' she asked.

It was extraordinary how much corrosive contempt Phoenix could convey, saying nothing. She felt it almost as an insult. Yet it was a relief to her.

'You know, I can't believe it. I can't believe Sir Henry would want to have St Mawr mutilated. I believe he'd rather shoot him.'

'You think so?' said Phoenix, with a faint grin.

Lou turned to Lewis.

'Lewis, will you tell me what you truly think?'

Lewis looked at her with a hard, straight, fearless British stare.

'That man Philips was in the "Moon and Stars" last night. He said Miss Manby told him she was buying St Mawr, and she asked him, if he thought it would be safe to cut him, and make a horse of him. He said it would be better, take some of the nonsense out of him. He's no good for a sire, anyhow –'

Lewis dropped his head again, and tapped a tattoo with the toe of his rather small foot.

'And what do you think?' said Lou. It occurred to her how sensible and practical Miss Manby was, so much more so than the Dean.

Lewis looked up at her with his pale eyes.

'It won't have anything to do with me,' he said. 'I shan't go to Corrabach Hall.'

'What will you do, then?'

Lewis did not answer. He looked at Phoenix.

'Maybe him and me go to America,' said Phoenix, looking at the void.

'Can he get in?' said Lou.

'Yes, he can. I know how,' said Phoenix.

'And the money?' she said.

'We got money.'

There was a silence, after which she asked of Lewis:

'You'd leave St Mawr to his fate?'

'I can't help his fate,' said Lewis. 'There's too many people in the world for me to help anything.'

'Poor St Mawr!'

She went indoors again, and up to her room: then higher, to the top rooms of the tall Georgian house. From one window she could see the fields in the rain. She could see St Mawr himself, alone as usual, standing with his head up, looking across the fences. He was streaked dark with rain. Beautiful, with his poised head and massive neck, and his supple hindquarters. He was neighing to Poppy. Clear on the wet wind came the sound of his bell-like, stallion's calling, that Mrs Vyner called cruel. It was a strange noise, with a splendour that belonged to another world-age. The mean cruelty of Mrs Vyner's humanitarianism, the barren cruelty of Flora Manby, the eunuch cruelty of Rico. Our whole eunuch civilization, nasty-minded as eunuchs are, with their kind of sneaking, sterilizing cruelty.

Yet even she herself, seeing St Mawr's conceited march along the fence, could not help addressing him:

'Yes, my boy! If you knew what Miss Flora Manby was preparing for you! *She'll* sharpen a knife that will settle you.'

And Lou called her mother.

The two American women stood high at the window, overlooking the wet, close, hedged-and-fenced English landscape. Everything enclosed, enclosed, to stifling. The very apples on the trees looked so shut in, it was impossible to imagine any speck of 'Knowledge' lurking inside them. Good to eat, good to cook, good even for show. But the wild sap of untameable and inexhaustible knowledge – no! Bred out of them. Geldings, even the apples.

Mrs Witt listened to Lou's half-humorous statements.

'You must admit, mother, Flora is a sensible girl,' she said.

'I admit it, Louise.'

'She goes straight to the root of the matter.'

'And eradicates the root. Wise girl! And what is your answer?'

'I don't know, mother. What would you say?'

'I know what *I* should say.'

'Tell me.'

'I should say: *Miss Manby, you may have my husband, but not my horse. My husband won't need emasculating, and my horse I*

*won't have you meddle with. I'll preserve one last male thing in
the museum of this world, if I can.'*

Lou listened, smiling faintly.

'That's what I will say,' she replied at length. 'The funny thing
is, mother, they think all their men with their bare faces or their
little quotation-mark moustaches *are* so tremendously male.
That fox-hunting one!'

'I know it. Like little male motor-cars. Give him a little gas,
and start him on the low gear, and away he goes: all his male gear
rattling, like a cheap motor-car.'

'I'm afraid I dislike men altogether, mother.'

'You may, Louise. Think of Flora Manby, and how you love
the fair sex.'

'After all, St Mawr is better. And I'm glad if he gives them
a kick in the face.'

'Ah, Louise!' Mrs Witt suddenly clasped her hands with
wicked passion. '*Ay, qué gozo!*⁴⁶ as our Juan used to say, on your
father's ranch in Texas.' She gazed in a sort of wicked ecstasy
out of the window.

They heard Lou's maid softly calling Lady Carrington from
below. Lou went to the stairs.

'What is it?'

'Lewis wants to speak to you, my Lady.'

'Send him into the sitting-room.'

The two women went down.

'What is it, Lewis?' asked Lou.

'Am I to bring in St Mawr, in case they send for him from
Corrabach?'

'No,' said Lou swiftly.

'Wait a minute,' put in Mrs Witt. 'What makes you think they
will send for St Mawr from Corrabach, Lewis?' she asked, suave
as a grey leopard cat.

'Miss Manby went up to Flints Farm with Dean Vyner this
morning, and they've just come back. They stopped the car, and
Miss Manby got out at the field gate, to look at St Mawr. I'm
thinking, if she made the bargain with Sir Henry, she'll be
sending a man over this afternoon, and if I'd better brush St
Mawr down a bit, in case.'

The man stood strangely still, and the words came like shadows of his real meaning. It was a challenge.

'I see,' said Mrs Witt slowly.

Lou's face darkened. She too saw.

'So that is her game,' she said. 'That is why they got me down here.'

'Never mind, Louise,' said Mrs Witt. Then to Lewis: 'Yes, please bring in St Mawr. You wish it, don't you, Louise?'

'Yes,' hesitated Lou. She saw by Mrs Witt's closed face that a counter-move was prepared.

'And Lewis,' said Mrs Witt, 'my daughter may wish you to ride St Mawr this afternoon – not to Corrabach Hall.'

'Very good, Mam.'

Mrs Witt sat silent for some time, after Lewis had gone, gathering inspiration from the wet, grisly gravestones.

'Don't you think it's time we made a move, daughter?' she asked.

'Any move,' said Lou desperately.

'Very well then. My dearest friends, and my *only* friends, in this country, are in Oxfordshire. I will set off to *ride* to Merriton this afternoon, and Lewis will ride with me on St Mawr.'

'But you can't ride to Merriton in an afternoon,' said Lou.

'I know it. I shall ride across country. I shall *enjoy* it, Louise. – Yes. – I shall consider I am on my way back to America. I am most deadly tired of this country. From Merriton I shall make my arrangements to go to America, and take Lewis and Phoenix and St Mawr along with me. I think they want to go. – You will decide for yourself.'

'Yes, I'll come too,' said Lou casually.

'Very well. I'll start immediately after lunch, for I can't *breathe* in this place any longer. Where are Henry's automobile maps?'

Afternoon saw Mrs Witt, in a large waterproof cape, mounted on her horse, Lewis, in another cape, mounted on St Mawr, trotting through the rain, splashing in the puddles, moving slowly southwards. They took the open country, and would pass quite near to Flints Farm. But Mrs Witt did not care. With great difficulty she had managed to fasten a small waterproof roll behind her, containing her night things. She seemed to breathe the first breath of freedom.

And sure enough, an hour or so after Mrs Witt's departure, arrived Flora Manby in a splashed-up motor-car, accompanied by her sister, and bringing a groom and a saddle.

'Do you know, Harry sold me St Mawr,' she said. 'I'm just wild to get that horse in hand.'

'How?' said Lou.

'Oh, I don't know. There are ways. Do you mind if Philips rides him over now, to Corrabach? – Oh, I forgot, Harry sent you a note.'

'Dearest Loulina: Have you been gone from here two days or two years? It seems the latter. You are terribly missed. Flora wanted so much to buy St Mawr, to save us further trouble, that I have sold him to her. She is giving me what we paid: rather, what you paid; so of course the money is yours. I am thankful we are rid of the animal, and that he falls into competent hands – I asked her please to remove him from your charge to-day. And I can't tell how much easier I am in my mind, to think of him gone. You are coming back to me to-morrow, aren't you? I shall think of nothing else but you, till I see you. Arrivederci, darling dear! R.'

'I'm so sorry,' said Lou. 'Mother went on horseback to see some friends, and Lewis went with her on St Mawr. He knows the road.'

'She'll be back this evening?' said Flora.

'I don't know. Mother is so uncertain. She may be away a day or two.'

'Well, here's the cheque for St Mawr.'

'No, I won't take it now – no, thank you – not till mother comes back with the goods.'

Flora was chagrined. The two women knew they hated one another. The visit was a brief one.

Mrs Witt rode on in the rain, which abated as the afternoon wore down, and the evening came without rain, and with a suffusion of pale yellow light. All the time she had trotted in silence, with Lewis just behind her. And she scarcely saw the heather-covered hills with the deep clefts between them, nor the oak-woods, nor the lingering foxgloves, nor the earth at all.

Inside herself she felt a profound repugnance for the English country: she preferred even the crudeness of Central Park in New York.

And she felt an almost savage desire to get away from Europe, from everything European. Now she was really *en route*, she cared not a straw for St Mawr or for Lewis or anything. Something just writhed inside her, all the time, against Europe. That closeness, that sense of cohesion, that sense of being fused into a lump with all the rest – no matter how much distance you kept – this drove her mad. In America the cohesion was a matter of choice and will. But in Europe it was organic, like the helpless particles of one sprawling body. And the great body in a state of incipient decay.

She was a woman of fifty-one: and she seemed hardly to have lived a day. She looked behind her – the thin trees and swamps of Louisiana, the sultry, sub-tropical excitement of decaying New Orleans, the vast bare dryness of Texas, with mobs of cattle in an illumined dust! The half-European thrills of New York! The false stability of Boston! A clever husband, who was a brilliant lawyer, but who was far more thrilled by his cattle ranch than by his law: and who drank heavily and died. The years of first widowhood in Boston, consoled by a self-satisfied sort of intellectual courtship from clever men. – For curiously enough, while she wanted it, she had always been able to compel men to pay court to her. All kinds of men. – Then a rather dashing time in New York – when she was in her early forties. Then the long *visual* philandering in Europe. She left off 'loving', save through the eye, when she came to Europe. And when she made her trips to America, she found it was finished there also, her 'loving'.

What was the matter? Examining herself, she had long ago decided that her nature was a destructive force. But then, she justified herself, she had only destroyed that which was destructible. If she could have found something indestructible, especially in men, though she would have fought against it, she would have been glad at last to be defeated by it.

That was the point. She really wanted to be defeated, in her own eyes. And nobody had ever defeated her. Men were never really her match. A woman of terrible strong health, she felt even

that in her strong limbs there was far more electric power than
in the limbs of any man she had met. That curious fluid electric
force, that could make any man kiss her hand, if she so willed
it. A queen, as far as she wished. And not having been very clever
at school, she always had the greatest respect for the mental
powers. Her own were not mental powers. Rather electric, as of
some strange physical dynamo within her. So she had been ready
to bow before Mind.

But alas! After a brief time, she had found Mind, at least the
man who was supposed to have the mind, bowing before her. Her
own peculiar dynamic force was stronger than the force of Mind.
She could make Mind kiss her hand.

And not by any sensual tricks. She did not really care about
sensualities, especially as a younger woman. Sex was a mere
adjunct. She cared about the mysterious, intense, dynamic
sympathy that could flow between her and some 'live' man – a
man who was highly conscious, a real live wire. That she cared
about.

But she had never rested until she had made the man she
admired – and admiration was the root of her attraction to any
man – made him kiss her hand. In both senses, actual and
metaphorical. Physical and metaphysical. Conquered his
country.

She had always succeeded. And she believed that, if she cared,
she always *would* succeed. In the world of living men. Because
of the power that was in her, in her arms, in her strong, shapely,
but terrible hands, in all the great dynamo of her body.

For this reason she had been so terribly contemptuous of Rico,
and of Lou's infatuation. Ye gods! what was Rico in the scale of
men!

Perhaps she despised the younger generation too easily.
Because she did not see its sources of power, she concluded it
was powerless. Whereas perhaps the power of accommodating
oneself to any circumstances and committing oneself to no
circumstance is the last triumph of mankind.

Her generation had had its day. She had had her day. The
world of her men had sunk into a sort of insignificance. And with
a great contempt she despised the world that had come into

place instead: the world of Rico and Flora Manby, the world represented, to her, by the Prince of Wales.[47]

In such a world there was nothing even to conquer. It gave everything and gave nothing to everybody and anybody all the time. *Dio benedetto!*[48] as Rico would say. A great complicated tangle of nonentities ravelled in nothingness. So it seemed to her.

Great God! This was the generation she had helped to bring into the world.

She had had her day. And, as far as the mysterious battle of life went, she had won all the way. Just as Cleopatra,[49] in the mysterious business of a woman's life, won all the way.

Though that bald tough Caesar had drawn his iron from the fire without losing much of its temper. And he had gone his way. And Antony surely was splendid to die with.

In her life there had been no tough Caesar to go his way in cold blood, away from her. Her men had gone from her like dogs on three legs, into the crowd. And certainly there was no gorgeous Antony to die for and with.

Almost she was tempted in her heart to cry: 'Conquer me, oh God, before I die!' – But then she had a terrible contempt for the God that was supposed to rule this universe. She felt she could make *Him* kiss her hand. Here she was a woman of fifty-one, past the change of life. And her great dread was to die an empty, barren death. Oh, if only Death might open dark wings of mystery and consolation. To die an easy, barren death. To pass out as she had passed in, without mystery or the rustling of darkness! That was her last, final, ashy dread.

'Old!' she said to herself. 'I am not *old*! I have lived many years, that is all. But I am as timeless as an hour-glass that turns morning and night, and spills the hours of sleep one way, the hours of consciousness the other way, without itself being affected. Nothing in all my life has ever truly affected me. – I believe Cleopatra only tried the asp, as she tried her pearls in wine, to see if it would really, really have any effect on her. Nothing had ever really had any effect on her, neither Caesar nor Antony nor any of them. Never once had she really been lost, lost to herself. Then try death, see if that trick would work. If she would lose herself that way. – Ah death –!'

But Mrs Witt mistrusted death too. She felt she might pass out as a bed of asters passes out in autumn, to mere nothingness. – And something in her longed to die, at least, *positively*: to be folded then at last into throbbing wings of mystery, like a hawk that goes to sleep. Not like a thing made into a parcel and put into the last rubbish-heap.

So she rode trotting across the hills, mile after mile, in silence. Avoiding the roads, avoiding everything, avoiding everybody, just trotting forwards, towards night.

And by nightfall they had travelled twenty-five miles. She had motored around this country, and knew the little towns and the inns. She knew where she would sleep.

The morning came beautiful and sunny. A woman so strong in health, why should she ride with the fact of death before her eyes? But she did.

Yet in sunny morning she must do something about it.

'Lewis!' she said. 'Come here and tell me something, please! Tell me,' she said, 'do you believe in God?'

'In God!' he said, wondering. 'I never think about it.'

'But do you say your prayers?'

'No, Mam!'

'Why don't you?'

He thought about it for some minutes.

'I don't like religion. My aunt and uncle were religious.'

'You don't like religion,' she repeated. 'And you don't believe in God. – Well then –'

'Nay!' he hesitated. 'I never said I didn't believe in God. – Only I'm sure I'm not a Methodist. And I feel a fool in a proper church. – And I feel a fool saying my prayers. – And I feel a fool when ministers and parsons come getting at me. – I never think about God, if folks don't try to make me.' He had a small, sly smile, almost gay.

'And you don't like feeling a fool?' She smiled rather patronizingly.

'No, Mam.'

'Do I make you feel a fool?' she asked, drily.

He looked at her without answering.

'Why don't you answer?' she said, pressing.

'I think you'd like to make a fool of me sometimes,' he said.

'Now?' she pressed.

He looked at her with that slow, distant look.

'Maybe!' he said, rather unconcernedly.

Curiously, she couldn't touch him. He always seemed to be watching her from a distance, as if from another country. Even if she made a fool of him, something in him would all the time be far away from her, not implicated.

She caught herself up in the personal game, and returned to her own isolated questions. A vicious habit made her start the personal tricks. She didn't want to, really.

There was something about this little man – sometimes, to herself, she called him *Little Jack Horner, Sat in a corner* – that irritated her and made her want to taunt him. His peculiar little inaccessibility, that was so tight and easy.

Then again, there was something, his way of looking at her as if he looked from out of another country, a country of which he was an inhabitant, and where she had never been: this touched her strangely. Perhaps behind this little man was the mystery. In spite of the fact that in actual life, in her world, he was only a groom, almost chétif, with his legs a little bit horsey and bowed; and of no education, saying *Yes Mam!* and *No Mam!* and accomplishing nothing, simply nothing at all on the face of the earth. Strictly a nonentity.

And yet, what made him perhaps the only real entity to her, his seeming to inhabit another world than hers. A world dark and still, where language never ruffled the growing leaves, and seared their edges like a bad wind.

Was it an illusion, however? Sometimes she thought it was. Just bunkum, which she had faked up, in order to have something to mystify about.

But then, when she saw Phoenix and Lewis silently together, she knew there *was* another communion, silent, excluding her. And sometimes when Lewis was alone with St Mawr: and once, when she saw him pick up a bird that had stunned itself against a wire: she had realized another world, silent, where each creature is alone in its own aura of silence, the mystery of power: as Lewis had power with St Mawr, and even with Phoenix.

The visible world, and the invisible. Or rather, the audible and the inaudible. She had lived so long, and so completely, in the visible, audible world. She would not easily admit that other, inaudible. She always wanted to jeer, as she approached the brink of it.

Even now, she wanted to jeer at the little fellow, because of his holding himself inaccessible within the inaudible, silent world. And she knew he knew it.

'Did you never want to be rich, and be a gentleman, like Sir Henry?' she asked.

'I would many times have liked to be rich. But I never exactly wanted to be a gentleman,' he said.

'Why not?'

'I can't exactly say. I should be uncomfortable if I was like they are.'

'And are you comfortable now?'

'When I'm let alone.'

'And do they let you alone? Does the world let you alone?'

'No, they don't.'

'Well then –!'

'I keep to myself all I can.'

'And are you comfortable, as you call it, when you keep to yourself?'

'Yes, I am.'

'But when you keep to yourself, what do you keep to? What precious treasure have you to keep to?'

He looked, and saw she was jeering.

'None,' he said. 'I've got nothing of that sort.'

She rode impatiently on ahead.

And the moment she had done so, she regretted it. She might put the little fellow, with contempt, out of her reckoning. But no, she would not do it.

She had put so much out of her reckoning: soon she would be left in an empty circle, with her empty self at the centre.

She reined in again.

'Lewis!' she said. 'I don't want you to take offence at anything I say.'

'No, Mam.'

'I don't want you to say just *No Mam!* all the time!' she cried impulsively. 'Promise me.'

'Yes, Mam!'

'But really! Promise me you won't be offended at whatever I say.'

'Yes, Mam!'

She looked at him searchingly. To her surprise, she was almost in tears. A woman of her years! And with a servant!

But his face was blank and stony, with a stony, distant look of pride that made him inaccessible to her emotions. He met her eyes again: with that cold distant look, looking straight into her hot, confused, pained self. So cold and as if merely refuting her. He didn't believe her, nor trust her, nor like her even. She was an attacking enemy to him. Only he stayed really far away from her, looking down at her from a sort of distant hill where her weapons could not reach: not quite.

And at the same time, it hurt him in a dumb, living way, that she made these attacks on him. She could see the cloud of hurt in his eyes, no matter how distantly he looked at her.

They bought food in a village shop, and sat under a tree near a field where men were already cutting oats, in a warm valley. Lewis had stabled the horses for a couple of hours, to feed and rest. But he came to join her under the tree, to eat. – He sat at a little distance from her, with the bread and cheese in his small brown hands, eating silently, and watching the harvesters. She was cross with him, and therefore she was stingy, would give him nothing to eat but dry bread and cheese. Herself, she was not hungry. – So all the time he kept his face a little averted from her. As a matter of fact, he kept his whole being averted from her, away from her. He did not want to touch her, nor to be touched by her. He kept his spirit there, alert, on its guard, but out of contact. It was as if he had unconsciously accepted the battle, the old battle. He was her target, the old object of her deadly weapons. But he refused to shoot back. It was as if he caught all her missiles in full flight, before they touched him, and silently threw them on the ground behind him. And in some essential part of himself he ignored her, staying in another world.

That other world! Mere male armour of artificial imperviousness! It angered her.

Yet she knew, by the way he watched the harvesters, and the grasshoppers popping into notice, that it was another world. And when a girl went by, carrying food to the field, it was at him she glanced. And he gave that quick, animal little smile that came from him unawares. Another world!

Yet also, there was a sort of meanness about him: a *suffisance*! A keep-yourself-for-yourself, and don't give yourself away.

Well! – she rose impatiently

It was hot in the afternoon, and she was rather tired. She went to the inn and slept, and did not start again till tea-time.

Then they had to ride rather late. The sun sank, among a smell of cornfields, clear and yellow-red behind motionless dark trees. Pale smoke rose from cottage chimneys. Not a cloud was in the sky, which held the upward-floating light like a bowl inverted on purpose. A new moon sparkled and was gone. It was beginning of night.

Away in the distance, they saw a curious pinkish glare of fire, probably furnaces. And Mrs Witt thought she could detect the scent of furnace smoke, or factory smoke. But then she always said that of the English air: it was never quite free of the smell of smoke, coal-smoke.

They were riding slowly on a path through fields, down a long slope. Away below was a puther of lights. All the darkness seemed full of half-spent crossing lights, a curious uneasiness. High in the sky a star seemed to be walking. It was an aeroplane with a light. Its buzz rattled above. Not a space, not a speck of this country that wasn't humanized, occupied by the human claim. Not even the sky.

They descended slowly through a dark wood, which they had entered through a gate. Lewis was all the time dismounting and opening gates, letting her pass, shutting the gate and mounting again.

So, in a while she came to the edge of the wood's darkness, and saw the open pale concave of the world beyond. The darkness was never dark. It shook with the concussion of many invisible lights, lights of towns, villages, mines, factories, furnaces, squatting in the valleys and behind all the hills.

Yet, as Rachel Witt drew rein at the gate emerging from the wood, a very big, soft star fell in heaven, cleaving the hubbub of this human night with a gleam from the greater world.

'See! a star falling!' said Lewis, as he opened the gate.

'I saw it,' said Mrs Witt, walking her horse past him.

There was a curious excitement of wonder, or magic, in the little man's voice. Even in this night something strange had stirred awake in him.

'You ask me about God,' he said to her, walking his horse alongside in the shadow of the wood's-edge, the darkness of the old Pan, that kept our artificially-lit world at bay. 'I don't know about God. But when I see a star fall like that out of long-distance places in the sky: and the moon sinking saying Good-bye! Good-bye! Good-bye! and nobody listening: I think I hear something, though I wouldn't call it God.'

'What then?' said Rachel Witt.

'And you smell the smell of oak-leaves now,' he said, 'now the air is cold. They smell to me more alive than people. The trees hold their bodies hard and still, but they watch and listen with their leaves. And I think they say to me: *Is that you passing there, Morgan Lewis? All right, you pass quickly, we shan't do anything to you. You are like a holly-bush.*'

'Yes,' said Rachel Witt, drily. '*Why?*'

'All the time, the trees grow, and listen. And if you cut a tree down without asking pardon, trees will hurt you some time in your life, in the night time.'

'I suppose,' said Rachel Witt, 'that's an old superstition.'

'They say that ash-trees don't like people. When the other people were most in the country – I mean like what they call fairies, that have all gone now – they liked ash-trees best. And you know the little green things with little small nuts in them, that come flying down from ash-trees – *pigeons*, we call them – they're the seeds – the other people used to catch them and eat them before they fell to the ground. And that made the people so they could hear trees living and feeling things. – But when all these people that there are now came to England, they liked the oak-trees best, because their pigs ate the acorns. So now you can

tell the ash-trees are mad, they want to kill all these people. But
the oak-trees are many more than the ash-trees.'

'And do you eat the ash-tree seeds?' she asked.

'I always ate them, when I was little. Then I wasn't frightened
of ash-trees, like most of the others. And I wasn't frightened of
the moon. If you didn't go near the fire all day, and if you didn't
eat any cooked food nor anything that had been in the sun, but
only things like turnips or radishes or pig-nuts, and then went
without any clothes on, in the full moon, then you could see the
people in the moon, and go with them. They never have fire, and
they never speak, and their bodies are clear almost like jelly.
They die in a minute if there's a bit of fire near them. But they
know more than we. Because unless fire touches them, they never
die. They see people live and they see people perish, and they
say, people are only like twigs on a tree, you break them off the
tree, and kindle fire with them. You made a fire of them, and they
are gone, the fire is gone, everything is gone. But the people of
the moon don't die, and fire is nothing to them. They look at it
from the distance of the sky, and see it burning things up, people
all appearing and disappearing like twigs that come in spring and
you cut them in autumn and make a fire of them and they are gone.
And they say: what do people matter? If you want to matter, you
must become a moon-boy. Then all your life, fire can't blind you
and people can't hurt you. Because at full moon you can join the
moon people, and go through the air and pass any cool places,
pass through rocks and through the trunks of trees, and when
you come to people lying warm in bed, you punish them.'

'How?'

'You sit on the pillow where they breathe, and you put a web
across their mouth, so they can't breathe the fresh air that comes
from the moon. So they go on breathing the same air again and
again, and that makes them more and more stupefied. The sun
gives out heat, but the moon gives out fresh air. That's what the
moon people do: they wash the air clean with moonlight.'

He was talking with a strange eager naïveté that amused
Rachel Witt, and made her a little uncomfortable in her skin.
Was he after all no more than a sort of imbecile?

'Who told you all this stuff?' she asked abruptly.

And, as abruptly, he pulled himself up.

'We used to say it, when we were children.'

'But you don't believe it? It *is* only childishness, after all.'

He paused a moment or two.

'No,' he said, in his ironical little day-voice. 'I know I shan't make anything but a fool of myself, with that talk. But all sorts of things go through our heads, and some seem to linger, and some don't. But you asking me about God put it into my mind, I suppose. I don't know what sort of things I believe in: only I know it's not what the chapel-folks believe in. We none of us believe in them when it comes to earning a living, or, with you people, when it comes to spending your fortune. Then we know that bread costs money, and even your sleep you have to pay for. – That's work. Or, with you people, it's just owning property and seeing you get your value for your money. – But a man's mind is always full of things. And some people's minds, like my aunt and uncle, are full of religion and hell for everybody except themselves. And some people's minds are all money, money, money, and how to get hold of something they haven't got hold of yet. And some people, like you, are always curious about what everybody else in the world is after. And some people are all for enjoying themselves and being thought much of, and some, like Lady Carrington, don't know what to do with themselves. Myself, I don't want to have in my mind the things other people have in their minds. I'm one that likes my own things best. And if, when I see a bright star fall, like to-night, I think to myself: *There's movement in the sky. The world is going to change again. They're throwing something to us from the distance, and we've got to have it, whether we want it or not. To-morrow there will be a difference for everybody, thrown out of the sky upon us, whether we want it or not:* then that's how I want to think, so let me please myself.'

'You know what a shooting star actually is, I suppose? – and that there are always many in August, because we pass through a region of them?'

'Yes, Mam, I've been told. But stones don't come at us from the sky for nothing. Either it's like when a man tosses an apple to you out of his orchard, as you go by. Or it's like when somebody shies a stone at you, to cut your head open. You'll never make me believe the sky is like an empty house with a slate falling from the roof. The world has its own life, the sky has a life of its own, and never is it like stones rolling down a rubbish heap and falling into a pond. Many things twitch and twitter within the sky, and many things happen beyond us. My own way of thinking is my own way.'

'I never knew you talk so much.'

'No, Mam. It's your asking me that about God. Or else it's the night-time. I don't believe in God and being good and going to Heaven. Neither do I worship idols, so I'm not a heathen as my aunt called me. Never from a boy did I want to believe the things they kept grinding in their guts at home, and at Sunday school, and at school. A man's mind has to be full of something, so I keep to what we used to think as lads. It's childish nonsense, I know it. But it suits me. Better than other people's stuff. Your man Phoenix is about the same, when he lets on. – Anyhow, it's my own stuff, that we believed as lads, and I like it better than other people's stuff. – You asking about God made me let on. But I would never belong to any club, or trades union, and God's the same to my mind.'

With this he gave a little kick to his horse, and St Mawr went dancing excitedly along the highway they now entered, leaving Mrs Witt to trot after as rapidly as she could.

When she came to the hotel, to which she had telegraphed for rooms, Lewis disappeared, and she was left thinking hard.

It was not till they were twenty miles from Merriton, riding through a slow morning mist, and she had a rather far-away, wistful look on her face, unusual for her, that she turned to him in the saddle and said:

'Now don't be surprised, Lewis, at what I am going to say. I am going to ask you, now, supposing I wanted to marry you, what should you say?'

He looked at her quickly, and was at once on his guard.

'That you didn't mean it,' he replied hastily.

'Yes' – she hesitated, and her face looked wistful and tired. – 'Supposing I *did* mean it. Supposing I did *really*, from my heart, want to marry you and be a wife to you –' she looked away across the fields – 'then what should you say?'

Her voice sounded sad, a little broken.

'Why, Mam!' he replied, knitting his brow and shaking his head a little. 'I should say you didn't mean it, you know. Something would have come over you.'

'But supposing I *wanted* something to come over me?'

He shook his head.

'It would never do, Mam! Some people's flesh and blood is kneaded like bread: and that's me. And some are rolled like fine pastry, like Lady Carrington. And some are mixed with gunpowder. They're like a cartridge you put in a gun, Mam.'

She listened impatiently.

'Don't talk,' she said, 'about bread and cakes and pastry, it all means nothing. You used to answer short enough, *Yes Mam! No Mam!* That will do now. Do you mean *Yes!* or *No?*'

His eyes met hers. She was again hectoring.

'No, Mam!' he said, quite neutral.

'Why?'

As she waited for his answer, she saw the foundations of his loquacity dry up, his face go distant and mute again, as it always used to be, till these last two days, when it had had a funny touch of inconsequential merriness.

He looked steadily into her eyes, and his look was neutral, sombre, and hurt. He looked at her as if infinite seas, infinite spaces divided him and her. And his eyes seemed to put her away beyond some sort of fence. An anger congealed cold like lava, set impassive against her and all her sort.

'No, Mam. I couldn't give my body to any woman who didn't respect it.'

'But I do respect it, I do!' – she flushed hot like a girl.

'No, Mam. Not as *I* mean it,' he replied.

There was a touch of anger against her in his voice, and a distance of distaste.

'And how do *you* mean it?' she replied, the full sarcasm coming back into her tones. She could see that, as a woman to touch and fondle he saw her as repellent: only repellent.

'I have to be a servant to women now,' he said, 'even to earn my wage. I could never touch with my body a woman whose servant I was.'

'You're not my servant: my daughter pays your wages. – And all that is beside the point, between a man and a woman.'

'No woman who I touched with my body should ever speak to me as you speak to me, or think of me as you think of me,' he said.

'But! –' she stammered. 'I think of you – with love. And can you be so unkind as to notice the way I speak? You know it's only my way.'

'You, as a woman,' he said, 'you have no respect for a man.'

'Respect! Respect!' she cried. 'I'm likely to lose what respect I have left. I know I can *love* a man. But whether a man can love a woman –'

'No,' said Lewis. 'I never could, and I think I never shall. Because I don't want to. The thought of it makes me feel shame.'

'What do you mean?' she cried.

'Nothing in the world,' he said, 'would make me feel such shame as to have a woman shouting at me, or mocking at me, as I see women mocking and despising the men they marry. No woman shall touch my body, and mock me or despise me. No woman.'

'But men must be mocked, or despised even, sometimes.'

'No. Not this man. Not by the woman I touch with my body.'

'Are you perfect?'

'I don't know. But if I touch a woman with my body, it must put a lock on her, to respect what I will never have despised: never!'

'What will you never have despised?'

'My body! And my touch upon the woman.'

'Why insist so on your body?' – And she looked at him with a touch of contemptuous mockery, raillery.

He looked her in the eyes, steadily, and coldly, putting her away from him, and himself far away from her.

'Do you expect that any woman will stay your humble slave, to-day?' she asked cuttingly.

But he only watched her, coldly, distant, refusing any connexion.

'Between men and women, it's a question of give and take. A man can't expect *always* to be humbly adored.'

He watched her still, cold, rather pale, putting her far from him. Then he turned his horse and set off rapidly along the road, leaving her to follow.

She walked her horse and let him go, thinking to herself: 'There's a little bantam cock. And a groom! Imagine it! Thinking he can dictate to a woman!'

She was in love with him. And he, in an odd way, was in love with her. She had known it by the odd, uncanny merriment in him, and his unexpected loquacity. But he would not have her come physically near him. Unapproachable there as a cactus, guarding his 'body' from her contact. As if contact with her would be mortal insult and fatal injury to his marvellous 'body'.

What a little cock-sparrow!

Let him ride ahead. He would have to wait for her somewhere.

She found him at the entrance to the next village. His face was pallid and set. She could tell he felt he had been insulted, so he had congealed into stiff insentience.

'At the bottom of all men is the same,' she said to herself: 'an empty, male conceit of themselves.'

She too rode up with a face like a mask, and straight on to the hotel.

'Can you serve dinner to myself and my servant?' she asked at the inn: which, fortunately for her, accommodated motorists, otherwise they would have said *No!*

'I think,' said Lewis as they came in sight of Merriton, 'I'd better give Lady Carrington a week's notice.'

A complete little stranger! And an impudent one.

'Exactly as you please,' she said.

She found several letters from her daughter at Marshal Place.

'Dear Mother: No sooner had you gone off than Flora appeared, not at all in the bud, but rather in full blow. She demanded her victim; Shylock demanding the pound of flesh:[50] and wanted to hand over the shekels.

'Joyfully I refused them. She said "Harry" was much better, and invited him and me to stay at Corrabach Hall till he was quite well: it would be less strain on your household, while he was still in bed and helpless. So the plan is, that he shall be brought down on Friday, if he is really fit for the journey, and we drive straight to Corrabach. I am packing his bags and mine, clearing up our traces: his trunks to go to Corrabach, mine to stay here and make up their minds. – I am going to Flints Farm again to-morrow, dutifully, though I am no flower for the bedside. – I do so want to know if Rico has already called her Fiorita: or perhaps Florecita. It reminds me of old William's joke: *Now yuh tell me, little Missy: which is the best posey that grow?* And the hushed whisper in which he said the answer: *The Collyposy!* Oh dear, I am so tired of feeling spiteful, but how else is one to feel?

'You looked most prosaically romantic, setting off in a rubber cape, followed by Lewis. Hope the roads were not very slippery, and that you had a good time, *à la Mademoiselle de Maupin.*[51] Do remember, dear, not to devour little Lewis before you have got half way –'

'Dear Mother: I half expected word from you before I left, but nothing came. Forrester drove me up here just before lunch. Rico seems much better, almost himself, and a little more than that. He broached our staying at Corrabach very tactfully. I told him Flora had asked me, and it seemed a good plan. Then I told him about St Mawr. He was a little piqued, and there was a pause of very disapproving silence. Then he said: *Very well, darling. If you wish to keep the animal, do so by all means. I make a present of him again.* Me: *That's so good of you, Rico. Because I know revenge is sweet.* Rico: *Revenge, Loulina! I don't think I was selling him for vengeance! Merely to get rid of him to Flora, who can keep better hold over him.* Me: *But you know, dear, she was going to geld him!* Rico: *I don't think anybody knew it. We only wondered if it were possible, to make him more amenable. Did she tell you?* Me: *No – Phoenix did. He had it from a groom.* Rico: *Dear me! A concatenation of grooms! So your mother rode off with Lewis, and carried St Mawr out of danger! I understand! Let us hope worse won't befall.* Me: *Whom?* Rico: *Never mind, dear! It's so lovely to see you. You are looking rested. I thought those Countess of Wilton roses the most marvellous things in the world, till you came, now they're quite in the background.* He had some very lovely red roses, in a crystal bowl: the room smelled of roses. Me: *Where did they*

come from? Rico: *Oh Flora brought them!* Me: *Bowl and all?* Rico:
Bowl and all! Wasn't it dear of her? Me: *Why yes! But then she's
the goddess of flowers, isn't she?* Poor darling, he was offended that
I should twit him while he is ill, so I relented. He has had a couple
of marvellous invalid's bed-jackets sent from London: one a
pinkish yellow, with rose-arabesque facings: this one in fine
cloth. But unfortunately he has already dropped soup on it. The
other is a lovely silvery and blue and green soft brocade. He had
that one on to receive me, and I at once complimented him on
it. He has got a new ring too: sent by Aspasia Weingartner, a
rather lovely intaglio of Priapus[52] under an apple bough, at least,
so he says it is. He made a naughty face, and said: *The Priapus
stage is rather advanced for poor me.* I asked what the Priapus stage
was, but he said *Oh, nothing!* Then nurse said: *There's a big
classical dictionary that Miss Manby brought up, if you wish to see
it.* So I have been studying the Classical Gods. The world always
was a queer place. It's a very queer one when Rico is the god
Priapus. He would go round the orchard painting life-like apples
on the trees, and inviting nymphs to come and eat them. And
the nymphs would pretend they were real: *Why, Sir Prippy, what
stunningly naughty apples!* There's nothing so artificial as sinning
nowadays. I suppose it once was real.

'I'm bored here: wish I had my horse.'

'Dear Mother: I'm so glad you are enjoying your ride. I'm sure
it is like riding into history, like the Yankee at the Court of King
Arthur,[53] in those old bye-lanes and Roman roads. They still
fascinate me: at least, more before I get there than when I am
actually there. I begin to feel real American and to resent the
past. Why doesn't the past decently bury itself, instead of sitting
waiting to be admired by the present?

'Phoenix brought Poppy. I am so fond of her: rode for five
hours yesterday. I was glad to get away from this farm. The
doctor came, and said Rico would be able to go down to Corrabach to-morrow. Flora came to hear the bulletin, and sailed back
full of zest. Apparently Rico is going to do a portrait of her,
sitting up in bed. What a mercy the bedclothes won't be mine,
when Priapus wields his palette from the pillow.

'Phoenix thinks you intend to go to America with St Mawr,

and that I am coming too, leaving Rico this side. – I wonder. I feel so unreal, nowadays, as if I too were nothing more than a painting by Rico on a millboard. I feel almost too unreal even to make up my mind to anything. It is terrible when the life-flow dies out of one, and everything is like cardboard, and oneself is like cardboard. I'm sure it is worse than being dead. I realized it yesterday when Phoenix and I had a picnic lunch by a stream. You see I must imitate you in all things. He found me some watercresses, and they tasted so damp and *alive*, I knew how deadened I was. Phoenix wants us to go and have a ranch in Arizona, and raise horses, with St Mawr, if willing, for Father Abraham.[54] I wonder if it matters what one does: if it isn't all the same thing over again? Only Phoenix, his funny blank face, makes my heart melt and go sad. But I believe he'd be cruel too. I saw it in his face when he didn't know I was looking. Anything though, rather than this deadness and this paint-Priapus business. Au revoir, mother dear! Keep on having a good time –'

'Dear Mother: I had your letter from Merriton: am so glad you arrived safe and sound in body and temper. There was such a funny letter from Lewis, too: I enclose it. What makes him take this extraordinary line? But I'm writing to tell him to take St Mawr to London, and wait for me there. I have telegraphed Mrs Squire to get the house ready for me. I shall go straight there.

'Things developed here, as they were bound to. I just couldn't bear it. No sooner was Rico put in the automobile than a self-conscious importance came over him, like when the wounded hero is carried into the middle of the stage. *Why so solemn, Rico dear?* I asked him, trying to laugh him out of it. *Not solemn, dear, only feeling a little transient.* I don't think he knew himself what he meant. Flora was on the steps as the car drew up, dressed in severe white. She only needed an apron, to become a nurse: or a veil to become a bride. Between the two, she had an unbearable air of a woman in seduced circumstances, as *The Times* said. She ordered two menservants about in subdued, you would have said hushed, but competent tones. And then I saw there was a touch of the priestess about her as well: Cassandra[55] preparing for her violation: Iphigenia,[56] with Rico for Orestes, on a stretcher: he looking like Adonis,[57] fully prepared to be an unconscionable time in dying.[58] They had given him a lovely room, downstairs, with doors opening on to a little garden all of its own. I believe it was Flora's boudoir. I left nurse and the men to put him to bed. Flora was hovering anxiously in the passage outside. *Oh what a marvellous room! Oh how colourful, how beautiful!* came Rico's tones, the hero behind the scenes. I must say, it was like a harvest festival, with roses and gaillardias in the shadow, and cornflowers in the light, and a bowl of grapes, and nectarines among leaves. *I'm so anxious that he should be happy*, Flora said to me in the passage. *You know him best. Is there anything else I could do for him?* Me: *Why, if you went to the piano and sang, I'm sure he'd love it. Couldn't you sing: Oh, my love is like a rred, rred rrose!*[59] – You know how Rico imitates Scotch!

'Thank goodness I have a bedroom upstairs: nurse sleeps in a little ante-chamber to Rico's room. The Edwards are still here, the blonde young man with some very futuristic plaster on his face. *Awfully good of you to come!* he said to me, looking at me out of one eye, and holding my hand fervently. How's that for cheek: *It's awfully good of Miss Manby to let me come*, said I. He: *Ah, but Flora is always a sport, a topping good sport!*

'I don't know what's the matter, but it just all put me into a fiendish temper. I felt I couldn't sit there at luncheon with that bright, youthful company, and hear about their tennis and their polo and their hunting and have their flirtatiousness making me sick. So I asked for a tray in my room. Do as I might, I couldn't help being horrid.

'Oh, and Rico! He really is too awful. Lying there in bed with every ear open, like Adonis waiting to be persuaded not to die. Seizing a hushed moment to take Flora's hand and press it to his lips, murmuring: *How awfully good you are to me, dear Flora!* And Flora: *I'd be better, if I knew how, Harry!* So cheerful with it all! No, it's too much. My sense of humour is leaving me: which means, I'm getting into too bad a temper to be able to ridicule it all. I suppose I feel in the minority. It's an awful thought, to think that most all the young people in the world are like this: so bright and cheerful, and *sporting*, and so brimming with libido. How awful!

'I said to Rico: *You're very comfortable here, aren't you?* He:

Comfortable! It's comparative heaven. Me: *Would you mind if I went away?* A deadly pause. He is deadly afraid of being left alone with Flora. He feels safe so long as I am about, and he can take refuge in his marriage ties. He: *Where do you want to go, dear?* Me: *To mother. To London. Mother is planning to go to America, and she wants me to go.* Rico: *But you don't want to go t – he – e – re – e!* You know, mother, how Rico can put a venomous emphasis on a word, till it suggests pure poison. It nettled me. *I'm not sure*, I said. Rico: *Oh, but you can't stand that awful America.* Me: *I want to try again.* Rico: *But Lou dear, it will be winter before you get there. And this is absolutely the wrong moment for me to go over there. I am only just making headway over here. When I am absolutely sure of a position in England, then we nip across the Atlantic and scoop in a few dollars, if you like. Just now, even when I am well, would be fatal. I've only just sketched in the outline of my success in London, and one ought to arrive in New York ready-made as a famous and important Artist.* Me: *But mother and I didn't think of going to New York. We thought we'd sail straight to New Orleans – if we could: or to Havana. And then go west to Arizona.* The poor boy looked at me in such distress. *But Loulina darling, do you mean you want to leave me in the lurch for the winter season? You can't mean it. We're just getting on so splendidly, really!* – I was surprised at the depth of feeling in his voice: how tremendously his career as an artist – a popular artist – matters to him. I can never believe it. – You know, mother, you and I feel alike about daubing paint on canvas: every possible daub that can be daubed has already been done, so people ought to leave off. Rico is so shrewd. I always think he's got his tongue in his cheek, and I'm always staggered once more to find that he takes it absolutely seriously. His career! The Modern British Society of Painters: perhaps even the Royal Academy! Those people we see in London, and those portraits Rico does! He may even be a second Laszlo,[60] or a thirteenth Orpen,[61] and die happy! Oh! mother! How can it really matter to *anybody*!

'But I was really rather upset, when I realized how his heart was fixed on his career, and that I might be spoiling everything for him. So I went away to think about it. And then I realized how unpopular you are, and how unpopular I shall be myself,

in a little while. A sort of hatred for people has come over me.
I hate their ways and their bunk, and I feel like kicking them in
the face, as St Mawr did that young man. Not that I should ever
do it. And I don't think I should ever have made my final
announcement to Rico, if he hadn't been such a beautiful pig in
clover, here at Corrabach Hall. He has known the Manbys all his
life; they and he are sections of one engine. He would be far
happier with Flora: or I won't say happier, because there is
something in him which rebels: but he would on the whole fit
much better. I myself am at the end of my limit, and beyond it.
I can't "mix" any more, and I refuse to. I feel like a bit of eggshell
in the mayonnaise: the only thing is to take it out, you can't beat
it in. I *know* I shall cause a fiasco, even in Rico's career, if I stay.
I shall go on being rude and hateful to people as I am at
Corrabach, and Rico will lose all his nerve.

'So I have told him. I said this evening, when no one was
about: *Rico dear, listen to me seriously. I can't stand these people.
If you ask me to endure another week of them, I shall either become
ill, or insult them, as mother does. And I don't want to do either.*
Rico: *But darling, isn't everybody perfect to you!* Me: *I tell you, I
shall just make a break, like St Mawr, if I don't get out. I simply
can't stand people.* – The poor darling, his face goes so blank and
anxious. He knows what I mean, because, except that they tickle
his vanity all the time, he hates them as much as I do. But his
vanity is the chief thing to him. He: *Lou darling, can't you wait
till I get up, and we can go away to the Tyrol or somewhere for a
spell?* Me: *Won't you come with me to America, to the South-West?
I believe it's marvellous country.* – I saw his face switch into hostility; quite vicious. He: *Are you so keen on spoiling everything for
me? Is that what I married you for? Do you do it deliberately?* Me:
*Everything is already spoilt for me. I tell you I can't stand people,
your Floras and your Aspasias, and your forthcoming young
Englishmen. After all, I am an American, like mother, and I've got
to go back.* He: *Really! And am I to come along as part of the
luggage? Labelled cabin!* Me: *You do as you wish, Rico.* He: *I wish
to God you did as you wished, Lou dear. I'm afraid you do as Mrs
Witt wishes. I always heard that the holiest thing in the world was
a mother.* Me: *No dear, it's just that I can't stand people.* He (with

a snarl): *And I suppose I'm lumped in as* PEOPLE! And when he'd said it, it was true. We neither of us said anything for a time. Then he said, calculating: *Very well, dear! You take a trip to the land of stars and stripes, and I'll stay here and go on with my work. And when you've seen enough of their stars and tasted enough of their stripes, you can come back and take your place again with me.* – We left it at that.

'You and I are supposed to have important business connected with our estates in Texas – it sounds so well – so we are making a hurried trip to the States, as they call them. I shall leave for London early next week –'

Mrs Witt read this long letter with satisfaction. She herself had one strange craving: to get back to America. It was not that she idealized her native country: she was a tartar of restlessness there, quite as much as in Europe. It was not that she expected to arrive at any blessed abiding place. No, in America she would go on fuming and chafing the same. But at least she would be in America, in her own country. And that was what she wanted.

She picked up the sheet of poor paper, that had been folded in Lou's letter. It was the letter from Lewis, quite nicely written. 'Lady Carrington, I write to tell you and Sir Henry that I think I had better quit your service, as it would be more comfortable all round. If you will write and tell me what you want me to do with St Mawr, I will do whatever you tell me. With kind regards to Lady Carrington and Sir Henry, I remain, Your obedient servant, Morgan Lewis.'

Mrs Witt put the letter aside, and sat looking out of the window. She felt, strangely, as if already her soul had gone away from her actual surroundings. She was there, in Oxfordshire, in the body, but her spirit had departed elsewhere. A listlessness was upon her. It was with an effort she roused herself, to write to her lawyer in London, to get her release from her English obligations. Then she wrote to the London hotel.

For the first time in her life she wished she had a maid, to do little things for her. All her life, she had had too much energy to endure anyone hanging round her, personally. Now she gave up. Her wrists seemed numb, as if the power in her were switched off.

When she went down they said Lewis had asked to speak to her. She had hardly seen him since they arrived at Merriton.

'I've had a letter from Lady Carrington, Mam. She says will I take St Mawr to London and wait for her there. But she says I am to come to you, Mam, for definite orders.'

'Very well, Lewis. I shall be going to London in a few days' time. You arrange for St Mawr to go up one day this week, and you will take him to the Mews. Come to me for anything you want. And don't talk of leaving my daughter. We want you to go with St Mawr to America, with us and Phoenix.'

'And your horse, Mam?'

'I shall leave him here at Merriton. I shall give him to Miss Atherton.'

'Very good Mam!'

'Dear Daughter: I shall be in my old quarters in Mayfair next Saturday, calling the same day at your house to see if everything is ready for you. Lewis has fixed up with the railway: he goes to town to-morrow. The reason of his letter was that I had asked him if he would care to marry me, and he turned me down with emphasis. But I will tell you about it. You and I are the scribe and the Pharisee;[62] I never could write a letter, and you could never leave off –'

'Dearest Mother: I smelt something rash, but I know it's no use saying: how *could* you? I only wonder, though, that you should think of marriage. You know, dear, I ache in every fibre to be left alone, from all that sort of thing. I feel all bruises, like one who has been assassinated. I do so understand why Jesus said: *Noli me tangere.* Touch me not, I am not yet ascended unto the Father.[63] Everything had hurt him so much, wearied him so beyond endurance, he felt he could not bear one little human touch on his body. I am like that. I can hardly bear even Elena to hand me a dress. As for a man – and marriage – ah no! *Noli me tangere, homine!* I am not yet ascended unto the Father. Oh, leave me alone, leave me alone! That is all my cry to all the world.

'Curiously, I feel that Phoenix understands what I feel. He leaves me so understandingly alone, he almost gives me my sheath of aloneness: or at least, he protects me in my sheath. I am grateful for him.

'Whereas Rico feels my aloneness as a sort of shame to himself. He wants at least a blinding *pretence* of intimacy. Ah intimacy! The thought of it fills me with aches, and the pretence of it exhausts me beyond myself.

'Yes, I long to go away to the west, to be away from the world like one dead and in another life, in a valley that life has not yet entered.

'Rico asked me: What are you doing with St Mawr? When I said we were taking him with us, he said: *Oh, the Corpus delicti!*[64] Whether that means anything I don't know. But he has grown sarcastic beyond my depth.

'I shall see you to-morrow –'

Lou arrived in town, at the dead end of August, with her maid and Phoenix. How wonderful it seemed to have London empty of all her set: her own little house to herself, with just the housekeeper and her own maid. The fact of being alone in those surroundings was so wonderful. It made the surroundings themselves seem all the more ghastly. Everything that had been actual to her was turning ghostly: even her little drawing-room was the ghost of a room, belonging to the dead people who had known it, or to all the dead generations that had brought such a room into being, evolved it out of their quaint domestic desires. And now, in herself, those desires were suddenly spent: gone out like a lamp that suddenly dies. And then she saw her pale, delicate room with its little green agate bowl and its two little porcelain birds and its soft, roundish chairs, turned into something ghostly, like a room set out in a museum. She felt like fastening little labels on the furniture: *Lady Louise Carrington Lounge Chair, Last used August 1923*. Not for the benefit of posterity: but to remove her own self into another world, another realm of existence.

'My house, my house, my house, how can I ever have taken so much pains about it!' she kept saying to herself. It was like one of her old hats, suddenly discovered neatly put away in an old hatbox. And what a horror: an old 'fashionable' hat.

Lewis came to see her, and he sat there in one of her delicate mauve chairs, with his feet on a delicate old carpet from Turkestan, and she just wondered. He wore his leather gaiters and khaki breeches as usual, and a faded blue shirt. But his beard and hair were trimmed, he was tidy. There was a certain fineness of contour about him, a certain subtle gleam, which made him seem, apart from his rough boots, not at all gross, or coarse, in that setting of rather silky, oriental furnishings. Rather he made the Asiatic, sensuous exquisiteness of her old rugs and her old white Chinese figures seem a weariness. Beauty! What was beauty, she asked herself? The Oriental exquisiteness seemed to her all like dead flowers whose hour had come, to be thrown away.

Lou could understand her mother's wanting, for a moment, to marry him. His detachedness and his acceptance of something in destiny which people cannot accept. Right in the middle of him he accepted something from destiny, that gave him a quality of eternity. He did not care about persons, people, even events. In his own odd way he was an aristocrat, inaccessible in his aristocracy. But it was the aristocracy of the invisible powers, the greater influences, nothing to do with human society.

'You don't really want to leave St Mawr, do you?' Lou asked him. 'You don't really want to quit, as you said?'

He looked at her steadily, from his pale grey eyes, without answering, not knowing what to say.

'Mother told me what she said to you. – But she doesn't mind, she says you are entirely within your rights. She has a real regard for you. But we mustn't let our regards run us into actions which are beyond our scope, must we? That makes everything unreal. But you will come with us to America with St Mawr, won't you? We depend on you.'

'I don't want to be uncomfortable,' he said.

'Don't be,' she smiled. 'I myself hate unreal situations – I feel I can't stand them any more. And most marriages are unreal situations. But apart from anything exaggerated, you like being with mother and me, don't you?'

'Yes, I do. I like Mrs Witt as well. But not –'

'I know. There won't be any more of that –'

'You see, Lady Carrington,' he said, with a little heat, 'I'm not by nature a marrying man. And I'd feel I was selling myself.'

'Quite! – Why do you think you are not a marrying man, though?'

'Me! I don't feel myself after I've been with women.' He spoke in a low tone, looking down at his hands. 'I feel messed up. I'm better to keep to myself. – Because –' and here he looked up with a flare in his eyes: 'women – they only want to make you give in to them, so that they feel almighty, and you feel small.'

'Don't you like feeling small?' Lou smiled. 'And don't you want to make them give in to you?'

'Not me,' he said. 'I don't want nothing. Nothing, I want.'

'Poor mother!' said Lou. 'She thinks if she feels moved by a man, it must result in marriage – or that kind of thing. Surely she makes a mistake. I think you and Phoenix and mother and I might live somewhere in a far-away wild place, and make a good life: so long as we didn't begin to mix up marriage, or love or that sort of thing into it. It seems to me men and women have really hurt one another so much, nowadays, that they had better stay apart till they have learned to be gentle with one another again. Not all this forced passion and destructive philandering. Men and women should stay apart, till their hearts grow gentle towards one another again. Now, it's only each one fighting for his own – or her own – underneath the cover of tenderness.'

'*Dear! – darling! – Yes my love!*' mocked Lewis, with a faint smile of amused contempt.

'Exactly. People always say *dearest!* when they hate each other most.'

Lewis nodded, looking at her with a sudden sombre gloom in his eyes. A queer bitterness showed on his mouth. But even then he was so still and remote.

The housekeeper came and announced The Honourable Laura Ridley. This was like a blow in the face to Lou. She rose hurriedly – and Lewis rose, moving to the door.

'Don't go please, Lewis,' said Lou – and then Laura Ridley appeared in the doorway. She was a woman a few years older than Lou, but she looked younger. She might have been a shy girl of twenty-two, with her fresh complexion, her hesitant manner, her round, startled brown eyes, her bobbed hair.

'Hello!' said the newcomer. 'Imagine your being back! I saw you in Paddington.'

Those sharp eyes would see everything.

'I thought everyone was out of town,' said Lou. 'This is Mr Lewis.'

Laura gave him a little nod, then sat on the edge of her chair.

'No,' she said. 'I did go to Ireland to my people, but I came back. I prefer London when I can be more or less alone in it. I thought I'd just run in for a moment, before you're gone again. – Scotland, isn't it?'

'No, mother and I are going to America.'

'America! Oh, I thought it was Scotland.'

'It was. But we have suddenly to go to America.'

'I see! – And what about Rico?'

'He is staying on in Shropshire. Didn't you hear of his accident?'

Lou told about it briefly.

'But how awful!' said Laura. 'But there! I knew it! I had a premonition when I saw that horse. We had a horse that killed a man. Then my father got rid of it. But ours was a mare, that one. Yours is a boy.'

'A full grown man I'm afraid.'

'Yes of course, I remember. – But how awful! I suppose you won't ride in the Row. The awful people that ride there nowadays, anyhow! Oh, aren't they awful! Aren't people monstrous, really! My word, when I see the horses crossing Hyde Park Corner, on a wet day, and coming down smash on those slippery stones, giving their riders a fractured skull! – No joke!'

She inquired details of Rico.

'Oh, I suppose I shall see him when he gets back,' she said. 'But I'm sorry you are going. I shall miss you, I'm afraid. Though you won't be staying long in America. No one stays there longer than they can help.'

'I think the winter through, at least,' said Lou.

'Oh, all the winter! So long? I'm sorry to hear *that*. You're one of the few, very few people one can talk *really* simply with. Extraordinary, isn't it, how few really simple people there are!

And they get fewer and fewer. I stayed a fortnight with my people, and a week of that I was in bed. It was really horrible. They really try to take the life out of one, *really!* Just because one won't be as they are, and play their game. I simply refused, and came away.'

'But you can't cut yourself off altogether,' said Lou.

'No, I suppose not. One has to see somebody. Luckily one has a few artists for friends. They're the only real people, anyhow –' She glanced round inquisitively at Lewis, and said, with a slight, impertinent elvish smile on her virgin face:

'Are you an artist?'

'No Mam!' he said. 'I'm a groom.'

'Oh, I see!' She looked him up and down.

'Lewis is St Mawr's master,' said Lou.

'Oh, the horse! the terrible horse!' She paused a moment. Then again she turned to Lewis with that faint smile, slightly condescending, slightly impertinent, slightly flirtatious.

'Aren't you afraid of him?' she asked.

'No, Mam.'

'Aren't you, *really!* – And can you always master him?'

'Mostly. He knows me.'

'Yes! I suppose that's it.' – She looked him up and down again, then turned away to Lou.

'What have you been painting lately?' said Lou. Laura was not a bad painter.

'Oh, hardly anything. I haven't been able to get on at all. This is one of my bad intervals.'

Here Lewis rose, and looked at Lou.

'All right,' she said. 'Come in after lunch, and we'll finish those arrangements.'

Laura gazed after the man, as he dived out of the room, as if her eyes were gimlets that could bore into his secret.

In the course of the conversation she said:

'What a curious little man that was!'

'Which?'

'The groom who was here just now. *Very* curious! Such peculiar eyes. I shouldn't wonder if he had psychic powers.'

'What sort of psychic powers?' said Lou.

'Could *see* things. – And hypnotic too. He might have hypnotic powers.'

'What makes you think so?'

'He gives me that sort of feeling. Very curious! Probably he hypnotizes the horse. – Are you leaving the horse here, by the way, in stable?'

'No, taking him to America.'

'Taking him to America! How extraordinary!'

'It's mother's idea. She thinks he might be valuable as a stock horse on a ranch. You know we still have interest in a ranch in Texas.'

'Oh, I see! Yes, probably he'd be very valuable, to improve the breed of the horses over there. – My father has some very lovely hunters. Isn't it disgraceful, he would never let me ride!'

'Why?'

'Because we girls weren't important, in his opinion. – So you're taking the horse to America! With the little man?'

'Yes, St Mawr will hardly behave without him.'

'I see! – I see – ee – ee! Just you and Mrs Witt and the little man. I'm sure you'll find he has psychic powers.'

'I'm afraid I'm not so good at finding things out,' said Lou.

'Aren't you? No, I suppose not. I am. I have a flair. I sort of *smell* things. – Then the horse is already here, is he? When do you think you'll sail?'

'Mother is finding a merchant boat that will go to Galveston, Texas, and take us along with the horse. She knows people who will find the right thing. But it takes time.'

'What a much nicer way to travel, than on one of those great liners! Oh, how awful they are! So vulgar! Floating palaces they call them! My word, the people inside the palaces! – Yes, I should say that would be a much pleasanter way of travelling: on a cargo boat.'

Laura wanted to go down to the Mews to see St Mawr. The two women went together.

St Mawr stood in his box, bright and tense as usual.

'Yes!' said Laura Ridley, with a slight hiss. 'Yes! Isn't he beautiful. Such very perfect legs!' – She eyed him round with those gimlet, sharp eyes of hers. 'Almost a pity to let him go out of England. We need some of his perfect *bone*, I feel. – But his eye! Hasn't he got a look in it, my word!'

'I can never see that he looks wicked,' said Lou.

'Can't you!' – Laura had a slight hiss in her speech, a sort of aristocratic decision in her enunciation, that got on Lou's nerves. – 'He looks wicked to me!'

'He's not *mean*,' said Lou. 'He'd never do anything mean to you.'

'Oh, mean! I daresay not. No! I'll grant him that, he gives fair warning. His eye says *Beware!* – But isn't he a beauty, *isn't* he!' Lou could feel the peculiar reverence for St Mawr's breeding, his show qualities. Herself, all she cared about was the horse himself, his real nature. 'Isn't it extraordinary,' Laura continued, 'that you never get a *really* perfectly satisfactory animal! There's always something wrong. And in men too. Isn't it curious? there's always something – something wrong – or something missing. Why is it?'

'I don't know,' said Lou. She felt unable to cope with any more. And she was glad when Laura left her.

The days passed slowly, quietly, London almost empty of Lou's acquaintances. Mrs Witt was busy getting all sorts of papers and permits: such a fuss! The battle light was still in her eye. But about her nose was a dusky, pinched look that made Lou wonder.

Both women wanted to be gone: they felt they had already flown in spirit, and it was weary, having the body left behind.

At last all was ready: they only awaited the telegram to say when their cargo-boat would sail. Trunks stood there packed, like great stones locked for ever. The Westminster house seemed already a shell. Rico wrote and telegraphed, tenderly, but there was a sense of relentless effort in it all, rather than of any real tenderness. He had taken his position.

Then the telegram came, the boat was ready to sail.

'There now!' said Mrs Witt, as if it had been a sentence of death.

'Why do you look like that, mother?'

'I feel I haven't an ounce of energy left in my body.'

'But how queer, for you, mother. Do you think you are ill?'

'No, Louise. I just feel that way: as if I hadn't an ounce of energy left in my body.'

'You'll feel yourself again, once you are away.'

'Maybe I shall.'

After all, it was only a matter of telephoning. The hotel and the railway porters and taxi-men would do the rest.

It was a grey, cloudy day, cold even. Mother and daughter sat in a cold first-class carriage and watched the little Hampshire countryside go past: little, old, unreal it seemed to them both, and passing away like a dream whose edges only are in consciousness. Autumn! Was this autumn? Were these trees, fields, villages? It seemed but the dim, dissolving edges of a dream, without inward substance.

At Southampton it was raining: and just a chaos, till they stepped on to a clean boat, and were received by a clean young captain, quite sympathetic, and quite a gentleman. Mrs Witt, however, hardly looked at him, but went down to her cabin and lay down in her bunk.

There, lying concealed, she felt the engines start, she knew the voyage had begun. But she lay still. She saw the clouds and the rain, and refused to be disturbed.

Lou had lunch with the young captain, and she felt she ought to be flirty. The young man was so polite and attentive. And she wished so much she were alone.

Afterwards, she sat on deck and saw the Isle of Wight pass shadowy, in a misty rain. She didn't know it was the Isle of Wight. To her, it was just the lowest bit of the British Isles. She saw it fading away: and with it, her life, going like a clot of shadow in a mist of nothingness. She had no feelings about it, none: neither about Rico, nor her London house, nor anything. All passing in a grey curtain of rainy drizzle, like a death, and she, with not a feeling left.

They entered the Channel, and felt the slow heave of the sea. And soon, the clouds broke in a little wind. The sky began to clear. By mid-afternoon it was blue summer, on the blue, running waters of the Channel. And soon, the ship steering for Santander, there was the coast of France, the rocks twinkling like some magic world.

The magic world! And back of it, that post-war Paris, which Lou knew only too well, and which depressed her so thoroughly. Or that post-war Monte Carlo, the Riviera still more depressing even than Paris. No, no one must land, even on magic coasts. Else you found yourself in a railway station and a 'centre of civilization' in five minutes.

Mrs Witt hated the sea, and stayed, as a rule, practically the whole time of the crossing, in her bunk. There she was now, silent, shut up like a steel trap, as in her tomb. She did not even read. Just lay and stared at the passing sky. And the only thing to do was to leave her alone.

Lewis and Phoenix hung on the rail, and watched everything. Or they went down to see St Mawr. Or they stood talking in the doorway of the wireless operator's cabin. Lou begged the Captain to give them jobs to do.

The queer, transitory, unreal feeling, as the ship crossed the great, heavy Atlantic. It was rather bad weather. And Lou felt, as she had felt before, that this grey, wolf-like, cold-blooded Ocean hated men and their ships and their smoky passage. Heavy grey waves, a low-sagging sky: rain: yellow, weird evenings with snatches of sun: so it went on. Till they got way South, into the westward-running stream. Then they began to get blue weather and blue water.

To go South! Always to go South, away from the arctic horror as far as possible! That was Lou's instinct. To go out of the clutch of greyness and low skies, of sweeping rain, and of slow, blanketing snow. Never again to see the mud and rain and snow of a northern winter, nor to feel the idealistic, Christianized tension of the now irreligious North.

As they neared Havana, and the water sparkled at night with phosphorus, and the flying-fishes came like drops of bright water, sailing out of the massive-slippery waves, Mrs Witt emerged once more. She still had that shut-up, deathly look on her face. But she prowled round the deck, and manifested at least a little interest in affairs not her own. Here at sea, she hardly remembered the existence of St Mawr or Lewis or Phoenix. She was not very deeply aware even of Lou's existence. – But of course, it would all come back, once they were on land.

They sailed in hot sunshine out of a blue, blue sea, past the castle into the harbour at Havana. There was a lot of shipping: and this was already America. Mrs Witt had herself and Lou put ashore immediately. They took a motor-car and drove at once to the great boulevard that is the centre of Havana. Here they saw a long rank of motor-cars, all drawn up ready to take a couple of hundred American tourists for one more tour. There were the tourists, all with badges in their coats, lest they should get lost.

'They get so drunk by night,' said the driver in Spanish, 'that the policemen find them lying in the road – turn them over, see the badge – and, hup! – carry them to their hotel.' He grinned sardonically.

Lou and her mother lunched at the Hotel d'Angleterre, and Mrs Witt watched transfixed while a couple of her countrymen, a stout successful man and his wife, lunched abroad. They had cocktails – then lobster – and a bottle of hock – then a bottle of champagne – then a half-bottle of port. – And Mrs Witt rose in haste as the liqueurs came. For that successful man and his wife had gone on imbibing with a sort of fixed and deliberate will, apparently tasting nothing, but saying to themselves: Now we're drinking Rhine wine! Now we're drinking 1912 champagne. Yah, Prohibition! Thou canst not put it over me. – Their complexions became more and more lurid. Mrs Witt fled, fearing a Havana débâcle. But she said nothing.

In the afternoon, they motored into the country, to see the great brewery gardens, the new villa suburb, and through the lanes past the old, decaying plantations with palm-trees. In one lane they met the fifty motor-cars with the two hundred tourists all with badges on their chests and self-satisfaction on their faces. Mrs Witt watched in grim silence.

'Plus ça change, plus c'est la même chose,' said Lou, with a wicked little smile. 'On n'est pas mieux ici, mother.'[65]

'I know it,' said Mrs Witt.

The hotels by the sea were all shut up: it was not yet the 'season'. Not till November. And then! – Why, then Havana would be an American city, in full leaf of green dollar bills. The green leaf of American prosperity shedding itself recklessly, from every roaming sprig of a tourist, over this city of sunshine and alcohol. Green leaves unfolded in Pittsburg and Chicago, showering in winter downfall in Havana.

Mother and daughter drank tea in a corner of the Hotel d'Angleterre once more, and returned to the ferry.

The Gulf of Mexico was blue and rippling, with the phantom of islands on the south. Great porpoises rolled and leaped, running in front of the ship in the clear water, diving, travelling in perfect motion, straight, with the tip of the ship touching the tip of their tails, then rolling over, cork-screwing, and showing their bellies as they went. Marvellous! The marvellous beauty and fascination of natural wild things! The horror of man's unnatural life, his heaped-up civilization!

The flying fishes burst out of the sea in clouds of silvery, transparent motion. Blue above and below, the Gulf seemed a silent, empty, timeless place where man did not really reach. And Lou was again fascinated by the glamour of the universe.

But bump! She and her mother were in a first-class hotel again, calling down the telephone for the bell-boy and ice-water. And soon they were in a Pullman, off to San Antonio.

It was America, it was Texas. They were at their ranch, on the great level of yellow autumn, with the vast sky above. And after all, from the hot wide sky, and the hot, wide, red earth, there *did* come something new, something not used-up. Lou *did* feel exhilarated.

The Texans were there, tall blonde people, ingenuously cheerful, ingenuously, childishly intimate, as if the fact that you had never seen them before was as nothing compared to the fact that you'd all been living in one room together all your lives, so that nothing was hidden from either of you. The one room being the mere shanty of the world in which we all live. Strange, un-inspired cheerfulness, filling, as it were, the blank of complete incomprehension.

And off they set in their motor-cars, chiefly high-legged Fords, rattling away down the red trails between yellow sunflowers or sere grass or dry cotton, away, away into great distances, cheerfully raising the dust of haste. It left Lou in a sort of blank amazement. But it left her amused, not depressed. The old screws of emotion and intimacy that had been screwed down so tightly upon her fell out of their holes, here. The Texan intimacy weighed no more on her than a postage stamp, even if, for the moment, it stuck as close. And there was a certain underneath recklessness, even a stoicism in all the apparently childish people, which left one free. They might appear childish: but they stoically depended on themselves alone, in reality. Not as in England, where every man waited to pour the burden of himself upon you.

St Mawr arrived safely, a bit bewildered. The Texans eyed him closely, struck silent, as ever, by anything pure-bred and beautiful. He was somehow too beautiful, too perfected, in this great open country. The long-legged Texan horses, with their elaborate saddles, seemed somehow more natural.

Even St Mawr felt himself strange, as it were naked and singled out, in this rough place. Like a jewel among stones, a pearl before swine, maybe. But the swine were no fools. They knew a pearl from a grain of maize, and a grain of maize from a pearl. And they knew what they wanted. When it was pearls, it was pearls; though chiefly, it was maize. Which shows good sense. They could see St Mawr's points. Only he needn't draw the point too fine, or it would just not pierce the tough skin of this country.

The ranch-man mounted him – just threw a soft skin over his back, jumped on, and away down the red trail, raising the dust among the tall wild yellow of sunflowers, in the hot wild sun. Then back again in a fume, and the man slipped off.

'He's got the stuff in him, he sure has,' said the man.

And the horse seemed pleased with this rough handling. Lewis looked on in wonder, and a little envy.

Lou and her mother stayed a fortnight on the ranch. It was all so queer: so crude, so rough, so easy, so artificially civilized, and so meaningless. Lou could not get over the feeling that it all meant nothing. There were no roots of reality at all. No consciousness below the surface, no meaning in anything save the obvious, the blatantly obvious. It was like life enacted in a mirror. Visually, it was wildly vital. But there was nothing behind it. Or like a cinematograph: flat shapes, exactly like men, but without any substance of reality, rapidly rattling away with talk, emotions, activity, all in the flat, nothing behind it. No deeper consciousness at all. So it seemed to her.

One moved from dream to dream, from phantasm to phantasm.

But at least, this Texan life, if it had no bowels, no vitals, at least it could not prey on one's own vitals. It was this much better than Europe.

Lewis was silent, and rather piqued. St Mawr had already made advances to the boss' long-legged, arch-necked, glossy-maned Texan mare. And the boss was pleased.

What a world!

Mrs Witt eyed it all shrewdly. But she failed to participate. Lou was a bit scared at the emptiness of it all, and the queer, phantasmal self-consciousness. Cowboys just as self-conscious as Rico, far more sentimental, inwardly vague and unreal. Cowboys that went after their cows in black Ford motor-cars: and who self-consciously saw Lady Carrington falling to them, as elegant young ladies from the East fall to the noble cowboy of the films, or in Zane Grey.[66] It was all film-psychology.

And at the same time, these boys led a hard, hard life, often dangerous and gruesome. Nevertheless, inwardly they were self-conscious film-heroes. The boss himself, a man over forty, long and lean and with a great deal of stringy energy, showed off before her in a strong silent manner, existing for the time being purely in his imagination of the sort of picture he made to her, the sort of impression he made on her.

So they all were, coloured up like a Zane Grey book-jacket, all of them living in the mirror. The kind of picture they made to somebody else.

And at the same time, with energy, courage, and a stoical grit getting their work done, and putting through what they had to put through.

It left Lou blank with wonder. And in the face of this strange cheerful living in the mirror – a rather cheap mirror at that – England began to seem real to her again.

Then she had to remember herself back in England. And no, oh God, England was not real either, except poisonously.

What was real? What under heaven was real?

Her mother had gone dumb and, as it were, out of range. Phoenix was a bit assured and bouncy, back more or less in his own conditions. Lewis was a bit impressed by the emptiness of everything, the *lack* of concentration. And St Mawr followed at the heels of the boss' long-legged black Texan mare, almost slavishly.

What, in heaven's name, was one to make of it all?

Soon, she could not stand this sort of living in a film-setting, with the mechanical energy of 'making good', that is, making money, to keep the show going. The mystic duty to 'make good', meaning to make the ranch pay a laudable interest on the 'owners'' investment. Lou herself being one of the owners. And the interest that came to her, from her father's will, being the money she spent to buy St Mawr and to fit up that house in Westminster. Then also the mystic duty to 'feel good'. Everybody had to *feel good, fine!* 'How are you this morning, Mr Latham?' – '*Fine!* Eh! Don't you feel good out here, eh? Lady Carrington?' – '*Fine!*' – Lou pronounced it with the same ringing conviction. It was Coué[67] all the time!

'Shall we stay here long, mother?' she asked.

'Not a day longer than you want to, Louise. I stay entirely for your sake.'

'Then let us go, mother.'

They left St Mawr and Lewis. But Phoenix wanted to come along. So they motored to San Antonio, got into the Pullman, and travelled as far as El Paso. Then they changed to go North. Santa Fé would be at least 'easy'. And Mrs Witt had acquaintances there.

They found the fiesta over in Santa Fé: Indians, Mexicans, artists had finished their great effort to amuse and attract the tourists. *Welcome Mr Tourist* said a great board on one side of the high-road. And on the other side, a little nearer to town: *Thank You, Mr Tourist*.

'Plus ça change –' Lou began.

'Ça ne change jamais[68] – except for the worse!' said Mrs Witt, like a pistol going off. And Lou held her peace, after she had sighed to herself, and said in her own mind: '*Welcome Also Mrs and Miss Tourist!*'

There was no getting a word out of Mrs Witt, these days. Whereas Phoenix was becoming almost loquacious.

They stayed a while in Santa Fé, in the clean, comfortable, 'homely' hotel, where 'every room had its bath': a spotless white bath, with very hot water night and day. The tourists and commercial travellers sat in the big hall down below, everybody living in the mirror! And of course, they knew Lady Carrington down to her shoe-soles. And they all expected her to know them down to their shoe-soles. For the only object of the mirror is to reflect images.

For two days mother and daughter ate in the mayonnaise intimacy of the dining-room. Then Mrs Witt struck, and telephoned down every meal-time, for her meal in her room. She got to staying in bed later and later, as on the ship. Lou became uneasy. This was worse than Europe.

Phoenix was still there, as a sort of half-friend, half-servant retainer. He was perfectly happy, roving round among the Mexicans and Indians, talking Spanish all day, and telling about England and his two mistresses, rolling the ball of his own importance.

'I'm afraid we've got Phoenix for life,' said Lou.

'Not unless we wish,' said Mrs Witt indifferently. And she picked up a novel which she didn't want to read, but which she was going to read.

'What shall we do next, mother?' Lou asked.

'As far as I am concerned, there is no next,' said Mrs Witt.

'Come, mother! Let's go back to Italy or somewhere, if it's as bad as that.'

'Never again, Louise, shall I cross that water. I have come home to die.'

'I don't see much home about it – the Gonsalez Hotel in Santa Fé.'

'Indeed not! But as good as anywhere else, to die in.'

'Oh mother, don't be silly! Shall we look for somewhere where we can be by ourselves?'

'I leave it to you, Louise. I have made my last decision.'

'What is that, mother?'

'Never, never to make another decision.'

'Not even to decide to die?'

'No, not even that.'

'Or *not* to die?'

'Not that either.'

Mrs Witt shut up like a trap. She refused to rise from her bed that day.

Lou went to consult Phoenix. The result was, the two set out to look at a little ranch that was for sale.

It was autumn, and the loveliest time in the south-west, where there is no spring, snow blowing into the hot lap of summer; and no real summer, hail falling in thick ice, from the thunderstorms: and even no very definite winter, hot sun melting the snow and giving an impression of spring at any time. But autumn there is, when the winds of the desert are almost still, and the mountains fume no clouds. But morning comes cold and delicate, upon the wild sunflowers and the puffing, yellow-flowered greasewood. For the desert blooms in autumn. In spring it is grey ash all the time, and only the strong breath of the summer sun, and the heavy splashing of thunder rain succeeds at last, by September, in blowing it into soft, puffy yellow fire.

It was such a delicate morning when Lou drove out with Phoenix towards the mountains, to look at this ranch that a Mexican wanted to sell. For the brief moment the high mountains had lost their snow: it would be back again in a fortnight: and stood dim and delicate with autumn haze. The desert stretched away pale, as pale as the sky, but silvery and sere, with hummock-mounds of shadow, and long wings of shadow, like the reflection of some great bird. The same eagle-shadows came like rude paintings of the outstretched bird, upon the mountains, where the aspens were turning yellow. For the moment, the brief moment, the great desert-and-mountain landscape had lost its certain cruelty, and looked tender, dreamy. And many, many birds were flickering around.

Lou and Phoenix bumped and hesitated over a long trail: then wound down into a deep canyon: and then the car began to climb, climb, climb, in steep rushes, and in long heart-breaking, uneven pulls. The road was bad, and driving was no joke. But it was the sort of road Phoenix was used to. He sat impassive and watchful, and kept on, till his engine boiled. He was *himself* in this country: impassive, detached, self-satisfied, and silently assertive. Guarding himself at every moment, but, on his guard, sure of himself. Seeing no difference at all between Lou or Mrs Witt and himself, except that they had money and he had none, while he had a native importance which they lacked. He depended on them for money, they on him for the power to live out here in the West. Intimately, he was as good as they. Money was their only advantage.

As Lou sat beside him in the front seat of the car, where it bumped less than behind, she felt this. She felt a peculiar tough-necked arrogance in him, as if he were asserting himself to put something over her. He wanted her to allow him to make advances to her, to allow him to suggest that he should be her lover. And then, finally, she would marry him, and he would be on the same footing as she and her mother.

In return, he would look after her, and give her his support and countenance, as a man, and stand between her and the world. In this sense, he would be faithful to her, and loyal. But as far as other women went, Mexican women or Indian women: why, that was none of her business. His marrying her would be a pact between two aliens, on behalf of one another, and he would keep his part of it all right. But himself, as a private man and a predative alien-blooded male, this had nothing to do with her. It didn't enter into her scope and count. She was one of these nervous white women with lots of money. She was very nice too. But as a *squaw* – as a real woman in a shawl whom a man went after for the pleasure of the night – why, she hardly counted. One of these white women who talk clever and know things like a man. She could hardly expect a half-savage male to acknowledge her as his female counterpart. – No! She had the bucks! And she had all the paraphernalia of the white man's civilization, which a savage can play with and so escape his own hollow boredom. But his own real female counterpart? – Phoenix would just have shrugged his shoulders, and thought the question not worth answering. How could there be any answer in *her*, to the phallic male in him? Couldn't! Yet it would flatter his vanity and his self-esteem immensely, to possess her. That would be possessing the very clue to the white man's overwhelming world. And if she would let him possess her, he would be absolutely loyal to her, as far as affairs and appearances went. Only, the aboriginal phallic male in him simply couldn't recognize her as a woman at all. In this respect, she didn't exist. It needed the shawled Indian or Mexican women, with their squeaky, plaintive voices, their shuffling, watery humility, and the dark glances of their big, knowing eyes. When an Indian woman looked at him from under her black fringe, with dark, half-secretive suggestion in her big eyes: and when she stood before him hugged in her shawl, in such apparently complete quiescent humility: and when she spoke to him in her mousey squeak of a high, plaintive voice, as if it were difficult for her female bashfulness even to emit so much sound: and when she shuffled away with her legs wide apart, because of her wide-topped, white, high buckskin boots with tiny white feet, and her dark-knotted hair so full of hard, yet subtle lure: and when he remembered the almost watery softness of the Indian woman's dark, warm flesh: then he was a male, an old, secretive, rat-like male. But before Lou's straight-forwardness and utter sexual incompetence, he just stood in contempt. And to him, even a French cocotte was utterly devoid of the right sort of sex. She couldn't really move him. She couldn't satisfy the furtiveness in him. He needed this plaintive, squeaky, dark-fringed Indian quality. Something furtive and soft and rat-like, really to rouse him.

Nevertheless he was ready to trade his sex, which, in his opinion, every white woman was secretly pining for, for the white woman's money and social privileges. In the daytime, all the thrill and excitement of the white man's motor-cars and moving pictures and ice-cream sodas and so forth. In the night, the soft, watery-soft warmth of an Indian or half-Indian woman. This was Phoenix's idea of life for himself.

Meanwhile, if a white woman gave him the privileges of the white man's world, he would do his duty by her as far as all that went.

Lou, sitting very, very still beside him as he drove the car – he was not a very good driver, not quick and marvellous as some white men are, particularly some French chauffeurs she had known, but usually a little behindhand in his movements – she knew more or less all that he felt. More or less she divined as a woman does. Even from a certain rather assured stupidity of his shoulders, and a certain rather stupid assertiveness of his knees, she knew him.

But she did not judge him too harshly. Somewhere deep, deep in herself she knew she too was at fault. And this made her sometimes inclined to humble herself, as a woman, before the furtive assertiveness of this underground, 'knowing' savage. He was so different from Rico.

Yet, after all, *was* he? In his rootlessness, his drifting, his real meaninglessness, was he different from Rico? And his childish, spellbound absorption in the motor-car, or in the moving-pictures, or in an ice-cream soda – was it very different from Rico? Anyhow, was it really any better? Pleasanter, perhaps, to a woman, because of the childishness of it.

The same with his opinion of himself as a sexual male! So childish, really, it was almost thrilling to a woman. But then, so stupid also, with that furtive lurking in holes and imagining it could not be detected. He imagined he kept himself dark, in his sexual rat holes. He imagined he was not detected!

No, no, Lou was not such a fool as she looked, in his eyes anyhow. She knew what she wanted. She wanted relief from the nervous tension and irritation of her life, she wanted to escape from the friction which is the whole stimulus in modern social life. She wanted to be still: only that, to be very, very still, and recover her own soul.

When Phoenix presumed she was looking for some secretly sexual male such as himself, he was ridiculously mistaken. Even the illusion of the beautiful St Mawr was gone. And Phoenix, roaming round like a sexual rat in promiscuous back yards! – *Merci, mon cher!* For that was all he was: a sexual rat in the great barn-yard of man's habitat, looking for female rats!

Merci, mon cher! You are had.

Nevertheless, in his very mistakenness, he was a relief to her. His mistake was amusing rather than impressive. And the fact that one half of his intelligence was a complete dark blank, that too was a relief.

Strictly, and perhaps in the best sense, he was a servant. His very unconsciousness and his very limitation served as a shelter, as one shelters within the limitations of four walls. The very decided limits to his intelligence were a shelter to her. They made her feel safe.

But that feeling of safety did not deceive her. It was the feeling one derived from having a *true* servant attached to one, a man whose psychic limitations left him incapable of anything but service, and whose strong flow of natural life, at the same time, made him need to serve.

And Lou, sitting there so very still and frail, yet self-contained, had not lived for nothing. She no longer wanted to fool herself. She had no desire at all to fool herself into thinking that a Phoenix might be a husband and a mate. No desire that way at all. His obtuseness was a servant's obtuseness. She was grateful to him for serving, and she paid him a wage. Moreover, she provided him with something to do, to occupy his life. In a sense, she gave him his life, and rescued him from his own boredom. It was a balance.

He did not know what she was thinking. There was a certain physical sympathy between them. His obtuseness made him think it was also a sexual sympathy.

'It's a nice trip, you and me,' he said suddenly, turning and looking her in the eyes with an excited look, and ending on a foolish little laugh.

She realized that she should have sat in the back seat.

'But it's a bad road,' she said. 'Hadn't you better stop and put the sides of the hood up? your engine is boiling.'

He looked away with a quick switch of interest to the red thermometer in front of his machine.

'She's boiling,' he said, stopping, and getting out with a quick alacrity to go to look at the engine.

Lou got out also, and went to the back seat, shutting the door decisively.

'I think I'll ride at the back,' she said, 'it gets so frightfully hot in front, when the engine heats up. – Do you think she needs some water? Have you got some in the canteen?'

'She's full,' he said, peering into the steaming valve.

'You can run a bit out, if you think there's any need. I wonder if it's much farther!'

'*Quién sabe!*'[69] said he, slightly impertinent.

She relapsed into her own stillness. She realized how careful, how very careful she must be of relaxing into sympathy, and reposing, as it were, on Phoenix. He would read it as a sexual appeal. Perhaps he couldn't help it. She had only herself to blame. He was obtuse, as a man and a savage. He had only one interpretation, sex, for any woman's approach to him.

And she knew, with the last clear knowledge of weary disillusion, that she did not want to be mixed up in Phoenix's sexual promiscuities. The very thought was an insult to her. The crude, clumsy servant-male: no, no, not that. He was a good fellow, a very good fellow, as far as he went. But he fell far short of physical intimacy.

'No, no,' she said to herself, 'I was wrong to ride in the front seat with him. I must sit alone, just alone. Because sex, mere sex, is repellent to me. I will never prostitute myself again. Unless something touches my very spirit, the very quick of me, I will stay alone, just alone. Alone, and give myself only to the unseen presences, serve only the other, unseen presences.'

She understood now the meaning of the Vestal Virgins,[70] the Virgins of the holy fire in the old temples. They were symbolic of herself, of woman weary of the embrace of incompetent men, weary, weary, weary of all that, turning to the unseen gods, the unseen spirits, the hidden fire, and devoting herself to that, and that alone. Receiving thence her pacification and her fulfilment.

Not these little, incompetent, childish self-opinionated men! Not these to touch her. She watched Phoenix's rather stupid shoulders, as he drove the car on between the *piñon* trees and the cedars of the narrow mesa ridge, to the mountain foot. He was a good fellow. But let him run among women of his own sort. Something was beyond him. And this something must remain beyond him, never allow itself to come within his reach. Otherwise he would paw it and mess it up, and be as miserable as a child that has broken its father's watch.

No, no! She had loved an American, and lived with him for a fortnight. She had had a long, intimate friendship with an

Italian. Perhaps it was love on his part. And she had yielded to him. Then her love and marriage to Rico.

And what of it all? Nothing. It was almost nothing. It was as if only the outside of herself, her top layers, were human. This inveigled her into intimacies. As soon as the intimacy penetrated, or attempted to penetrate inside her, it was a disaster. Just a humiliation and a breaking down.

Within these outer layers of herself lay the successive inner sanctuaries of herself. And these were inviolable. She accepted it.

'I am not a marrying woman,' she said to herself. 'I am not a lover nor a mistress nor a wife. It is no good. Love can't really come into me from the outside, and I can never, never mate with any man, since the mystic new man will never come to me. No, no, let me know myself and my rôle. I am one of the eternal Virgins, serving the eternal fire. My dealings with men have only broken my stillness and messed up my doorways. It has been my own fault. I ought to stay virgin, and still, very, very still, and serve the most perfect service. I want my temple and my loneliness and my Apollo mystery[71] of the inner fire. And with men, only the delicate, subtler, more remote relations. No coming near. A coming near only breaks the delicate veils, and broken veils, like broken flowers, only lead to rottenness.'

She felt a great peace inside herself as she made this realization. And a thankfulness. Because, after all, it seemed to her that the hidden fire was alive and burning in this sky, over the desert, in the mountains. She felt a certain latent holiness in the very atmosphere, a young, spring-fire of latent holiness, such as she had never felt in Europe, or in the East. 'For me,' she said, as she looked away at the mountains in shadow and the pale-warm desert beneath, with wings of shadow upon it: 'For me, this place is sacred. It is blessed.'

But as she watched Phoenix: as she remembered the motor-cars and tourists, and the rather dreary Mexicans of Santa Fé, and the lurking, invidious Indians, with something of a rat-like secretiveness and defeatedness in their bearing, she realized that the latent fire of the vast landscape struggled under a great weight of dirt-like inertia. She had to mind the dirt, most carefully and vividly avoid it and keep it away from her, here in this place that at last seemed sacred to her.

The motor-car climbed up, past the tall pine-trees, to the foot of the mountains, and came at last to a wire gate, where nothing was to be expected. Phoenix opened the gate, and they drove on, through more trees, into a clearing where dried up bean-plants were yellow.

'This man got no water for his beans,' said Phoenix. 'Not got much beans this year.'

They climbed slowly up the incline, through more pine trees, and out into another clearing, where a couple of horses were grazing. And there they saw the ranch itself, little low cabins with patched roofs, under a few pine-trees, and facing the long twelve-acre clearing, or field, where the michaelmas daisies were purple mist, and spangled with clumps of yellow flowers.

'Not got no alfalfa here neither!' said Phoenix, as the car waded past the flowers. 'Must be a dry place up here. Got no water, sure they haven't.'

Yet it was the place Lou wanted. In an instant, her heart sprang to it. The instant the car stopped, and she saw the two cabins inside the rickety fence, the rather broken corral beyond, and behind all, tall, blue balsam pines, the round hills, the solid uprise of the mountain flank: and getting down, she looked across the purple and gold of the clearing, downwards at the ring of pine-trees standing so still, so crude and untameable, the motionless desert beyond the bristles of the pine crests, a thousand feet below: and beyond the desert, blue mountains, and far, far-off blue mountains in Arizona: '*This is the place,*' she said to herself.

This little tumble-down ranch, only a homestead of a hundred-and-sixty acres, was, as it were, man's last effort to-wards the wild heart of the Rockies, at this point. Sixty years before, a restless schoolmaster had wandered out from the East, looking for gold among the mountains. He found a very little, then no more. But the mountains had got hold of him, he could not go back.

There was a little trickling spring of pure water, a thread of treasure perhaps better than gold. So the schoolmaster took up a homestead on the lot where this little spring arose. He struggled, and got himself his log cabin erected, his fence put up, sloping at the mountain-side through the pine-trees and dropping into the hollows where the ghost-white mariposa lilies stood leafless and naked in flower, in spring, on tall invisible stems. He made the long clearing for alfalfa.

And fell so into debt, that he had to trade his homestead away, to clear his debt. Then he made a tiny living teaching the children of the few American prospectors who had squatted in the valleys, beside the Mexicans.

The trader who got the ranch tackled it with a will. He built another log cabin, and a big corral, and brought water from the canyon two miles and more across the mountain slope, in a little runnel ditch, and more water, piped a mile or more down the little canyon immediately above the cabins. He got a flow of water for his houses: for being a true American, he felt he could not *really* say he had conquered his environment till he had got running water, taps, and wash-hand basins inside his house.

Taps, running water and wash-hand basins he accomplished. And, undaunted through the years, he prepared the basin for a fountain in the little fenced-in enclosure, and he built a little bath-house. After a number of years, he sent up the enamelled bath-tub to be put in the little log bath-house on the little wild ranch hung right against the savage Rockies, above the desert.

But here the mountains finished him. He was a trader down below, in the Mexican village. This little ranch was, as it were, his hobby, his ideal. He and his New England wife spent their summers there: and turned on the taps in the cabins and turned them off again, and felt really that civilization had conquered.

All this plumbing from the savage ravines of the canyons – one of them nameless to this day – cost, however, money. In fact, the ranch cost a great deal of money. But it was all to be got back. The big clearing was to be irrigated for alfalfa, the little clearing for beans, and the third clearing, under the corral, for potatoes. All these things the trader could trade to the Mexicans, very advantageously.

And moreover, since somebody had started a praise of the famous goats' cheese made by Mexican peasants in New Mexico, goats there should be.

Goats there were: five hundred of them, eventually. And they fed chiefly in the wild mountain hollows, the no-man's-land. The Mexicans call them fire-mouths, because everything they nibble dies. Not because of their flaming mouths, really, but because they nibble a live plant down, down to the quick, till it can put forth no more.

So, the energetic trader, in the course of five or six years, had got the ranch ready. The long three-roomed cabin was for him and his New England wife. In the two-roomed cabin lived the Mexican family who really had charge of the ranch. For the trader was mostly fixed to his store, seventeen miles away, down in the Mexican village.

The ranch lay over eight thousand feet up, the snows of winter came deep and the white goats, looking dirty yellow, swam in snow with their poor curved horns poking out like dead sticks. But the corral had a long, cosy, shut-in goat-shed all down one side, and into this crowded the five hundred, their acrid goat-smell rising like hot acid over the snow. And the thin, pock-marked Mexican threw them alfalfa out of the log barn. Until the hot sun sank the snow again, and froze the surface, when patter-patter went the two thousand little goat-hoofs, over the silver-frozen snow, up at the mountain. Nibble, nibble, nibble, the fire-mouths, at every tender twig. And the goat-bell climbed, and the baa-ing came from among the dense and shaggy pine-trees. And sometimes, in a soft drift under the trees, a goat, or several goats, went through, into the white depths, and some were lost thus, to reappear dead and frozen at the thaw.

By evening, they were driven down again, like a dirty yellowish-white stream carrying dark sticks on its yeasty surface, tripping and bleating over the frozen snow, past the bustling dark green pine-trees, down to the trampled mess of the corral. And everywhere, everywhere over the snow, yellow stains and dark pills of goat-droppings melting into the surface crystal. On still, glittering nights, when the frost was hard, the smell of goats came up like some uncanny acid fire, and great stars sitting on the mountain's edge seemed to be watching like the eyes of a mountain lion, brought by the scent. Then the coyotes in the near canyon howled and sobbed, and ran like shadows over the snow. But the goat corral had been built tight.

In the course of years the goat-herd had grown from fifty to five hundred, and surely that was increase. The goat-milk cheeses sat drying on their little racks. In spring, there was a great flowing and skipping of kids. In summer and early autumn, there was a pest of flies, rising from all that goat-smell and that cast-out whey of goats'-milk, after the cheese making. The rats came, and the pack-rats, swarming.

And after all, it was difficult to sell or trade the cheeses, and little profit to be made. And in dry summers, no water came down in the narrow ditch-channel, that straddled in wooden runnels over the deep clefts in the mountain side. No water meant no alfalfa. In winter the goats scarcely drank at all. In summer they could be watered at the little spring. But the thirsty land was not so easy to accommodate.

Five hundred fine white Angora goats, with their massive handsome padres![72] They were beautiful enough. And the trader made all he could of them. Come summer, they were run down into the narrow tank filled with the fiery dipping fluid. Then their lovely white wool was clipped. It was beautiful, and valuable, but comparatively little of it.

And it all cost, cost, cost. And a man was always let down. At one time no water. At another a poison-weed. Then a sickness. Always, some mysterious malevolence fighting, fighting against the will of man. A strange invisible influence coming out of the livid rock-fastnesses in the bowels of those uncreated Rocky Mountains, preying upon the will of man, and slowly wearing down his resistance, his onward-pushing spirit. The curious, subtle thing, like a mountain fever, got into the blood, so that the men at the ranch, and the animals with them, had bursts of queer, violent, half-frenzied energy, in which, however, they were wont to lose their wariness. And then, damage of some sort. The horses ripped and cut themselves, or they were struck by lightning, the men had great hurts, or sickness. A curious disintegration working all the time, a sort of malevolent breath, like a stupefying, irritant gas, coming out of the unfathomed mountains.

The pack-rats with their bushy tails and big ears came down

out of the hills, and were jumping and bouncing about: symbols of the curious debasing malevolence that was in the spirit of the place. The Mexicans in charge, good honest men, worked all they could. But they were like most of the Mexicans in the south-west, as if they had been pithed, to use one of Kipling's[73] words. As if the invidious malevolence of the country itself had slowly taken all the pith of manhood from them, leaving a hopeless sort of corpus of a man.

And the same happened to the white men, exposed to the open country. Slowly, they were pithed. The energy went out of them. And more than that, the interest. An inertia of indifference invading the soul, leaving the body healthy and active, but wasting the soul, the living interest, quite away.

It was the New England wife of the trader who put most energy into the ranch. She looked on it as her home. She had a little white fence put all round the two cabins: the bright brass water-taps she kept shining in the two kitchens: outside the kitchen door she had a little kitchen garden and nasturtiums, after a great fight with invading animals, that nibbled everything away. And she got so far as the preparation of the round concrete basin which was to be a little pool, under the few enclosed pine-trees between the two cabins, a pool with a tiny fountain jet.

But this, with the bath-tub, was her limit, as the five hundred goats were her man's limit. Out of the mountains came two breaths of influence: the breath of the curious, frenzied energy, that took away one's intelligence as alcohol or any other stimulus does: and then the most strange invidiousness that ate away the soul. The woman loved her ranch, almost with passion. It was she who felt the stimulus, more than the men. It seemed to enter her like a sort of sex passion, intensifying her ego, making her full of violence and of blind female energy. The energy, and the blindness of it! A strange blind frenzy, like an intoxication while it lasted. And the sense of beauty that thrilled her New England woman's soul.

Her cabin faced the slow downslope of the clearing, the alfalfa field: her long, low cabin, crouching under the great pine-tree that threw up its trunk sheer in front of the house, in the yard. That pine-tree was the guardian of the place. But a bristling, almost demonish guardian, from the far-off crude ages of the world. Its great pillar of pale, flakey-ribbed copper rose there in strange callous indifference, and the grim permanence, which is in pine-trees. A passionless, non-phallic column, rising in the shadows of the pre-sexual world, before the hot-blooded ithyphallic column ever erected itself. A cold, blossomless, resinous sap surging and oozing gum, from that pallid brownish bark. And the wind hissing in the needles, like a vast nest of serpents. And the pine cones falling plump as the hail hit them. Then lying all over the yard, open in the sun like wooden roses, but hard, sexless, rigid with a blind will.[74]

Past the column of that pine-tree, the alfalfa field sloped gently down, to the circling guard of pine-trees, from which silent, living barrier isolated pines rose to ragged heights at intervals, in blind assertiveness. Strange, those pine-trees! In some lights all their needles glistened like polished steel, all subtly glittering with a whitish glitter among darkness, like real needles. Then again, at evening, the trunks would flare up orange red, and the tufts would be dark, alert tufts like a wolf's tail touching the air. Again, in the morning sunlight they would be soft and still, hardly noticeable. But all the same, present, and watchful. Never sympathetic, always watchfully on their guard, and resistant, they hedged one in with the aroma and the power and the slight horror of the pre-sexual primeval world. The world where each creature was crudely limited to its own ego, crude and bristling and cold, and then crowding in packs like pine-trees and wolves.

But beyond the pine-trees, ah, there beyond, there was beauty for the spirit to soar in. The circle of pines, with the loose trees rising high and ragged at intervals, this was the barrier, the fence to the foreground. Beyond was only distance, the desert a thousand feet below, and beyond.

The desert swept its great fawn-coloured circle around, away beyond and below like a beach, with a long mountainside of pure blue shadow closing in the near corner, and strange bluish hummocks of mountains rising like wet rock from a vast strand, away in the middle distance, and beyond, in the farthest distance, pale blue crests of mountains looking over the horizon, from the west, as if peering in from another world altogether.

Ah, that was beauty! – perhaps the most beautiful thing in the world. It was pure beauty, *absolute* beauty! There! That was it. To the little woman from New England, with her tense, fierce soul and her egoistic passion of service, this beauty was absolute, a *ne plus ultra*.[75] From her doorway, from her porch, she could watch the vast, eagle-like wheeling of the daylight, that turned as the eagles which lived in the near rocks overhead in the blue, turning their luminous, dark-edged-patterned bellies and under-wings upon the pure air, like winged orbs. So the daylight made the vast turn upon the desert, brushing the farthest outwatching mountains. And sometimes, the vast strand of the desert would float with curious undulations and exhalations amid the blue fragility of mountains, whose upper edges were harder than the floating bases. And sometimes she would see the little brown adobe[76] houses of the village Mexicans, twenty miles away, like little cube crystals of insect-houses dotting upon the desert, very distinct, with a cotton-wood tree or two rising near. And some-times she would see the far-off rocks, thirty miles away, where the canyon made a gateway between the mountains. Quite clear, like an open gateway out of a vast yard, she would see the cut-out bit of the canyon-passage. And on the desert itself, curious puckered folds of mesa-sides.[77] And a blackish crack which in places revealed the otherwise invisible canyon of the Rio Grande. And beyond everything, the mountains like icebergs showing up from an outer sea. Then later, the sun would go down blazing above the shallow cauldron of simmering darkness, and the round mountains of Colorado would lump up into uncanny significance, northwards. That was always rather frightening. But morning came again, with the sun peeping over the mountain slopes and lighting the desert away in the distance long, long before it lighted on her yard. And then she would see another valley, like magic and very lovely, with green fields and long tufts of cotton-wood trees, and a few long-cubical adobe houses, lying floating in shallow light below, like a vision.

Ah! it was beauty, beauty absolute, at any hour of the day: whether the perfect clarity of morning, or the mountains beyond the simmering desert at noon, or the purple lumping of northern mounds under a red sun at night. Or whether the dust whirled in tall columns, travelling across the desert far away, like pillars of cloud by day, tall, leaning pillars of dust hastening with ghostly haste: or whether, in the early part of the year, suddenly in the morning a whole sea of solid white would rise rolling below, a solid mist from melted snow, ghost-white under the mountain sun, the world below blotted out: or whether the black rain and cloud streaked down, far across the desert, and lightning stung down with sharp white stings on the horizon: or the cloud travelled and burst overhead, with rivers of fluid blue fire running out of heaven and exploding on earth, and hail coming down like a world of ice shattered above: or the hot sun rode in again: or snow fell in heavy silence: or the world was blinding white under a blue sky, and one must hurry under the pine-trees for shelter against that vast, white, back-beating light which rushed up at one and made one almost unconscious, amid the snow.

It was always beauty, *always*! It was always great, and splendid, and, for some reason, natural. It was never grandiose or theatrical. Always, for some reason, perfect. And quite simple, in spite of it all.

So it was, when you watched the vast and living landscape. The landscape lived, and lived as the world of the gods, unsullied and unconcerned. The great circling landscape lived its own life, sumptuous and uncaring. Man did not exist for it.

And if it had been a question simply of living through the eyes, into the *distance*, then this would have been Paradise, and the little New England woman on her ranch would have found what she was always looking for, the earthly paradise of the spirit.

But even a woman cannot live only into the distance, the beyond. Willy-nilly she finds herself juxtaposed to the near things, the thing in itself. And willy-nilly she is caught up into the fight with the immediate object.

The New England woman had fought to make the nearness as perfect as the distance: for the distance was absolute beauty. She had been confident of success. She had felt quite assured, when the water came running out of her bright brass taps, the wild water of the hills caught, tricked into the narrow iron pipes, and led tamely to her kitchen, to jump out over her sink, into her

wash-basin, at her service. *There!* she said. I have tamed the
waters of the mountain to my service.

So she had, for the moment.

At the same time, the invisible attack was being made upon
her. While she revelled in the beauty of the luminous world that
wheeled around and below her, the grey, rat-like spirit of the
inner mountains was attacking her from behind. She could not
keep her attention. And, curiously, she could not keep even her
speech. When she was saying something, suddenly the next word
would be gone out of her, as if a pack-rat had carried it off. And
she sat blank, stuttering, staring in the empty cupboard of her
mind, like Mother Hubbard, and seeing the cupboard bare. And
this irritated her husband intensely.

Her chickens, of which she was so proud, were carried away.
Or they strayed. Or they fell sick. At first she could cope with
their circumstances. But after a while, she couldn't. She couldn't
care. A drug-like numbness possessed her spirit, and at the very
middle of her, she couldn't care what happened to her chickens.

The same when a couple of horses were struck by lightning.
It frightened her. The rivers of fluid fire that suddenly fell out
of the sky and exploded on the earth near by, as if the whole earth
had burst like a bomb, frightened her from the very core of her,
and made her know, secretly and with cynical certainty, *that there
was no merciful God in the heavens.* A very tall, elegant pine-tree
just above her cabin took the lightning, and stood tall and elegant
as before, but with a white seam spiralling from its crest, all down
its tall trunk, to earth. The perfect scar, white and long as
lightning itself. And every time she looked at it, she said to
herself, in spite of herself: *There is no Almighty loving God. The
God there is shaggy as the pine-trees, and horrible as the lightning.*
Outwardly, she never confessed this. Openly, she thought of her
dear New England Church as usual. But in the violent undercurrent of her woman's soul, after the storms, she would look at
that living seamed tree, and the voice would say in her, almost
savagely: *What nonsense about Jesus and a God of Love, in a place
like this! This is more awful and more splendid. I like it better.* The
very chipmunks, in their jerky helter-skelter, the blue jays
wrangling in the pine-tree in the dawn, the grey squirrel un-

dulating to the tree-trunk, then pausing to chatter at her and scold her, with a shrewd fearlessness, as if she were the alien, the outsider, the creature that should not be permitted among the trees, all destroyed the illusion she cherished, of love, universal love. There was no love on this ranch. There was life, intense, bristling life, full of energy, but also, with an undertone of savage sordidness.

The black ants in her cupboard, the pack-rats bouncing on her ceiling like hippopotamuses in the night, the two sick goats: there was a peculiar undercurrent of squalor, flowing under the curious *tussle* of wild life. That was it. The wild life, even the life of the trees and flowers, seemed one bristling, hair-raising tussle. The very flowers came up bristly, and many of them were fang-mouthed, like the dead-nettle: and none had any real scent. But they were very fascinating, too, in their very fierceness. In May, the curious columbines of the stream-beds, columbines scarlet outside and yellow in, like the red and yellow of a herald's uniform – farther from the dove nothing could be: then the beautiful rosy-blue of the great tufts of the flower they called blue-bell, but which was really a flower of the snap-dragon family: these grew in powerful beauty in the little clearing of the pine-trees, followed by the flower the settlers had mysteriously called herb honeysuckle: a tangle of long drops of pure fire-red, hanging from slim invisible stalks of smoke colour. The purest, most perfect vermilion scarlet, cleanest fire colour, hanging in long drops like a shower of fire-rain that is just going to strike the earth. A little later, more in the open, there came another sheer fire-red flower, sparking, fierce red stars running up a bristly grey ladder, as if the earth's fire-centre had blown out some red sparks, white-speckled and deadly inside, puffing for a moment in the day air.

So it was! The alfalfa field was one raging, seething conflict of plants trying to get hold. One dry year, and the bristly wild things had got hold: the spiky, blue-leaved thistle-poppy with its moon-white flowers, the low clumps of blue nettle-flower, the later rush, after the sereneness of June and July, the rush of red sparks and michaelmas daisies, and the tough wild sun-flowers, strangling and choking the dark, tender green of the clover-like alfalfa! A battle, a battle, with banners of bright scarlet and yellow.

When a really defenceless flower did issue, like the moth-still, ghost-centred mariposa lily, with its inner moth-dust of yellow, it came invisible. There was nothing to be seen, but a hair of greyish grass near the oak-scrub. Behold, this invisible long stalk was balancing a white, ghostly, three-petalled flower, naked out of nothingness. A mariposa lily!

Only the pink wild roses smelled sweet, like the old world. They were sweet-briar roses. And the dark blue hare-bells among the oak-scrub, like the ice-dark bubbles of the mountain flowers in the Alps, the Alpenglocken.

The roses of the desert are the cactus flowers, crystal of translucent yellow or of rose-colour. But set among spines the devil himself must have conceived in a moment of sheer ecstasy.

Nay, it was a world before and after the God of Love. Even the very humming-birds hanging about the flowering squaw-berry bushes, when the snow had gone, in May, they were before and after the God of Love. And the blue jays were crested dark with challenge, and the yellow-and-dark woodpecker was fearless like a warrior in war-paint, as he struck the wood. While on the fence hawks sat motionless, like dark fists clenched under heaven, ignoring man and his ways.

Summer, it was true, unfolded the tender cotton-wood leaves, and the tender aspen. But what a tangle and a ghostly aloofness in the aspen thickets high up on the mountains, the coldness that is in the eyes and the long cornelian talons of the bear.

Summer brought the little wild strawberries, with their savage aroma, and the late summer brought the rose-jewel raspberries in the valley cleft. But how lonely, how harsh-lonely and menacing it was, to be alone in that shadowy, steep cleft of a canyon just above the cabins, picking raspberries, while the thunder gathered thick and blue-purple at the mountain tops. The many wild raspberries hanging rose-red in the thickets. But the stream bed below all silent, waterless. And the trees all bristling in silence, and waiting like warriors at an out-post. And the berries waiting for the sharp-eyed, cold, long-snouted bear to come rambling and shaking his heavy sharp fur. The berries grew for the bears, and the little New England woman, with her uncanny sensitiveness to underlying influences, felt all the time she was stealing. Stealing the wild raspberries in the secret little canyon behind her home. And when she had made them into jam, she could almost taste the theft in her preserves.

She confessed nothing of this. She tried even to confess nothing of her dread. But she was afraid. Especially she was conscious of the prowling, intense aerial electricity all the summer, after June. The air was thick with wandering currents of fierce electric fluid, waiting to discharge themselves. And almost every day there was the rage and battle of thunder. But the air was never cleared. There was no relief. However the thunder raged, and spent itself, yet, afterwards, among the sunshine was the strange lurking and wandering of the electric currents, moving invisible, with strange menace, between the atoms of the air. She knew. Oh, she knew!

And her love for her ranch turned sometimes into a certain repulsion. The underlying rat-dirt, the everlasting bristling tussle of the wild life, with the tangle and the bones strewing. Bones of horses struck by lightning, bones of dead cattle, skulls of goats with little horns: bleached, unburied bones. Then the cruel electricity of the mountains. And then, most mysterious but worst of all, the animosity of the spirit of place: the crude, half-created spirit of place, like some serpent-bird for ever attacking man, in a hatred of man's onward-struggle towards further creation.

The seething cauldron of lower life, seething on the very tissue of the higher life, seething the soul away, seething at the marrow. The vast and unrelenting will of the swarming lower life, working for ever against man's attempt at a higher life, a further created being.

At last, after many years, the little woman admitted to herself that she was glad to go down from the ranch, when November came with snows. She was glad to come to a more human home, her house in the village. And as winter passed by, and spring came again, she knew she did not want to go up to the ranch again. It had broken something in her. It had hurt her terribly. It had maimed her for ever in her hope, her belief in paradise on earth. Now, she hid from herself her own corpse, the corpse of her New England belief in a world ultimately all for love. The belief, and herself with it, was a corpse. The gods of those inner mountains were grim and invidious and relentless, huger than man, and lower than man. Yet man could never master them.

The little woman in her flower-garden away below, by the stream-irrigated village, hid away from the thought of it all. She would not go to the ranch any more.

The Mexicans stayed in charge, looking after the goats. But the place didn't pay. It didn't pay, not quite. It had paid. It might pay. But the effort, the effort! And as the marrow is eaten out of a man's bones and the soul out of his belly, contending with the strange rapacity of savage life, the lower stage of creation, he cannot make the effort any more.

Then also, the war came, making many men give up their enterprises at civilization.

Every new stroke of civilization has cost the lives of countless brave men, who have fallen defeated by the 'dragon', in their efforts to win the apples of the Hesperides, or the fleece of gold.[78] Fallen in their efforts to overcome the old, half-sordid savagery of the lower stages of creation, and win to the next stage.

For all savagery is half-sordid. And man is only himself when he is fighting on and on, to overcome the sordidness.

And every civilization, when it loses its inward vision and its cleaner energy, falls into a new sort of sordidness, more vast and more stupendous than the old savage sort. An Augean stables of metallic filth.[79]

And all the time, man has to rouse himself afresh, to cleanse the new accumulations of refuse. To win from the crude wild nature the victory and the power to make another start, and to cleanse behind him the century-deep deposits of layer upon layer of refuse: even of tin cans.

The ranch dwindled. The flock of goats declined. The water ceased to flow. And at length the trader gave it up.

He rented the place to a Mexican, who lived on the handful of beans he raised, and who was being slowly driven out by the vermin.

And now arrived Lou, new blood to the attack. She went back

to Santa Fé, saw the trader and a lawyer, and bought the ranch for twelve hundred dollars. She was so pleased with herself.

She went upstairs to tell her mother.

'Mother, I've bought a ranch.'

'It is just as well, for I can't stand the noise of automobiles outside here another week.'

'It is quiet on my ranch, mother: the stillness simply speaks.'

'I had rather it held its tongue. I am simply drugged with all the bad novels I have read. I feel as if the sky was a big cracked bell and a million clappers were hammering human speech out of it.'

'Aren't you interested in my ranch, mother?'

'I hope I may be, by and by.'

Mrs Witt actually got up the next morning, and accompanied her daughter in the hired motor-car driven by Phoenix, to the ranch: which was called Las Chivas.[80] She sat like a pillar of salt, her face looking what the Indians call a False Face, meaning a mask. She seemed to have crystallized into neutrality. She watched the desert with its tufts of yellow greasewood go lurching past: she saw the fallen apples on the ground in the orchards near the adobe cottages: she looked down into the deep arroyo,[81] and at the stream they forded in the car, and at the mountains blocking up the sky ahead, all with indifference. High on the mountains was snow: lower, blue-grey livid rock: and below the livid rock the aspens were expiring their daffodil yellow, this year, and the oak-scrub was dark and reddish, like gore. She saw it all with a sort of stony indifference.

'Don't you think it's lovely?' said Lou.

'I can *see* it is lovely,' replied her mother.

The michaelmas daisies in the clearing as they drove up to the ranch were sharp-rayed with purple, like a coming night.

Mrs Witt eyed the two log cabins, one of which was dilapidated and practically abandoned. She looked at the rather ricketty corral, whose long planks had silvered and warped in the fierce sun. On one of the roof-planks a pack-rat was sitting erect like an old Indian keeping watch on a pueblo roof. He showed his white belly, and folded his hands and lifted his big ears, for all the world like an old immobile Indian.

'Isn't it for all the world as if *he* were the real boss of the place, Louise?' she said cynically.

And turning to the Mexican, who was a rag of a man but a pleasant, courteous fellow, she asked him why he didn't shoot the rat.

'Not worth a shell!' said the Mexican, with a faint hopeless smile.

Mrs Witt paced round and saw everything: it did not take long. She gazed in silence at the water of the spring, trickling out of an iron pipe into a barrel, under the cotton-wood tree in an arroyo.

'Well, Louise,' she said. 'I am glad you feel competent to cope with so much hopelessness and so many rats.'

'But, mother, you must admit it is beautiful.'

'Yes, I suppose it is. But to use one of your Henry's phrases, beauty is a cold egg, as far as I am concerned.'

'Rico never would have said that beauty was a cold egg to him.'

'No, he wouldn't. He sits on it like a broody old hen on a china imitation. – Are you going to bring him here?'

'*Bring* him! – No. But he can come if he likes,' stammered Lou.

'*Oh –h!* won't it be beau – ti –ful!' cried Mrs Witt, rolling her head and lifting her shoulders in savage imitation of her son-in-law.

'Perhaps he won't come, mother,' said Lou, hurt.

'He will most certainly come, Louise, to see what's doing: unless you tell him you don't want him.'

'Anyhow, I needn't think about it till spring,' said Lou, anxiously pushing the matter aside.

Mrs Witt climbed the steep slope above the cabins, to the mouth of the little canyon. There she sat on a fallen tree, and surveyed the world beyond: a world not of men. She could not fail to be roused.

'What is your idea in coming here, daughter?' she asked.

'I love it here, mother.'

'But what do you expect to achieve by it?'

'I was rather hoping, mother, to escape achievement. I'll tell you – and you mustn't get cross if it sounds silly. As far as people go, my heart is quite broken. As far as people go, I don't want any more. I can't stand any more. What heart I ever had for it — for life with people — is quite broken. I want to be alone, mother: with you here, and Phoenix perhaps to look after horses and drive a car. But I want to be by myself, really.'

'With Phoenix in the background! Are you sure he won't be coming into the foreground before long?'

'No, mother, no more of that. If I've got to say it, Phoenix is a servant: he's really placed, as far as I can see. Always the same, playing about in the old back-yard. I can't take those men seriously. I can't fool round with them, or fool myself about them. I can't and I won't fool myself any more, mother, especially about men. They don't count. So why should you want them to pay me out?'

For the moment, this silenced Mrs Witt. Then she said:

'Why, *I* don't want it. Why should I! But after all you've got to live. You've never *lived* yet: not in my opinion.'

'Neither, mother, in my opinion, have you,' said Lou drily.

And this silenced Mrs Witt altogether. She had to be silent, or angrily on the defensive. And the latter she wouldn't be. She couldn't, really, in honesty.

'What do you call life?' Lou continued. 'Wriggling half-naked at a public show, and going off in a taxi to sleep with some half-drunken fool who thinks he's a man because — Oh, mother, I don't even want to think of it. I know you have a lurking idea that *that is life*. Let it be so then. But leave me out. Men in that aspect simply nauseate me: so grovelling and ratty. Life in that aspect simply drains all my life away. I tell you, for all that sort of thing, I'm broken, absolutely broken: if I wasn't broken to start with.'

'Well, Louise,' said Mrs Witt after a pause, 'I'm convinced that ever since men and women were men and women, people who took things seriously, and had time for it, got their hearts broken. Haven't I had mine broken! It's as sure as having your virginity broken: and it amounts to about as much. It's a beginning rather than an end.'

'So it is, mother. It's the beginning of something else, and the end of something that's done with. I *know*, and there's no altering it, that I've got to live differently. It sounds silly, but I don't know how else to put it. I've got to live for something that matters, way, way down in me. And I think sex would matter, to my very soul, if it was really sacred. But cheap sex kills me.'

'You have had a fancy for rather cheap men, perhaps.'

'Perhaps I have. Perhaps I should always be a fool, where people are concerned. Now I want to leave off that kind of foolery. There's something else, mother, that I want to give myself to. I know it. I know it absolutely. Why should I let myself be shouted down any more?'

Mrs Witt sat staring at the distance, her face a cynical mask.

'What is the something bigger? And *pray*, what is it bigger than?' she asked, in that tone of honied suavity which was her deadliest poison. 'I want to learn. I am out to know. I'm terribly intrigued by it. Something bigger! Girls in my generation occasionally entered convents, for *something bigger*. I always wondered if they found it. They seemed to me inclined in the imbecile direction, but perhaps that was because I was *something less* –'

There was a definite pause between the mother and daughter, a silence that was a pure breach. Then Lou said:

'You know quite well I'm not conventy, mother, whatever else I am – even a bit of an imbecile. But that kind of religion seems to me the other half of men. Instead of running after them you run away from them, and get the thrill that way. I don't hate men *because* they're men, as nuns do. I dislike them because they're not men enough: babies, and playboys, and poor things showing off all the time, even to themselves. I don't say I'm any better. I only wish, with all my soul, that some men *were* bigger and stronger and *deeper* than I am . . .'

'How do you know they're not? –' asked Mrs Witt.

'How *do* I know? –' said Lou mockingly.

And the pause that was a breach resumed itself. Mrs Witt was teasing with a little stick the bewildered black ants among the fir-needles.

'And no doubt you are right about men,' she said at length.

'But at your age, the only sensible thing is to try and keep up the illusion. After all, as you say, you may be no better.'

'I may be no better. But keeping up the illusion means fooling myself. And I won't do it. When I see a man who is even a bit attractive to me – even as much as Phoenix – I say to myself: *Would you care for him afterwards? Does he really mean anything to you, except just a sensation?* – And I know he doesn't. No, mother, of this I am convinced: either my taking a man shall have a meaning and a mystery that penetrates my very soul, or I will keep to myself. – And what I *know* is, that the time has come for me to keep to myself. No more messing about.'

'Very well, daughter. You will probably spend your life keeping to yourself.'

'Do you think I mind! There's something else for me, mother. There's something else even that loves me and wants me. I can't tell you what it is. It's a spirit. And it's here, on this ranch. It's here, in this landscape. It's something more real to me than men are, and it soothes me, and it holds me up. I don't know what it is, definitely. It's something wild, that will hurt me sometimes and will wear me down sometimes. I know it. But it's something big, bigger than men, bigger than people, bigger than religion. It's something to do with wild America. And it's something to do with me. It's a mission, if you like. I am imbecile enough for that! – But it's my mission to keep myself for the spirit that is wild, and has waited so long here: even waited for such as me. Now I've come! Now I'm here. Now I am where I want to be: with the spirit that wants me. – And that's how it is. And neither Rico nor Phoenix nor anybody else really matters to me. They are in the world's back-yard. And I am here, right deep in America, where there's a wild spirit wants me, a wild spirit more than men. And it doesn't want to save me either. It needs me. It craves for me. And to it, my sex is deep and sacred, deeper than I am, with a deep nature aware deep down of my sex. It saves me from cheapness, mother. And even you could never do that for me.'

Mrs Witt rose to her feet, and stood looking far, far away, at the turquoise ridge of mountains half sunk under the horizon.

'How much did you say you paid for Las Chivas?' she asked.

'Twelve hundred dollars,' said Lou, surprised.

'Then I call it cheap, considering all there is to it: even the name.'

The Princess

To her father, she was The Princess. To her Boston aunts and uncles she was just *Dollie Urquhart, poor little thing*.

Colin Urquhart was just a bit mad. He was of an old Scottish family, and he claimed royal blood. The blood of Scottish kings flowed in his veins. On this point, his American relatives said, he was just a bit 'off'. They could not bear any more to be told *which* royal blood of Scotland blued his veins. The whole thing was rather ridiculous, and a sore point. The only fact they remembered was that it was not Stuart.

He was a handsome man, with a wide-open blue eye that seemed sometimes to be looking at nothing, soft black hair brushed rather low on his low, broad brow, and a very attractive body. Add to this a most beautiful speaking voice, usually rather hushed and diffident, but sometimes resonant and powerful like bronze, and you have the sum of his charms. He looked like some old Celtic hero. He looked as if he should have worn a greyish kilt and a sporran, and shown his knees. His voice came direct out of the hushed Ossianic past.[1]

For the rest, he was one of those gentlemen of sufficient but not excessive means who fifty years ago wandered vaguely about, never arriving anywhere, never doing anything, and never definitely being anything, yet well received and familiar in the good society of more than one country.

He did not marry till he was nearly forty, and then it was a wealthy Miss Prescott, from New England. Hannah Prescott at twenty-two was fascinated by the man with the soft black hair not yet touched by grey, and the wide, rather vague blue eyes. Many women had been fascinated before her. But Colin Urquhart, by his very vagueness, had avoided any decisive connection.

Mrs Urquhart lived three years in the mist and glamour of her husband's presence. And then it broke her. It was like living with a fascinating spectre. About most things he was completely, even ghostlily oblivious. He was always charming, courteous, perfectly gracious in that hushed, musical voice of his. But absent. When all came to all, he just wasn't there. 'Not all there,' as the vulgar say.

He was the father of the little girl she bore at the end of the first year. But this did not substantiate him the more. His very beauty and his haunting musical quality became dreadful to her after the first few months. The strange echo: he was like a living echo! His very flesh, when you touched it, did not seem quite the flesh of a real man.

Perhaps it was that he was a little bit mad. She thought it definitely the night her baby was born.

'Ah, so my little princess has come at last!' he said, in his throaty, singing Celtic voice, like a glad chant, swaying absorbed.

It was a tiny, frail baby, with wide, amazed blue eyes. They christened it Mary Henrietta. She called the little thing *My Dollie*. He called it always *My Princess*.

It was useless to fly at him. He just opened his wide blue eyes wider, and took a childlike, silent dignity there was no getting past.

Hannah Prescott had never been robust. She had no great desire to live. So when the baby was two years old she suddenly died.

The Prescotts felt a deep but unadmitted resentment against Colin Urquhart. They said he was selfish. Therefore they discontinued Hannah's income, a month after her burial in Florence, after they had urged the father to give the child over to them, and he had courteously, musically, but quite finally refused. He treated the Prescotts as if they were not of his world, not realities to him: just casual phenomena, or gramophones, talking-machines that had to be answered. He answered them. But of their actual existence he was never once aware.

They debated having him certified unsuitable to be guardian of his own child. But that would have created a scandal. So they did the simplest thing, after all – washed their hands of him. But they wrote scrupulously to the child, and sent her modest presents of money at Christmas, and on the anniversary of the death of her mother.

To The Princess her Boston relatives were for many years just a nominal reality. She lived with her father, and he travelled continually, though in a modest way, living on his moderate income. And never going to America. The child changed nurses all the time. In Italy it was a contadina; in India she had an ayah; in Germany she had a yellow-haired peasant girl.

Father and child were inseparable. He was not a recluse. Wherever he went he was to be seen paying formal calls going out to luncheon or to tea, rarely to dinner. And always with the child. People called her Princess Urquhart, as if that were her christened name.

She was a quick, dainty little thing with dark gold hair that went a soft brown, and wide, slightly prominent blue eyes that were at once so candid and so knowing. She was always grown up; she never really grew up. Always strangely wise, and always childish.

It was her father's fault.

'My little Princess must never take too much notice of people and the things they say and do,' he repeated to her. 'People don't know what they are doing and saying. They chatter-chatter, and they hurt one another, and they hurt themselves very often, till they cry. But don't take any notice, my little Princess. Because it is all nothing. Inside everybody there is another creature, a demon which doesn't care at all. You peel away all the things they say and do and feel, as cook peels away the outside of the onions. And in the middle of everybody there is a green demon which you can't peel away. And this green demon never changes, and it doesn't care at all about all the things that happen to the outside leaves of the person, all the chatter-chatter, and all the husbands and wives and children, and troubles and fusses. You peel everything away from people, and there is a green, upright demon in every man and woman; and this demon is a man's real self, and a woman's real self. It doesn't really care about anybody, it belongs to the demons and the primitive fairies, who never care. But, even so, there are big demons and mean demons, and splendid demonish fairies, and vulgar ones. But there are no royal fairy women left. Only you, my little Princess. You are the last of the royal race of the old people; the last, my Princess.

There are no others. You and I are the last. When I am dead there will only be you. And that is why, darling, you will never care for any of the people in the world very much. Because their demons are all dwindled and vulgar. They are not royal. Only you are royal, after me. Always remember that. And always remember, it is a *great secret*. If you tell people, they will try to kill you, because they will envy you for being a Princess. It is our great secret, darling. I am a prince, and you a princess, of the old, old blood. And we keep our secret between us, all alone. And so, darling, you must treat all people very politely, because *noblesse oblige*.[2] But you must never forget that you alone are the last of Princesses, and that all others are less than you are, less noble, more vulgar. Treat them politely and gently and kindly, darling. But you are the Princess, and they are commoners. Never try to think of them as if they were like you. They are not. You will find, always, that they are lacking, lacking in the royal touch, which only you have –'

The Princess learned her lesson early – the first lesson, of absolute reticence, the impossibility of intimacy with any other than her father; the second lesson, of naïve, slightly benevolent politeness. As a small child, something crystallized in her character, making her clear and finished, and as impervious as crystal.

'Dear child!' her hostess said of her. 'She is so quaint and old-fashioned; such a lady, poor little mite!'

She was erect, and very dainty. Always small, nearly tiny in physique, she seemed like a changeling beside her big, handsome, slightly mad father. She dressed very simply, usually in blue or delicate greys, with little collars of old Milan point, or very finely-worked linen. She had exquisite hands that made the piano sound like a spinet when she played. She was rather given to wearing cloaks and capes, instead of coats, out of doors, and little eighteenth-century sort of hats. Her complexion was pure apple-blossom.

She looked as if she had stepped out of a picture. But no one, to her dying day, ever knew exactly the strange picture her father had framed her in and from which she never stepped.

Her grandfather and grandmother and her Aunt Maud

demanded twice to see her, once in Rome and once in Paris. Each time they were charmed, piqued, and annoyed. She was so exquisite and such a little virgin. At the same time so knowing and so oddly assured. That odd, assured touch of condescension, and the inward coldness, infuriated her American relations.

Only she really fascinated her grandfather. He was spell-bound; in a way, in love with the little faultless thing. His wife would catch him brooding, musing over his grandchild, long months after the meeting, and craving to see her again. He cherished to the end the fond hope that she might come to live with him and her grandmother.

'Thank you so much, grandfather. You are so very kind. But Papa and I are such an old couple, you see, such a crotchety old couple, living in a world of our own.'

Her father let her see the world – from the outside. And he let her read. When she was in her teens she read Zola and Maupassant,[3] and with the eyes of Zola and Maupassant she looked on Paris. A little later she read Tolstoy and Dostoevsky.[4] The latter confused her. The others, she seemed to understand with a very shrewd, canny understanding, just as she understood the Decameron[5] stories as she read them in their old Italian, or the Nibelung poems.[6] Strange and *uncanny*, she seemed to understand things in a cold light perfectly, with all the flush of fire absent. She was something like a changeling, not quite human.

This earned her, also, strange antipathies. Cabmen and railway porters, especially in Paris and Rome, would suddenly treat her with brutal rudeness, when she was alone. They seemed to look on her with sudden violent antipathy. They sensed in her curious impertinence, an easy, sterile impertinence towards the things *they* felt most. She was so assured, and her flower of maidenhood was so scentless. She could look at a lusty, sensual Roman cabman as if he were a sort of grotesque, to make her smile. She knew all about him, in Zola. And the peculiar condescension with which she would give him her order, as if she, frail, beautiful thing, were the only reality, and he, coarse monster, were a sort of Caliban[7] floundering in the mud on the margin of the pool of the perfect lotus, would suddenly enrage the fellow, the real Mediterranean who prided himself on his *beauté mâle*, and to whom the phallic mystery was still the only mystery. And he would turn a terrible face on her, bully her in a brutal, coarse fashion – hideous. For to him she had only the blasphemous impertinence of her own sterility.

Encounters like these made her tremble, and made her know she must have support from the outside. The power of her spirit did not extend to these low people, and they had all the physical power. She realized an implacability of hatred in their turning on her. But she did not lose her head. She quietly paid out money and turned away.

Those were dangerous moments, though, and she learned to be prepared for them. The Princess she was, and the fairy from the north, she could never understand the volcanic phallic rage with which coarse people could turn on her in a paroxysm of hatred. They never turned on her father like that. And quite early she decided it was the New England mother in her whom they hated. Never for one minute could she see with the old Roman eyes, see herself as sterility, the barren flower taking on airs and an intolerable impertinence. This was what the Roman cabman saw in her. And he longed to crush the barren blossom. Its sexless beauty and its authority put him in a passion of brutal revolt.

When she was nineteen her grandfather died, leaving her a considerable fortune in the safe hands of responsible trustees. They would deliver her her income, but only on condition that she resided for six months in the year in the United States.

'Why should they make me conditions?' she said to her father. 'I refuse to be imprisoned for six months in the year in the United States. We will tell them to keep their money.'

'Let us be wise, my little Princess, let us be wise. No, we are almost poor, and we are never safe from rudeness. I cannot allow anybody to be rude to me. I hate it, I hate it!' His eyes flamed as he said it. 'I could kill any man or woman who is rude to me. But we are in exile in the world. We are powerless. If we were really poor, we should be quite powerless, and then I should die. No, my Princess. Let us take their money, then they will not dare to be rude to us. Let us take it, as we put on clothes, to cover ourselves from their aggressions.'

There began a new phase, when the father and daughter spent their summers on the Great Lakes, or in California, or in the South-West. The father was something of a poet, the daughter something of a painter. He wrote poems about the lakes or the redwood trees, and she made dainty drawings. He was physically a strong man, and he loved the out-of-doors. He would go off with her for days, paddling in a canoe and sleeping by a campfire. Frail little Princess, she was always undaunted. She would ride with him on horseback over the mountain trails till she was so tired she was nothing but a bodiless consciousness sitting astride her pony. But she never gave in. And at night he folded her in her blankets on a bed of balsam pine twigs, and she lay and looked at the stars unmurmuring. She was fulfilling her role.

People said to her as the years passed, and she was a woman of twenty-five, then a woman of thirty, and always the same virgin dainty Princess, 'knowing' in a dispassionate way, like an old woman, and utterly intact:

'Don't you ever think what you will do when your father is no longer with you?'

She looked at her interlocutor with that cold, elfin detachment of hers:

'No, I never think of it,' she said.

She had a tiny, but exquisite little house in London, and another small, perfect house in Connecticut, each with a faithful housekeeper. Two homes, if she chose. And she knew many interesting literary and artistic people. What more?

So the years passed imperceptibly. And she had that quality of the sexless fairies, she did not change. At thirty-three she looked twenty-three.

Her father, however, was ageing, and becoming more and more queer. It was now her task to be his guardian in his private madness. He spent the last three years of life in the house in Connecticut. He was very much estranged, sometimes had fits of violence which almost killed the little Princess. Physical violence was horrible to her; it seemed to shatter her heart. But she found a woman a few years younger than herself, well-educated and sensitive, to be a sort of nurse-companion to the mad old man. So the fact of madness was never openly admitted.

Miss Cummins, the companion, had a passionate loyalty to the Princess, and a curious affection, tinged with love, for the handsome, white-haired, courteous old man, who was never at all aware of his fits of violence once they had passed.

The Princess was thirty-eight years old when her father died. And quite unchanged. She was still tiny, and like a dignified, scentless flower. Her soft brownish hair, almost the colour of beaver fur, was bobbed, and fluffed softly round her apple-blossom face, that was modelled with an arched nose like a proud old Florentine portrait. In her voice, manner and bearing she was exceedingly still, like a flower that has blossomed in a shadowy place. And from her blue eyes looked out the Princess's eternal laconic challenge, that grew almost sardonic as the years passed. She was the Princess, and sardonically she looked out on a princeless world.

She was relieved when her father died, and at the same time, it was as if everything had evaporated around her. She had lived in a sort of hot-house, in the aura of her father's madness. Suddenly the hot-house had been removed from around her, and she was in the raw, vast, vulgar open air.

Quoi faire? What was she to do? She seemed faced with absolute nothingness. Only she had Miss Cummins, who shared with her the secret, and almost the passion for her father. In fact, the Princess felt that her passion for her mad father had in some curious way transferred itself largely to Charlotte Cummins during the last years. And now Miss Cummins was the vessel that held the passion for the dead man. She herself, the Princess, was an empty vessel.

An empty vessel in the enormous warehouse of the world.

Quoi faire? What was she to do? She felt that, since she could not evaporate into nothingness, like alcohol from an unstoppered bottle, she must *do* something. Never before in her life had she felt the incumbency. Never, never had she felt she must *do* anything. That was left to the vulgar.

Now her father was dead, she found herself on the *fringe* of the vulgar crowd, sharing their necessity to *do* something. It was a little humiliating. She felt herself becoming vulgarized. At the same time she found herself looking at men with a shrewder eye:

an eye to marriage. Not that she felt any sudden interest in men, or attraction towards them. No. She was still neither interested nor attracted towards men vitally. But *marriage*, that peculiar abstraction, had imposed a sort of spell on her. She thought that *marriage*, in the blank abstract, was the thing she ought to *do*. That *marriage* implied a man she also knew. She knew all the facts. But the man seemed a property of her own mind rather than a thing in himself, another being.

Her father died in the summer, the month after her thirty-eighth birthday. When all was over, the obvious thing to do, of course, was to travel. With Miss Cummins. The two women knew each other intimately, but they were always Miss Urquhart and Miss Cummins to one another, and a certain distance was instinctively maintained. Miss Cummins, from Philadelphia, of scholastic stock, and intelligent but untravelled, four years younger than the Princess, felt herself immensely the junior of her 'lady'. She had a sort of passionate veneration for the Princess, who seemed to her ageless, timeless. She could not see the rows of tiny, dainty, exquisite shoes in the Princess's cupboard without feeling a stab at the heart, a stab of tenderness and reverence, almost of awe.

Miss Cummins also was virginal, but with a look of puzzled surprise in her brown eyes. Her skin was pale and clear, her features well modelled, but there was a certain blankness in her expression, where the Princess had an odd touch of Renaissance grandeur. Miss Cummins's voice was also hushed almost to a whisper; it was the inevitable effect of Colin Urquhart's room. But the hushedness had a hoarse quality.

The Princess did not want to go to Europe. Her face seemed turned west. Now her father was gone, she felt she would go west, westwards, as if for ever. Following, no doubt, the March of Empire, which is brought up rather short on the Pacific coast, among swarms of wallowing bathers.

No, not the Pacific coast. She would stop short of that. The South-West was less vulgar. She would go to New Mexico.

She and Miss Cummins arrived at the Rancho del Cerro Gordo towards the end of August, when the crowd was beginning to drift back east. The ranch lay by a stream on the desert some four miles from the foot of the mountains, a mile away from the Indian pueblo of San Cristobal.[8] It was a ranch for the rich; the Princess paid thirty dollars a day for herself and Miss Cummins. But then she had a little cottage to herself, among the apple trees of the orchard, with an excellent cook. She and Miss Cummins, however, took dinner at evening in the large guest-house. For the Princess still entertained the idea of *marriage*.

The guests at the Rancho del Cerro Gordo were of all sorts, except the poor sort. They were practically all rich, and many were romantic. Some were charming, others were vulgar, some were movie people, quite quaint and not unattractive in their vulgarity, and many were Jews. The Princess did not care for Jews, though they were usually the most interesting to *talk* to. So she talked a good deal with the Jews, and painted with the artists, and rode with the young men from college, and had altogether quite a good time. And yet she felt something of a fish out of water, or a bird in the wrong forest. And *marriage* remained still completely in the abstract. No connecting it with any of these young men, even the nice ones.

The Princess looked just about twenty-five. The freshness of her mouth, the hushed, delicate-complexioned virginity of her face gave her not a day more. Only a certain laconic look in her eyes was disconcerting. When she was *forced* to write her age, she put twenty-eight, making the figure *two* rather badly, so that it just avoided being a three.

Men hinted marriage at her. Especially boys from college suggested it from a distance. But they all failed before the look of sardonic ridicule in the Princess's eyes. It always seemed to her rather preposterous, quite ridiculous, and a tiny bit impertinent on their part.

The only man that intrigued her at all was one of the guides, a man called Romero – Domingo Romero. It was he who had sold the ranch itself to the Wilkiesons, ten years before, for two thousand dollars. He had gone away, then reappeared at the old place. For he was the son of the old Romero, the last of the Spanish family that had owned miles of land around San Cristobal. But the coming of the white man and the failure of the vast flocks of sheep, and the fatal inertia which overcomes all men, at last, on the desert near the mountains, had finished the Romero family. The last descendants were just Mexican peasants.

Domingo, the heir, had spent his two thousand dollars, and was working for white people. He was now about thirty years old, a tall, silent fellow, with a heavy closed mouth and black eyes that looked across at one almost sullenly. From behind he was handsome, with a strong, natural body, and the back of his neck very dark and well-shapen, strong with life. But his dark face was long and heavy, almost sinister, with that peculiar heavy meaninglessness in it, characteristic of the Mexicans of his own locality. They are strong, they seem healthy. They laugh and joke with one another. But their physique and their natures seem static, as if there were nowhere, nowhere at all for their energies to go, and their faces, degenerating to misshapen heaviness, seem to have no *raison d'être*,[9] no radical meaning. Waiting either to die or to be aroused into passion and hope. In some of the black eyes a queer, haunting mystic quality, sombre and a bit gruesome, the skull-and-crossbones look of the Penitentes.[10] They had found their *raison d'être* in self-torture and death-worship. Unable to wrest *positive* significance for themselves from the vast, beautiful, but vindictive landscape they were born into, they turned on their own selves, and worshipped death through self-torture. The mystic gloom of this showed in their eyes.

But as a rule the dark eyes of the Mexicans were heavy and half-alive, sometimes hostile, sometimes kindly, often with the fatal Indian glaze on them, or the fatal Indian glint.

Domingo Romero was *almost* a typical Mexican to look at, with the typical heavy, dark, long face, clean-shaven, with an almost brutally heavy mouth. His eyes were black and Indian-looking. Only, at the centre of their hopelessness was a spark of pride, of self-confidence, of dauntlessness. Just a spark in the midst of the blackness of static despair.

But this spark was the difference between him and the mass of men. It gave a certain alert sensitiveness to his bearing and a certain beauty to his appearance. He wore a low-crowned black hat, instead of the ponderous headgear of the usual Mexican, and his clothes were thinnish and graceful. Silent, aloof, almost imperceptible in the landscape, he was an admirable guide, with a startling quick intelligence that anticipated difficulties about to rise. He could cook, too, crouching over the camp-fire and moving his lean deft brown hands. The only fault he had was that he was not forthcoming, he wasn't chatty and cosy.

'Oh, don't send Romero with us,' the Jews would say. 'One can't get any response from him.'

Tourists come and go, but they rarely *see* anything, inwardly. None of them ever saw the spark at the middle of Romero's eye; they were not alive enough to see it.

The Princess caught it one day, when she had him for a guide. She was fishing for trout in the canyon, Miss Cummins was reading a book, the horses were tied under the trees, Romero was fixing a proper fly on her line. He fixed the fly and handed her the line, looking up at her. And at that moment she caught the spark in his eye. And instantly she knew that he was a gentleman, that his 'demon', as her father would have said, was a fine demon. And instantly her manner towards him changed.

He had perched her on a rock over a quiet pool, beyond the cotton-wood trees. It was early September, and the canyon already cool, but the leaves of the cotton-woods were still green. The Princess stood on her rock, a small but perfectly-formed figure, wearing a soft, close grey sweater and neatly-cut grey riding-breeches, with tall black boots, her fluffy brown hair straggling from under a little grey felt hat. A woman? Not quite. A changeling of some sort, perched in outline there on the rock, in the bristling wild canyon. She knew perfectly well how to handle a line. Her father had made a fisherman of her.

Romero, in a black shirt and with loose black trousers pushed into wide black riding-boots, was fishing a little farther down. He had put his hat on a rock behind him; his dark head was bent a little forward, watching the water. He had caught three trout. From time to time he glanced up-stream at the Princess, perched there so daintily. He saw she had caught nothing.

Soon he quietly drew in his line and came up to her. His keen eye watched her line, watched her position. Then, quietly, he suggested certain changes to her, putting his sensitive brown hand before her. And he withdrew a little, and stood in silence,

leaning against a tree, watching her. He was helping her across
the distance. She knew it, and thrilled. And in a moment she had
a bite. In two minutes she had landed a good trout. She looked
round at him quickly, her eyes sparkling, the colour heightened
in her cheeks. And as she met his eyes a smile of greeting went
over his dark face, very sudden, with an odd sweetness.

She knew he was helping her. And she felt in his presence
a subtle, insidious male *kindliness* she had never known before waiting upon her. Her cheek flushed, and her blue eyes
darkened.

After this, she always looked for him, and for that curious dark
beam of a man's kindliness which he could give her, as it were,
from his chest, from his heart. It was something she had never
known before.

A vague, unspoken intimacy grew up between them. She liked
his voice, his appearance, his presence. His natural language was
Spanish; he spoke English like a foreign language, rather slow,
with a slight hesitation, but with a sad, plangent sonority lingering over from his Spanish. There was a certain subtle correctness
in his appearance; he was always perfectly shaved; his hair was
thick and rather long on top, but always carefully groomed
behind. And his fine black cashmere shirt, his wide leather belt,
his well-cut, wide black trousers going into the embroidered
cowboy boots had a certain inextinguishable elegance. He wore
no silver rings or buckles. Only his boots were embroidered and
decorated at the top with an inlay of white suède. He seemed
elegant, slender, yet he was very strong.

And at the same time, curiously, he gave her the feeling that
death was not far from him. Perhaps he too was half in love with
death. However that may be, the sense she had that death was
not far from him made him 'possible' to her.

Small as she was, she was quite a good horsewoman. They
gave her at the ranch a sorrel mare, very lovely in colour, and
well-made, with a powerful broad neck and the hollow back that
betokens a swift runner. Tansy, she was called. Her only fault
was the usual mare's failing, she was inclined to be hysterical.

So that every day the Princess set off with Miss Cummins and
Romero, on horseback, riding into the mountains. Once they

went camping for several days, with two more friends in the party.

'I think I like it better,' the Princess said to Romero, 'when we three go alone.'

And he gave her one of his quick, transfiguring smiles.

It was curious no white man had ever showed her this capacity for subtle gentleness, this power to *help* her in silence across a distance, if she were fishing without success, or tired of her horse, or if Tansy suddenly got scared. It was as if Romero could send her *from his heart* a dark beam of succour and sustaining. She had never known this before, and it was very thrilling.

Then the smile that suddenly creased his dark face, showing the strong white teeth. It creased his face almost into a savage grotesque. And at the same time there was in it something so warm, such a dark flame of kindliness for her, she was elated into her true Princess self.

Then that vivid, latent spark, in his eye, which she had seen, and which she knew he was aware she had seen. It made an inter-recognition between them, silent and delicate. Here he was delicate as a woman in this subtle inter-recognition.

And yet his presence only put to flight in her the *idée fixe* of 'marriage'. For some reason, in her strange little brain, the idea of *marrying* him could not enter. Not for any definite reason. He was in himself a gentleman, and she had plenty of money for two. There was no actual obstacle. Nor was she conventional.

No, now she came down to it, it was as if their two 'demons' could marry, were perhaps married. Only their two *selves*, Miss Urquhart and Señor Domingo Romero, were for some reason incompatible. There was a peculiar subtle intimacy of inter-recognition between them. But she did not see in the least how it would lead to marriage. Almost she could more easily marry one of the nice boys from Harvard or Yale.

The time passed, and she let it pass. The end of September came, with aspens going yellow on the mountain heights, and oak-scrub going red. But as yet the cotton-woods in the valley and canyons had not changed.

'When will you go away?' Romero asked her, looking at her fixedly, with a blank black eye.

'By the end of October,' she said. 'I have promised to be in Santa Barbara at the beginning of November.'

He was hiding the spark in his eye from her. But she saw the peculiar sullen thickening of his heavy mouth.

She had complained to him many times that one never saw any wild animals, except chipmunks and squirrels, and perhaps a skunk and a porcupine. Never a deer, or a bear, or a mountain lion.

'Are there no bigger animals in these mountains?' she asked, dissatisfied.

'Yes,' he said. 'There are deer – I see their tracks. And I saw the tracks of a bear.'

'But why can one never see the animals themselves?' She looked dissatisfied and wistful like a child.

'Why, it's pretty hard for you to see them. They won't let you come close. You have to keep still, in a place where they come. Or else you have to follow their tracks a long way.'

'I can't bear to go away till I've seen them: a bear, or a deer –'

The smile came suddenly on his face, indulgent.

'Well, what do you want? Do you want to go up into the mountains to some place, to wait till they come?'

'Yes,' she said, looking up at him with a sudden naïve impulse of recklessness.

And immediately his face became sombre again, responsible.

'Well,' he said, with slight irony, a touch of mockery of her. 'You will have to find a house. It's very cold at night now. You would have to stay all night in a house.'

'And there are no houses up there?' she said.

'Yes,' he replied. 'There is a little shack that belongs to me, that a miner built a long time ago, looking for gold. You can go there and stay one night, and maybe you see something. Maybe! I don't know. Maybe nothing come.'

'How much chance is there?'

'Well, I don't know. Last time when I was there I see three deer come down to drink at the water, and I shot two raccoons. But maybe this time we don't see anything.'

'Is there water there?' she asked.

'Yes, there is a little round pond, you know, below the spruce trees. And the water from the snow runs into it.'

'Is it far away?' she asked.

'Yes, pretty far. You see that ridge there' – and turning to the mountains he lifted his arm in the gesture which is somehow so moving, out in the West, pointing to the distance – 'that ridge where there are no trees, only rock' – his black eyes were focused on the distance, his face impassive, but as if in pain – 'you go round that ridge, and along, then you come down through the spruce trees to where that cabin is. My father bought that placer claim from a miner who was broke, but nobody ever found any gold or anything, and nobody ever goes there. Too lonesome!'

The Princess watched the massive, heavy-sitting, beautiful bulk of the Rocky Mountains. It was early in October, and the aspens were already losing their gold leaves; high up, the spruce and pine seemed to be growing darker; the great flat patches of oak scrub on the heights were red like gore.

'Can I go over there?' she asked, turning to him and meeting the spark in his eye.

His face was heavy with responsibility.

'Yes,' he said, 'you can go. But there'll be snow over the ridge, and it's awful cold, and awful lonesome.'

'I should like to go,' she said, persistent.

'All right,' he said. 'You can go if you want to.'

She doubted, though, if the Wilkiesons would let her go; at least alone with Romero and Miss Cummins.

Yet an obstinacy characteristic of her nature, an obstinacy tinged perhaps with madness, had taken hold of her. She wanted to look over the mountains into their secret heart. She wanted to descend to the cabin below the spruce trees, near the tarn of bright green water. She wanted to see the wild animals move about in their wild unconsciousness.

'Let us say to the Wilkiesons that we want to make the trip round the Frijoles canyon,' she said.

The trip round the Frijoles canyon was a usual thing. It would not be strenuous, nor cold, nor lonely: they could sleep in the log house that was called an hotel.

Romero looked at her quickly.

'If you want to say that,' he replied, 'you can tell Mrs Wilkieson. Only I know she'll be mad with me if I take you up in the mountains to that place. And I've got to go there first with a pack-horse, to take lots of blankets and some bread. Maybe Miss Cummins can't stand it. Maybe not. It's a hard trip.'

He was speaking, and thinking, in the heavy, disconnected Mexican fashion.

'Never mind!' The Princess was suddenly very decisive and stiff with authority. 'I want to do it. I will arrange with Mrs Wilkieson. And we'll go on Saturday.'

He shook his head slowly.

'I've got to go up on Sunday with a pack-horse and blankets,' he said. 'Can't do it before.'

'Very well!' she said, rather piqued. 'Then we'll start on Monday.'

She hated being thwarted even the tiniest bit.

He knew that if he started with the pack on Sunday at dawn he would not be back until late at night. But he consented that they should start on Monday morning at seven. The obedient Miss Cummins was told to prepare for the Frijoles trip. On Sunday Romero had his day off. He had not put in an appearance when the Princess retired on Sunday night, but on Monday morning, as she was dressing, she saw him bringing in the three horses from the corral. She was in high spirits.

The night had been cold. There was ice at the edges of the irrigation ditch, and the chipmunks crawled into the sun and lay with wide, dumb, anxious eyes, almost too numb to run.

'We may be away two or three days,' said the Princess.

'Very well. We won't begin to be anxious about you before Thursday, then,' said Mrs Wilkieson, who was young and capable: from Chicago. 'Anyway,' she added, 'Romero will see you through. He's so trustworthy.'

The sun was already on the desert as they set off towards the mountains, making the greasewood and the sage pale as pale-grey sands, luminous the great level around them. To the right glinted the shadows of the adobe pueblo, flat and almost invisible on the plain, earth of its earth. Behind lay the ranch and the tufts of tall, plumy cotton-woods, whose summits were yellowing under the perfect blue sky.

Autumn breaking into colour in the great spaces of the South-West.

But the three trotted gently along the trail, towards the sun that sparkled yellow just above the dark bulk of the ponderous mountains. Side-slopes were already gleaming yellow, flaming with a second light, under the coldish blue of the pale sky. The front slopes were in shadow, with submerged lustre of red oak scrub and dull-gold aspens, blue-black pines and grey-blue rock. While the canyon was full of deep blueness.

They rode single file, Romero first, on a black horse. Himself in black, made a flickering black spot in the delicate pallor of the great landscape, where even pine trees at a distance take a film of blue paler than their green. Romero rode on in silence past the tufts of furry greasewood. The Princess came next, on her sorrel mare. And Miss Cummins, who was not quite happy on horseback, came last, in the pale dust that the others had kicked up. Sometimes her horse sneezed, and she started.

But on they went at a gentle trot. Romero never looked round. He could hear the sound of the hoofs following, and that was all he wanted.

For the rest, he held ahead. And the Princess, with that black, unheeding figure always travelling away from her, felt strangely helpless, withal elated.

They neared the pale, round foot-hills, dotted with the round dark piñon[11] and cedar shrubs. The horses clinked and clattered among stones. Occasionally a big round greasewood held out fleecy tufts of flowers, pure gold. They wound into blue shadow, then up a steep stony slope, with the world lying pallid away behind and below. Then they dropped into the shadow of the San Cristobal canyon.

The stream was running full and swift. Occasionally the horses snatched at a tuft of grass. The trail narrowed and became rocky; the rocks closed in; it was dark and cool as the horses climbed and climbed upwards, and the tree trunks crowded in the shadowy, silent tightness of the canyon. They were among cottonwood trees that ran up straight and smooth and round to an extraordinary height. Above, the tips were gold, and it was sun. But away below, where the horses struggled up the rocks and wound among the trunks, there was still blue shadow by the sound of waters and an occasional grey festoon of old man's beard, and here and there a pale, dipping cranesbill flower among the tangle and the débris of the virgin place. And again the chill entered the Princess's heart as she realized what a tangle of decay and despair lay in the virgin forests.

They scrambled downwards, splashed across stream, up rocks and along the trail of the other side. Romero's black horse stopped, looked down quizzically at the fallen trees, then stepped over lightly. The Princess's sorrel followed, carefully. But Miss Cummins's buckskin made a fuss, and had to be got round.

In the same silence, save for the clinking of the horses and the splashing as the trail crossed stream, they worked their way upwards in the tight, tangled shadow of the canyon. Sometimes, crossing stream, the Princess would glance upwards, and then always her heart caught in her breast. For high up, away in heaven, the mountain heights shone yellow, dappled with dark spruce firs, clear almost as speckled daffodils against the pale turquoise blue lying high and serene above the dark-blue shadow where the Princess was. And she would snatch at the blood-red leaves of the oak as her horse crossed a more open slope, not knowing what she felt.

They were getting fairly high, occasionally lifted above the canyon itself, in the low groove below the speckled, gold-sparkling heights which towered beyond. Then again they dipped and crossed stream, the horses stepping gingerly across a tangle of fallen, frail aspen stems, then suddenly floundering in a mass of rocks. The black emerged ahead, his black tail waving. The Princess let her mare find her own footing; then she too emerged from the clatter. She rode on after the black. Then came a great frantic rattle of the buckskin behind. The Princess was aware of Romero's dark face looking round, with a strange, demon-like watchfulness, before she herself looked round, to see the buckskin scrambling rather lamely beyond the rocks, with one of his pale buff knees already red with blood.

'He almost went down!' called Miss Cummins.

But Romero was already out of the saddle and hastening down the path. He made quiet little noises to the buckskin, and began examining the cut knee.

'Is he hurt?' cried Miss Cummins anxiously, and she climbed hastily down.

'Oh, my goodness!' she cried, as she saw the blood running down the slender buff leg of the horse in a thin trickle. 'Isn't that *awful*?' She spoke in a stricken voice, and her face was white.

Romero was still carefully feeling the knee of the buckskin. Then he made him walk a few paces. And at last he stood up straight and shook his head.

'Not very bad!' he said. 'Nothing broken.'

Again he bent and worked at the knees. Then he looked up at the Princess.

'He can go on,' he said. 'It's not bad.'

The Princess looked down at the dark face in silence.

'What, go on right up here?' cried Miss Cummins. 'How many hours?'

'About five!' said Romero simply.

'Five hours!' cried Miss Cummins. 'A horse with a lame knee! And a steep mountain! Why-y!'

'Yes, it's pretty steep up there,' said Romero, pushing back his hat and staring fixedly at the bleeding knee. The buckskin stood in a stricken sort of dejection. 'But I think he'll make it all right,' the man added.

'Oh!' cried Miss Cummins, her eyes bright with sudden passion of unshed tears. 'I wouldn't think of it. I wouldn't ride him up there, not for any money.'

'Why wouldn't you?' asked Romero.

'It *hurts* him.'

Romero bent down again to the horse's knee.

'Maybe it hurts him a little,' he said. 'But he can make it all right, and his leg won't get stiff.'

'What! Ride him five hours up the steep mountains?' cried Miss Cummins. 'I couldn't. I just couldn't do it. I'll lead him a little way and see if he can go. But I *couldn't* ride him again. I couldn't. Let me walk.'

'But Miss Cummins, dear, if Romero says he'll be all right?' said the Princess.

'I know it hurts him. Oh, I just couldn't bear it.'

There was no doing anything with Miss Cummins. The thought of a hurt animal always put her into a sort of hysterics.

They walked forward a little, leading the buckskin. He limped rather badly. Miss Cummins sat on a rock.

'Why, it's agony to see him!' she cried. 'It's *cruel*!'

'He won't limp after a bit, if you take no notice of him,' said Romero. 'Now he plays up, and limps very much, because he wants to make you see.'

'I don't think there can be much playing up,' said Miss Cummins bitterly. 'We can *see* how it must hurt him.'

'It don't hurt much,' said Romero.

But now Miss Cummins was silent with antipathy.

It was a deadlock. The party remained motionless on the trail, the Princess in the saddle, Miss Cummins seated on a rock, Romero standing black and remote near the drooping buckskin.

'Well!' said the man suddenly at last. 'I guess we go back, then.'

And he looked up swiftly at his horse, which was cropping at the mountain herbage and treading on the trailing reins.

'No!' cried the Princess. 'Oh no!' Her voice rang with a great wail of disappointment and anger. Then she checked herself.

Miss Cummins rose with energy.

'Let me lead the buckskin home,' she said, with cold dignity, 'and you two go on.'

This was received in silence. The Princess was looking down at her with a sardonic, almost cruel gaze.

'We've only come about two hours,' said Miss Cummins. 'I don't mind a bit leading him home. But I *couldn't* ride him. I *couldn't* have him ridden with that knee.'

This again was received in dead silence. Romero remained impassive, almost inert.

'Very well, then,' said the Princess. 'You lead him home. You'll be quite all right. Nothing can happen to you, possibly. And say to them that we have gone on and shall be home tomorrow – or the day after.'

She spoke coldly and distinctly. For she could not bear to be thwarted.

'Better all go back, and come again another day,' said Romero – non-committal.

'There will never *be* another day,' cried the Princess. 'I want to go on.'

She looked at him square in the eyes, and met the spark in his eye.

He raised his shoulders slightly.

'If you want it,' he said. 'I'll go on with you. But Miss Cummins can ride my horse to the end of the canyon, and I lead the buckskin. Then I come back to you.'

It was arranged so. Miss Cummins had her saddle put on Romero's black horse, Romero took the buckskin's bridle, and they started back. The Princess rode very slowly on, upwards, alone. She was at first so angry with Miss Cummins that she was blind to everything else. She just let her mare follow her own inclinations.

The peculiar spell of anger carried the Princess on, almost unconscious, for an hour or so. And by this time she was beginning to climb pretty high. Her horse walked steadily all the time. They emerged on a bare slope, and the trail wound through frail aspen stems. Here a wind swept, and some of the aspens were already bare. Others were fluttering their discs of pure, solid yellow leaves, so *nearly* like petals, while the slope ahead was one soft, glowing fleece of daffodil yellow; fleecy like a golden fox-skin, and yellow as daffodils alive in the wind and the high mountain sun.

She paused and looked back. The near great slopes were mottled with gold and the dark hue of spruce, like some unsinged eagle, and the light lay gleaming upon them. Away through the gap of the canyon she could see the pale blue of the egg-like desert, with the crumpled dark crack of the Rio Grande Canyon. And far, far off, the blue mountains like a fence of angels on the horizon.

And she thought of her adventure. She was going on alone with Romero. But then she was very sure of herself, and Romero was not the kind of man to do anything to her against her will.

This was her first thought. And she just had a fixed desire to go over the brim of the mountains, to look into the inner chaos of the Rockies. And she wanted to go with Romero, because he had some peculiar kinship with her; there was some peculiar link between the two of them. Miss Cummins anyhow would have been only a discordant note.

She rode on, and emerged at length in the lap of the summit. Beyond her was a great concave of stone and stark, dead-grey trees, where the mountain ended against the sky. But nearer was the dense black, bristling spruce, and at her feet was the lap of the summit, a flat little valley of sere grass and quiet-standing yellow aspens, the stream trickling like a thread across.

It was a little valley or shell from which the stream was gently poured into the lower rocks and trees of the canyon. Around her was a fairy-like gentleness, the delicate sere grass, the groves of delicate-stemmed aspens dropping their flakes of bright yellow. And the delicate, quick little stream threading through the wild, sere grass.

Here one might expect deer and fawns and wild things, as in a little paradise. Here she was to wait for Romero, and they were to have lunch.

She unfastened her saddle and pulled it to the ground with a crash, letting her horse wander with a long rope. How beautiful Tansy looked, sorrel, among the yellow leaves that lay like a patina on the sere ground. The Princess herself wore a fleecy sweater of a pale, sere buff, like the grass, and riding-breeches of a pure orange-tawny colour. She felt quite in the picture.

From her saddle-pouches she took the packages of lunch, spread a little cloth, and sat to wait for Romero. Then she made a little fire. Then she ate a devilled egg. Then she ran after Tansy, who was straying across-stream. Then she sat in the sun, in the stillness near the aspens, and waited.

The sky was blue. Her little alp was soft and delicate as fairyland. But beyond and up jutted the great slopes, dark with the pointed feathers of spruce, bristling with grey dead trees among grey rock, or dappled with dark and gold. The beautiful, but fierce, heavy cruel mountains, with their moments of tenderness.

She saw Tansy start, and begin to run. Two ghost-like figures on horseback emerged from the black of the spruce across the stream. It was two Indians on horseback, swathed like seated mummies in their pale-grey cotton blankets. Their guns jutted beyond the saddles. They rode straight towards her, to her thread of smoke.

As they came near, they unswathed themselves and greeted her, looking at her curiously from their dark eyes. Their black hair was somewhat untidy, the long rolled plaits on their shoulders were soiled. They looked tired.

They got down from their horses near her little fire – a camp was a camp – swathed their blankets round their hips, pulled the saddles from their ponies and turned them loose, then sat down. One was a young Indian whom she had met before, the other was an older man.

'You all alone?' said the younger man.

'Romero will be here in a minute,' she said glancing back along the trail.

'Ah, Romero! You with him? Where are you going?'

'Round the ridge,' she said. 'Where are you going?'

'We going down to Pueblo.'

'Been out hunting? How long have you been out?'

'Yes. Been out five days.' The young Indian gave a little meaningless laugh.

'Got anything?'

'No. We see tracks of two deer – but not got nothing.'

The Princess noticed a suspicious-looking bulk under one of the saddles – surely a folded-up deer. But she said nothing.

'You must have been cold,' she said.

'Yes, very cold in the night. And hungry. Got nothing to eat since yesterday. Eat it all up.' And again he laughed his little meaningless laugh. Under their dark skins, the two men looked peaked and hungry. The Princess rummaged for food among the saddle-bags. There was a lump of bacon – the regular stand-back – and some bread. She gave them this, and they began toasting slices of it on long sticks at the fire. Such was the little camp Romero saw as he rode down the slope: the Princess in her orange breeches, her head tied in a blue-and-brown silk kerchief, sitting opposite the two dark-headed Indians across the camp-fire, while one of the Indians was leaning forward toasting bacon, his two plaits of braid-swathed hair dangling as if wearily.

Romero rode up, his face expressionless. The Indians greeted him in Spanish. He unsaddled his horse, took food from the bags, and sat down at the camp to eat. The Princess went to the stream for water, and to wash her hands.

'Got coffee?' asked the Indians.

'No coffee this outfit,' said Romero.

They lingered an hour or more in the warm midday sun. Then Romero saddled the horses. The Indians still squatted by the fire. Romero and the Princess rode away, calling *Adios!* to the Indians over the stream and into the dense spruce whence two strange figures had emerged.

When they were alone, Romero turned and looked at her curiously, in a way she could not understand, with such a hard glint in his eyes. And for the first time she wondered if she was rash.

'I hope you don't mind going alone with me,' she said.

'If you want it,' he replied.

They emerged at the foot of the great bare slope of rocky summit, where dead spruce trees stood sparse and bristling like bristles on a grey dead hog. Romero said the Mexicans, twenty years back, had fired the mountains, to drive out the whites. This grey concave slope of summit was corpse-like.

The trail was almost invisible. Romero watched for the trees which the Forest Service had blazed. And they climbed the stark corpse slope, among dead spruce, fallen and ash-grey, into the wind. The wind came rushing from the west, up the funnel of the canyon, from the desert. And there was the desert, like a vast mirage tilting slowly upwards towards the west, immense and pallid, away beyond the funnel of the canyon. The Princess could hardly look.

For an hour their horses rushed the slope, hastening with a great working of the haunches upwards, and halting to breathe, scrambling again, and rowing their way up length by length, on the livid, slanting wall. While the wind blew like some vast machine.

After an hour they were working their way on the incline, no longer forcing straight up. All was grey and dead around them; the horses picked their way over the silver-grey corpses of the spruce. But they were near the top, near the ridge.

Even the horses made a rush for the last bit. They had worked round to a scrap of spruce forest near the very top. They hurried in, out of the huge, monstrous, mechanical wind, that whistled inhumanly and was palely cold. So stepping through the dark screen of trees, they emerged over the crest.

In front now was nothing but mountains, ponderous, massive, down-sitting mountains, in a huge and intricate knot, empty of life or soul. Under the bristling black feathers of spruce near by lay patches of white snow. The lifeless valleys were concaves of rock and spruce, the rounded summits and the hog-backed summits of grey rock crowded one behind the other like some monstrous herd in arrest.

It frightened the Princess, it was *so* inhuman. She had not thought it could be so inhuman, so, as it were, anti-life. And yet now one of her desires was fulfilled. She had seen it, the massive, gruesome, repellant core of the Rockies. She saw it there beneath her eyes, in its gigantic, heavy gruesomeness.

And she wanted to go back. At this moment she wanted to turn back. She had looked down into the intestinal knot of these mountains. She was frightened. She wanted to go back.

But Romero was riding on, on the lee side of the spruce forest, above the concaves of the inner mountains. He turned round to her and pointed at the slope with a dark hand.

'Here a miner has been trying for gold,' he said. It was a grey scratched-out heap near a hole – like a great badger hole. And it looked quite fresh.

'Quite lately?' said the Princess.

'No, long ago – twenty, thirty years.' He had reined in his horse and was looking at the mountains. 'Look!' he said. 'There goes the Forest Service trail – along those ridges, on the top, way over there till it comes to Lucytown, where is the Government road. We go down there – no trail – see behind that mountain – you see the top, no trees, and some grass?'

His arm was lifted, his brown hand pointing, his dark eyes piercing into the distance, as he sat on his black horse twisting round to her. Strange and ominous, only the demon of himself, he seemed to her. She was dazed and a little sick, at that height, and she could not see any more. Only she saw an eagle turning in the air beyond, and the light from the west showed the pattern on him underneath.

'Shall I ever be able to go so far?' asked the Princess faintly, petulantly.

'Oh yes! All easy now. No more hard places.'

They worked along the ridge, up and down, keeping on the lee side, the inner side, in the dark shadow. It was cold. Then the trail laddered up again, and they emerged on a narrow ridge-track, with the mountain slipping away enormously on either side. The Princess was afraid. For one moment she looked out, and saw the desert, the desert ridges, more desert, more blue ridges, shining pale and very vast, far below, vastly palely tilting to the western horizon. It was ethereal and terrifying in its gleaming, pale, half-burnished immensity, tilted at the west. She could not bear it. To the left was the ponderous, involved mass of mountains all kneeling heavily.

She closed her eyes and let her consciousness evaporate away. The mare followed the trail. So on and on, in the wind again.

They turned their backs to the wind, facing inwards to the mountains. She thought they had left the trail; it was quite invisible.

'No,' he said, lifting his hand and pointing. 'Don't you see the blazed trees?'

And making an effort of consciousness, she was able to perceive on a pale-grey dead spruce stem the old marks where an axe had chipped a piece away. But with the height, the cold, the wind, her brain was numb.

They turned again and began to descend; he told her they had left the trail. The horses slithered in the loose stones, picking their way downward. It was afternoon, the sun stood obtrusive and gleaming in the lower heavens – about four o'clock. The horses went steadily, slowly, but obstinately onwards. The air was getting colder. They were in among the lumpish peaks and steep concave valleys. She was barely conscious at all of Romero.

He dismounted and came to help her from her saddle. She tottered, but would not betray her feebleness.

'We must slide down here,' he said. 'I can lead the horses.'

They were on a ridge, and facing a steep bare slope of pallid, tawny mountain grass on which the western sun shone full. It was steep and concave. The Princess felt she might start slipping, and go down like a toboggan into the great hollow.

But she pulled herself together. Her eye blazed up again with excitement and determination. A wind rushed past her; she could hear the shriek of spruce trees far below. Bright spots came on her cheeks as her hair blew across. She looked a wild, fairy-like little thing.

'No,' she said. 'I will take my horse.'

'Then mind she doesn't slip down on top of you,' said Romero. And away he went, nimbly dropping down the pale, steep incline, making from rock to rock, down the grass, and following any little slanting groove. His horse hopped and slithered after him, and sometimes stopped dead, with forefeet pressed back, refusing to go farther. He, below his horse, looked up and pulled the reins gently, and encouraged the creature. Then the horse once more dropped his forefeet with a jerk, and the descent continued.

The Princess set off in blind, reckless pursuit, tottering and yet nimble. And Romero, looking constantly back to see how she was faring, saw her fluttering down like some queer little bird, her orange breeches twinkling like the legs of some duck, and her head, tied in the blue and buff kerchief, bound round and round like the head of some blue-topped bird. The sorrel mare rocked and slipped behind her. But down came the Princess in a reckless intensity, a tiny, vivid spot on the great hollow flank of the tawny mountain. So tiny! Tiny as a frail bird's egg. It made Romero's mind go blank with wonder.

But they had to get down, out of that cold and dragging wind. The spruce trees stood below, where a tiny stream emerged in stones. Away plunged Romero, zigzagging down. And away behind, up the slope, fluttered the tiny, bright-coloured Princess, holding the end of the long reins, and leading the lumbering, four-footed, sliding mare.

At last they were down. Romero sat in the sun, below the wind, beside some squaw-berry bushes. The Princess came near, the colour flaming in her cheeks, her eyes dark blue, much darker than the kerchief on her head, and glowing unnaturally.

'We made it,' said Romero.

'Yes,' said the Princess, dropping the reins and subsiding on to the grass, unable to speak, unable to think.

But, thank heaven, they were out of the wind and in the sun.

In a few minutes her consciousness and her control began to come back. She drank a little water. Romero was attending to the saddles. Then they set off again, leading the horses still a little farther down the tiny stream-bed. Then they could mount.

They rode down a bank and into a valley grove dense with aspens. Winding through the thin, crowding, pale-smooth stems, the sun shone flickering beyond them, and the disc-like aspen leaves, waving queer mechanical signals, seemed to be splashing the gold light before her eyes. She rode on in a splashing dazzle of gold.

Then they entered shadow and the dark, resinous spruce trees. The fierce boughs always wanted to sweep her off her horse. She had to twist and squirm past.

But there was a semblance of an old trail. And all at once they emerged in the sun on the edge of a spruce grove, and there was a little cabin, and the bottom of a small, naked valley with a grey rock and heaps of stones, and a round pool of intense green water, dark green. The sun was just about to leave it.

Indeed, as she stood, the shadow came over the cabin and over herself; they were in the lower gloom, a twilight. Above, the heights still blazed.

It was a little hole of a cabin, near the spruce trees, with an earthen floor and an unhinged door. There was a wooden bed-bunk, three old sawn-off log-lengths to sit on as stools, and a sort of fireplace; no room for anything else. The little hole would hardly contain two people. The roof had gone – but Romero had laid on thick spruce boughs.

The strange squalor of the primitive forest pervaded the place, the squalor of animals and their droppings, the squalor of the wild. The Princess knew the peculiar repulsiveness of it. She was tired and faint.

Romero hastily got a handful of twigs, set a little fire going in the stove grate, and went out to attend to the horses. The Princess vaguely, mechanically, put sticks on the fire, in a sort of stupor, watching the blaze, stupefied and fascinated. She could not make much fire – it would set the whole cabin alight. And smoke oozed out of the dilapidated mud-and-stone chimney.

When Romero came in with the saddle-pouches and saddles, hanging the saddles on the wall, there sat the little Princess on her stump of wood in front of the dilapidated fire-grate, warming her tiny hands at the blaze, while her orange breeches glowed almost like another fire. She was in a sort of stupor.

'You have some whisky now, or some tea? Or wait for some soup?' he asked.

She rose and looked at him with bright, dazed eyes, half comprehending; the colour glowing hectic in her cheeks.

'Some tea,' she said, 'with a little whisky in it. Where's the kettle?'

'Wait,' he said. 'I'll bring the things.' She took her cloak from the back of her saddle, and followed him into the open. It was a deep cup of shadow. But above the sky was still shining, and the heights of the mountains were blazing with aspen like fire blazing.

Their horses were cropping the grass among the stones. Romero clambered up a heap of grey stones and began lifting away logs and rocks, till he had opened the mouth of one of the miner's little old workings. This was his cache. He brought out bundles of blankets, pans for cooking, a little petrol camp-stove, an axe, the regular camp outfit. He seemed so quick and energetic and full of force. This quick force dismayed the Princess a little.

She took a saucepan and went down the stones to the water. It was very still and mysterious, and of a deep green colour, yet pure, transparent as glass. How cold the place was! How mysterious and fearful.

She crouched in her dark cloak by the water, rinsing the saucepan, feeling the cold heavy above her, the shadow like a vast weight upon her, bowing her down. The sun was leaving the mountain-tops, departing, leaving her under profound shadow. Soon it would crush her down completely.

Sparks? – or eyes looking at her across the water? She gazed, hypnotized. And with her sharp eyes she made out in the dusk the pale form of a bob-cat crouching by the water's edge, pale as the stones among which it crouched, opposite. And it was watching her with cold, electric eyes of strange intentness, a sort of cold, icy wonder and fearlessness. She saw its *museau*[12] pushed forward, its tufted ears pricking intensely up. It was watching her with cold animal curiosity, something demonish and conscience-less.

She made a swift movement, spilling her water. And in a flash the creature was gone, leaping like a cat that is escaping; but strange and soft in its motion, with its little bob-tail. Rather fascinating. Yet that cold, intent, demonish watching! She shivered with cold and fear. She knew well enough the dread and repulsiveness of the wild.

Romero carried in the bundles of bedding and the camp outfit. The windowless cabin was already dark inside. He lit a lantern, and then went out again with the axe. She heard him chopping wood as she fed sticks to the fire under her water. When he came in with an armful of oak-scrub faggots, she had just thrown the tea into the water.

'Sit down,' she said, 'and drink tea.'

He poured a little bootleg whisky[13] into the enamel cups, and in the silence the two sat on the log-ends, sipping the hot liquid and coughing occasionally from the smoke.

'We burn these oak sticks,' he said. 'They don't make hardly any smoke.'

Curious and remote he was, saying nothing except what had to be said. And she, for her part, was as remote from him. They seemed far, far apart, worlds apart, now they were so near.

He unwrapped one bundle of bedding, and spread the blankets and the sheepskin in the wooden bunk.

'You lie down and rest,' he said, 'and I make the supper.'

She decided to do so. Wrapping her cloak round her, she lay down in the bunk, turning her face to the wall. She could hear him preparing supper over the little petrol stove. Soon she could smell the soup he was heating; and soon she heard the hissing of fried chicken in a pan.

'You eat your supper now?' he said.

With a jerky, despairing movement, she sat up in the bunk, tossing back her hair. She felt cornered.

'Give it me here,' she said.

He handed her first the cupful of soup. She sat among the blankets, eating it slowly. She was hungry. Then he gave her an enamel plate with pieces of fried chicken and currant jelly, butter and bread. It was very good. As they ate the chicken he made the coffee. She said never a word. A certain resentment filled her. She was cornered.

When supper was over he washed the dishes, dried them, and put everything away carefully, else there would have been no room to move in the hole of a cabin. The oak-wood gave out a good bright heat.

He stood for a few moments at a loss. Then he asked her:

'You want to go to bed soon?'

'Soon,' she said. 'Where are you going to sleep?'

'I make my bed here –' he pointed to the floor along the wall. 'Too cold out of doors.'

'Yes,' she said. 'I suppose it is.'

She sat immobile, her cheeks hot, full of conflicting thoughts. And she watched him while he folded the blankets on the floor, a sheepskin underneath. Then she went out into the night.

The stars were big. Mars sat on the edge of a mountain, for all the world like the blazing eye of a crouching mountain lion. But she herself was deep, deep below in a pit of shadow. In the intense silence she seemed to hear the spruce forest crackling with electricity and cold. Strange, foreign stars floated on that unmoving water. The night was going to freeze. Over the hills came the far sobbing-singing howling of coyotes. She wondered how the horses would be.

Shuddering a little, she turned to the cabin. Warm light showed through its chinks. She pushed at the rickety, half-opened door.

'What about the horses?' she said.

'My black, he won't go away. And your mare will stay with him. You want to go to bed now?'

'I think I do.'

'All right. I feed the horses some oats.'

And he went out into the night.

He did not come back for some time. She was lying wrapped up tight in the bunk.

He blew out the lantern, and sat down on his bedding to take off his clothes. She lay with her back turned. And soon, in the silence, she was asleep.

She dreamed it was snowing, and the snow was falling on her through the roof, softly, softly, helplessly, and she was going to be buried alive. She was growing colder and colder, the snow was weighing down on her. The snow was going to absorb her.

She awoke with a sudden convulsion, like pain. She was really very cold; perhaps the heavy blankets had numbed her. Her heart seemed unable to beat, she felt she could not move.

With another convulsion she sat up. It was intensely dark. There was not even a spark of fire, the light wood had burned right away. She sat in thick oblivious darkness. Only through a chink she could see a star.

What did she want? Oh, what did she want? She sat in bed and rocked herself woefully. She could hear the steady breathing of the sleeping man. She was shivering with cold; her heart seemed as if it could not beat. She wanted warmth, protection, she wanted to be taken away from herself. And at the same time, perhaps more deeply than anything, she wanted to keep herself intact, intact, untouched, that no one should have any power over her, or rights to her. It was a wild necessity in her that no one, particularly no man, should have any rights or power over her, that no one and nothing should possess her.

Yet that other thing! And she was so cold, so shivering, and her heart could not beat. Oh, would not someone help her heart to beat?

She tried to speak, and could not. Then she cleared her throat.

'Romero,' she said strangely, 'it is so cold.'

Where did her voice come from, and whose voice was it, in the dark?

She heard him at once sit up, and his voice, startled, with a resonance that seemed to vibrate against her, saying:

'You want to me to make you warm?'

'Yes.'

As soon as he had lifted her in his arms, she wanted to scream to him not to touch her. She stiffened herself. Yet she was dumb.

And he was warm, but with a terrible animal warmth that seemed to annihilate her. He panted like an animal with desire. And she was given over to this thing.

She had never, never wanted to be given over to this. But she had *willed* that it should happen to her. And according to her will, she lay and let it happen. But she never wanted it. She never wanted to be thus assailed and handled, and mauled. She wanted to keep herself to herself.

However, she had willed it to happen, and it had happened. She panted with relief when it was over.

Yet even now she had to lie within the hard, powerful clasp of this other creature, this man. She dreaded to struggle to go away. She dreaded almost too much the icy cold of that other bunk.

'Do you want to go away from me?' asked his strange voice. Oh, if it could only have been a thousand miles away from her! Yet she had willed to have it thus close.

'No,' she said.

And she could feel a curious joy and pride surging up again in him: at her expense. Because he had got her. She felt like a victim there. And he was exulting in his power over her, his possession, his pleasure.

When dawn came, he was fast asleep. She sat up suddenly.

'I want a fire,' she said.

He opened his brown eyes wide, and smiled with a curious tender luxuriousness.

'I want you to make a fire,' she said.

He glanced at the chinks of light. His brown face hardened to the day.

'All right,' he said. 'I'll make it.'

She did her face while he dressed. She could not bear to look at him. He was so suffused with pride and luxury. She hid her face almost in despair. But feeling the cold blast of air as he opened the door, she wriggled down into the warm place where he had been. How soon the warmth ebbed, when he had gone!

He made a fire and went out, returning after a while with water.

'You stay in bed till the sun comes,' he said. 'It's very cold.'

'Hand me my cloak.'

She wrapped the cloak fast round her, and sat up among the blankets. The warmth was already spreading from the fire.

'I suppose we will start back as soon as we've had breakfast?'

He was crouching at his camp-stove making scrambled eggs. He looked up suddenly, transfixed, and his brown eyes, so soft and luxuriously widened, looked straight at her.

'You want to?' he said.

'We'd better get back as soon as possible,' she said, turning aside from his eyes.

'You want to get away from me?' he asked, repeating the question of the night in a sort of dread.

'I want to get away from here,' she said decisively. And it was true. She wanted supremely to get away, back to the world of people.

He rose slowly to his feet, holding the aluminium frying-pan.

'Don't you like last night?' he asked.

'Not really,' she said. 'Why? Do you?'

He put down the frying-pan and stood staring at the wall. She could see she had given him a cruel blow. But she did not relent. She was getting her own back. She wanted to regain possession of all herself, and in some mysterious way she felt that he possessed some part of her still.

He looked round at her slowly, his face greyish and heavy.

'You Americans,' he said, 'you always want to do a man down.'

'I am not American,' she said. 'I am British. And I don't want to do any man down. I only want to go back, now.'

'And what will you say about me, down there?'

'That you were very kind to me, and very good.'

He crouched down again, and went on turning the eggs. He gave her her plate, and her coffee, and sat down to his own food.

But again he seemed not to be able to swallow. He looked up at her.

'You don't like last night?' he asked.

'Not really,' she said, though with some difficulty. 'I don't care for that kind of thing.'

A blank sort of wonder spread over his face at these words, followed immediately by a black look of anger, and then a stony, sinister despair.

'You don't?' he said, looking her in the eyes.

'Not really,' she replied, looking back with steady hostility into his eyes.

Then a dark flame seemed to come from his face.

'I make you,' he said, as if to himself.

He rose and reached her clothes, that hung on a peg: the fine linen underwear, the orange breeches, the fleecy jumper, the blue-and-buff kerchief; then he took up her riding-boots and her bead moccasins. Crushing everything in his arms, he opened the door. Sitting up, she saw him stride down to the dark-green pool in the frozen shadow of that deep cup of a valley. He tossed the clothing and the boots out on the pool. Ice had formed. And on the pure, dark green mirror, in the slaty shadow, the Princess saw her things lying, the white linen, the orange breeches, the black boots, the blue moccasins, a tangled heap of colour. Romero picked up rocks and heaved them out at the ice till the surface broke and the fluttering clothing disappeared in the rattling water, while the valley echoed and shouted again with the sound.

She sat in despair among the blankets, hugging tight her pale-blue cloak. Romero strode straight back to the cabin.

'Now you stay here with me,' he said.

She was furious. Her blue eyes met his. They were like two demons watching one another. In his face, beyond a sort of unrelieved gloom, was a demonish desire for death.

He saw her looking round the cabin, scheming. He saw her eyes on his rifle. He took the gun and went out with it. Returning, he pulled out her saddle, carried it to the tarn, and threw it in. Then he fetched his own saddle, and did the same.

'Now will you go away?' he said, looking at her with a smile.

She debated within herself whether to coax him and wheedle him. But she knew he was already beyond it. She sat among her blankets in a frozen sort of despair, hard as hard ice with anger.

He did the chores, and disappeared with the gun. She got up in her blue pyjamas, huddled in her cloak, and stood in the doorway. The dark-green pool was motionless again, the stony slopes were pallid and frozen. Shadow still lay, like an after-death, deep in this valley. Always in the distance she saw the horses feeding. If she could catch one! The brilliant yellow sun was half-way down the mountain. It was nine o'clock.

All day she was alone, and she was frightened. What she was frightened of she didn't know. Perhaps the crackling in the dark spruce wood. Perhaps just the savage, heartless wildness of the mountains. But all day she sat in the sun in the doorway of the cabin, watching, watching for hope. And all the time her bowels were cramped with fear.

She saw a dark spot that probably was a bear, roving across the pale grassy slope in the far distance, in the sun.

When, in the afternoon, she saw Romero approaching, with silent suddenness, carrying his gun and a dead deer, the cramp in her bowels relaxed, then became colder. She dreaded him with a cold dread.

'There is deer-meat,' he said, throwing the dead doe at her feet.

'You don't want to go away from here,' he said. 'This is a nice place.'

She shrank into the cabin.

'Come into the sun,' he said, following her. She looked up at him with hostile, frightened eyes.

'Come into the sun,' he repeated, taking her gently by the arm, in a powerful grasp.

She knew it was useless to rebel. Quietly he led her out, and seated himself in the doorway, holding her still by the arm.

'In the sun it is warm,' he said. 'Look, this is a nice place. You are such a pretty white woman, why do you want to act mean to me? Isn't this a nice place! Come! Come here! It is sure warm here.'

He drew her to him, and in spite of her stony resistance, he took her cloak from her, holding her in her thin blue pyjamas.

'You sure are a pretty little white woman, small and pretty,' he said. 'You sure won't act mean to me – you don't want to, I know you don't.'

She, stony and powerless, had to submit to him. The sun shone on her white, delicate skin.

'I sure don't mind hell fire,' he said. 'After this.'

A queer, luxurious good humour seemed to possess him again. But though outwardly she was powerless, inwardly she resisted him, absolutely and stonily.

When later he was leaving her again, she said to him suddenly:

'You think you can conquer me this way. But you can't. You can never conquer me.'

He stood arrested, looking back at her, with many emotions conflicting in his face – wonder, surprise, a touch of horror, and an unconscious pain that crumpled his face till it was like a mask. Then he went out without saying a word, hung the dead deer on a bough, and started to flay it. While he was at this butcher's work, the sun sank and cold night came on again.

'You see,' he said to her as he crouched, cooking the supper, 'I ain't going to let you go. I reckon you called to me in the night, and I've some right. If you want to fix it up right now with me, and say you want to be with me, we'll fix it up now and go down to the ranch tomorrow and get married or whatever you want. But you've got to say you want to be with me. Else I shall stay right here, till something happens.'

She waited a while before she answered:

'I don't want to be with anybody against my will. I don't dislike you; at least, I didn't, till you tried to put your will over mine. I won't have anybody's will put over me. You can't succeed. Nobody could. You can never get me under your will. And you won't have long to try, because soon they will send someone to look for me.'

He pondered this last, and she regretted having said it. Then, sombre, he bent to the cooking again.

He could not conquer her, however much he violated her. Because her spirit was hard and flawless as a diamond. But he could shatter her. This she knew. Much more, and she would be shattered.

In a sombre, violent excess he tried to expend his desire for her. And she was racked with an agony, and felt each time she would die. Because, in some peculiar way, he had got hold of her, some unrealized part of her which she never wished to realize. Racked with a burning, tearing anguish, she felt that the thread of her being would break, and she would die. The burning heat that racked her inwardly.

If only, only she could be alone again, cool and intact! If only she could recover herself again, cool and intact! Would she ever, ever, ever be able to bear herself again?

Even now she did not hate him. It was beyond that. Like some racking, hot doom. Personally he hardly existed.

The next day he would not let her have any fire, because of attracting attention with the smoke. It was a grey day, and she was cold. He stayed round, and heated soup on the petrol stove. She lay motionless in the blankets.

And in the afternoon she pulled the clothes over her head and broke into tears. She had never really cried in her life. He dragged the blankets away and looked to see what was shaking her. She sobbed in helpless hysterics. He covered her over again and went outside, looking at the mountains, where clouds were dragging and leaving a little snow. It was a violent, windy, horrible day, the evil of winter rushing down.

She cried for hours. And after this a great silence came between them. They were two people who had died. He did not touch her any more. In the night she lay and shivered like a dying dog. She felt that her very shivering would rupture something in her body, and she would die.

At last she had to speak.

'Could you make a fire? I am so cold,' she said, with chattering teeth.

'Want to come over here?' came his voice.

'I would rather you made me a fire,' she said, her teeth knocking together and chopping the words in two.

He got up and kindled a fire. At last the warmth spread, and she could sleep.

The next day was still chilly, with some wind. But the sun shone. He went about in silence, with a dead-looking face. It was now so dreary and so like death she wished he would do anything rather than continue in this negation. If now he asked her to go down with him to the world and marry him, she would do it. What did it matter? Nothing mattered any more.

But he would not ask her. His desire was dead and heavy like ice within him. He kept watch around the house.

On the fourth day as she sat huddled in the doorway in the sun, hugged in a blanket, she saw two horsemen come over the crest of the grassy slope – small figures. She gave a cry. He looked up quickly and saw the figures. The men had dismounted. They were looking for the trail.

'They are looking for me,' she said.

'Muy bien,'[14] he answered in Spanish.

He went and fetched his gun, and sat with it across his knees.

'Oh!' she said. 'Don't shoot!'

He looked across at her.

'Why?' he said. 'You like staying with me?'

'No,' she said. 'But don't shoot.'

'I ain't going to Pen,'[15] he said.

'You won't have to go to Pen,' she said. 'Don't shoot!'

'I'm going to shoot,' he muttered.

And straightway he kneeled and took very careful aim. The Princess sat on in an agony of helplessness and hopelessness.

The shot rang out. In an instant she saw one of the horses on the pale grassy slope rear and go rolling down. The man had dropped in the grass, and was invisible. The second man clambered on his horse, and on that precipitous place went at a gallop in a long swerve towards the nearest spruce tree cover. Bang! Bang! went Romero's shots. But each time he missed, and the running horse leaped like a kangaroo towards cover.

It was hidden. Romero now got behind a rock; tense silence, in the brilliant sunshine. The Princess sat on the bunk inside the cabin, crouching, paralysed. For hours, it seemed, Romero knelt behind this rock, in his black shirt, bare-headed, watching. He had a beautiful, alert figure. The Princess wondered why she did not feel sorry for him. But her spirit was hard and cold, her heart could not melt. Though now she would have called him to her, with love.

But no, she did not love him. She would never love any man. Never! It was fixed and sealed in her, almost vindictively.

Suddenly she was so startled she almost fell from the bunk. A shot rang out quite close from behind the cabin. Romero leaped straight into the air, his arms fell outstretched, turning as he leaped. And even while he was in the air, a second shot rang out, and he fell with a crash, squirming, his hands clutching the earth towards the cabin door.

The Princess sat absolutely motionless, transfixed, staring at the prostrate figure. In a few moments the figure of a man in the Forest Service appeared close to the house; a young man in a broad-brimmed Stetson hat, dark flannel shirt, and riding-boots, carrying a gun. He strode over to the prostrate figure.

'Got you, Romero!' he said aloud. And he turned the dead man over. There was already a little pool of blood where Romero's breast had been.

'H'm!' said the Forest Service man. 'Guess I got you nearer than I thought.'

And he squatted there, staring at the dead man.

The distant calling of his comrade aroused him. He stood up.

'Hullo, Bill!' he shouted. 'Yep! Got him! Yep! Done him in, apparently.'

The second man rode out of the forest on a grey horse. He had a ruddy, kind face, and round brown eyes, dilated with dismay.

'He's not passed out?' he asked anxiously.

'Looks like it,' said the first young man coolly.

The second dismounted and bent over the body. Then he stood up again, and nodded.

'Yea-a!' he said. 'He's done in all right. It's him all right, boy! It's Domingo Romero.'

'Yep! I know it!' replied the other.

Then in perplexity he turned and looked into the cabin, where the Princess squatted, staring with big owl eyes from her red blanket.

'Hello!' he said, coming towards the hut. And he took his hat off. Oh, the sense of ridicule she felt! Though he did not mean any.

But she could not speak, no matter what she felt.

'What'd this man start firing for?' he asked.

She fumbled for words, with numb lips.

'He had gone out of his mind!' she said, with solemn, stammering conviction.

'Good Lord! You mean to say he'd gone out of his mind? Whew! That's pretty awful! That explains it then. H'm!'

He accepted the explanation without more ado.

With some difficulty they succeeded in getting the Princess down to the ranch. But she, too, was not a little mad.

'I'm not quite sure where I am,' she said to Mrs Wilkieson, as she lay in bed. 'Do you mind explaining?'

Mrs Wilkieson explained tactfully.

'Oh yes!' said the Princess. 'I remember. And I had an accident in the mountains, didn't I? Didn't we meet a man who'd gone mad, and who shot my horse from under me?'

'Yes, you met a man who had gone out of his mind.'

The real affair was hushed up. The Princess departed east in a fortnight's time, in Miss Cummins's care. Apparently she had recovered herself entirely. She was the Princess, and a virgin intact.

But her bobbed hair was grey at the temples, and her eyes were a little mad. She was slightly crazy.

'Since my accident in the mountains, when a man went mad and shot my horse from under me, and my guide had to shoot him dead, I have never felt quite myself.'

So she put it.

Later, she married an elderly man, and seemed pleased.

The Virgin and the Gipsy

I

WHEN the vicar's wife went off with a young and penniless man the scandal knew no bounds. Her two little girls were only seven and nine years old respectively. And the vicar was such a good husband. True, his hair was grey. But his moustache was dark, he was handsome, and still full of furtive passion for his unrestrained and beautiful wife.

Why did she go? Why did she burst away with such an *éclat*[1] of revulsion, like a touch of madness?

Nobody gave any answer. Only the pious said she was a bad woman. While some of the good women kept silent. They knew.

The two little girls never knew. Wounded, they decided that it was because their mother found them negligible.

The ill wind that blows nobody any good swept away the vicarage family on its blast. Then lo and behold! the vicar, who was somewhat distinguished as an essayist and a controversialist, and whose case had aroused sympathy among the bookish men, received the living of Papplewick.[2] The Lord had tempered the wind of misfortune with a rectorate in the north country.

The rectory was a rather ugly stone house down by the river Papple, before you come into the village. Further on, beyond where the road crosses the stream, were the big old stone cotton-mills, once driven by water. The road curved up-hill, into the bleak stone streets of the village.

The vicarage family received decided modification, upon its transference into the rectory. The vicar, now the rector, fetched up his old mother and his sister, and a brother from the city. The two little girls had a very different milieu from the old home.

The rector was now forty-seven years old; he had displayed an intense and not very dignified grief after the flight of his wife. Sympathetic ladies had stayed him from suicide. His hair was

472 The Virgin and the Gipsy

almost white, and he had a wide-eyed, tragic look. You had only to look at him, to know how dreadful it all was, and how he had been wronged.

Yet somewhere there was a false note. And some of the ladies, who had sympathised most profoundly with the vicar, secretly rather disliked the rector. There was a certain furtive self-righteousness about him, when all was said and done.

The little girls, of course, in the vague way of children, accepted the family verdict. Granny, who was over seventy and whose sight was failing, became the central figure in the house. Aunt Cissie, who was over forty, pale, pious, and gnawed by an inward worm, kept house. Uncle Fred, a stingy and grey-faced man of forty, who just lived dingily for himself, went into town every day. And the rector, of course, was the most important person, after Granny.

They called her The Mater. She was one of those physically vulgar, clever old bodies who had got her own way all her life by buttering the weaknesses of her men-folk. Very quickly she took her cue. The rector still 'loved' his delinquent wife, and would 'love her' till he died. Therefore hush! The rector's feeling was sacred. In his heart was enshrined the pure girl he had wedded and worshipped.

Out in the evil world, at the same time, there wandered a disreputable woman who had betrayed the rector and abandoned his little children. She was now yoked to a young and despicable man, who no doubt would bring her the degradation she deserved. Let this be clearly understood, and then hush! For in the pure loftiness of the rector's heart still bloomed the pure white snow-flower of his young bride. This white snow-flower did not wither. That other creature, who had gone off with that despicable young man, was none of his affair.

The Mater, who had been somewhat diminished and insignificant as a widow in a small house, now climbed into the chief arm-chair in the rectory, and planted her old bulk firmly again. She was not going to be dethroned. Astutely she gave a sigh of homage to the rector's fidelity to the pure white snowflower, while she pretended to disapprove. In sly reverence for her son's great love, she spoke no word against that nettle which flourished in the evil world, and which had once been called Mrs Arthur Saywell. Now, thank heaven, having married again, she was no more Mrs Arthur Saywell. No woman bore the rector's name. The pure white snow-flower bloomed *in perpetuum*, without nomenclature. The family even thought of her as She-who-was-Cynthia.

All this was water on the Mater's mill. It secured her against Arthur's ever marrying again. She had him by his feeblest weakness, his skulking self-love. He had married an imperishable white snow-flower. Lucky man! He had been injured. Unhappy man! He had suffered. Ah, what a heart of love! And he had – forgiven! Yes, the white snow-flower was forgiven. He even had made provision in his will for her, when that other scoundrel – But hush! Don't even *think* too near to that horrid nettle in the rank outer world! She-who-was-Cynthia. Let the white snow-flower bloom inaccessible on the heights of the past. The present is another story.

The children were brought up in this atmosphere of cunning self-sanctification and of unmentionability. They too, saw the snow-flower on inaccessible heights. They too knew that it was throned in lone splendour aloft their lives, never to be touched.

At the same time, out of the squalid world sometimes would come a rank, evil smell of selfishness and degraded lust, the smell of that awful nettle, She-who-was-Cynthia. This nettle actually contrived, at intervals, to get a little note through to the girls, her children. And at this the silver-haired Mater shook inwardly with hate. For if She-who-was-Cynthia ever came back, there wouldn't be much left of the Mater. A secret gust of hate went from the old granny to the girls, children of that foul nettle of lust, that Cynthia who had had such an affectionate contempt for the Mater.

Mingled with all this, was the children's perfectly distinct recollection of their real home, the vicarage in the south, and their glamorous but not very dependable mother, Cynthia. She had made a great glow, a flow of life, like a swift and dangerous sun in the home, forever coming and going. They always associated her presence with brightness, but also with danger; with glamour, but with fearful selfishness.

Now the glamour was gone, and the white snow-flower, like a porcelain wreath, froze on its grave. The danger of instability, the peculiarly *dangerous* sort of selfishness, like lions and tigers, was also gone. There was now a complete stability, in which one could perish safely.

But they were growing up. And as they grew, they became more definitely confused, more actively puzzled. The Mater, as she grew older, grew blinder. Somebody had to lead her about. She did not get up till towards midday. Yet blind or bed-ridden, she held the house.

Besides, she wasn't bed-ridden. Whenever the *men* were present, the Mater was in her throne. She was too cunning to court neglect. Especially as she had rivals.

Her great rival was the younger girl, Yvette. Yvette had some of the vague, careless blitheness of She-who-was-Cynthia. But this one was more docile. Granny perhaps had caught her in time. Perhaps!

The rector adored Yvette, and spoiled her with a doting fondness; as much as to say: am I not a soft-hearted, indulgent old boy! He liked to have this opinion of himself, and the Mater knew his weaknesses to a hair's breadth. She knew them, and she traded on them by turning them into decorations for him, for his character. He wanted, in his own eyes, to have a fascinating character, as women want to have fascinating dresses. And the Mater cunningly put beauty-spots over his defects and deficiencies. Her mother-love gave her the clue to his weaknesses, and she hid them for him with decorations. Whereas She-who-was-Cynthia —! But don't mention *her*, in this connexion. In her eyes, the rector was almost hump-backed and an idiot.

The funny thing was, Granny secretly hated Lucille, the elder girl, more than the pampered Yvette. Lucille, the uneasy and irritable, was more conscious of being under Granny's power, than was the spoilt and vague Yvette.

On the other hand, Aunt Cissie hated Yvette. She hated her very name. Aunt Cissie's life had been sacrificed to the Mater, and Aunt Cissie knew it, and the Mater knew she knew it. Yet as the years went on, it became a convention. The convention of Aunt Cissie's sacrifice was accepted by everybody, including

the self-same Cissie. She prayed a good deal about it. Which also
showed that she had her own private feelings somewhere, poor
thing. She had ceased to be Cissie, she had lost her life and her
sex. And now, she was creeping towards fifty, strange green
flares of rage would come up in her, and at such times, she was
insane.

But Granny held her in her power. And Aunt Cissie's one
object in life was to look after the Mater.

Aunt Cissie's green flares of hellish hate would go up against
all young things, sometimes. Poor thing, she prayed and tried to
obtain forgiveness from heaven. But what had been done to her,
she could not forgive, and the vitriol would spurt in her veins
sometimes.

It was not as if the Mater were a warm, kindly soul. She wasn't.
She only seemed it, cunningly. And the fact dawned gradually
on the girls. Under her old-fashioned lace cap, under her silver
hair, under the black silk of her stout, short, forward-bulging
body, this old woman had a cunning heart, seeking for ever her
own female power. And through the weakness of the unfresh,
stagnant men she had bred, she kept her power, as her years
rolled on, from seventy to eighty, and from eighty on the new
lap, towards ninety.

For in the family there was a whole tradition of 'loyalty':
loyalty to one another, and especially to the Mater. The Mater,
of course, was the pivot of the family. The family was her own
extended ego. Naturally she covered it with her power. And her
sons and daughters, being weak and disintegrated, naturally were
loyal. Outside the family, what was there for them but danger
and insult and ignominy? Had not the rector experienced it, in
his marriage? So now, caution! Caution and loyalty, fronting the
world! Let there be as much hate and friction *inside* the family,
as you like. To the outer world, a stubborn fence of unison.

II

But it was not until the girls finally came home from school that
they felt the full weight of Granny's dead old hand on their lives.
Lucille was now nearly twenty-one, and Yvette nineteen. They

had been to a good girls' school, and had had a finishing year in Lausanne, and were quite the usual thing, tall young creatures with fresh, sensitive faces and bobbed hair and young-manly, deuce-take-it manners.

'What's so awfully *boring* about Papplewick,' said Yvette, as they stood on the Channel boat watching the grey, grey cliffs of Dover draw near, 'is that there are no *men* about. Why doesn't Daddy have some good old sports for friends? As for Uncle Fred, he's the limit!'

'Oh, you never know what will turn up,' said Lucille, more philosophic.

'You jolly well know what to expect,' said Yvette. 'Choir on Sundays, and I hate mixed choirs. Boys' voices are *lovely*, when there are no women. And Sunday School and Girls' Friendly, and socials, all the dear old souls that inquire after Granny! Not a decent young fellow for miles.'

'Oh, I don't know!' said Lucille. 'There's always the Framleys. And you know Gerry Somercotes *adores* you.'

'Oh but I *hate* fellows who adore me!' cried Vvette, turning up her sensitive nose. 'They *bore* me. They hang on like lead.'

'Well what *do* you want, if you can't stand being adored? *I* think it's perfectly all right to be adored. You know you'll never marry them, so why not let them go on adoring, if it amuses them.'

'Oh but I *want* to get married,' cried Yvette.

'Well in that case, let them go on adoring you till you find one that you can *possibly* marry.'

'I never should, that way. Nothing puts me off like an adoring fellow. They *bore* me so! They make me feel beastly.'

'Oh, so they do me, if they get pressing. But at a distance, I think they're rather nice.'

'I should like to fall *violently* in love.'

'Oh, very likely! I shouldn't! I should hate it. Probably so would you, if it actually happened. After all, we've got to settle down a bit, before we know what we want.'

'But don't you *hate* going back to Papplewick?' cried Yvette, turning up her young, sensitive nose.

'No, not particularly. I suppose we shall be rather bored. I wish Daddy would get a car. I suppose we shall have to drag the old bikes out. Wouldn't you like to get up to Tansy Moor?'

'Oh, *love* it! Though it's an awful *strain*, shoving an old push-bike up those hills.'

The ship was nearing the grey cliffs. It was summer, but a grey day. The two girls wore their coats with fur collars turned up, and little *chic* hats pulled down over their ears. Tall, slender, fresh-faced, naïve, yet confident, too confident, in their schoolgirlish arrogance, they were so terribly English. They seemed so free, and were as a matter of fact so tangled and tied up, inside themselves. They seemed so dashing and unconventional, and were really so conventional, so, as it were, shut up indoors inside themselves. They looked like bold, tall young sloops, just slipping from the harbour, into the wide seas of life. And they were, as a matter of fact, two poor young rudderless lives, moving from one chain anchorage to another.

The rectory struck a chill into their hearts as they entered. It seemed ugly, and almost sordid, with the dank air of that middle-class, degenerated comfort which has ceased to be comfortable and has turned stuffy, unclean. The hard, stone house struck the girls as being unclean, they could not have said why. The shabby furniture seemed somehow sordid, nothing was fresh. Even the food at meals had that awful dreary sordidness which is so repulsive to a young thing coming from abroad. Roast beef and wet cabbage, cold mutton and mashed potatoes, sour pickles, inexcusable puddings.

Granny, who 'loved a bit of pork', also had special dishes, beef-tea and rusks, or a small savoury custard. The grey-faced Aunt Cissie ate nothing at all. She would sit at table, and take a single lonely and naked boiled potato on to her plate. She never ate meat. So she sat in sordid durance, while the meal went on, and Granny quickly slobbered her portion – lucky if she spilled nothing on her protuberant stomach. The food was not appetizing in itself: how could it be, when Aunt Cissie hated food herself, hated the fact of eating, and never could keep a maid-servant for three months? The girls ate with repulsion, Lucille bravely bearing up, Yvette's tender nose showing her disgust. Only the rector, white-haired, wiped his long grey moustache with his serviette, and cracked jokes. He too was getting heavy and inert, sitting in his study all day, never taking exercise. But he cracked sarcastic little jokes all the time, sitting there under the shelter of the Mater.

The country, with its steep hills and its deep, narrow valleys, was dark and gloomy, yet had a certain powerful strength of its own. Twenty miles away was the black industrialism of the north. Yet the village of Papplewick was comparatively lonely, almost lost, the life in it stony and dour. Everything was stone, with a hardness that was almost poetic, it was so unrelenting.[3]

It was as the girls had known: they went back into the choir, they helped in the parish. But Yvette struck absolutely against Sunday School, the Band of Hope,[4] the Girls' Friendlies – indeed against all those functions that were conducted by determined old maids and obstinate, stupid elderly men. She avoided church duties as much as possible, and got away from the rectory whenever she could. The Framleys, a big, untidy, jolly family up at the Grange, were an enormous stand-by. And if anybody asked her out to a meal, even if a woman in one of the workmen's houses asked her to stay to tea, she accepted at once. In fact, she was rather thrilled. She liked talking to the working men, they had often such fine, hard heads. But of course they were in another world.

So the months went by. Gerry Somercotes was still an adorer. There were others, too, sons of farmers or mill-owners. Yvette really ought to have had a good time. She was always out to parties and dances, friends came for her in their motor-cars, and off she went to the city, to the afternoon dance in the chief hotel, or in the gorgeous new Palais de Danse, called the Pally.

Yet she always seemed like a creature mesmerized. She was never free to be quite jolly. Deep inside her worked an intolerable irritation, which she thought she *ought* not to feel, and which she hated feeling, thereby making it worse. She never understood at all whence it arose.

At home, she truly was irritable, and outrageously rude to Aunt Cissie. In fact Yvette's awful temper became one of the family by-words.

Lucille, always more practical, got a job in the city as private secretary to a man who needed somebody with fluent French and shorthand. She went back and forth every day, by the same train as Uncle Fred. But she never travelled with him, and wet or fine, bicycled to the station, while he went on foot.

The two girls were both determined that what they wanted was a really jolly social life. And they resented with fury that the rectory was, for their friends, impossible. There were only four rooms downstairs: the kitchen, where lived the two discontented maid-servants: the dark dining-room: the rector's study: and the big, 'homely', dreary living-room or drawing-room. In the dining-room there was a gas fire. Only in the living-room was a good hot fire kept going. Because of course, here Granny reigned.

In this room the family was assembled. At evening, after dinner, Uncle Fred and the rector invariably played cross-word puzzles with Granny.

'Now, Mater, are you ready? N blank blank blank blank W: a Siamese functionary.'

'Eh? Eh? M blank blank blank blank W?'

Granny was hard of hearing.

'No Mater. Not M! N blank blank blank blank W: a Siamese functionary.'

'N blank blank blank blank W: a Chinese functionary.'

'SIAMESE.'

'Eh?'

'SIAMESE! SIAM!'

'A Siamese functionary! Now what can that be?' said the old lady profoundly, folding her hands on her round stomach. Her two sons proceeded to make suggestions, at which she said Ah! Ah! The rector was amazingly clever at cross-word puzzles. But Fred had a certain technical vocabulary.

'This certainly is a hard nut to crack,' said the old lady, when they were all stuck.

Meanwhile Lucille sat in a corner with her hands over her ears, pretending to read, and Yvette irritably made drawings, or hummed loud and exasperating tunes, to add to the family concert. Aunt Cissie continually reached for a chocolate, and her jaws worked ceaselessly. She literally lived on chocolates. Sitting in the distance, she put another into her mouth, then looked again at the parish magazine. Then she lifted her head, and saw it was time to fetch Granny's cup of Horlicks.

While she was gone, in nervous exasperation Yvette would open the window. The room was never fresh, she imagined it smelt: smelt of Granny. And Granny, who was hard of hearing, heard like a weasel when she wasn't wanted to.

'Did you open the window, Yvette? I think you might remember there are older people than yourself in the room,' she said.

'It's stifling! It's unbearable! No wonder we've all of us always got colds.'

'I'm sure the room is large enough, and a good fire burning.' The old lady gave a little shudder. 'A draught to give us all our death.'

'Not a draught at all,' roared Yvette. 'A breath of fresh air.'

The old lady shuddered again, and said: 'Indeed!'

The rector, in silence, marched to the window and firmly closed it. He did not look at his daughter meanwhile. He hated thwarting her. But she must know what's what!

The cross-word puzzles, invented by Satan himself, continued till Granny had had her Horlicks, and was to go to bed. Then came the ceremony of Goodnight! Everybody stood up. The girls went to be kissed by the blind old woman. The rector gave his arm, and Aunt Cissie followed with a candle.

But this was already nine o'clock, although Granny was really getting old, and should have been in bed sooner. But when she was in bed, she could not sleep, till Aunt Cissie came.

'You see,' said Granny, 'I have *never* slept alone. For fifty-four years I never slept a night without the Pater's arm round me. And when he was gone, I tried to sleep alone. But as sure as my eyes closed to sleep, my heart nearly jumped out of my body, and I lay in a palpitation. Oh, you may think what you will, but it was a fearful experience, after fifty-four years of perfect married life! I would have prayed to be taken first, but the Pater, well, no I don't think he would have been able to bear up.'

So Aunt Cissie slept with Granny. And she hated it. She said *she* could never sleep. And she grew greyer and greyer, and the food in the house got worse, and Aunt Cissie had to have an operation.

But The Mater rose as ever, towards noon, and at the midday meal, she presided from her arm-chair, with her stomach protruding; her reddish, pendulous face, that had a sort of horrible majesty, dropping soft under the wall of her high brow, and her blue eyes peering unseeing. Her white hair was getting scanty, it was altogether a little indecent. But the rector jovially cracked his jokes to her, and she pretended to disapprove. But she was perfectly complacent, sitting in her ancient obesity, and after meals, getting the wind from her stomach, pressing her bosom with her hand as she 'rifted' in gross physical complacency.

What the girls minded most was that, when they brought their young friends to the house, Granny always was there, like some awful idol of old flesh, consuming all the attention. There was only the one room for everybody. And there sat the old lady, with Aunt Cissie keeping an acrid guard over her. Everybody must be presented first to Granny: she was ready to be genial, she liked company. She had to know who everybody was, where they came from, every circumstance of their lives. And then, when she was *au fait*,[5] she could get hold of the conversation.

Nothing could be more exasperating to the girls. 'Isn't old Mrs Saywell wonderful! She takes *such* an interest in life, at nearly ninety!'

'She does take an interest in people's affairs, if that's life,' said Yvette.

Then she would immediately feel guilty. After all, it *was* wonderful to be nearly ninety, and have such a clear mind! And Granny never *actually* did anybody any harm. It was more that she was in the way. And perhaps it was rather awful to hate somebody because they were old and in the way.

Yvette immediately repented, and was nice. Granny blossomed forth into reminiscences of when she was a girl, in the little town in Buckinghamshire. She talked and talked away, and was *so* entertaining. She really *was* rather wonderful.

Then in the afternoon Lottie and Ella and Bob Framley came, with Leo Wetherell.

'Oh, come in!' – and in they all trooped to the sitting-room, where Granny, in her white cap, sat by the fire.

'Granny, this is Mr Wetherell.'

'Mr what-did-you-say? You must excuse me, I'm a little deaf!'

Granny gave her hand to the uncomfortable young man, and gazed silently at him, sightlessly.

'You are not from our parish?' she asked him.

'Dinnington!' he shouted.

'We want to go a picnic tomorrow, to Bonsall Head, in Leo's car. We can all squeeze in,' said Ella, in a low voice.

'Did you say Bonsall Head?' asked Granny.

'Yes!'

There was a blank silence.

'Did you say you were going in a car?'

'Yes! In Mr Wetherell's.'

'I hope he's a good driver. It's a very dangerous road.'

'He's a *very* good driver.'

'Not a very good driver?'

'Yes! He *is* a very good driver.'

'If you go to Bonsall Head, I think I must send a message to Lady Louth.'

Granny always dragged in this miserable Lady Louth, when there was company.

'Oh, we shan't go that way,' cried Yvette.

'Which way?' said Granny. 'You must go by Heanor.'

The whole party sat, as Bob expressed it, like stuffed ducks, fidgeting on their chairs.

Aunt Cissie came in – and then the maid with the tea. There was the eternal and everlasting piece of bought cake. Then appeared a plate of little fresh cakes. Aunt Cissie had actually sent to the baker's.

'Tea, Mater!'

The old lady gripped the arms on her chair. Everybody rose and stood, while she waded slowly across, on Aunt Cissie's arm, to her place at table.

During tea Lucille came in from town, from her job. She was simply worn out, with black marks under her eyes. She gave a cry, seeing all the company.

As soon as the noise had subsided, and the awkwardness was resumed, Granny said:

'You have never mentioned Mr Wetherell to me, have you, Lucille?'

'I don't remember,' said Lucille.

'You can't have done. The name is strange to me.'

Yvette absently grabbed another cake, from the now almost empty plate. Aunt Cissie, who was driven almost crazy by Yvette's vague and inconsiderate ways, felt the green rage fuse in her heart. She picked up her own plate, on which was the one cake she allowed herself, and said with vitriolic politeness, offering it to Yvette:

'Won't you have mine?'

'Oh thanks!' said Yvette, starting in her angry vagueness. And with an appearance of the same insouciance, she helped herself to Aunt Cissie's cake also, adding as an afterthought: 'If you're sure you don't want it.'

She now had two cakes on her plate. Lucille had gone white as a ghost, bending to her tea. Aunt Cissie sat with a green look of poisonous resignation. The awkwardness was an agony.

But Granny, bulkily enthroned and unaware, only said, in the centre of the cyclone:

'If you are motoring to Bonsall Head tomorrow, Lucille, I wish you would take a message from me to Lady Louth.'

'Oh!' said Lucille, giving a queer look across the table at the sightless old woman. Lady Louth was the King Charles' Head[6] of the family, invariably produced by Granny for the benefit of visitors. 'Very well!'

'She was so very kind last week. She sent her chauffeur over with a Cross-word Puzzle book for me.'

'But you thanked her then,' cried Yvette.

'I should like to send her a note.'

'We can post it,' cried Lucille.

'Oh no! I should like you to take it. When Lady Louth called last time . . .'

The young ones sat like a shoal of young fishes dumbly mouthing at the surface of the water, while Granny went on about Lady Louth. Aunt Cissie, the two girls knew, was still helpless, almost unconscious in a paroxysm of rage about the cake. Perhaps, poor thing, she was praying.

It was a mercy when the friends departed. But by that time the two girls were both haggard-eyed. And it was then that Yvette, looking round, suddenly saw the stony, implacable will-to-power in the old and motherly-seeming Granny. She sat there bulging backwards in her chair, impassive, her reddish, pendulous old face rather mottled, almost unconscious, but implacable, her face like a mask that hid something stony, relentless. It was the static inertia of her unsavoury power. Yet in a minute she would open her ancient mouth to find out every detail about Leo Wetherell. For the moment she was hibernating in her oldness, her agedness. But in a minute her mouth would open, her mind would flicker awake, and with her insatiable greed for life, other people's life, she would start on her quest for every detail. She was like the old toad which Yvette had watched, fascinated, as it sat on the ledge of the bee-hive, immediately in front of the little entrance by which the bees emerged, and which, with a demonish lightning-like snap of its pursed jaws, caught every bee as it came out to launch into the air, swallowed them one after the other, as if it could consume the whole hive-full, into its aged, bulging, purse-like wrinkledness. It had been swallowing bees as they launched into the air of spring, year after year, year after year, for generations.

But the gardener, called by Yvette, was in a rage, and killed the creature with a stone.

' 'Appen tha *art* good for th' snails,' he said, as he came down with the stone. 'But tha 'rt none goin' ter emp'y th' bee-'ive into thy guts.'

III

The next day was dull and low, and the roads were awful, for it had been raining for weeks, yet the young ones set off on their trip, without taking Granny's message either. They just slipped out while she was making her slow trip upstairs after lunch. Not for anything would they have called at Lady Louth's house. That widow of a knighted doctor, a harmless person indeed, had become an obnoxity in their lives.

Six young rebels, they sat very perkily in the car as they swished through the mud. Yet they had a peaked look too. After all, they had nothing really to rebel against, any of them. They were left so very free in their movements. Their parents let them do almost entirely as they liked. There wasn't really a fetter to break, nor a prison-bar to file through, nor a bolt to shatter. The keys of their lives were in their own hands. And there they dangled inert.

It is very much easier to shatter prison bars than to open undiscovered doors to life. As the younger generation finds out, somewhat to its chagrin. True, there was Granny. But poor old Granny, you couldn't actually say to her: 'Lie down and die, you old woman!' She might be an old nuisance, but she never really *did* anything. It wasn't fair to hate her.

So the young people set off on their jaunt, trying to be very full of beans. They could really do as they liked. And so, of course, there was nothing to do but sit in the car and talk a lot of criticism of other people, and silly flirty gallantry that was really rather a bore. If there had only been a few 'strict orders' to be disobeyed! But nothing: beyond the refusal to carry the message to Lady Louth, of which the rector would approve, because he didn't encourage King Charles' Head either.

They sang, rather scrappily, the latest would-be comic songs, as they went through the grim villages. In the great park the deer were in groups near the road, roe deer and fallow, nestling in the gloom of the afternoon under the oaks by the road, as if for the stimulus of human company.

Yvette insisted on stopping and getting out to talk to them. The girls, in their Russian boots, tramped through the damp grass, while the deer watched them with big, unfrightened eyes. The hart trotted away mildly, holding back his head, because of the weight of the horns. But the doe, balancing her big ears, did not rise from under the tree, with her half-grown young ones, till the girls were almost in touch. Then she walked light-foot away, lifting her tail from her spotted flanks, while the young ones nimbly trotted.

'Aren't they awfully dainty and nice!' cried Yvette. 'You'd wonder they could lie so cosily in this horrid wet grass.'

'Well I suppose they've got to lie down *sometime*,' said Lucille. 'And it's *fairly* dry under the tree.' She looked at the crushed grass, where the deer had lain.

Yvette went and put her hand down, to feel how it felt.

'Yes!' she said, doubtfully, 'I believe it's a bit warm.'

The deer had bunched again a few yards away, and were standing motionless in the gloom of the afternoon. Away below the slopes of grass and trees, beyond the swift river with its balustraded bridge, sat the huge ducal house, one or two chimneys smoking bluely.[7] Behind it rose purplish woods.

The girls, pushing their fur collars up to their ears, dangling one long arm, stood watching in silence, their wide Russian boots protecting them from the wet grass. The great house squatted square and creamy-grey below. The deer, in little groups, were scattered under the old trees close by. It all seemed so still, so unpretentious, and so sad.

'I wonder where the Duke is now,' said Ella.

'Not here, wherever he is,' said Lucille. 'I expect he's abroad where the sun shines.'

The motor horn called from the road, and they heard Leo's voice:

'Come on, boys! If we're going to get to the Head and down to Amberdale[8] for tea, we'd better move.'

They crowded into the car again, with chilled feet, and set off through the park, past the silent spire of the church, out through the great gates and over the bridge, on into the wide, damp, stony village of Woodlinkin,[9] where the river ran. And thence, for a long time, they stayed in the mud and dark and dampness of the valley, often with sheer rock above them; the water brawling on one hand, the steep rock or dark trees on the other.

Till, through the darkness of overhanging trees, they began to climb, and Leo changed the gear. Slowly the car toiled up through the whitey-grey mud, into the stony village of Bolehill,[10] that hung on the slope, round the old cross, with its steps, that stood where the road branched, on past the cottages whence came a wonderful smell of hot tea-cakes, and beyond, still upwards, under dripping trees and past broken slopes of bracken, always climbing. Until the cleft became shallower, and the trees finished, and the slopes on either side were bare, gloomy grass, with low dry-stone walls. They were emerging on to the Head.

The party had been silent for some time. On either side the road was grass, then a low stone fence, and the swelling curve of the hill-summit, traced with the low, dry-stone walls. Above this, the low sky.

The car ran out, under the low, grey sky, on the naked tops.

'Shall we stay a moment?' called Leo.

'Oh yes!' cried the girls.

And they scrambled out once more, to look around. They knew the place quite well. But still, if one came to the Head, one got out to look.

The hills were like the knuckles of a hand, the dales were below, between the fingers, narrow, steep, and dark. In the deeps a train was steaming, slowly pulling north: a small thing of the under-world. The noise of the engine re-echoed curiously upwards. Then came the dull, familiar sound of blasting in a quarry.

Leo, always on the go, moved quickly.

'Shall we be going?' he said. 'Do we *want* to get down to Amberdale for tea? Or shall we try somewhere nearer?'

They all voted for Amberdale, for the Marquis of Grantham.

'Well, which way shall we go back? Shall we go by Codnor and over Crosshill, or shall we go by Ashbourne?'

There was the usual dilemma. Then they finally decided on the Codnor top road. Off went the car, gallantly.

They were on the top of the world, now, on the back of the fist. It was naked, too, as the back of your fist, high under heaven, and dull, heavy green. Only it was veined with a network of old stone walls, dividing the fields, and broken here and there with ruins of old lead-mines and works. A sparse stone farm bristled with six naked sharp trees. In the distance was a patch of smoky grey stone, a hamlet. In some fields grey, dark sheep fed silently, sombrely. But there was not a sound nor a movement. It was the roof of England, stony and arid as any roof. Beyond, below, were the shires.

' "And see the coloured counties –" ' [11] said Yvette to herself.

Here anyhow they were not coloured. A stream of rooks trailed out from nowhere. They had been walking, pecking, on a naked field that had been manured. The car ran on between the grass and the stone walls of the upland lane, and the young people were silent, looking out over the far network of stone fences, under the sky, looking for the curves downward that indicated a drop to one of the underneath, hidden dales.

Ahead was a light cart, driven by a man, and trudging along at the side was a woman, sturdy and elderly, with a pack on her back. The man in the cart had caught her up, and now was keeping pace.

The road was narrow. Leo sounded the horn sharply. The man on the cart looked round, but the woman on foot only trudged steadily, rapidly forward, without turning her head.

Yvette's heart gave a jump. The man on the cart was a gipsy, one of the black, loose-bodied, handsome sort. He remained seated on his cart, turning round and gazing at the occupants of the motor-car, from under the brim of his cap. And his pose was loose, his gaze insolent in its indifference. He had a thin black moustache under his thin, straight nose, and a big silk handkerchief of red and yellow tied round his neck. He spoke a word to the woman. She stood a second, solid, to turn round and look at the occupants of the car, which had now drawn quite close. Leo honked the horn again, imperiously. The woman, who had a grey-and-white kerchief tied round her head, turned sharply, to keep pace with the cart, whose driver also had settled back, and was lifting the reins, moving his loose, light shoulders. But still he did not pull aside.

Leo made the horn scream, as he put the brakes on and the car slowed up near the back of the cart. The gipsy turned round at the din, laughing in his dark face under his dark-green cap, and said something which they did not hear, showing white teeth under the line of black moustache, and making a gesture with his dark, loose hand.

'Get out o' the way then!' yelled Leo.

For answer, the man delicately pulled the horse to a standstill, as it curved to the side of the road. It was a good roan horse, and a good, natty, dark-green cart.

Leo, in a rage, had to jam on the brake and pull up too.

'Don't the pretty young ladies want to hear their fortunes?' said the gipsy on the cart, laughing except for his dark, watchful eyes, which went from face to face, and lingered on Yvette's young, tender face.

She met his dark eyes for a second, their level search, their insolence, their complete indifference to people like Bob and Leo, and something took fire in her breast. She thought: 'He is stronger than I am! He doesn't care!'

'Oh yes! let's!' cried Lucille at once.

'Oh yes!' chorused the girls.

'I say! What about the time?' cried Leo.

'Oh bother the old time! Somebody's always dragging in time by the forelock,' cried Lucille.

'Well, if you don't mind *when* we get back, *I* don't!' said Leo heroically.

The gipsy man had been sitting loosely on the side of his cart, watching the faces. He now jumped softly down from the shaft, his knees a bit stiff. He was apparently a man something over thirty, and a beau in his way. He wore a sort of shooting-jacket, double-breasted, coming only to the hips, of dark green-and-black frieze; rather tight black trousers, black boots, and a dark-green cap; with the big yellow-and-red bandanna handkerchief round his neck. His appearance was curiously elegant, and quite expensive in its gipsy style. He was handsome, too, pressing in his chin with the old, gipsy conceit, and now apparently not heeding the strangers any more, as he led his good roan horse off the road, preparing to back his cart.

The girls saw for the first time a deep recess in the side of the road, and two caravans smoking. Yvette got quickly down. They had suddenly come upon a disused quarry, cut into the slope of the road-side, and in this sudden lair, almost like a cave, were three caravans, dismantled for the winter. There was also, deep at the back, a shelter built of boughs, as a stable for the horse. The grey, crude rock rose high above the caravans, and curved round towards the road. The floor was heaped chips of stone, with grasses growing among. It was a hidden, snug winter camp.

The elderly woman with the pack had gone into one of the

caravans, leaving the door open. Two children were peeping out, showing black heads. The gipsy man gave a little call, as he backed his cart into the quarry, and an elderly man came out to help him untackle.

The gipsy himself went up the steps into the newest caravan, that had its door closed. Underneath, a tied-up dog ranged forth. It was a white hound spotted liver-coloured. It gave a low growl as Leo and Bob approached.

At the same moment, a dark-faced gipsy-woman with a pink shawl or kerchief round her head and big gold ear-rings in her ears, came down the steps of the newest caravan, swinging her flounced, voluminous green skirt. She was handsome in a bold, dark, long-faced way, just a bit wolfish. She looked like one of the bold, loping Spanish gipsies.

'Good-morning, my ladies and gentlemen,' she said, eyeing the girls from her bold, predative eyes. She spoke with a certain foreign stiffness.

'Good afternoon!' said the girls.

'Which beautiful little lady like to hear her fortune? Give me her little hand?'

She was a tall woman, with a frightening way of reaching forward her neck like a menace. Her eyes went from face to face, very active, heartlessly searching out what she wanted. Meanwhile the man, apparently her husband, appeared at the top of the caravan steps smoking a pipe, and with a small, black-haired child in his arms. He stood on his limber legs, casually looking down on the group, as if from a distance, his long black lashes lifted from his full, conceited, impudent black eyes. There was something peculiarly transfusing in his stare. Yvette felt it, felt it in her knees. She pretended to be interested in the white-and-liver-coloured hound.

'How much do you want, if we all have our fortunes told?' asked Lottie Framley, as the six fresh-faced young Christians hung back rather reluctantly from this pagan pariah woman.

'All of you? ladies and gentlemen, all?' said the woman shrewdly.

'I don't want mine told! You go ahead!' cried Leo.

'Neither do I,' said Bob. 'You four girls.'

'The four ladies?' said the gipsy woman, eyeing them shrewdly, after having looked at the boys. And she fixed her price. 'Each one give me a sheeling, and a little bit more for luck? a little bit!' She smiled in a way that was more wolfish than cajoling, and the force of her will was felt, heavy as iron beneath the velvet of her words.

'All right,' said Leo. 'Make it a shilling a head. Don't spin it out too long.'

'Oh, *you*!' cried Lucille at him. 'We want to hear it *all*.'

The woman took two wooden stools, from under a caravan, and placed them near the wheel. Then she took the tall, dark Lottie Framley by the hand, and bade her sit down.

'You don't care if everybody hear?' she said, looking up curiously into Lottie's face.

Lottie blushed dark with nervousness, as the gipsy woman held her hand, and stroked her palm with hard, cruel-seeming fingers.

'Oh, I don't mind,' she said.

The gipsy woman peered into the palm, tracing the lines of the hand with a hard, dark forefinger. But she seemed clean.

And slowly she told the fortune, while the others, standing listening, kept on crying out: 'Oh, that's Jim Baggaley! Oh, I don't believe it! Oh, that's not true! A fair woman who lives beneath a tree! Why whoever's that?' until Leo stopped them with a manly warning:

'Oh, hold on, girls! You give everything away.'

Lottie retired blushing and confused, and it was Ella's turn. She was much more calm and shrewd, trying to read the oracular words. Lucille kept breaking out with: Oh, I say. The gipsy man at the top of the steps stood imperturbable, without any expression at all. But his bold eyes kept staring at Yvette, she could feel them on her cheek, on her neck, and she dared not look up. But Framley would sometimes look up at him, and got a level stare back, from the handsome face of the male gipsy, from the dark conceited proud eyes. It was a peculiar look, in the eyes that belonged to the tribe of the humble: the pride of the pariah, the half-sneering challenge of the outcast, who sneered at law-abiding men, and went his own way. All the time, the gipsy man stood there, holding his child in his arms, looking on without being concerned.

Lucille was having her hand read – 'You have been across the sea, and there you met a man – a brown-haired man – but he was too old –'

'Oh, I *say*!' cried Lucille, looking round at Yvette.

But Yvette was abstracted, agitated, hardly heeding: in one of her mesmerized states.

'You will marry in a few years – not now, but a few years – perhaps four – and you will not be rich, but you will have plenty – enough – and you will go away, a long journey.'

'With my husband, or without?' cried Lucille.

'With him –'

When it came to Yvette's turn, and the woman looked up boldly, cruelly, searching for a long time in her face, Yvette said nervously:

'I don't think I want mine told. No, I won't have mine told! No I won't, really!'

'You are afraid of something?' said the gipsy woman cruelly.

'No, it's not that –' Yvette fidgeted.

'You have some secret. You are afraid I shall say it. Come, would you like to go in the caravan, where nobody hears?'

The woman was curiously insinuating; while Yvette was always wayward, perverse. The look of perversity was on her soft, frail young face now, giving her a queer hardness.

'Yes!' she said suddenly. 'Yes! I might do that!'

'Oh, I say!' cried the others. 'Be a sport!'

'I don't think you'd *better*!' cried Lucille.

'Yes!' said Yvette, with that hard little way of hers. 'I'll do that. I'll go in the caravan.'

The gipsy woman called something to the man on the steps. He went into the caravan for a moment or two, then re-appeared, and came down the steps, setting the small child on its uncertain feet, and holding it by the hand. A dandy, in his polished black boots, tight black trousers and tight dark-green jersey, he walked slowly across, with the toddling child, to where the elderly gipsy was giving the roan horse a feed of oats, in the bough shelter between pits of grey rock, with dry bracken upon the stone-chip floor. He looked at Yvette as he passed, staring her full in the eyes, with his pariah's bold yet dishonest stare. Something hard inside her met his stare. But the surface of her body seemed to turn to water. Nevertheless, something hard in her registered the peculiar pure lines of his face, of his straight, pure nose, of his cheeks and temples. The curious dark, suave purity of all his body, outlined in the green jersey: a purity like a living sneer.

And as he loped slowly past her, on his flexible hips, it seemed to her still that he was stronger than she was. Of all the men she had ever seen, this one was the only one who was stronger than she was, in her own kind of strength, her own kind of understanding.

So, with curiosity, she followed the woman up the steps of the caravan, the skirts of her well-cut tan coat swinging and almost showing her knees, under the pale-green cloth dress. She had long, long-striding, fine legs, too slim rather than too thick, and she wore curiously-patterned pale-and-fawn stockings of fine wool, suggesting the legs of some delicate animal.

At the top of the steps she paused and turned, debonair, to the others, saying in her naïve, lordly way, so off-hand:

'I won't let her be long.'

Her grey fur collar was open, showing her soft throat and pale green dress, her little plaited tan-coloured hat came down to her ears, round her soft, fresh face. There was something soft and yet overbearing, unscrupulous, about her. She knew the gipsy man had turned to look at her. She was aware of the pure dark nape of his neck, the black hair groomed away. He watched as she entered his house.

What the gipsy told her, no one ever knew. It was a long time to wait, the others felt. Twilight was deepening on the gloom, and it was turning raw and cold. From the chimney of the second caravan came smoke and a smell of rich food. The horse was fed, a yellow blanket strapped round him, and two gipsy men talked together in the distance, in low tones. There was a peculiar feeling of silence and secrecy in that lonely, hidden quarry.

At last the caravan door opened, and Yvette emerged, bending forward and stepping with long, witch-like slim legs down the steps. There was a stooping, witch-like silence about her as she emerged on the twilight.

'Did it seem long?' she said vaguely, not looking at anybody and keeping her own counsel hard within her soft, vague waywardness. 'I hope you weren't bored! Wouldn't tea be nice! Shall we go?'

'You get in!' said Bob. 'I'll pay.'

The gipsy-woman's full, metallic skirts of jade-green alpaca came swinging down the steps. She rose to her height, a big, triumphant-looking woman with a dark-wolf face. The pink cashmere kerchief, stamped with red roses, was slipping to one side over her black and crimped hair. She gazed at the young people in the twilight with bold arrogance.

Bob put two half-crowns in her hand.

'A little bit more, for luck, for your young lady's luck,' she wheedled, like a wheedling wolf. 'Another bit of silver, to bring you luck.'

'You've got a shilling for luck, that's enough,' said Bob calmly and quietly, as they moved away to the car.

'A little bit of silver! Just a little bit, for your luck in love!'

Yvette, with the sudden long, startling gestures of her long limbs, swung round as she was entering the car, and with long arm outstretched, strode and put something into the gipsy's hand, then stepped, bending her height, into the car.

'Prosperity to the beautiful young lady, and the gipsy's blessing on her,' came the suggestive, half-sneering voice of the woman.

The engine *birred!* then *birred!* again more fiercely, and started. Leo switched on the lights, and immediately the quarry with the gipsies fell back into the blackness of night.

'Good night!' called Yvette's voice, as the car started. But hers was the only voice that piped up, chirpy and impudent in its nonchalance. The headlights glared down the stone lane.

'Yvette, you've got to tell us what she said to you,' cried Lucille, in the teeth of Yvette's silent will *not* to be asked.

'Oh, nothing at *all* thrilling,' said Yvette, with false warmth. 'Just the usual old thing: a dark man who means good luck, and a fair one who means bad: and a death in the family, which if it means Granny, won't be so *very* awful: and I shall marry when I'm twenty-three, and have heaps of money and heaps of love, and two children. All sounds very nice, but it's a bit too much of a good thing, you know.'

'Oh, but why did you give her more money?'

'Oh well, I wanted to! You *have* to be a bit lordly with people like that —.'

IV

There was a terrific rumpus down at the rectory, on account of Yvette and the Window Fund. After the war, Aunt Cissie had set her heart on a stained glass window in the church, as a memorial for the men of the parish who had fallen. But the bulk of the fallen had been non-conformists, so the memorial took the form of an ugly little monument in front of the Wesleyan chapel.

This did not vanquish Aunt Cissie. She canvassed, she had bazaars, she made the girls get up amateur theatrical shows, for her precious window. Yvette, who quite liked the acting and showing-off part of it, took charge of the farce called *Mary in the Mirror*, and gathered in the proceeds, which were to be paid to the Window Fund when accounts were settled. Each of the girls was supposed to have a money-box for the Fund.

Aunt Cissie, feeling that the united sums must now almost suffice, suddenly called in Yvette's box. It contained fifteen shillings. There was a moment of green horror.

'Where is all the rest?'

'Oh!' said Yvette casually. 'I just borrowed it. It wasn't so awfully much.'

'What about the three pounds thirteen for *Mary in the Mirror*?' asked Aunt Cissie, as if the jaws of Hell were yawning.

'Oh quite! I just borrowed it. I can pay it back.'

Poor Aunt Cissie! The green tumour of hate burst inside her, and there was a ghastly, abnormal scene, which left Yvette shivering with fear and nervous loathing.

Even the rector was rather severe.

'If you needed money, why didn't you tell me?' he said coldly. 'Have you ever been refused anything in reason?'

'I — I thought it didn't matter,' stammered Yvette.

'And what have you done with the money?'

'I suppose I've spent it,' said Yvette, with wide, distraught eyes and a peaked face.

'Spent it, on what?'

'I can't remember everything: stockings and things, and I gave some of it away.'

Poor Yvette! Her lordly airs and ways were already hitting back at her, on the reflex. The rector was angry: his face had a snarling, doggish look, a sort of sneer. He was afraid his daughter was developing some of the rank, tainted qualities of She-who-was-Cynthia.

'You *would* do the large with somebody else's money, wouldn't you?' he said, with a cold, mongrel sort of sneer, which showed what an utter unbeliever he was, at the heart. The inferiority of a heart which has no core of warm belief in it, no pride in life. He had utterly no belief in her.

Yvette went pale, and very distant. Her pride, that frail, precious flame which everybody tried to quench, recoiled like a flame blown far away, on a cold wind, as if blown out, and her face, white now and still like a snowdrop, the white snow-flower of his conceit, seemed to have no life in it, only this pure, strange abstraction.

'He has no belief in me!' she thought in her soul. 'I am really nothing to him. I am nothing, only a shameful thing. Everything is shameful, everything is shameful!'

A flame of passion or rage, while it might have overwhelmed or infuriated her, would not have degraded her as did her father's unbelief, his final attitude of a sneer against her.

He became a little afraid, in the silence of sterile thought. After all, he needed the *appearance* of love and belief and bright life, he would never dare to face the fat worm of his own unbelief, that stirred in his heart.

'What have you to say for yourself?' he asked.

She only looked at him from that senseless snowdrop face which haunted him with fear, and gave him a helpless sense of guilt. That other one, She-who-was-Cynthia, she had looked back at him with the same numb, white fear, the fear of his degrading unbelief, the worm which was his heart's core. He *knew* his heart's core was a fat, awful worm. His dread was lest anyone else should know. His anguish of hate was against anyone who knew, and recoiled.

He saw Yvette recoiling, and immediately his manner changed to the worldly old good-humoured cynic which he affected.

'Ah well!' he said. 'You have to pay it back, my girl, that's all. I will advance you the money out of your allowance. But I shall charge you four per-cent a month interest. Even the devil himself must pay a percentage on his debts. Another time, if you can't trust yourself, don't handle money which isn't your own. Dishonesty isn't pretty.'

Yvette remained crushed, and deflowered and humiliated. She crept about, trailing the rays of her pride. She had a revulsion even from herself. Oh, why had she ever touched the leprous money! Her whole flesh shrank as if it were defiled. Why was that? Why, why was that?

She admitted herself wrong in having spent the money. 'Of course I shouldn't have done it. They are quite right to be angry,' she said to herself.

But where did the horrible wincing of her flesh come from? Why did she feel she had caught some physical contagion?

'Where you're so *silly*, Yvette,' Lucille lectured her: poor Lucille was in great distress – 'is that you give yourself away to them all. You might *know* they'd find out. I could have raised the money for you, and saved all this bother. It's perfectly awful! But you never will think beforehand where your actions are going to land you! Fancy Aunt Cissie saying all those things to you! How *awful*! Whatever would Mamma have said, if she'd heard it?'

When things went very wrong, they thought of their mother, and despised their father and all the low brood of the Saywells. Their mother, of course, had belonged to a higher, if more dangerous and 'immoral' world. More selfish, decidedly. But with a showier gesture. More unscrupulous and more easily moved to contempt: but not so humiliating.

Yvette always considered that she got her fine, delicate flesh from her mother. The Saywells were all a bit leathery, and grubby somewhere inside. But then the Saywells never let you down. Whereas the fine She-who-was-Cynthia had let the rector down with a bang, and his little children along with him. Her little children! They could not quite forgive her.

Only dimly, after the row, Yvette began to realize the other sanctity of herself, the sanctity of her sensitive, clean flesh and blood, which the Saywells with their so-called morality, succeeded in defiling. They always wanted to defile it. They were the life unbelievers. Whereas, perhaps She-who-was-Cynthia had only been a moral unbeliever.

Yvette went about dazed and peaked and confused. The rector paid in the money to Aunt Cissie, much to that lady's rage. The helpless tumour of her rage was still running. She would have liked to announce her niece's delinquency in the parish magazine. It was anguish to the destroyed woman that she could not publish the news to all the world. The selfishness! The selfishness! The selfishness!

Then the rector handed his daughter a little account with himself: her debt to him, interest thereon, the amount deducted from her small allowance. But to her credit he had placed a guinea, which was the fee he had to pay for complicity.

'As father of the culprit,' he said humorously, 'I am fined one guinea. And with that I wash the ashes out of my hair.'

He was always generous about money. But somehow, he seemed to think that by being free about money he could absolutely call himself a generous man. Whereas he used money, even generosity, as a hold over her.

But he let the affair drop entirely. He was by this time more amused than anything, to judge from appearances. He thought still he was safe.

Aunt Cissie, however, could not get over her convulsion. One night when Yvette had gone rather early, miserably, to bed, when Lucille was away at a party, and she was lying with soft, peaked limbs aching with a sort of numbness and defilement, the door softly opened, and there stood Aunt Cissie, pushing her grey-green face through the opening of the door. Yvette started up in terror.

'Liar! Thief! Selfish little beast!' hissed the maniacal face of Aunt Cissie. 'You little hypocrite! You liar! You selfish beast! You greedy little beast!'

There was such extraordinary impersonal hatred in that grey-green mask, and those frantic words, that Yvette opened her mouth to scream with hysterics. But Aunt Cissie shut the door as suddenly as she had opened it, and disappeared. Yvette leaped from her bed and turned the key. Then she crept back, half demented with fear of the squalid abnormal, half numbed with paralysis of damaged pride. And amid it all, up came a bubble of distracted laughter. It *was* so filthy ridiculous!

Aunt Cissie's behaviour did not hurt the girl so very much. It was after all somewhat fantastic. Yet hurt she was: in her limbs, in her body, in her sex, hurt. Hurt, numbed, and half destroyed, with only her nerves vibrating and jangled. And still so young, she could not conceive what was happening.

Only she lay and wished she were a gipsy. To live in a camp, in a caravan, and never set foot in a house, not know the existence of a parish, never look at a church. Her heart was hard with repugnance, against the rectory. She loathed these houses with their indoor sanitation and their bathrooms, and their extra-ordinary repulsiveness. She hated the rectory, and everything it implied. The whole stagnant, sewerage sort of life, where sewerage is never mentioned, but where it seems to smell from the centre to every two-legged inmate, from Granny to the servants, was foul. If gipsies had no bathrooms, at least they had no sewerage. There was fresh air. In the rectory there was *never* fresh air. And in the souls of the people, the air was stale till it stank.

Hate kindled her heart, as she lay with numbed limbs. And she thought of the words of the gipsy woman: 'There is a dark man who never lived in a house. He loves you. The other people are treading on your heart. They will tread on your heart till you think it is dead. But the dark man will blow the one spark up into fire again, good fire. You will see what good fire.'

Even as the woman was saying it, Yvette felt there was some duplicity somewhere. But she didn't mind. She hated with the cold, acrid hatred of a child the rectory interior, the sort of putridity in the life. She liked that big, swarthy, wolf-like gipsy-woman, with the big gold rings in her ears, the pink scarf over her wavy black hair, the tight bodice of brown velvet, the green, fan-like skirt. She liked her dusky, strong, relentless hands, that had pressed so firm, like wolf's paws, in Yvette's own soft palm. She liked her. She liked the danger and the covert fearlessness of her. She liked her covert, unyielding sex, that was immoral, but with a hard, defiant pride of its own. Nothing would ever get that woman under. She would despise the rectory and the rectory morality, utterly! She would strangle Granny with one hand. And she would have the same contempt for Daddy and for Uncle Fred, as men, as she would have for fat old slobbery Rover, the Newfoundland dog. A great, sardonic female contempt, for such domesticated dogs, calling themselves men.

And the gipsy man himself! Yvette quivered suddenly, as if she had seen his big, bold eyes upon her, with the naked insinuation of desire in them. The absolutely naked insinuation of desire made her lie prone and powerless in the bed, as if a drug had cast her in a new, molten mould.

She never confessed to anybody that two of the ill-starred Window Fund pounds had gone to the gipsy woman. What if Daddy and Aunt Cissie knew *that*! Yvette stirred luxuriously in the bed. The thought of the gipsy had released the life of her limbs, and crystallized in her heart the hate of the rectory: so that now she felt potent, instead of impotent.

When, later, Yvette told Lucille about Aunt Cissie's dramatic interlude in the bedroom doorway, Lucille was indignant.

'Oh, hang it all!' cried she. 'She might let it drop now. I should think we've heard enough about it by now! Good heavens, you'd think Aunt Cissie was a perfect bird of paradise! Daddy's dropped it, and after all, it's his business if it's anybody's. Let Aunt Cissie shut up!'

It was the very fact that the rector had dropped it, and that he again treated the vague and inconsiderate Yvette as if she were some specially-licensed being, that kept Aunt Cissie's bile flowing. The fact that Yvette really was most of the time unaware of other people's feelings, and being unaware, couldn't care about them, nearly sent Aunt Cissie mad. Why should that young creature, with a delinquent mother, go through life as a privileged being, even unaware of other people's existence, though they were under her nose.

Lucille at this time was very irritable. She seemed as if she simply went a little unbalanced, when she entered the rectory. Poor Lucille, she was so thoughtful and responsible. She did all the extra troubling, thought about doctors, medicines, servants, and all that sort of thing. She slaved conscientiously at her job all day in town, working in a room with artificial light from ten till five. And she came home to have her nerves rubbed almost to frenzy by Granny's horrible and persistent inquisitiveness and parasitic agedness.

The affair of the Window Fund had apparently blown over, but there remained a stuffy tension in the atmosphere. The weather continued bad. Lucille stayed at home on the afternoon of her half holiday, and did herself no good by it. The rector was in his study, she and Yvette were making a dress for the latter young woman, Granny was resting on the couch.

The dress was of blue silk velours, French material, and was going to be very becoming. Lucille made Yvette try it on again: she was nervously uneasy about the hang, under the arms.

'Oh bother!' cried Yvette, stretching her long, tender, childish arms, that tended to go bluish with the cold. 'Don't be so frightfully *fussy*, Lucille! It's quite all right.'

'If that's all the thanks I get, slaving my half day away making dresses for you, I might as well do something for myself!'

'Well, Lucille! You know I never *asked* you! You know you can't bear it unless you *do* supervise,' said Yvette, with that irritating blandness of hers, as she raised her naked elbows and peered over her shoulder into the long mirror.

'Oh yes! you never *asked* me!' cried Lucille. 'As if I didn't know what you meant, when you started sighing and flouncing about.'

'I!' said Yvette, with vague surprise. 'Why, when did I start sighing and flouncing about?'

'Of course you know you did.'

'Did I? No, I didn't know! When was it?' Yvette could put a peculiar annoyance into her mild, straying questions.

'I shan't do another thing to this frock, if you don't stand still and *stop* it,' said Lucille, in her rather sonorous, burning voice.

'You know you are most awfully nagging and irritable, Lucille,' said Yvette, standing as if on hot bricks.

'Now Yvette!' cried Lucille, her eyes suddenly flashing in her sister's face, with wild flashes. 'Stop it at once! Why should everybody put up with your abominable and overbearing temper!'

'Well, I don't know about *my* temper,' said Yvette, writhing slowly out of the half-made frock, and slipping into her dress again.

Then, with an obstinate little look on her face, she sat down again at the table, in the gloomy afternoon, and began to sew at the blue stuff. The room was littered with blue clippings, the scissors were lying on the floor, the workbasket was spilled in chaos all over the table, and a second mirror was perched perilously on the piano.

Granny, who had been in a semi-coma, called a doze, roused herself on the big, soft couch and put her cap straight.

'I don't get much peace for my nap,' she said, slowly feeling her thin white hair, to see that it was in order. She had heard vague noises.

Aunt Cissie came in, fumbling in a bag for a chocolate.

'I never saw such a mess!' she said. 'You'd better clear some of that litter away, Yvette.'

'All right,' said Yvette. 'I will in a minute.'

'Which means never!' sneered Aunt Cissie, suddenly darting and picking up the scissors.

There was silence for a few moments, and Lucille slowly pushed her hands in her hair, as she read a book.

'You'd better clear away, Yvette,' persisted Aunt Cissie.

'I will, before tea,' replied Yvette, rising once more and pulling the blue dress over her head, flourishing her long, naked arms through the sleeveless armholes. Then she went between the mirrors, to look at herself once more.

As she did so, she sent the second mirror, that she had perched carelessly on the piano, sliding with a rattle to the floor. Luckily it did not break. But everybody started badly.

'She's smashed the mirror!' cried Aunt Cissie.

'Smashed a mirror! Which mirror! Who smashed it?' came Granny's sharp voice.

'I haven't smashed anything,' came the calm voice of Yvette. 'It's quite all right.'

'You'd better not perch it up there again,' said Lucille.

Yvette, with a little impatient shrug at all the fuss, tried making the mirror stand in another place. She was not successful.

'If one had a fire in one's own room,' she said crossly, 'one needn't have a lot of people fussing when one wants to sew.'

'Which mirror are you moving about?' asked Granny.

'One of our own, that came from the vicarage,' said Yvette rudely.

'Don't break it in *this* house, wherever it came from,' said Granny.

There was a sort of family dislike for the furniture that had belonged to She-who-was-Cynthia. It was most of it shoved into the kitchen, and the servants' bedrooms.

'Oh, *I'm* not superstitious,' said Yvette, 'about mirrors or any of that sort of thing.'

'Perhaps you're not,' said Granny. 'People who never take the responsibility for their own actions usually don't care what happens.'

'After all,' said Yvette, 'I may say it's my own looking-glass, even if I did break it.'

'And I say,' said Granny, 'that there shall be no mirrors broken in *this* house, if we can help it; no matter who they belong to, or did belong to. Cissie, have I got my cap straight?'

Aunt Cissie went over and straightened the old lady. Yvette loudly and irritatingly trilled a tuneless tune.

'And now, Yvette, will you please clear away,' said Aunt Cissie.

'Oh bother!' cried Yvette angrily. 'It's simply *awful* to live with a lot of people who are always nagging and fussing over trifles.'

'What people, may I ask?' said Aunt Cissie ominously.

Another row was imminent. Lucille looked up with a queer cast in her eyes. In the two girls, the blood of She-who-was-Cynthia was roused.

'Of course you may ask! You know quite well I mean the people in this beastly house,' said the outrageous Yvette.

'At least,' said Granny, 'we don't come of half-depraved stock.'

There was a second's electric pause. Then Lucille sprang from her low seat, with sparks flying from her.

'You shut up!' she shouted, in a blast full upon the mottled majesty of the old lady.

The old woman's breast began to heave with heaven knows what emotions. The pause this time, as after the thunderbolt, was icy.

Then Aunt Cissie, livid, sprang upon Lucille, pushing her like a fury.

'Go to your room!' she cried hoarsely. 'Go to your room!'

And she proceeded to push the white but fiery-eyed Lucille from the room. Lucille let herself be pushed, while Aunt Cissie vociferated:

'Stay in your room till you've apologized for this! – till you've apologized to the Mater for this!'

'I shan't apologize!' came the clear voice of Lucille, from the passage, while Aunt Cissie shoved her.

Aunt Cissie drove her more wildly upstairs.

Yvette stood tall and bemused in the sitting-room, with the air of offended dignity, at the same time bemused, which was so odd on her. She still was bare-armed, in the half-made blue dress. And even *she* was half-aghast at Lucille's attack on the majesty of age. But also, she was coldly indignant against Granny's aspersion of the maternal blood in their veins.

'Of course I meant no offence,' said Granny.

'Didn't you!' said Yvette coolly.

'Of course not. I only said we're not depraved, just because we happen to be superstitious about breaking mirrors.'

Yvette could hardly believe her ears. Had she heard right? Was it possible! Or was Granny, at her age, just telling a barefaced lie?

Yvette knew that the old woman was telling a cool, barefaced lie. But already, so quickly, Granny believed her own statement.

The rector appeared, having left time for a lull.

'What's wrong?' he asked cautiously, genially.

'Oh nothing!' drawled Yvette. 'Lucille told Granny to shut up, when she was saying something. And Aunt Cissie drove her up to her room. *Tant de bruit pour une omelette!*[12] Though Lucille *was* a bit over the mark, that time.'

The old lady couldn't quite catch what Yvette said.

'Lucille really will have to learn to control her nerves,' said the old woman. 'The mirror fell down, and it worried me. I said so to Yvette, and she said something about superstitions and the people in the beastly house. I told her the people in the house were not depraved, if they happened to mind when a mirror was broken. And at that Lucille flew at me and told me to shut up. It really is disgraceful how these children give way to their nerves. I know it's nothing but nerves.'

Aunt Cissie had come in during this speech. At first even she was dumb. Then it seemed to her, it was as Granny had said.

'I have forbidden her to come down until she comes to apologize to the Mater,' she said.

'I doubt if she'll apologize,' said the calm, queenly Yvette, holding her bare arms.

'And I don't want any apology,' said the old lady. 'It is merely nerves. I don't know what they'll come to, if they have nerves like that, at their age! She must take Vibrofat. – I am sure Arthur would like his tea, Cissie.'

Yvette swept her sewing together, to go upstairs. And again she trilled her tune, rather shrill and tuneless. She was trembling inwardly.

'More glad rags!' said her father to her, genially.

'More glad rags!' she re-iterated sagely, as she sauntered upstairs, with her day dress over one arm. She wanted to console Lucille, and ask her how the blue stuff hung now.

At the first landing, she stood as she nearly always did, to gaze through the window that looked to the road and the bridge. Like the Lady of Shalott, she seemed always to imagine that someone would come along singing *Tirra-lirra!* or something equally intelligent, by the river.[13]

V

It was nearly tea-time. The snow-drops were out by the short drive going to the gate from the side of the house, and the gardener was pottering at the round, damp flower-beds, on the wet grass that sloped to the stream. Past the gate went the whitish muddy road, crossing the stone bridge almost immediately, and winding in a curve up to the steep, clustering, stony, smoking northern village, that perched over the grim stone mills which Yvette could see ahead down the narrow valley, their tall chimneys long and erect.

The rectory was on one side the Papple, in the rather steep valley, the village was beyond and above, further down, on the other side the swift stream. At the back of the rectory the hill went up steep, with a grove of dark, bare larches, through which the road disappeared. And immediately across stream from the rectory, facing the house, the river-bank rose steep and bushy, up to the sloping, dreary meadows, that sloped up again to dark hillsides of trees, with grey rock cropping out.

But from the end of the house, Yvette could only see the road curving round past the wall with its laurel hedge, down to the bridge, then up again round the shoulder to that first hard cluster of houses in Papplewick village, beyond the dry-stone walls of the steep fields.

She always expected *something* to come down the slant of the road from Papplewick, and she always lingered at the landing window. Often a cart came, or a motor-car, or a lorry with stone, or a labourer, or one of the servants. But never anybody who sang *Tirra-lirra!* by the river. The tirralirraing days seem to have gone by.

This day, however, round the corner on the white-grey road, between the grass and the low stone walls, a roan horse came stepping bravely and briskly down-hill, driven by a man in a cap, perched on the front of his light cart. The man swayed loosely to the swing of the cart, as the horse stepped down-hill, in the silent sombreness of the afternoon. At the back of the cart, long long duster-brooms of reed and feather stuck out, nodding on their stalks of cane.

Yvette stood close to the window, and put the casement-cloth curtains behind her, clutching her bare upper arms with her hands.

At the foot of the slope the horse started into a brisk trot to the bridge. The cart rattled on the stone bridge, the brooms bobbed and flustered, the driver sat as if in a kind of dream, swinging along. It was like something seen in a sleep.

But as he crossed the end of the bridge, and was passing along the rectory wall, he looked up at the grim stone house that seemed to have backed away from the gate, under the hill. Yvette moved her hands quickly on her arms. And as quickly, from under the peak of his cap, he had seen her, his swarthy predative face was alert.

He pulled up suddenly at the white gate, still gazing upwards at the landing window; while Yvette, always clasping her cold and mottled arms, still gazed abstractedly down at him, from the window.

His head gave a little, quick jerk of signal, and he led his horse well aside, on to the grass. Then, limber and alert, he turned back the tarpaulin of the cart, fetched out various articles, pulled forth two or three of the long brooms of reed or turkey-feathers, covered the cart, and turned towards the house, looking up at Yvette as he opened the white gate.

She nodded to him, and flew to the bathroom to put on her dress, hoping she had disguised her nod so that he wouldn't be sure she had nodded. Meanwhile she heard the hoarse deep roaring of that old fool, Rover, punctuated by the yapping of that young idiot, Trixie.

She and the housemaid arrived at the same moment at the sitting-room door.

'Was it the man selling brooms?' said Yvette to the maid. 'All right!' and she opened the door. 'Aunt Cissie, there's a man selling brooms. Shall I go?'

'What sort of a man?' said Aunt Cissie, who was sitting at tea with the rector and the Mater: the girls having been excluded for once from the meal.

'A man with a cart,' said Yvette.

'A gipsy,' said the maid.

Of course Aunt Cissie rose at once. She had to look at him.

The gipsy stood at the back door, under the steep dark bank where the larches grew. The long brooms flourished from one hand, and from the other hung various objects of shining copper and brass: a saucepan, a candlestick, plates of beaten copper. The man himself was neat and dapper, almost rakish, in his dark green cap and double-breasted green check coat. But his manner was subdued, very quiet: and at the same time proud, with a touch of condescension and aloofness.

'Anything today, lady?' he said, looking at Aunt Cissie with dark, shrewd, searching eyes, but putting a very quiet tenderness into his voice.

Aunt Cissie saw how handsome he was, saw the flexible curve of his lips under the line of black moustache, and she was fluttered. The merest hint of roughness or aggression on the man's part would have made her shut the door contemptuously in his face. But he managed to insinuate such a subtle suggestion of submission into his male bearing, that she began to hesitate.

'The candlestick is lovely!' said Yvette. 'Did you make it?'

And she looked up at the man with her naïve, childlike eyes, that were as capable of double meanings as his own.

'Yes lady!' He looked back into her eyes for a second, with that naked suggestion of desire which acted on her like a spell, and robbed her of her will. Her tender face seemed to go into a sleep.

'It's awfully nice!' she murmured vaguely.

Aunt Cissie began to bargain for the candlestick: which was a low, thick stem of copper, rising from a double bowl. With patient aloofness the man attended to her, without ever looking at Yvette, who leaned against the doorway and watched in a muse.

'How is your wife?' she asked him suddenly, when Aunt Cissie had gone indoors to show the candlestick to the rector, and ask him if he thought it was worth it.

The man looked fully at Yvette, and a scarcely discernible smile curled his lips. His eyes did not smile: the insinuation in them only hardened to a glare.

'She's all right. When are you coming that way again?' he murmured, in a low, caressive, intimate voice.

'Oh, I don't know,' said Yvette vaguely.

'You come Fridays, when I'm there,' he said.

Yvette gazed over his shoulder as if she had not heard him. Aunt Cissie returned, with the candlestick and the money to pay for it. Yvette turned nonchalant away, trilling one of her broken tunes, abandoning the whole affair with a certain rudeness.

Nevertheless, hiding this time at the landing window, she stood to watch the man go. What she wanted to know, was whether he really had any power over her. She did not intend him to see her this time.

She saw him go down to the gate, with his brooms and pans, and out to the cart. He carefully stowed away his pans and his brooms, and fixed down the tarpaulin over the cart. Then with a slow, effortless spring of his flexible loins, he was on the cart again, and touching the horse with the reins. The roan horse was away at once, the cart-wheels grinding uphill, and soon the man was gone, without looking round. Gone like a dream which was only a dream, yet which she could not shake off.

'No, he hasn't any power over me!' she said to herself: rather disappointed really, because she wanted somebody, or something to have power over her.

She went up to reason with the pale and overwrought Lucille scolding her for getting into a state over nothing.

'What does it *matter*,' she expostulated, 'if you told Granny to shut up! Why, everybody ought to be told to shut up, when they're being beastly. But she didn't mean it, you know. No, she didn't mean it. And she's quite sorry she said it. There's absolutely no reason to make a fuss. Come on, let's dress ourselves up and sail down to dinner like duchesses. Let's have our own back that way. Come on, Lucille!'

There was something strange and mazy, like having cobwebs over one's face, about Yvette's vague blitheness; her queer, misty side-stepping from an unpleasantness. It was cheering too. But it was like walking in one of those autumn mists, when gossamer strands blow over your face. You don't quite know where you are.

She succeeded, however, in persuading Lucille, and the girls got out their best party frocks: Lucille in green and silver, Yvette in a pale lilac colour with turquoise chenille threading. A little rouge and powder, and their best slippers, and the gardens of paradise began to blossom. Yvette hummed and looked at herself, and put on her most *dégagé*[14] airs of one of the young marchionesses. She had an odd way of slanting her eyebrows and pursing her lips, and to all appearances detaching herself from every earthly consideration, and floating through the cloud of her own pearl-coloured reserves. It was amusing, and not quite convincing.

'Of course I am beautiful, Lucille,' she said blandly. 'And you're perfectly lovely, now you look a bit reproachful. Of course you're the most aristocratic of the two of us, with your nose! And now your eyes look reproachful, that adds an appealing look, and you're perfect, perfectly lovely. But I'm more *winning*, in a way. – Don't you agree?' She turned with arch, complicated simplicity to Lucille.

She was truly simple in what she said. It was just what she thought. But it gave no hint of the very different *feeling* that also preoccupied her: the feeling that she had been looked upon, not from the outside, but from the inside, from her secret female self. She was dressing herself up and looking her most dazzling, just to counteract the effect that the gipsy had had on her, when he had looked at her, and seen none of her pretty face and her pretty ways, but just the dark, tremulous, potent secret of her virginity.

The two girls started downstairs in state when the dinner-gong rang: but they waited till they heard the voices of the men. Then they sailed down and into the sitting-room, Yvette preening herself in her vague, debonair way, always a little bit absent; and Lucille shy, ready to burst into tears.

'My goodness gracious!' exclaimed Aunt Cissie, who was still wearing her dark-brown knitted sports coat. 'What an apparition! Wherever do you think you're going?'

'We're dining with the family,' said Yvette naïvely, 'and we've put on our best gewgaws in honour of the occasion.'

The rector laughed aloud, and Uncle Fred said:

'The family feels itself highly honoured.'

Both the elderly men were quite gallant, which was what Yvette wanted.

'Come and let me feel your dresses, do!' said Granny. 'Are they your best? It *is* a shame I can't see them.'

'Tonight, Mater,' said Uncle Fred, 'we shall have to take the young ladies in to dinner, and live up to the honour. Will you go with Cissie?'

'I certainly will,' said Granny. 'Youth and beauty must come first.'

'Well, tonight Mater!' said the rector, pleased.

And he offered his arm to Lucille, while Uncle Fred escorted Yvette.

But it was a draggled, dull meal, all the same. Lucille tried to be bright and sociable, and Yvette really was most amiable, in her vague, cobwebby way. Dimly, at the back of her mind, she was thinking: Why are we all only like mortal pieces of furniture? Why is nothing *important*?

That was her constant refrain to herself: Why is nothing important? Whether she was in church, or at a party of young people, or dancing in the hotel in the city, the same little bubble of a question rose repeatedly on her consciousness: Why is nothing important?

There were plenty of young men to make love to her: even devotedly. But with impatience she had to shake them off. Why were they so unimportant? – so irritating!

She never even thought of the gipsy. He was a perfectly negligible incident. Yet the approach of Friday loomed strangely significant. 'What are we doing on Friday?' she said to Lucille. To which Lucille replied that they were doing nothing. And Yvette was vexed.

Friday came, and in spite of herself she thought all day of the quarry off the road up high Bonsall Head. She wanted to be there. That was all she was conscious of. She wanted to be there. She had not even a dawning idea of going there. Besides, it was raining again. But as she sewed the blue dress, finishing it for the party up at Lambley Close, tomorrow, she just felt that her soul was up there, at the quarry, among the caravans, with the gipsies. Like one lost, or whose soul was stolen, she was not present in her body, the shell of her body. Her intrinsic body was away at the quarry, among the caravans.

The next day, at the party, she had no idea that she was being sweet to Leo. She had no idea that she was snatching him away from the tortured Ella Framley. Not until, when she was eating her pistachio ice, he said to her:

'Why don't you and me get engaged, Yvette? I'm absolutely sure it's the right thing for us both.'

Leo was a bit common, but good-natured, and well-off. Yvette quite liked him. But engaged! How perfectly silly! She felt like offering him a set of her silk underwear, to get engaged to.

'But, I thought it was Ella!' she said, in wonder.

'Well! It might ha' been, but for you. It's your doings, you know! Ever since those gipsies told your fortune, I felt it was me or nobody, for you, and you or nobody, for me.'

'Really!' said Yvette, simply lost in amazement. 'Really!'

'Didn't you feel a bit the same?' he asked.

'Really!' Yvette kept on gasping softly, like a fish.

'You felt a bit the same, didn't you?' he said.

'What? About what?' she asked, coming to.

'About me, as I feel about you.'

'Why? What? Getting engaged, you mean? I? No! Why how *could* I? I could never have dreamed of such an impossible thing.'

She spoke with her usual heedless candour, utterly un-occupied with his feelings.

'What was to prevent you?' he said, a bit nettled. 'I thought you did.'

'Did you *really now*?' she breathed in amazement, with that soft, virgin, heedless candour which made her her admirers and her enemies.

She was so completely amazed, there was nothing for him to do but twiddle his thumbs in annoyance.

The music began, and he looked at her.

'No! I won't dance any more,' she said, drawing herself up and gazing away rather loftily over the assembly, as if he did not exist. There was a touch of puzzled wonder on her brow, and her soft, dim virgin face did indeed suggest the snowdrop of her father's pathetic imagery.

'But of course *you* will dance,' she said, turning to him with young condescension. 'Do ask somebody to have this with you.'

He rose, angry, and went down the room.

She remained soft and remote in her amazement. Expect Leo to propose to her! She might as well have expected old Rover the Newfoundland dog to propose to her. Get engaged, to any man on earth? No, good heavens, nothing more ridiculous could be imagined!

It was then, in a fleeting side-thought, that she realized that the gipsy existed. Instantly, she was indignant. Him, of all things! Him! Never!

'Now why?' she asked herself, again in hushed amazement. 'Why? It's *absolutely* impossible: absolutely! So why is it?'

This was a nut to crack. She looked at the young men dancing, elbows out, hips prominent, waists elegantly in. They gave her no clue to her problem. Yet she did particularly dislike the forced elegance of the waists and the prominent hips, over which the well-tailored coats hung with such effeminate discretion.

'There is something about me which they don't see and never would see,' she said angrily to herself. And at the same time, she was relieved that they didn't and couldn't. It made life so very much simpler.

And again, since she was one of the people who are conscious in visual images, she saw the dark-green jersey rolled on the black trousers of the gipsy, his fine, quick hips, alert as eyes. They were elegant. The elegance of these dancers seemed so stuffed, hips merely wadded with flesh. Leo the same, thinking himself such a fine dancer! and a fine figure of a fellow!

Then she saw the gipsy's face; the straight nose, the slender mobile lips, and the level, significant stare of the black eyes, which seemed to shoot her in some vital, undiscovered place, unerring.

She drew herself up angrily. How dared he look at her like that? So she gazed glaringly at the insipid beaux on the dancing floor. And she despised them. Just as the raggle-taggle gipsy women[15] despise men who are not gipsies, despise their dog-like walk down the streets, she found herself despising this crowd. Where among them was the subtle, lonely, insinuating challenge that could reach her?

She did not want to mate with a house-dog.

Her sensitive nose turned up, her soft brown hair fell like a soft sheath round her tender, flower-like face, as she sat musing. She seemed so virginal. At the same time, there was a touch of the tall young virgin *witch* about her, that made the house-dog men shy off. She might metamorphose into something uncanny before you knew where you were.

This made her lonely, in spite of all the courting. Perhaps the courting only made her lonelier.

Leo, who was a sort of mastiff among the house-dogs, returned after his dance, with fresh cheery-o! courage.

'You've had a little think about it, haven't you?' he said, sitting down beside her: a comfortable, well-nourished, determined sort of fellow. She did not know why it irritated her so unreasonably, when he hitched up his trousers at the knee, over his good-sized but not very distinguished legs, and lowered himself assuredly on to a chair.

'Have I?' she said vaguely. 'About what?'

'You know what about,' he said. 'Did you make up your mind?'

'Make up my mind about what?' she asked, innocently.

In her upper consciousness, she truly had forgotten.

'Oh!' said Leo, settling his trousers again. 'About me and you getting engaged, you know.' He was almost as off-hand as she.

'Oh that's *absolutely* impossible,' she said, with mild amiability, as if it were some stray question among the rest. 'Why I never even thought of it again. Oh, don't talk about that sort of nonsense! That sort of thing is *absolutely* impossible,' she reiterated like a child.

'That sort of thing is, is it?' he said, with an odd smile at her calm, distant assertion. 'Well, what sort of thing *is* possible, then? You don't want to die an old maid, do you?'

'Oh I don't mind,' she said absently.

'I do,' he said.

She turned round and looked at him in wonder.

'Why?' she said. 'Why should you mind if I was an old maid?'

'Every reason in the world,' he said, looking up at her with a bold, meaningful smile, that wanted to make its meaning blatant, if not patent.

But instead of penetrating into some deep, secret place, and shooting her there, Leo's bold and patent smile only hit her on the outside of the body, like a tennis ball, and caused the same kind of sudden irritated reaction.

'I think this sort of thing is awfully silly,' she said, with minx-like spite. 'Why, you're practically engaged to – to –' she pulled herself up in time – 'probably half a dozen other girls. I'm not flattered by what you've said. I should hate it if anybody knew! – Hate it! – I shan't breathe a word of it, and I hope you'll have the sense not to. – There's Ella!'

And keeping her face averted from him, she sailed away like a tall, soft flower, to join poor Ella Framley.

Leo flapped his white gloves.

'Catty little bitch!' he said to himself. But he was of the mastiff type, he rather liked the kitten to fly in his face. He began definitely to single her out.

VI

The next week it poured again with rain. And this irritated Yvette with strange anger. She had intended it should be fine. Especially she insisted it should be fine towards the weekend. Why, she did not ask herself.

Thursday, the half-holiday, came with a hard frost, and sun. Leo arrived with his car, the usual bunch. Yvette disagreeably and unaccountably refused to go.

'No thanks, I don't feel like it,' she said.

She rather enjoyed being Mary-Mary-quite-contrary.

Then she went for a walk by herself, up the frozen hills, to the Black Rocks.

The next day also came sunny and frosty. It was February, but in the north country the ground did not thaw in the sun. Yvette announced that she was going for a ride on her bicycle, and taking her lunch as she might not be back till afternoon.

She set off, not hurrying. In spite of the frost, the sun had a touch of spring. In the park, the deer were standing in the distance, in the sunlight, to be warm. One doe, white spotted, walked slowly across the motionless landscape.

Cycling, Yvette found it difficult to keep her hands warm, even when bodily she was quite hot. Only when she had to walk up the long hill, to the top, and there was no wind.

The upland was very bare and clear, like another world. She had climbed on to another level. She cycled slowly, a little afraid of taking the wrong lane, in the vast maze of stone fences. As she passed along the lane she thought was the right one, she heard a faint tapping noise, with a slight metallic resonance.

The gipsy man was seated on the ground with his back to the cart-shaft, hammering a copper bowl. He was in the sun, bare-headed, but wearing his green jersey. Three small children were moving quietly round, playing in the horse's shelter: the horse and cart were gone. An old woman, bent, with a kerchief round her head, was cooking over a fire of sticks. The only sound was the rapid, ringing tap-tap-tap! of the small hammer on the dull copper.

The man looked up at once, as Yvette stepped from her bicycle, but he did not move, though he ceased hammering. A delicate, barely discernible smile of triumph was on his face. The old woman looked round, keenly, from under her dirty grey hair. The man spoke a half-audible word to her, and she turned again to her fire. He looked up at Yvette.

'How are you all getting on?' she asked politely.

'All right, eh! You sit down a minute?' He turned as he sat, and pulled a stool from under the caravan for Yvette. Then, as she wheeled her bicycle to the side of the quarry, he started hammering again, with that bird-like, rapid light stroke.

Yvette went to the fire to warm her hands.

'Is this the dinner cooking?' she asked childishly, of the old gipsy, as she spread her long, tender hands, mottled red with the cold, to the embers.

'Dinner, yes!' said the old woman. 'For him! And for the children.'

She pointed with the long fork at the three black-eyed, staring children, who were staring at her from under their black fringes. But they were clean. Only the old woman was not clean. The quarry itself they had kept perfectly clean.

Yvette crouched in silence, warming her hands. The man

rapidly hammered away with intervals of silence. The old hag slowly climbed the steps to the third, oldest caravan. The children began to play again, like little wild animals, quiet and busy.

'Are they your children?' asked Yvette, rising from the fire and turning to the man.

He looked her in the eyes, and nodded.

'But where's your wife?'

'She's gone out with the basket. They've all gone out, cart and all, selling things. I don't go selling things. I make them, but I don't go selling them. Not often. I don't often.'

'You make all the copper and brass things?' she said.

He nodded, and again offered her the stool. She sat down.

'You said you'd be here on Fridays,' she said. 'So I came this way, as it was so fine.'

'Very fine day!' said the gipsy, looking at her cheek, that was still a bit blanched by the cold, and the soft hair over her reddened ear, and the long, still mottled hands on her knee.

'You get cold, riding a bicycle?' he asked.

'My hands!' she said, clasping them nervously.

'You didn't wear gloves?'

'I did, but they weren't much good.'

'Cold comes through,' he said.

'Yes!' she replied.

The old woman came slowly, grotesquely down the steps of the caravan, with some enamel plates.

'The dinner cooked, eh?' he called softly.

The old woman muttered something, as she spread the plates near the fire. Two pots hung from a long iron horizontal bar, over the embers of the fire. A little pan seethed on a small iron tripod. In the sunshine, heat and vapour wavered together.

He put down his tools and the pot, and rose from the ground.

'You eat something along of us?' he asked Yvette, not looking at her.

'Oh, I brought my lunch,' said Yvette.

'You eat some stew?' he said. And again he called quietly, secretly to the old woman, who muttered in answer, as she slid the iron pot towards the end of the bar.

'Some beans, and some mutton in it,' he said.

'Oh, thanks awfully!' said Yvette. Then, suddenly taking courage, added: 'Well yes, just a very little, if I may.'

She went across to untie her lunch from her bicycle, and he went up the steps to his own caravan. After a minute, he emerged, wiping his hands on a towel.

'You want to come up and wash your hands?' he said.

'No, I think not,' she said. 'They are clean.'

He threw away his wash-water, and set off down the road with a high brass jug, to fetch clean water from the spring that trickled into a small pool, taking a cup to dip it with.

When he returned, he set the jug and the cup by the fire, and fetched himself a short log, to sit on. The children sat on the floor, by the fire, in a cluster, eating beans and bits of meat with spoon or fingers. The man on the log ate in silence, absorbedly. The woman made coffee in the black pot on the tripod, hobbling upstairs for the cups. There was silence in the camp. Yvette sat on her stool, having taken off her hat and shaken her hair in the sun.

'How many children have you?' Yvette asked suddenly.

'Say five,' he replied slowly, as he looked up into her eyes.

And again the bird of her heart sank down and seemed to die. Vaguely, as in a dream, she received from him the cup of coffee. She was aware only of his silent figure, sitting like a shadow there on the log, with an enamel cup in his hand, drinking his coffee in silence. Her will had departed from her limbs, he had power over her: his shadow was on her.

And he, as he blew his hot coffee, was aware of one thing only, the mysterious fruit of her virginity, her perfect tenderness in the body.

At length he put down his coffee-cup by the fire, then looked round at her. Her hair fell across her face, as she tried to sip from the hot cup. On her face was that tender look of sleep, which a nodding flower has when it is full out. Like a mysterious early flower, she was full out, like a snowdrop which spreads its three white wings in a flight into the waking sleep of its brief blossoming. The waking sleep of her full-opened virginity, entranced like a snowdrop in the sunshine, was upon her.

The gipsy, supremely aware of her, waited for her like the substance of shadow, as shadow waits and is there.

At length his voice said, without breaking the spell:

'You want to go in my caravan, now, and wash your hands?'

The childlike, sleep-waking eyes of her moment of perfect virginity looked into his, unseeing. She was only aware of the dark, strange effluence of him bathing her limbs, washing her at last purely will-less. She was aware of *him*, as a dark, complete power.

'I think I might,' she said.

He rose silently, then turned to speak, in a low command, to the old woman. And then again he looked at Yvette, and putting his power over her, so that she had no burden of herself, or of action.

'Come!' he said.

She followed simply, followed the silent, secret, overpowering motion of his body in front of her. It cost her nothing. She was gone in his will.

He was at the top of the steps, and she at the foot, when she became aware of an intruding sound. She stood still, at the foot of the steps. A motor-car was coming. He stood at the top of the steps, looking round strangely. The old woman harshly called something, as with rapidly increasing sound, a car rushed near. It was passing.

Then they heard the cry of a woman's voice, and the brakes on the car. It had pulled up, just beyond the quarry.

The gipsy came down the steps, having closed the door of the caravan.

'You want to put your hat on,' he said to her.

Obediently she went to the stool by the fire, and took up her hat. He sat down by the cart-wheel, darkly, and took up his tools. The rapid tap-tap-tap of his hammer, rapid and angry now like the sound of a tiny machine-gun, broke out just as the voice of the woman was heard crying:

'May we warm our hands at the camp fire?'

She advanced, dressed in a sleek but bulky coat of sable fur. A man followed, in a blue great-coat; pulling off his fur gloves and pulling out a pipe.

'It looked so tempting,' said the woman in the coat of many dead little animals, smiling a broad, half-condescending, half-hesitant simper, round the company.

No one said a word.

She advanced to the fire, shuddering a little inside her coat, with the cold. They had been driving in an open car.

She was a very small woman, with a rather large nose: probably a Jewess. Tiny almost as a child, in that sable coat she looked much more bulky than she should, and her wide, rather resentful brown eyes of a spoilt Jewess gazed oddly out of her expensive get-up.

She crouched over the low fire, spreading her little hands, on which diamonds and emeralds glittered.

'Ugh!' she shuddered. 'Of course we ought not to have come in an open car! But my husband won't even let me say I'm cold!' She looked round at him with her large, childish, reproachful eyes, that had still the canny shrewdness of a bourgeois Jewess: a rich one, probably.

Apparently she was in love, in a Jewess's curious way, with the big, blond man. He looked back at her with his abstracted blue eyes, that seemed to have no lashes, and a small smile creased his smooth, curiously naked cheeks. The smile didn't mean anything at all.

He was a man one connects instantly with winter sports, skiing and skating. Athletic, unconnected with life, he slowly filled his pipe, pressing in the tobacco with long, powerful reddened finger.

The Jewess looked at him to see if she got any response from him. Nothing at all, but that odd, blank smile. She turned again to the fire, tilting her eyebrows and looking at her small, white, spread hands.

He slipped off his heavily-lined coat, and appeared in one of the handsome, sharp-patterned knitted jerseys, in yellow and grey and black, over well-cut trousers, rather wide. Yes, they were both expensive! And he had a magnificent figure, an athletic, prominent chest. Like an experienced camper, he began building the fire together, quietly: like a soldier on campaign.

'D'you think they'd mind if we put some fir-cones on, to make a blaze?' he asked of Yvette, with a silent glance at the hammering gipsy.

'Love it, I should think,' said Yvette, in a daze, as the spell of the gipsy slowly left her, feeling stranded and blank.

The man went to the car, and returned with a little sack of cones, from which he drew a handful.

'Mind if we make a blaze?' he called to the gipsy.

'Eh?'

'Mind if we make a blaze with a few cones?'

'You go ahead!' said the gipsy.

The man began placing the cones lightly, carefully on the red embers. And soon, one by one, they caught fire, and burned like roses of flame, with a sweet scent.

'Ah lovely! lovely!' cried the little Jewess, looking up at her man again. He looked down at her quite kindly, like the sun on ice. 'Don't you love fire! Oh, I love it!' the little Jewess cried to Yvette, across the hammering.

The hammering annoyed her. She looked round with a slight frown on her fine little brows, as if she would bid the man stop. Yvette looked round too. The gipsy was bent over his copper bowl, legs apart, head down, lithe arm lifted. Already he seemed so far from her.

The man who accompanied the little Jewess strolled over to the gipsy, and stood in silence looking down on him, holding his pipe to his mouth. Now they were two men, like two strange male dogs, having to sniff one another.

We're on our honeymoon,' said the little Jewess, with an arch, resentful look at Yvette. She spoke in a rather high, defiant voice, like some bird, a jay, or a rook, calling.

'Are you really?' said Yvette.

'Yes! Before we're married! Have you heard of Simon Fawcett?' – she named a wealthy and well-known engineer of the north country. 'Well, I'm Mrs Fawcett, and he's just divorcing me!' She looked at Yvette with curious defiance and wistfulness.

'Are you really!' said Yvette.

She understood now the look of resentment and defiance in the little Jewess's big, childlike brown eyes. She was an honest little thing, but perhaps her honesty was *too* rational. Perhaps it partly explained the notorious unscrupulousness of the well-known Simon Fawcett.

'Yes! As soon as we get the divorce, I'm going to marry Major Eastwood.'

Her cards were now all on the table. She was not going to deceive anybody.

Behind her, the two men were talking briefly. She glanced round, and fixed the gipsy with her big brown eyes.

He was looking up, as if shyly, at the big fellow in the sparkling jersey, who was standing pipe in mouth, man to man, looking down.

'With the horses back of Arras,'¹⁶ said the gipsy, in a low voice.

They were talking war. The gipsy had served with the artillery teams, in the Major's own regiment.

'Ein schöner Mensch!' said the Jewess. 'A handsome man, eh?'

For her, too, the gipsy was one of the common men, the Tommies.¹⁷

'Quite handsome!' said Yvette.

'You are cycling?' asked the Jewess in a tone of surprise.

'Yes! Down to Papplewick. My father is rector of Papplewick: Mr Saywell!'

'Oh!' said the Jewess. 'I know! A clever writer! Very clever! I have read him.'

The fir-cones were all consumed already, the fire was a tall pile now of crumbling, shattering fire-roses. The sky was clouding over for afternoon. Perhaps towards evening it would snow.

The major came back, and slung himself into his coat.

'I thought I remembered his face!' he said. 'One of our grooms, A1 man with horses.'

'Look!' cried the Jewess to Yvette. 'Why don't you let us motor you down to Normanton. We live in Scoresby. We can tie the bicycle on behind.'

'I think I will,' said Yvette.

'Come!' called the Jewess to the peeping children, as the blond man wheeled away the bicycle. 'Come! Come here!' and taking out her little purse, she held out a shilling.

'Come!' she cried. 'Come and take it!'

The gipsy had laid down his work, and gone into his caravan. The old woman called hoarsely to the children, from her enclosure. The two elder children came stealing forward. The Jewess gave them the two bits of silver, a shilling and a florin, which she had in her purse, and again the hoarse voice of the unseen old woman was heard.

The gipsy descended from his caravan and strolled to the fire. The Jewess searched his face with the peculiar bourgeois bold-ness of her race.

'You were in the war, in Major Eastwood's regiment!' she said.

'Yes, lady!'

'Imagine you both being here now! – It's going to snow –' She looked up at the sky.

'Later on,' said the man, looking at the sky.

He too had gone inaccessible. His race was very old, in its peculiar battle with established society, and had no conception of winning. Only now and then it could score.

But since the war, even the old sporting chance of scoring now and then, was pretty well quenched. There was no question of yielding. The gipsy's eyes still had their bold look: but it was hardened and directed far away, the touch of insolent intimacy was gone. He had been through the war.

He looked at Yvette.

'You're going back in the motor-car?' he said.

'Yes!' she replied, with a rather mincing mannerism. 'The weather is so treacherous!'

'Treacherous weather!' he repeated, looking at the sky.

She could not tell in the least what his feelings were. In truth, she wasn't very much interested. She was rather fascinated, now, by the little Jewess, mother of two children, who was taking her wealth away from the well-known engineer and transferring it to the penniless, sporting young Major Eastwood, who must be five or six years younger than she. Rather intriguing!

The blond man returned.

'A cigarette, Charles!' cried the little Jewess, plaintively.

He took out his case, slowly, with his slow, athletic movement. Something sensitive in him made him slow, cautious, as if he had hurt himself against people. He gave a cigarette to his wife, then one to Yvette, then offered the case, quite simply, to the gipsy. The gipsy took one.

'Thank you sir!'

And he went quietly to the fire, and stooping, lit it at the red embers. Both women watched him.

'Well goodbye!' said the Jewess, with her old bourgeois freemasonry. 'Thank you for the warm fire.'

'Fire is everybody's,' said the gipsy.

The young child came toddling to him.

'Goodbye!' said Yvette. 'I hope it won't snow for you.'

'We don't mind a bit of snow,' said the gipsy.

'Don't you?' said Yvette. 'I should have thought you would!'

'No!' said the gipsy.

She flung her scarf royally over her shoulder, and followed the fur coat of the Jewess, which seemed to walk on little legs of its own.

VII

Yvette was rather thrilled by the Eastwoods, as she called them. The little Jewess had only to wait three months now, for the final decree. She had boldy rented a small summer cottage, by the moors up at Scoresby, not far from the hills. Now it was dead winter, and she and the Major lived in comparative isolation, without any maid-servant. He had already resigned his commission in the regular army, and called himself Mr Eastwood. In fact, they were already Mr and Mrs Eastwood, to the common world.

The little Jewess was thirty-six, and her two children were both over twelve years of age. The husband had agreed that she should have the custody, as soon as she was married to Eastwood.

So there they were, this queer couple, the tiny, finely-formed little Jewess with her big, resentful reproachful eyes, and her mop of carefully-barbered black, curly hair, an elegant little thing in her way; and the big, pale-eyed young man, powerful and wintry, the remnant, surely of some old uncanny Danish stock: living together in a small modern house near the moors and the hills, and doing their own housework.

It was a funny household. The cottage was hired furnished, but the little Jewess had brought along her dearest pieces of furniture. She had an odd little taste for the rococo, strange curving cupboards inlaid with mother of pearl, tortoiseshell, ebony, heaven knows what; strange tall flamboyant chairs, from Italy, with sea-green brocade: astonishing saints with wind-blown, richly-coloured carven garments and pink faces: shelves of weird old Saxe and Capo di Monte figurines: and finally, a strange assortment of astonishing pictures painted on the back of glass, done probably in the early years of the nineteenth century, or in the late eighteenth.

In this crowded and extraordinary interior she received Yvette, when the latter made a stolen visit. A whole system of stoves had been installed into the cottage, every corner was warm, almost hot. And there was the tiny rococo figurine of the Jewess herself, in a perfect little frock, and an apron, putting slices of ham on the dish, while the great snow-bird of a major, in a white sweater and grey trousers, cut bread, mixed mustard, prepared coffee, and did all the rest. He had even made the dish of jugged hare which followed the cold meats and caviare.

The silver and the china were really valuable, part of the bride's trousseau. The major drank beer from a silver mug, the little Jewess and Yvette had champagne in lovely glasses, the major brought in coffee. They talked away. The little Jewess had a burning indignation against her first husband. She was intensely moral, so moral, that she was a divorcée. The major too, strange wintry bird, so powerful, handsome too in his way, but pale round the eyes as if he had no eyelashes, like a bird, he too had a curious indignation against life, because of the false morality. That powerful, athletic chest hid a strange, snowy sort of anger. And his tenderness for the little Jewess was based on his sense of outraged justice, the abstract morality of the north blowing him, like a strange wind, into isolation.

As the afternoon drew on, they went to the kitchen, the major pushed back his sleeves, showing his powerful athletic white arms, and carefully, deftly washed the dishes, while the women wiped. It was not for nothing his muscles were trained. Then he went round attending to the stoves of the small house, which only needed a moment or two of care each day. And after this, he brought out the small, closed car and drove Yvette home, in the rain, depositing her at the back gate, a little wicket among the larches, through which the earthen steps sloped downwards to the house.

She was really amazed by this couple.

'Really, Lucille!' she said. 'I do meet the most extraordinary people!' And she gave a detailed description.

'I think they sound rather nice!' said Lucille. 'I like the Major doing the housework, and looking so frightfully Bond-streety with it all. I should think, *when they're married*, it would be rather fun knowing them.'

'Yes!' said Yvette vaguely. 'Yes! Yes, it would!'

The very strangeness of the connexion between the tiny Jewess and that pale-eyed, athletic young officer made her think again of her gipsy, who had been utterly absent from her consciousness, but who now returned with sudden painful force.

'What is it, Lucille,' she asked, 'that brings people together? People like the Eastwoods, for instance? and Daddy and Mamma, so frightfully unsuitable? – and that gipsy woman who told my fortune, like a great horse, and the gipsy man, so fine and delicately cut? What is it?'

'I suppose it's sex, whatever that is,' said Lucille.

'Yes, what is it? It's not really anything *common*, like common sensuality, you know, Lucille. It really isn't!'

'No, I suppose not,' said Lucille. 'Anyhow I suppose it needn't be.'

'Because you see the *common* fellows, you know, who make a girl feel *low*: nobody cares much about them. Nobody feels any connexion with them. Yet they're supposed to be the sexual sort.'

'I suppose,' said Lucille, 'there's the low sort of sex, and there's the other sort, that isn't low. It's frightfully complicated, really! I *loathe* common fellows. And I never feel anything *sexual* –' she laid a rather disgusted stress on the word – 'for fellows who aren't common. Perhaps I haven't got any sex.'

'That's just it!' said Yvette. 'Perhaps neither of us has. Perhaps we haven't really *got* any sex, to connect us with men.'

'How horrible it sounds: *connect us with men*!' cried Lucille, with revulsion. 'Wouldn't you hate to be connected with men that way? Oh I think it's an awful pity there has to *be* sex! It would be so much better if we could still be men and women, without that sort of thing.'

Yvette pondered. Far in the background was the image of the gipsy as he had looked round at her, when she had said: 'The weather is so treacherous.' She felt rather like Peter when the cock crew, as she denied him.[18] Or rather, she did not deny the gipsy; she didn't care about his part in the show, anyhow. It was some hidden part of herself which she denied: that part which mysteriously and unconfessedly responded to him. And it was a strange, lustrous black cock which crew in mockery of her.

'Yes!' she said vaguely. 'Yes! Sex is an awful bore, you know Lucille. When you haven't got it, you feel you *ought* to have it, somehow. And when you've got it – or *if* you have it –' she lifted her head and wrinkled her nose disdainfully – 'you hate it.'

'Oh, I don't know!' cried Lucille. 'I think I should *like* to be awfully in love with a man.'

'You think so!' said Yvette, again wrinkling her nose. 'But if you were you wouldn't.'

'How do you know?' asked Lucille.

'Well, I don't really,' said Yvette. 'But I think so! Yes, I think so.'

'Oh, it's very likely!' said Lucille disgustedly. 'And anyhow one would be sure to get out of love again, and it would be merely disgusting.'

'Yes,' said Yvette. 'It's a problem.' She hummed a little tune.

'Oh hang it all, it's not a problem for us two yet. We're neither of us really in love, and we probably never shall be, so the problem is settled that way.'

'I'm not so sure!' said Yvette sagely. 'I'm not so sure. I believe, one day, I shall fall *awfully* in love.'

'Probably you never will,' said Lucille brutally. 'That's what most old maids are thinking all the time.'

Yvette looked at her sister from pensive but apparently insouciant eyes.

'Is it?' she said. 'Do you really think so, Lucille? How perfectly awful for them, poor things! Why ever do they *care*?'

'Why do they?' said Lucille. 'Perhaps they don't, really. –

Probably it's all because people say: *Poor old girl, she couldn't catch a man.*'

'I suppose it is!' said Yvette. 'They get to mind the beastly things people always do say about old maids. What a shame!'

'Anyhow we have a good time, and we do have lots of boys who make a fuss of us,' said Lucille.

'Yes!' said Yvette. 'Yes! But I couldn't possibly marry any of them.'

'Neither could I,' said Lucille. 'But why shouldn't we! Why should we bother about marrying, when we have a perfectly good time with the boys who are awfully good sorts, and you must say, Yvette, awfully sporting and *decent* to us.'

'Oh, they are!' said Yvette absently.

'I think it's time to think of marrying somebody,' said Lucille, 'when you feel you're *not* having a good time any more. Then marry, and just settle down.'

'Quite!' said Yvette.

But now, under all her bland, soft amiability, she was annoyed with Lucille. Suddenly she wanted to turn her back on Lucille.

Besides, look at the shadows under poor Lucille's eyes, and the wistfulness in the beautiful eyes themselves. Oh, if some awfully nice, kind, protective sort of man would but marry her! And if the sporting Lucille would let him!

Yvette did not tell the rector, nor Granny, about the Eastwoods. It would only have started a lot of talk which she detested. The rector wouldn't have minded, for himself, privately. But he too knew the necessity of keeping as clear as possible from that poisonous, many-headed serpent, the tongue of the people.

'But I don't *want* you to come if your father doesn't know,' cried the little Jewess.

'I suppose I'll have to tell him,' said Yvette. 'I'm sure he doesn't mind, really. But if he knew, he'd have to, I suppose.'

The young officer looked at her with an odd amusement, bird-like and unemotional, in his keen eyes. He too was by way of falling in love with Yvette. It was her peculiar virgin tenderness, and her straying, absent-minded detachment from things, which attracted him.

She was aware of what was happening, and she rather preened

herself. Eastwood piqued her fancy. Such a smart young officer, awfully good class, so calm and amazing with a motor-car, and quite a champion swimmer, it was intriguing to see him quietly, calmly washing dishes, smoking his pipe, doing his job so alert and skilful. Or, with the same interested care with which he made his investigation into the mysterious inside of an automobile, concocting jugged hare in the cottage kitchen. Then going out in the icy weather and cleaning his car till it looked like a live thing, like a cat when she has licked herself. Then coming in to talk so unassumingly and responsively, if briefly, with the little Jewess. And apparently, never bored. Sitting at the window with his pipe, in bad weather, silent for hours, abstracted, musing, yet with his athletic body alert in its stillness.

Yvette did not flirt with him. But she *did* like him.

'But what about your future?' she asked him.

'What about it?' he said, taking his pipe from his mouth, the unemotional point of a smile in his bird's eyes.

'A career! Doesn't every man have to carve out a career? – like some huge goose with gravy?' She gazed with odd naïveté into his eyes.

'I'm perfectly all right today, and I shall be all right to-morrow,' he said, with a cold, decided look. 'Why shouldn't my future be continuous todays and tomorrows?'

He looked at her with unmoved searching.

'Quite!' she said. 'I hate jobs, and all that side of life.' But she was thinking of the Jewess's money.

To which he did not answer. His anger was of the soft, snowy sort, which comfortably muffles the soul.

They had come to the point of talking philosophically together. The little Jewess looked a bit wan. She was curiously naïve and not possessive in her attitude to the man. Nor was she at all catty with Yvette. Only rather wan, and dumb.

Yvette, on a sudden impulse, thought she had better clear herself.

'I think life's *awfully* difficult,' she said.

'Life is!' cried the Jewess.

'What's so beastly, is that one is supposed to *fall in love*, and get married!' said Yvette, curling up her nose.

'Don't you *want* to fall in love and get married?' cried the Jewess, with great glaring eyes of astounded reproach.

'No, not particularly!' said Yvette. 'Especially as one feels there's nothing else to do. It's an awful chicken-coop one has to run into.'

'But you don't know what love is?' cried the Jewess.

'No!' said Yvette. 'Do you?'

'I!' bawled the tiny Jewess. 'I! My goodness, don't I!' She looked with reflective gloom at Eastwood, who was smoking his pipe, the dimples of his disconnected amusement showing on his smooth, scrupulous face. He had a very fine, smooth skin, which yet did not suffer from the weather, so that his face looked naked as a baby's. But it was not a round face: it was characteristic enough, and took queer ironical dimples, like a mask which is comic but frozen.

'Do you mean to say you don't know what love is?' insisted the Jewess.

'No!' said Yvette, with insouciant candour. 'I don't believe I do! Is it awful of me, at my age?'

'Is there never any man that makes you feel quite, quite different?' said the Jewess, with another big-eyed look at Eastwood. He smoked, utterly unimplicated.

'I don't think there is,' said Yvette. 'Unless – yes! – unless it is that gipsy' – she had put her head pensively sideways.

'Which gipsy?' bawled the little Jewess.

'The one who was a Tommy and looked after horses in Major Eastwood's regiment in the war,' said Yvette coolly.

The little Jewess gazed at Yvette with great eyes of stupor.

'You're not in love with that *gipsy*!' she said.

'Well!' said Yvette. 'I don't know. He's the only one that makes me feel – different! He really is!'

'But how? How? Has he ever *said* anything to you?'

'No! No!'

'Then how? What has he done?'

'Oh, just looked at me!'

'How?'

'Well you see, I don't know. But different! Yes, different! Different, quite different from the way any man ever looked at me.'

'But *how* did he look at you?' insisted the Jewess.

'Why – as if he really, but *really, desired* me,' said Yvette, her meditative face looking like the bud of a flower.

'What a vile fellow! What *right* had he to look at you like that?' cried the indignant Jewess.

'A cat may look at a king,' calmly interposed the Major, and now his face had the smiles of a cat's face.

'You think he oughtn't to?' asked Yvette, turning to him.

'Certainly not! A gipsy fellow, with half a dozen dirty women trailing after him! Certainly not!' cried the tiny Jewess.

'I wondered!' said Yvette. 'Because it *was* rather wonderful, really! And it *was* something quite different in my life.'

'I think,' said the Major, taking his pipe from his mouth, 'that desire is the most wonderful thing in life. Anybody who can really feel it, is a king, and I envy nobody else!' He put back his pipe.

The Jewess looked at him stupefied.

'But Charles!' she cried. 'Every common low man in Halifax feels nothing else!'

He again took his pipe from his mouth.

'That's merely appetite,' he said.

And he put back his pipe.

'You think the gipsy is the real thing?' Yvette asked him.

He lifted his shoulders.

'It's not for me to say,' he replied. 'If I were you, I should know, I shouldn't be asking other people.'

'Yes – but –' Yvette trailed out.

'Charles! You're wrong! How *could* it be a real thing! As if she could possibly marry him and go round in a caravan!'

'I didn't say marry him,' said Charles.

'Or a love affair! Why it's monstrous! What would she think of herself! – That's not love! That's – that's prostitution!'

Charles smoked for some moments.

'That gipsy was the best man we had, with horses. Nearly died of pneumonia. I thought he *was* dead. He's a resurrected man to me. I'm a resurrected man myself, as far as that goes.' He looked at Yvette. 'I was buried for twenty hours under snow,' he said. 'And not much the worse for it, when they dug me out.'

There was a frozen pause in the conversation.

'Life's awful!' said Yvette.

'They dug me out by accident,' he said.

'Oh! —' Yvette trailed slowly. 'It might be destiny, you know.'

To which he did not answer.

VIII

The rector heard about Yvette's intimacy with the Eastwoods, and she was somewhat startled by the result. She had thought he wouldn't care. Verbally, in his would-be humorous fashion, he was so entirely unconventional, such a frightfully good sport. As he said himself, he was a conservative anarchist; which meant he was like a great many more people, a mere unbeliever. The anarchy extended to his humorous talk, and his secret thinking. The conservatism, based on a mongrel fear of the anarchy, controlled every action. His thoughts, secretly, were something to be scared of. Therefore, in his life, he was fanatically afraid of the unconventional.

When his conservatism and his abject sort of fear were uppermost, he always lifted his lip and bared his teeth a little, in a dog-like sneer.

'I hear your latest friends are the half-divorced Mrs Fawcett and the *maquereau*[19] Eastwood,' he said to Yvette.

She didn't know what a *maquereau* was, but she felt the poison in the rector's fangs.

'I just know them,' she said. 'They're awfully nice, really. And they'll be married in about a month's time.'

The rector looked at her insouciant face with hatred. Somewhere inside him, he was cowed, he had been born cowed. And those who are born cowed are natural slaves, and deep instinct makes them fear with poisonous fear those who might suddenly snap the slave's collar round their necks.

It was for this reason the rector had so abjectly curled up, still so abjectly curled up before She-who-was-Cynthia: because of his slave's fear of her contempt, the contempt of a born-free nature for a base-born nature.

Yvette too had a free-born quality. She too, one day, would

know him, and clap the slave's collar of her contempt round his neck.

But should she? He would fight to the death, this time, first. The slave in him was cornered this time, like a cornered rat, and with the courage of a cornered rat.

'I suppose they're your sort!' he sneered.

'Well, they are, really,' she said, with that blithe vagueness. 'I do like them awfully. They seem so solid, you know, so honest.'

'You've got a peculiar notion of honesty!' he sneered. 'A young sponge going off with a woman older than himself, so that he can live on her money! The woman leaving her home and her children! I don't know where you get your idea of honesty. Not from me, I hope. – And you seem to be very well acquainted with them, considering you say you just know them. Where did you meet them?'

'When I was out bicycling. They came along in their car, and we happened to talk. She told me at once who she was, so that I shouldn't make a mistake. She *is* honest.'

Poor Yvette was struggling to bear up.

'And how often have you seen them since?'

'Oh, I've just been over twice.'

'Over where?'

'To their cottage in Scoresby.'

He looked at her in hate, as if could kill her. And he backed away from her, against the window-curtains of his study, like a rat at bay. Somewhere in his mind he was thinking unspeakable depravities about his daughter, as he had thought them of She-who-was-Cynthia. He was powerless against the lowest insinuations of his own mind. And these depravities which he attributed to the still-uncowed, but frightened girl in front of him, made him recoil, showing all his fangs in his handsome face.

'So you just know them, do you?' he said. 'Lying is in your blood, I see. I don't believe you get it from me.'

Yvette half averted her mute face, and thought of Granny's bare-faced prevarication. She did not answer.

'What takes you creeping round such couples?' he sneered. 'Aren't there enough decent people in the world for you to know? Anyone would think you were a stray dog, having to run round indecent couples, because the decent ones wouldn't have you. Have you got something worse than lying in your blood?'

'What have I got, worse than lying in my blood?' she asked. A cold deadness was coming over her. Was she abnormal, one of the semi-criminal abnormals? It made her feel cold and dead.

In his eyes, she was just brazening out the depravity that underlay her virgin, tender, bird-like face. She-who-was-Cynthia had been like this: a snow-flower. And he had convulsions of sadistic horror, thinking what might be the *actual* depravity of She-who-was-Cynthia. Even his *own* love for her, which had been the lust-love of the born cowed, had been a depravity, in secret, to him. So what must an illegal love be?

'You know best yourself, what you have got,' he sneered. 'But it is something you had best curb, and quickly, if you don't intend to finish in a criminal-lunacy asylum.'

'Why?' she said, pale and muted, numbed with frozen fear. 'Why criminal lunacy? What have I done?'

'That is between you and your Maker,' he jeered. 'I shall never ask. But certain tendencies end in criminal lunacy, unless they are curbed in time.'

'Do you mean like knowing the Eastwoods?' asked Yvette, after a pause of numb fear.

'Do I mean like nosing round such people as Mrs Fawcett, a Jewess, and ex-Major Eastwood, a man who goes off with an older woman for the sake of her money? Why yes, I do!'

'But you *can't* say that,' cried Yvette. 'He's an awfully simple, straightforward man.'

'He is apparently one of your sort.'

'Well! – In a way, I thought he was. I thought you'd like him too,' she said, simply, hardly knowing what she said.

The rector backed into the curtains, as if the girl menaced him with something fearful.

'Don't say any more,' he snarled, abject. 'Don't say any more. You've said too much, to implicate you. I don't want to learn any more horrors.'

'But what horrors?' she persisted.

The very naïveté of her unscrupulous innocence repelled him, cowed him still more.

'Say no more!' he said, in a low, hissing voice. 'But I will kill you before you shall go the way of your mother.'

She looked at him, as he stood there backed against the velvet curtains of his study, his face yellow, his eyes distraught like a rat's with fear and rage and hate, and a numb, frozen loneliness came over her. For her, too, the meaning had gone out of everything.

It was hard to break the frozen, sterile silence that ensued. At last, however, she looked at him. And in spite of herself, beyond her own knowledge, the contempt for him was in her young, clear, baffled eyes. It fell like the slave's collar over his neck, finally.

'Do you mean I mustn't know the Eastwoods?' she said.

'You can know them if you wish,' he sneered. 'But you must not expect to associate with your Granny, and your Aunt Cissie, and Lucille, if you do. I cannot have *them* contaminated. Your Granny was a faithful wife and a faithful mother, if ever one existed. She has already had one shock of shame and abomination to endure. She shall never be exposed to another.'

Yvette heard it all dimly, half hearing.

'I can send a note and say you disapprove,' she said dimly.

'You follow your own course of action. But remember, you have to choose between clean people, and reverence for your Granny's blameless old age, and people who are unclean in their minds and their bodies.'

Again there was a silence. Then she looked at him, and her face was more puzzled than anything. But somewhere at the back of her perplexity was that peculiar calm, virgin contempt of the free-born for the base-born. He, and all the Saywells, were base-born.

'All right,' she said. 'I'll write and say you disapprove.'

He did not answer. He was partly flattered, secretly triumphant, but abjectly.

'I have tried to keep this from your Granny and Aunt Cissie,' he said. 'It need not be public property, since you choose to make your friendship clandestine.'

There was a dreary silence.

'All right,' she said. 'I'll go and write.'

And she crept out of the room.

She addressed her little note to Mrs Eastwood. 'Dear Mrs Eastwood, Daddy doesn't approve of my coming to see you. So you will understand if we have to break it off. I'm awfully sorry –.' That was all.

Yet she felt a dreary blank when she had posted her letter. She was now even afraid of her own thoughts. She wanted, now, to be held against the slender, fine-shaped breast of the gipsy. She wanted him to hold her in his arms, if only for once, for once, and comfort and confirm her. She wanted to be confirmed by him, against her father, who had only a repulsive fear of her.

And at the same time she cringed and winced, so that she could hardly walk, for fear the thought was obscene, a criminal lunacy. It seemed to wound her heels as she walked, the fear. The fear, the great cold fear of the base-born, her father, everything human and swarming. Like a great bog humanity swamped her, and she sank in, weak at the knees, filled with repulsion and fear of every person she met.

She adjusted herself, however, quite rapidly to her new conception of people. She had to live. It is useless to quarrel with one's bread and butter. And to expect a great deal out of life is puerile. So, with the rapid adaptability of the post-war generation, she adjusted herself to the new facts. Her father was what he was. He would always play up to appearances. She would do the same. She too would play up to appearances.

So, underneath the blithe, gossamer-straying insouciance, a certain hardness formed, like rock crystallizing in her heart. She lost her illusions in the collapse of her sympathies. Outwardly, she seemed the same. Inwardly she was hard and detached, and, unknown to herself, revengeful.

Outwardly she remained the same. It was part of her game. While circumstances remained as they were, she must remain, at least in appearance, true to what was expected of her.

But the revengefulness came out in her new vision of people. Under the rector's apparently gallant handsomeness, she saw the weak, feeble nullity. And she despised him. Yet still, in a way, she liked him too. Feelings are so complicated.

It was Granny whom she came to detest with all her soul. That obese old woman, sitting there in her blindness like some great red-blotched fungus, her neck swallowed between her heaped-up shoulders and her rolling, ancient chins, so that she was neckless as a double potato, her Yvette really hated, with that pure, sheer hatred which is almost a joy. Her hate was so clear, that while she was feeling strong, she enjoyed it.

The old woman sat with her big, reddened face pressed a little back, her lace cap perched on her thin white hair, her stub nose still assertive, and her old mouth shut like a trap. This motherly old soul, her mouth gave her away. It always had been one of the compressed sort. But in her great age, it had gone like a toad's, lipless, the jaw pressing up like the lower jaw of a trap. The look Yvette most hated, was the look of that lower jaw pressing relentlessly up, with an ancient prognathous thrust, so that the snub nose in turn was forced to press upwards, and the whole face was pressed a little back, beneath the big, wall-like forehead. The will, the ancient, toad-like, obscene *will* in the old woman, was fearful, once you saw it: a toad-like self-will that was godless, and less than human! It belonged to the old, enduring race of toads, or tortoises. And it made one feel that Granny would never die. She would live on like these higher reptiles, in a state of semi-coma, for ever.

Yvette dared not even suggest to her father that Granny was not perfect. He would have threatened his daughter with the lunatic asylum. That was the threat he always seemed to have up his sleeve: the lunatic asylum. Exactly as if a distaste for Granny and for that horrible house of relatives was in itself a proof of lunacy, dangerous lunacy.

Yet in one of her moods of irritable depression, she did once fling out:

'How perfectly beastly, this house is! Aunt Lucy comes, and Aunt Nell, and Aunt Alice, and they make a ring like a ring of crows, with Granny and Aunt Cissie, all lifting their skirts up and warming their legs at the fire, and shutting Lucille and me out. We're nothing but outsiders in this beastly house!'

Her father glanced at her curiously. But she managed to put a petulance into her speech, and a mere cross rudeness into her look, so that he could laugh, as at a childish tantrum. Somewhere, though, he knew that she coldly, venomously meant what she said, and he was wary of her.

Her life seemed now nothing but an irritable friction against the unsavoury household of the Saywells, in which she was immersed. She loathed the rectory with a loathing that consumed her life, a loathing so strong, that she could not really go away from the place. While it endured, she was spell-bound to it, in revulsion.

She forgot the Eastwoods again. After all, what was the revolt of the little Jewess, compared to Granny and the Saywell bunch! A husband was never more than a semi-casual thing! But a family! – an awful, smelly family that would never disperse, stuck half dead round the base of a fungoid old woman! How was one to cope with that?

She did not forget the gipsy entirely. But she had no time for him. She, who was bored almost to agony, and who had nothing at all to do, she had not time to think even, seriously, of anything. Time being, after all, only the current of the soul in its flow.

She saw the gipsy twice. Once he came to the house, with things to sell. And she, watching him from the landing window, refused to go down. He saw her too, as he was putting his things back into his cart. But he too gave no sign. Being of a race that exists only to be harrying the outskirts of our society, for ever hostile and living only by spoil, he was too much master of himself, and too wary, to expose himself openly to the vast and gruesome clutch of our law. He had been through the war. He had been enslaved against his will, that time.

So now, he showed himself at the rectory, and slowly, quietly busied himself at his cart outside the white gate, with that air of silent and forever-unyielding outsideness which gave him his lonely, predative grace. He knew she saw him. And she should see him unyielding, quietly hawking his copper vessels, on an old, old war-path against such as herself.

Such as herself? Perhaps he was mistaken. Her heart, in its stroke, now rang hard as his hammer upon his copper, beating against circumstances. But he struck stealthily on the outside, and she still more secretly on the inside of the establishment. She liked him. She liked the quiet, noiseless clean-cut presence of

him. She liked that mysterious endurance in him, which endures
in opposition, without any idea of victory. And she liked that
peculiar added relentlessness, the disillusion in hostility, which
belongs to after the war. Yes, if she belonged to any side, and
to any clan, it was to his. Almost she could have found it in her
heart to go with him, and be a pariah gipsy-woman.

But she was born inside the pale. And she liked comfort, and
a certain prestige. Even as a mere rector's daughter, one did have
a certain prestige. And she liked that. Also she liked to chip
against the pillars of the temple, from the inside. She wanted to
be safe under the temple roof. Yet she enjoyed chipping fragments off the supporting pillars. Doubtless many fragments had
been whittled away from the pillars of the Philistine, before
Samson pulled the temple down.[20]

'I'm not sure one shouldn't have one's fling till one is twenty-
six, and then give in, and marry!'

This was Lucille's philosophy, learned from older women.
Yvette was twenty-one. It meant she had five more years in
which to have this precious fling. And the fling meant, at the
moment, the gipsy. The marriage, at the age of twenty-six, meant
Leo or Gerry.

So, a woman could eat her cake and have her bread and
butter.[21]

Yvette, pitched in gruesome, deadlocked hostility to the Saywell household, was very old and very wise: with the agedness
and the wisdom of the young, which always overleaps the agedness and the wisdom of the old, or the elderly.

The second time, she met the gipsy by accident. It was March,
and sunny weather, after unheard-of rains. Celandines were
yellow in the hedges, and primroses among the rocks. But still
there came a smell of sulphur from far-away steel-works, out of
the steel-blue sky.

And yet it was spring.

Yvette was cycling slowly along by Codnor Gate, past the lime
quarries, when she saw the gipsy coming away from the door of
a stone cottage. His cart stood there in the road. He was returning
with his brooms and copper things, to the cart.

She got down from her bicycle. As she saw him, she loved with curious tenderness, the slim lines of his body in the green jersey, the turn of his silent face. She felt she knew him better than she knew anybody on earth, even Lucille, and belonged to him, in some way, for ever.

'Have you made anything new and nice?' she asked innocently, looking at his copper things.

'I don't think,' he said, glancing back at her.

The desire was still there, still curious and naked, in his eyes. But it was more remote, the boldness diminished. There was a glint, as if he might dislike her. But this dissolved again, as he saw her looking among his bits of copper and brasswork. She searched them diligently.

There was a little oval brass plate, with a queer figure like a palm-tree beaten upon it.

'I like that,' she said. 'How much is it?'

'What you like,' he said.

This made her nervous: he seemed off-hand, almost mocking.

'I'd rather you said,' she told him, looking up at him.

'You give me what you like,' he said.

'No!' she said, suddenly. 'If you won't tell me I won't have it.'

'All right,' he said. 'Two shilling.'

She found half-a-crown, and he drew from his pocket a handful of silver, from which he gave her sixpence.

'The old gipsy dreamed something about you,' he said, looking at her with curious, searching eyes.

'Did she!' cried Yvette, at once interested. 'What was it?'

'She said: Be braver in your heart, or you lose your game. She said it this way: Be braver in your body, or your luck will leave you. And she said as well: Listen for the voice of water.'

Yvette was very much impressed.

'And what does it mean?' she asked.

'I asked her,' he said. 'She says she don't know.'

'Tell me again what it was,' said Yvette.

' "Be braver in your body, or your luck will go." And: "Listen for the voice of water." '

He looked in silence at her soft, pondering face. Something almost like a perfume seemed to flow from her young bosom direct to him, in a grateful connexion.

'I'm to be braver in my body, and I'm to listen for the voice of water! All right!' she said. 'I don't understand, but perhaps I shall.'

She looked at him with clear eyes. Man or woman is made up of many selves. With one self, she loved this gipsy man. With many selves, she ignored him or had a distaste for him.

'You're not coming up to the Head no more?' he asked.

Again she looked at him absently.

'Perhaps I will,' she said, 'some time. Some time!'

'Spring weather!' he said, smiling faintly and glancing round at the sun. 'We're going to break camp soon, and go away.'

'When?' she said.

'Perhaps next week.'

'Where to?'

Again he made a move with his head.

'Perhaps up north,' he said.

She looked at him.

'All right!' she said. 'Perhaps I *will* come up before you go, and say Goodbye! to your wife and to the old woman who sent me the message.'

IX

Yvette did not keep her promise. The few March days were lovely, and she let them slip. She had a curious reluctance, always, towards taking action, or making any real move of her own. She alway wanted someone else to make a move for her, as if she did not want to play her own game of life.

She lived as usual, went out to her friends, to parties, and danced with the undiminished Leo. She wanted to go up and say goodbye! to the gipsies. She wanted to. And nothing prevented her.

On the Friday afternoon especially she wanted to go. It was sunny, and the last yellow crocuses down the drive were in full blaze, wide open, the first bees rolling in them. The Papple rushed under the stone bridge, uncannily full, nearly filling the arches. There was the scent of a mezereon tree.

And she felt too lazy, too lazy, too lazy. She strayed in the garden by the river, half dreamy, expecting something. While the gleam of spring sun lasted, she would be out of doors. Indoors Granny, sitting back like some awful old prelate, in her bulk of black silk and her white lace cap, was warming her feet by the fire, and hearing everything that Aunt Nell had to say. Friday was Aunt Nell's day. She usually came for lunch, and left after an early tea. So the mother and the large, rather common daughter, who was a widow at the age of forty, sat gossiping by the fire, while Aunt Cissie prowled in and out. Friday was the rector's day for going to town: it was also the housemaid's half day.

Yvette sat on a wooden seat in the garden, only a few feet above the bank of the swollen river, which rolled a strange, uncanny mass of water. The crocuses were passing in the ornamental beds, the grass was dark green where it was mown, the laurels looked a little brighter. Aunt Cissie appeared at the top of the porch steps, and called to ask if Yvette wanted that early cup of tea. Because of the river just below, Yvette could not hear what Aunt Cissie said, but she guessed, and shook her head. An early cup of tea, indoors, when the sun actually shone? No thanks!

She was conscious of her gipsy, as she sat there musing in the sun. Her soul had the half painful, half easing knack of leaving her, and straying away to some place, to somebody that had caught her imagination. Some days she would be at the Framleys', even though she did not go near them. Some days, she was all the time in spirit with the Eastwoods. And today it was the gipsies. She was up at their encampment in the quarry. She saw the man hammering his copper, lifting his head to look at the road; and the children playing in the horse-shelter: and the women, the gipsy's wife and the strong, elderly woman, coming home with their packs, along with the elderly man. For this afternoon, she felt intensely that *that* was home for her: the gipsy camp, the fire, the stool, the man with the hammer, the old crone.

It was part of her nature, to get these fits of yearning for some place she knew; to be in a certain place; with somebody who meant home to her. This afternoon it was the gipsy camp. And the man in the green jersey made it home to her. Just to be where he was, that was to be at home. The caravans, the brats, the other women: everything was natural to her, her home, as if she had been born there. She wondered if the gipsy was aware of her: if he could see her sitting on the stool by the fire; if he would lift his head and see her as she rose, looking at him slowly and significantly, turning towards the steps of his caravan. Did he know? Did he know?

Vaguely she looked up the steep of dark larch trees north of the house, where unseen the road climbed, going towards the Head. There was nothing, and her glance strayed down again. At the foot of the slope the river turned, thrown back harshly, ominously, against the low rocks across stream, then pouring past the garden to the bridge. It was unnaturally full, and whitey-muddy, and ponderous. 'Listen for the voice of the water,' she said to herself. 'No need to listen for it, if the voice means the noise!'

And again she looked at the swollen river breaking angrily as it came round the bend. Above it the black-looking kitchen garden hung, and the hard-natured fruit trees. Everything was on the tilt, facing south and south-west, for the sun. Behind, above the house and the kitchen garden hung the steep little wood of withered-seeming larches. The gardener was working in the kitchen garden, high up there, by the edge of the larch-wood.

She heard a call. It was Aunt Cissie and Aunt Nell. They were on the drive, waving Goodbye! Yvette waved back. Then Aunt Cissie, pitching her voice against the waters, called:

'I shan't be long. Don't forget Granny is alone!'

'All right!' screamed Yvette rather ineffectually.

And she sat on her bench and watched the two undignified, long-coated women walk slowly over the bridge and begin the curving climb on the opposite slope, Aunt Nell carrying a sort of suit-case in which she brought a few goods for Granny and took back vegetables or whatever the rectory garden or cupboard was yielding. Slowly the two figures diminished, on the whitish, up-curving road, labouring slowly towards Papplewick village. Aunt Cissie was going as far as the village for something.

The sun was yellowing to decline. What a pity! Oh what a pity the sunny day was going, and she would have to turn indoors, to those hateful rooms, and Granny! Aunt Cissie would be back directly: it was past five. And all the others would be arriving from town, rather irritable and tired, soon after six.

As she looked uneasily round, she heard, across the running water, the sharp noise of a horse and cart rattling on the road hidden in the larch-trees. The gardener was looking up too. Yvette turned away again, lingering, strolling by the full river a few paces, unwilling to go in; glancing up the road to see if Aunt Cissie were coming. If she saw her, she would go indoors.

She heard somebody shouting, and looked round. Down the path through the larch-trees the gipsy was bounding. The gardener, away beyond, was also running. Simultaneously she became aware of a great roar, which, before she could move, accumulated to a vast deafening snarl. The gipsy was gesticulating. She looked round, behind her.

And to her horror and amazement, round the bend of the river she saw a shaggy, tawny wave-front of water advancing like a wall of lions. The roaring sound wiped out everything. She was powerless, too amazed and wonder-struck, she wanted to see it.

Before she could think twice, it was near, a roaring cliff of water. She almost fainted with horror. She heard the scream of the gipsy, and looked up to see him bounding upon her, his black eyes starting out of his head.

'Run!' he screamed, seizing her arm.

And in the instant the first wave was washing her feet from under her, swirling, in the insane noise, which suddenly for some reason seemed like stillness, with a devouring flood over the garden. The horrible mowing of water!

The gipsy dragged her heavily, lurching, plunging, but still keeping foot-hold both of them, towards the house. She was barely conscious: as if the flood was in her soul.

There was one grass-banked terrace of the garden, near the path round the house. The gipsy clawed his way up this terrace to the dry level of the path, dragging her after him, and sprang with her past the windows to the porch steps. Before they got there, a new great surge of water came mowing, mowing trees down even, and mowed them down too.

Yvette felt herself gone in an agonizing mill-race of icy water, whirled, with only the fearful grip of the gipsy's hand on her wrist. They were both down and gone. She felt a dull but stunning bruise somewhere.

Then he pulled her up. He was up, streaming forth water, clinging to the stem of the great wisteria that grew against the wall, crushed against the wall by the water. Her head was above water, he held her arm till it seemed dislocated: but she could not get her footing. With a ghastly sickness like a dream, she struggled and struggled, and could not get her feet. Only his hand was locked on her wrist.

He dragged her nearer till her one hand caught his leg. He nearly went down again. But the wisteria held him, and he pulled her up to him. She clawed at him, horribly, and got to her feet, he hanging on like a man torn in two, to the wisteria trunk.

The water was above her knees. The man and she looked into each other's ghastly streaming faces.

'Get to the steps!' he screamed.

It was only just round the corner: four strides! She looked at him: she could not go. His eyes glared on her like a tiger's, and he pushed her from him. She clung to the wall, and the water seemed to abate a little. Round the corner she staggered, but staggering, reeled and was pitched up against the cornice of the balustrade of the porch steps, the man after her.

They got on to the steps, when another roar was heard amid the roar, and the wall of the house shook. Up heaved the water round their legs again, but the gipsy had opened the hall door. In they poured with the water, reeling to the stairs. And as they did so, they saw the short but strange bulk of Granny emerge in the hall, away down from the dining-room door. She had her hands lifted and clawing, as the first water swirled round her legs, and her coffin-like mouth was opened in a hoarse scream.

Yvette was blind to everything but the stairs. Blind, unconscious of everything save the steps rising beyond the water, she clambered up like a wet, shuddering cat, in a state of unconsciousness. It was not till she was on the landing, dripping and shuddering till she could not stand erect, clinging to the bannisters, while the house shook and the water raved below, that she was aware of the sodden gipsy, in paroxysms of coughing at the head of the stairs, his cap gone, his black hair over his eyes, peering between his washed-down hair at the sickening heave of water below, in the hall. Yvette, fainting, looked too and saw Granny bob up, like a strange float, her face purple, her blind blue eyes bolting, spume hissing from her mouth. One old purple hand clawed at a banister rail, and held for a moment, showing the glint of a wedding ring.

The gipsy, who had coughed himself free and pushed back his hair, said to that awful float-like face below:

'Not good enough! Not good enough!'

With a low thud like thunder, the house was struck again, and shuddered, and a strange cracking, rattling, spitting noise began. Up heaved the water like a sea. The hand was gone, all sign of anything was gone, but upheaving water.

Yvette turned in blind unconscious frenzy, staggering like a wet cat to the upper stair-case, and climbing swiftly. It was not till she was at the door of her room that she stopped, paralysed by the sound of a sickening, tearing crash, while the house swayed.

'The house is coming down!' yelled the green-white face of the gipsy, in her face.

He glared into her crazed face.

'Where is the chimney? the back chimney? – which room? The chimney will stand –'

He glared with strange ferocity into her face, forcing her to understand. And she nodded with a strange, crazed poise, nodded quite serenely, saying:

'In here! In here! It's all right.'

They entered her room, which had a narrow fire-place. It was a back room with two windows, one on each side the great chimney-flue. The gipsy, coughing bitterly and trembling in every limb, went to the window to look out.

Below, between the house and the steep rise of the hill, was a wild mill-race of water rushing with refuse, including Rover's green dog-kennel. The gipsy coughed and coughed, and gazed down blankly. Tree after tree went down, mown by the water, which must have been ten feet deep.

Shuddering and pressing his sodden arms on his sodden breast, a look of resignation on his livid face, he turned to Yvette.

A fearful tearing noise tore the house, then there was a deep, watery explosion. Something had gone down, some part of the house, the floor heaved and wavered beneath them. For some moments both were suspended, stupefied. Then he roused.

'Not good enough! Not good enough! This will stand – This here will stand. See – that chimney! – like a tower. Yes! All right! All right. You take your clothes off and go to bed. You'll die of the cold.'

'It's all right! It's quite all right!' she said to him, sitting on a chair and looking up into his face with her white, insane little face, round which the hair was plastered.

'No!' he cried. 'No! Take your things off and I rub you with this towel. I rub myself. If the house falls then die warm. If it don't fall, then live, not die of pneumonia.'

Coughing, shuddering violently, he pulled up his jersey hem and wrestled with all his shuddering, cold-racked might, to get off his wet, tight jersey.

'Help me!' he cried, his face muffled.

She seized the edge of the jersey, obediently, and pulled with all her might. The garment came over his head, and he stood in his braces.

'Take your things off! Rub with this towel!' he commanded ferociously, the savageness of the war on him. And like a thing obsessed, he pushed himself out of his trousers, and got out of his wet, clinging shirt, emerging slim and livid, shuddering in every fibre with cold and shock.

He seized a towel, and began quickly to rub his body, his teeth chattering like plates rattling together. Yvette dimly saw it was wise. She tried to get out of her dress. He pulled the horrible wet death-gripping thing off her, then, resuming his rubbing, went to the door, tip-toeing on the wet floor.

There he stood, naked, towel in hand, petrified. He looked west, towards where the upper landing window had been, and was looking into the sunset, over an insane sea of waters, bristling with uptorn trees and refuse. The end corner of the house, where porch had been, and the stairs, had gone. The wall had fallen, leaving the floors sticking out. The stairs had gone.

Motionless, he watched the water. A cold wind blew in upon

him. He clenched his rattling teeth with a great effort of will, and turned into the room again, closing the door.

Yvette, naked, shuddering so much that she was sick, was trying to wipe herself dry.

'All right!' he cried. 'All right! The water don't rise no more! All right!'

With his towel he began to rub her, himself shaking all over, but holding her gripped by the shoulder, and slowly, numbedly rubbing her tender body, even trying to rub up into some dryness the pitiful hair of her small head.

Suddenly he left off.

'Better lie in the bed,' he commanded, 'I want to rub myself.'

His teeth went snap-snap-snap-snap, in great snaps, cutting off his words. Yvette crept shaking and semi-conscious into her bed. He, making strained efforts to hold himself still and rub himself warm, went again to the north window, to look out.

The water had risen a little. The sun had gone down, and there was a reddish glow. He rubbed his hair into a black, wet tangle, then paused for breath, in a sudden access of shuddering, then looked out again, then rubbed again on his breast, and began to cough afresh, because of the water he had swallowed. His towel was red: he had hurt himself somewhere: but he felt nothing.

There was still the strange huge noise of water, and the horrible bump of things bumping against the walls. The wind was rising with sundown, cold and hard. The house shook with explosive thuds, and weird, weird frightening noises came up.

A terror creeping over his soul, he went again to the door. The wind, roaring with the waters, blew in as he opened it. Through the awesome gap in the house he saw the world, the waters, the chaos of horrible waters, the twilight, the perfect new moon high above the sunset, a faint thing, and clouds pushing dark into the sky, on the cold, blustery wind.

Clenching his teeth again, fear mingling with resignation, or fatalism, in his soul, he went into the room and closed the door, picking up her towel to see if it were drier than his own, and less blood-stained, again rubbing his head, and going to the window.

He turned away, unable to control his spasms of shivering. Yvette had disappeared right under the bedclothes, and nothing of her was visible but a shivering mound under the white quilt. He laid his hand on this shivering mound, as if for company. It did not stop shivering.

'All right!' he said. 'All right! Water's going down.'

She suddenly uncovered her head and peered out at him from a white face. She peered into his greenish, curiously calm face, semi-conscious. His teeth were chattering unheeded, as he gazed down at her, his black eyes still full of the fire of life and a certain vagabond calm of fatalistic resignation.

'Warm me!' she moaned, with chattering teeth. 'Warm me! I shall die of shivering.'

A terrible convulsion went through her curled-up white body, enough indeed to rupture her and cause her to die.

The gipsy nodded, and took her in his arms, and held her in a clasp like a vice, to still his own shuddering. He himself was shuddering fearfully, and only semi-conscious. It was the shock.

The vice-like grip of his arms round her seemed to her the only stable point in her consciousness. It was a fearful relief to her heart, which was strained to bursting. And though his body, wrapped round her strange and lithe and powerful, like tentacles, rippled with shuddering as an electric current, still the rigid tension of the muscles that held her clenched steadied them both, and gradually the sickening violence of the shuddering, caused by shock, abated, in his body first, then in hers, and the warmth revived between them. And as it roused, their tortured, semi-conscious minds became unconscious, they passed away into sleep.

X

The sun was shining in heaven before men were able to get across the Papple with ladders. The bridge was gone. But the flood had abated, and the house, that leaned forwards as if it were making a stiff bow to the stream, stood now in mud and wreckage, with a great heap of fallen masonry and debris at the south-west corner. Awful were the gaping mouths of rooms!

Inside, there was no sign of life. But across-stream the gardener had come to reconnoitre, and the cook appeared, thrilled with curiosity. She had escaped from the back door and up through the larches to the high-road, when she saw the gipsy bound past the house: thinking he was coming to murder somebody. At the little top gate she had found his cart standing. The gardener had led the horse away to the Red Lion up at Darley, when night had fallen.

This the men from Papplewick learned when at last they got across the stream with ladders, and to the back of the house. They were nervous, fearing a collapse of the building, whose front was all undermined and whose back was choked up. They gazed with horror at the silent shelves of the rector's rows of books, in his torn-open study; at the big brass bed-stead of Granny's room, the bed so deep and comfortably made, but one brass leg of the bed-stead perching tentatively over the torn void; at the wreckage of the maid's room upstairs. The housemaid and the cook wept. Then a man climbed in cautiously through a smashed kitchen window, into the jungle and morass of the ground floor. He found the body of the old woman: or at least he saw her foot, in its flat black slipper, muddily protruding from a mud-heap of debris. And he fled.

The gardener said he was sure that Miss Yvette was not in the house. He had seen her and the gipsy swept away. But the policeman insisted on a search, and the Framley boys rushing up at last, the ladders were roped together. Then the whole party set up a loud yell. But without result. No answer from within.

A ladder was up, Bob Framley climbed, smashed a window, and clambered into Aunt Cissie's room. The perfect homely familiarity of everything terrified him like ghosts. The house might go down any minute.

They had just got the ladder up to the top floor, when men came running from Darley, saying the old gipsy had been to the Red Lion for the horse and cart, leaving word that his son had seen Yvette at the top of the house. But by that time the policeman was smashing the window of Yvette's room.

Yvette, fast asleep, started from under the bed-clothes with a scream, as the glass flew. She clutched the sheets round her nakedness. The policeman uttered a startled yell, which he converted into a cry of: Miss Yvette! Miss Yvette!

He turned round on the ladder, and shouted to the faces below:

'Miss Yvette's in bed! – in bed!'

And he perched there on the ladder, an unmarried man, clutching the window in peril, not knowing what to do.

Yvette sat up in bed, her hair in a matted tangle, and stared with wild eyes, clutching up the sheets at her naked breast. She had been so very fast asleep, that she was still not there.

The policeman, terrified at the flabby ladder, climbed into the room, saying:

'Don't be frightened, Miss! Don't you worry any more about it. You're safe now.'

And Yvette, so dazed, thought he meant the gipsy. Where was the gipsy? This was the first thing in her mind. Where was her gipsy of this world's-end night?

He was gone! He was gone! And a policeman was in the room! A policeman!

She rubbed her hand over her dazed brow.

'If you'll get dressed, Miss, we can get you down to safe ground. The house is likely to fall. I suppose there's nobody in the other rooms?'

He stepped gingerly into the passage and gazed in terror through the torn-out end of the house, and far-off saw the rector coming down in a motor-car, on the sunlit hill.

Yvette, her face gone numb and disappointed, got up quickly, closing the bedclothes, and looked at herself a moment, then opened her drawers for clothing. She dressed herself, then looked in a mirror, and saw her matted hair with horror. Yet she did not care. The gipsy was gone, anyhow.

Her own clothes lay in a sodden heap. There was a great sodden place on the carpet where his had been, and two blood-stained filthy towels. Otherwise there was no sign of him.

She was tugging at her hair when the policeman tapped at her door. She called him to come in. He saw with relief that she was dressed and in her right senses.

'We'd better get out of the house as soon as possible, Miss,' he reiterated. 'It might fall any minute.'

'Really!' said Yvette calmly. 'Is it as bad as that?'

There were great shouts. She had to go to the window. There, below, was the rector, his arms wide open, tears streaming down his face.

'I'm perfectly all right, Daddy!' she said, with the calmness of her contradictory feelings. She would keep the gipsy a secret from him. At the same time, tears ran down her face.

'Don't you cry, Miss, don't you cry! The rector's lost his mother, but he's thanking his stars to have his daughter. We all thought you were gone as well, we did that!'

'Is Granny drowned?' said Yvette.

'I'm afraid she is, poor lady!' said the policeman, with a grave face.

Yvette wept away into her hanky, which she had had to fetch from a drawer.

'Dare you go down that ladder, Miss?' said the policeman.

Yvette looked at the sagging depth of it, and said promptly to herself: No! Not for anything! – But then she remembered the gipsy's saying: 'Be braver in the body.'

'Have you been in all the other rooms?' she said, in her weeping, turning to the policeman.

'Yes, Miss! But you was the only person in the house, you know, save the old lady. Cook got away in time, and Lizzie was up at her mother's. It was only you and the poor old lady we was fretting about. Do you think you dare go down that ladder?'

'Oh yes!' said Yvette, with indifference. The gipsy was gone anyway.

And now the rector in torment watched his tall, slender daughter slowly stepping backwards down the sagging ladder, the policeman, peering heroically from the smashed window, holding the ladder's top end.

At the foot of the ladder Yvette appropriately fainted in her father's arms, and was borne away with him, in the car, by Bob, to the Framley home. There the poor Lucille, a ghost of ghosts, wept with relief till she had hysterics, and even Aunt Cissie cried out among her tears: 'Let the old be taken and the young spared! Oh I *can't* cry for the Mater, now Yvette is spared!'

And she wept gallons.

The flood was caused by the sudden bursting of the great

reservoir, up in Papple Highdale, five miles from the rectory. It was found out later that an ancient, perhaps even a Roman mine tunnel, unsuspected, undreamed of, beneath the reservoir dam, had collapsed, undermining the whole dam. That was why the Papple had been, for that last day, so uncannily full. And then the dam had burst.

The rector and the two girls stayed on at the Framleys', till a new home could be found. Yvette did not attend Granny's funeral. She stayed in bed.

Telling her tale, she only told how the gipsy had got her inside the porch, and she had crawled to the stairs out of the water. It was known that he had escaped: the old gipsy had said so, when he fetched the horse and cart from the Red Lion.

Yvette could tell little. She was vague, confused, she seemed hardly to remember anything. But that was just like her.

It was Bob Framley who said:

'You know, I think that gipsy deserves a medal.'

The whole family suddenly was struck.

'Oh, we *ought* to thank him!' cried Lucille.

The rector himself went with Bob in the car. But the quarry was deserted. The gipsies had lifted camp and gone, no one knew whither.

And Yvette, lying in bed, moaned in her heart: Oh, I love him! I love him! I love him! The grief over him kept her prostrate. Yet practically, she too was acquiescent in the fact of his disappearance. Her young soul knew the wisdom of it.

But after Granny's funeral, she received a little letter, dated from some unknown place.

'Dear Miss, I see in the paper you are all right after your ducking, as is the same with me. I hope I see you again one day, maybe at Tideswell cattle fair, or maybe we come that way again. I come that day to say Goodbye! and I never said it, well, the water give no time, but I live in hopes. Your obdt. servant Joe Boswell.'

And only then she realized that he had a name.

The Escaped Cock

I

THERE was a peasant near Jerusalem who acquired a young gamecock which looked a shabby little thing, but which put on brave feathers as spring advanced, and was resplendent with arched and orange neck by the time the fig-trees were letting out leaves from their end-tips.

This peasant was poor, he lived in a cottage of mud-brick and had only a dirty little inner courtyard with a tough fig-tree for all his territory. He worked hard among the vines and olives and wheat of his master, then came home to sleep in the mud-brick cottage by the path. But he was proud of his young rooster. In the shut-in yard were three shabby hens which laid small eggs, shed the few feathers they had, and made a disproportionate amount of dirt. There was also, in a corner under a straw roof, a dull donkey that often went with the peasant to work, but sometimes stayed at home. And there was the peasant's wife, a black-browed youngish woman who did not work too hard. She threw a little grain, or the remains of the porridge mess, to the fowls, and she cut green fodder with a sickle, for the ass.

The young cock grew to a certain splendour. By some freak of destiny, he was a dandy rooster, in that dirty little yard with three patchy hens. He learned to crane his neck and give shrill answers to the crowing of other cocks, beyond the walls, in a world he knew nothing of. But there was a special fiery colour to his crow, and the distant calling of other cocks roused him to unexpected outbursts.

'How he sings,' said the peasant, as he got up and pulled his day-shirt over his head.

'He is good for twenty hens,' said the wife.

The peasant went out and looked with pride at his young rooster. A saucy, flamboyant bird, that had already made the final acquaintance of the three tattered hens. But the cockerel was tipping his head, listening to the challenge of far-off unseen cocks, in the unknown world. Ghost voices, crowing at him mysteriously out of limbo. He answered with a ringing defiance, never to be daunted.

'He will surely fly away one of these days,' said the peasant's wife.

So they lured him with grain, caught him, though he fought with all his wings and feet, and they tied a cord round his shank, fastening it against the spur; and they tied the other end of the cord to the post that held up the donkey's straw pent-roof.

The young cock, freed, marched with a prancing stride of indignation away from the humans, came to the end of his string, gave a tug and a hitch of his tied leg, fell over for a moment, scuffled frantically on the unclean earthen floor, to the horror of the shabby hens, then with a sickening lurch, regained his feet, and stood to think. The peasant and the peasant's wife laughed heartily, and the young cock heard them. And he knew, with a gloomy, foreboding kind of knowledge, that he was tied by the leg.

He no longer pranced and ruffled and forged his feathers. He walked within the limits of his tether sombrely. Still he gobbled up the best bits of food. Still, sometimes, he saved an extra-best bit for his favourite hen of the moment. Still he pranced with quivering, rocking fierceness upon such of his harem as came nonchalantly within range, and gave off the invisible lure. And still he crowed defiance to the cock-crows that showered up out of limbo, in the dawn.

But there was now a grim voracity in the way he gobbled his food, and a pinched triumph in the way he seized upon the shabby hens. His voice, above all, had lost the full gold of its clangour. He was tied by the leg, and he knew it. Body soul and spirit were tied by that string.

Underneath, however, the life in him was grimly unbroken. It was the cord that should break. So one morning, just before the light of dawn, rousing from his slumbers with a sudden wave of strength, he leaped forward on his wings, and the string snapped. He gave a wild strange squawk, rose in one lift to the top of the wall, and there he crowed a loud and splitting crow. So loud, it woke the peasant.

At the same time, at the same hour before dawn, on the same morning, a man awoke from a long sleep in which he was tied up. He woke numb and cold, inside a carved hole in the rock. Through all the long sleep his body had been full of hurt, and it was still full of hurt. He did not open his eyes. Yet he knew that he was awake, and numb, and cold, and rigid, and full of hurt, and tied up. His face was banded with cold bands, his legs were bandaged together. Only his hands were loose.

He could move if he wanted: he knew that. But he had no want. Who would want to come back from the dead? A deep, deep nausea stirred in him, at the premonition of movement. He resented already the fact of the strange, incalculable moving that had already taken place in him: the moving back into consciousness. He had not wished it. He had wanted to stay outside, in the place where even memory is stone dead.

But now, something had returned him, like a returned letter, and in the return he lay overcome with a sense of nausea. Yet suddenly his hands moved. They lifted up, cold, heavy and sore. Yet they lifted up, to drag away the cloth from his face, and to push at the shoulder-bands. Then they fell again, cold, heavy, numb, and sick with having moved even so much, unspeakably unwilling to move further.

With his face cleared and his shoulders free, he lapsed again, and lay dead, resting on the cold nullity of being dead. It was the most desirable. And almost, he had it complete: the utter cold nullity of being outside.

Yet when he was most nearly gone, suddenly, driven by an ache at the wrists, his hands rose and began pushing at the bandages of his knees, his feet began to stir, even while his breast lay cold and dead still.

And at last, the eyes opened. On to the dark. The same dark! yet perhaps there was a pale chink, of the all-disturbing light, prising open the pure dark. He could not lift his head. The eyes closed. And again it was finished.

Then suddenly he leaned up, and the great world reeled. Bandages fell away. And narrow walls of rock closed upon him, and gave the new anguish of imprisonment. There were chinks of light. With a wave of strength that came from revulsion, he leaned forward, in that narrow cell of rock, and leaned frail hands on the rock near the chinks of light.

Strength came from somewhere, from revulsion; there was a crash and a wave of light, and the dead man was crouching in his lair, facing the animal onrush of light. Yet it was hardly dawn. And the strange, piercing keenness of daybreak's sharp breath was on him. It meant full awakening.

Slowly, slowly he crept down from the cell of rock with the caution of the bitterly wounded. Bandages and linen and perfume fell away, and he crouched on the ground against the wall of rock, to recover oblivion. But he saw his hurt feet touching the earth again, with unspeakable pain, the earth they had meant to touch no more, and he saw his thin legs that had died, and pain unknowable, pain like utter bodily disillusion, filled him so full that he stood up, with one torn hand on the ledge of the tomb.

To be back! To be back again, after all that! He saw the linen swathing-bands fallen round his dead feet, and stooping, he picked them up, folded them, and laid them back in the rocky cavity from which he had emerged. Then he took the perfumed linen sheet, wrapped it round him as a mantle, and turned away, to the wanness of the chill dawn.

He was alone; and having died, was even beyond loneliness.

Filled still with the sickness of unspeakable disillusion, the man stepped with wincing feet down the rocky slope, past the sleeping soldiers, who lay wrapped in their woollen mantles under the wild laurels. Silent, on naked scarred feet, wrapped in a white linen shroud, he glanced down for a moment on the inert, heap-like bodies of the soldiers. They were repulsive, a slow squalor of limbs, yet he felt a certain compassion. He passed on towards the road, lest they should wake.

Having nowhere to go, he turned away from the city that stood on her hills. He slowly followed the road away from the town, past the olives, under which purple anemones were drooping in the chill of dawn, and rich-green herbage was pressing thick. The world, the same as ever, the natural world, thronging with greenness, a nightingale winsomely, wistfully, coaxingly calling from the bushes beside a runnel of water, in the world, the natural world of morning and evening, for ever undying, from which he had died.

He went on, on scarred feet, neither of this world nor of the next. Neither here nor there, neither seeing nor yet sightless, he passed dimly on, away from the city and its precincts, wondering why he should be travelling, yet driven by a dim, deep nausea of disillusion, and a resolution of which he was not even aware.

Advancing in a kind of half-consciousness under the dry stone wall of the olive orchard, he was roused by the shrill, wild crowing of a cock just near him, a sound which made him shiver as if electricity had touched him. He saw a black and orange cock on a bough above the road, then running through the olives of the upper level, a peasant in a grey woollen shirt-tunic. Leaping out of greenness, came the black and orange cock with the red comb, his tail-feathers streaming lustrous.

'O stop him, Master!' called the peasant. 'My escaped cock!'

The man addressed, with a sudden flicker of smile, opened his great white wings of a shroud in front of the leaping bird. The cock fell back with a squawk and a flutter, the peasant jumped forward, there was a terrific beating of wings, and whirring of feathers, then the peasant had the escaped cock safely under his arm, its wings shut down, its face crazily craning forward, its round eyes goggling from its white chops.

'It's my escaped cock!' said the peasant, soothing the bird with his left hand, as he looked perspiringly up into the face of the man wrapped in white linen.

The peasant changed countenance, and stood transfixed, as he looked into the dead-white face of the man who had died. That dead-white face, so still, with the black beard growing on it as if in death; and those wide-open, black, sombre eyes, that had died! and those washed scars on the waxy forehead! The slow-blooded man of the fields let his jaw drop, in childish inability to meet the situation.

'Don't be afraid,' said the man in the shroud. 'I am not dead. They took me down too soon.[1] So I have risen up. Yet if they discover me, they will do it all over again.'

He spoke in a voice of old disgust. Humanity! Especially

humanity in authority! There was only one thing it could do. He looked with black, indifferent eyes into the quick, shifty eyes of the peasant. The peasant quailed, and was powerless under the look of deathly indifference, and strange, cold resoluteness. He could only say the one thing he was afraid to say:

'Will you hide in my house, Master?'

'I will rest there. But if you tell anyone, you know what will happen. You too will have to go before a judge.'

'Me! I shan't speak. Let us be quick!'

The peasant looked round in fear, wondering sulkily why he had let himself in for this doom. The man with scarred feet climbed painfully up to the level of the olive garden, and followed the sullen, hurrying peasant across the green wheat among the olive trees. He felt the cool silkiness of the young wheat under his feet that had been dead, and the roughishness of its separate life was apparent to him. At the edges of rocks, he saw the silky, silvery-haired buds of the scarlet anemone bending downwards. And they too, were in another world. In his own world he was alone, utterly alone. These things around him were in a world that had never died. But he himself had died, or had been killed from out of it, and all that remained now was the great void nausea of utter disillusion.

They came to a clay cottage, and the peasant waited dejectedly for the other man to pass.

'Pass!' he said. 'Pass! We have not been seen.'

The man in white linen entered the earthen room, taking with him the aroma of strange perfumes. The peasant closed the door, and passed through the inner doorway into the yard, where the ass stood within the high walls, safe from being stolen. There the peasant, in great disquietude, tied up the cock. The man with the waxen face sat down on a mat near the hearth, for he was spent and barely conscious. Yet he heard outside the whispering of the peasant to his wife, for the woman had been watching from the roof.

Presently they came in, and the woman hid her face. She poured water, and put bread and dried figs on a wooden platter.

'Eat, Master!' said the peasant. 'Eat! No one has seen.'

But the stranger had no desire for food. Yet he moistened a

little bread in the water, and ate it, since life must be. But desire was dead in him, even for food and drink. He had risen without desire, without even the desire to live, empty save for the all-overwhelming disillusion that lay like nausea where his life had been. Yet perhaps, deeper even than disillusion, was a desireless resoluteness, deeper even than consciousness.

The peasant and his wife stood near the door, watching. They saw with terror the livid wounds on the thin, waxy hands and the thin feet of the stranger, and the small lacerations in the still-dead forehead. They smelled with terror the scent of rich perfumes that came from him, from his body. And they looked at the fine, snowy, costly linen. Perhaps really he was a dead king, from the region of terrors. And he was still cold and remote in the region of death, with perfumes coming from his transparent body as if from some strange flower.

Having with difficulty swallowed some of the moistened bread, he lifted his eyes to them. He saw them as they were: limited, meagre in their life, without any splendour of gesture and of courage. But they were what they were, slow inevitable parts of the natural world. They had no nobility, but fear made them compassionate.

And the stranger had compassion on them again, for he knew that they would respond best to gentleness, giving back a clumsy gentleness again.

'Do not be afraid,' he said to them gently. 'Let me stay a little while with you. I shall not stay long. And then I shall go away for ever. But do not be afraid. No harm will come to you through me.'

They believed him at once, yet the fear did not leave them. And they said:

'Stay, Master, while ever you will. Rest! Rest quietly!'

But they were afraid.

So he let them be, and the peasant went away with the ass. The sun had risen bright, and in the dark house with the door shut, the man was again as if in the tomb. So he said to the woman: 'I would lie in the yard.'

And she swept the yard for him, and laid him a mat, and he lay down under the wall in the morning sun. There he saw the first green leaves spurting like flames from the ends of the enclosed fig tree, out of the bareness to the sky of spring above. But the man who had died could not look, he only lay quite still in the sun which was not yet too hot, and had no desire in him, not even to move. But he lay with his thin legs in the sun, his black, perfumed hair falling into the hollows of his neck, and his thin, colourless arms utterly inert. As he lay there, the hens clucked and scratched, and the escaped cock, caught and tied by the leg again, cowered in a corner.

The peasant woman was frightened. She came peeping, and, seeing him never move, feared to have a dead man in the yard. But the sun had grown stronger, he opened his eyes and looked at her. And now she was frightened of the man who was alive, but spoke nothing.

He opened his eyes, and saw the world again bright as glass. It was life, in which he had no share any more. But it shone outside him, blue sky, and a bare fig tree with little jets of green leaf. Bright as glass, and he was not of it, for desire had failed.

Yet he was there, and not extinguished. The day passed in a kind of coma, and at evening, he went into the house. The peasant man came home, but he was frightened, and had nothing to say. The stranger too ate of the mess of beans, a little. Then he washed his hands and turned to the wall, and was silent. The peasants were silent too. They watched their guest sleep. Sleep was so near death, he could still sleep.

Yet when the sun came up, he went again to lie in the yard. The sun was the one thing that drew him and swayed him, and he still wanted to feel the cool air of the morning in his nostrils, see the pale sky overhead. He still hated to be shut up.

As he came out, the young cock crowed. It was a diminished, pinched cry, but there was that in the voice of the bird stronger than chagrin. It was the necessity to live, and even to cry out the triumph of life. The man who had died stood and watched the cock who had escaped and been caught, ruffling himself up, rising forward on his toes, throwing up his head, and parting his beak in another challenge from life to death. The brave sounds rang out, and though they were diminished by the cord round the bird's leg, they were not cut off. The man who had died looked nakedly on life, and saw a vast resoluteness everywhere flinging itself up in stormy or subtle wave-crests, foam-tips emerging out of the blue invisible, a black and orange cock, or the green flame-tongues out of the extremes of the fig tree. They came forth, these things and creatures of spring, glowing with desire and with assertion. They came like crests of foam, out of the blue flood of the invisible desire, out of the vast invisible sea of strength, and they came coloured and tangible, evanescent, yet deathless in their coming. The man who had died looked on the great swing into existence of things that had not died, but he saw no longer their tremulous desire to exist and to be. He heard instead their ringing, ringing, defiant challenge to all other things existing.

The man lay still, with eyes that had died now wide open and darkly still, seeing the everlasting resoluteness of life. And the cock, with the flat, brilliant glance, glanced back at him, with a bird's half-seeing look. And always the man who had died saw not the bird alone, but the short, sharp wave of life of which the bird was the crest. He watched the queer, beaky motion of the creature as it gobbled into itself the scraps of food; its glancing of the eye of life, ever alert and watchful, overweening and cautious, and the voice of its life, crowing triumph and assertion, yet strangled by a cord of circumstance. He seemed to hear the queer speech of very life, as the cock triumphantly imitated the clucking of the favourite hen, when she had laid an egg, a clucking which still had, in the male bird, the hollow chagrin of the cord round his leg. And when the man threw a bit of bread to the cock, it called with an extraordinary cooing tenderness, tousling and saving the morsel for the hens. The hens ran up greedily, and carried the morsel away beyond the reach of the string.

Then, walking complacently after them, suddenly the male bird's leg would hitch at the end of his tether, and he would yield with a kind of collapse. His flag fell, he seemed to diminish, he would huddle in the shade. And he was young, his tail-feathers, glossy as they were, were not fully grown. It was not till evening again that the tide of life in him made him forget. Then when his favourite hen came strolling unconcernedly near him, emit-

ting the lure, he pounced on her with all his feathers vibrating.
And the man who had died watched the unsteady, rocking
vibration of the bent bird, and it was not the bird he saw, but
one wave-tip of life overlapping for a minute another, in the tide
of the swaying ocean of life. And the destiny of life seemed more
fierce and compulsive to him even than the destiny of death. The
doom of death was a shadow compared to the raging destiny of
life, the determined surge of life.

At twilight the peasant came home with the ass, and he said:
'Master! It is said that the body was stolen from the garden, and
the tomb is empty, and the soldiers are taken away, accursed
Romans! And the women are there to weep.'

The man who had died looked at the man who had not died.

'It is well,' he said. 'Say nothing, and we are safe.'

And the peasant was relieved. He looked rather dirty and
stupid, and even as much flaminess as that of the young cock,
which he had tied by the leg, would never glow in him. He was
without fire. But the man who had died thought to himself:

'Why, then, should he be lifted up? Clods of earth are turned
over for refreshment, they are not to be lifted up. Let the earth
remain earthy, and hold its own again the sky. I was wrong to
seek to lift it up. I was wrong to try to interfere. The ploughshare
of devastation will be set in the soil of Judaea, and the life of this
peasant will be overturned like the sods of the field. No man can
save the earth from tillage. It is tillage, not salvation . . .'

So he saw the man, the peasant, with compassion; but the man
who had died no longer wished to interfere in the soul of the man
who had not died, and who could never die, save to return to
earth. Let him return to earth in his own good hour, and let no
one try to interfere when the earth claims her own.

So the man with scars let the peasant go from him, for the
peasant had no re-birth in him. Yet the man who had died said
to himself: 'He is my host.'

And at dawn, when he was better, the man who had died rose
up, and on slow, sore feet retraced his way to the garden. For
he had been betrayed in a garden,[2] and buried in a garden. And
as he turned round the screen of laurels, near the rock-face, he
saw a woman hovering by the tomb, a woman in blue and

yellow.[3] She peeped again into the mouth of the hole, that was like a deep cupboard. But still there was nothing. And she wrung her hands and wept. And as she turned away, she saw the man in white, standing by the laurels, and she gave a cry, thinking it might be a spy, and she said:

'They have taken him away!'

So he said to her:

'Madeleine!'

Then she reeled as if she would fall, for she knew him. And he said to her:

'Madeleine! Do not be afraid. I am alive. They took me down too soon, so I came back to life. Then I was sheltered in a house.'

She did not know what to say, but fell at his feet, to kiss them.

'Don't touch me, Madeleine,' he said. 'Not yet! I am not yet healed and in touch with men.'

So she wept because she did not know what to do. And he said:

'Let us go aside, among the bushes, where we can speak unseen.'

So in her blue mantle and her yellow robe, she followed him among the trees, and he sat down under a myrtle bush. And he said:

'I am not yet quite come to. Madeleine, what is to be done next?'

'Master!' she said. 'Oh, we have wept for you! And will you come back to us?'

'What is finished is finished, and for me the end is past,' he said. 'The stream will run till no more rains fill it, then it will dry up. For me, that life is over.'

'And will you give up your triumph?' she said sadly.

'My triumph,' he said, 'is that I am not dead. I have outlived my mission, and know no more of it. It is my triumph. I have survived the day and the death of my interference, and am still a man. I am young still, Madeleine, not even come to middle age.[4] I am glad all that is over. It had to be. But now I am glad it is over, and the day of my interference is done. The teacher and the saviour are dead in me; now I can go about my own business, into my own single life.'

She heard him, and did not fully understand. But what he said made her feel disappointed.

'But you will come back to us?' she said, insisting.

'I don't know what I shall do,' he said. 'When I am healed, I shall know better. But my mission is over, and my teaching is finished, and death has saved me from my own salvation. Oh, Madeleine, I want to take my single way in life, which is my portion. My public life is over, the life of my self-importance. Now I can wait on life, and say nothing, and have no one betray me. I wanted to be greater than the limits of my hands and feet, so I brought betrayal on myself. And I know I wronged Judas, my poor Judas. For I have died, and now I know my own limits. Now I can live without striving to sway others any more. For my reach ends in my finger-tips, and my stride is no longer than the ends of my toes. Yet I would embrace multitudes, I who have never truly embraced even one. But Judas and the high priests saved me from my own salvation, and soon I can turn to my destiny like a bather in the sea at dawn, who has just come down to the shore alone.'

'Do you want to be alone henceforward?' she asked. 'And was your mission nothing? Was it all untrue?'

'Nay!' he said. 'Neither were your lovers in the past nothing. They were much to you, but you took more than you gave. Then you came to me for salvation from your own excess. And I, in my mission, I too ran to excess. I gave more than I took, and that also is woe and vanity. So Judas and the high priests saved me from my own excessive salvation. Don't run to excess now in giving, Madeleine. It only means another death.'

She pondered bitterly, for the need for excessive giving was in her, and she could not bear to be denied.

'And will you not come back to us?' she said. 'Have you risen for yourself alone?'

He heard the sarcasm in her voice, and looked at her beautiful face which still was dense with excessive need for salvation from the woman she had been, the female who had caught men with her will. The cloud of necessity was on her, to be saved from the old, wilful Eve, who had embraced many men, and taken more than she gave. Now the other doom was on her. She wanted to give without taking. And that too is hard, and cruel to the warm body.

'I have not risen from the dead in order to seek death again,' he said.

She glanced up at him, and saw the weariness settling again on his waxy face, and the vast disillusion in his dark eyes, and the underlying indifference. He felt her glance, and said to himself:

'Now my own followers will want to do me to death again, for having risen up different from their expectation.'

'But you will come to us, to see us, us who love you?' she said.

He laughed a little and said:

'Ah yes!' Then he added: 'Have you a little money? Will you give me a little money? I owe it.'

She had not much, but it pleased her to give it to him.

'Do you think,' he said to her, 'that I might come and live with you in your house?'

She looked up at him with large blue eyes, that gleamed strangely.

'Now?' she said, with peculiar triumph.

And he, who shrank now from triumph of any sort, his own or another's, said:

'Not now! Later, when I am healed, and . . . and I am in touch with the flesh.'

The words faltered in him. And in his heart, he knew he would never go to live in her house. For the flicker of triumph had gleamed in her eyes; the greed of giving. But she murmured in a humming rapture:

'Ah, you know I would give up everything to you.'

'Nay!' he said. 'I didn't ask that.'

A revulsion from all the life he had known came over him again, the great nausea of disillusion, and the spear-thrust through his bowels. He crouched under the myrtle bushes, without strength. Yet his eyes were open. And she looked at him again, and she saw that it was not the Messiah. The Messiah had not risen. The enthusiasm and the burning purity were gone, and the rapt youth. His youth was dead. This man was middle-aged and disillusioned, with a certain terrible indifference, and a resoluteness which love would never conquer. This was not the Master she had so adored, the young, flamy, unphysical exalter of her soul. This was nearer to the lovers she had known of old, but with a greater indifference to the personal issue, and a lesser susceptibility.

She was thrown out of the balance of her rapturous, anguished adoration. This risen man was the death of her dream.

'You should go now,' he said to her. 'Do not touch me, I am in death. I shall come again here, on the third day. Come if you will, at dawn. And we will speak again.'

She went away, perturbed and shattered. Yet as she went, her mind discarded the bitterness of the reality, and she conjured up rapture and wonder, that the Master was risen and was not dead. He was risen, the Saviour, the exalter, the wonder-worker! He was risen, but not as man; as pure God, who should not be touched by flesh, and who should be rapt away into Heaven. It was the most glorious and most ghostly of the miracles.

Meanwhile the man who had died gathered himself together at last, and slowly made his way to the peasants' house. He was glad to go back to them, and away from Madeleine and his own associates. For the peasants had the inertia of earth and would let him rest, and as yet, would put no compulsion on him.

The woman was on the roof, looking for him. She was afraid that he had gone away. His presence in the house had become like gentle wine to her. She hastened to the door, to him.

'Where have you been?' she said. 'Why did you go away?'

'I have been to walk in a garden, and I have seen a friend, who gave me a little money. It is for you.'

He held out his thin hand, with the small amount of money, all that Madeleine could give him. The peasant's wife's eyes glistened, for money was scarce, and she said:

'Oh, Master! And is it truly mine?'

'Take it!' he said. 'It buys bread, and bread brings life.'

So he lay down in the yard again, sick with relief at being alone again. For with the peasants he could be alone, but his own friends would never let him be alone. And in the safety of the yard, the young cock was dear to him, as it shouted in the helpless zest of life, and finished in the helpless humiliation of being tied by the leg. This day the ass stood swishing her tail under the shed. The man who had died lay down, and turned utterly away from life, in the sickness of death in life.

But the woman brought wine and water, and sweetened cakes, and roused him, so that he ate a little, to please her. The day was hot, and as she crouched to serve him, he saw her breasts sway from her humble body, under her smock. He knew she wished he would desire her, and she was youngish, and not unpleasant. And he, who had never known a woman, would have desired her if he could. But he could not want her, though he felt gently towards her soft, crouching, humble body. But it was her thoughts, her consciousness, he could not mingle with. She was pleased with the money, and now she wanted to take more from him. She wanted the embrace of his body. But her little soul was hard, and short-sighted, and grasping, her body had its little greed, and no gentle reverence of the return gift. So he spoke a quiet, pleasant word to her, and turned away. He could not touch the little, personal body, the little, personal life in this woman, nor in any other. He turned away from it without hesitation.

Risen from the dead, he had realized at last that the body, too, has its little life, and beyond that, the greater life. He was virgin, in recoil from the little, greedy life of the body. But now he knew that virginity is a form of greed; and that the body rises again to give and to take, to take and to give, ungreedily. Now he knew that he had risen for the woman, or women, who knew the greater life of the body, not greedy to give, not greedy to take, and with whom he could mingle his body. But having died, he was patient, knowing there was time, an eternity of time. And he was driven by no greedy desire, either to give himself to others, or to grasp anything for himself. For he had died.

The peasant came home from work, and said:

'Master, I thank you for the money. But we did not want it. And all I have is yours.'

But the man who had died was sad, because the peasant stood there in the little, personal body, and his eyes were cunning and sparkling with the hope of greater rewards in money, later on. True, the peasant had taken him in free, and had *risked* getting no reward. But the hope was cunning in him. Yet even this was as men are made. So when the peasant would have helped him to rise, for night had fallen, the man who had died said:

'Don't touch me, brother. I am not yet risen to the Father.'[5]

The sun burned with greater splendour, and burnished the young cock brighter. But the peasant kept the string renewed, and the bird was a prisoner. Yet the flame of life burned up to a sharp point in the cock, so that it eyed askance and haughtily the man who had died. And the man smiled and held the bird dear, and he said to it:

'Surely thou art risen to the Father, among birds.'

And the young cock, answering, crowed.

When at dawn on the third morning the man went to the garden, he was absorbed, thinking of the greater life of the body, beyond the little, narrow, personal life. So he came through the thick screen of laurel and myrtle bushes, near the rock, suddenly, and he saw three women near the tomb. One was Madeleine, and one was the woman who had been his mother, and the third was a woman he knew, called Joan. He looked up, and saw them all, and they saw him, and they were all afraid.

He stood arrested in the distance, knowing they were there to claim him back, bodily. But he would in no wise return to them. Pallid, in the shadow of a grey morning that was blowing to rain, he saw them, and turned away. But Madeleine hastened towards him.

'I did not bring them,' she said. 'They have come of themselves. See, I have brought you money! ... Will you not speak to them?'

She offered him some gold pieces, and he took them, saying:

'May I have this money? I shall need it! – I cannot speak to them, for I am not yet ascended to the Father. And I must leave you now.'

'Ah! Where will you go?' she cried.

He looked at her, and saw she was clutching for the man in him who had died and was dead, the man of his youth and his mission, of his chastity and his fear, of his little life, his giving without taking.

'I must go to my Father!' he said.

'And you will leave us? There is your mother!' she cried,

turning round with the old anguish, which yet was sweet to her.

'But now I must ascend to my Father,' he said, and he drew back into the bushes, and so turned quickly, and went away, saying to himself:

'Now I belong to no one, and have no connexion, and my mission or gospel is gone from me. Lo! I cannot make even my own life, and what have I to save? ... I can learn to be alone.'

So he went back to the peasants' house, to the yard where the young cock was tied by the leg, with a string. And he wanted no one, for it was best to be alone; for the presence of people made him lonely. The sun and the subtle salve of spring healed his wounds, even the gaping wound of disillusion through his bowels was closing up. And his need of men and women, his fever to save them and to be saved by them, this too was healing in him. Whatever came of touch between himself and the race of men, henceforth, should come without trespass or compulsion. For he said to himself:

'I tried to compel them to live, so they compelled me to die. It is always so, with compulsion. The recoil kills the advance. Now is my time to be alone.'

Therefore he went no more to the garden, but lay still and saw the sun, or walked at dusk across the olive slopes, among the green wheat, that rose a palm-breadth higher every sunny day. And always he thought to himself:

'How good it is to have fulfilled my mission, and to be beyond it. Now I can be alone, and leave all things to themselves, and the fig tree may be barren if it will, and the rich may be rich. My way is my own alone.'

So the green jets of leaves unspread on the fig tree, with the bright, translucent, green blood of the tree. And the young cock grew brighter, more lustrous with the sun's burnishing; yet always tied by the leg with a string. And the sun went down more and more in pomp, out of the gold and red-flushed air. The man who had died was aware of it all, and he thought:

'The Word is but the midge that bites at evening. Man is tormented with words like midges, and they follow him right into the tomb. But beyond the tomb they cannot go. Now I have passed the place where words can bite no more and the air is clear, and there is nothing to say, and I am alone within my own skin, which is the walls of all my domain.'

So he healed of his wounds, and enjoyed his immortality of being alive without fret. For in the tomb he had slipped that noose which we call care. For in the tomb he had left his striving self, which cares and asserts itself. Now his uncaring self healed and became whole within his skin, and he smiled to himself with pure aloneness, which is one sort of immortality.

Then he said to himself: 'I will wander the earth, and say nothing. For nothing is so marvellous as to be alone in the phenomenal world, which is raging, and yet apart. And I have not seen it, I was too much blinded by my confusion within it. Now I will wander among the stirring of the phenomenal world, for it is the stirring of all things among themselves which leaves me purely alone.'

So he communed with himself, and decided to be a physician. Because the power was still in him to heal any man or child who touched his compassion. Therefore he cut his hair and his beard after the right fashion, and smiled to himself. And he bought himself shoes, and the right mantle, and put the right cloth over his head, hiding all the little scars. And the peasant said:

'Master, will you go forth from us?'

'Yes, for the time is come for me to return to men.'

So he gave the peasant a piece of money, and said to him:

'Give me the cock that escaped and is now tied by the leg. For he shall go forth with me.'

So for a piece of money the peasant gave the cock to the man who had died, and at dawn the man who had died set out into the phenomenal world, to be fulfilled in his own aloneness in the midst of it. For previously he had been too much mixed up in it. Then he had died. Now he must come back, to be alone in the midst. Yet even now he did not go quite alone, for under his arm, as he went, he carried the cock, whose tail fluttered gaily behind, and who craned his head excitedly, for he too was adventuring out for the first time into the wider phenomenal world, which is the stirring of the body of cocks also. And the peasant woman shed a few tears, but then went indoors, being a peasant, to look again at the pieces of money. And it seemed to her, a gleam came out of the pieces of money, wonderful.

The man who had died wandered on, and it was a sunny day. He looked around as he went, and stood aside as the pack-train passed by, towards the city. And he said to himself:

'Strange is the phenomenal world, dirty and clean together! And I am the same. Yet I am apart! And life bubbles variously. Why should I ever have wanted it to bubble all alike? What a pity I preached to them! A sermon is so much more likely to cake into mud, and to close the fountains, then is a psalm or a song. I made a mistake. I understand that they executed me for preaching to them. Yet they could not finally execute me, for now I am risen in my own aloneness, and inherit the earth, since I lay no claim on it. And I will be alone in the seethe of all things; first and foremost, for ever, I shall be alone. But I must toss this bird into the seethe of phenomena, for he must ride his wave. How hot he is with life! Soon, in some place, I shall leave him among the hens. And perhaps one evening I shall meet a woman who can lure my risen body, yet leave me my aloneness. For the body of my desire has died, and I am not in touch anywhere. Yet how do I know! All at least is life. And this cock gleams with bright aloneness, though he answers the lure of hens. And I shall hasten on to that village on the hill ahead of me; already I am tired and weak, and want to close my eyes to everything.'

Hastening a little with the desire to have finished going, he overtook two men going slowly, and talking. And being soft-footed, he heard they were speaking of himself. And he remembered them, for he had known them in his life, the life of his mission. So he greeted them, but did not disclose himself in the dusk, and they did not know him.[6] He said to them:

'What then of him who would be king, and was put to death for it?'

They answered, suspiciously: 'Why ask you of him?'

'I have known him, and thought much about him,' he said.

So they replied: 'He is risen.'

'Yea! And where is he, and how does he live?'

'We know not, for it is not revealed. Yet he is risen, and in a little while will ascend unto the Father.'

'Yea! And where then is his Father?'

'Know ye not? You are then of the Gentiles! The Father is in Heaven, above the cloud and the firmament.'

'Truly? Then how will he ascend?'

'As Elijah the Prophet, he shall go up in a glory.'

'Even into the sky.'

'Into the sky.'

'Then he is not risen in the flesh?'

'He is risen in the flesh.'

'And will he take flesh up into the sky?'

'The Father in Heaven will take him up.'

The man who had died said no more, for his say was over, and words beget words, even as gnats. But the man asked him: 'Why do you carry a cock?'

'I am a healer,' he said, 'and the bird hath virtue.'

'You are not a believer?'

'Yea! I believe the bird is full of life and virtue.'

They walked on in silence after this, and he felt they disliked his answer. So he smiled to himself, for a dangerous phenomenon in the world is a man of narrow belief, who denies the right of his neighbour to be alone. And as they came to the outskirts of the village, the man who had died stood still in the gloaming and said in his old voice:

'Know ye me not?'

And they cried in fear: 'Master!'

'Yea!' he said, laughing softly. And he turned suddenly away, down a side lane, and was gone under the wall before they knew.

So he came to an inn where the asses stood in the yard. And he called for fritters, and they were made for him. So he slept under a shed. But in the morning he was wakened by a loud crowing, and his cock's voice ringing in his ears. So he saw the rooster of the inn walking forth to battle, with his hens, a goodly number, behind him. Then the cock of the man who had died sprang forth, and a battle began between the birds. The man of the inn ran to save his rooster, but the man who had died said:

'If my bird wins, I will give him thee. And if he lose, thou shalt eat him.'

So the birds fought savagely, and the cock of the man who had died killed the common cock of the yard. Then the man who had died said to his young cock:

'Thou at least hast found thy kingdom, and the females to thy body. Thy aloneness can take on splendour, polished by the lure of thy hens.'

And he left his bird there, and went on deeper into the phenomenal world, which is a vast complexity of entanglements and allurements. And he asked himself a last question:

'From what, and to what, could this infinite whirl be saved?'

So he went his way, and was alone. But the way of the world was past belief, as he saw the strange entanglement of passions and circumstance and compulsion everywhere, but always the dread insomnia of compulsion. It was fear, the ultimate fear of death, that made men mad. So always he must move on, for if he stayed, his neighbours wound the strangling of their fear and bullying round him. There was nothing he could touch, for all, in a mad assertion of the ego, wanted to put a compulsion on him, and violate his intrinsic solitude. It was the mania of cities and societies and hosts, to lay a compulsion upon a man, upon all men. For men and women alike were mad with the egoistic fear of their own nothingness. And he thought of his own mission, how he had tried to lay the compulsion of love on all men. And the old nausea came back on him. For there was no contact without a subtle attempt to inflict a compulsion. And already he had been compelled even into death. The nausea of the old wound broke out afresh, and he looked again on the world with repulsion, dreading its mean contacts.

II

The wind came cold and strong from inland, from the invisible snows of Lebanon. But the temple, facing south and west, towards Egypt, faced the splendid sun of winter as he curved down towards the sea, and warmth and radiance flooded in between the pillars of painted wood. But the sea was invisible, because of the trees, though its dashing sounded among the hum of pines. The air was turning golden to afternoon. The woman who served Isis[7] stood in her yellow robe, and looked up at the steep slopes coming down to the sea, where the olive-trees silvered under the wind like water splashing. She was alone; save for the goddess. And in the winter afternoon the light stood erect and magnificent off the invisible sea, filling the hills of the coast. She went towards the sun, through the grove of Mediterranean pine-trees and evergreen oaks, in the midst of which the temple stood, on a little, tree-covered tongue of land between two bays.

It was only a very little way, and then she stood among the dry trunks of the outermost pines, on the rocks under which the sea smote and sucked, facing the open where the bright sun gloried in winter. The sea was dark, almost indigo, running away from the land, and crested with white. The hand of the wind brushed it strangely with shadow, as it brushed the olives of the slopes with silver. And there was no boat out.

The three boats were drawn high up on the steep shingle of the little bay, by the small grey tower. Along the edge of the shingle ran a high wall, inside which was a garden occupying the brief flat of the bay, then rising in terraces up the steep slope of the coast. And there, some little way up, within another wall, stood the low white villa, white and alone as the coast, over-looking the sea. But higher, much higher up, where the olives had given way to pine-trees again, ran the coast road, keeping to the height to be above the gullies that came down to the bays.

Upon it all poured the royal sunshine of the January after-noon. Or rather, all was part of the great sun, glow and substance and immaculate loneliness of the sea, and pure brightness.

Crouching in the rocks above the dark water which only swung up and down, two slaves, half-naked, were dressing pigeons for the evening meal. They pierced the throat of a blue, live bird, and let the drops of blood fall into the heaving sea, with curious concentration. They were performing some sacrifice, or working some incantation. The woman of the temple, yellow and white and alone like a winter narcissus, stood between the pines of the small, humped peninsula where the temple secretly hid, and watched.

A black-and-white pigeon, vividly white, like a ghost, sud-denly escaped over the low dark sea, sped out, caught the wind, tilted, rose, soared and swept over the pine-trees, and wheeled away, a speck, inland. It had escaped. The priestess heard the cry of the boy slave, a garden slave of about seventeen. He raised his arms to heaven in anger as the pigeon wheeled away, naked and angry and young he held out his arms. Then he turned and seized the girl in an access of rage, and beat her with his fist that was stained with pigeon's blood. And she lay down with her face hidden, passive and quivering. The woman who owned them watched. And as she watched, she saw another onlooker, a stranger, in a low, broad hat, and a cloak of grey homespun, a dark-bearded man standing on the little causeway of rock that was the neck of her temple peninsula. By the blowing of his dark-grey cloak, she saw him. And he saw her, on the rocks like a white-and-yellow narcissus, because of the flutter of her white linen tunic, below the yellow mantle of wool. And both of them watched the two slaves.

The boy suddenly left off beating the girl. He crouched over her, touching her, trying to make her speak. But she lay quite inert, face down on the smoothed rock. And he put his arms round her and lifted her, but she slipped back to earth like one dead, yet far too quick for anything dead. The boy, desperate, caught her by the hips and hugged her to him, turning her over there. There she seemed inert, all her fight was in her shoulders. He twisted her over, intent and unconscious, and pushed his hands between her thighs, to push them apart. And in an instant he was covering her in the blind, frightened frenzy of a boy's first passion. Quick and frenzied his young body quivered naked on hers, blind, for a minute. Then it lay quite still, as if dead.

And then, in terror, he peeped up. He peeped round, and drew slowly to his feet, adjusting his loin-rag. He saw the stranger, and then he saw, on the rocks beyond, the lady of Isis, his mistress. And as he saw her, his whole body shrank and cowed, and with a strange, cringing motion he scuttled lamely towards the door in the wall.

The girl sat up and looked after him. When she had seen him disappear, she too looked round. And she saw the stranger and the priestess. Then with a sullen movement she turned away, as if she had seen nothing, to the four dead pigeons and the knife, which lay there on the rock. And she began to strip the small feathers, so that they rose on the wind like dust.

The priestess turned away. Slaves! Let the overseer watch them. She was not interested. She went slowly through the pines again, back to the temple, which stood in the sun in a small clearing, at the centre of the tongue of land. It was a small temple of wood, painted all pink and white and blue, having at the front four wooden pillars rising like stems to the swollen lotus-bud of Egypt at the top, supporting the roof and the open, spiky lotus-flowers[8] of the outer frieze, which went round under the eaves. Two low steps of stone led up to the platform before the pillars, and the chamber behind the pillars was open. There a low stone altar stood, with a few embers in its hollow, and the dark stain of blood in its end groove.

She knew her temple so well, for she had built it at her own expense, and tended it for seven years. There it stood, pink and white like a flower in the little clearing, backed by blackish evergreen oaks; and the shadow of afternoon was already washing over its pillar-bases.

She entered slowly, passing through to the dark inner chamber, lighted by a perfumed oil-flame. And once more she pushed shut the door, and once more she threw a few grains of incense on a brazier before the goddess, and once more she sat down before her goddess, in the almost-darkness, to muse, to go away into the dream of the goddess.

It was Isis; but not Isis, Mother of Horus.[9] It was Isis Bereaved, Isis in Search. The goddess in painted marble lifted her face, and strode, one thigh forward, through the frail fluting of her robe, in the anguish of bereavement and of search. She was looking for the fragments of the dead Osiris, dead and scattered asunder, dead, torn apart, and thrown in fragments over the wide world. And she must find his hands and his feet, his heart, his thighs, his head, his belly, she must gather him together and fold her arms round the re-assembled body till it became warm again, and roused to life, and could embrace her and could fecundate her womb. And the strange rapture and anguish of search went on through the years, as she lifted her throat, and her hollowed eyes looked inward, in the tormented ecstasy of seeking, and the delicate navel of her bud-like belly showed through the frail, girdled robe with the eternal asking, asking, of her search. And through the years she found him bit by bit, heart and head and limbs and body. And yet she had not found the last reality, the final clue to him, that alone could bring him really back to her. For she was Isis of the subtle lotus, the womb which waits submerged and in bud, waits for the touch of that other, inward sun that streams its rays from the loins of the male Osiris.

This was the mystery the woman had served alone for seven years, since she was twenty, till now she was twenty-seven. Before, when she was young, she had lived in the world, in Rome, in Ephesus, in Egypt. For her father had been one of Anthony's captains and comrades, had fought with Anthony and had stood with him when Caesar was murdered, and through to the days of shame. Then he had come again across to Asia, out of favour with Rome, and had been killed in the mountains beyond Lebanon. The widow, having no favour to hope for from Octavius, had retired to her small property on the coast under Lebanon, taking her daughter from the world, a girl of nineteen, beautiful but unmarried.

When she was young the girl had known Caesar, and had shrunk from his eagle-like rapacity. The golden Anthony[10] had sat with her many a half-hour, in the splendour of his great limbs and glowing manhood, and talked with her of the philosophies and the gods. For he was fascinated as a child by the gods, though he mocked at them, and forgot them in his own vanity. But he said to her:

'I have sacrificed two doves for you, to Venus, for I am afraid you make no offering to the sweet goddess.[11] Beware, you will offend her. Come, why is the flower of you so cool within? Does never a ray nor a glance find its way through? Ah, come, a maid should open to the sun, when the sun leans towards her to caress her.'

And the big, bright eyes of Anthony laughed down on her, bathing her in his glow. And she felt the lovely glow of his male beauty and his amorousness bathe all her limbs and her body. But it was as he said: the very flower of her womb was cool, was almost cold, like a bud in shadow of frost, for all the flooding of his sunshine. So Anthony, respecting her father, who loved her, had left her.

And it had always been the same. She saw many men, young and old. And on the whole, she liked the old ones best, for they talked to her still and sincere, and did not expect her to open like a flower to the sun of their maleness. Once she asked a philosopher: 'Are all women born to be given to men?' To which the old man answered slowly:

'Rare women wait for the re-born man. For the lotus, as you know, will not answer to all the bright heat of the sun. But she curves her dark, hidden head in the depths, and stirs not. Till, in the night, one of these rare invisible suns that have been killed and shine no more, rises among the stars in unseen purple, and like the violet, sends its rare, purple rays out into the night. To these the lotus stirs as to a caress, and rises upwards through the flood, and lifts up her bent head, and opens with an expansion such as no other flower knows, and spreads her sharp rays of bliss, and offers her soft, gold depths such as no other flower possesses, to the penetration of the flooding, violet-dark sun that has died and risen and makes no show. But for the golden brief day-suns of show, such as Anthony, and for the hard winter suns of power, such as Caesar, the lotus stirs not, nor will ever stir. Those will only tear open the bud. Ah, I tell you, wait for the re-born and wait for the bud to stir.'

So she had waited. For all the men were soldiers or politicians in the Roman spell, assertive, manly, splendid apparently, but of an inward meanness, an inadequacy. And Rome and Egypt alike, had left her alone, unroused. And she was a woman to herself, she would not give herself for a surface glow, nor marry for reasons. She would wait for the lotus to stir.

And then, in Egypt, she had found Isis, in whom she spelled her mystery, she brought Isis to the shores of Sidon, and lived with her in the mystery of search; whilst her mother, who loved affairs, controlled the small estate and the slaves, with a free hand.

When the woman had roused from her muse and risen to perform the last brief ritual to Isis, she replenished the lamp and

left the sanctuary, locking the door. In the outer world, the sun
had already set, and twilight was chill among the humming trees,
which hummed still, though the wind was abating.

A stranger in a dark, broad hat rose from the corner of the
temple steps, holding his hat in the wind. He was dark-faced,
with a black pointed beard.

'O madam, whose shelter may I implore?' he said to the
woman who stood in her yellow mantle on a step above him,
beside a pink-and-white painted pillar. Her face was rather long
and pale, her dusky blonde hair was held under a thin gold net.
She looked down on the vagabond with indifference. It was the
same she had seen watching the slaves.

'Why come you down from the road?' she asked.

'I saw the temple like a pale flower on the coast, and would
rest among the trees of the precincts, if the lady of the goddess
permits.'

'It is Isis in Search,' she said, answering his first question.

'The goddess is great,' he replied.

She looked at him still with mistrust. There was a faint, remote
smile in the dark eyes lifted to her, though the face was hollow
with suffering. The vagabond divined her hesitation, and was
mocking her.

'Stay here upon the steps,' she said. 'A slave shall show you
the shelter.'

'The lady of Egypt is gracious.'

She went down the rocky path of the humped peninsula, in
her gilded sandals. Beautiful were her ivory feet, beneath the
white tunic, and above the saffron mantle her dusky-blonde head
bent as with endless musings. A woman entangled in her own
dream. The man smiled a little, half-bitterly, and sat again on
the step to wait, drawing his mantle round him, in the cold
twilight.

At length a slave appeared, also in hodden grey.

'Seek ye the shelter of our lady?' he said insolently.

'Even so.'

'Then come.'

With the brusque insolence of a slave waiting on a vagabond,
the young fellow led through the trees and down into a little gully

in the rock, where, almost in darkness, was a small cave, with a litter of the tall heaths that grew on the waste places of the coast, under the stone-pines. The place was dark, but absolutely silent from the wind. There was still a faint odour of goats.

'Here sleep!' said the slave. 'For the goats come no more on this half-island. And there is water!' He pointed to a little basin of rock where the maidenhair fern fringed a dripping mouthful of water.

Having scornfully bestowed his patronage, the slave departed. The man who had died climbed out to the tip of the peninsula, where the waves thrashed. It was rapidly getting dark, and the stars were coming out. The wind was abating for the night. Inland, the steep grooved upslope was dark, to the long wavering outline of the crest against the translucent sky. Only now and then, a lantern flickered towards the villa.

The man who had died went back to the shelter. There he took bread from his leather pouch, dipped it in the water of the tiny spring, and slowly ate. Having eaten and washed his mouth, he looked once more at the bright stars in the pure, windy sky, then settled the heath for his bed. Having laid his hat and his sandals aside, and put his pouch under his cheek for a pillow, he slept, for he was very tired. Yet during the night the cold woke him, pinching wearily through his weariness. Outside was brilliantly starry, and still windy. He sat and hugged himself in a sort of coma, and towards dawn went to sleep again.

In the morning, the coast was still chill in shadow, though the sun was up behind the hills, when the woman came down from the villa towards the goddess. The sea was fair and pale-blue, lovely in newness, and at last the wind was still. Yet the waves broke white in the many rocks, and tore in the shingle of the little bay. The woman came slowly, towards her dream. Yet she was aware of an interruption.

As she followed the little neck of rock on to her peninsula, and climbed the slope between the trees to the temple, a slave came down and stood, making his obeisance. There was a faint insolence in his humility. 'Speak!' she said.

'Lady, the man is there, he still sleeps. Lady, may I speak?'

'Speak!' she said, repelled by the fellow.

'Lady, the man is an escaped malefactor.'

The slave seemed to triumph in imparting the unpleasant news.

'By what sign?'

'Behold, his hands and feet! Will the Lady look on him?'

'Lead on!'

The slave led quickly over the mound of the hill down to the tiny ravine. There he stood aside, and the woman went into the crack towards the cave. Her heart beat a little. Above all, she must preserve her temple inviolate.

The vagabond was asleep with his cheek on his scrip, his mantle wrapped round him, but his bare, soiled feet curling side by side, to keep each other warm, and his hand lying loosely clenched in sleep. And in the pale skin of his feet, usually covered by sandal-straps, she saw the scars, and in the palm of the loose hand.

She had no interest in men, particularly in the servile class. Yet she looked at the sleeping face. It was worn, hollow, and rather ugly. But, a true priestess, she saw the other kind of beauty in it, the sheer stillness of the deeper life. There was even a sort of majesty in the dark brows, over the still, hollow cheeks. She saw that his black hair, left long, in contrast to the Roman fashion, was touched with grey at the temples, and the black pointed beard had threads of grey. But that must be suffering or misfortune, for the man was young. His dusky skin had the silvery glisten of youth still.

There was a beauty of much suffering, and the strange calm candour of finer life in the whole delicate ugliness of the face. For the first time, she was touched on the quick at the sight of a man, as if the tip of a fine flame of living had touched her. It was the first time. Men had roused all kinds of feeling in her, but never had touched her with the flame-tip of life.

She went back under the rock to where the slave waited.

'Know!' she said. 'This is no malefactor, but a free citizen of the east. Do not disturb him. But when he comes forth, bring him to me, tell him I would speak with him.'

She spoke coldly, for she found slaves invariably repellent, a little repulsive. They were so embedded in the lesser life, and their appetites and their small consciousness were a little disgusting. So she wrapped her dream round her, and went to the temple, where a slave-girl brought winter roses and jasmine, for the altar. But to-day, even in her ministrations, she was disturbed.

The sun rose over the hill, sparkling, the light fell triumphantly on the little pine-covered peninsula of the coast, and on the pink temple, in pristine newness. The man who had died woke up, and put on his sandals. He put on his hat too, slung his scrip under his mantle, and went out, to see the morning in all its blue and its new gold. He glanced at the little yellow-and-white narcissus sparkling gaily in the rocks. And he saw the slave waiting for him, like a menace.

'Master!' said the slave. 'Our Lady would speak with you at the house of Isis.'

'It is well,' said the wanderer.

He went slowly, staying to look at the pale-blue sea, like a flower in unruffled bloom, and the white fringes among the rocks, like white rock-flowers, the hollow slopes sheering up high from the shore, grey with olive-trees and green with bright young wheat, and set with the white small villa. All fair and pure in the January morning.

The sun fell on the corner of the temple, he sat down on the step, in the sunshine, in the infinite patience of waiting. He had come back to life, but not the same life that he had left, the life of little people and the little day. Re-born, he was in the other life, the greater day of the human consciousness. And he was alone and apart from the little day, and out of contact with the daily people. Not yet he had accepted the irrevocable *noli me tangere*[12] which separates the re-born from the vulgar. The separation was absolute, as yet here at the temple he felt peace, the hard, bright pagan peace with hostility of slaves beneath.

The woman came into the dark inner doorway of the temple, from the shrine, and stood there hesitating. She could see the dark figure of the man sitting in that terrible stillness that was portentous to her, had something almost menacing in its patience.

She advanced across the outer chamber of the temple, and the man, becoming aware of her, stood up. She addressed him in Greek, but he said: 'Madam, my Greek is limited. Allow me to speak vulgar Syrian.'

'Whence come you? Whither go you?' she asked, with the hurried preoccupation of a priestess.

'From the east beyond Damascus – and I go west as the road goes,' he replied, slowly.

She glanced at him with sudden anxiety and shyness.

'But why do you have the marks of a malefactor?' she asked abruptly.

'Did the Lady of Isis spy upon me in my sleep?' he asked, with a grey weariness.

'The slave warned me – your hands and feet –' she said.

He looked at her. Then he said:

'Will the Lady of Isis allow me to bid her farewell, and go up to the road?'

The wind came in a sudden puff, lifting his mantle and his hat. He put up his hand to hold the brim, and she saw again the thin brown hand with its scar.

'See! the scar!' she said, pointing.

'Even so!' he said. 'But farewell, and to Isis my homage and my thanks for sleep.'

He was going. But she looked up at him with her wondering blue eyes.

'Will you not look on Isis?' she said, with sudden impulse. And something stirred in him, like pain.

'Where then?' he said.

'Come!'

He followed her into the inner shrine, into the almost darkness. When his eyes got used to the faint glow of the lamp, he saw the goddess striding like a ship, eager in the swirl of her gown, and he made his obeisance.

'Great is Isis!' he said. 'In her search she is greater than death. Wonderful is such walking in a woman, wonderful the goal. All men praise thee, Isis, thou greater than the mother unto man.'

The woman of Isis heard, and threw incense on the brazier. Then she looked at the man.

'Is it well with thee here?' she asked him. 'Has Isis brought thee home to herself?'

He looked at the priestess in wonder and trouble.

'I know not,' he said.

But the woman was pondering, that this was the lost Osiris. She felt in the quick of her soul. And her agitation was intense.

He could not stay in the close, dark, perfumed shrine. He went out again to the morning, to the cold air. He felt something approaching to touch him, and all his flesh was still woven with pain and the wild commandment: *Noli me tangere*! Touch me not! Oh, don't touch me!

The woman followed into the open with timid eagerness. He was moving away.

'Oh stranger, do not go! O stay a while with Isis!'

He looked at her, at her face open like a flower, as if a sun had risen in her soul. And again his loins stirred.

'Would you detain me, girl of Isis?' he said.

'Stay! I am sure you are Osiris!' she said.

He laughed suddenly.

'Not yet!' he said. Then he looked at her wistful face. 'But I will sleep another night in the cave of the goats, if Isis wills it,' he added.

She put her hands together with a priestess' childish happiness.

'Ah, Isis will be glad!' she said.

So he went down to the shore, in great trouble, saying to himself: Shall I give myself into this touch? Shall I give myself into this touch? Men have tortured me to death with their touch. Yet this girl of Isis is a tender flame of healing. I am a physician, yet I have no healing like the flame of this tender girl. The flame of this tender girl! Like the first pale crocus of the spring. How could I have been blind to the healing and the bliss in the crocus-like body of a tender woman! Ah tenderness! more terrible and lovely than the death I died –

He prised small shell-fish from the rocks, and ate them with relish and wonder for the simple taste of the sea. And inwardly, he was tremulous, thinking: Dare I come into touch? For this is farther than death. I have dared to let them lay hands on me and put me to death. But dare I come into this tender touch of life? Oh this is harder –

But the woman went into the shrine again, and sat rapt in pure muse, through the long hours, watching the swirling stride of the yearning goddess, and the navel of the bud-like belly, like a seal on the virgin urge of the search. And she gave herself to the woman-flow and to the urge of Isis in Search.

Towards sundown she went on the peninsula to look for him. And she found him gone towards the sun, as she had gone the day before, and sitting on the pine-needles at the foot of the tree, where she had stood when first she saw him. Now she approached tremulously and slowly, afraid lest he did not want her. She stood near him unseen, till suddenly he glanced up at her from under his broad hat, and saw the westering sun on her netted hair. He was startled, yet he expected her.

'Is that your home?' he said, pointing to the white low villa on the slope of olives.

'It is my mother's house. She is a widow, and I am her only child.'

'And are these all her slaves?'

'Except those that are mine.'

Their eyes met for a moment.

'Will you too sit to see the sun go down?' he said.

He had not risen to speak to her. He had known too much pain. So she sat on the dry brown pine-needles, gathering her saffron mantle round her knees. A boat was coming in, out of the open glow into the shadow of the bay, and slaves were lifting small nets, their babble coming off the surface of the water.

'And this is home to you,' he said.

'But I serve Isis in Search,' she replied.

He looked at her. She was like a soft, musing cloud, somehow remote. His soul smote him with passion and compassion.

'Mayst thou find thy desire, Maiden,' he said, with sudden earnestness.

'And art thou not Osiris?' she asked.

He flushed suddenly.

'Yea, if thou wilt heal me!' he said. 'For the death-aloofness is still upon me, and I cannot escape it.'

She looked at him for a moment in fear, from the soft, blue sun of her eyes. Then she lowered her head, and they sat in silence in the warmth and glow of the western sun: the man who had died, and the woman of the pure search.

The sun was curving down to the sea, in grand winter splendour. It fell on the twinkling, naked bodies of the slaves, with their ruddy broad hams and the small black heads, as they ran spreading the nets on the pebble beach. The all-tolerant Pan watched over them. All-tolerant Pan should be their god for ever.[13]

The woman rose as the sun's rim dipped, saying:

'If you will stay, I shall send down victual and covering.'

'The lady your Mother, what will she say?'

The woman of Isis looked at him strangely, but with a tinge of misgiving.

'It is my own,' she said.

'It is good,' he said, smiling faintly, and foreseeing difficulties.

He watched her go, with her absorbed, strange motion of the self-dedicate. Her dun head was a little bent, the white linen swung about her ivory ankles. And he saw the naked slaves stand to look at her, with a certain wonder, and even a certain mischief. But she passed intent through the door in the wall, on the bay.

But the man who had died sat on at the foot of the tree overlooking the strand, for on the little shore everything happened. At the small stream which ran in round the corner of the property wall, women slaves were still washing linen, and now and again came the hollow chock! chock! chock! as they beat it against the smooth stones, in the dark little hollow of the pool. There was a smell of olive-refuse on the air; and sometimes still the faint rumble of the grindstone that was milling the olives, inside the garden, and the sound of the slave calling to the ass at the mill. Then through the doorway a woman stepped, a grey-haired woman in a mantle of whitish wool, and there followed her a bare-headed man in a toga, a Roman: probably her steward or overseer. They stood on the high shingle above the sea, and cast round a rapid glance. The broad-hammed, ruddy-bodied slaves bent absorbed and abject over the nets, picking them clean, the women washing linen thrust their palms with energy down on the wash, the old slave bent absorbed at the water's edge, washing the fish and the polyps of the catch. And the woman and the overseer saw it all, in one glance. They also saw, seated at the foot of the tree on the rocks of the peninsula, the strange man silent and alone. And the man who had died saw that they spoke of him. Out of the little sacred world of the peninsula he looked on the common world, and saw it still hostile.

The sun was touching the sea, across the tiny bay stretched the shadow of the opposite humped headland. Over the shingle, now blue and cold in shadow, the elderly woman trod heavily, in shadow too, to look at the fish spread in the flat basket of the old man crouching at the water's edge: a naked old slave with fat hips and shoulders, on whose soft, fairish-orange body the last sun twinkled, then died. The old slave continued cleaning the fish absorbedly, not looking up: as if the lady were the shadow of twilight falling on him.

Then from the gateway stepped two slave-girls with flat baskets on their heads, and from one basket the terra-cotta wine-jar and the oil-jar poked up, leaning slightly. Over the massive shingle, under the wall, came the girls, and the woman of Isis in her saffron mantle stepped in twilight after them. Out at sea, the sun still shone. Here was shadow.

The mother with grey head stood at the sea's edge and watched the daughter, all yellow and white, with dun blonde head, swinging unseeing and unheeding after the slave-girls, towards the neck of rock of the peninsula: the daughter, travelling in her absorbed other-world. And not moving from her place, the elderly mother watched that procession of three file up the rise of the headland, between the trees, and disappear, shut in by trees. No slave had lifted a head to look. The grey-haired woman still watched the trees where her daughter had disappeared. Then she glanced again at the foot of the tree, where the man who had died was still sitting, inconspicuous now, for the sun had left him; and only the far blade of the sea shone bright. It was evening. Patience! Let destiny move!

The mother plodded with a stamping stride up the shingle: not long and swinging and rapt, like the daughter, but short and determined. Then down the rocks opposite came two naked slaves trotting with huge bundles of dark green on their shoulders, so their broad, naked legs twinkled underneath like insects' legs, and their heads were hidden. They came trotting across the shingle, heedless and intent on their way, when suddenly the man, the Roman-looking overseer, addressed them, and they stopped dead. They stood invisible under their loads, as if they might disappear altogether, now they were arrested. Then a hand came out and pointed to the peninsula. Then the two green-heaped slaves trotted on, towards the temple precincts. The grey-haired woman joined the man, and slowly the two passed through the door again, from the shingle of the sea to the property of the villa. Then the old, fat-shouldered slave rose, pallid in the shadow, with his tray of fish from the sea, and the women rose from the pool, dusky and alive, piling the wet linen in a heap on to the flat baskets, and the slaves who had cleaned the net gathered its whitish folds together. And the old slave with the fish-basket on his shoulder, and the women slaves with heaped baskets of wet linen on their heads, and the two slaves with the folded net, and the slave with oars on his shoulders, and the boy with the folded sail on his arm, gathered in a naked group near the door, and the man who had died heard the low buzz of their chatter. Then as the wind wafted cold, they began to pass through the door.

It was the life of the little day, the life of little people. And the man who had died said to himself: Unless we encompass it in the greater day, and set the little life in the circle of the greater life, all is disaster.

Even the tops of the hills were in shadow. Only the sky was still upwardly radiant. The sea was a vast milky shadow. The man who had died rose a little stiffly, and turned into the grove.

There was no one at the temple. He went on to his lair in the rock. There, the slave-men had carried out the old heath of the bedding, swept the rock floor, and were spreading with nice art the myrtle, then the rougher heath, then the soft, bushy heath-tips on top, for a bed. Over it all they put a well-tanned white ox-skin. The maids had laid folded woollen covers at the head of the cave, and the wine-jar, the oil-jar, a terra-cotta drinking-cup, and a basket containing bread, salt cheese, dried figs and eggs stood neatly arranged. There was also a little brazier of charcoal. The cave was suddenly full, and a dwelling-place.

The woman of Isis stood in the hollow by the tiny spring.

Only one slave at a time could pass. The girl-slaves waited at the entrance to the narrow place. When the man who had died appeared, the woman sent the girls away. The men-slaves still arranged the bed, making the job as long as possible. But the woman of Isis dismissed them too. And the man who had died came to look at his house.

'Is it well?' the woman asked him.

'It is very well,' the man replied. 'But the lady your mother, and he who is no doubt the steward, watched while the slaves brought the goods. Will they not oppose you?'

'I have my own portion! Can I not give of my own? Who is going to oppose me and the gods?' she said, with a certain soft fury, touched with exasperation. So that he knew her mother would oppose her, and that the spirit of the little life would fight against the spirit of the greater. And he thought: Why did the woman of Isis relinquish her portion in the daily world? She should have kept her goods fiercely! —

'Will you eat and drink?' she said. 'On the ashes are warm eggs. And I will go up to the meal at the villa. But in the second hour of the night I shall come down to the temple. O, then, will you too come to Isis?' She looked at him, and a queer glow dilated her eyes. This was her dream, and it was greater than herself. He could not bear to thwart her or hurt her in the least thing now. She was in the full glow of her woman's mystery.

'Shall I wait at the temple?' he said.

'O, wait in the second hour, and I shall come.' He heard the humming supplication in her voice, and his fibres quivered.

'But the lady, your mother?' he said gently.

The woman looked at him, startled.

'She will not thwart me!' she said.

So she knew that the mother would thwart the daughter, for the daughter had left her goods in the hands of her mother, who would hold fast to this power.

But she went, and the man who had died lay reclining on his couch, and ate the eggs from the ashes, and dipped his bread in oil, and ate it, for his flesh was dry; and he mixed wine and water, and drank. And so he lay still, and the lamp made a small bud of light.

He was absorbed and enmeshed in new sensations. The woman of Isis was lovely to him, not so much in form, as in the wonderful womanly glow of her. Suns beyond suns had dipped her in mysterious fire, the mysterious fire of a potent woman, and to touch her was like touching the sun. Best of all was her tender desire for him, like sunshine, so soft and still.

'She is like sunshine upon me,' he said to himself, stretching his limbs. 'I have never before stretched my limbs in such sunshine, as her desire for me. The greatest of all gods granted me this.'

At the same time, he was haunted by the fear of the outer world. 'If they can, they will kill us,' he said to himself. 'But there is a law of the sun which protects us.'

And he said again to himself: 'I have risen naked and branded. But if I am naked enough for this contact, I have not died in vain. Before, I was clogged.'

He rose and went out. The night was chill and starry, and of a great wintry splendour. 'There are destinies of splendour,' he said to the night, 'after all our doom of littleness and meanness and pain.'

So he went up silently to the temple, and waited in darkness against the inner wall, looking out on grey darkness, stars, and rims of trees. And he said again to himself: There are destinies of splendour, and there is a greater power.

So at last he saw the light of her silk lanthorn swinging, coming intermittent between the trees, yet coming swiftly. She was alone, and near, the light softly swishing on her mantle-hem. And he trembled with fear and with joy, saying to himself: I am almost more afraid of this touch than I was of death. For I am more nakedly exposed to it.

'I am here, Lady of Isis,' he said softly out of the dark.

'Ah!' she cried, in fear also, yet in rapture. For she was given to her dream.

She unlocked the door of the shrine, and he followed after her. Then she latched the door shut again. The air inside was warm and close and perfumed. The man who had died stood by the closed door, and watched the woman. She had come first to the goddess. And dim-lit the goddess-statue stood surging forward, a little fearsome, like a great woman-presence urging.

The priestess did not look at him. She took off her saffron mantle and laid it on a low couch. In the dim light she was bare-armed, in her girdled white tunic. But she was still hiding herself away from him. He stood back in shadow, and watched her softly fan the brazier and fling on incense. Faint clouds of sweet aroma arose on the air. She turned to the statue in the ritual of approach, softly swaying forward with a slight lurch, like a moored boat, tipping towards the goddess.

He watched the strange rapt woman, and he said to himself: I must leave her alone in her rapture, her female mysteries. – So she tipped in her strange forward-swaying rhythm before the goddess. Then she broke into a murmur of Greek, which he could not understand. And, as she murmured, her swaying softly subsided, like a boat on a sea that grows still. And as he watched her, he saw her soul in its aloneness, and its female difference. He said to himself: How different she is from me, how strangely different! She is afraid of me, and my male difference. She is getting herself naked and clear of her fear. How sensitive and softly alive she is! How alive she is, with a life so different from mine! How beautiful, with a soft, strange courage of life, so different from my courage of death! What a beautiful thing, like the heart of a rose, like the core of a flame. She is making herself completely penetrable. Ah, how terrible to fail her, or to trespass on her!

She turned to him, her face glowing from the goddess.

'You are Osiris, aren't you?' she said naïvely.

'If you will,' he said.

'Will you let Isis discover you? Will you not take off your things?'

He looked at the woman, and lost his breath. And his wounds, and especially the death-wound through his belly, began to cry again.

'It has hurt so much!' he said. 'You must forgive me if I am still held back.'

But he took off his cloak and his tunic, and went naked towards the idol, his breast panting with the sudden terror of over-whelming pain, memory of overwhelming pain, and grief too bitter.

'They did me to death!' he said in excuse of himself, turning his face to her for a moment.

And she saw the ghost of the death in him as he stood there thin and stark before her, and suddenly she was terrified, and she felt robbed. She felt the shadow of the grey, grisly wing of death triumphant.

'Ah Goddess,' he said to the idol, in the vernacular. 'I would be so glad to live, if you would give me my clue again.'

For here again he felt desperate, faced by the demand of life, and burdened still by his death.

'Let me anoint you!' the woman said to him softly, 'let me anoint the scars! Show me, and let me anoint them!'

He forgot his nakedness in this re-evoked old pain. He sat on the edge of the couch, and she poured a little ointment into the palm of his hand. And as she chafed his hand, it all came back, the nails, the holes, the cruelty, the unjust cruelty against him who had offered only kindness. The agony of injustice and cruelty came over him again, as in his death-hour. But she chafed the palm, murmuring: 'What was torn becomes a new flesh, what was a wound is full of fresh life, this scar is the eye of the violet.'

And he could not help smiling at her, in her naïve priestess' absorption. This was her dream, and he was only a dream-object to her. She would never know or understand what he was. Especially she would never know the death that was gone before in him. But what did it matter? She was different. She was woman: her life and her death were different from his. Only she was good to him.

When she chafed his feet with oil and tender healing, he could not refrain from saying to her:

'Once a woman washed my feet with tears, and wiped them with her hair, and poured on precious ointment.'

The woman of Isis looked up at him from her earnest work, interrupted again.

'Were they hurt then?' she said. 'Your feet?'

'No no! It was while they were whole.'

'And did you love her?'

'Love had passed in her. She only wanted to serve,' he replied. 'She had been a prostitute.'

'And did you let her serve you?' she asked.

'Yea.'

'Did you let her serve you with the corpse of her love?'

'Ay!'

Suddenly it dawned on him: I asked them all to serve me with the corpse of their love. And in the end I offered them only the corpse of my love. This is my body – take and eat – my corpse –

A vivid shame went through him. – After all, he thought, – I wanted them to love with dead bodies. If I had kissed Judas with live love, perhaps he would never have kissed me with death. Perhaps he loved me in the flesh, and I willed that he should love me bodilessly, with the corpse of love –

There dawned on him the reality of the soft warm love which is in touch, and which is full of delight. – And I told them, blessed are they that mourn, – he said to himself. Alas, if I mourned even this woman here, now I am in death, I should have to remain dead, and I want so much to live. Life has brought me to this woman with warm hands. And her touch is more to me now than all my words. For I want to live –

'Go then to the Goddess!' she said softly, gently pushing him towards Isis. And as he stood there dazed and naked as an unborn thing, he heard the woman murmuring to the goddess, murmuring, murmuring with a plaintive appeal. She was stooping now, looking at the scar in the soft flesh of the socket of his side, a scar deep and like an eye sore with endless weeping, just in the soft socket above the hip. It was here that his blood had left him, and his essential seed. The woman was trembling softly and murmuring in Greek. And he, in the recurring dismay of having died, and in the anguished perplexity of having tried to force life, felt his wounds crying aloud, and the deep places of his body howling again: I have been murdered, and I lent myself to murder. They murdered me, but I lent myself to murder. –

The woman, silent now, but quivering, laid oil in her hand and put her palm over the wound in his right side. He winced, and the wound absorbed his life again, as thousands of times before. And in the dark, wild pain and panic of his consciousness rang only one cry: Oh, how can she take this death out of me? How can she take from me this death? She can never know! She can never understand! She can never equal it! . . .

In silence, she softly rhythmically chafed the scar with oil, absorbed now in her priestess' task, softly, softly gathering power, while the vitals of the man howled in panic. But as she gradually gathered power, and passed in a girdle round him to the opposite scar, gradually warmth began to take the place of the cold terror, and he felt: I am going to be flushed warm again, I am going to be whole! I shall be warm like the morning. I shall be a man. It doesn't need understanding. It needs newness. She brings me newness —

And he listened to the faint, ceaseless wail of distress, of his wounds, sounding as if for ever under the horizons of his consciousness. But the wail was growing dim, more dim.

He thought of the woman toiling over him: she does not know! she does not realize the death in me. But she has another consciousness. She comes to me from the opposite end of the night.

Having chafed all his lower body with oil, having worked with her slow intensity of a priestess, so that the sound of his wounds grew dimmer and dimmer, suddenly, she put her breast against the wound in his left side, and her arms round him, folding over the wound in his right side, and she pressed him to her, in a power of living warmth, like in the folds of a river. And the wailing died out altogether, and there was stillness, and darkness in his soul, unbroken dark stillness, wholeness.

Then slowly, slowly, in the perfect darkness of his inner man, he felt the stir of something coming: a dawn, a new sun. A new sun was coming up in him, in the perfect inner darkness of himself. He waited for it breathless, quivering with fearful hope . . . 'Now I am not myself — I am something new . . .'

And as it rose, he felt, with a cold breath of disappointment, the girdle of the living woman slip from him, the warmth and the glow slipped down from him, leaving him stark. She crouched spent at the feet of the goddess, hiding her face.

Stooping, he laid his hand softly on her warm, bright shoulder, and the shock of desire went through him, shock after shock, so that he wondered if it were another sort of death: but full of magnificence.

Now all his consciousness was there in the crouching, hidden woman. He stooped beside her and caressed her softly, blindly, murmuring inarticulate things. And his death and his passion of sacrifice were all as nothing to him now, he knew only the crouching fullness of the woman there, the soft white rock of life ... 'On this rock I built my life' – The deep-folded, penetrable rock of the living woman! the woman, hiding her face. Himself bending over, powerful and new like dawn.

He crouched to her, and he felt the blaze of his manhood and his power rise up in his loins, magnificent.

'I am risen!'

Magnificent, blazing indomitable in the depths of his loins, his own sun dawned, and sent its fire running along his limbs, so that his face shone unconsciously.

He untied the string on the linen tunic, and slipped the garment down, till he saw the white glow of her white-gold breasts. And he touched them, and he felt his life go molten. – Father! he said, – why did you hide this from me? – And he touched her with the poignancy of wonder, and the marvellous piercing transcendence of desire. – Lo! he said. – This is beyond prayer. – It was the deep, interfolded warmth, warmth living and penetrable, the woman, the heart of the rose! – My mansion is the intricate warm rose, my joy is this blossom! –

She looked up at him suddenly, her face like a lifted light, wistful, tender, her eyes like many wet flowers. And he drew her to his breast with a passion of tenderness and consuming desire, and a last thought: – My hour is upon me, I am taken unawares –

So he knew her, and was one with her.

Afterwards, with a dim wonder, she touched the great scars in his sides with her finger-tips, and said:

'But they no longer hurt?'

'They are suns!' he said. 'They shine from your touch. They are my atonement with you.'

And when they left the temple, it was the coldness before dawn. As he closed the door, he looked again at the goddess, and he said: 'Lo, Isis is a kindly goddess; and full of tenderness. Great gods are warm-hearted, and have tender goddesses.'

The woman wrapped herself in her mantle and went home in silence, sightless, brooding like the lotus softly shutting again, with its gold core full of fresh life. She saw nothing, for her own petals were a sheath to her. Only she thought: I am full of Osiris. I am full of the risen Osiris! ...

But the man looked at the vivid stars before dawn, as they rained down to the sea, and the dog-star[14] green towards the sea's rim. And he thought: How plastic it is, how full of curves and folds like an invisible rose of dark-petalled openness, that shows where dew touches its darkness! How full it is, and great beyond all gods. How it leans around me, and I am part of it, the great rose of Space. I am like a grain of its perfume, and the woman is a grain of its beauty. Now the world is one flower of many-petalled darknesses, and I am in its perfume as in a touch.

So, in the absolute stillness and fullness of touch, he slept in his cave while the dawn came. And after the dawn, the wind rose and brought a storm, with cold rain. So he stayed in his cave in the peace and the delight of being in touch, delighting to hear the sea, and the rain on the earth, and to see one white-and-gold narcissus bowing wet, and still wet. And he said: This is the great atonement, the being in touch. The grey sea and the rain, the wet narcissus and the woman I wait for, the invisible Isis and the unseen sun are all in touch, and at one.

He waited at the temple for the woman, and she came in the rain. But she said to him:

'Let me sit awhile with Isis. And come to me, will you come to me, in the second hour of night?'

So he went back to the cave and lay in stillness and in the joy of being in touch, waiting for the woman who would come with the night, and consummate again the contact. Then when night came the woman came, and came gladly, for her great yearning too was upon her, to be in touch, to be in touch with him, nearer.

So the days came, and the nights came, and days came again, and the contact was perfected and fulfilled. And he said: I will ask her nothing, not even her name, for a name would set her apart.

And she said to herself: He is Osiris. I wish to know no more.

Plum-blossom blew from the trees, the time of the narcissus was past, anemones lit up the ground and were gone, the perfume of bean-fields was in the air. All changed, the blossom of the universe changed its petals and swung round to look another way. The spring was fulfilled, a contact was established, the man and the woman were fulfilled of one another, and departure was in the air.

One day he met her under the trees, when the morning sun was hot, and the pines smelled sweet, and on the hills the last pear-bloom was scattering. She came slowly towards him, and in her gentle lingering, her tender hanging back from him, he knew a change in her.

'Hast thou conceived?' he asked her.

'Why?' she said.

'Thou art like a tree whose green leaves follow the blossom, full of sap. And there is a withdrawing about thee.'

'It is so,' she said. 'I am with young by thee. Is it good?'

'Yea!' he said. 'How should it not be good? So the nightingale calls no more from the valley-bed. But where wilt thou bear the child, for I am naked of all but life.'

'We will stay here,' she said.

'But the lady your mother?'

A shadow crossed her brow. She did not answer.

'What when she knows?' he said.

'She begins to know.'

'And would she hurt you?'

'Ah, not me! What I have is all my own. And I shall be big with Osiris ... But thou, do you watch her slaves.'

She looked at him, and the peace of her maternity was troubled by anxiety.

'Let not your heart be troubled!' he said. 'I have died the death once.'

So he knew the time was come again, for him to depart. He would go alone, with his destiny. Yet not alone, for the touch would be upon him, even as he left his touch on her. And invisible suns would go with him.

Yet he must go. For here on the bay the little life of jealousy and property was resuming sway again, as the suns of passionate fecundity relaxed their sway. In the name of property, the widow and her slaves would seek to be revenged on him for the bread he had eaten, and the living touch he had established, the woman he had delighted in. But he said: Not twice! They shall not now profane the touch in me. My wits against theirs.

So he watched. And he knew they plotted. So he moved from the little cave, and found another shelter, a tiny cove of sand by the sea, dry and secret under the rocks.

He said to the woman:

'I must go now soon. Trouble is coming to me from the slaves. But I am a man, and the world is open. But what is between us is good, and is established. Be at peace. And when the nightingale calls again from your valley-bed, I shall come again, sure as spring.'

She said: 'O don't go! Stay with me on half the island, and I will build a house for you and me under the pine-trees by the temple, where we can live apart.'

Yet she knew that he would go. And even she wanted the coolness of her own hair around her, and the release from anxiety.

'If I stay,' he said, 'they will betray me to the Romans and to their justice. But I will never be betrayed again. So when I am gone, live in peace with the growing child. And I shall come again; all is good between us, near or apart. The suns come back in their seasons: and I shall come again.'

'Do not go yet,' she said. 'I have set a slave to watch at the neck of the peninsula. Do not go yet, till the harm shows.'

But as he lay in his little cove, on a calm, still night, he heard the soft knock of oars, and the bump of the boat against the rock. So he crept out to listen. And he heard the Roman overseer say:

'Lead softly to the goat's den. And Lysippus shall throw the net over the malefactor while he sleeps, and we will bring him before justice, and the Lady of Isis shall know nothing of it . . .'

The man who had died caught a whiff of flesh from the oiled and naked slaves as they crept up, then the faint perfume of the Roman. He crept nearer to the sea. The slave who sat in the boat, sat motionless, holding the oars, for the sea was quite still. And the man who had died knew him.

So out of the deep cleft of a rock he said, in a clear voice:

'Art thou not that slave who possessed the maiden under the eyes of Isis? Art thou not the youth? Speak!'

The youth stood up in the boat in terror. His movement sent the boat bumping against the rock. The slave sprang out in wild fear, and fled up the rocks. The man who had died quickly seized the boat and stepped in, and pushed off. The oars were yet warm with the unpleasant warmth of the hands of slaves. But the man pulled slowly out, to get into the current which set down the coast, and would carry him in silence. The high coast was utterly dark against the starry night. There was no glimmer from the peninsula: the priestess came no more at night. The man who had died rowed slowly on, with the current, and laughed to himself: I have sowed the seed of my life and my resurrection, and put my touch for ever upon the choice woman of this day, and I carry her perfume in my flesh like essence of roses. She is dear to me in the middle of my being. But the gold and flowing serpent is coiling up again, to sleep at the root of my tree.[15]

'So let the boat carry me. Tomorrow is another day.'

Notes

1 (p. 47). German: 'Yes.' 'Where are you?' 'Here.' 'Where's that?'

2 (p. 47). On 25 October 1921 Lawrence wrote to Donald Carswell for information about Scots military dress: 'I want a man in those tight trews in a story.' (*Collected Letters*, p. 668.)

3 (p. 50). French: '– never – never, you understand.'

4 (p. 58). German: 'But of course not.'

5 (p. 58). The story is set in the Rhineland, occupied by the allies after the First World War as one of the terms of the Treaty of Versailles. The occupation was to last for fifteen years, and the treaty imposed economic penalties on Germany which caused hardship and resentment. Various remarks in the story refer to the post-war condition of Germany and Austria, and Lawrence was critical of the terms of the treaty, seeing the dangers of a Germany alienated from the rest of Western Europe. See 'Letter from Germany', *Phoenix*, p. 107.

6 (p. 61). German: literally, 'the place where you are not'; colloquially, 'the grass is always greener on the other side of the fence'.

7 (p. 64). French: impressive feat.

8 (p. 68). French: 'it's all the same'.

9 (p. 69). French: 'the done thing'.

10 (p. 71). *Hanneles Himmelfahrt* (1892), by Gerhart Hauptmann.

11 (p. 72). Lawrence is probably thinking of 'Les Bons Proupos des Religieuses de Poissy' from *Cent Contes Drolatiques*.

12 (p. 74). Italian: a kind of fine lace.

13 (p. 75). Emperor Charles V (1500–1558) was King of Spain (as Charles I) from 1516, and Holy Roman Emperor from 1519, thus bringing under one rule these two vast empires.

14 (p. 81). Caius Julius Caesar (*c*. 101–44 B.C.) conquered Gaul, invaded Britain, and re-established Cleopatra as Queen of Egypt. Germanicus (15 B.C.–19 A.D.), also called Julius Caesar, was great-nephew to Augustus and adopted son of Tiberius. He acquired the name Germanicus for victories in Germany, which, however, had no lasting effect.

15 (p. 84). British common soldiers were known as Tommies because the War Office used the imaginary name Tommy Atkins in its example of how to fill in the pay-book issued to each soldier.

16 (p. 89). French: trinkets.

17 (p. 93). An aureole or nimbus; the circle of light often represented as surrounding the head or whole figure of Christ.

18 (p. 94). German: Countess.

19 (p. 95). German: Senior Civil Servant or leading figure in the local administration. Lawrence based this character on Max von Schreibershofen, the first husband of Frieda's younger sister Johanna.

20 (p. 96). French: large gesture.

21 (p. 96). French: upstart.

22 (p. 98). German: local government offices.

23 (p. 102). German: 'Coffee, Madam!'

24 (p. 102). German: 'Yes! I'm coming.'

25 (p. 102). German: 'We're waiting for you'.

26 (p. 102). German: 'It was lovely! The water is good!'

27 (p. 102). German: hot.

28 (p. 103). French: composure, self-possession.

29 (p. 108). German: 'Good climbing!'

30 (p. 109). German: 'Good day.'

31 (p. 110). German: 'Hello.'

32 (p. 110). Tannhäuser (1205–68): German poet and wandering minstrel; legendary hero of popular stories and of Wagner's opera of that name. Siegfried: slayer of monsters in Teutonic mythology; also a Wagnerian hero. Balder: in Teutonic mythology the son of Odin and a god of light, whose early life was filled with harmony and happiness, he being the favourite of the gods.

33 (p. 111). French: heart-broken.

34 (p. 115). German: 'This rain isn't the sort to last long.'

35 (p. 122). Beads made of borax (the acid borate of sodium or biborate of soda) are used in blowpipe analysis to distinguish the metallic oxides, and to test minerals by the characteristic colours they give in the flame. (*Shorter Oxford English Dictionary*.)

36 (p. 128). German: 'Yes.'

37 (p. 131). Griselda is the heroine of the last tale in Boccaccio's *Decameron*. Her husband, the Marquis de Saluzzo, subjected her to various severe trials, all of which she suffered without protest. She has therefore come to be regarded as the archetype of enduring patience and conjugal obedience.

38 (p. 132). In 1921 Lawrence did contemplate going to Africa to join his friend, the painter Jan Juta.

39 (p. 134). 'Yes. Here I am. Yes, it was wonderful.'

40 (p. 134). 'Did it rain? How was the weather? Did you go on the glacier?'

41 (p. 134). 'No – not much rain. Wonderful! Yes, he was right on the glacier.'

THE FOX

1 (p. 137). The Daylight Saving Bill, instituting British Summer Time, came into effect on 21 May 1916.

2 (p. 138). The White Horse Hills in Berkshire are so called because of the great figure of a white horse cut into the chalk of a hillside near Wantage. It is 374 feet long and visible from a distance of fifteen miles.

3 (p. 158). Thomas Mayne Reid (1818–83), Irish writer of adventure stories.

THE LADYBIRD

1 (p. 206). Latin: sorrowing mother; a common depiction of Mary weeping over the body of Christ.

2 (p. 210). Three figures from Greek mythology famous for their fierce chastity. Artemis was a nature deity, traditionally the virgin huntress, daughter of Zeus and twin of Apollo. She was worshipped as a moon goddess. In Ephesus she was a very different figure – a many-breasted goddess of fertility. Atlanta was also a virgin huntress, but not an immortal. She was famed for her running, and in order to avoid marriage, she refused to accept any but the man who could outrun her. Many failed, but at last Melanion succeeded by dropping three golden apples during the race, which Atlanta paused to pick up. Daphne was a nymph desired by the god Apollo. She was able to escape his embrace only by being changed into a laurel tree.

3 (p. 213). Italian: wan, ashen.

4 (p. 215). French: literally, false step; colloquially, social blunder.

5 (p. 226). Cerberus in Greek mythology was a monstrous many-headed dog, guardian of Hades. He would allow entry to the under-world, but not escape. He could, however, be appeased by a gift of honey cakes.

6 (p. 228). Nickname of a type of German cannon in the First World War.

7 (p. 234). Dionysos is most widely known as the Greek god of wine and revelry. The cradle of his cult was in Thrace, to the north, so he is often considered to originate from there. Legends tell of his wander-ings through the known world, spreading the culture of the vine and acquiring, as he went, characteristics of the regions through which he passed. From Asia he acquired the youthful, somewhat effeminate

appearance which is the usual depiction of him. The major tradition of his birth is that he was the son of Semele and Zeus. Semele pleaded with Zeus to appear before her in his full glory; but she, being mortal, was unable to endure the sight, and was consumed as by fire. Zeus saved the as yet unborn Dionysos by grafting him into his own thigh until he was ready to be born. Thus he was twice born. See Introduction for an account of a different Dionysos – Dionysos Zagreus, a destroyed and resurrected god of the underworld.

8 (p. 235). A German folksong.

9 (p. 241). Aphrodite, goddess of love in Greek mythology. According to Hesiod, she was born from the foam which gathered round the severed phallus of the sky-god Ouranos, and rose naked from the sea near the island of Cythera. Thus she is always associated with both sea and sky. She was worshipped in Asia as Ishtar or Ashtaroth, and Astarte, a moon-goddess. Her Roman name is Venus.

10 (p. 244). Cybele was a great Phrygian earth-goddess, also worshipped as a moon-goddess. The Greeks identified her with the Hellenic Rhea, but she retained much of her Asiatic character. Her followers sometimes practised self-castration as part of their orgiastic rites. She is often identified with Aphrodite.

Isis was a moon- and fertility-goddess in Egyptian mythology. See note 7 to 'The Escaped Cock'.

11 (p. 244). Astarte was a Syrian earth-goddess associated also with the moon because it was believed to govern growth, decay and rebirth.

12 (p. 246). Proserpine, or Persephone, was, in Greek mythology, the daughter or underworld counterpart of Demeter, goddess of the fruitful earth. She was seized by Hades (Pluto), god of the underworld, and taken to be queen of his kingdom. Demeter managed to procure the return of her daughter for half the year, during which time the earth could once more bear fruit. See also Introduction.

13 (p. 247). Latin: in the highest.

14 (p. 254). Kaiser Wilhelm II (1859–1941), King of Prussia and Emperor of Germany. His military ambitions helped to precipitate the First World War, at the end of which he abdicated.

15 (p. 254). The Hohenzollerns were the German dynasty which held the royal or imperial crown from 1701 to 1918. The Habsburgs were the great ruling dynasty of Austria from 1282 to 1918. The murder of the heir to the Habsburg empire at Sarajevo in 1914 had been the immediate provocation of the outbreak of war.

16 (p. 255). Judas Iscariot was the disciple who betrayed Jesus with a kiss, and who has therefore come to be the archetype of the traitor.

17 (p. 257). The Romanovs were the ruling dynasty in Russia from

1613 to 1917, when revolution deposed them. The entire family was shot in July 1918.

18 (p. 262). Jean Henri Fabre (1823–1915), a French naturalist whose studies of insect behaviour were recorded in his *Souvenirs entomologiques*. Lawrence may have been familiar with his work as early as 1911, when reports of it appeared in *The English Review*, of which he was a regular reader.

19 (p. 270). The story of Paolo and Francesca is told in the fifth canto of Dante's *Inferno*. Francesca di Rimini and Paolo, brother of her husband Gianciotto Malatesta, Lord of Rimini, were put to death in 1389 for adultery. In Dante, this crime assigns them to Hell, but because their love is genuine and mutual, they are allowed to share their wanderings there.

In Greek mythology, Hades is the name of the underworld and of its king. The place was conceived as a vague and shadowy region to which all souls retired after death. At first it was not the equivalent of the Christian idea of Hell, having nothing to do with sin and damnation. Gradually, however, the idea of judgement entered in, and souls were thought of as being consigned either to Tartarus, a place of unending torment, or to Elysium, a place of eternal happiness, according to a person's conduct during life.

ST MAWR

1 (p. 276). French: muzzle of an animal; colloquial for face.

2 (p. 277). French: street-urchin, hoyden.

3 (p. 278). Paul Cézanne (1839–1906) and Auguste Renoir (1841–1919), major French Impressionist painters.

4 (p. 278). Unredeemed and uncivilized man.

5 (p. 280). French: domestic arrangements.

6 (p. 281). French: Parisian tough or hooligan.

7 (p. 281). Rotten Row is an avenue in Hyde Park where members of high society traditionally ride.

8 (p. 281). French: high society.

9 (p. 281). The fashionable park for riding in Paris.

10 (p. 281). The equivalent in Rome, in the gardens of the Villa Borghese.

11 (p. 282). In Greek fable Argus had a hundred eyes and was employed by Juno as a spy who never missed anything.

12 (p. 282). Abraham Lincoln (1809–65), the sixteenth President of the U.S.A., who in 1862 declared all slaves to be free.

13 (p. 282). Arthur Balfour (1848–1930) was a philosopher who became Prime Minister of England from 1902 to 1905.

14 (p. 283). French: living people arranged to resemble a statuary group or painting.

15 (p. 284). Welsh: big, great. Pronounced with a short 'a' and rolled 'r'. For the significance of the name, see Introduction.

16 (p. 291). French: complacency, conceit.

17 (p. 291). 'Mahomet made the people believe that he would call a hill to him, and from the top of it offer up his prayers for the observers of his law. The people assembled: Mahomet called the hill to come to him again and again; and when the hill stood still, he was never a whit abashed, but said, "If the hill will not come to Mahomet, Mahomet will go to the hill."' (Bacon, *Essays*, p. 12, 'Boldness'.)

18 (p. 292). Hippolytus, a son of Theseus, whose name means 'of the stampeding horses', was dragged to his death by wild horses as a punishment for pride. See Euripides, *Hippolytus*.

19 (p. 294). Medusa in Greek myth was the chief of the Gorgons. Her hair was made of snakes, which turned to stone anyone who looked on her.

20 (p. 296). Queen Alexandra (1844–1925) was the widow of Edward VII and mother of George V.

21 (p. 296). An attendant in a Pullman car, a railway carriage designed by George M. Pullman as a saloon and sleeping-car.

22 (p. 298). Both Sèvres (France) and Dresden (Germany) were famous for delicate ornamental porcelain.

23 (p. 299). French: thrill, stimulus.

24 (p. 299). Claridge's and the Carlton were exclusive London hotels.

25 (p. 300). Barmecide is a character in *The Arabian Nights* who invites a starving beggar to dinner, then sets before him empty plates. Thus the word has come to signify all illusory hopes and empty pleasures.

26 (p. 302). A Non-conformist temperance union to which the Lawrence children had belonged: 'They also belonged to the Band of Hope and signed the pledge, and sang "There's a serpent in the glass dash it down!" and "Dare to be a Daniel, dare to stand alone", with fervent enthusiasm.' (Ada Lawrence, *The Early Life of D. H. Lawrence*.)

27 (p. 302). i.e. she was an Anglican, not a Non-conformist.

28 (p. 303). Quoted from Gabriele D'Annunzio (1863–1938), *Il Trionfo della Morte*.

29 (p. 307). French: mother-in-law.

30 (p. 316). In Greek myth the three Fates were Clotho, who held the distaff, Lachesis, who span the thread of life, and Atropos, who cut it, bringing life to an end.

31 (p. 320). See note 13.

32 (p. 323). French: fussy, over-zealous.

33 (p. 323). See Introduction p. 30.

34 (p. 325). The artist-astrologer Cartwright is based on Lawrence's friend Frederick Carter. See Introduction pp. 29–30.

35 (p. 325). Pan, the Greek god of Nature and of all created things, was usually depicted as a goat from the waist down to signify fertility and closeness to the rank earth. Sometimes, like his Celtic equivalent the Horned God Cernunnos, he also had the horns of a goat. The sight of him was supposed to produce panic. He became the Devil in Christian mythology. See Introduction pp. 30–31.

36 (p. 325). King Edward VII (1841–1910) kept several mistresses.

37 (p. 326). H. G. Wells (1866–1946) had published his *Outline of History* in 1920. Wells's assumption that all human history was progress infuriated Lawrence, who wrote in 1925: 'Hadn't somebody better write Mr Wells' History backwards, to prove how we've degenerated, in our stupid visionlessness, since the cave-men?' (*Phoenix II*, p. 434). The suggestion was eventually taken up by William Golding in *The Inheritors*.

38 (p. 336). French: joy of living.

39 (p. 346). French: non-interference, drift.

40 (p. 349). Local Spanish names for varieties of pine. The piñon (*Pinus cembroides*) is a very common, not very attractive shrub, but the pine-nuts it produces are an important food for the Indians.

41 (p. 356). A line from a First World War soldiers' song which parodies the verse from 1 Corinthians xv, 55, used in the Church of England service, the Burial of the Dead: 'O death, where is thy sting? O grave, where is thy victory?'

42 (p. 356). American: raincoat.

43 (p. 357). A reference to Thomas Gray (1716–1771), 'Elegy Written in a Country Churchyard'.

44 (p. 357). In Greek legend the Amazons were a nation of very warlike women. Hence, any aggressive or manly woman, a virago.

45 (p. 359). French: pursing of the lips.

46 (p. 362). Spanish: 'Oh, what joy!'

47 (p. 367). Edward, Prince of Wales (1894–1972), who later became, briefly, Edward VIII and then, after his abdication, the Duke of Windsor, represented to Lawrence democratic service rather than aristocratic leadership. See Lawrence's poem 'Elephant'. Lawrence had seen the Prince of Wales in Ceylon in 1922: 'We were down at the Perahera at night – were just opposite the Prince. Poor devil, he is so thin and nervy: all twitchy: and seems worn out and disheartened. No

wonder, badgered about like a doll among a mob of children. A woman threw a bouquet and he nearly jumped out of his skin.' (*Collected Letters*, p. 696.)

48 (p. 367). Italian: 'blessed god!'

49 (p. 367). Cleopatra, Queen of Egypt, had Julius Caesar as her lover. After his assassination, she had her more celebrated love-affair with Mark Antony, which ended with their simultaneous suicides.

50 (p. 379). Shakespeare, *The Merchant of Venice*.

51 (p. 380). Novel by Théophile Gautier (1811–72) in which the hero and heroine go riding together every day. She is disguised as a man, but he falls in love with her nevertheless.

52 (p. 381). Priapus, in Greek mythology, was a misbegotten son of Aphrodite, with huge tongue, belly and phallus, who became a fertility god. Many obscene stories were told of him. He later degenerated into a grotesque garden-god.

53 (p. 381). A reference to the novel *A Connecticut Yankee in King Arthur's Court* by Mark Twain (1835–1910), in which a modern American is imagined time-travelling into the Arthurian past.

54 (p. 382). Abraham, according to Genesis xvii, 1–8, was the progenitor of the Jews.

55 (p. 382). Cassandra, a prophetess and daughter of Priam, King of Troy, was raped by Ajax during the sack of Troy, then taken by Agamemnon as his concubine.

56 (p. 382). Iphegenia, younger daughter of Agamemnon and Clytemnestra, sister of Orestes and Electra, was sacrificed by her father in order to procure fair winds to take his fleet to Troy.

57 (p. 382). 'Of the death of Adonis, which every year carried him off to Persephone in the Underworld, it was most commonly said that he was wounded by a boar while hunting . . . Aphrodite was thus compelled to mourn for Adonis before she could truly possess him. The festivals at which her woeful love was celebrated were held in commemoration of the love-goddess's parting from her young lord. He lay there wounded unto death, loved and wept over by Aphrodite. In vain she tried to hold him back. On the next day he soared away through sea and air. It used to be said, however, that he was still alive. Women brought him little "gardens" – a symbol and picturesque expression, which was common in our tongue, as in others, for their own femininity.' (Kerenyi, *The Gods of the Greeks*.)

58. (p. 383). Charles II is reputed to have apologized for being 'an unconscionable time dying'.

59 (p. 383). Song by the Scottish poet Robert Burns (1759–96).

60 (p. 384). Philip Alexius de Laszlo de Lombos (1869–1937). Fashionable portrait-painter, born in Budapest, naturalized English.

61 (p. 384). Sir William Orpen (1878–1931), a prominent painter of portraits and conversation pieces, was to be one of the leading defenders of Lawrence's paintings when they were confiscated by the police in 1929.

62 (p. 387). The Pharisee regarded himself as so superior to other men that he would refuse to have any intercourse with them, and stood aloof. In the Bible scribes are professional interpreters of the Law often associated with Pharisees as upholders of ceremonial tradition; but Mrs Witt is here using the word scribe in its modern sense, as one who is in the habit of writing.

63 (p. 387). Christ's words to Mary Magdalen after the Resurrection. See 'The Escaped Cock', p. 564.

64 (p. 388). Latin: the substance of a crime. A legal term meaning the basic evidence that a crime has actually been committed, i.e. a body in the case of a murder.

65 (p. 397). French: 'The more it changes, the more it is the same thing.' 'One is no better here.'

66 (p. 400). Zane Grey (1875–1939), popular American adventure novelist.

67 (p. 401). Émile Coué (1857–1926), French psychologist whose name was particularly associated with a method of healing by auto-suggestion. Lawrence is referring to the idea that if you tell yourself often enough, with sufficient conviction, that you feel good, you will actually do so.

68 (p. 401). French: 'It never changes.'

69 (p. 408). Spanish: 'Who knows!'

70 (p. 408). The Vestal Virgins were spotless maidens serving the goddess Vesta by keeping the sacred fire burning day and night in the temple.

71 (p. 409). The Pythia, Apollo's priestess at Delphi, was regarded as the god's mystical bride.

72 (p. 413). Spanish: sires, mature males.

73 (p. 414). Rudyard Kipling (1856–1936), who wrote about the British in India.

74 (p. 415). Lawrence wrote at greater length about this same pine-tree in 'Pan in America' (*Phoenix*).

75 (p. 416). Latin: nothing more beyond, i.e. ultimate perfection.

76 (p. 416). Spanish: baked mud.

77 (p. 416). Spanish: high tableland between canyons.

78 (p. 422). One of the tasks of Hercules was to obtain the apples of

the Hesperides which were guarded by the dragon Ladon. Jason and his Argonauts passed through many dangers on their way to steal the golden fleece, which was also guarded day and night by a dragon.

79 (p. 422). Another of Hercules' labours was to clean the stables of King Augeas, in which he kept three thousand oxen. The stables had not been cleaned for thirty years.

80 (p. 423). Spanish: The Goats.

81 (p. 423). Spanish: gully.

THE PRINCESS

1 (p. 429). Ossian was the son of Fingal, a Scottish warrior-bard of the third century A.D.

2 (p. 432). French: noble birth carries the obligation to behave nobly.

3 (p. 433). Émile Zola (1840–1902), French novelist concerned with social realism, notorious at one time for his preoccupation with vice. Guy de Maupassant (1850–1893) was also regarded as risqué in the earthy sexuality of his novels and short stories.

4 (p. 433). Leo Tolstoy (1828–1910) and Fyodor Dostoevsky (1821–81) were the two outstanding nineteenth-century Russian novelists. Dostoevsky is more concerned with abnormal psychology and the darker areas of spiritual experience.

5 (p. 433). *The Decameron* is a cycle of a hundred stories, many of them frankly erotic, by the Florentine writer Giovanni Boccaccio (1313–75). The point is that all the writers mentioned in this paragraph would have been considered highly improper reading for a teenage girl.

6 (p. 433). *The Nibelungenlied* is a German epic of the thirteenth century telling in thirty-nine lays of nearly ten thousand lines the story of Siegfried and his widow Kriemhild. Siegfried conquers Nibelungenland (Norway) and steals the Nibelungen Hoard of gold and jewels.

7 (p. 433). Caliban is a deformed savage who attempts to deflower the beautiful Miranda in Shakespeare's *The Tempest*.

8 (p. 438). Lawrence's own ranch was near the village of San Cristobal; but he seems to have given the Rancho del Cerro Gordo a location more like that of Mabel Luhan's ranch in Taos.

9 (p. 439). French: reason for existing.

10 (p. 439). The Penitentes are societies of flagellants practising scourging of the body for religious purposes. They are found in Mexico, New Mexico and Colorado.

11 (p. 446). See note 40 to 'St Mawr'.

12 (p. 459). French: muzzle.

13 (p. 459). This was the era of Prohibition in many states. Illicit

liquor was often secreted in bootlegs and those who traded in it were therefore called bootleggers.

14 (p. 468). Spanish: very good.

15 (p. 468). The State Penitentiary.

THE VIRGIN AND THE GIPSY

1 (p. 471). French: outburst, flash.

2 (p. 471). Lawrence took only the name from Papplewick in Nottinghamshire: 'No doubt the whole setting is a combination of Lawrence's memories of his stay in Middleton-by-Wirksworth from May 1918 to February 1919 and his travels through Derbyshire with Ada Lawrence in October 1925. He uses obvious features of this countryside, the numerous quarries, the presence of old Roman mine workings, and the deep-wooded valleys with swiftly-flowing streams, as integral parts of the story. It is possible that he has Cromford in mind when he describes Papplewick. Lawrence describes "black industrialisation" (possibly of Sheffield) twenty miles to the north. The town has a stone bridge, and the Arkwright mills are also of stone. St Mary's Cromford is situated by a swiftly-flowing river, although it is without a rectory. Willersley Castle just beside it has many of the features of the setting described by Lawrence, although the house itself sounds rather like the home of the Weekleys, No. 32 Victoria Crescent, Mapperley Park, Nottingham.' (Bridget Pugh in *A D. H. Lawrence Handbook*, ed. K. Sagar, Manchester University Press, 1982.)

3 (p. 478). See note 2.

4 (p. 478). See note 26 to 'St Mawr'.

5 (p. 481). French: in possession of the facts.

6 (p. 483). A monomania; a subject introduced on any occasion, *ad nauseam*. Named after the topic which Mr Dick in Charles Dickens's *David Copperfield* introduced into all conversations.

7 (p. 486). Chatsworth House.

8 (p. 486). Ambergate.

9 (p. 486). Wirksworth.

10 (p. 486). Bonsall.

11 (p. 487). From *A Shropshire Lad* by A. E. Housman (1859–1936): 'Here of a Sunday morning/My love and I would lie,/And see the coloured counties,/And hear the larks so high/About us in the sky.'

12 (p. 505). French: 'So much noise over an omelette.' We should say, a trifle.

13 (p. 505). The Lady of Shalott, in Tennyson's poem of that name, is cut off from life, condemned to remain in her fusty room weaving what

she sees in her mirror reflected through the window. She is finally drawn to enter the real world (which is death to her) when Sir Lancelot rides by with his 'coal-black curls', singing 'Tirra lirra'.

14 (p. 510). French: pert, free-and-easy.

15 (p. 513). From 'The Wraggle-Taggle Gipsies', by an unknown author: 'What care I for my house and my land?/What care I for my money, O?/What care I for my new-wedded lord?/I'm off with the wraggle-taggle gipsies, O.'

16 (p. 522). In the spring of 1917 the British took a month to advance four miles at Arras (in France), but eventually broke the Hindenburg Line there. Horses were still used to haul the guns.

17 (p. 522). See note 15 to 'The Captain's Doll'.

18 (p. 527). Christ said to Peter: 'This night, before the cock crow, thou shalt deny me thrice.' (Matthew xxvi, 34.)

19 (p. 532). French: man who lives off the earnings of prostitutes.

20 (p. 539). Judges xvi. Matthew Arnold applied the term Philistine to the English middle class, which is, he said, 'ignorant, narrow-minded, and deficient in great ideas'.

21 (p. 539). Lawrence is playing on the saying: 'You cannot have your cake and eat it.'

THE ESCAPED COCK

1 (p. 558). i.e. from the cross. The man is clearly Christ. The first part is based on the biblical account of the Resurrection.

2 (p. 563). Gethsemane, where Judas betrayed his master with a kiss for thirty pieces of silver.

3 (p. 564). Mary Magdalene, who had been a prostitute before she met Jesus. See John xx, 11–17.

4 (p. 564). According to modern dating, Christ was about thirty-five at His crucifixion in A.D. 29.

5 (p. 569). In the Bible, these words are spoken to Mary Magdalene: 'Touch me not, for I am not yet ascended to my Father.' (John xx, 17.)

6 (p. 572). The biblical account of this meeting is in Luke xxiv, 13–31.

7 (p. 574). Lawrence had probably got most of his knowledge of Isis and Osiris from Frazer's *The Golden Bough*, which he had read at least twice, in 1915 and 1922. Gerald Lacy summarizes Frazer: 'Osiris was the offspring of the earth-god Seb and the sky-goddess Nut. He had several brothers and sisters, among them Set (who was later to betray him) and Isis (whom he later married). Osiris was a god of special

importance to the Egyptians, for it was believed that he taught his people the cultivation of grains and that he was directly connected with the yearly rising and falling of the Nile, an event on which the Egyptians depended for their very lives. Set became jealous of his brother and arranged to have a special coffin built exactly to the measurements of Osiris' body. At a banquet, as a sort of game, each male in attendance attempted to fit into the coffin, but only Osiris could fit easily. When he stretched out in the coffin, Set and his followers slammed the lid shut and flung the sealed coffin into the Nile. Isis immediately went on a search for her dead husband and finally found the coffin, miraculously grown into the trunk of a tall tree which had been cut and used as a pillar for the palace of one of the kings on the coast of Syria. Through various stratagems, Isis arranged to retrieve the coffin from the pillar and returned to Egypt with the body. Set then discovered the body and cut it into fourteen pieces and scattered them throughout Egypt. Again Isis ("Isis in Search", as Lawrence pointedly calls her) dutifully sought to gather all the pieces together and to reassemble her husband's body. She found all the parts except the genitals, which had been eaten by the fish of the Nile. Isis therefore had to make an image of the phallus. Ra, the sun-god, took pity on mourning Isis and arranged to have the re-assembled Osiris rise from the dead. Henceforth Osiris reigned as Lord of the Underworld, Lord of Eternity, and Ruler of the Dead. It is thus easy to understand why Osiris became a promise of resurrection and everlasting life for the Egyptians. He also functioned as a corn-god (bringing yearly the return of flood waters and the prosperity of the crops), a tree-spirit, a god of fertility (both of nature and of man), and as a general god of the dead.' (Gerald Lacy, *The Escaped Cock*, pp. 124–5.)

8 (p. 577). The lotus, the Egyptian waterlily, grew with the rising of the Nile, and became a fertility symbol associated with sun-worship. In *Etruscan Places* Lawrence speaks of 'the eternal quick of all things, which yet divides and sub-divides, so that it becomes the sun of the firmament and the lotus of the waters under the earth, and the rose of all existence upon the earth.'

9 (p. 577). In Egyptian myth Isis was supernaturally impregnated by the dead Osiris to become the mother of Horus, a bringer of harmony; but in Lawrence's version she can become pregnant only after a physical union with the resurrected Osiris/Christ.

10 (p. 578). Marcus Antonius was a friend of Julius Caesar. After Caesar's death he succeeded him as the lover of Cleopatra, Queen of Egypt, neglecting both his wife and the affairs of the Empire. He committed suicide in 30 B.C., and was not therefore a contemporary of Christ.

11 (p. 578). The dove was sacred to the love-goddess Venus and to the moon-goddess Isis.

12 (p. 583). Latin: touch me not.

13 (p. 587). Pan was the Greek god who represented the sacredness of all created things.

14 (p. 597). The dog-star Sirius is the brightest star in the heavens: 'And the sign of the rising waters on earth was accompanied by a sign in heaven. For in the early days of Egyptian history, some three or four thousand years before the beginning of our era, the splendid star of Sirius, the brightest of all the fixed stars, appeared at dawn in the east just before sunrise about the time of the summer solstice, when the Nile begins to rise. The Egyptians called it Sothis, and regarded it as the star of Isis.' (J. G. Frazer, *The Golden Bough*, 'The Ritual of Osiris'.)

15 (p. 600). In *Apocalypse*, written a year and a half after the second part of 'The Escaped Cock', Lawrence wrote: 'A hero was a hero, in the great past, when he had conquered the hostile dragon, when he had the power of the dragon *with him* in his limbs and breast ... the liberation within the self of the gleaming bright serpent of gold, golden fluid life within the body, the rousing of the splendid divine dragon within a man, or within a woman ... For in his good aspect, the dragon is the great vivifier, the great enhancer of the whole universe ... It is the same dragon which, according to the Hindus, coils quiescent at the base of the spine of a man, and unfolds sometimes lashing along the spinal way: and the yogi is only trying to set this dragon in controlled motion.' (*Apocalypse*, Cambridge University Press, 1980, pp. 124–5.)

In her introduction to that edition Mara Kalnins writes: 'Lawrence had been particularly influenced by the Dublin theosophist James Pryse, whose *The Apocalypse Unsealed* he had read. He liked Pryse's notion of a latent power within a man that could be liberated through the controlled awakening of the seven principal nerve centres or "chakras" along the spine. The "chakra" – generally translated as "plexus", a term Lawrence used in *Fantasia of the Unconscious* though elsewhere he also calls it a "primary affective centre" – is a vortex or centre of psychic energy. In yoga this power is called *kundalini* and is symbolically represented as a dragon or a serpent curled at the base of the spine; it is that "startled life which runs through us like a serpent, or coils within us potent and waiting, like a serpent". When awakened this serpent releases a life-giving force by moving upward and gaining power with the "conquest" of each "chakra".' (ibid. pp. 5–6.)

Select Bibliography

I. TEXTUAL

Harry T. Moore, ed., *A D. H. Lawrence Miscellany* (Southern Illinois University Press, 1959). Contains the early version of 'The Fox'.

D. H. Lawrence, *The Escaped Cock*, ed. Gerald M. Lacy (Black Sparrow Press, 1973). Contains early and definitive texts, full textual commentary and related letters.

2. REFERENCE

Keith Sagar, *D. H. Lawrence: A Calendar of his Works* (Manchester University Press, 1979).

3. BIOGRAPHICAL

Harry T. Moore, *The Priest of Love* (Penguin, 1976).

Edward Nehls, *D. H. Lawrence: A Composite Biography*, 3 vols (Madison: University of Wisconsin Press, 1957–9).

Keith Sagar, *The Life of D. H. Lawrence* (Eyre Methuen, 1980).

4. CRITICAL

David Cavitch, *D. H. Lawrence and the New World* (Oxford University Press, 1969). On 'St Mawr' and 'The Princess'.

James C. Cowan, *D. H. Lawrence's American Journey* (Case Western Reserve University Press, 1970). On 'St Mawr' and 'The Princess'. 'The Function of Allusions and Symbols in D. H. Lawrence's *The Man Who Died*', *American Imago* XVII (1960), pp. 241–53.

H. M. Daleski, 'Aphrodite of the Foam and *The Ladybird* Tales', in *D. H. Lawrence*, ed. Gomme (Harvester, 1978).

Eugene W. Dawson, 'Love Among the Mannikins: "The Captain's Doll"', *D. H. Lawrence Review* I (1968), pp. 137–48.

R. P. Draper, ed., *D. H. Lawrence: The Critical Heritage* (Routledge & Kegan Paul, 1970; revised 1979). Contains contemporary reviews of 'The Ladybird' and 'St Mawr'.

Ian Gregor, ' "The Fox": a Caveat', *Essays in Criticism*, Vol. 9 (1959), pp. 10–21.

F. R. Leavis, *D. H. Lawrence: Novelist* (Chatto & Windus, 1955; Penguin, 1964). On all the short novels except 'The Escaped Cock'. *Thought, Words and Creativity: Art and Thought in Lawrence* (Chatto & Windus, 1976). On 'The Captain's Doll'.

Larry V. Ledoux, 'Christ and Isis: The Function of the Dying and Reviving God in *The Man Who Died*', *D. H. Lawrence Review*, Vol. 5, pp. 132–48.

Robert H. MacDonald, 'The Union of Fire and Water: An Examination of the Imagery of *The Man Who Died*', *D. H. Lawrence Review*, Vol. 10, pp. 34–51.

Elgin W. Mellown, ' "The Captain's Doll": Its Origins and Literary Allusions', *D. H. Lawrence Review*, Vol. 9, pp. 226–35.

Julian Moynahan, *The Deed of Life* (Oxford University Press, 1963). On 'The Fox' and 'The Virgin and the Gipsy'.

Keith Sagar, *The Art of D. H. Lawrence* (Cambridge University Press, 1966). On 'St Mawr' and 'The Escaped Cock'.

Mark Spilka, *The Love Ethic of D. H. Lawrence* (Indiana University Press, 1955). On 'The Escaped Cock'.

John B. Vickery, 'Myth and Ritual in the Shorter Fiction of D. H. Lawrence', *Modern Fiction Studies*, Vol. 5, pp. 65–82. On 'The Fox' and 'The Virgin and the Gipsy'. Reprinted, enlarged, in *The Literary Impact of the Golden Bough* (Princeton University Press, 1973).

S. Ronald Weiner, 'Irony and Symbolism in "The Princess" ', in *A D. H. Lawrence Miscellany*, ed. Moore (Southern Illinois University Press, 1959).

Kingsley Widmer, *The Art of Perversity: D. H. Lawrence's Shorter Fictions* (Washington University Press, 1962).

FOR THE BEST IN PAPERBACKS, LOOK FOR THE

In every corner of the world, on every subject under the sun, Penguin represents quality and variety – the very best in publishing today.

For complete information about books available from Penguin – including Pelicans, Puffins, Peregrines and Penguin Classics – and how to order them, write to us at the appropriate address below. Please note that for copyright reasons the selection of books varies from country to country.

In the United Kingdom: For a complete list of books available from Penguin in the U.K., please write to *Dept E.P., Penguin Books Ltd, Harmondsworth, Middlesex, UB7 0DA*

In the United States: For a complete list of books available from Penguin in the U.S., please write to *Dept BA, Penguin, 299 Murray Hill Parkway, East Rutherford, New Jersey 07073*

In Canada: For a complete list of books available from Penguin in Canada, please write to *Penguin Books Canada Ltd, 2801 John Street, Markham, Ontario L3R 1B4*

In Australia: For a complete list of books available from Penguin in Australia, please write to the *Marketing Department, Penguin Books Australia Ltd, P.O. Box 257, Ringwood, Victoria 3134*

In New Zealand: For a complete list of books available from Penguin in New Zealand, please write to the *Marketing Department, Penguin Books (NZ) Ltd, Private Bag, Takapuna, Auckland 9*

In India: For a complete list of books available from Penguin, please write to *Penguin Overseas Ltd, 706 Eros Apartments, 56 Nehru Place, New Delhi, 110019*

In Holland: For a complete list of books available from Penguin in Holland, please write to *Penguin Books Nederland B.V., Postbus 195, NL–1380AD Weesp, Netherlands*

In Germany: For a complete list of books available from Penguin, please write to *Penguin Books Ltd, Friedrichstrasse 10 – 12, D–6000 Frankfurt Main 1, Federal Republic of Germany*

In Spain: For a complete list of books available from Penguin in Spain, please write to *Longman Penguin España, Calle San Nicolas 15, E–28013 Madrid, Spain*

D. H. LAWRENCE

D. H. Lawrence is now acknowledged as one of the greatest writers of the twentieth century. Nearly all his works have been published in Penguins.

Novels

Aaron's Rod   Lady Chatterley's Lover
The Lost Girl   The Plumed Serpent
The Rainbow   Sons and Lovers
The Trespasser   The White Peacock
Women in Love   Kangaroo
The First Lady Chatterley   John Thomas and Lady Jane
The Boy in the Bush

Short Stories

The Prussian Officer   England, My England
Love Among the Haystacks
The Woman Who Rode Away
Three Novellas:
The Fox, The Ladybird, The Captain's Doll
St Mawr *and* The Virgin and the Gipsy
The Princess and Other Stories
The Mortal Coil and Other Stories

Travel Books and Other Works

Mornings in Mexico *and* Etruscan Places
Sea and Sardinia   Twilight in Italy
Selected Essays
Fantasia of the Unconscious *and* Psychoanalysis
and the Unconscious
Studies in Classic American Literature

Poetry

D. H. Lawrence: The Complete Poems
Edited and introduced by Vivian de Sola Pinto
and F. Warren Roberts

Plays

Three Plays: A Collier's Friday Night/
The Daughter-in-Law/The Widowing of Mrs Holroyd

Matthew Arnold	**Selected Prose**
Jane Austen	**Emma**
	Lady Susan, The Watsons, Sanditon
	Mansfield Park
	Northanger Abbey
	Persuasion
	Pride and Prejudice
	Sense and Sensibility
Anne Brontë	**The Tenant of Wildfell Hall**
Charlotte Brontë	**Jane Eyre**
	Shirley
	Villette
Emily Brontë	**Wuthering Heights**
Samuel Butler	**Erewhon**
	The Way of All Flesh
Thomas Carlyle	**Selected Writings**
Wilkie Collins	**The Moonstone**
	The Woman in White
Charles Darwin	**The Origin of Species**
Charles Dickens	**American Notes for General Circulation**
	Barnaby Rudge
	Bleak House
	The Christmas Books
	David Copperfield
	Dombey and Son
	Great Expectations
	Hard Times
	Little Dorrit
	Martin Chuzzlewit
	The Mystery of Edwin Drood
	Nicholas Nickleby
	The Old Curiosity Shop
	Oliver Twist

Benjamin Disraeli	**Sybil**
George Eliot	**Adam Bede**
	Daniel Deronda
	Felix Holt
	Middlemarch
	The Mill on the Floss
	Romola
	Scenes of Clerical Life
	Silas Marner
Elizabeth Gaskell	**Cranford** and **Cousin Phillis**
	The Life of Charlotte Brontë
	Mary Barton
	North and South
	Wives and Daughters
Edward Gibbon	**The Decline and Fall of the Roman Empire**
George Gissing	**New Grub Street**
Edmund Gosse	**Father and Son**
Richard Jefferies	**Landscape with Figures**
Thomas Macaulay	**The History of England**
Henry Mayhew	**Selections from London Labour** and **The London Poor**
John Stuart Mill	**On Liberty**
William Morris	**News from Nowhere** and **Selected Writings and Designs**
Walter Pater	**Marius the Epicurean**
John Ruskin	**'Unto This Last' and Other Writings**
Sir Walter Scott	**Ivanhoe**
Robert Louis Stevenson	**Dr Jekyll and Mr Hyde**
William Makepeace Thackeray	**The History of Henry Esmond**
	Vanity Fair
Anthony Trollope	**Barchester Towers**
	Framley Parsonage
	Phineas Finn